VATICAN

Books by Malachi Martin

THE SCRIBAL CHARACTER
OF THE DEAD SEA SCROLLS

THE PILGRIM
(under the pseudonym Michael Serafian)

THE ENCOUNTER

THREE POPES AND THE CARDINAL

JESUS NOW

THE NEW CASTLE

HOSTAGE TO THE DEVIL

THE FINAL CONCLAVE

KING OF KINGS

THE DECLINE AND FALL
OF THE ROMAN CHURCH

THERE IS STILL LOVE

RICH CHURCH, POOR CHURCH

VATICAN

Malachi Martin

VATICAN

a novel

HARPER & ROW, PUBLISHERS, New York

Cambridge, Philadelphia,
San Francisco, London
Mexico City, São Paulo,
Singapore, Sydney

 For information address Harper & Row, Publishers, Inc., 10 East 53rd Street, New York, N.Y. 10022. Published simultaneously in Canada by Fitzhenry & Whiteside Limited, Toronto.

FIRST EDITION

Designed by Ruth Bornschlegel

Library of Congress Cataloging in Publication Data
Martin, Malachi.
Vatican.

I. Title.
PS3563.A725V3 1986 813'.54 85-42645
ISBN 0-06-015478-0

---

86 87 88 89 90 RRD 10 9 8 7 6 5 4 3 2 1

For the Assumption

Contents

This is a work of fiction. In order to create a dramatic climate that imitates reality, the author has used the correct names of certain offices and posts in the Catholic Church and elsewhere. However, it is not the author's intention to suggest that the real occupants, past or present, living or dead, of any such office, engaged in any activity mentioned or suggested in this book.

Part One

THE SEASON BEFORE

[1]

IN THAT LATE, cheerless spring of 1945, blood still stained the great rivers of Europe. Along a radius of thousands of miles, whole countries lay in such deep ruins and despair that the future seemed to belong only to the young and the undisillusioned. The whole world was at war, and no one could predict when the millions of men would stop the killing.

In that world at war, the ancient city of Rome with its Vatican resembled nothing more than an antique topaz hanging on the neck of the bedraggled whore Italy had become at the hands of Fascist, Nazi, and Communist. *"Il solo bel paese"*—the only beautiful country—the Italians used to call her. Now, in the ruin of total defeat, she was ugly.

In money, she was one extended poorhouse. In politics, she was a tangled ruin: Only the Communist Party was intact, backed by a quarter of a million seasoned partisan fighters. In war, she was pinned beneath two foreign fighting machines. The American Third Army held two-thirds of the country, everything south of a line running from Livorno on the Ligurian Sea in the west over to Ancona on the Adriatic in the east. Nazi General Kesselring faced that line. With one million of the Wehrmacht's finest and with far superior strategy, he had pounded the Allies to a halt.

And so on that April 27 it was, as Lord Byron said of his own days there, "a damned peculiar time" for anyone to come to Italy. A damned peculiar time for a six-passenger Portuguese commercial plane to nose in through the cold mists that wound like a morning shroud around Rome's Ciampino Airport. The metal hulk made a rough landing and taxied noisily, growling, trailing long lanyards of mist like spittle from the mouth of a rabid beast. At the end of the runaway, a grim U.S. Army lieutenant sitting in a personnel carrier with four heavily armed GI's checked his watch. O-five-thirty. No chance to make Rome under cover of dark.

He waited for the plane to come to a stop and, without cutting its engines, disgorge its solitary passenger with his two suitcases, then turn tail immediately, give a roar of sudden warning and flee from sight, gashing an invisible passage for itself through the mist and into the western sky.

The passenger left behind in the dank silence was young—just twenty-four—and straight out of Chicago, Illinois. The only relief to the stark black of his clericals was provided by the white Roman collar and the violet rabat—a biblike garment tucked beneath the collar's edge and covering his chest—that showed rank as clearly as the single bar painted on the soldier's helmet.

The young monsignor showed a tired stiffness in his step as he went over to the personnel carrier and handed his travel orders up to the lieutenant. They were of about the same age, those two, born in the same isolated peace of far-off America, reared probably in the same openness of living and the same pursuit of happiness. But war had dug a deep difference between them. The young cleric was cold and tired after thirty-one hours of travel. Barely a day ago, a lumbering military transport had taken him in twenty-two hours from Andrews Air force Base, Maryland, to Lisbon, Portugal. The commercial plane had flown him practically without rest across the Mediterranean to Italy, skimming almost at surface level to avoid detection by German Messerschmitts. That was the closest Richard Lansing had come to war. Nothing that a good, long sleep and a hot meal would not cure. The lieutenant, a very old young man after three years of carnage, was cold from killing and tired from trying to stay alive. He would never be the same again.

A grunt, a glance at Lansing's face to confirm identity. "Okay, Padre. Gimme your luggage. Climb up and let's get outa here. It's gonna be fast. And rough." Then, over his shoulder as he swung behind the wheel, "Pack it in, boys."

No one said anything more as they sped out of the airport and on to the three-thousand-year-old Roman road. Quickly they were clear of the swampy mist that forever clung to Ciampino, then hurtled along at seventy and eighty miles an hour through territory only recently liberated from the Germans and still infested with snipers left behind to harass the conquerors, and with Communist partisans hunting everything that moved. "Morgue Alley," the GI's called it, so many of their dead had lain unburied for weeks along the sides of that road and in among the gnarled olive groves and immemorial cypress trees planted there by Julius Caesar's forefathers.

Hanging on to keep from being tossed from his seat beside the lieutenant, Lansing still managed to drink in the lovely blue of the Tyrrhenian Sea lying in a morning haze to the right. To their left, as he bounced about, he could see the Alban Hills. His companions were watching from their different world for death from bullets, bazookas, or grenades. Speed, the maximum speed, was the guardian angel they relied on in their dash for Rome.

When they entered Rome itself, the carrier slowed very little. The lieutenant turned on the military siren to scream the "let pass" signal. Everywhere the steel sinews of war wound around the arteries of a city not yet securely in Allied hands. The breakneck speed of the personnel carrier allowed no casual view of anything. Army patrols and armored pickets that gripped each square and street were a blur of guns and khaki. The Baths of Caracalla fled past, an unfocused series of jagged teeth, brown with ancient decay. As they curved around it on screeching tires, the Circo Massimo melted in their vision into the form of some long-dead monster. They pelted up the east bank of the Tiber; the fragmented walls, the standing columns, the shattered pavements and headless statues of the Roman Forum, all were of one piece with all the other bombed-out cities of Italy. The boarded-up shops, the deserted streets, the frightened faces behind the windows here and there, all told the silent story of a people cowed by war. For the ninth time in its long history, the eternal city was under the fist of a foreign invader. And the people hid as though from their own fate being decided at alien hands.

Only when the personnel carrier had raced across the Victor Emmanuel Bridge and was heading straight up the Via della Conciliazione did the pace slacken. Suddenly then, without warning, a vista of solid and beautifully symmetrical peace and strength replaced everything else; St. Peter's domed basilica seemed to have been waiting there always like an unchanging, promised land atop Vatican Hill.

The soldiers relaxed the grip on their weapons a little. The lieutenant sighed almost out loud, and pushed his helmet back on his head. He glanced at the young cleric, and half smiled, half grimaced at his rapt expression. A few minutes more, and they crossed into St. Peter's Piazza, past the Egyptian obelisk and the two fountains in the piazza's center. The lieutenant veered skillfully to the right, then, mumbling a curse under his breath, braked to a sudden stop outside the gate of the courtyard of St. Damasus in front of the Apostolic Palace. A black Mercedes-Benz, motor running, blocked his path into the smaller courtyard and the entrance to the Secretariat of State.

A man carrying a briefcase had got out of the limousine and was chatting with a woman sitting in the back. Both looked around unhurriedly, curious to see what was this rumbling interruption of the early-morning quiet.

After the breakneck dash from the airport, Lansing was struck first by the ease and leisure of the man who turned to look at him, and then by the brilliance of that look, blue-green and clear. The man turned back, waved goodbye to the woman, moved easily up the steps, and pushed through the swinging doors of the Secretariat. The darkened back window of the Mercedes closed while the limousine edged its way through the gate and past the personnel carrier, picking up speed as it headed silently across St. Peter's Piazza toward the Via della Conciliazione.

Without waiting for the lieutenant to pull inside the gate, Lansing climbed stiffly down from his seat. The lieutenant handed him his two suitcases and saluted. Lansing, a man of few words at best, thanked him with a look. In any event, there were no words he could say to melt the tension in the young officer's eyes or rid him of his weariness. The lieutenant acknowledged the thanks with a small jerk of his head, then backed from the gate, made a quick U-turn, and roared across the piazza, leaving the newcomer quite alone for the first time in the early Roman sun.

Richard Cooper Lansing, the youngest ranking monsignor of the Chicago archdiocese, had arrived in one piece to begin what clerics of that time familiarly called his "Roman stint." In Chicago, he had dreamed of this place. All his life, it seemed, he had heard about it. From the nuns in kindergarten, from his Jesuit teachers in high school, from his professors in the seminary. This Vatican! This Rome of the popes! Now that he was here, it was all he ever dreamed it would be, more exciting than he had ever imagined. This cluster of buildings and monuments lazing silently in the early sunlight around the wide arc of St. Peter's Piazza appeared somehow immune to the racking pain of the world he had just crossed, independent of the killing and dying and tears and fatigue and eyes like that young lieutenant's eyes.

There was no way Lansing could even begin to imagine what cruel tensions were housed within that Renaissance Apostolic Palace, or what destiny of his own lay hidden from his sight behind the weather-beaten faces of the Twelve Apostles staring out sightlessly at him from the topmost balcony.

He took a few paces out from the gate to get a better view, first of the basilica with its great floating dome and, beside it, the peaked, red-tiled roof of the Sistine Chapel, where popes were elected. He slowly saw it all. The sweep of Bernini's colonnade around the piazza. The massive Portoni di Bronzo, the famous Bronze Doors, opening on an unimaginable flight of stairs that was a path into the heart of the Vatican. The long, high, crenellated buildings of the museums. Up there on the Janiculum Hill, the American College. Each building was massive, and their total appearance was overwhelming in its weight. Yet the proportions devised by the geniuses who put it all together were in such perfect symmetry that, above all, the place seemed made for peace.

He listened to the plashing of the two fountains whispering to one another the hidden secrets of their tranquillity, rested his gaze on the Apostolic Palace, took in the outsize height and delicate ornamentation of the windows, the fluted pillars of the balconies, even the cobbled ground, and wondered at the strangely inviolate silence that seemed to protect it all.

The two-door Fiat that drove up barely distracted Lansing. Almost without thinking, he watched a small, black-robed cleric, his broad-brimmed Roman hat in one hand and his briefcase in the other, get out of the car at the main door of the Secretariat. Lansing had a brief glimpse of a swarthy complexion, a large hooked nose, a burning glance in his direction from deep-set eyes, a face whose severity was at odds with the tide of Lansing's awe. But the man's glance was as quick as his step, and he was lost from view inside the Secretariat doors almost at once.

Lansing forgot him as quickly as he went, so intimate to him was the sense of longing fulfilled here and now on this Vatican Hill. His gaze returned to the Renaissance facade of the Apostolic Palace. And as it did, the tiniest flash of brilliant light just caught his glance. Perhaps the sun on the glass, a window opening to the morning? Or was it just his imagination? But no! See there! Curtains falling back into place. He stared at that window for some moments. It was odd, he thought, that an actual movement made by a human hand made everything seem so utterly remote and unattainable, made all seem in a twinkling to be clad in such a special privacy as to be totally disinterested in what went on down here below in the piazza where he stood.

"Reverendo! Reverendo!"

Lansing turned in the direction of the voice. There, in the midst of all this immensity, he saw the tiniest old man he could ever remember seeing, wearing a blue smock over his clothes and a black beret on his head. The man stood at the main door of the Secretariat, smiling and beckoning him.

"Please, *Reverendo!* Take the trouble to enter here and announce yourself at the reception. I am Amadeo, Amadeo Solimando, the *portiere.*"

The American laughed with pure pleasure. All sense of remoteness fled. All his young life in Chicago he had come across thousands of stocky little Italian men with similar accents on the city's west side. He picked up his luggage and walked across the courtyard.

Amadeo's already large eyes grew a little larger as he caught sight of that little patch of violet under Lansing's collar. He snatched the beret off an utterly bald head. *"Ma, scusi, Monsignore!"* He prudently fell into the most formal Italian at his command. "Welcome to the eternal city of our Caesars and popes! *Scusi! Scusi tanto!"* He opened his arms as wide as nature would permit and bowed a little—a movement at once deferential and exploratory.

Few people had served longer in the Vatican than Amadeo Solimando. "I've served four popes," he would often tell visitors to the apartment he shared with his patient wife, "and I've seen thousands of dignitaries come and go." And so it was that this fellow citizen of the Caesars had developed a quick and careful eye for all the signs of clerical rank. A lot depended on that ability. In the context of Amadeo's world, authority was everything. And he somehow shared in its dignity. Take the color of the rabat, for example. For Amadeo, a glance was enough to differentiate among all the shades of violet and lavender and purple that distinguished one grade of monsignor from another; and all of them from all the grades of bishops; and all the bishops from all the archbishops; and *all* of them from the cardinals.

Still, Amadeo also knew that with some of these unschooled foreigners you could be fooled. As Lansing strode up and deposited his luggage, there was a discreet glance at his right hand. No. No ring. Not a bishop. Lansing introduced himself, thankful for once that his mother, a New York Sammartino by birth, had insisted her children learn Italian.

Little Amadeo smiled again, plopped his beret back on his head, and with that happy dignity he shared with popes and princes, picked up the two suitcases and led the way up the steps.

It was Lansing's turn to push through the swinging doors and into the Vatican Secretariat of State. Inside, Amadeo's fast steps were silent; but Lansing's echoed on the parquet flooring of a long entry hall flanked on either side with busts of dead popes. Ahead of him, Amadeo stopped at a small table and whispered something to a round-shouldered, chubby-cheeked, black-eyed cleric sitting there. Amadeo turned back then, beret in hand, gestured Lansing toward the seated cleric, bestowed another full-toothed and quite genuine smile on the American, and finally bowed his way past him, presumably to take up again his post by the main door.

The cleric at the little reception desk could not have been more completely Amadeo's opposite. He peered up at Lansing through thick lenses that magnified a look of the most profound misery, then down at a photograph in a manila folder on his table, then back at Lansing again. His eyes flickered without shame or apology over every inch of the American's well-tanned face, the reddish-brown hair, his black suit, his immaculate collar, the shoes, the fine leather of his suitcases, and finally, perhaps longingly, back up to the violet rabat. He sighed as if his misery had deepened (though that hardly seemed possible), closed the manila folder, stood up—he was no taller than Amadeo—and at last removed the three-cornered biretta from his head.

"Buon giorno, Monsignore." The voice was as mournful as the face, but the accents were velvet. "Pasquinelli, at Your Reverence's service."

"Buon giorno, Reverendo." Lansing looked down at Pasquinelli. "I am Richard Lansing of Chicago. Archbishop Da Brescia is expecting me."

"Documents, please, Monsignore." Lansing opened one of his suitcases and took out a manila envelope. Pasquinelli mournfully indicated a chair for him, and disappeared into an inner office.

Pasquinelli? Pasquinelli? Lansing rummaged in his mind for the name as he sat down to wait. He had a remarkable memory, and Cardinal Krementz of Chicago had given him some thorough briefings before sending him over here. Old "Blackjack"—that was what everyone who knew the cardinal called him, but not to his face—old Blackjack had mentioned a lot of names. But no, not Pasquinelli's. Lansing was sure of that. Still, he thought again. His mind flashed back over that farewell visit he had paid the cardinal, accompanied by his parents and his twin sister, Netta. He could see them all, sitting in the drawing room of the old man's residence overlooking Lake Michigan, listening while Krementz threw out bits of candid information and salty advice for Richard.

"Now, Da Brescia. He's an archbishop. Head of the Bureau of Internal Affairs at the Secretariat. Officially, you'll be working for him. Watch that one. He has plans. And power. Manages all the legacies, trusts, mortgages on property willed to the Holy See, administration of Holy See property, the tax exemptions of the Holy See, and all that folderol. . . ." Then there was Archbishop Morandi, head of the Bureau of External Affairs in the Secretariat. "An honest fellow, that," was Blackjack's comment. "Should be a cardinal someday. All heart. No brains. . . . Da Brescia and Morandi are called pro-secretaries of state. The Pope doesn't trust anyone as Secretary. You might say he's his own Secretary. Those two men merely do the paperwork for him. . . . By the way, Da Brescia has a sidekick, a man called Casaregna. A careful type, that. Never lost a battle yet. But watch his aide, Carnatiu. A Romanian . . . Doesn't smell quite right, somehow. . . ."

At that last meeting, and at one or two before, Krementz had thrown out a welter of names and comments, a beginner's who's who of the Vatican—Dell'Angelo, Bernardino, Serena, Lanser, Solaccio, Mangano, Arnulfo, de this and della that—hurrying through descriptions and crusty remarks and a mother lode of useful information. Richard was unused to the clerical familiarity of all this talk about Roman prelates, but Basil

Lansing, his father, had learned to relish the intimate style of this man over years of association with him. Beloved old Blackjack! Richard wasn't sure what his mother, Margaret, thought of it all.

"When I proposed the lad's name for bishop," Krementz confided to Basil and Margaret, "the Romans thought he should do a stint with them. And so did I. Better now than never. Who knows when this damn war will really be over."

The "lad" had sat quietly by, paying close attention when the cardinal rattled out names and information, and the rest of the time trying not to laugh at the teasing faces Netta made at him. Even as young adults, twin sister and brother retained a remarkably close resemblance: the same coloring, eyes, high cheekbones, mouth and chin. The same gestures. Even something the same about the way they spoke. Richard and Netta had always understood each other, even without words. They were on some shared wavelength of feeling and thought. And yet the very traits that made them so alike seemed somehow to underline Netta's appealing femininity and Richard's gentle, handsome masculinity.

"They owed me a big one for the loan we arranged for them back in the twenties." Richard remembered the way Krementz had winked at his father. In 1929, with Basil's help as board chairman at First National of Chicago, Krementz had floated a loan of one million dollars through twenty-year bonds collateralized with millions of dollars' worth of Church property in Chicago. The move was intended to save the almost bankrupt papacy. And it had worked. "I've fixed it so the lad returns here in a couple of years. He'll be my auxiliary bishop with right of succession as AB of Chicago, when I pass on. But they want to make sure he's kosher. And anyway, if he's going to run a diocese as big as this someday, he's got to know his way around with those bureaucrats, know who can do what for whom for how much. He can use my apartment in the Vatican until he gets settled into his own place.

"Ah!" Krementz had walked over to Richard then and looked down into his face. "He'll become more Roman than the Romans themselves in no time! You'll see, lad. You'll see! But listen to me now. You've been first among the brightest of your generation. That's intellect. What counts over there is intelligence—not the same thing as high marks in the seminary! So keep your wits about you, and learn to cook Roman spaghetti, if you get my meaning." Lansing thought he did. "Stay simple." Krementz had almost whispered that, at the very end. "Don't let them get you down, lad. Stay simple."

Richard remembered it all, as though watching a film frame by frame. There had been no mention of the sad-faced little priest called Pasquinelli.

In an inner office, Monsignore Gian Solaccio, the security officer on duty that morning, verified Lansing's passport and the letters of introduction from Krementz. That much was in order. He took Lansing's dental records into an adjacent office lined with filing cabinets, and closed the door carefully behind him.

Certainly Lansing and maybe even old Blackjack would have been surprised at some of the intelligence the files in that office contained—remarkably thorough information that many a government would have moved mountains to get its hands on. War and technology had made changes here since Krementz's time. Long experience with impostors and "moles" of all kinds and from all sides had imposed strict rules on Vatican security. And in a shooting war, the neutral ground of the Vatican could be a God-sent haven, a discreet base of operations, and a ready source of intelligence. Information was an element in Vatican service. But the authorities liked to know who benefited by that service.

Solaccio ran through the *L*'s, pulled a file, and removed the dental records from the papers. He placed both sets against a lighted frame, and studied them with a practiced eye until he was satisfied.

Back again at his desk, Solaccio scribbled illegibly across the manila envelope, and handed it back to Pasquinelli.

"Take him to Casaregna. Da Brescia has cut his orders. He begins next Monday. In Passports. Speaks Italian?"

"Chicagoese with adenoids," Pasquinelli joked, without a crack in that woebegone look.

Solaccio's eyes glistened with humor for both of them.

Monsignore Agostino Casaregna's was a name Lansing did remember. And Blackjack's description had been perfect, right down to the hollow cheeks, thin lips, sallow complexion, and those watchful eyes of a fox glinting behind steel-rimmed spectacles. Casaregna spoke very correct English. His office was large and airy, his desk tidy. He shook Lansing's hand perfunctorily, welcomed him to the Vatican "in the name of the Holy Father," introduced him to his secretary, Father Roman Carnatiu, and had Lansing sign the register of Secretariat employees. Lansing recognized Casaregna for the dedicated bureaucrat he was. But the sloe-eyed Romanian, Carnatiu, made him feel uneasy. It wasn't just his imagination. *"Watch him"*—Lansing played back Blackjack's warning. *"Doesn't smell quite right somehow. . . ."*

"Now"—Casaregna moved forward briskly with the formalities—"we will say hello to Monsignore Da Brescia. Leave your things here." He pressed a bell twice to alert Da Brescia that he was coming with a visitor, then led his charge to a tiny elevator furnished with old-fashioned ormolu and painted wood.

Da Brescia's office, a long, narrow, high-ceilinged room with deep carpeting, was on the third floor of the Secretariat. Casaregna took Lansing just inside the door and then stepped back. Lansing supposed that was the way things were done here.

Da Brescia's desk was at the far end of the room, placed diagonally across one corner. "They say Da Brescia likes to see how his visitors negotiate that long walk between the door and the desk—coming in *and* going out," Krementz had said. "Tells him a lot about their character, they say." No surprises so far.

Da Brescia was in conference with two clerical colleagues. Still, after a look at Casaregna, who was no help at all, Lansing decided he was supposed to "negotiote that long walk" alone.

As he took his first steps, the three men at the desk stood up, less in welcome, it seemed, than to gaze at the tall, gawky American. They were quick to note the steady blue eyes that gave them a stare of appraisal as good as their own. And his walk—self-assured, almost casual, as if in fact every patch of ground he covered belonged to him. An alarm bell rang in their ecclesiastical brains. Independence! The only real threat! All three had the basic Roman instinct for survival within a system built on grades of absolute authority.

Outwardly, however, they were imperturbable, urbane, smiling, speaking soft Italian syllables of welcome.

Lansing was startled for a quick moment when he seemed to recognize those deep-set, piercing eyes of Da Brescia's. And then he remembered the Fiat down there in the piazza. The powerful Da Brescia, head of the Vatican's Bureau of Internal Affairs, was the small, black-robed cleric he had barely paid attention to less than an hour before.

De Brescia caught the look of recognition but did not return it. He inquired after Lansing's physical condition, asked about that great servant of the Church Cardinal Krementz. He introduced the two others. The squat, pug-nosed one with iron-gray hair and owlish glasses was Aldo Morandi. Dell'Angelo was youngish, handsome in a diabolic way, seemed affable. When he spoke, his voice was more like his name than were his looks; it was soft and angelic.

Dell'Angelo was sure Monsignore Lansing needed a good rest.

Indeed, Da Brescia agreed; he had until next Monday to recuperate from that exhausting journey. The cardinal had given him permission to use his Vatican apartment? Why, splendid! The American wanted to know if he could possibly get a message to his parents that he had arrived safely? Well, that had already been done. They already knew! At least Cardinal Krementz did. Surely, he would alert the monsignore's parents. The three Romans laughed pleasantly at the openly puzzled expression on Lansing's face. It would be some time before he learned about the coded messages broadcast every morning over Radio Vatican to Vatican listening posts throughout the world.

"Monsignore Casaregna," Da Brescia called out. "Have Pasquinelli show the monsignore to the cardinal's apartment. Tomorrow, Monsignore Lansing, Pasquinelli will be your guide until you find your Vatican legs!" His tones were solicitous.

Lansing thanked him, smiled at the other two. All three watched the American turn and walk back the length of the office to the door where Casaregna still waited.

"Krementz's *bambino,* eh?" Morandi asked, when it was just the three Romans again.

Dell'Angelo nodded. "Due back in Chicago as auxiliary and with right of succession. Krementz is close to the fourth floor." He raised his eyes in the general direction of the papal apartment.

"Close or not, it makes no difference." Morandi was not impressed. "They're so far away, those Americans. Krementz included."

Only Da Brescia was silent. He could still see the way Lansing had walked toward him from the door.

"He takes long steps," he remarked finally.

[2]

They used to say about His Holiness, Papa Eugenio Profumi, two hundred sixty-third successor to Blessed Peter the Apostle, that nothing happened down there on "Our piazza," as he called it, that he did not notice from his papal apartments on the fourth floor of the Apostolic Palace. Not that anyone, even with cotton-stuffed ears, could have ignored the gunning engine and the screeching halt of the U.S. Army personnel carrier that exploded the after-dawn silence of St. Peter's Piazza.

The Pope finished the sentence he was writing at the desk in his study. He pressed a bell button; then he went to the window and pulled the curtains aside, letting the morning light flood over the yellow walls and white ceiling of his private study. The face of the Pope, gaunt and bespectacled, was probably only one of many that craned down to see the new arrival.

The strain that showed in the Pope's eyes, the tight lines of his mouth, softened just a little, almost to a smile, as he watched the young cleric clamber down from his perch beside the American soldier and come under the spell of the peace that settled upon the place again. The Pope removed his hand to let the curtains fall back into place, just as that distant young face of Richard Lansing turned upward and the bright spring sun played a parting game with the single jewel in the papal ring, coaxing from it the tiniest flash of brilliant light.

Of above medium height, slim and long-boned, bald, brown-eyed, endowed with the typical "Roman" nose—straight with narrow nostrils and a slight hump in its middle—Profumi was Italian of the Italians, hot-blooded, realistic, witty, ruthless if power demanded it, indirect in any close infighting, charming or icily forbidding, depending on the circumstances. Profumi could hypnotize a visitor, friend or foe, with the keen vivacity of his look, the powerful understatement of his remarks, and the eloquent images those slender hands of his drew in the air. But no one ever missed the strength of his mouth and chin, even when a smile relaxed his face.

Born of an old, established Catholic family, Eugenio Profumi became a cleric and ecclesiastic in his sixteenth year, was deep in affairs of state by the age of twenty-four, elected pope at sixty, had been acquainted in adult life with nearly all the greats of his mid-twentieth-century world, and was a man with only one aim in life.

"To maintain the greatness of the Roman Church" would have been his unequivocal reply to any question about that unique aim. As a child, as a young man, as priest, as bishop, as cardinal, as pope, Profumi had always wanted exactly that.

He had a specific meaning for that phrase. The rock-bottom fact for this man was a geographical one—as, indeed, it had been for 262 popes before him. The only personal representative of God on earth was the Pope. And the Pope was the bishop of one particular church that stood in the city of Rome, Italy. That church was in Rome because God had willed it so. The Roman fact, he called it, the geographical association between this one special man and this one place.

Every other church, every other bishop and diocese and congregation, ruled itself only. But the Bishop of Rome, with his bureaucracy—the Vatican—as his instrument, ruled over every one of them, wherever they might be. For Profumi, the Roman fact was Rome's unique greatness; Rome's rule was uniquely universal; Rome's unique offer was God and his salvation.

Until this spring of 1945, there had been no doubt in his mind about the principal means of Roman rule; it was the clerical bureaucracy of his Vatican, with its honeycomb of ministries and offices and bureaucrats housed on that quiet Roman hill, its emissaries and legates and representatives all over the world. Within that context, Profumi had until very recently subordinated all of himself to being the ideal embodiment of Christ's vicar on earth.

On this spring morning, though still carried forward by that sure sense of destiny he had never lost, as sure as always of God in heaven above his head and of the Enemy condemned to hell beneath his feet, sustained by the saints, devoted to the Virgin, now this strong man was caught in a vortex of doubts that no raw newcomer such as Richard Lansing could ever have suspected churned within the graceful tranquillity of the Apostolic Palace.

About one thing Profumi had no doubt. Roman rule by the Bishop of Rome was paramount. But the instrument of that rule—the Vatican with its immersion in the politics, the diplomacy, and the economics of the nations—that had become another matter. At the heel of this terrible six-year war, nearly every facet of politics and diplomacy and economics appeared increasingly so godless, so irreligious, that merely to remain immersed in them by all the traditional means was to become as godless and irreligious as the nations.

To be sure, there were many in the Vatican—most, perhaps—who would not dare agree with this dawning realization of Profumi's. But for this Pope, one question had become relentless in his mind. Wasn't it fast becoming evident that Rome, as things stood, could no longer leaven that mounting godlessness and irreligion with its spiritual message?

And yet if he broke away, withdrew his Vatican and his Church from that immersion—what was the alternative? The catacombs? He could find no answer to those questions. He needed some light from God, some sign. . . .

"Guten Morgen, Heilige Vater." In answer to Profumi's bell, Father Joachim Lanser had come quietly, quickly up the spiral staircase from the radio room below. He and the other Germans in the household always spoke their native language with Profumi. Crew-cut, ascetic-faced, above medium height, dressed in a simple black cassock with a sash, never without dark-tinted sunglasses day or night, Lanser was one of two Jesuits who were Profumi's close and trusted collaborators in the day-to-day routine of the papacy. The other, Father Kensich, remained down in the radio room.

That pair made up half the number of people whose entire lives revolved about this slight papal figure. Bavarian Sister Philomena, his housekeeper, and Commendatore Stefanori, his valet, filled out the number. Faithful servants, all knew every detail of Profumi's life, all of his moods, his habits, quirks, tics, reactions, dislikes, how long he slept, his taste in food and wine and humor and books and people. They had made it their business and their life's preoccupation to know all that, as though they had no life but his and wanted no other. They communicated with few words, seemed to sense Profumi's wishes and needs, and then moved to do what was necessary.

Profumi crossed the rust-colored Persian carpet to his desk. He scanned the appointment pad that lay open on one side. Lanser knew what was weighing on the Pontiff's mind, but he waited silently for His Holiness to come to it.

There was a mission in progress, initiated by Papa Profumi. Perhaps "gamble" was a better word. But, either way, the matter was closely connected with the Pope's deepest concerns. Despite the danger involved, no one less trusted or less powerful than his intimate colleague and old friend, Maestro Guido de la Valle, could be charged with it.

The Maestro had left for Milan two days before. Surely he had arrived safely; and surely he was still in that region. But no radio signal had been received.

Profumi straightened in his high-backed chair. He was not nearly ready to consider the darkest possibilities.

"Now! When will the Maestro be back, do you think? This morning, perhaps . . . ?" The note of hope was clear in the question.

"I don't think so, Holiness. More probably late this evening. There are difficulties and dangers. . . ."

"Yes, yes." Profumi seemed embarrassed by his show of anxiety. He had known there would be no pretense in the Jesuit's answer, but he appeared to shrink at the words. His mind raced yet again along the sharp edges of all the policy gambles and forecasts that had etched tension and worry like visible pain on his features these last few weeks.

He stood up and paced the study with slow steps as he so often did when conferring with familiar visitors. "Yes, perhaps. . . . Well, we will have to wait, Father. Let us keep praying. And have patience! Prayer and patience. The Maestro will return as soon as he can. Let us pray he succeeds. If he fails . . ." Profumi broke off, as doubts rushed at him again.

Lanser's eyes met the Pontiff's. He nodded, and went down again to the radio room.

[3]

Guido de la Valle's skull seemed to vibrate beneath his scalp. An uncontrolled shivering ran through him, as if draining something vital and irretrievable from the core of his being.

"I tried." He hardly whispered the words in the back of the smoothly riding sedan.

The driver heard, and responded with a glance into the rearview mirror. In his five years of service with this man, Franze Sagastume had never seen such a look of distraught apprehension on the Maestro's face; and perhaps he saw something more there as well. It was hard to tell.

Sagastume, his own features unchanged, turned his eyes back to the road that led down from the hills toward Milan. He braked a little. It wouldn't do to follow the van too closely. He took one hand from the steering wheel and placed it on the weapon lying across his lap.

The Maestro, looking much older now than his forty-seven years, barely noticed the changing landscape as the car he had commandeered two days before from the Cardinal of Milan tracked the van with the miniature red flags flying on its roof. His mind was riveted elsewhere. On that farmhouse. He could not pull his thoughts away. "I did try. . . ."

The Pope's commission had been unusual, even unwelcome in some ways. But it had been clear. And from the beginning, Guido saw certain advantages that could come from it.

In terms of mere field intelligence, the Pope knew what all the world knew: The defeated dictator Benito Mussolini, known in headier days as Il Duce, The Leader, was fleeing for his life. With him were more than a dozen of his closest aides, and his mistress, Clara Petacci. He carried in his possession a heavy and slowing load of tens of millions in Italy's gold reserves. And he had with him a pouch crammed full of important state papers. He had fled north. He would try to make it into neutral Switzerland, with its haven banks, and its promise of sanctuary, or perhaps make a last stand in the mountains. The dictator, pursued by angry bands of armed men who wanted to tear him to pieces, had finally found a secure refuge for himself and Petacci in an isolated farmhouse near the high rocky mountain village of Bonzanigo, overlooking Lake Como. There he awaited an armed escort. But the Pope knew the impossible odds against Mussolini's even surviving, let alone making it across the Swiss border. Dead, he would serve no purpose; or, at least, he would hold no wolves at bay. Alive, in the Vatican, in Profumi's hands, Mussolini could still be a political pawn—perhaps, in the Pope's skilled hands, even be used to halt the warring armies and bring the Allies to the negotiating table instead of their forcing an unconditional surrender on Italy.

Profumi wanted to avoid other consequences, even more dire than unconditional surrender.

"Il Duce will be slaughtered and bled like a pig by the Communist partisans." Those had been the very words Profumi had used. "He must be saved, Maestro, from the hate he has created. Not for his own sake. For the sake of Italy. And for the sake of much more. If there is a public spectacle of killing, vengeful killing, if Italians acquiesce in such a blasphemy, it will be just that extra ounce added to the caldron of evil already boiling. The brew will spill over and corrode all of life's goodness. Italy will become the Devil's Workshop. Worse still may happen. I see a horrible specter on the human horizon, attracted by such public evil. The councils of nations will be the salons of Satan."

Profumi's reasons, as Guido understood very well, were complex. But they boiled down to one thing: In the Pope's mind, Guido's success or failure would have echoes in history for millions who would know little or nothing of what would happen in these coming days. In the Pope's view, failure now would be directly linked to that specter of evil—Profumi talked of it as if he could almost see its shadow looming over the world horizon, even as everyone else was beginning to talk about victory or defeat; at any rate, about peace at last.

The Maestro had listened to Profumi carefully. He had missed nothing; he never did. Still, in his own mind the most important thing was that looming peace. And perhaps his own thoughts had been more fixed on the plans he had to make and to put in motion in order to keep the Vatican strong in the scramble for power that would soon be born out of this war. The interruption of this mission to snatch Il Duce from his deserved fate was unwelcome delay. Still, he had thought even then, if he was successful, there would be the Fascist gold. And the papers; doubtless they would be useful too. A rare prize, even.

In any case, unwelcome delay or unexpected opportunity, Guido would do as the Pope had asked. Guido de la Valle had been as faithful a servant to popes as his father and grandfather had been before him. Never had any of them refused a papal summons or request. Seldom had any of them, Guido above all, returned without securing the goal—or some part of it. It all lay in what you thought of as success.

The mission had gone easily enough at the start. A few discreet calls, a blunt conversation or two, and Guido, with the huge Sagastume at his side as bodyguard and driver as always, was aboard a small unmarked plane, courtesy of the German High Command, hedge-hopping the three hundred miles from Rome to Milan. Once there, another quiet conversation at the cardinal archbishop's residence had secured the black four-door sedan with the SCV license plates marking it as a Vatican-registered vehicle.

After that, it was a matter of learning all he could of Mussolini's whereabouts. Milan was a city without government or order by then;

whole sectors were controlled by whoever could keep the upper hand—Germans, Allies, Communists, partisans, bandits, thugs, Mafia. Guido spoke to all of them, traced and retraced the trail Mussolini tried to camouflage as he doubled back and forth over his tracks like the hunted fox he had become.

It had taken two days and one fateful deal before Guido finally reached Mussolini. The deal was with a man Guido had known before only by reputation, a veteran Communist fighter known in the underground as "Colonel Valerio"—a fanatic but a realist, Guido decided, as they faced one another by the stone wall that edged the road below the high mountain village of Bonzanigo. A man he could deal with, if need be.

Bonzanigo overlooked Lake Como. In the early light by the roadside, Valerio described for Guido the isolated farmhouse where Il Duce and Petacci and the others awaited an armed escort and prepared for the final dash across the lake and into Switzerland.

"But he will not make it, Maestro. Not to Switzerland. And not to Rome, whatever the Pope may say! We are determined to give him a people's trial. It will be best if he puts himself in our safekeeping. You want his state papers? You have made arrangements for the gold he is carrying? Fine by us! All we want is Benito Mussolini. Arrange that, and then do what you like!"

"No violence to Il Duce," Guido had said. He *had* tried.

"Rest assured, Maestro. All justice will be done."

Valerio's directions to the farmhouse had been pinpoint accurate. Further proof, if proof were needed, that Valerio, and probably others who knew these mountains, would have closed in anyway, in time.

Il Duce's aides had been armed, as had Mussolini himself. But the SCV license plates were Guido's safe-pass as Sagastume drove up to the house.

Inside, Guido presented the Pope's offer first. His manner was intense. Time was short. He mentioned the love of Christ and the Pope's love. He repeated it all several times. Safe-conduct to Rome. Sanctuary guaranteed by the Pope himself. The dictator's debt to Italy, to the people. Avoid further horrors. The Pope's own protection: he repeated the point, though with Valerio's threat still clear in his memory.

"Thank the Holy Father." Mussolini's reply was weary. Resigned, even, Guido thought. But not hesitant. "It is too late. I am in the hands of history. I have my destiny."

Despite the contempt and disdain Guido felt for this despot who refused to bargain, he was impressed by the impassive confidence expressed in those words. History. Destiny.

Unexpectedly, though, it was Petacci who made the deepest impression on Guido. He would never forget her role in that day's events, from first to last. He would never forget her eyes on him, her look that said she read his hate for her beloved, recognized the lack of enthusiasm in his dutiful presentation of the papal offer of safety for them all—for she was included in the offer; her parents had made a special plea to the Pope in her behalf. But no. She had decided, she said, to follow Mussolini. "There is no dealing with hate, Maestro. Papa Profumi is wrong. I have only a woman's love to fight with. This is how I want it."

Well, he had tried. Hadn't he?

The conversation turned to other matters, to things one might think of as last arrangements. The dictator's estate. His state documents. The Fascist Party gold.

And then, finally, Guido presented Valerio's offer, his promise to "help Mussolini on his journey."

"Do *you* believe him, Maestro?" Guido could not tell from Mussolini's voice if that was a question or a cynical commentary.

Either way, Guido's answer was a simple statement of fact. "There seems little other choice for you now."

It was agreed then. On Valerio's word to Guido. On Guido's word to Mussolini. Mussolini and Petacci would accept transport in the van with the miniature red flags fluttering on its roof.

By the time it was all settled and Guido left the farmhouse, the morning was bright. Sagastume drove him the mile or so down the mountain to where the stone wall separated the road from a grand mansion called Villa Belmonte. There Valerio waited. A word with the colonel. The van departed up the road toward the farmhouse. The wait. Five minutes. Ten. Fifteen. Never had Lake Como seemed so blue, so beautiful, so calm as on that morning, in those moments. Never did the peaks of the distant Alps beckon with such promise of peace. Never was the silence so golden.

Guido turned at the soft sound of tires on the road. He watched from morning's long shadows as the van stopped. First Valerio got out, his men gathering behind. Someone opened the van's rear doors. Valerio ordered Mussolini and his woman out. The partisan's eyes shone now with the full blazing light of fanaticism and hate and vengeance and victory. He pushed the pair against the wall. Guido made no move, no sound, from where he stood.

For just an instant all seemed frozen. Even the morning breeze held its breath. Petacci was the first to understand. She shattered the crystal of stopped time with a scream, stepped in front of Mussolini, screaming and screaming at Valerio, at the guerrillas. She never saw Guido standing in the shadow.

They leveled their automatic weapons. Petacci turned her back to the executioners, clung to Mussolini, threw her arms around his neck. He held her and planted his feet wide apart. His chin jutted out. His eyes stared defiantly at Valerio. Abruptly Petacci's screams mixed with the explosions of firing guns in an ear-splitting chorus of death. The first bullets that hit Mussolini passed through her body.

For a few seconds, the two of them, still alive, lay writhing on the ground in their agony, Petacci's face above Mussolini's, her arms still around him. And then there was an orgy of firing and shouting and noise and blood. Round after round of bullets struck heads, torsos, legs, forcing them to move and jerk as though they could never die, until finally the shouting and the shooting had stopped and blood was everywhere and all movement had ceased.

At what moment the partisans had gone back to the farmhouse, Guido was not certain. At what moment he thought he heard the echo of more firing in the mountain, or how much time passed before the van returned again with the corpses of Mussolini's aides, he was not certain. He remembered clearly only one thought as he turned from the carnage and waited for all to be finished in this bargain. His gaze wandered out over Lake Como, that bluest of lakes in the morning time. "Everything bloody in Italy takes place in golden sunlight."

It was the first killing Guido had ever seen. Even for a man accustomed to wielding enormous power from great distances, the power of killing one man, and one woman, the power of death from only yards away, was a shocking thing. It was that first shock, surely, that made him shiver so; but as he got control of it, almost forced it to drain away by strength of will, it took something with it. The ability to be shocked at all is a great defense against evil; it was that ability, perhaps, that lessened for Guido.

All the way down the mountain road as they followed that van, he fought for control, reasoning with himself about it all. Profumi was not here, on the spot. His Holiness could not judge the situation at a distance. Anyway, there had been no possibility of saving Mussolini. One way or the other, Valerio, or any of a dozen others, was going to get him and his companions. No one, papal emissary or not, could have done more. And at least he had secured those important papers and the gold. Others wouldn't have salvaged even that.

Perhaps the worst of it was that none of this was his choice. If he had had his way, oh so long ago, he would never have seen these killings at all, never would have been here in Milan these two days, or in Rome. The life he had wanted was a different one, isolated from everyone but his God in a monastery on the barest cliffs of Mount Athos in northern Greece. He had spent eight years there in his youth. That, he always thought, had been the only truly happy time he had ever passed. It had ended too soon, and abruptly. His uncle, who was in his time the Keeper of the Bargain that was the family trust, had suddenly found out that he had only months to live. He had come and fetched Guido down from those heights of prayer and peaceful living. It was Guido's turn, his uncle said. It was Guido's obligation and trust now to become Keeper of the Bargain, and then to pass that trust intact to the next de la Valle when his own time should come to die. Guido was reminded that the Vatican and his Church could not survive without the strength of money and worldly power at their disposal. He was reminded that his was a singular trust; that everything that mattered depended greatly on his keeping that trust; that it was not possible for him to refuse. And he did not.

But dear God, it plunged him too deeply into the world. With what nostalgia did he sometimes long for that peace and ecstasy he had found in prayer at Athos. Now all that remained to him was isolation. Because so much of what he did must be completely secret, it kept him apart from everyone. Even those closest to him, even his beloved sister, Agathi, could not know it all. Only Helmut, his nephew and his heir; and his chauffeur-bodyguard, Sagastume, who was with him everywhere: they were the only ones who had some little idea. Yet even Helmut would not know of his part in this murderous day. Only Valerio. And Sagastume. And God.

"Maestro . . ."

Sagastume's even voice from the driver's seat pulled Guido away from his tangled thoughts. He was calmer now. His head still throbbed, though, and he passed a steady hand over his silvery hair as if to banish the pain. He would see the whole thing through to the end, whatever that end might be. It would be important to know what was done with the bodies; he could not report to the Pontiff with only half the matter done. And there were the details concerning the gold to arrange as well, the banks in Milan and Switzerland to be contacted before he could return to Rome.

The van was slowing in front of Guido's car. They were in a part of Milan unfamiliar to the Maestro, approaching a little-known square, the Piazzale Loreto, in the heart of the sector of the city under Valerio's control. Guido indicated a narrow street, an alleyway almost, off to one side of the square; Sagastume pulled the sedan into its shadows and left the engine running. Standing on the running board of the car, Guido could see all that was happening on the opposite side of the Piazza.

It became clear in a matter of moments that the bestial insanity of that day was not over. Valerio's van circled the piazzale once, twice, horn blaring, Valerio shouting from its window, waving bystanders to follow, to gather in. Storekeepers and customers ran to see what the sudden excitement was about. The name of Mussolini was heard, and repeated, and then ran like wildfire. "Mussolini is dead! Valerio has killed Il Duce!" Women ran down from flats, children in tow. Word spread in every direction. By the time the van pulled to a halt near a ruined gas station, crowds filled the square, and every balcony and rooftop was chock-full of anxious, excited spectators. Was it true? Did anybody know? Was Il Duce dead? Everywhere Guido could see members of the partisans, armed and grim men, come to taste the final triumph of five years of fighting. Cameras seemed to appear from nowhere. There was even an artist perched atop a nearby car, sketching everything in hurried charcoal strokes. The Piazzale Loreto, named for the house of the Holy Family, had become a colosseum, and in the frenzy of expectation, the desecration seemed to cross no one's mind.

Colonel Valerio, clad in his tattered uniform, his automatic weapon strapped across his back, jumped from the cab of the van to the ground. At his brisk command, one of his men threw open the back doors of the van, and a dozen more began heaving bodies out.

The crowd hushed suddenly. And then, as with the Colosseum crowds of centuries before, began a chorus as each body was hurled from the vehicle.

"Uno!" At first it was a few voices only. Then more. "Due! . . . Tre! . . ." It became a roaring ocean of sound: *". . . Dieci! . . .* DODICI! *. . . SEDICI!*

The sixteenth corpse was the last; as it hit the cement, Valerio raised his arms in triumph and circled the grisly pile, basking in the cheers.

Guido's face hardened as he watched every move.

When Valerio stopped his circling and lowered his arms, the crowd hushed as on a signal. Valerio scrutinized each body, reaching down to twist the heads of some that were face down. On his command, six of the bodies, one a woman's, were seized brusquely by arms or legs—the woman's by its hair—and dragged into a row beneath what was left of the roof of the bombed-out gas station, a single steel girder still in place between two ragged walls.

The first in the row was the body of a stocky, barrel-chested, bald and big-headed man dressed in jackboots and riding breeches, naked now from the waist up, bullet holes and caked blood clear on his torso. Murmurs rippled through the crowd from front to back: Il Duce! It was true, then! Next to him, the body of the woman, shoeless, in a blouse and skirt, her black hair matted with dirt and blood. More murmurs, like growls: Claretta! Clara Petacci!

Beside the woman's body, four Fascist leaders, all of them known by sight to everyone in the piazzale, to everyone in Italy.

A new ripple of expectation traveled through the crowd.

"Show us! Show us! Show us the Fascist pig and his whore! Show us!" A fresh wave of roaring demand grew as each of the six "special" corpses was tied by the feet and then hoisted, one after the other, to hang head down, strung from that steel girder.

"Mussolini . . . !" The shout became a crescendo as Il Duce's body was jerked upward.

Then, *"Petacci . . . !"*—but a sudden hush as her skirt fell over her head. She was naked beneath it. "NO!" they screamed. They wanted to see her face, read her suffering. Her body was quickly lowered and her skirt tied to her legs with a length of rope. Then up again to hateful jeers. *"Petacci . . . !"*

Then the others—*"Barracu! . . . Pavolini! . . . Mezzasomma! . . . Zerbino! . . ."*—until they all hung there, the greats of the Italian Fascists, swaying and spinning in a ghastly laziness. Petacci's eyes were closed tightly, the lips clamped, as if in death she would not give up one secret of her love. Mussolini's big eyes were wide open and staring, an expression of terror still stamped on them, seeming to watch as the ten bodies of the lesser aides were piled on the pavement beneath his head, almost as an afterthought of indignity. Il Duce's great lower jaw was agape, his scream of agony in his last moment of life frozen in a soundless and never-ending cry.

By now the crowd was caught in a delirium of excess. People laughed into each other's faces, shook hands and clapped one another on the back, embraced, jostled and shoved, clambered over each other to get a better view. Children on their parents' shoulders waved little flags that seemed to pop up from nowhere like sudden flowers and added their shrill cries: "Death!" "They are dead!" "All dead!"

The sustained cascade of jeers and catcalls and curses was not sufficient for the hate. Stones and lumps of mortar began flying through the air. Mud, pieces of wood, old shoes, bricks, pelted like filth onto the miserable remains of the once glorious emperor, head of the ludicrous Third Roman Empire; onto his faithful mistress and his fellow Fascists. There were even occasional bursts of small-arms fire. It was a public celebration of joy in the letting of human blood, of revenge for its own sake, of pain and public disgrace for the sake of ugly delight that comes from other men's misery.

The Devil's Workshop. The Pontiff's words had been uncannily accurate. The Maestro had seen enough. He knew everything there was to be known. He knew that he had connived in this. He knew that, like this crowd, no responsible group of Italians would repudiate it. He knew that none of the warring Allies—British, French, Soviet, American—would repudiate it.

Hadn't he himself talked with representatives of each of them in his two-day hunt? Hadn't some of them actually used their authority to connive along with him, to plot to this very end? They would have done it themselves. Guido thought, if they had had Valerio's nerve. They would all accept it as a stepping-stone in the progress of their plans. Only one public authority, only the slight figure in the white robe, waiting in his Vatican, with no armored divisions at his command, and with only the moral authority and spiritual armor guaranteed him from heaven, only he would refuse to regard this public blasphemy as a step forward.

Guido thought again, still painfully, of Profumi's warning of that hideous shadow slouching over the horizon. Part of his mission had been to stop it, or at least to slow its progress, to gain a little time, a little leverage to use against it. *"Il Duce will be slaughtered and bled like a pig by the Communist partisians. . . . He must be saved, Maestro . . . For the sake of Italy. And for the sake of much more."*

Guido could not answer even the memory of that warning now. He could not even whisper, "I tried. . . ."

He stepped down heavily from the running board of the sedan. Sagastume opened the door to the rear seat for him.

"You had no part in this, Maestro. You have no guilt in this. You did what had to be done. It could not be helped." Sagastume's words, far more than the still unchanging expression of his face, told of his worry for his master.

When Guido did not reply, the chauffeur closed the door behind him and slid behind the wheel, his weapon on the seat beside him. The greatest danger was past. The sedan, unnoticed in the shadowed alleyway, moved quietly away from the Piazzale Loreto, regained a main boulevard, and headed toward downtown Milan.

[4]

That day of waiting appeared ordinary on the surface. Papa Profumi had his usual conferences with officials of the Secretariat of State. He went through all six pages of *Osservatore Romano,* the Vatican newspaper. He studied the day's batch of documents, and noticed among them the routine memorandum from Da Brescia about the arrival of Richard Lansing; Profumi required such memoranda from his subordinates. He read his Breviary and spent some time in the chapel, praying. He had a few private audiences with some panicky South American diplomats. He did not take the usual siesta. He had another round of interviews—Professore Soldi, editor of *Osservatore Romano;* Cardinal Rivali, administrator of St. Peter's Basilica; Giuseppe Tambroni, the Vatican cobbler, who bustled about for some moments fitting His Holiness with a new pair of walking shoes. There were some few others. The routine of work and prayer served to move him through the hours.

Evening was another matter. Sister Philomena laid out an early dinner. A scant serving of beef, a few vegetables, a glass of red wine mixed with water, a digestive biscuit. But when she came to clear away the things, she found the Pontiff had hardly touched it. Philomena, with her solid Bavarian peasant face, her starched white wimple and all-enveloping black clothes, moved like a knowing angel in Profumi's life. She removed the meal, a curling upward of her left eyebrow the only visible expression of her concern. Like the others in Profumi's household, she knew when to say nothing.

As the evening wore on, Philomena and the others could hear Profumi's restless footsteps. He prayed in the light-green chapel; rummaged in the white-walled bedroom to find a pen he had left there the previous morning; went down the inner stairway, holding on to its brass railing as it creaked and shook, to speak a few words with Lanser and Kensich, who were working late in the radio room; then back again to his study. He tried for a time to work at his desk by the shaded light of a small desk lamp—wartime imposed some blackout precautions even on a pope. But he could not put his mind to anything except the expected return of Guido de la Valle, and the endless repetition of possible events and probable happenings, playing out as though triggered by so many automatic trip wires. The weight of such thoughts made the slow hours increasingly oppressive.

Finally, when Rome was deep in night darkness, Profumi's valet, Commendatore Stefanori, admitted a solitary visitor to the high-ceilinged anteroom outside the papal study. A moment more and the Maestro's tall and bulky form appeared in the shadow of the study's doorway.

"Maestro . . . ?" Profumi compressed all his questions into the one word.

"Holiness." Guido stepped forward into the pool of soft light surrounding the shaded desk lamp and knelt to kiss the Fisherman's Ring.

When he straightened, the answers to all the Pope's questions could be read clearly on the Maestro's face, white with the words he was suppressing.

It was the Pope who spoke the truth he saw there. "Il Duce is dead."

Guido nodded, almost imperceptibly. "It was all that Your Holiness had hoped to avoid." Guido did not fill in the details; he did not think he had the strength to live that horror over again so soon. In a matter of hours, they would show Profumi the actual photographs. That would be time enough.

The Pope turned away. "What did he say to our offer?" Profumi's voice was a hoarse whisper. "What were his words?"

"That it came too late, Holiness."

"And the woman?"

The scene forced itself into Guido's mind. Petacci stepping in front of Mussolini, screaming at the partisans, the first bursts of gunfire, her scream choking on the blood gushing up into her throat . . .

"She would not leave him, Holiness." Guido kept his voice level with some effort.

"He did not get the grace of God to accept our offer." Profumi spoke as though to himself.

"Holiness, I don't think he'd have had the nerve to face the Almighty if he had begged mercy from any man alive—even from Your Holiness."

"He didn't get the grace, Maestro."

"No, of course not, Holiness. He did wish the Holy See to receive the bulk of his estate and the Party funds and some documents." It was all he had retrieved, all he had to offer.

The Pope dismissed the subject with a wave of his right hand. He walked toward one of the windows giving onto the piazza, and looked out as if surveying his Church, his beloved Italy, and the whole world under the blanket of night. In a way, he was doing just that, in typical Profumi fashion—piercing the surrounding gloom with little stabs of hardheaded realistic logic, peering at effects and consequences one, two, ten, twenty years from now.

So. Mussolini was dead. Obviously with everybody's connivance. Victorious Allies. Retreating Germans. Vengeful partisans. Ravening Communists bent on fashioning their most useful tool, chaos. For all he knew, even with the Maestro's connivance, although . . . He glanced around at Guido, then turned back to the window. No. He had worked with this man for decades, had learned to trust him implicitly. The Maestro had followed instructions, he was sure.

All he had hoped to avoid, Guido had said. "Was it—was it a public spectacle?"

"In every sense of the word, a human blasphemy, Holiness. A national blasphemy." Guido drew in a deep breath, hoping that was the end of it, at least for now.

Profumi's face took on a new grimness. Mussolini himself in his heyday had behaved like an animal. Nothing but sheer horror would have satisfied the blood lust of the other animals who mauled him. Profumi had written them all off long ago, Mussolini and his friends and his enemies. But such a death! A blasphemy. That was the word the Maestro had used. Not a death for defense. Certainly not for strategy; that should have kept him alive! Not for any cause of war or of peace or of morality. No cause, in fact, but death's own. And wasn't that the very point now, the single thing that riveted his attention, that dictated the policy of every nation on earth?

Beyond the night darkness, about fifty million men were fighting this war. Not for any moral values. No longer even for patriotic values. Just for power. Destroy your enemy. Totally. Without mercy. Foment war, hate, revenge, and use it for power's sake. Even when your enemy is prostrate. Destroy him. Bloodily. That principle of power, stripped of all other function, was washing away the last few grains of traditional decency, honesty, fear of God, love of neighbor. What was left was like an ugly skeleton without flesh to make it splendid or beautiful or provide it with any motive beyond itself. That was the stark portrait of power now. Without mercy or compassion to temper it, or so much as a glance of love to soften it. In the new postwar world, only that power would count, that skeleton stripped of all the ancient dreams.

Profumi scrutinized the shifting shadows of the Roman night. What weapons had he, the vicar of Christ on earth, to fight against this new thing? It had about it the stench of death from which it sprang. Evil incarnate. Satan unleashed. Could this Vatican as it was today contend successfully against that? Had this universal bureaucracy that so many had learned to think of as "the Church" been built in order to pit power against power? Where would that lead? His mind returned to Mussolini's death and to the only answer he could see to his question:

"You said a human blasphemy, Maestro." He spoke without turning from the window.

"Yes, Holiness. Just one more sign of what this war has let loose among the nations."

"Well." Profumi turned slowly, then, drawing each word out along the lines of his thought: "How can this Holy See carry on as it has up to now?" It was a theme he and the Maestro had talked over before, not a favorite topic for Guido, the Pontiff knew; but not one that would disappear on that account. "We maintain diplomatic and political, financial and cultural relations with this world of nations—all, of course, with one aim: to promote our spiritual and religious mission. That was fine, Maestro, for as long as it was possible for us to exercise that mission among the nations, however indirectly. But now, can we go on and be a part of this system?"

"But, Holiness, the Church . . ."

"Ah, the Church!" Profumi raised a hand. "You mean the clerical bureaucracy here and abroad." Profumi turned back to the window, putting both white-sleeved arms out and resting his hands on the sill. "The house of Our Catholicism." There was almost a wistful note in his tone for a moment. "It was solid, Maestro. *Dio!* But that house of ours seemed so solid."

Profumi's fingers opened and closed on the rim of the sill, as if to feel that solidity just one more time. "But somewhere, at certain times, in little things and in great things, we in the Church didn't take a stand of our own, a Catholic stand. We conformed to the system because we were part of the system. Our bishops didn't take a stand. Our priests didn't. Our theologians and teachers didn't. We in the Vatican didn't. We went along with it all. We told ourselves we were missioners. But it was the world and its system that missionized us, converted us to its way of thinking. We became like the rest. We failed because we became like them."

"Holiness," Guido answered, "that is the past. We have built up such a strength now: our prestige is so high, our diplomatic power is so strong, our finances are perhaps the soundest in the whole world. We cannot abandon that strength, that"—he stuttered, reaching for the proper word—"that preponderance. If we don't use that, how do we proceed, Holiness?"

Guido's aim in life was no different from Profumi's—to maintain the greatness of the Catholic Church. But he was persuaded that everything would crumble—the whole edifice, the entire bureaucracy, all that made faith real for millions—if it were not for the solidity they had worked so hard to achieve. He had sacrificed everything for that solidity. He and others. The Church reached everywhere because of those sacrifices, because of that solidity. The Pope himself knew that. A hundred popes before this one had known that. When this topic had arisen between them before, Guido had been sure that, with time, as the strains imposed by the war faded, Profumi would become again the champion of that old, traditional solidity they had both accepted as their trust, each in his own way, each in the role assigned him. But now? Perhaps it was his weariness, the horrors of his past few days, that allowed a feeling of foreboding to shake him. His voice began to rise.

"We must be prepared, Holiness. The world after this war is going to be rebuilt on money and technology, run by money managers and technocrats. We are perfectly positioned to be their equals, members of their club, and wield our strength for great accomplishments." He faltered; a freezing chill swept his body and made him realize he had been sweating.

Profumi, surprised at the change in the Maestro's tone, turned to look at his old friend. A wonderful smile of warmth and concern immediately melted the stern lines on his face. "Maestro, I have kept you too long. You have been through much. It will be all right. We'll make the right decisions, you and I. If we have to make some fundamental change, then that change will be the least of our worries.

"And I'm not even sure we'll have to do that. I've prayed for a sign, Maestro. Some small sign from God. He will do his part." The Pontiff's smile was as steadying as his faith. "And we will do ours. Now your part is to go and take some rest."

"Holiness, my tiredness doesn't matter." Guido was reluctant to leave just yet. "A few hours of sleep will make me a new man. There are things we must discuss."

"Indeed, there are. But not tonight, Maestro. Tomorrow."

"Tomorrow, permit me to remind Your Holiness, there will be special visitors."

Profumi knitted his brows. "Special visitors? Ah, yes! *Dio!* Now, of all times!" He made the words sound like an indignant rejection of some unseemly proposition. But yes, he did remember. The commander of all Allied forces in Italy, together with the principal officers in his GHQ, was to pay a formal visit tomorrow, the twenty-ninth. "There will be no change in Allied stubbornness; but We will see them. We will try one more time." Profumi used the papal "We" now, as if already rehearsing for that formal visit on the morrow.

There was one more thing, one more promise Guido had made. "As Your Holiness knows, it was by courtesy of German General Kesselring, and in the general's own plane, that I was finally able to reach Il Duce this morning. The general wishes Your Holiness to receive Obergruppenführer Wolff one more time. Tomorrow at the latest. Later may be too late for the general."

Profumi's face was a picture of revolt. Guido kept on. "Kesselring is holding about fourteen thousand prisoners, Jews and Christians—some ten priests among them. He wants to negotiate an exchange. A quid pro quo." He waited for the explosion. Profumi stood there for a few seconds, taut, staring; then he half turned away.

"As you arrange it, Maestro. Let's see this miserable business through to the end."

Guido did not mention the matter of the "Swiss Windfall." Tomorrow would do. "Tomorrow, then, Holiness. First the Allied commander, at five o'clock in the afternoon. Then the German."

Profumi nodded. Guido kissed the Pope's ring, backed away a few steps in the customary fashion, then turned and stepped through the doorway.

In the anteroom, Sister Philomena, keeping vigil now, sat at her desk, saying her Rosary. Guido glanced his farewell at her. Commendatore Stefanori escorted him as far as the elevator. On the ground floor, Amadeo Solimando, beret in hand, was waiting to check out this last and most important of all papal visitors. Guido could not miss the concern on his face. He told him what he could. Mussolini was dead. There was much to be done. Much trouble to be faced.

Amadeo watched from the door as the Maestro walked heavily toward the limousine. The giant, Sagastume, stood holding the door open for him. To the tiny Amadeo, the solidly built, seven-foot frame of the bodyguard-chauffeur seemed like a work of sinister masonry turned to flesh. As Sagastume closed the door behind his master, he turned heavy-lidded black eyes toward the door, the teeth in his small mouth bared in a quick smile. Amadeo hastily shut the door and touched his scrotum to ward off the evil eye. *"Ni italiano ni umano,"* he murmured. Neither Italian nor human.

Four hundred yards or so from the Apostolic Palace, Richard Lansing suddenly came wide awake in his temporary quarters. It took him a moment to remember that he was lying in the huge, canopied four-poster in Cardinal Krementz's bedroom.

He got up, a not unpleasant excitement—Roman fever, it was called here—drawing him to the window. Silver-clean moonlight flowed in around him, as fragments of his first day in Rome flooded his thoughts. In his mind, he saw the piazza of St. Peter's in the morning light. He smiled at the memory of little Amadeo's welcome and of Pasquinelli's mournful face. He remembered those piercing eyes of Monsignore Da Brescia, and almost felt the presence of Morandi and Dell'Angelo as they had watched him from the far end of that long office. How small in size these men of great power are, he thought; and then he thought how odd a thought that was. As odd as the thought that everyone he had met that day seemed so naturally a part of this place, this hub of his world where he was still a stranger. Even their dress seemed different. Or something about the way they wore their collars and cassocks. As though they had been born to them, the way princes had once been born to crowns and diadems. Would he ever be like that? Did he want to be like that? So naturally a part of this place?

Although he could not imagine it at that moment, all those little men of power who seemed to belong here so naturally had gone through their own bouts of Roman fever too, once upon a time, before they lost their innocence to a system in which they had resolved to flourish at any cost.

Lansing stayed for some time, looking at the twinkling diamond stars set out on the velvet of the sky, as though they were incandescent tea leaves in which he might read what promise this Rome held out to him.

Amadeo made certain all the doors were secure, the alarm system turned on, and the master switch for the lights turned off. Then he crossed himself and muttered a prayer under his breath for the Holy Father, as he finally climbed the stairs to the apartment he shared with his wife and family above the main door of the Secretariat. He gave one more glance out of the parlor window to see that the courtyard of St. Damasus was clear, and up at the light that still shone dimly from the Pope's study. Then he tiptoed into the bedroom.

He needn't have taken such care to be quiet; Martha, his wife, was never able to sleep until Amadeo was safe beside her.

"You are very late tonight, Amadino. Is there trouble?"

"Sì, sì. Grande guai," Amadeo sighed as he kicked off his shoes and began to undress. "Much grief and trouble. For the poor Holy Father. For our Rome. For the Church. For Italy. For the whole world."

"God is still God, *caro?*" she asked as they lay in bed. Martha had her little sarcasms.

"Sometimes, *cara,* I think even the Lord and the Holy Father are too busy with the *pezzi grossi,* the big bananas of this world, to be able to care for us, the little ones."

"We'll have to pray to the Virgin," Martha said firmly. "He always does what his mother tells him."

"You do that, woman." Amadeo turned on his side and closed his eyes. "We men must think."

"Santa Maria!" Martha grumbled contentedly under her breath. "Think, the man says, and already he's halfway to sleep and snoring. Men!"

The moon rode through the heavens of the night and dipped toward the horizon. The diamond stars were plucked from the eastern sky by morning's finger. And still the solitary light burned in the papal window.

[5]

Word of Mussolini's death began to spread with the early risers the way news always has among the Romans, quietly at first, like an electric charge: in whispers from window to window; in a name mouthed silently, with an across-the-throat gesture from rooftop to rooftop; with children sent scampering by their parents to alert relatives up the street; in a word from penitent to priest in the darkened confessionals of little back-street chapels, or from street vendors to buyers over wheelbarrows filled with last week's produce, or from prostitute to client; in messages chalked in death white on the walls of the Capitol and the sad-faced masonry of the Colosseum.

Il Duce is dead! . . . The tyrant has paid! . . . The Republic has been assassinated! . . . Italians! Victory is impossible! Prepare to die for Italy! . . . The Communists are coming to government! . . .

The reactions formed more slowly in the wake of the news, a mixtum-gatherum of fear, elation, foreboding, all mingling as tentative undercurrents that increased with the advancing hours.

By midafternoon, with the sad-faced Pasquinelli to guide him, Richard Lansing had accomplished miracles. What would have taken him a week by himself, the two men did in a single whirlwind day. They had started with an early-morning visit to the Vatican Bank. *"La bottega del Papa,"* Pasquinelli called it—the Pope's store. Pasquinelli didn't even crack a smile. Lansing had deposited his own funds, and entrusted Cardinal Krementz's moneys and instructions to an efficient cleric.

With the Krementz name behind Richard and with Pasquinelli's insider connections, in another couple of hours they had secured an apartment of ample size for Richard's needs and rank on the Via della Conciliazione, which ran between the Tiber and St. Peter's Piazza, just a short walk from the Secretariat of State. Pasquinelli helped him find some pieces of furniture, then drove him to the far side of the city in order to buy the Roman clothes he would need—cassocks, sashes, broad-brimmed hats, cape, shirts, gloves. All, even a briefcase, had to be *alla romana.* Pasquinelli would not have any charge of his making a poor showing.

It must have been well after three in the afternoon when Lansing and Pasquinelli finally paused long enough for the news to catch up with them. The kindly-eyed, bald-headed proprietor of the fourth haberdashery they entered that day spoke softly as he fitted the American for the round, wide-brimmed Roman clerical hat.

"Hung them up by the feet in a Milano gas station. Il Duce and the other Fascisti with him. And the woman too! I heard it from my neighbor, who heard it over the American Army network. Like pigs! To drain them of their blood!"

The man's agitation was something new and unsettling for Lansing. Not fear. Not horror. As though this man with the appearance of a loving grandfather was accustomed to bloodshed by now, tolerated it without either approval or condemnation, like a neighbor he would rather not have, but had no power to banish.

Pasquinelli showed no outward reaction to the news beyond a simple remark as he peered critically at the Roman hat sitting on Lansing's head. He couldn't see, Pasquinelli said, how Mussolini and Petacci could have escaped. He was a Roman, though, and had surely sensed the rising emotional charge that had been building as the day progressed. Still, he gave no hint to Lansing.

"Now you look like a real Roman cleric!" He gave his approval to this final purchase. "So, Monsignore, now that you are respectable, and before you become weak with hunger, we will have a bite to eat."

The late-day sun shone through a hundred windows of the Apostolic Palace. Promptly at 5 P.M., just as had been agreed by the Pontiff and Guido de la Valle, the double doors at one end of the immense Sala delle Benedizioni in that ancient building were opened by two *camerieri segreti* clad in black tunics and hose. His Holiness entered. He was preceded by a detachment of four Noble Guards in high cavalry boots, shining cuirasses, and plumed helmets, sabers held vertically at the ready. Then came Profumi's pro-secretaries of state, Morandi and Da Brescia, dressed in their most formal cloaks and robes; and an assortment of Vatican chamberlains and notables fluttering in purple and white like exotic orchids. Before the doors were closed, the Maestro entered the room and stood apart from the gathering.

Papa Profumi was led to the papal throne which stood at the middle of one long, ornate wall. Waiting at attention before the throne and flanked in a semicircle by the officers of his GHQ stood the commander in chief of all Allied forces in Italy, a Britisher.

Profumi was grave, smooth, controlled as he read his address from papers held in front of him by Morandi. He congratulated the Allies on their victories, and asked for God's blessings on their endeavors. The general greeting accomplished, a papal chamberlain led each officer forward singly and presented him to the Holy Father. Profumi, excellently briefed and genuinely concerned, had a special word for each. He inquired about this man's wife, that man's son who was fighting in the Pacific or European theater, promised prayers for another officer's son killed in action.

The commander was the last to be ushered forward. Profumi exchanged good wishes with him personally, then came quickly to what was for him the object of the papal audience.

"The end of hostilities is near, General. Will the Allies still insist on unconditional surrender from Germany and Japan?" The tone was blunt.

The commander confirmed that that was so; there had been no change in the decision. While he knew the Holy Father's objections, he was only a soldier. When he gave battle orders, millions obeyed. When it came to political decisions and overall strategy, he, too, deferred to higher authority.

As the commander talked, Profumi's dismay at the loss of Mussolini was a bitter taste in his mind. If only now he had the defeated dictator securely in sanctuary within this same Apostolic Palace, he would not be asking for information from the mere commander of Allied armies. He would be parleying with the political oligarchs who ran the affairs of the world. Instead, he knew, for this military man he was a religious potentate isolated in the middle of a country that had lost a fight and then cannibalized itself in front of the whole world. It was as if the very hand of the Evil One had whisked away that invaluable pawn Benito Mussolini. Profumi showed no sign of his chagrin and bitterness, however. The commander and his officers all bore themselves like men who were bent on pummeling their enemies until the very end. He knew their arguments: They had not asked for this war or the Blitzkrieg or the death camps. But once they were in it, total and absolute victory was the only goal.

"May We take the liberty of repeating to you what We have been saying over and over again for a year, to the Allied governments?" Profumi's voice remained low-key but imperious. "There will be no real peace unless vengeance and hate are excluded. The demand for unconditional surrender is incompatible with both the doctrine of Christ and the dignity of the human being, even if he is your mortal enemy. History will bear out the accuracy of that judgment, General."

The commander said he would transmit the Pope's remarks to London and Washington. But realistically both men knew that the general's words were accurate. There had been no change of heart among the Allies; and there would be none.

The commander bowed, stepped away from the throne, and stood at attention with his officers. As if on some invisible signal, Profumi's cortege formed again. The Holy Father blessed the general and his staff, and then left them in the care of a papal chamberlain.

It was like a chain that could not be broken, Profumi reflected to himself as he walked away. One blasphemy committed in Milan in the name of victory meant that another, greater one—a prolonged war—could not now be avoided. Nor could the humiliation of the next audience be altered. He had not been able to break that chain.

Accompanied now only by Guido and two security men, Papa Profumi entered a private, windowless room immediately off the Sala delle Benedizioni. At once, Obergruppenführer Wolff stood up from his seat at the table where he had been waiting, straightened his shoulders, removed his officer's cap, bowed, and clicked his heels smartly. The tightly cropped gingerbread hair, the porcelain-blue eyes with that glint of contempt behind steel-rimmed spectacles, the spotless field-gray uniform, the shining military boots, the Iron Cross that hung between the lapels of his military collar, all bespoke the spit-and-polish of Germany's Wehrmacht at its best—defeat or no defeat. Because the Allies occupied Rome, Wolff had been forced to arrive in civilian clothes, but he had insisted on changing into his sacred uniform for this, his last papal interview. Wolff was a proud and incurable romantic. The empty cigarette holder he sported in one hand had the same purpose. It was a gesture, at least.

A slight, stiff bow from the waist, the blue eyes never leaving the Pope's face. The Pope sat down, then Wolff. The Maestro remained standing between the Pontiff and the German. Profumi's expression was like stone. On the German's face, telltale lines of hardship muted the acquired look of arrogance that all Wehrmacht officers displayed.

Wolff came to his point without ceremony. General Kesselring wanted to buy something only the Vatican had for sale: temporary refuge and, ultimately, valid Vatican passports and safe-conduct for some dozen key German officers so that they could escape the Allied pincers closing in around them. Eventually, once the dust of war had settled, these officers would emigrate to friendly South American countries. If they were taken prisoner by the Allies, they would certainly die.

Wolff paused as though waiting for some reaction. Guido glanced at the Pope, saw the vein in his right temple throbbing, saw him nod his head once. Profumi was disgusted and angry and humiliated, but willing to hear the man out.

Yes, Guido answered dryly, they could arrange for temporary refuge, safe-conduct, new identities, valid passports, all of that. But at what price? The lives of those fourteen thousand prisoners Kesselring held—men and women, priests and Jews, he had rounded up barbarously as hostages? Let's be sensible—Guido spat the words at Wolff. General Kesselring was not going to add to his war crimes by harming them. Besides, the Holy See did not barter in human lives. No. The release of the fourteen thousand must be a foregone conclusion to all discussion of terms. But what then could Kesselring offer to pay, if there was a bargain?

"In that case, a bargain we can have," Wolff said with grim deliberation. He opened one button of his uniform and took out a thick envelope.

"Several prominent leaders in the Wehrmacht and the Party took the precaution years ago of building up private accounts in Switzerland, and of transferring their valuable art acquisitions to private storage vaults in that same land. This envelope contains all the information: the numbers of the accounts and the location and the numbers of the vault deposits of art objects in Basel and Zurich. None of the objects was stolen"—he glanced at Profumi—"and all the money was legitimately acquired."

Profumi gave no sign.

The Maestro stretched out his hand. "Your envelope also contains a complete list of names of your prisoners and their location, and the names of the commanding officers in charge of them?"

"Of course! Ah, but one instant, Maestro!" Wolff withheld the envelope; he had not quite finished. "There is one condition. Once the original owners of these moneys are relocated abroad, you must arrange for regular and secure drawing facilities on the ordinary interest accruing from the deposited sums into foreign accounts. I repeat: the interest of the original deposited sums. The capital, of course, is yours to invest. Anything accruing above the ordinary interest earned on the original sums is likewise yours. Have I a guarantee?"

"Obergruppenführer, our guarantee is our word. Accept it or reject it."

Smiling mirthlessly, Wolff handed him the envelope. Profumi glanced at the Maestro as he examined its contents. The Maestro nodded to the Pope, then turned to Wolff. The Pope and Wolff stood up almost simultaneously. The German gave one more stiff bow. The Maestro opened the door for the Pope and let him pass into the corridor where the two security men awaited His Holiness. Then he turned to the German, and indicated another door.

"My personal bodyguard, Sagastume, will see you to a safe house. You understand, I'm sure, that we must do some preliminary verification." He held the envelope up. "It will all be done by morning, I'm sure."

"Of course." Wolff had his cigarette holder back in his mouth. "Auf Wiedersehen, Maestro. By the way, full documentation could be made available to the Swiss and American governments. In case of default, I mean."

The Maestro inclined his head. *"Keine Sorge,* Obergruppenführer. Not to worry. We also have our recourse." He smiled at the German, and nodded. "In case of default."

[[6]]

By the time Lansing and Pasquinelli left the small trattoria at the other side of the city, and began the drive back across to the Vatican, Rome had been transformed. Despite all the buzzing and growing tension, traffic and street crowds had been sparse all morning and even into the siesta hour.

Little by little, however, the Romans had begun to emerge from behind the boarded-up shops and cafés, from the shuttered houses and the curtained tenement rooms, to look into each other's eyes, exchange their fears, argue about what they should do. All the little shopkeepers and artisans of the Trastevere, the laborers with their wives and children along the Esquiline and Via Casilina, the middle-class professional men with their families out on Monte Mario, the rich and well-to-do in the suburbs of Prati and Parioli, the monks and nuns out on the Via Aurelia, the small farmers living along the Via Appia Antica and the Villa Ada, and all the others from beyond the roads running down to the sea in the west and up to the Alban Hills in the east.

Everywhere small groups formed and dispersed, re-formed into larger ones which shifted and moved in a contagious agitation. An almost palpable fear of the near future in this headless vacuum of power and order was the only binding force.

And then a curious rhythm was supplied. Old men, first a few, and then many, sitting in low doorways in forgotten alleys and little piazzas, began tapping their rough walking sticks: three shorts, a pause, two longs. The Roman "echo of fate" that the old men had learned from their fathers and grandfathers seventy years before in the war of Italian independence. *"Roma o Morte,"* that rhythm said. Rome or Death. Three shorts . . . two longs. Three shorts . . . two longs. Again and again, the sound pounded and echoed through the brittle tufa, the volcanic ash on which the city is built.

It was an unnerving sound. Richard Lansing glanced uneasily at Pasquinelli, who seemed alert but calm enough as he drove through the narrow streets. It wasn't long, however, before the hard, rhythmic, tapping echo was challenged by a sort of murmuring, a rising sound of voices, but with no shouts or screams. They could see little groups of men and women and children moving forward, stopping, joining with other groups, starting off again. As they moved across the city, the groups became a crowd until, by the time they reached the Via Nazionale at the center of the city, they realized that all of Rome was in the streets and squares, moving ponderously up toward Vatican Hill and St. Peter's Piazza. Voices were beginning to repeat certain words and slogans to the unending rhythm that was like thunder under foot. The rising, gathering sound took on a voice and a plea all its own. The forward edges of the crowds were already gathering up around St. Peter's, clamoring for the Pope and crying out: *"Liberatore! . . . Papa Profumi! . . . Liberatore nostro! . . . Viva il Papa! . . ."*

The path of Pasquinelli's car across the Victor Emmanuel Bridge and up the Via della Conciliazione became slower, tortuous, at times frightening for Lansing. They were able to inch forward only because the car bore Vatican plates. Lansing had never seen anything like it. As the car crept along, it was surrounded by the stifling density of the mobs. Some made out that there were two priests in the automobile, and knelt or held babies up for a blessing or kissed the windows or touched the doors. What on earth possessed them? Lansing asked himself.

Pasquinelli seemed to understand exactly what was happening and what needed to be done. "Monsignore, these are Romans. They speak with the voice of Rome. Wave back to them, Monsignore. No, no! Not like that! Don't smile at them! It's a grave moment. Don't tip your hat like that. You're not saying good-day-thank-you-nice-to-see-you-all! You're not their serf or their equal. You represent the Church and the Holy Father for them right now. Wave, Monsignore. As if you were about to make the sign of the cross. In fact, make the sign of the cross now and again. There! That's it! Go on, Monsignore!"

Imperceptibly, Lansing's apprehension and shyness evaporated. Every pair of eyes that met his, every face that pressed against the window, all the weeping, the cries and pleas, all produced a change in him. Between him and every man and woman who reached out to him with their hands or their eyes, between him and every mother who held up an infant and cried for a blessing, some exhilarating message passed. His breath started coming in deep drafts. His throat contracted with silent sobs. Tears filled his eyes. It was a pure, bittersweet experience, a painful breaking of bonds that had tied down an inner power in him, and over which he now had no conscious control.

At the top of the Via della Conciliazione, just outside the white line demarcating the beginning of St. Peter's Piazza, American MP's sat helplessly in their jeeps. Unable to maintain control, or even to part the crowd and enter St. Peter's Piazza, totally overcome in a sea of unarmed, nonviolent citizens, they had finally been put under strict orders not to budge or make one untoward gesture. Some wise officer at headquarters knew events had overleaped every one of the directives in his manual of operations.

Lansing was dripping with sweat by the time they finally broke across the white lines separating Vatican City from greater Rome, and entered St. Peter's Piazza. The light of day was fading into darkness. The square was already packed tight, but the Vatican police and the Swiss Guards had somehow managed to impose a semblance of order on that entwining mass of bodies.

The main lights in the Basilica and the great arc lights over Bernini's colonnade had been switched on, wartime or no. Pasquinelli halted on the north side of the colonnade. From there, he and Lansing had a clear view of Profumi's windows on the third and fourth floors of the Apostolic Palace. There they listened to the steady rumble of cries around them rise into a deafening roar.

"Papa! . . . Papa! . . . Papa! . . ." On and on the cry went, gathering the momentum and power of thousands—seventy, ninety, one hundred thousand voices—striking those two syllables together like cosmic cymbals: *"Pa-pa!"* The fresh and green American from the New World and the little Roman-born cleric who had never left Rome looked up to where all eyes were drawn.

"Papa! . . . Papa! . . . Papa! . . ."

Lansing saw that all the windows of the Apostolic Palace were shuttered and dark, save one. At a certain moment, framed in the warm yellow light from that window, there stood the slim, white-robed figure of Papa Profumi, almost ethereal in the counterplay of ivory brightness and subtle shadows. For just a second, the crowd hushed. Would the Pope speak? But no, no word was needed. That became clear to Lansing as he watched the Pope raise both hands in the traditional Roman gesture of greeting and encouragement. It was the simplest of gestures, each arm bent upward at the elbow, the fingers of each hand held together, the backs of the hands toward the crowd, the arms moving up and down slowly. And yet the power it transmitted was unmistakable. "Rise up!" the gesture said. "Be lifted in spirit and mind! Hope! Look up toward the hope in your sky, Romans!"

A renewed frenzy of cheering was the great Roman response. They understood. *"Papa! Papa!"* Lansing found himself joining in the cries. Even the mournful-faced Pasquinelli was drawn out of himself.

After some moments, the Pope left the window. There was a boiling-up of expectation in the piazza until the Pope reappeared a second time. And a third time. And a fourth. How could anyone who was not present here begin to imagine this night, Lansing wondered as tears filled his eyes and ran down his face. How could anyone who had not been part of it ever begin to understand what was taking place between Papa Profumi and that immense crowd? Over and above the cries and shouts, the fears and pleas, beyond Profumi's ethereal appearance and his eloquent gestures, the practiced theatricality of the setting, over and beyond all that, something was being transacted between Profumi and that gathered host of Romans. Lansing knew he was witnessing not just a mob of cheering, desperately pleading Catholic Italians. Some process was taking place between Pope and Romans: they were communicating together on some upper avenue of spirit; something special was passing between them in that exchange.

He should have known what it was. Lansing was a child of American democracy. The first Americans had rediscovered an ancient Roman principle going back to the childhood of the Catholic Church: "The voice of the people is the voice of God." The people as the *channel* of power and authority that came to each successive government. Only, by the time Lansing was born into that democracy, he and his generation were taught that the people were the ultimate source of power and authority. God was eliminated—or at least outlawed. Lansing, like most of his contemporaries, had lost sight of that otherworldly font of worldly power and authority.

Even with his faith and all his priestly training, he could barely grasp now what he was perceiving. Some transom of spirit had opened, and the intangible light of God enshrouded Pope and people, calming, sweetening, uniting, encouraging, comforting. Papa Profumi and that crowd seemed to live such a moment prolonged into hours. This wasn't a congregation worshiping in a church. This was the ordinary citizenry of Rome, Lansing marveled.

Yet, if he didn't understand it, there were others who seemed farther still from understanding. Obergruppenführer Wolff, S.S., watching from the safe house, breathed an enormous sigh. *"Ein echter Führer!"* he muttered. "A real leader!"

Sometime before nine o'clock, Profumi came out for the last time to renewed, untiring cries. *"Papa!"* He stood in the flood of sound, his head raised, his eyes scanning the crowds, the left hand laid slantingly on his chest, the right raised up, the long delicate fingers together.

The crowd hushed in quick understanding. He was going to bless them and their world. The thin, reedlike sound of Profumi's voice with its high, almost singsong tone reached surprisingly far, as far as it had to. *"Ego vos benedico . . . in nomine Patris . . . et Filii . . . et Spiritus Sancti . . ."* The Fisherman's Ring on the fourth finger scintillated in the light of the lamps as the right hand traced three crosses in the air, one for each of the Divine Persons.

He remained for only a minute more, then disappeared. The window was closed. The lights were put out. Within half an hour, the piazza and the adjoining streets were clear of crowds. The dark silence betrayed no trace of that night's events. But the mood of Rome was changed. And young Richard Lansing had the first of many new discoveries to ponder.

Once back in his office overlooking the Belvedere courtyard, Guido worked with an effortless and remarkable efficiency. First, he telephoned the Vatican Central Exchange and gave them a number in Geneva. It would take an hour to put the call through, he was told. He opened the envelope Wolff had handed him, and studied the information about the fourteen thousand German-held prisoners. He spoke briefly on the phone with Monsignore Da Brescia, then placed the information in a separate envelope for Da Brescia to pick up later.

Finally, he turned his attention to the other documents in Wolff's envelope. A series of lists. One contained some sixty-three names, each with a bank account number beside it. Another named five banks, two in Basel, three in Lugano. A third list consisted of twelve names—the German officers whose escape from Allied capture was to be facilitated by the Holy See. A short, impersonally worded, unsigned note typewritten in German indicated where the officers were now hiding and how they could be contacted. All twelve were no more than half a mile from where Guido was sitting in his Vatican office. The Maestro smiled grimly. So much for the alert Allied occupation of Rome!

Next, he took from his breast pocket a slim notebook with a gold-embossed red-leather cover and a locked clasp. He opened the notebook with a key attached to his watch chain, and turned to a certain page on which was a handwritten list of ciphers. He took a clean sheet of paper and wrote the heading "Swiss Windfall" at the top. Within forty minutes, he had transcribed each of the sixty-three bank account numbers into a cipher. He did likewise for the names of the five banks. He retrieved a folder from a locked drawer where he had placed it earlier in the day, opened it, and quickly transcribed the information Mussolini had given him about the Fascist Party gold deposits in Milan.

When his call to Geneva came through, there was no chitchat. Just a curt word of recognition to verify that it was his agent, Klaus Fabian. Guido read out his list of ciphers in a slow monotone, then hung up and settled back to wait. It would take Fabian a little time to verify the total sum of money involved in those accounts. He closed and locked the red notebook, and sat there, head bowed, running his forefinger lightly over the two sets of arms emblazoned on it—the papal arms of tiara and crossed keys, and the Lodge's triangle with the All-Seeing Eye. As he fingered it, he mused over the gold lettering that ran beneath each coat of arms. He drew in a deep breath, as he returned the notebook to his inner pocket.

His gaze wandered out the window and over the rooftops toward the dome of St. Peter's. He let his mind seesaw back over his recent conversations with Profumi and over the papal audiences of this afternoon. Of course, the manner of Il Duce's death and the public display that followed it amounted to a blasphemy—but only one of hundreds, thousands even, in this war. The whole war was a blasphemy, for that matter! And, of course, the Allies were going to bear the burden of needless slaughter by their insistence on unconditional surrender. Another penalty of war. Guido could not see in any of this a reason for—what had His Holiness called it?—a fundamental change.

At that moment, the first waves of rhythmic cheering from the gathering Romans reached his ears. He lifted his head to listen more intently. He pressed a bell button. Sagastume appeared at the door. It was nothing to be worried about, he said. The police and Vatican guards had the situation under control. There was going to be a demonstration outside the Basilica. No need to worry.

Guido was not worried; he wanted to find out what was behind it. But the telephone purred softly and Sagastume retired.

Klaus Fabian again. Guido listened, copying down two pages of ciphers from the agent, and then replaced the receiver. Quickly, he deciphered Fabian's message. The total of all the accounts on Wolff's list ran to slightly over $400 million. The assessed market value of the antiques, objets d'art, and paintings would approach $50 million at prewar prices.

The second series of ciphers told him about the Fascist gold.

Guido sat for a long time, poring over the figures, the currencies involved, and the individual accounts, to each of which he could now attach a name. He looked up some data about the banks and storage vaults where this Swiss Windfall was presently kept.

By the time he was satisfied that he understood what the Swiss Windfall meant in terms of hard cash and realizable assets, three things were clear to Guido. First, the moneys must be invested as soon as possible. Second, the "goods" would have to be disposed of without fanfare and over an extended period of time. And, third, for both operations he needed the advice and the practical help of his longtime associates, a group of thirteen men in powerful positions about the world. War had kept them from several but not all of their accustomed and always confidential meetings. The present matters were too serious to wait until war's end for another plenary session. The Vatican wheels themselves would be in motion very soon concerning this Swiss Windfall; Guido must be ready to respond. He knew the perfect event to serve as a suitable occasion for assembling his associates. Such quiet caution and care would always continue to be Guido's way in these matters.

He put in another call to Klaus Fabian and instructed him to invite his associates to Villa Cerulea for the weekend of July 14. Annually, at that time, Guido gave his Ferragosto dinner party, an old Roman custom before everyone dispersed for the vacation time of August. Fabian was perfectly positioned in Switzerland to make the necessary arrangements.

It remained only to deal with Monsignore Da Brescia's end of the matter. Guido glanced at the envelope with the names of the fourteen thousand prisoners that still waited on his desk for the monsignore. Obviously, Da Brescia was making his presence precious and would not come to Guido's office just because he received one telephone call. Little men always fought with little arms, the Maestro reflected.

As soon as Guido could make the necessary travel arrangements with the military authorities, it would be Da Brescia who would go north as His Holiness' personal emissary to ensure the liberation, the safe-conduct, and the care of the prisoners. The Maestro picked up the phone one last time that day, and with a note of dislike barely disguised in his voice asked to be put through again to the tardy monsignore. Someday, he thought while he waited for Da Brescia to come on the line, he would have to settle several scores with that reverend gentleman.

[7]

Rome proceeded to take Richard Lansing to itself as only Rome can.

When he arrived promptly at 8 A.M. for his first workaday Monday, little Amadeo Solimando seemed agreeably more familiar as he guided "the new man" through the Secretariat doors. Pasquinelli, somber-faced as always at his reception desk, gave a more approving glance at the lanky American, dressed now as a proper Roman cleric. Without any ado, the Italian showed Lansing to the entrance of a small chapel on the ground floor and told him to enter and wait. "Archbishop Morandi and Monsignore Da Brescia will join you here momentarily."

Lansing recognized the chaste style of the chapel as Romanesque: yellow walls hung with carved cameos of the fourteen Stations of the Cross, raised sanctuary platform, small domed ceiling over the altar, narrow stained-glass windows.

A slight sound made him turn back toward the door. It was Morandi who entered, but without Da Brescia.

"The archbishop will be here in a moment." Morandi made Richard feel more at ease than he might have under Da Brescia's hard stare; but maybe Cardinal Krementz's briefing had something to do with that. Morandi is all heart, the cardinal had said.

"I thought I would give you an idea of how you will be spending your 'Roman stint,' or at least the first few weeks, anyway." Morandi strolled a few steps to one side of the chapel and sat on one of the chairs arranged by the wall. He motioned Lansing to take one beside him.

All personnel assigned to the Secretariat, Morandi explained, swore an oath of office. "I have it here somewhere. . . ." Morandi reached into the folds of his cassock and produced a card, which he handed to the younger man. "You will read the oath printed there, and then make a solemn profession of faith in the beliefs of the Church—something you doubtless do every day in any case." Morandi acknowledged Richard's nod of assent with a quick, pleasant smile and went on. There would be one final oath, he said, against the heresy of Modernism. "You are familiar with Modernism, of course, Monsignore."

Richard was. He had had many a heated argument with seminarians who flirted with the Modernist wish to abolish the papacy and change all the dogmatic beliefs of the Church according as the mentality and culture of the world changed.

"Now as to your work assignment, you will replace Monsignore Novarese as head of the Passport Section. Novarese is a good man, as you will see for yourself; but the strain of the work has taken its toll on his health. He will be leaving for a lighter assignment in about a month. That should give you time to find your legs here.

"You will begin in the trenches, so to say. With the Work of St. Raphael. 'The St. Raphael,' it's generally called. The war has displaced millions of people. Can you imagine that, Monsignore? It's a hard thing to grasp until you have seen it! Most of them are Europeans, but not all, by any means. We are uniquely placed to help them. But you will see that for yourself too. Of course, now that much of Europe has been liberated, the flood of people looking for their loved ones and hoping to return to their own countryside to begin life again—well, all I can say is that the work now is nearly overwhelming in every sense of the word. You are much needed here, Monsignore! Much needed."

For another ten minutes or so, Archbishop Morandi sketched out for Richard what needed to be done, and some of the resources he could call upon for help. There was the regular lay and clerical staff, of course. There was also the Secretariat's pool of translators for forty-two languages and dialects. Most important of all, there was a remarkable system, one not to be found anywhere else in the world, for the recording and the retrieval of information about missing and displaced persons.

"You will find it amazing, Monsignore Lansing. It sometimes seems that every family ever torn apart by one horror of war or another has come to some priest or some papal legate or some church somewhere. Every scrap of information from every possible source has been channeled here, by Papa Profumi's orders, to the St. Raphael. For over six years now, Vatican representatives in every war-torn country of the world have been sending names, aliases, prison numbers, addresses, personal histories, family descriptions, newspaper reports, government lists. Floods of disjointed information have flowed in here from Europe and from Africa and Southeast Asia, from China and the U.S.S.R. From forgotten places you may never have heard of, Monsignore.

"Early on, we enlisted the help of professors of mathematics from our Italian universities to devise our system of organizing and retrieving all that information handily. I assure you, if a clue is to be found anywhere in this world that could reunite any person with his loved ones, it will be found in the millions upon millions of names our professors have marshaled into order for us. . . .

"Ah, but here is Monsignore Da Brescia!" Morandi rose and led Lansing forward. "It is time to leave the talk and begin the work!"

The three priests gathered before a small shrine of the Virgin Mary. Monsignore Da Brescia held out a fourteenth-century copy of the Gospels. Richard placed his right hand upon it and read aloud in Latin the oath Morandi had given him:

" 'In the name of Our Lord, Jesus Christ, I, Richard Cooper Lansing, do agree, promise, and swear to be at all times obedient to Blessed Peter the Apostle and to our superior, Papa Profumi, and his lawful successors; to perform diligently the tasks that may be entrusted to me by this Secretariat; and religiously to guard professional secrets. I promise also I will not accept gratuities, not even in the form of gifts. So help me God and likewise the Holy Gospels upon which I place my hand.' "

Then he made his profession of faith solemnly and with all his heart, and just as solemnly repeated after Morandi the oath forswearing the Modernist heresy. By turns, then, Da Brescia and Morandi shook Lansing's hand in congratulations. The formalities were over. Richard Cooper Lansing was one of them now.

Morandi had been right. It was not possible to grasp the reality of an ocean of miserable, displaced souls until you were engulfed by it. Helpful though the briefing in the chapel had been, nothing could possibly have prepared Lansing for the St. Raphael. Nor could any other work so completely have diluted his comfortable and very American idea of the Church as a neatly arranged hierarchy of privileged clerics. The hard reality of the Church, he began to see, was that in its greatest part it was a very un-neat profusion of ordinary souls whose physical needs must be taken care of if their spiritual needs were to be tended in time.

Each day, no matter how early Richard arrived at his office, visitors already filled the outer room beyond the glazed doors, patiently waiting to be called for their appointments. One or another of the ushers in black frock coats generally had a pile of telephone messages for him. From the waiting room he would pass into a high, vaulted corridor, striding beneath the arabesques and birds of paradise painted there four hundred years earlier by Raphael's pupils. At the far end, he entered the work area proper and found his office, a moderate-size room with white rough-cast walls. And, however early the hour, Novarese would almost always be waiting for him. Together they would begin the day's work.

National boundaries, race, creed, politics, social position—all such distinctions were ignored at the St. Raphael. Lansing's section, or the section he would be taking over from Novarese, dealt mainly with Poland and Czechoslovakia. When the war in Germany itself was over, "whenever that may be," Novarese said wearily, that sector, too, would be Richard's responsibility. "So brace yourself, Monsignore."

Richard couldn't imagine anything worse than he was seeing already; and even if worse came along, there was no bracing himself more than he did now as each new refugee came wearily or tearfully into his office. Every day was filled with endless repetitions in two dozen languages and dialects of the same man-made universe of miseries. Exile was the least of it, all too often. Wives had been raped and taken away. Whole families had been dispersed. Children were missing. Parents had been deported. Husbands had been snatched away in labor trains. Poverty, despair, helplessness, hopelessness came in every form, stared from every face.

With Novarese to help him at first, but within a day or two alone, Lansing would take down the particulars, calling on interpreters as needed. Secretaries already acquainted with the filing system then took Lansing's notes and sought to find some information about the problem.

Richard found the heartache and the noise and the bustle all left him tired in body and raw in spirit.

He was still finding his legs, as Morandi had said, when he was given an additional assignment. Every cleric at the Vatican has a spiritual function, whatever his work may be. Richard was to say daily Mass for the Polish Sisters in the Via Sistina. The Vatican car pool assigned him a car. Each morning he was to drive across town to say Mass for the Sisters at six o'clock. That would give him just enough time to have a quick meal and be back at his desk in the Secretariat by eight o'clock.

Those early-morning trips across the city, when Rome was bathed in golden sunlight and utterly quiet, were moments of revelation for Lansing. Without traffic and crowds, the quiet and ancient voice of Rome spoke to his soul, soundlessly, spoke about an eternity of existence and an unruffled destiny that he found mirrored in the peace of the convent, the rapt quietude of the Sisters and the atmosphere of serene confidence that shrouded their lives. Hidden from the rough, fighting, dying world around them, totally dedicated to a life of piety and obscure work, they seemed already to be enjoying the sort of peace that Richard always associated with the privileged, the saints in heaven, and that Rome itself seemed to possess.

For the first weeks, understandably, he had no time to get to know anyone in the Vatican beyond the dozen or so people who worked most closely with him. They were mainly laymen placed under his direction.

Each evening he was so drained, he barely managed to eat an evening meal at some trattoria or other, and say his prayers, before he fell into bed to dream through each night of the horrors he had witnessed the preceding day. He almost began to think he could never return to a normal routine either in Rome or in Chicago. But then two seemingly minor things happened to change the stark pattern of his life at the Secretariat.

The first was a startling phone call from Morandi. Lansing usually did not take calls while he was with a client. But when an usher knocked on his office door early one morning and said earnestly that "the archbishop seems upset," Lansing picked up his phone.

Morandi, it seemed, had tried to reach Richard that morning at home. The matter he had wished to confide to Lansing had been taken care of since. That was not the reason for this call! How could it be, Morandi wanted to know, that the monsignore had no one to answer his phone, whether he was at the Sisters' or anywhere else? "Where on earth was your valet at that time of the morning?" Morandi's voice was indignation itself.

"My what?" Richard could not believe his ears. In the midst of this misery, with a tearful old man waiting in the chair at the other side of the desk, and a hundred more like him in the outer room, and his office filled with folders detailing who knew how many more desperate cases, here was Archbishop Morandi, the man who was all heart, asking about a valet! "My what, Monsignore?" Richard asked again, something between laughter and despair edging into his voice.

"Your valet, man! Your valet!" Clearly, Morandi was dead serious. "Doesn't he ever stay at home?"

"Excellency, I haven't got a valet. . . ."

That possibility was so outrageously impossible that it had never entered Morandi's head. Did these young Americans understand nothing? He was speechless for a moment as he pondered the idea of coping with Vatican life without a valet. Suppressing a shudder, he announced that this was an important matter, and one he would take into his own hands. "As of this coming weekend, Monsignore, you will have a valet. I'll choose him myself."

Morandi was not being so frivolous as Richard first thought. In fact, he was not being frivolous at all. A Roman dignitary without a valet was as anomalous as a bishop without a violet rabat or a cardinal without a red hat. Anybody above the rank of simple priest who had any pretensions to *romanità*—that distinctive and distinguished quality of being "Roman"—had his personal valet.

The reason was as obvious as it was practical: the Holy See couldn't function on a day-to-day basis without the valets.

Most significant details of inner Roman news traveled like mercury through what could only be thought of as the "valet system." The most efficient and discreet way to alert a cardinal or any high official to some situation or need or problem was to whisper it in the ear of his valet, who, if he was worth his salt, could plant viewpoints and news in the mind of his master as he fed him in the morning or served him dinner in the evening. It was well known that careers had been made or unmade simply by skillful if somewhat unscrupulous use of the whispering gallery provided by the valet system. After all, the reasoning went, if half the highly placed valets in the Holy City kept repeating a certain name as absolutely certain soon to be attached to a certain position, their patrons came to believe that the thing had been decided behind their backs and at the highest level, and that they themselves had better confirm it with their own consent.

Papa Profumi had Stefanori, who had the right to the exalted title of Commendatore, as had the valets of such highly placed cardinals as Rivali and Padrone, who sat on the Vatican City maintenance commission with Prince Carlo Profumi, the Pope's nephew.

Those men were keystones in the system. Through their patrons, they knew exactly how much oil, wine, vegetables, sugar, cigarettes, alcohol, bread, gasoline, cloth-of-gold, silk—how much of anything, in fact—was available to the 150 households within Vatican City. Cardinal Rivali also presided over the administration of the Ordinary Assets of the Holy See—an invaluable source of financial information. His man and others of such rank knew much that was precious and vital.

Valets of lesser personalities were called Professore, a title they shared with the coach of Rome's crack soccer team, or Capo, along with the head chefs of Rome's fashionable restaurants. Below that level, they went either as simple Signore or, even worse, by their family names. Roman valets, in other words, reproduced exactly the pecking order of their patrons; and to know a prelate's valet was to know the prelate.

And so it was that Vittorio Benfatti, *supremo* of intermediate-quality valets, arrived on Lansing's doorstep, all ready to take over. Vittorio had done his apprenticeship for fourteen years with doddering Cardinal Posti. A prime man in his class, he had been the object of much watchful care by more than one Roman prelate, all of whom followed Posti's declining health inch by inch. There would be only the shortest time in which Benfatti could be successfully snatched from the grasp of other like-minded watchers the moment Posti breathed his last. The rough-and-ready Morandi stepped in brusquely. After all, one of *his* key prelates, Monsignore Lansing, lacked a man. That was enough.

The chagrin of the other contenders for Benfatti's hands trickled from valet to valet, finally reaching Papa Profumi through Commendatore Stefanori.

"They tell me, Maestro," Profumi said with mock solemnity to Guido de la Valle one day, "that the Americans are taking over not only political and economic leadership of our Europe, but also our entire Roman valet system!"

Guido's flashing blue-green eyes sparkled. "Yes, Holiness. Monsignore Lansing must be destined for great things. When he returns to Chicago as 'residential,' perhaps the Church in the U.S.A. will adopt our valet system. And thus we may yet convert America!"

As if he had been doing it all his life, Vittorio Benfatti organized Lansing's life. Every morning, dressed impeccably in gray trousers, white shirt, black waistcoat, and shining black shoes, he got his American master up, shaved him, ran his bath, drove him to Mass and back home again, fed him breakfast, and had him at the door of the Secretariat of State at seven-fifty sharp.

From his former exalted position with Cardinal Posti, Vittorio had been able to establish a network of connections with the valets of all the important men of Rome and the Vatican. The fact that he had been snatched for this young, simple American by none other than Archbishop Morandi himself, coupled with Richard's connection with Cardinal Krementz, precluded any impression of a lowering of status in the valet system. Vittorio remained one of the few who could sit down and drink wine with the all-knowing valets of Cardinals Rivali and Padrone. The rumor was that he could speak even to the all-powerful Sister Philomena, because, as the rumor went on, Vittorio's sister, Beatrice, was the seamstress Sister Philomena called in for all work done on His Holiness's clothes, household linen, and liturgical vestments. Vittorio also knew the best chefs and restaurateurs of Rome on a first-name basis. Vittorio, in other words, was a godsend.

Benfatti had all the characteristics of his ancestors, valets all. He had inherited the slight build, rounded shoulders, flat feet. The rest he had learned from his earliest days: the measured tones, and the ease with which he could and did cook, sew, market, clean, drive, repair anything, keep accounts, deal with even the most delicate personal correspondence, file papers, catalogue books. He chatted in five languages, was somewhat pompous, somewhat deferential, took personal pride in his position, and had a quietly fierce attachment to his master.

Each day, while Lansing dealt with the tide of human tragedies, Vittorio set about his own work. The ordinary house supplies he bought cut-rate at the Vatican State Stores and at the State pharmacy. He generally dropped in to the laundry, then to one of the four post offices, or to the Swiss Guards canteen for a chat over a cup of coffee with the captain in charge. In the afternoon, after a siesta, he often went for a little visit with his particular friends at the Vatican firehouse in the Belvedere courtyard. From the firehouse, Vittorio went to Lansing's office to deliver any home mail, packages, or messages that he judged too important to wait until evening. Then, fortified with all the current news and whisperings, he would head back home for more household chores and to prepare for the evening.

There was a gentle clockwork character to this new mode of life. Lansing liked it, and settled into it long before he fully understood it. For whether he knew it or not, Vittorio made the difference—at least in social life—between living on the outer periphery of Roman interests and being an identifiable part of it. Vittorio was a key element in the young American's "Roman stint," one more subtle part of Rome's possessive filament that fell gently around him.

The second seemingly minor occurrence that changed Richard's life announced itself in the form of a message.

"Helmut de la Valle." Vittorio repeated the name as he served Richard's evening meal. Then, as the monsignore looked blank, and as he was Vittorio's enterprise now, to be schooled (though Vittorio would never say this in so many words) in the ways and manners not only of a Roman cleric of standing but of a Roman gentleman, the valet supplied the essentials implicit in the name de la Valle, and those particular to Helmut.

"He is, Monsignore, the nephew of Maestro Guido de la Valle. He lives with the Maestro and Signora Agathi, the Maestro's sister—a beautiful woman, but a sad story, if I may say so—at their estate some miles from the city. An invitation to Villa Cerulea is more coveted than a papal audience by most Vatican officials."

Richard listened to Vittorio's easy voice, grateful for the diversion from the more grisly aspects of his life during the day. By the time Vittorio served dessert, he had finally got back to the message.

"Signor Helmut, Monsignore, is head of one important section of the Banco." Lansing remembered: *"La bottega del Papa,"* Pasquinelli had called it the day they went to deposit his funds.

"The very same sacred place, Monsignore!" Vittorio smiled. "And the very reason for the call. Signor Helmut apologizes for not welcoming you in person at the Banco that day. He has only just returned from a business trip. He asks that you dine with him at your earliest convenience so that he can make amends, and perhaps suggest certain investments for your funds."

"Kind of him." Richard reflected that it was probably his connection with old Blackjack Krementz that brought such attention his way. Still, Vittorio approved, and Lansing was neither unaware of nor ungrateful for the education that came with his services.

Of course, the restaurant where Lansing waited for Helmut de la Valle was probably the most expensive in the Rome of that time. Pietro's, in the Piazza Navona. It was de la Valle's choice, and Vittorio had said he could not have chosen better himself.

Richard smiled to himself as he waited at the table for his host. This was, he mused, a little like his coming-out party.

"Not many men doing the work of St. Raphael smile when they are alone, Monsignore! It's a good sign!"

Startled, Richard looked up as the captain held out a chair. Helmut de la Valle was far different from what Lansing had imagined an important director of the Banco would be. He was quite young—about Lansing's own age, in fact—and almost as tall, with auburn hair and ruddy features. But it was de la Valle's eyes, blue-green and shining, that were his special feature.

A tableau flashed across Lansing's memory. His first morning in Rome . . . The sunlit, peaceful piazza . . . A limousine parked outside the Secretariat . . . The lustrous eyes that had turned in his direction . . .

"You . . ." Richard exclaimed with obvious surprise, as he stood up.

"Yes." Helmut laughed. "I try to be me as often as possible!"

Richard apologized for his apparent rudeness, and explained himself, as they settled into their places under the awning.

Helmut remembered the noisy entry of the army personnel carrier; that was the morning he himself had left for his trip. "For Waidhofen," he said, "on family business. Otherwise, I would have welcomed you myself at the Banco."

"No apologies, please, Signor de la Valle . . ."

"Helmut. I like the American custom of first names."

"Richard." The American smiled.

"Richard." Helmut tested the name and shook his head in disapproval. "That will never do in Rome! Rico. That's better. May I call you Rico?"

"No one ever has, but why not?"

"Rico it is, then."

Helmut had apparently ordered their menu beforehand, for waiters began pouring a delightful Bardolino, and serving the first course without so much as interrupting a sentence as the two young men got to know something about each other. By the time they were halfway through the meal, Lansing had almost forgotten this was their first meeting. He had the feeling that creates friendship—that he had known de la Valle for years. Helmut talked on about Rome—he obviously loved the place—and the various officials of the Secretariat with whom Lansing worked; and as he did, the American had time to observe him. Clearly well-educated, his English too cultured to allow otherwise. Also, a certain sophistication was obvious in his clothes and manners. The hands were carefully manicured. The bearing was polished. And yet the smoothness and ease that could be taken for arrogance was tempered by a most genuine candor and openness in the way he talked about himself.

He had spent five years of his life in English public schools, Helmut told his new friend. Then his family pulled him back on the eve of the outbreak of war. He finished in the University of Basel, and then came to work under his uncle at the Banco. "But I was born in an obscure village that nobody has ever heard of. Waidhofen-an-der-Ybbs. In Austria. My family, however, has lived for a long time at our place in Foligno in Umbria, northeast of here."

With the same candor and ease, Helmut asked questions about Lansing. He learned that Rico had moved with his family to Chicago as a young boy, but that he had been born in a town as obscure as his own Waidhofen.

"Peculiar, Kentucky!" Helmut let out a loud guffaw of laughter at the name of Rico's birthplace. He had a thousand questions about Peculiar, and at least that many about Rico's youth in Chicago and his seminary days. It became increasingly obvious to him that Rico was exactly what he seemed to be: a very simple, intelligent man whose heart was totally devoted to his priesthood—something Helmut admired but had not always found in Roman clerics.

They talked on and on, sharing stories, comparing notes, discovering similar likes and dislikes, contrasting impressions and common hopes centered on Rome and the Vatican and Papa Profumi. What had been planned as a short courtesy meal stretched far beyond the couple of hours Helmut had foreseen, as they chatted over *espressi* in the calm night air.

It was the first time the American had talked about himself with anybody since he took up his post at Rome, and it was a welcome relief from his status as stranger and sojourner. Even his new Roman name made him feel more at home.

They were almost the last patrons left, when Helmut remembered that this was supposed to have been a business dinner. He made up for the lack in a quick, clear explanation. He told Rico that his funds had been invested in Switzerland "through third-party associates," and that he would be receiving regular report sheets. A checking account had been opened in his name at the Banco. "But," he suggested, "you would do well to leave the funds untouched as far as possible."

Rico said that would be no problem. His starting salary of $180 at the Secretariat plus the $30 a month his chaplaincy at the Polish Sisters brought him was ample to cover his rent of $12 plus the maintenance tax of 48 cents. Gas was free, and everything purchased at Vatican stores was tax-free. He had no time, inclination, or need to spend much more. Even Benfatti's salary of $48 a month was not a difficulty.

"Ah!" Helmut's eyes lit up at the valet's name. "You caused a stir getting Vittorio into your service," he teased. "My uncle Guido says even the Holy Father was impressed!"

Rico was genuinely surprised, almost refused to believe that Papa Profumi knew or cared about his existence or his valet.

"You will begin to see otherwise, when you meet His Holiness." Helmut tried to correct Lansing's impression. But that idea seemed even more outlandish to Lansing, until de la Valle explained that all new arrivals at the Secretariat were granted a short private audience with the Pontiff, and received his personal blessing. And on top of that, the work of the St. Raphael was of special interest to Papa Profumi.

"He will be at Castel Gandolfo for the summer. But when he gets back, I think you'll find he knows about you."

Rico walked Helmut to his car and suggested that they have dinner again soon, this time a meal prepared by the valet who was making him so famous.

That would be something to look forward to, Helmut agreed. He held out his hand to shake Rico's in parting. "And you must come out to Villa Cerulea. My aunt Agathi loves nothing more than making new friends welcome. In fact, there is to be a party soon. *The* party, I should say. The Ferragosto. Save the evening of July fifteenth, will you?"

"It's saved."

For the first time since he had begun at the St. Raphael, Rico's thoughts were all pleasant ones. Maybe it *was* only because of his connection with the powerful cardinal in Chicago; but he felt he had his first true friend in Rome, and that made him happy. A whole new vista seemed to open up before him, a world to be tasted, to be experienced.

As he approached his apartment, he saw the lights still on in the windows. Vittorio was waiting, even at this late hour, to see his master to bed. He would be all curiosity, Rico knew; and he would certainly take the invitation to Ferragosto at Villa Cerulea as his personal accomplishment.

That unexpected thought tickled Lansing, and he laughed softly to himself as he closed the elevator doors.

[8]

While Richard Lansing was beginning "in the trenches," as Morandi had so aptly said, Maestro Guido de la Valle was laboring at a far different but not unrelated level. In the Vatican, everything is intertwined, and nobody works in a vacuum.

The war had been a steady backdrop for the Maestro's activities for six years, as it had been for everyone else, from Papa Profumi to the youngest chamberlain and the rawest guard. For Guido, as for his Pope, the object of all his work had been to make certain that the Church would be the phoenix that rose from the man-made ashes of war's conflagration. The greater the conflagration, the more important and urgent was the work to be done.

A man of lesser purpose than the current Keeper of the Bargain would long since have thrown his hands up in despair. Guido, however, had planned well, had used all of his contacts in that planning, and had fostered more contacts still. All of Italy would need rebuilding. Barely a bridge or a factory still stood in normal operating order. And the ruins of Italy were mirrored in every country within a thousand miles of Rome.

Before Italy entered the war, Guido and his associates had already invested extensively in the principal sectors of the industrial and agricultural life of Italy. Steel, cement, home industries, food packaging, cosmetics, construction, chemicals, timber, coal, electricity and gas, telephones, a long list of luxury goods, farming, mining, transport—the list of holdings was interminable.

All this infrastructure of investment was backed up by solid ventures in banking, insurance, and reinsurance. True, the damage to plant and equipment was extensive. But Guido and his associates still possessed funds ample enough to start the whole operation in motion again. His forte, however, lay in developing and orchestrating overseas operations. For Guido, "overseas" meant anyplace outside Italy. During hostilities, his associate Michael Manley of Australia took care of the Far East holdings. His two North American associates and the three in Latin America were in charge of affairs in the Western Hemisphere. Except for the last year and a half of the war in the European theater, even investments in

Western Europe had paid off. Everywhere now, of course, repair and reconstruction were needed. But the bulk of the moneys in his care and under his supervision had been invested through Switzerland. In principle, he had lost very little. In fact, he was owed much.

At the moment, therefore, when the war in Europe's ancient heartland came to a crashing stop, no institution was better prepared to take the reins of the future in hand than the Vatican's Istituto per le Opere di Religione, the Banco, "the Pope's store." Its director, Guido, intended to do just that.

Obergruppenführer Wolff's negotiations with Papa Profumi were just successfully completed, when all fighting in Italy ceased. Within two days of Mussolini's death, the world heard the news of another dictator's inglorious end: Adolf Hitler killed himself on April 30. General Kesselring surrendered his million troops one day later. Within six days, the remaining German generals signed the formal instruments of unconditional surrender. Within two months, the Potsdam Conference would open, and the Allies would impose their own peace conditions. The European front was history. Troops and civilians alike emerged from the rubble to gaze on the pathetic meaning of victory.

War still raged in the Pacific theater. Dire foreboding filled the minds of planners as they contemplated the probable losses in men and materiel it would cost to take the home islands of the empire of Japan. The Maestro, however, took consolation from the fact that the European theater was pacified. The dreadful specter that Papa Profumi had spoken of so often in these past months, as the Allies had prolonged the war, was halted at last. Surely there would be no need now for the deep changes in policy and operations that the Pope had been flirting with. Hadn't Profumi himself admitted that there might be no need for drastic changes? Profumi still waited for his sign; Guido knew that. But for the Maestro, the signs were already plain enough all around him. Rebuilding was the need now. Rebuilding Italy and Europe. The power to participate in all that would place the Church, with its message and its mission, more strongly in the midst of the world and its people than ever before. It was the managing of that rebuilding process that must be their prime goal now, Guido was certain. Profumi would see the wisdom of that, surely.

And yet, in meeting after meeting, Profumi had still refused to give his final approval for the needed expansion of Guido's activities. Reconstruction must begin, of course, he conceded. Not only of roads and bridges and cities, but of government itself. Profumi had no intention of *letting* things happen to Italy. He was intent on *making* them happen in the political arena. One of his deliberate plans was to refinance and refurbish the People's Party, give it a new name, Christian Democrats, supply it with ample funds, organize a ready source of votes by means of a Catholic social organization which he had already named: Catholic Action. When national elections came, he intended the Democristiani to win by an absolute majority. That much seemed necessary. And surely it would cost money. But expansion beyond what was immediately needed for the survival of Italy and the Vatican, expansion in real terms of finance and power—on that the Pope had not yet given the nod.

The bargain the Pope had allowed to be struck with Wolff would be honored. The passports for the twelve German officers were to be prepared against the day when they could safely make their way by sea to Latin America. The Swiss Windfall, however, was to be kept in place, Profumi insisted, and no extraordinary use was to be made of it. Papa Profumi clung stubbornly to the growing conviction that a great and unwelcome change had already entered the working of the international world. If that was so—and he would know for sure only by means of the sign he was so confident would come—then business as usual would not be the boon it seemed. On the contrary, it could well mark the undoing of the Church.

"Just as wood has a grain," Profumi said, "so with human history. Religion and love have formed that grain; but now rude hands are splitting the tree."

Guido had taken up the simile for his own argument. "Then we will use the wood for fire to destroy our enemies, Holiness."

But no. Profumi would wait for his sign. "It will come, Maestro. Soon. The sign will come. The Blessed Mother will not fail me."

Perhaps, the Maestro thought. But May gave way to June, and when the Pope left for his summer residence at Castel Gandolfo, Guido felt he could wait no longer. They were not alone in the world, after all. The opportunity that was theirs now, thanks to all of Guido's foresight and careful planning and hard work, could easily slip into other hands. And where would be the advantage in that?

With Papa Profumi at Castel Gandolfo, it was not necessary for Guido to spend as much time at the Vatican himself. He had everything he needed at Villa Cerulea. Apart from his former hermitage at Mount Athos, which was the haven of his memory, nothing in the Maestro's daily life consoled and restored him to peace of soul as that great estate, surrounded by the Alban Hills as by so many cowled heads bowed in prayer. All of Guido's history after Mount Athos, all that had made him what he had become, all that he wished to be, was symbolized by Villa Cerulea.

Not that Guido himself was responsible for the splendor of the place. The credit for that belonged to his sixteenth-century ancestor. Gottfried, the Austrian Jew, had come down to Italy, converted, changed his name to Guido, and amassed a fortune as business manager for three popes. His portrait, complete with ruffles, hose, and doublet of a Renaissance *cortegiano,* a gentleman of leisure and achievement, hung in its rich gilt frame over the great fireplace in the upstairs library. He had been the one who had planned the sweep and the majesty of Villa Cerulea and named it after the blue-green color of his wife's eyes. From the intricate cellars that honeycombed its basement, through its Great Hall, its massive and proudly curving staircases leading to its upper floors, its scores of rooms topped by painted concave ceilings, and right up to the four rounded towers that pointed toward heaven with the stalwart certainty of the Evangelists themselves, Villa Cerulea had stood ever since like a promise fulfilled.

It was the Maestro's grandfather, Guido by name as well, who had at last framed the magnificent house in its setting of graceful acres—lightsome gardens and restful woods; winding paths; the massive entry gate set in a high granite wall; the breathless arc of the drive that swept visitors between hillocks and wooded entrenchments until suddenly they were at the foot of blue limestone steps leading to the great oaken doors of the de la Valle home.

That Guido's portrait immortalized him wearing the insignia of the Vatican Noble Guard and holding a red book identical in every way with the one the Maestro always kept with him.

The man the Maestro had called Uncle had added less to the splendor of Villa Cerulea than others, perhaps because he had died so uncharacteristically early for a de la Valle. While his portrait showed him in more somber dress, as befit a gentleman of Edwardian times, the eyes were the same startling blue-green, and his right hand held the same red book embossed in gold, its secrets locked beneath its clasp. That was the man who had gone and fetched the Maestro from the peace of his hermitage and committed to him the family trust, the sacred Bargain.

It was at least a symbolic contradiction that the Maestro's rooms, set off in the east tower, were stark by comparison with the rest of the house. Still, his study, where he did most of his work, and the conference room adjoining it, had every conceivable contrivance and convenience to help him in the management both of his personal affairs and of the far vaster affairs of the Holy See. And for all its simplicity of decor and furnishings, it was much more comfortable in feeling than any office he had been in anywhere else in the world.

The Maestro's days in that June of 1945 began long before his sister, Agathi, had wakened. He had left the preparations for the coming Ferragosto celebration in her hands as always, and she was glad not to have her brother underfoot as she made her plans for the huge party and for the special guests who would be staying over. By the time Helmut drove off each day for the Banco, Guido had already spoken by phone to a dozen bankers on the daylight side of the globe. By eight, he was ringing phones in the Vatican Secretariat and the Banco, where clerics and lay workers were just coming in to work. Every call, every letter, every memorandum, every directive, put another piece of his wide-sweeping plans in action.

Franze Sagastume took on much of the sensitive legwork, transferring securities, depositing checks, carrying personal communications from the Maestro around Rome. On some days he drove Guido in to his Vatican office, or to a business luncheon, or, occasionally, to Castel Gandolfo if there were matters to discuss with His Holiness that could not be confided on the telephone or in writing. During those weeks, Guido often labored until long after the house was deep again in sleep around him.

Even with all this activity, however, it was clear to Guido that until the basic question of whether to expand the Holy See's activities was decided yea or nay, he could not forge ahead on a clear path. A yea decision would mean he could use not only Mussolini's gold and the Swiss Windfall, but everything else at his command. It was an opportunity that would not come again.

July upon him, Guido did what had to be done. Through Sagastume, he first sent a brief but carefully worded memorandum to Papa Profumi at Castel Gandolfo, suggesting that the time had come to put the matter of expansion, and therefore of the Swiss Windfall, before the Council of State of the Vatican at its next weekly meeting. "To wait any longer," he wrote, "would be to run a greater risk than seems prudent."

At Castel Gandolfo, Sagastume was instructed to wait; His Holiness would send a reply.

Guido read the Pontiff's words alone in his study later that day.

> We remind you, Maestro, that what has come to be called the Banco must not become what that name implies. When We established it, We called it the Institute for Religious Agencies. As *that* name implies, Our intent was to have a Vatican institute responsible for and capable of sponsoring religious works. Truly works of religion, for religion, through religion. It freed Us from the need to seek patronage from any other banking system in Italy or abroad. And for that We have you to thank, Maestro, Our true servant, and servant of Holy Mother Church. It has allowed Us to remain independent of Axis powers and Allies alike in this war. And it has made Our Vatican State a solid fact in the world and the marketplace of men. For that, too, We have you to thank.
>
> Now, Maestro, We face a question together. When does Our Institute for the Works of Religion cease to be that in fact as well as in name? When does it become what it is so often called: a bank, pure and simple? When do the Children of Light become the very same as the Children of Mammon?
>
> We face that question now more urgently than ever We might have thought. Within the past twenty-five years, first the Soviets, then the Nazis, carried out social revolutions that destroyed traditional loyalties, norms, and values. Within the last two weeks, Mussolini's death carried the portents of those revolutions into Our own Italy. The Allied insistence on unconditional surrender was and remains, in Our view, a worldwide portent of that same destructive revolution. There is an evil abroad in the world, as We have said to you, Maestro; an evil that makes society into its own pawn. When there is no basis at all for continuing civilization except a lie that makes evil into good, then that civilization cannot hold. And so the question of when the Children of Light become the Children of Mammon is made urgent in this very time.
>
> In our lifetime, Maestro, you and We will face the answer to that question. As you judge it necessary to place the issue of the Swiss Windfall before the State Council without further delay, do so. Father Lanser will represent Us there in the usual manner.

Guido found Papa Profumi's letter clearly unsettling, there was no denying that. Nevertheless, at long last, he had the permission he needed. Under his direction, the papers were prepared, summarizing clearly for the cardinal members of the Vatican State Council the opportunities, the dangers, and the choices that faced the Pope and the Vatican with summary urgency, just as a new postwar world was being born.

[9]

On the morning of July 13, the Governing Council of the State of Vatican City met in the central conference room of the Secretariat of State.

As absolute monarch in the Church, the Pope has a personal mandate to govern that Church, with or without the Vatican State. However, as head of that State, it is often said, the Pope reigns, and the Council governs.

As with most clichés, of course, that is not the whole of the matter. While it is true in practice that no pope today can govern without a State Council, the checks and balances between them are delicate, long-tried, and effective. Neither one is dependent upon, or independent of, the other. The Council's business is politics, insofar as politics touches the vital interest of the Church. The Council's function is to make political decisions, give political advisements, and express political opinions about important situations that may arise at any time in any sector of Church life and activity: in situations that have clear and vital implications for the Vatican itself or for the Church as a whole—the Church Universal, according to the time-honored phrase.

The Council's power, meanwhile, is far more subtle than either its business or its function. In principle, it has no executive power. It gives no mandate. It forbids. It permits. It advises. It suggests. It recommends. It is not created, renewed, or maintained by any one pope; in fact, it precedes and outlives all popes, each of whom approves but does not appoint new members of the Council once their names are placed before him by the existing members. Only death or heresy or election to the papacy removes a member from the Council. Each member is chosen on the strength of certain qualifications. One of the most important is his political leaning; for each main faction of the College of Cardinals is represented by at least one member. Another is the importance of the interests he represents. Yet, no matter how weighty the qualifications of each, all Council members are on an equal footing. Chairmanship is rotated.

While the papacy embodies the absolute mandate of a single man, the Council embodies the republicanism of the papacy. And together its members have managed for centuries to embody Rome's equilibrium in the exercise of authority and power.

The Council chairman on that July morning was Cardinal Falconieri of Bologna. In terms of political leanings, he spoke for the conservatives among Profumi's cardinals. In terms of power, he was the ranking member of the Secretariat of State. Just as Cardinal Krementz had explained to Richard Lansing, Papa Profumi had chosen not to name an actual secretary; but in the event of Profumi's death, it would be Falconieri who would guide the Church through the conclave that would elect his successor.

There were four other cardinal members in the Council, each powerful, and each representing one of three main factions among the larger body of cardinals. Cardinal Arnulfo of Naples, a traditionalist, was head of the all-powerful Holy Office, which watched over purity of doctrine. Cardinal Ferragamo-Duca of Rome represented the progressives among the cardinals; he was in charge of the Propagation of the Faith, a Vatican congregation or ministry with ramifications in every part of the Church. Cardinal Hans Hoffeldt of Munich represented the radical point of view, as well as specifically European interests, all of which had a vital stake in today's agenda. Absent from today's meeting was Cardinal Krementz. The old man represented American interests. But he had sent word that illness kept him from traveling. Monsignor Kieran O'Mahoney, his agent in Rome, had been briefed and would represent the cardinal's views.

There were two non-cardinals who had been granted permission to attend this July 13 meeting. Monsignore Alberto Di Lorio, a big football of a man with stunning girth, a pince-nez always askew at the end of his nose, represented the Vatican Bank, as well as Guido de la Valle and his collaborators. In his day, he had been the butt of a variety of nicknames, but "Sphinx" was the one that best described his unchanging, unrevealing, stone-faced expression.

Finally, Father Lanser was there, as he was at nearly every weekly meeting, on behalf of the Holy Father. What Lanser did or did not relate to His Holiness about each Council meeting depended on that good Jesuit's judgment. The Council, in its own unspoken way, depended on that judgment.

With practiced efficiency, the Council members took care of the more routine matters on this week's agenda. Without comment, Cardinal Falconieri as chairman nodded to Di Lorio. Everyone had studied the papers Guido de la Valle had so carefully prepared. Quickly and succinctly, Di Lorio added only one dimension to the facts and figures: In the Maestro's view, he said, the Fascist gold, the Swiss Windfall, and the other "sources" he expected to tap in the near and more distant future should be used to make the Church independently viable in the postwar world.

The Council listened attentively. When the Sphinx had finished, Falconieri turned to Father Lanser; they would have Papa Profumi's view of the issue.

Through his shaded spectacles, Lanser glanced at each Council member in turn as he explained the Holy Father's view: The Church was faced now with a totally new situation, where religion and morality were banished from international relations and the national life of states. The Church needed to refurbish not merely her image but her behavior, even if that meant forgoing the use of material competitiveness.

Falconieri, a practical man, asked Lanser by what means the Church would carry on its work in the world.

Lanser could respond only that the answer would come. Such a shift, if it became necessary, would take time, of course. But it was the Holy Father's view that the Council's decision in this matter should be deferred; the Holy Father would have a sign. This was a moment in the Church's history when impatient action might well move the Church in the wrong direction.

"I repeat"—Di Lorio did not wait for Falconieri's permission to speak —"we can rely on the integrity of Guido de la Valle and his associates. They will not prostitute the wealth of the Church."

Cardinal Falconieri laughed at the staid Di Lorio's use of that particular metaphor. "Alberto! You're like life—full of surprises!" He brushed back a rebellious lock of gray hair that was straying on his forehead. That lock was known to his colleagues as Falconieri's barometer; if it stayed in place, they said, he was tense, anxious; if it strayed, he was relaxed. He turned to his fellow cardinals, still smiling. "I think we can be satisfied that the Maestro makes good sense."

The others nodded. Arnulfo spoke the mind of the group. "We are satisfied that profits can legitimately be made."

"And that the Church needs them," Ferragamo-Duca added, glancing at Hoffeldt and O'Mahoney. "We cannot wait for signs from heaven. We've done quite well without one till now, thank you very much!" Ferragamo-Duca was not much of a believer, but he was an ardent Roman.

"Then I suppose," Falconieri said with his usual tact, "the only remaining question concerns the Holy Father and his knowledge of the Maestro's position." All three turned to Father Lanser.

"He knows," Lanser said shortly from behind the dark glasses. "He disagrees. But he knows."

"That's sufficient." Ferragamo-Duca was ready to close the discussion in the Maestro's favor.

"Your Eminences." Lanser was quietly insistent. "You are quite certain you do not go along with His Holiness's opinion?"

There were a few moments of silence. Falconieri exchanged glances with the other cardinals. " 'Quite certain' is too strong a phrase, Father. We understand His Holiness' mind, but it doesn't seem practical right now. If His Holiness does receive a sign, that's another story. Meantime, life goes on. We are responsible for the continuities of policy. When His Holiness dies, it is we who have to go on. He will be in heaven. We cannot see our way, if we adopt his opinion."

"I see." Lanser paused. He would make one more try. "His Holiness has a point of view difficult to explain. It's a radical view. 'Go slow with change in our Church,' says the conservative." A glance at Falconieri. " 'Hurry up and change,' says the progressive." Lanser's eyes met Ferragamo-Duca's. " 'Don't change at all,' says the traditionalist." He caught Arnulfo's eyes. "Yet the change being talked about by all three is change merely in order to conform with what is happening in the world around us, change in order to keep up with that world, in order to be acceptable in that world.

"His Holiness is neither conservative, nor progressive, nor traditionalist. 'Don't conform. Don't be acceptable. Don't "keep up." ' That is what he says. 'Transform both the Church and the world by a radically new approach.' "

Ferragamo-Duca looked at Lanser disbelievingly. "I don't understand, Father. . . ."

"Your Eminence," Falconieri broke in, knowing full well the cardinal's viciousness. "A moment, please." He turned then to Lanser: "Absolute certainty is a rare thing, Father. Even His Holiness is not certain; as you say, he waits for a sign. Perhaps the decision and recommendation of this Council will itself be that sign. Who can say? The hard facts remain that Maestro de la Valle's plans and intentions are clear, and that we have decades of experience to indicate the soundness of his judgment."

Falconieri turned then to Di Lorio. "You will inform the Maestro of our support for his decisions." The Sphinx did not change expression.

It was not even ten o'clock when Di Lorio returned to his office and made an entry in his office log. In an hour, Lanser would arrive at Castel Gandolfo to relate the Council's proceedings to Papa Profumi. In the days to come, the word would filter out to each level of authority, through the mass of differing viewpoints, nationalities, ideologies, and ambitions, through the carefully constructed interlocking directorate of the Church hierarchy. Those at each level would learn as much as was needed for their particular functions and participation.

The delicate balance between the cardinals who elect the pope, and the pope who makes the cardinals, had swung for this moment away from the pope. And yet they remained as always in lockstep, held within that unique balance of authority, obedience, and participative government by which Vatican State politics and the governance of the Church Universal are determined.

[10]

Germany's collapse and surrender brought still more starved and beaten and homeless thousands out of prison and labor camps to join the millions already desperate for help of every kind. They needed clothes, money, and food. They needed temporary shelter, word about their families, or comfort if no one else had survived. Thousands needed transit papers; thousands more sought a country to take them in. All needed some peg on which to hang a hope. Many organizations increased their efforts to keep up with the flood; but it was to the St. Raphael, with its unparalleled records and its unflagging expertise, that individuals and governments alike turned most often for help.

Despite the pressure and the spiritual and physical toll it took of him, Rico Lansing, in the view of more than one Vatican watcher, seemed born for such work as this. After Father Novarese had left, all but broken by the St. Raphael and relieved to depart, Rico was in full charge of the section that dealt with the most devastated areas of the European heartland. Nevertheless, the hallmarks of his work became and remained uncommon humanity and uncommon efficiency. Even with the endless number of cases he saw personally or at least reviewed with his staff, he rarely forgot a face or confused the facts that went with each one. Though his almost photographic memory impressed a lot of people, the most frequent comment about him was that he had a cool, accurate eye and a deep compassion—and that one never interfered with the other.

Rico quickly learned that salted away among the bona fide refugees were a certain number of scoundrels—turncoat spies, drug dealers, black marketeers, refugees from justice, common criminals—a dark assortment of characters who had wile and reason enough to con some softhearted priest into handing over the coveted Vatican identity papers. Those papers, without anything else required, would open ships' gangways and national borders alike. The lanky American from Peculiar, Kentucky, began to understand that things are sometimes genuinely desperate; but misery—real misery of the kind the world had harvested in a bumper crop out of the war—that was unique, and it couldn't be counterfeited. There would be some misstep or misstatement, something in the story, something in the voice, something in the eyes. Lansing was not a pushover.

Archbishop Morandi and Monsignore Da Brescia were not the only ones impressed with the new man in the Secretariat. Through his work, Lansing caught the attention of a number of Vatican hands, and the respect of more than a few. Trust, however, was another matter. That could come only with time, and rarely from every quarter.

Because his days were rough on the spirit, Rico was that much more grateful for his early Mass each morning. There he found the peace of mind and the nourishment of soul that made it possible for him to function under stress. Vittorio Benfatti added one more element for which he was intensely thankful: his daily routine was efficiently organized for him. The growing friendship with Helmut de la Valle was another bright side to life. Circumstances brought them together in meetings at the Banco concerning urgent funding matters for the St. Raphael; Rico was not surprised to find Helmut quick to see a point and clever in solving problems. The dinner he had promised Helmut was another relaxed, long talkfest for them both. And it was a positive triumph for Vittorio, who basked in its glow for days afterward during his daily rounds in the Vatican, where, after his own dignified and modest way, he made sure everyone knew about it. It was not everyone's master, after all, who received a de la Valle for dinner at home.

For the last few days before the Ferragosto party at Villa Cerulea, Benfatti's not entirely subtle coaching was meant to prepare Lansing for such an exceptional invitation. Along with dinner each evening, Rico was served a generous portion of lore about that great estate in the Alban Hills and the ancient family that called Villa Cerulea home. There was, for example, the tragic marriage of Signora Agathi: "He was a drunk and a wastrel, Monsignore, and insane, to boot," Benfatti confided. "Killed himself and their only child, they say, a boy not yet six, in a car crash. Right off the side of a cliff. Some say he meant to do it. God knows! That was when the Maestro brought Signora Agathi to live at Villa Cerulea. They are devoted to one another; but people who know her well always speak about a sadness in her—if I am not being too personal, Monsignore."

And about the Maestro himself: "They say Maestro Guido has always observed his vow of celibacy. He is as single-minded a servant of the Holy Father as the most enclosed monk anywhere in the whole Church. Single-minded, Monsignore."

There was even a word—a discreet one, to be sure—about the Maestro's unusual chauffeur-valet, Franze Sagastume. "It would be hard to miss noticing him, Monsignore. A giant of a man! No one seems to know where he comes from. Some say he's Greek. Guards and cares for the Maestro like the crown jewels. All in all, he gives a peculiar impression. Anyway, the Maestro trusts him implicitly."

Rico gradually pieced it all together, and by the time Helmut picked him up early on the evening of July 14, three things were clear, if Benfatti was to be believed. Whether in Rome or anywhere else, there was no family quite like the de la Valles; there was no estate as grand as Villa Cerulea; and Lansing would never attend a more sparkling celebration than this Ferragosto dinner party, "unless it might be the coronation festivities for a new pope."

Even with all that coaching, Rico was not fully prepared for the magnificence that opened out before him, as Helmut guided his car slowly up the giant drive already lined for a mile with the parked limousines of guests who had arrived before them. Little groups of liveried chauffeurs in shining boots and uniforms of gray and black and blue stood about gossiping and settling in for the evening's long wait. There were quite a number of silent and watchful men in tuxedos who were obviously not moving toward the house. Guards, Helmut explained. The countryside was not rid of robbers and thieves. "Don't let the fancy dress fool you; they know their business." Rico didn't doubt it for a moment.

As Helmut brought the car around the slant of a hillside, Lansing caught his breath at the first sight of the great house. Every Palladian window along the huge facade was ablaze with light. Two flags fluttered atop the eastern tower. One, Rico supposed, was the family coat of arms. The other was the yellow and white papal flag with the tiara and keys.

Helmut turned his car over to a footman, and the two friends climbed the broad steps, bathed in the golden glow that splashed over them from the massive open doors. There must have been a hundred guests already inside, but the Great Hall was not nearly filled. Rico tried to take it all in at once. The enormous room seemed to run from the front of the house to the back, where glass doors opened onto a long terrace and gardens. The ceiling was two stories high, its concave shape covered with frescoes. The walls were richly paneled and decorated with quattrocento paintings. The cornicework was as delicate as a spider's web.

The sound of soft music starting brought Rico's eyes up to the gallery, which lay in shadows. Near one of the huge staircases he saw the little group of musicians, and just caught a glimpse of a very large uniformed man surveying the crowd of guests. Sagastume, Rico surmised, guarding his master's kingdom just as Benfatti had said. Had he shared superstitions with the little doorman Amadeo, doubtless Rico would have touched his scrotum to ward off the evil eye. As it was, he simply looked away.

Everywhere his eyes turned in that room, he saw women aglitter in jewels and tiaras, and distinguished-looking men in evening clothes adorned with medals and gala sashes, mingling and gossiping with prelates of every grade and many nationalities. There were cardinals in ermine-trimmed copes, bishops in gleaming robes, monsignori in ritual magenta. Rico nervously fingered his own violet rabat and sash as his eyes traveled over the guests and back up toward the vaulted ceiling.

"Rico"—Helmut laughed—"you'll get a crick in your neck!"

A little embarrassed at his own gawking, Rico followed Helmut toward a receiving line. He was still gawking a little, though trying hard to be less obvious, when he felt Helmut's hand on his shoulder, impelling him forward.

"Aunt Agathi," he heard his friend say, "I've told you about Rico Lansing. . . ."

Agathi de la Valle was very simply one of the most beautiful women Richard Lansing had ever seen. Whatever picture Vittorio's description had painted in his mind was wiped away by the reality before him. She couldn't have been more than ten years older than he was. Her blond hair was swept back and caught by a gleaming tiara. Her eyes were like Helmut's but of a deeper blue and more shining, if that were possible. They seemed exactly to match her gown and the exquisite stones of her necklace and bracelets. Rico could not see any sadness on that face.

"Monsignore Lansing!" Her warmth was spontaneous. "At last we have the pleasure of welcoming you to our home." Rico bowed and took her hand gently. "We will have a long chat this evening, Monsignore, if at all possible. But now let me introduce you to your host." She took Rico's hand and led him a few steps to where her brother stood. "Guido *caro*, this is Monsignore Richard Lansing from your Secretariat, who has become such a dear friend of Helmut's."

If Agathi had been a surprise, Guido de la Valle was exactly what Rico would have imagined. Taller than Helmut, with a big frame and a barrel chest, white hair brushed back from a strong face, a long straight nose with a slight hump, flaring nostrils, a long and full mouth—the Maestro riveted Rico's attention immediately. And those eyes. The color might vary in shading, but the de la Valle eyes were unmistakable. And yet within Guido's there was a fire that neither Helmut nor Agathi displayed. All in all, the man seemed clad in a palpable aura of command and power.

Guido's welcome was less effusive but clearly as genuine as his sister's.

He gave Rico a firm, quick handshake. "Monsignore, I'm glad you have come." The English was almost perfect, with a slight drawl. "May this be the first of many enjoyable visits to Villa Cerulea."

The press of more guests arriving made it clear that this was not the moment for small talk. Rico was relieved. He needed time to adjust. Helmut promised to deliver his friend back to his aunt and uncle later in the evening, then led him off for his first taste of the social life the Vatican community conducted with the secular Roman world that surrounded it.

As Helmut introduced him to guest after guest, names tumbled at Rico in an endless cascade. Monsignore Bacci, Cardinal Mangano, Luigi Garganelli, Regice Bernardo, Contessa Maria di Parma, Jean-Pierre Duchesne, Michael Manley, Duchesse Guyon de Rochefoucauld, General Montefalcone, Ambassador Orzuk of Turkey, Signorina Ciaretta Profumi, Professore Orlandi . . . And so it went, name after name, group after group, all chatting and talking and laughing.

After some ten weeks of intimate daily contact with sad-faced, weeping souls, the flotsam and jetsam of war's cruelty, with their eternally woebegone stories and abiding loneliness, it was almost shocking for Rico to find himself with people possessed, it seemed, of undisturbed happiness and well-being. Even their beautiful clothes jarred on him, after the worn and miserable rags he had seen on his clients at the St. Raphael. The well-nourished bodies and satisfied voices of the men, the perfumes of the women, had an almost heady effect on him.

He shook hands, bowed, chatted, sipped his wine, laughed and smiled. But truth to tell, Rico found he was lost in the quick flow of conversation. Without Helmut to guide him through the first half hour or so, he wasn't sure what he would have made of it all.

"The first thing to remember," Helmut confided in a not entirely serious voice as they moved away from one group and toward another, "is that these great old halls were built so that all your friends and all your enemies could be gathered in plain sight, in one place. That way, there are no surprises!"

Rico laughed. Perhaps that was so when these places were built, he guessed. But the idea seemed outdated now.

"Not quite. You'll see it's still a useful system. Take old Cardinal Lisserant over there, talking to the French ambassador, who is very anti-Turk, and with the Turkish ambassador, who is very anti-French. Neither one of those two would be unhappy if the Vatican went up in a puff of smoke. Right now, the Holy See needs the Turks and the French need the Holy See. Nobody can make that situation pay off as well as the old tiger Lisserant. In fact, right now there are a dozen little international dramas being played out all around us.

"It takes a while to learn. But the point you must grasp is that what's important is never said in so many words. The trick is to fill in the blanks, and not to say too much until you *can* fill them in."

A short time later, and Helmut felt he really should relieve Agathi and Guido in receiving the late arrivals. Dinner would be soon, he said. "Just circulate a bit and enjoy yourself."

Rico did look confident enough, as he made his way about the hall, mixing with the guests. He saw a few people he knew from the Secretariat. Archbishop Morandi caught his eye and smiled. Even Monsignore Da Brescia looked almost affable. But a nagging sense of being in the wrong place pursued Rico; and, now and again, it made him study for an instant the face of some cardinal or bishop, drink in hand, holding forth to an impressive and impressed circle of lay people. "Does he really belong in this gathering?" Rico caught himself wondering once or twice. "In fact, do I belong in it?"

As the evening progressed, he realized the one subject he had not heard even mentioned was the war. Not that anyone avoided it or refused to talk about it. It just did not seem to be in the world or on the mind of anyone in this glittering assembly.

It was perhaps ten o'clock when Helmut, who, like his aunt and uncle, always seemed to know where everyone was, came to collect his friend again. Dinner was about to begin. The tables were arranged around the walls. Agathi, a knowledgeable hostess, had managed as always to group people who were at least reasonably congenial to each other. The object was to do as much as possible for the right people; and to avoid matching those who might cause anything from indigestion to an international incident. For all Signora Agathi's warmth and smiles and gracious beauty, a cool rational eye assessed every situation meticulously.

Rico had already met most of his dinner companions. Monsignore Cipullo resembled a chirrupy sparrow in voice as well as in the sound of his name. Regice Bernardo was an old and good friend of Guido de la Valle. While he wasn't a young man, his body looked remarkably fit—broad-shouldered and flat-bellied. A stubby, swarthy, bemedaled little man with a brilliant red and gold sash across his chest was presented as Count Saramati di Saramate. There were two cardinals, Felicità and Garronio, both youngish and both argumentative. Rico sat opposite Francis Xavier Kelly, who, as he discovered, was chairman of the Boston Immigrant Savings Bank and a distant acquaintance of his father's. As at any party where churchmen made up much of the guest list, there were relatively few women. Rico's table had only one. A florid-faced lady with a kindly voice and a great deal of jewelry introduced herself to Rico in impeccable English as Signora Benelli. She seemed already to know everyone else.

Except for answering a few questions about his own work at the St. Raphael, Rico had little to say; he wasn't sure he could fill in those blanks Helmut had mentioned.

He did listen with great interest, however, and decided that his earlier impression had been correct in a way. Conversation still did not center on the war or its aftermath; but not for the frivolous reasons Rico had assumed. Bernardo and Kelly and the others seemed already to be living in the future, as though they had access to a magic time machine. After Guido de la Valle, in fact, Bernardo turned out to be the most impressive man Rico had met that evening. He painted so brilliant a picture of a rejuvenated Europe that Lansing was tempted to ask if he had forgotten about the bombed-out streets of Rome. But it was he, not Regice Bernardo, who was odd man out at the table; everyone else appeared accustomed to assessing and planning and sowing seeds for times that seemed far distant to the young American.

After dinner, it was not with Agathi that Rico had the chat she had promised, but with the Maestro, who found him taking a breath of fresh air near the open glass doors of the terrace. A stroll in the garden, Guido suggested, would be just the right thing after eating. He was a master at making others feel at ease. In fact, despite the solitary nature of his work and his desire for discretion always, in social situations Guido de la Valle was the best of good and charming company. He placed a gently guiding hand on the younger man's shoulder. As they set foot on one of the dimly lighted paths that wound through the fragrant flower beds, the Maestro talked in a full but quiet voice about Rome and the Holy Father. Rico thought he glimpsed someone on the path nearest to them. He assumed it was the ever-cautious Franze Sagastume stalking silently in the shadows.

The Maestro knew, of course, that Rico was slated to return to Chicago and eventually to head that diocese. He chatted easily and amusingly about Cardinal Krementz and the greatness of the Catholic Church in the U.S.A. The monsignore would make a fine administrator, Guido was sure of that; he himself knew a little something about administration, and about the abilities Rico had already shown at the Secretariat. They stopped now and again as the Maestro made a point or drew his young guest out on one subject or another.

All in all, their time alone together could not have been more than a quarter of an hour. But at the end of that time, Guido de la Valle had become a puzzlement for Lansing. Rico enjoyed the company of the man; but he was sure of only one thing: he hadn't begun to understand one-tenth of his character or mind.

By the end of their stroll, on the other hand, the Maestro had no such uncertainties about Richard Lansing. He liked the way the younger man spoke his mind, liked the tough mettle he had shown at the St. Raphael. He would have to be tested further, of course. He had faith and he had character; but that wasn't always enough. Guido would bet on it, though: the American would come through any test they threw at him with flying colors. You could work with such a man at your side. Guido de la Valle rarely was wrong in such judgments. Empires sometimes depended on it.

"You must come back." Agathi gave Rico a wonderful smile as he and Helmut left for the drive back to Rome. "I never once had a chance to talk with you."

"Yes." Guido came up behind his sister and linked her arm easily in his. "You must come often, Monsignore. You must think of yourself as one of us."

11

On the morning after the Ferragosto party, Agathi de la Valle was up and dressed by six-thirty, and striding through the downstairs rooms toward the kitchens. A house such as Villa Cerulea did not run by magic. Since her arrival a decade before, Agathi had, little by little and most ably, taken over first the management of the household and then, increasingly, much of the day-to-day decisionmaking and the operation of the full estate. There was very little Agathi felt she did not understand about Villa Cerulea; and, in fact, it was she who solved most of the problems connected with the live-in staff and the tenant families on the property. She discussed the overall planning with Guido on the quiet evenings they managed to spend together in the upstairs library. Helmut, too, was wonderfully helpful, when called upon for advice in Guido's absences.

Agathi did not concern herself with her brother's work, or her nephew's career at the Banco. For all the centuries, since their ancestor Gottfried as the Pope's financier had established the de la Valle connection with the Holy See, one male issue in each generation was selected as the Keeper of that trust. No other member of the family was or could be directly involved. Guido was the Keeper now. Helmut would be his successor; but even he knew very little, for barring accidents, his day was yet far off.

And Agathi did not concern herself, either, about her personal wealth. Guido always directed the family finances, including hers, with a touch of genius that had made their inherited fortunes and holdings as solid as the Rock of Gibraltar. As solid as Villa Cerulea!

On this July morning, in addition to her normally full schedule, she and Guido had houseguests—a baker's dozen of them—who had stayed on after the Ferragosto for an important meeting with her brother. Some of them had traveled very far—from Canada and the U.S.A., even from Australia and South America. All of them must be tired; and all of them, she reasoned, would be grateful to have breakfast served in their rooms before being "locked up," as she thought of it, in Guido's study for what would surely be a long session of work.

Agathi quickly arranged the logistics of the day with Mariella, the housekeeper, and the other house servants. Agathi had trained Mariella personally, and she knew that this farmer's daughter from the Abruzzi, with the big black eyes, wide-waisted body, and powerful hands, had become as attached to her and to Villa Cerulea as though she herself were a de la Valle.

Breakfast, Agathi instructed, would be light—melon from their own fields, ham from the smokehouse, fresh bread from the farm ovens, "and plenty of that wonderful coffee Claro Trujillo brought with him all the way from Colombia." The guests, she continued, should be awakened and served within the hour. They should be told that the Maestro would await them in his private conference room at nine o'clock. "They know the way." She glanced at one or two of the newer servants. "They have all been here often before. Later, lunch will be brought up to the library. Sagastume will let you know the hour, Mariella, but have everything in readiness."

The day begun, Agathi strolled into the sunlit breakfast room. To her surprise and pleasure, Helmut was there, already halfway through his meal. She saw by the empty plate that Guido had already eaten.

"Sì, zia." Helmut confirmed his aunt's observation. "He went to an early Mass in the village. Sphinx Di Lorio arrived a few minutes ago—you should have seen him! All dressed up, bright-purple buttons from chin to toe, a furry Roman hat on him, shoes so polished you could use them as a mirror! He and Uncle Guido have gone up to his study. Your ears should have been burning, though. We were talking about how well things went last evening, at Ferragosto. You outdid yourself!"

Agathi knew her nephew was not flattering her. For one thing, she knew Ferragosto had indeed been a marvelous success, even by her brother's high standards. And she knew that by now Helmut understood the uses of such affairs almost as well as Guido did. Neither man ever made light of them.

She smiled at the compliment, but was worried to hear how early Guido's day had begun. He had been working too much lately, sometimes twenty out of twenty-four hours. She knew there must be a crisis; but not even Guido was strong enough to keep up that kind of schedule much longer. She said as much to Helmut, but he brushed aside such worry with a kiss on her cheek as he rose to start his own day. "Don't worry, Aunt Agathi. Uncle knows what he is doing!"

"Perhaps . . ."

Helmut did not wait for her to finish her thought, and so she did not. "Perhaps . . ." She whispered her worry again to herself.

Up in the large room adjoining the Maestro's private study, the Sphinx, bright-purple buttons and all, solemnly placed a thick leather folder at each of thirteen places around the long, polished conference table. Each folder was embossed with a name, and each contained several reports neatly typed in the language of the man for whom it had been prepared. This was merely a courtesy, for each man who would attend the meeting there spoke more than one language; and all spoke at least English and Italian—whether with a good or a bad accent was beside the point.

Two of the reports in those folders were financial summaries prepared under Guido's general guidance by the investment wizard of the group, Regice Bernardo. The first summary, labeled "Account A," dealt entirely with Vatican moneys invested outside the active war zones over the past several years. The second, "Account B," summarized the handling of another $632 million that had been paid to the Vatican by Mussolini's government, ostensibly in exchange for a large amount of moribund securities belonging to three "branches" acquired by the Vatican's Banco—the Banco di Roma, the Banco di Santo Spirito, and the Sardinian Land

Credit. The Fascist government of Mussolini had generously paid face value for those securities, Guido's associates were aware, as a tangible "thank you" for munitions for his Abyssinian campaign.

There were additional papers in each folder. A brief summary of the Swiss Windfall and the Fascist Party gold. A summary of the Holy Father's position concerning the future involvement of the Church and the Vatican in commercial and political affairs. And, finally, the minutes of the most recent meeting of the Vatican State Council, at which its members had thrown their weight against the Pontiff's position, at least in regard to finances.

It was the Council vote, its mandate, if you will, that had come to dominate Guido's thinking day and night. *"We can rely on . . . Guido de la Valle and his associates. . . ."* He had read those words a hundred times in the past day or so. Had he been a different man, a mere corporate tiger, for example, or minister of some secular state, such a blank check placed in his hand would have been a triumph. But the Maestro was neither of those things, and did not even remotely equate himself with anything so ordinary in worldly affairs.

The letter the Pontiff had written from Castel Gandolfo had been on target. The Banco had been founded, just three years before, only with papal approval. Officially, it was called the Institute for Religious Agencies—the IRA, for short. But everyone except Profumi called it the Banco. It had been buttressed from the start with the power of the Pope—power, then, that could not be changed or withdrawn except by the most cumbersome of Vatican machinery and by a truly revolutionary papal decision. And it had been established only and precisely to continue into the rapidly changing modern world the work Guido's ancestors had done before him. That was work for, and in the name of, the Vicar of Christ, the Keeper of the Keys and of Christ's Church. With good reason, then, Guido like all the Keepers of this trust before him had always done his work within the stated policies and purposes of the Pope. Oh, yes, there had been deviations in the past; situations that had forced things off the main course. But never, either before or since the Banco was formed, had any de la Valle purposefully set out to go against the Pontiff's expressed wishes.

What was troubling Guido now wasn't a question of disobedience in faith or morals; in such matters, Guido would not have had a moment's doubt. It wasn't even a question of more mundane disobedience. Guido knew Profumi's character well enough. When this Pope meant to be imperative, the order was given and there was no deviation tolerated. No excuse or exception was acceptable to Profumi. If the Pope had given an order, Guido would not even be discussing "Should we?" but only "How shall we?"

For the Maestro, that was the problem. The Pope had given no order. He had expressed an opinion: Summary evil is abroad among men. And a wish produced by that opinion: We of Christ's Church must not immerse ourselves in, or connive at, that summary evil. But no order. And no plan. No way to proceed. Or even survive. Except the plan that Guido had devised and had now brought to the brink of such success that he could almost see its very outlines on the near horizons of power—outlines that loomed greater than anything he had conceived before.

"And yet . . ." How many times had he said those two words, as he paced his rooms in the darkest night hours? "And yet, if I proceed alone, without papal blessing for the first time . . ." Guido would stop his pacing at such a thought, and stare ahead as though at some limit he had never thought to brush against. There was no area of the Church not already touched by the infant Banco. Just three years, and already there was no country, no diocese, no religious order that was not included in some way within the lengthening shadow of the IRA. If he went forward now, within ten years its power and its influence would be as great as—no, greater than—those of any institution on earth. By papal order already in place, no one would be able to interfere with it. He, or Helmut if that was the way of things—at any rate, the Keeper of the de la Valle bargain—would be dealing on a plane that would concern, if not govern, every facet of Church and salvation.

At such a thought, Guido's mind would almost stop functioning, and he would begin pacing again, as if to get his head going anew in some productive way. The words of Profumi's letter would often force themselves forward again at such a moment. *"We remind you, Maestro, that what has come to be called the Banco must not become what that name implies. . . . When do the Children of Light become . . . the Children of Mammon? . . . The question . . . is made urgent in this very time."*

He had tried and tried, but Guido could not answer that question. Would it be better to wait, then? To see the opportunities that now were ripe soften and slip away forever? No. It seemed clear enough that waiting was not what it seemed in this matter. To wait was to make a choice against seizing and making the most of this unique moment of history. To wait could prove fatal.

It was a question of balance, then. Could Guido keep the power, the enormous power the Banco could amass, under control? The Vatican State Council had said they trusted him to do just that. *". . . Guido de la Valle and his associates. . . ."*

And so he waited with some impatience for those associates to gather on this July 15 morning. He would have one last counsel, that of his closest, most experienced men of trust. By the end of this day, the matter would be decided. If it was yes for Guido's plans, then he would move forward without delay and without tremor. If it was no, then the work of the orderly dismantling of the carefully laid foundations would begin.

And then? The Maestro did not know. He could not see how his Pope and his Church could thread their way on another path in the coming world. But still, he would not go lightly against the papal wish.

Dr. Regice Bernardo, who had so impressed Rico Lansing the previous evening, was generally the first of the group to arrive at any meeting. That morning of July 15 was no exception. Bernardo was Guido's oldest associate, both in age—he was a hale and hearty sixty-five—and in service. He was the only one of the group who could be described as an employee of the Vatican. Guido had got to know him fifteen years before, in 1930, as a financial genius, and had tapped him at once as overall manager for the investment of Vatican moneys. As usual, Guido's quick assessment of the man had proved accurate. Over the years, Regice had become almost like one of Guido's family, a favorite dinner and weekend guest at Villa Cerulea.

Guido, still in the adjoining office, on the telephone as he so often was, waved to his old friend to take his accustomed chair. Regice did so, with a good morning word to the Sphinx, who by then had taken his own place in a chair near the wall, his open Breviary in hand, the pince-nez askew on his nose, his expression as blank as it always was, his lips moving soundlessly in prayer.

Within moments, Luigi Garganelli and Daniel Loredan came through the door, squabbling good-naturedly. Garganelli was built like a bear, with wide shoulders, stocky frame, huge hands, a head of thick black curls framing a heavily jowled face. A Sicilian and a self-made millionaire in publishing, mining, and wheat, Garganelli always knew he would get a ribbing from Daniel. Loredan, tall, skinny, and suntanned, had a smile that showed much gold in his teeth. He was heir to old and solid money, from the elite classes of Venice, and he was caustic in a kindly way about new money, about Sicilians in general, and about his good friend Garganelli in particular.

Regice greeted both men warmly, and then Franco Graziani as well, the aristocratic and always impeccably dressed head of the fabulously powerful state-owned Industrial Reconstruction Institute, the IRI, who followed behind the other two Italians. Graziani was a man of few words, a warm heart, and *occhi di ghiaccio,* eyes of ice. He raised a hand in greeting —an effusive gesture for Graziani—and found his place at the table.

The other nine members of the group came in almost together, one after the other, and almost on the dot of nine. Wiry little Philippe Dominique, with his foxlike features, loquacious nature, and rapier wit, president of the Banque Commerciale de Dijon, was in fine fettle, as he always was.

Philippe's five-foot-four-inch frame seemed even smaller as he sat beside the huge Australian industrialist Michael Manley, whose three newspapers, some said, gave the news to Australia and half the world "down under," and then told them what to think about it all.

In spite of the Irish brogue he liked to use, Francis Xavier Kelly was "pure second-generation American," as Helmut sometimes teased him. Red hair now graying, freckled skin, a certain impish look in the blue eyes, and the quicksilver reactions marked him indelibly as Irish. It was not his brogue or his lineage, but his loyalty to the Church and his expertise as chairman of the Boston Immigrant Savings Bank, that had caught Guido's attention shortly before the war exploded in Poland in 1939. Kelly knew his way around American banking circles and the Federal Reserve.

Kelly and Dominique were not the only bankers there. Carlo Benelli was president of the Banco di Venezia; and though he looked more like a playboy and ladies' man—in his forties, very good-looking in a dangerous way, with dark hair, black eyes, liquid accents, and a pleasing smile—he would perhaps understand the complex reports in the folder that awaited him more quickly than anyone except Bernardo and Guido himself.

Count Adolfo Sarimati di Sarimate, "the Turk," was the only member who used his title; everyone else ignored it. Julio Montt, the Peruvian, and Carlo Trujillo of Colombia looked enough alike to be brothers or at least first cousins. Both were sallow, with shining black hair and handlebar mustaches. Although Trujillo was shorter than the Peruvian, they were both lean and athletic-looking. The third Latin American of the group, Ari Potamianos, though born and bred in Panama City, was Greek by blood. He had that sort of face—heavily lined, with hooked nose, thick-lipped mouth, and clever eyes—that you can find all over the eastern portion of the Mediterranean wherever the lingua franca of Arab, Jew, Greek, and Italian is understood. His type had been there since the time Homer spun the tale of the wily adventurous trader Ulysses.

All three Latin Americans, Julio Montt, Claro Trujillo, and Aristotle Potamianos, talked at once as they found their places. Frank Kelly couldn't see how the Latins could talk and listen at the same time, but he wished he had that gift. One of these days, he resolved, he would have to get Ari to tell him the secret. Ari could explain anything.

Jean-Pierre Duchesne came in last, as he generally contrived to do, his bright eyes gleaming in competition with his totally bald head. He was a high-powered character, a Canadian lumber king and newspaper owner with a husky figure usually dressed, as on this morning, in a very expensive version of lumberjack's clothes.

"Outrageous!" the impeccably dressed Graziani said.

"Thank you." Jean-Pierre rightly took the words as greeting.

Mariella bustled in with a large urn of Trujillo's gift of coffee. She placed it on the credenza beside the cups already laid out, and left as quickly as she had come. Franze Sagastume appeared from nowhere, glanced about the room, then left and closed the door behind him.

By the time Guido entered quickly from his office, the coffee urn was half empty and the room was silent as each man in the group read quickly and with sharp eyes through the papers in the leather folders. Because of the difficulty of travel during the war, they had not all met together in some time. Still, though only the Italians had been able to gather regularly during the war for each semiannual meeting, Guido had contrived to keep them all generally informed.

Each of them had been chosen by the Maestro himself; and each had been intimately associated with him for a considerable time in managing all financial transactions that did not concern the day-to-day administration of Vatican City itself.

Guido had satisfied himself that each associate was as devoted to the Church and to the papacy as he was, and that each could and would devote himself, as he did, to expanding a pool of wealth solely for the sake of that Church and that papacy. Together, their only aim in this world had to be the success of the social and political policies of the Holy See.

Once formed, the group went by no name, and needed none. There was occasional banter about *l'impero,* the empire, but that was more a recognition that their service was to a Vatican whose empire existed no longer; that, in fact, was why their group was needed—to keep the Holy See afloat without its former temporal power and wealth.

All of these men saw one another socially, too, without regard to the work at *l'impero.* They visited one another's homes, sometimes did business together, often vacationed in the same exclusive playgrounds of the ultrarich. Their children and nieces and nephews even intermarried. But this small collection of men shared a common mentality, possessed a common identity of aims that constituted a greater bond than any social or business relationship, a loyalty deeper than any oath or formal membership could possibly have evoked. They made up a smoothly working team. Their discussions were always low-key, in the tones used by men of substance who have perfect confidence in their own abilities and resources and are burdened with no fear of the future.

No such wide-ranging organization as *l'impero* had been needed for many years. But in 1929, Mussolini and the Vatican had signed the Lateran Pacts. The Holy See, in reparation for the loss of its Papal State sixty years before, was awarded ninety million prewar dollars by the Italian government, together with other sums and assets, whose value was less widely known. The Holy See had received further reparation as well in the form of the greatest tax exemption possible. In effect, any corporation in which the Vatican had or would acquire a major equity holding was tax exempt. Through the thirties, further tax exemptions followed—exemptions from the war tax, for example, and from the graduated tax on capital stock, and from sales taxes, and from taxes on certain assessments and dividends. But, basically, it was as a direct result of the Lateran Pacts that Guido had seen the need to found a bank of its own for the Holy See. As the reparation moneys, once wisely invested, started to yield fruit, it became more readily clear that in war and in peace what the Holy See needed again was what it had once had for centuries: its own bank, and its own professional financial agency. By 1942, with the war fast becoming global, Guido's reasoning ran, the Vatican's economic well-being should not be tied to the banking system of any one country. Together he and these associates had established the Vatican's own bank, with Papa Profumi's blessing. It had rapidly become the main channel of their combined efforts.

As pages turned quickly, there were occasional questions about this acquisition or investment, that figure or date. But even with the lapse in regular meetings, all thirteen were familiar with the general lines of the data in the financial summaries A and B. The lists of companies that had been gobbled up were impressive—telephone, communications, cement, artificial textile fibers, electric power, agricultural implements, chemical products, gas, construction, pasta, literally hundreds of urban and rural banks and credit institutions, insurance. All in all, Regice Bernardo's expert execution of the investment plans had led to an eightfold increase in the Lateran Pacts' assets—Account A—which had been put to work outside the active war zones. Account B, meanwhile, had just about quadrupled.

The clever interlocking of directorates among companies that the Holy See had established did not escape any of the group. They had, in fact, helped to develop the system by which trusted Vatican representatives, *uomini di fiducia,* were placed in every sector where substantial Vatican sums were invested. Names they all knew—Sentini, Carelli, de la Valle, Raperato, Whitmore, de la Coste, Grundsbacher—perhaps two dozen of them, cropped up with orderly regularity.

The Vatican's favored position in the Industrial Reconstruction Institute headed by Graziani had obviously been of enormous advantage in the whole process of growth and diversification. Established by Mussolini in 1933, the Institute was government owned and subsidized; and it controlled close to one-third of all investments in Italy through bonds issued in the open money markets. Guido saw to it that the Vatican had become the single largest investor in those bonds and thereby exercised control over more than one hundred major companies in the country.

Banking strengths, as the reports indicated, lay mainly in the north, in the Veneto and Lombardy provinces. But there were already indications in the reports of some movement to establish mutual business interests with houses of credit and banking in Switzerland, Liechtenstein, and Panama, and to expand interests in small but promising northern Italian banks such as the Banco Agostiniano of Milan.

From his chair at the head of the table, Guido watched each face as his associates passed from the financial summaries to the matter of the Swiss Windfall and Fascist Party gold. He watched expressions change to surprise and concern as, one after another, the group moved on to the paper summarizing Papa Profumi's position concerning the Banco and what it should and should not be doing in a radically changing world. Guido could see that, to a man, the *impero* was taken aback, as he had been when the Pontiff had first begun to share his deepening misgivings with the Maestro. As he had expected, four of the thirteen seemed especially tight-lipped. The Turk, the Colombian Montt, Kelly of Boston, and Loredan of Venice had always been the stalwart guardians against any move to cross the Pope even in the slightest detail.

Finally, everyone turned silently to the minutes of the Vatican State Council meeting of two days before. By the time they had all finished the last page, it was clear on every face that each understood, at least in broad terms, the huge decisions that had impelled the Maestro to call them all together. Not one of them would have wanted to decide these matters alone.

"Well, my friends!" Michael Manley heaved a sigh as he pushed his great frame out of his chair. "The fat's in the fire for us now." He poured himself some coffee, and returned to his place beside Philippe Dominique.

Guido chose to be more to the point. "The decisions we make here today, by their very nature and magnitude, will take on a momentum that will not easily be changed. So let us all be clear about just whose fat is in what fire.

"As you have all seen by the reports, the guidelines we have set for carrying out our work, and Regice's expert management of day-to-day investments, have borne fruit exactly as we planned. Reports A and B make the details clear enough. If there are any surprises, they are all on the plus side.

"Now, I take it you all understand the details of the Swiss Windfall and Mussolini's Party gold. Their sources are clear, are they not?" Guido glanced about the table. There were no questions. "And it is clear that the minimum sum we are dealing with from those two sources is roughly half a billion dollars." Again, no questions.

"Well, then," Guido went on methodically, "financially we stand at a watershed moment. We are perfectly positioned, both in our widespread connections laid out in these reports, and by the arrival of these new assets into our hands at this precise moment, to enter into the higher realms of money and economic expansion, to create a higher stake for the Church in wealth and power than even we envisioned fifteen years ago.

"We have the blessing of Cardinal Falconieri and the others on the Vatican State Council, as you read in the minutes of their meeting."

"But"—Frank Kelly held up the summary of Profumi's position—"we do not have the blessing of the Holy Father, Guido!" Predictably, Kelly was joined in his objection by the Turk, by Julio Montt, and by Daniel Loredan. "The financial activity of the *impero* should follow the guidelines of the Pope to the letter."

"Exactly!" Guido welcomed the point. It was not that they had sought or felt they needed His Holiness' approval for every detail of their work and administration of funds. That was both unnecessary and impractical. "But in this case, we have guidelines. I think you can all see, as clearly as I, that waiting—whether for a sign or for any reason—is to make the decision to pull back. Waiting means time. And time is the essential factor in success just now."

That, however, was only one new element facing them today. Guido pointed out that they themselves had never been in a situation such as this, where the Pontiff's wishes and those of the Vatican State Council's members had been at such loggerheads on so basic and vital an issue. "The entire choice has de facto been left to the *impero.* To us, gentlemen!"

Guido looked around at each of his associates. "If we decide to use the Swiss Windfall and the money from the Fascist source for expansion of our operations, there is no doubt that we will put into motion a whole galaxy of activities that will not merely make things possible for the Church to achieve, but may well carry the Church along on their tide.

"And *that*, gentlemen, is the crux of the major decision that faces us today. Not merely to go against the advice and opinion of the Holy Father. But whether we should—or perhaps 'must' is the word—become now more than a mere appendage of the Holy See. For it seems clear to me that if we expand our operations and our capital growth in a manner even approaching what is possible for us at this moment, we will be leaving behind any thought of ourselves as a closely controlled operation, working directly at the will of those who normally govern and regulate each important segment of this Holy See."

"Guido, a few questions before you go on." It was Graziani, who as the hard-fisted chief of the IRI had always been one of the most intensely practical of the *impero* members. "Does Papa Profumi intend to stop all political activity? And does he have alternate means of financing the Holy See and its staff? And what of the financing of charitable works? If we decide to run in place—never move ahead—will the Vatican not be forced to cannibalize its capital to meet expenses? And if we disband altogether, the Vatican will be bankrupt in short order, indeed! Or am I wrong?"

Guido answered as completely as he could. No, he said to Graziani's first question, the Pontiff did not intend to cease all efforts to influence political life, particularly in Italy. In fact, the Pontiff had plans on the drawing boards for a broad and energetic strategy to refinance and resurrect the old moribund People's Party. The plan was to rename the Party, and create an ancillary organization, Catholic Action, throughout every village, hamlet, town, and city in Italy, in order to garner votes. The object of the plan was to head off the Communist power play that was certain to come, and to make sure that Italy's first postwar government, at least, was Christian and democratic. "The Democristian Party will be Profumi's baby," Guido explained, "and the Catholic Action organization the means by which a plurality of votes will be assured for that Party's victory. Both organizations will need money. Much money."

"So, then"—Graziani looked about with those eyes of ice—"we must look at the practicalities of the Holy Father's position."

Guido took the point. "Regice has a tentative estimate, I believe, of how much the Holy Father's political initiatives are expected to cost over a ten-year period."

Regice was ready. "These are difficult figures to fix precisely in advance. You can understand that, I'm sure. But within general lines, I would foresee that the initial outlays will be in the region of $20 to $30 million. After that, perhaps, some $5 to $8 million each year. That's a bare minimum. Over five years, calculate something in the region of $50 to $60 million."

"I have been making notes from Regice's figures on the report of normal income and expenditures of the Vatican State," Garganelli broke in. In most *impero* decisions, this tough-minded Sicilian had often backed and admired Guido's vision. "If I understand you, Regice, the rundown of expenditures you've just given will be in addition to the increasing yearly deficit of the Vatican. True?"

"True. For the ordinary upkeep and running of the Vatican, income derives from bequests, contributions—in a good year, both yield anything up to $5 million. Add in Peter's Pence for another $1.5 million every June 29. Postage stamps average about $200,000 annually. Land revenues never bring in more than a quarter of a million. And . . . hmm, at present, let me see, the annual payroll runs to a little more than $4.5 million, and that takes in everything from cardinals, lawyers, secretaries, librarians, Latinists, throne-bearers, down through stonemasons, seamstresses, florists, carpenters, plumbers, archivists, cobblers, ushers, and simple cleaners.

"The cost of the big items such as the diplomatic corps, the sixty-unit car pool, the seven-day newspaper, the radio station . . . add in special accounts—the Holy Father's own Number 10, the Special Administration's Number 2, and suchlike—all that brings total operating expenses to more than $14 million. . . . There's a continual deficit mounting each year, side by side with other mounting costs. The State cannot make up that deficit of itself. Currently, of course, the deficit is made up by voluntary tax-exempt contributions from corporations in which we have a substantial equity participation."

Regice stopped his financial summary abruptly, and shook his head. "It can't be done, my friends. I don't see how the Holy Father can run the Church and the Vatican unless we can increase the funds available on a reliable and predictable basis. Oh, I know as well as anyone here—as well as Frank, Daniel, and all of you—that the handling of Accounts A and B, the reinvestment of acquired funds, the opening of foreign accounts, the acquisition of fresh equity positions—all this has nothing directly to do with the Vatican's income. Not only is the Banco—the Institute for Religious Agencies—merely one Vatican office; it has a separate and special papal charter all its own. All of us here function as a group in lockstep with the Banco, not with any other part of the Papal State of the Vatican. Nor were we conceived to be the tail that wags the dog, if I may use that expression.

"But we do have a supplementary function vis-à-vis the other parts of the Vatican City State. That of quiet cushion. For that reason, the sovereign Pontiff entrusted to our care the nourishment of the Holy See's special funds, so that in the banks associated with the Holy See, the various drawing accounts needed for the different sectors of Vatican City State will never go dry. For public consumption and in law, those different accounts must be kept separate. Deficits they always will have. The Propaganda Fide Congregation will go on losing money, as will the Congregation of the Council, and Vatican Radio, and *Osservatore Romano.* But please! These are deficits in single and separate accounts."

"Well, that may seem like a lot of red ink," the Turk intervened. "But in our present state we can afford it all. So what is the difficulty?"

"Prescisely, Excellency," Regice answered. "We can stand still where we stand. We do pay the bills, don't we? But as Graziani rightly said earlier, if we stand still and stop expanding altogether, we shall shortly be forced to eat into our capital. We shall thus once again mortgage our future, if we just stand pat.

"That is exactly what happened to the Holy See in the past, especially between 1900 and 1929—it literally ate up its capital resources. If it hadn't been for Cardinal Krementz of Chicago and our good friend Basil Lansing, bankruptcy would have been inevitable. Life is already more expensive, and in the postwar world it is not going to get any cheaper.

"Now, the opportunity we have at present will not come knocking at our door again. Can any of you foresee at the end of this cursed war a repetition of the circumstances that put us in the way of such an increment of funds? No, history does not repeat itself in that fashion, at least not in the same century. And we live in this century. This is no rehearsal. This is it, gentlemen!"

"I think, my friends," Guido said slowly, "that this is not a decision we can make on the ground of money alone. That's important, and I for one cannot see how to overcome the problem Regice has outlined, unless we take new steps to finance even what Papa Profumi wants to do in the near future in Italy alone. But that financial need has to be coupled with the equally grave matter Frank Kelly raised earlier. We do not have the blessing of the Holy Father. That's a first for me. And for the *impero.* And yet our decisions will carry over into every crevice of the Church Universal. Have we the right . . . ?"

"With all due respect, Guido, it seems to me your question is the wrong one." Philippe Dominique had followed the points with clear logic, and had made up his mind. "The 'right,' as you call it, has been forced on us. We all had better remember Papa Profumi's character. He is as gifted at analyzing situations as any man here—as any man in the world, in fact. And he is courageous; we've all seen evidence of that. And he's not afraid to give orders and see that they're obeyed. Now, if you put all that together in this situation, you have to say certain things. First, he understands the financial situation; he even created the Banco to deal with it, after all. Second, he has given no order to stop our activities. Those activities have always meant growth, investment, reinvestment. It is only the matter of degree that is at issue here."

Kelly and Loredan were both ready to counter Dominique's view. It was Loredan who spoke first. "Matters of degree, Philippe, make the difference between a birdbath and an ocean. Papa Profumi has not given an order, you say. But I see Guido's dilemma. In a sense, for Papa Profumi, the Beast has been let loose among men. And apparently he sees the manifestation of that Beast clearly in the modern uses of material power. And in all that goes along with materialism—lies, killing, mercilessness, pride, irreligion. And if the Pontiff's wish is not an order, still it seems clear—and bold, by the way; even courageous. Shed all dependence on the material wealth we have and can accumulate. Turn to other ways of sustaining the needs of the Church."

"*What* other ways?" Benelli's tone was measured, but his words were blunt. "And by what means, Daniel? It is not just that the Pontiff hasn't given orders or expressed a wish. It's that with or without a sign, he has no plan, even in general terms; at least not beyond his plans to keep Italy out of Marxist hands, if he can. Granted he is courageous. And granted the very thought of shedding dependence on what people think of as 'wordly power' is bold. But how? Concretely, how?

"Just being courageous and bold does not make it correct or wise or even godly, my friends. Not in my opinion. Not even in his. Otherwise, he *would* have imposed an order, and not expressed a mere wish. So we are not offending against our faith, which tells us that this man is the Vicar of Christ, of God Himself on earth. In fact, we are not dealing with matters of faith here. Only with the *means* of *propagating* the faith among our fellow human beings. And, in this matter, there have always been differences of opinion between pontiffs and their servants in the government of the Vatican. We all know that.

"In other words, we are faced with a situation in which we have the liberty of implementing what we think is the best course of action. The Holy Father disagrees profoundly, but he leaves us our liberty. The worst thing we could do is to do nothing, to let the Vatican founder in ten or twenty years' time, to let the Holy See become dependent on outside agencies for its very physical survival."

Throughout the discussion, Guido was uncharacteristically silent. Through the rest of the morning, through lunch in the library, and into the afternoon, he listened, he prodded for new ideas, for assessments of the future, in greater and greater detail. Often it was like listening again to his own warring thoughts in the days and nights just past. Finally, in the early afternoon, it was clear a consensus had been reached in the *impero.* They didn't take a vote; they never did that. There was nothing so formal as a concluding statement or a summing up. But at some point, even "the Pope's four" (that was how Garganelli, at least, thought of Kelly, Loredan, Montt, and the Turk), even they began to turn their attention to the details of implementation in what they all knew would be the greatest leap the Church had taken in material well-being since that far-off day in A.D. 315 when the emperor Constantine endowed the infant Church with its first riches.

By evening, each man knew his part, at least for now, for each would be deeply involved in a process that bid fair to make one agency of the Holy See—the Banco, the Institute for Religious Agencies—the dominant element in papal policy and Vatican actions on the international plane. Into the center of the centuries-old bureaucracy of the Pope, there had now been introduced an utterly novel aim: to attain equal pride of place at the green-topped tables of power, side by side with a host of nations and individuals who shared no ethical or moral or religious ideal or purpose with the Vatican.

[[12]]

In his retreat at Castel Gandolfo, by July of that year, Papa Profumi was deeply preoccupied with a different sort of balance sheet from those Regice Bernardo had analyzed for the *impero* associates.

Each ripe summertime, once Profumi retired to the papal villa, his life was stripped of its year-long garment of activity. He left behind him in Rome the day-to-day contentions of curial clashes, the constant performance for visitors, the parading from one place to another in pomp and ceremony, the stress of talking to immense crowds, the demands of humoring the arrogance of princes, of pampering the pride of politicians. Here he had leisure for refreshment of his soul, long hours of relative privacy that afforded him deep drafts of thought, analysis, and prayer.

For sixteen consecutive years, six of those years as pope, Profumi had spent his summer months in this little town nestled in the crook of an ancient volcanic crater that now rippled with the bright mountain waters of Lake Albano. The papal villa was encased like an enormous jewel within its own park of flowering gardens and landscaped walks lined with evergreens. The peace of castle and grounds invaded his soul with the serenity of ordered parts and the symmetry of lovingly tended nature in tree and bush and flower and pool. The air itself seemed to clear the eye and the mind. The soundlessness was so profound and welcome that often Profumi would stop on his frequent strolls and say to Father Lanser or whoever might be his companion, "Listen! Can't you hear it? The silence! Listen to it!"

In those summer days and nights of 1945, surrounded only by his most intimate collaborators, and tended by a much reduced household and security staff, Profumi did not set his reckonings down on paper as Regice Bernardo did. Still, if there had been columns ruled on his mental ledger, they would not have carried the headings of debits and credits, but of time and events. And even those headings were a measure of a different sort. For, in terms of time, while the *impero* dealt in moments to be seized, popes dealt in decades, even in centuries, they would not live to see on this earth. Events were the fruits of time past that bore within themselves the sweet or bitter seeds of future harvests.

Papa Profumi was especially grateful for this summer's quiet time. Facing him in the very near future were huge decisions. There was the urgent matter of the political fate of Italy, for one. Only his old enemies, the Communists, were sufficiently organized to sweep into power by the ballot, or even to seize power, once peace was declared; and that day was fast approaching. Well, the Church had faced worse in its day; and problems of this magnitude had always struck sparks from his papal spirit. He fully intended to be more than a spectator in this quarter, as in others, and spent great blocks of quiet time refining the details of his plans.

There loomed as well the vast work of restoring the structure and organization of the Church in the many places where war had torn it apart, especially in northern and eastern Europe. Because he had to choose carefully the men who would do that work, he spent many days and nights studying reports and dossiers, conferring, now with Father Lanser or Father Kensich, now with special visitors who knew not only Vatican personnel but clerics in every part of the world.

In the Far East, meanwhile, there was a whole gamut of totally new problems to be analyzed and met. Postwar Asia, Profumi realized, was going to be an alphabet of revolutions and new regimes. He found Father Youn of Korea to be of considerable help in his thinking here. But, as many visitors told him and report after report illustrated for him, there was no need to travel so far afield from the heartland of Europe in order to find problems. In France, Belgium, Holland, Germany, Italy, an ugly bouquet of false doctrines had sprouted, a little like those hardy weeds that popped up everywhere in the rubble of war. The heresies were clear; the harder question to answer was, Why there? Why did he get the strongest smell of the decadence of faith in those five countries, but not from much more likely places—from Poland or Czechoslovakia or Lithuania or Hungary, for example? Why that difference?

All these things and dozens more Profumi tackled with the clarity and directness and faith that were hallmarks of the man and of his papacy. But yet, oddly enough, as he himself thought more than once, it was the recalcitrance of the Vatican Council of State in its vote the week before that most troubled him and cast an unaccustomed darkness on his spirit.

It was not the Council's opposition in itself that bothered him, he reflected. Profumi was used to the give-and-take of Vatican government affairs. He had cut his ecclesiastical teeth on them, after all. He had spent his life, as priest, bishop, archbishop, cardinal, and pope, dealing expertly with bureaucracy. But in this case, and in the quiet of deep reflection, Profumi began to feel that this time, in this vote, the cardinals of the Council had unwisely turned aside from a deep responsibility. Coupled as it now was with the decision taken by the Maestro and his associates, the Council's vote against the Pope's wish to go slowly in this one matter cast a long shadow over all his other thoughts and plans, which seemed to promise so well.

"In all honesty," he confided a little tartly to Father Lanser while they chatted after early-morning Mass in his private chapel that July 16, "We did not ask the Council to take a very heroic stand. Not even a permanent one. We asked them only to pause. Could they not have found the grace to do even *that?*"

Father Lanser thought he understood the Council's reasons. As one of Profumi's closest aides and representatives, he was forced to understand and tackle more than one faction at odds with the Pope on all sorts of issues. In fact, he sometimes thought, he understood too many sides of too many questions. This morning was one of those times, for immediately an unwelcome thought rose in his mind: that partisan Colonel Valerio, too, had refused to pause in his brutal plans for Il Duce; and the Allies had refused to pause in a war they had already won. Like anxious lovers, nobody wanted to wait.

He said a silent prayer that the Council's decision would not one day be seen in so bad a light; and he changed the subject by reminding Papa Profumi of the special Benediction ceremony scheduled for ten-thirty that morning. "In honor of the feast of Our Lady of Mount Carmel, Holiness."

Profumi's mood seemed to brighten at once; he smiled a little. This day in the Church calendar was special to him, in part because he always celebrated it with the simple townfolk—mostly farmers and artisans—in the peace of Castel Gandolfo, and partly because of his own uncomplicated and pious devotion to this honorable title of the Mother of God. July 16 had been chosen by a previous pope to solemnize the Catholic belief that Mary had been appointed by God as a special channel of divine knowledge. Often in Profumi's life it had been a day of rich consolation in spirit. Not so on this day, however—at least not so far.

Ah, well. It was early yet. Not even eight o'clock.

"You will celebrate this Benediction with me, Father." The two were nearly at the door of Profumi's study on the second floor of Castel Gandolfo. "We will pray together for special blessings. And for light to see our way."

Profumi entered his large, high-ceilinged study alone. A light morning wind ruffled the curtains at the three Palladian windows giving out on the park. The red damask wallpaper dated from an earlier pope's time, as did the Persian carpet. But the large desk, the bookcases, the easy chairs, were Profumi's. He glanced over at the small table by the window, tempted for a moment by the open book he had been reading the night before. But no. There was work to be done.

Seated at his desk, he quickly digested the contents of the papers that had already come in that morning's pouch from the Apostolic Palace in Rome. There was nothing remarkable in the report from his observer at the Cecilienhof Palace in Potsdam, where President Truman and his Secretary of War, Stimson, were doing their best with the Soviet dictator Stalin—but it looked as though Stalin was all over the Americans. A series of memoranda from Archbishop Morandi summarized the latest reports that had come from Africa. There were a half-dozen requests and as many recommendations from Polish and German bishops, all grappling with the utter confusion that reigned in the dioceses there. A short briefing document from Guido de la Valle gave him the Maestro's schedule for the next two months, and included a request to see Profumi in the next day or two.

The several reports from the United States held nothing new; but he did pause for a time over the brief communiqué from Bishop McSorley of San Francisco: no visible developments yet in the Manhattan Project, but assurances had been given that it was only a matter of time now.

"Assurances." Papa Profumi fixed on that word as an odd one to use in this situation. He was one of a handful of world leaders who had some official intelligence from the Americans about their frantic efforts to be the first to split the atom. The Manhattan Project, as the Americans referred to their effort, appeared to be progressing. So close, in fact, did the Americans see themselves to success that it had already been arranged for representatives of a few friendly powers to be summoned on a moment's notice to witness the first test of the new atomic device. "Fat Man," it was called. Everything seemed to have a code name these days.

Bishop McSorley of San Francisco would be Profumi's representative when the moment came. The test would take place somewhere near a town called Alamogordo in New Mexico. Of course, no one knew in advance just what "success" would mean in this case. Even the best-informed—the prestigious director of the whole operation, Dr. Robert Oppenheimer himself—had no way of predicting whether the device would work at all. Or worse still, if it did work, whether it might run wild, destroying scientists and observers along with everything for hundreds or perhaps thousands of miles in every direction. No one knew the nature or the force of the power they were struggling to let loose. "It might outshine the sun," they had told McSorley, "or it might fizzle like a Chinese cracker."

In the face of such profound uncertainty, McSorley had devised not one code to send to Papa Profumi after the test of Fat Man (assuming McSorley would survive, of course); he had decided on a coded scale. For complete failure of the test he had for a moment considered "Chinese cracker"; but it was not a time for jokes, he decided. The code word flashed to Rome would be *natura inviolata.* Untainted nature. There were three or four intermediate code words ranging over that many possibilities, and ending with one that would indicate complete "success"—the arrival of a weapon of destruction beyond human comprehension: *Sol exsolita est.* The sun has been outsunned.

Papa Profumi was relieved that McSorley had not yet been called to New Mexico. But he knew the moment had to come.

He was about to place the bishops' report aside in a folder, as if to banish the worry of it for as long as possible, when Lanser knocked once on the study door and entered. Profumi glanced at his watch; it was not quite time to prepare for Benediction.

"Morandi has just phoned from the Secretariat," Lanser said in answer to the Pontiff's questioning look. "He has deciphered a message just in by radio from the San Francisco chancellery."

Lanser handed Profumi the message Morandi had dictated. It was terse, clear. *Am spending a week in New Mexico. Suggest you wait for news about sunshine.*

The old Catholic ceremony of Benediction was among the most beautiful acts of devotion that had evolved in the Church over the centuries. It was a triumph of ceremonial craft that blended light and incense and chant, a sweet celebration of Christ's continual union with His Church by his bodily presence.

On this feast day, as on most Saturdays and Sundays while he was at Castel Gandolfo, the Pope celebrated Benediction at the Church of St. Thomas of Villanova, a little treasure of a place designed by Bernini and built just across the town square from the entrance to the papal villa.

As always for such moments, the church sanctuary brimmed with a profusion of fresh flowers. The six great candles on the altar and the smaller candelabra at both sides below it formed a half circle, enclosing the tabernacle, beckoning with their little fingers of light as if to encourage each arriving worshiper to draw close.

Near the tabernacle, a monstrance had already been placed, a metal stand, perhaps two feet high and crowned with a circle of rays, fashioned in gold, which gleamed outward from the round, central eye that was empty now, but where the Host would soon be placed for adoration.

By the time the first pure notes sounded on the organ, at ten-thirty sharp, the church was crowded from front to back. Two little boys, scrubbed to a shine for the occasion and with all the unconscious gravity of children, led Father Lanser and Papa Profumi in procession from sacristy to altar. Alone, the Pope, in gold-colored vestments, mounted the three altar steps, opened the tabernacle, and removed from it the Sacred Host, which he placed in the waiting monstrance so that all could see.

The small village choir began the first Benediction hymn, a gentle cascade of sound in praise of the Bread of Salvation, composed by one of the greatest minds the Catholic Church ever produced, Thomas of Aquin. *"O Salutaris Hostia . . ."* The Pontiff took his place at the lowest altar step, and soon, as though in heightened sensory accompaniment to the song, he sent incense smoke, blue and sweet-smelling, rising about the monstrance, entwining among kneeling forms and bowed heads, and up to the bright mosaics of Christ the King set in the cupola overhead.

Quickly the moment came for Father Lanser to rise from his knees and drape the Pontiff's shoulders with a cloth-of-gold veil, and for Profumi to mount the altar steps again, this time for the blessing of the people.

There was no sound. Everything that came before and everything that followed was a frame of faith for this moment. The moment of Benediction.

Careful that both hands were covered in the veil as a physical token of reverence, the Pope lifted the heavy gold monstrance and turned to face the gathering. Every eye was on the gleaming white Host, drawn to Christ in his body and blood as to the sun of life, as to the hope and glory of the wide world; drawn as to a sun that does not burn or blind or threaten, but gathers all life and all minds gently to sacrament.

Papa Profumi raised the monstrance high and lowered it slowly, tracing with it the Cross of Christ. It was just when he reached the center point of the invisible Cross that the very light of the candles seemed to recede from his presence. Though he continued to guide it in its tracing, he no longer felt the weight of the monstrance. Everything on the natural plane, though still present, became as background.

His first emotion was a sweet peace, a calm so profound that he felt his soul infused with such fortitude and courage as would sustain him against the whole world.

He knew what was happening; it had happened before, to him and to others. One of those brief moments in which the soul experiences God directly, for God's purposes. It was not a vision—at least, not as people normally think of visions. There were no wraithlike figures looming about and no hollow voices echoing through corridors of the mind. Anything of that sort Profumi would have fought off with all his strength.

It was, rather, one of those moments in which God speaks by means of truth itself to those who can hear it, and light is shed directly upon the darkness of the mind; an infinite second during which Christ is present and makes it impossible not to know who he is.

Profumi heard no words with his bodily ear, true; but the sense of God's message was clearer than if words had been perfectly formed. And though he did not "see" him, either, in any usual sense, still he knew his Lord was very close, addressing his servant and reassuring him.

The first thing Profumi knew at once, in a way he could only speak of later as the simple essence of knowing, was that now he would be granted the sign he had been promised and had awaited. A sign in the sun so great as to challenge even Fatima would be placed in his hands before he left this church today.

Beyond that, and as nearly as he was able to explain it afterward, Profumi understood three principal things with an unshakable certainty that never left him.

First, he knew he had been only partially correct in his assessment that evil had been loosed with special force into the world. Not only had it been unchained; it had been welcomed in Christendom, and it had been accepted within Christ's very Church.

Second, he knew that history had literally been severed in two. A new epoch was now begun, in which the people of Christ's Church would have to rely on different and untried means of survival.

And third, he knew that one profoundly important thing had not changed: Even with this new certainty, neither Profumi nor those who came after him as Vicars of Christ would be able to bypass the dawning epoch of history. Instead, he and those who followed were to persevere in seeking and developing those new means, to build foundations for the future. Time and events were still the right headings for the papal ledger, still the raw stuff of salvation.

Profumi understood all this, all he needed to know in order to proceed as Christ's Vicar, in one glance of his soul, as it were. As complex as it was for him to relate later, it could not have occupied more than two or three seconds. For when it was over, he still held the monstrance before him, his hands were still draped in the cloth-of-gold veil, and he was just completing the sign of the cross.

Around him, all was the same. Father Lanser was kneeling on the altar steps, the scrubbed-faced altar boys behind him. Even the babies and small children of the congregation were quiet, as men and women crossed themselves and prayed. But within Papa Profumi himself there was a change. Though what he now knew confirmed the fears that had perturbed him in these past months, his spirit was so confident that it seemed there was no means, no torture even, that could drain it of its power.

Profumi turned and rested the monstrance again upon the altar. The ceremony was nearly completed. He descended the steps. Father Lanser rose and took the veil from his shoulders. Then they knelt again, side by side, as Profumi led a vibrant chanting of the divine praises: "Blessed be God," he began. "Blessed be His Holy Name . . ."

When it was 10 A.M. on July 16 at Castel Gandolfo, the time in New Mexico was still only 5 A.M. Bishop McSorley had already changed his watch to Central Daylight Time.

The setting in which he waited bore only a single ironic resemblance to the one at St. Thomas' Church in Castel Gandolfo; and McSorley would later describe even that resemblance as a blasphemy: this place, which had no name on any map, had somehow been dubbed Trinity. It lay at the center of a valley the first Spanish conquistadores had called and cursed as Jornada del Muerto. Dead Man's Way. Some names just don't let go. The closest town was a few miles away, a little dot of a community called Alamogordo.

There was no church at Trinity, of course; only some shallow trenches and three ugly dirt-and-concrete bunkers marking the north, west, and south extremes of a triangular bit of real estate that wasn't much to look at, either. As far as the eye could see, it was all parched shrubs and sand.

Perhaps there was a monstrance of sorts, if you chose to think of it that way; or something that might pass for one in this situation. A spindly tower had been erected roughly equidistant from those three bunkers, at the center of the triangle. Atop that tower sat Fat Man.

Admittedly, neither Fat Man nor his monstrance was very beautiful. No one who had come here expected that. He was all nose and torso, covered with a dull gray skin of metal. But gathered inside that skin, what strength was stored! And speed, as well! And trigger-point obedience to the one command he had been created to obey: Destroy! What a revelation Fat Man held silently in store!

All the previous day while McSorley waited, the sun had beat down mercilessly on Trinity at 110 degrees. Late that night of the fifteenth, a torrential rain and lightning storm lashed the area. Neither one nor the other affected Fat Man.

Finally, all was peaceful and desert cool. The bunkers filled with observers. The trenches held still more men, who lay on their backs, their eyes closed, feet toward Trinity's center. That seemed to be the safest way anyone could figure to venerate Fat Man. Fearfully. Over to the southwest, along the gypsum dunes of White Sands National Monument, the wildlife was quiet in the night darkness. Alamogordo, a few miles away, and Albuquerque, some 120 miles farther north, were asleep.

Sometime before three or three-thirty, it must have been, over on

Compañía Hill, additional busloads of dignitaries and notables arrived. Clocks ticked and all eyes turned toward Trinity, all hopes pinned on Fat Man.

One would naturally not have expected candlelight flickering on mosaics here, or gently wafting clouds of incense smoke or lilting chants in sweet Latin cadences. It wasn't that kind of celebration. Instead, at 4 A.M., men switched on banks of searchlights, which illuminated Fat Man and Trinity and the scrubs of Jornada del Muerto for miles. In one bunker, a single hand abruptly threw a single silent switch. Through the umbilical cord that ran from bunker to tower, current raced to touch Fat Man's electronic entrails. A totally new, unheard-of circuitry alerted him that his glory was at hand.

His triumph began with a blinding burst of intensely fierce light that outshone any noonday sun a thousand times, instantly bathing everything within a radius of fifteen miles in dazzling brilliance—the Tularosa desert valley and the San Andres Mountains away to the west and south, Sierra Blanca to the north, the Sacramento mountains to the east.

Immediately, Fat Man generated temperatures in the region of one million degrees Fahrenheit; he vaporized his tower, and for a radius of eight hundred yards around him he burned the desert to glass. And talk of music! Fat Man composed a wholly new score, roaring with sounds never before heard on earth. It opened with a loud, ugly crack, and a rumbling, threatening accompaniment to heavy shock waves that lashed out along the valley and echoed against the blind faces of distant mountains.

But that was only the beginning. It wouldn't do to speak in Fat Man's presence of beckoning fingers of candle flame. Rather, he spewed up a huge, irregular billowing ball of fire, foul, angry, writhing within itself, rising within a hundredth of a second to eight hundred feet, belching with color—reds, sickly oranges, dirty yellows—all changing into a swirling mass of purple clouds boiling with flames, swelling, rising up and up.

One minute passed. Two. Until Fat Man's visible greatness shone to a height of forty thousand feet, cooled to a mere eight-thousand degrees Fahrenheit. And there, transfigured at last before the eyes of his beholders, he towered and swayed, boomed and rumbled and belched like an obscene monster with mushroom head and churning belly.

Where were the words to praise *this* great power? What litany could possibly serve tribute to Fat Man's terrible epiphany?

At first, in the bunkers and trenches that surrounded Trinity, witnesses only stood up and gazed. Moments passed before the principal celebrants began to cheer and congratulate one another.

"Now we're all sons of bitches," a man called Bainbridge said. No Hail Marys here.

The scientist who led the Manhattan Project seemed stunned. His mind turned to the Hindu Bhagavad Gita, and out loud he spoke its words as though they were the gospel of Fat Man himself. "I am become death. I am now a shatterer of worlds."

As the day progressed, official observers sent coded messages chattering off to certain heads of state, few of whom added more memorable phrases to the new litany than Bainbridge had.

Not everything in such matters is planned, of course. So, ironically, at Potsdam, it was Stalin who learned of Fat Man before Truman did. Spying may not be the oldest profession in the world, but the Soviet leader often found it the most useful. By the time the American President told him, "We have a superbomb," the Russian was able to make his reply seem nonchalant: *"Khorosho."* He smiled. "Good."

Winston Churchill was in London that day when he heard the news that men now had the means to incinerate the world. He added his pungent verse to Fat Man's litany. "The idiot child has the matches now."

". . . Blessed be God in his angels and his saints." Papa Profumi came to the end of the Divine Praises. He rose from the altar steps, a signal for organ and chorus. *"Tantum ergo sacramentum . . ."* The ancient words of the second great Benediction hymn were sung: "Let us therefore venerate so great a Sacrament . . ." The Pontiff removed the Sacred Host from the monstrance and placed it in the tabernacle behind the altar. Benediction was over.

As he entered the sacristy, where he would remove his ceremonial garb, the effects of Papa Profumi's personal experience at Benediction lay like a soothing cloak upon his mind and spirit. He was not surprised to see an anxious-faced Father Kensich waiting for him with some impatience; he seemed to know Kensich would be there, and why he had come.

"Another message from Bishop McSorley?" He framed his knowledge in a question.

In answer, Kensich placed a slip of paper in the Pontiff's hands. "From Morandi," he said. "Just moments ago."

Profumi read the words of the prearranged signal. The sign. Placed in his hands before he had left this church today. *"Sol exsolita est."* The sun has been outsunned.

When he stepped from the shadowed shelter of the church out onto the portico, the day seemed like any other. A cluster of townspeople waited for him, drew around him as he came forward. He knew them all, of course, except for the half-dozen or so infants who had been born since the previous summer. He had blessed these same families so many times that he and they had long since lost count. He chatted with storekeepers and wizened farmers, with patient wives and harried mothers. He blessed each of them, as he always did. In a little while the small crowd began to break apart, as it always did, each little group chatting along its way.

Once inside the gates of the villa, Papa Profumi paused to look back toward the church. A few families lingered in the square. Impatient children tugged at their parents' hands or chased about in improvised games. He watched the blessed ordinariness of the scene for a moment or two and was thankful for it. But at last he turned and walked unhurriedly up the drive between the shaped cypresses toward the villa. Lanser and Kensich strolled behind.

Somewhere along the way, Profumi raised his eyes toward the almost mystical Latio sky that had supplied Dante with his immortal images of Paradise. *"Sol exsolita est,"* he whispered.

A new epoch had begun.

Part Two

THE LONG LAST AUTUMN

[13]

THE MONTH OF September dawned upon peace. Or upon what passed for peace in 1945. The High Mass celebrated by Papa Profumi on his seventy-sixth birthday filled St. Peter's Basilica with happy and grateful thousands come to wish the Pope health and success at this new beginning. That month, all the enthusiasm seemed appropriate. Had not autumn always been for Romans the time for wise counsel and perpetual beginnings? Had not even the ancient Latins celebrated September as the month when the goddess Lavinia showered her most fruitful gifts of law and empire on infant Rome? How much more cause did these Romans have to rejoice and to hope!

"Evviva!" the crowds chanted in Profumi's praise. Behind him, they could see, lay his greatest triumph. Nations had spent seven years beating the world into a sodden mass of lost dreams and wasted pasts in the most devastating war of all human history. Yet, at great personal toll, Profumi had guided his Church through it all. It seemed enough for one man's achievement. *"Evviva Papa Liberatore!"*

As always, however, Papa Profumi saw it all differently. This autumn of dawning peace, this autumn time of his own life and of his papacy, were not days of triumph. Far from it! The future spread before his mind's eye like one of those enormous cartoon sketches done by Raphael in preparation for a great narrative tapestry; the details were not yet clear, but the outlines were already becoming distinct. Profumi intended to cram every hour of the time left to him, whether short or long, with the work of shaping those outlines to embrace some measure of God's grace before the busy weavers of history's details made revision impossible. He intended to set in motion very long-term events, so that even after they had buried his body with the remains of other popes beneath the great High Altar of St. Peter's, his hands would still reach out from beyond death and mold future events. That, he knew, was the privilege of genuine papal strategy. And that was the greatness of truly great popes.

Of course, his summer's work at Castel Gandolfo had assured that even before those shouts of *Evviva!* welcomed him back to Rome, he had some of his plans in place and had even an opening agenda set on several fronts.

First on that agenda were his plans for Italy. Time was shortest and dangers clearest here. Great swaths of the country were already solidly in Communist control. The "Roman fact" was uppermost in his mind always. Rome and its Vatican lay in Italy; Italy must be secured. Yet even now enormous "red belts," as they were called, enfolded parts of Bologna, Sicily, Milan, Naples, and a dozen other major cities. The Communists might not yet have an absolute majority, but there was no doubt that, even if elections were held that very year, the Communists could already block anyone else from getting that majority. By that token alone, they could at the very least wield their ever-ready weapon of threatening chaos.

Of course, there was no question of elections so soon. Even the most basic political organization did not exist in the country. The people still had to decide if Italy would be a monarchy or a republic. Either way, however, there would be at least an elected national parliament and elected local governments. And either way, the Communists were not about to wait upon such decisions. Neither was Profumi.

By the time the Allies handed Italy back to the Italians and political life was organized, the Pope intended to ensure that Christian Democrats *would* command an absolute majority. Profumi reckoned he had about two years at the outside to pull off that major miracle of state.

He was not a dreamer, and he acknowledged it as not a minor point that in 1945 there existed no such thing as a Christian Democratic party in Italy. Or, for that matter, any organized party, except the Communists. The first part of Profumi's miracle, in fact, was to be the creation of the Democristiani. And the starting point of its creation would be its leader.

"Daniele Della Croce." Father Lanser's tone echoed the Pope's resoluteness of mind as he repeated the name to the surprised members of the Vatican Council of State. "Papa Profumi's decision is firm. There is not time to waste in argument or debate. Della Croce will be the head of the Christian Democratic Party. And Fabrizio Menda will be head of Catholic Action; he will deliver the vote, when the time comes. But only if we prepare, only if we use every moment we have to build."

There was no objection from the Council. They were surprised only because neither of Profumi's two choices for leadership had been heard or thought of for several years; and, to put it mildly, neither man had made much of a go of his earlier political career.

Della Croce was an economist by training. Menda's background was in sociology and business management. Both had been active in politics during the thirties, and both had fallen foul of Dictator Mussolini's will. Profumi was still only Cardinal Secretary of State to Papa Ambrosiano at the time, of course. But then, as now, he seemed to know everything that was going on. In fact, only the timely appearance of Profumi's personal representatives—one at Della Croce's house, and another at Menda's—on the very night Il Duce's Blackshirt bullyboys came to get them, had saved the two men from being kidnapped. And it had only been Profumi's personal intervention at the highest level that had saved the two from certain torture and probable death.

"Release both men into my personal custody," Profumi had urbanely told Mussolini in the course of a midnight phone conversation, "and I will personally ensure that they will be harmless to Your Excellency's regime."

Mussolini had fumed at the accuracy of this cleric's intelligence service and at his smooth arrogance. On the other hand—there was always a way of reaching an accommodation. Mussolini was just about to invade Tunisia, and the Vatican could render the dictator certain favors.

In the end, Menda and Della Croce had become Vatican citizens and spent all these intervening war years working demurely as filing clerks in the Vatican Library.

"Well!" Cardinal Falconieri smiled at the other members of the Council, and then again at Lanser. He had to admire Papa Profumi's plan, he said. "They will certainly be loyal, those two. And their names will still carry political clout." All in all, Profumi's general scheme fit very well with the exuberant mood of Curia and Council. The moment was theirs to seize. No wait-and-see attitudes this time. None of that hesitation or waiting for signs. This was more like the Profumi of old, planning with visionary foresight, swinging into unhesitating action. This time, the Council was with him.

By December's end, everything seemed in place for the opening gambit. Menda and Della Croce had been "called out of retirement" and their Italian citizenship had been restored. Menda had put his long-dormant talents to use in whirlwind fashion, establishing an intricate network of organized Catholics-for-the-vote. The Catholic Action group about which Guido had briefed the *impero* associates the prior summer was a reality aborning now. No hamlet or village or town, no city, no province, from the northern Alps of Lombardy down to Ragusa at the southernmost tip of Sicily, would be without its branch of Catholic Action.

Della Croce, too, had his Democristiani Party staff in place on a national scale. True, it was only a skeleton staff at the moment; but it was a solid network, a true beginning.

The funds needed by both Catholic Action and the Christian Democrats were assured by the Maestro. Thanks to his foresight, it would all be done in a timely and perfectly legal manner through voluntary campaign contributions and charitable donations from a host of companies in which the *impero* exercised equity control. Cardinal Falconieri threw his might and vast influence into the effort outside the Council as well as in it, and by early 1946, he had made what he modestly termed "great progress" in bringing to heel those churchmen, priests and bishops, who had "wandered for a moment into the wrong political field."

As head of the powerful Holy Office, meanwhile, Cardinal Arnulfo, not one to take chances, had prepared a decree of excommunication for any Catholic who voted Communist or who joined the Communist Party. "To be used just in case," as he explained at one of the many meetings in which the complex strategies of Profumi's campaign were dovetailed and checked and pushed forward inch by carefully prepared inch.

That still left the impenetrable "red belts" to be dealt with. The object, as everyone understood, was for the Democristiani to achieve an absolute majority in the national government. Any amateur could see that all the planning and organization in the world would come up short of that goal as long as the votes in the "red belt" areas, still solidly for the Communist ticket, entered the national calculations. And Profumi's collaborators were no amateurs.

Ordinary politicking was out of the question in the "red belts." After all, if even a priest couldn't walk the streets safely in those zones, any ordinary person spouting the Democristiani line would be boiled in oil on a charitable day. Votes couldn't be bought there, either, because, as the Maestro put it, "they already have been." The Communists were being financed to a fare-thee-well with Soviet gold.

It was decided to call on two members of the Secretariat of State who, in the cryptic phrase used to cover such delicate matters, had "friends who had friends." *Amici degli amici.* There were—and had been for a long time—two ranking monsignori of the Secretariat of State who also entered the Lodge as full-fledged members. This arrangement was part and parcel of the old, old Bargain struck in the infancy of the Italian State between the "Catholic" and "secular" classes. The Church and the Lodge had divided Italy's raw power between them. Guido de la Valle was now Keeper of that Bargain.

At this moment, the members of the "Catholic" class who sat formally with the Lodge were Archbishop Giovanni Da Brescia and Monsignore Annibale Sugnini.

Guido did not relish working so closely with either man for a long period of time. But there was no other way he could see to blindside the "red belt" vote. Da Brescia and Sugnini both had remarkably effective relationships with powerful Lodge members; and powerful Lodge members could exercise a remarkable skill when it came to counting and discounting ballots.

Da Brescia received his instructions from Guido with no particular objection, and no particular enthusiasm. Sugnini, a Sardinian by birth, tubby, gregarious, a self-proclaimed expert on Catholic ceremonial, grinned mischievously at the Maestro. "By hook or by crook, eh?"

Sugnini wasn't far off the mark, but Guido felt like punching him anyway. "Can you do it, Excellency?" He controlled his temper, and turned to Da Brescia, who nodded. He could.

"And you, Monsignore?"

"Viva la partita democristiana!" Sugnini rarely answered a question with a direct "yes" or "no." This was about as close as he could be expected to come to commitment.

Guido sighed and shook his head. Who had ever understood a Sard? he wondered.

"Who can understand the Soviets, Holy Father?" Father Pantelleimon Lysenko, sitting in Profumi's private study in early 1946, was no stranger to the Pontiff. Over the nearly ten years since Lysenko had fled the Soviet Union and appeared in Rome, Profumi had tested and then trusted and finally helped Lysenko on the road to his dream. Profumi had first taken an interest in this émigré Russian at just about the time he had rescued Menda and Della Croce from Il Duce's assassination squads.

From their first encounter when Profumi was secretary of state in 1936, Lysenko had been clear about that dream of his. He wanted to be a priest. That was why he had left the Soviet Union, for there was no priestly training there. And that was why he had come to Rome. Further, he wanted someday to find a way to go back into the Soviet Union as a priest. "I want to priest my people," he had said in his thick, unsure Italian. "They have no one now. The state is the church, and so there is no real church. Priests, bishops, all are licensed by the secret police, the NKVD. All are first and foremost government functionaries, ultimately responsible to the NKVD and the Politburo."

None of that had been news to Profumi even then. Not just because he had read deeply in Marxist and Leninist writings, or because of necessity he had had countless meetings with so many of Stalin's representatives. No. He himself had had close personal dealings with the Soviets after they had strong-armed their way into control of Munich, where he was papal nuncio in the 1920s. He had told Lysenko some of his experiences. His residence had been sprayed with machine-gun fire. He himself had almost been killed by a mob of those red bullies one day as he was returning to his residence. They had halted his car, screamed at him to get out so they could kill him. But he had stood up in the back of the open car and challenged the attackers. "I represent not man, but God. *This* God." He held up the crucifix he always wore around his neck. "Make way for this car in the name of my Divine Master." Reluctantly—miraculously, some said—the armed mob had parted to let his car pass on into safety.

Lysenko had understood at once. It was that same religious faith in Christ and his power, he said, his somber eyes ablaze, that he wanted to teach his own Russian people. "I want to priest my people. In my Holy Mother Russia. I know it will mean spending my life underground. Always moving. Always one step ahead of the NKVD. Never at peace. Slowly building a silent network of believers throughout my native land. Finally, in all probability, I shall end up in the hands of those NKVD wolves, who will tear me to pieces alive. But I want to do it."

Profumi had seen to it that Lysenko was accepted into the Russian College in Rome, which had been founded precisely to train priests for Russia. He had watched the man closely, tested him relentlessly and without apology, was present at his ordination, called upon him for information that time and time again checked out and more than once proved invaluable.

When the war finally broke out, Lysenko took a special and understandable interest in Profumi's Work of St. Raphael. "My people are coming for help there too," he pleaded. "I want to help them."

Profumi thought it better to keep Lysenko behind the scenes as much as possible. Careful though Morandi and his staff were, with tens of thousands coming for help, some were bound to be unfriendly "plants" come to see what they could see. And there were those Romans who weren't so sure of Lysenko, either.

Nevertheless, Lysenko pitched in wherever he was assigned—verifying identities of people and places, testing reports, assessing stories told by the refugees, translating documents, teaching Russian and Lithuanian to members of the Raphael staff charged with those populations. At war's end, when the senior Raphael staff were at last able to travel in order to hunt down records and locate missing persons, Lysenko's information and guidelines proved as helpful as they always had.

And so it was that, if Lysenko had been regarded as a valuable prize in 1936, by late 1945 his importance in Profumi's eyes had been magnified a hundred times over. In him, the Pope had a genuine Russian of the Russians on his side, thoroughly Romanized, thoroughly tested and proven, intelligent, zealous, raring to go. As with the agenda in Italy, it was time to begin preparations for Profumi's Soviet plan.

It was no coincidence that the Pope so often reached back far into his past to find the men he needed. During his entire Vatican career, he had always planned for the future. Now he was planning for a future when he would no longer be alive on earth, and he wanted to rely, insofar as possible, on men he had the deepest reasons to trust. Men he had tried and tested for years. Men such as Della Croce and Menda. And Lysenko.

"Who can understand the Soviets, Holy Father?" Lysenko repeated his question as if to examine a puzzle more closely. "Or at any rate, the Soviet leaders. Stalin and *his* brand of bullyboys. As Your Holiness says, they have obviously been cleverer than their Western Allies. The war is not yet six months over; and from what Your Holiness tells me, they have already secured every Slav country. Hungary too, I suppose. In fact, all land between the Baltic and the Adriatic."

As he sat there, dejected at the summary the Pontiff had given him of the current "zones of influence" secured by Stalin, Lysenko cut a figure as unmistakable as the Pontiff himself. In fact, many in Rome had long come to recognize the Russian when he walked its streets. With his conical hat and the flowing robes of the traditional Russian monk, his long black hair and fulsome beard, the high rounded cheekbones, expressive hands, Lysenko might have stepped out of one of those old Muscovite icons. In fact, the intense eyes and his ever-present seriousness seemed to draw upon deep inner pools of both sadness and power. He reminded many, Profumi among them, of ancient Orthodox paintings of Christ Pantocrator, Christ the All-Powerful, frozen in his humanness nearly to the point of distortion by the fearful piety of long-dead artists.

"But the people, Holiness!" The Russian persisted in his own cause. "The people are a breed apart from the leaders. And yet they have no one to offer them a choice."

"Ah!" Profumi rose from his chair opposite Lysenko and began to pace slowly in his customary way. "Exactly the point, Father. What has come out of the shooting war is merely another kind of war, but for the same kind of power: raw and brute, political and economic. That's not new in the world, granted. But at this moment, when so much of the world has been devastated and decimated, it is Our intention, Father, to do everything We can to see that there will be room in the inn of the world for devotion to God and his love and his grace. Those spiritual things, too, exercise huge power. But unlike the power of Hitler or Il Duce or Stalin, such spiritual things cannot be imposed. They must be chosen. That much has been made clear to Us again and again. But it is also obvious that, to be chosen, they must be available."

Profumi stopped his pacing and looked at the monk. "So. We will be fighting a war for power too, Father. But the war We fight and the power We seek are not ones the world will easily see or understand."

"Yes, Holy Father!" Lysenko seemed less brooding, almost excited for a tiny moment. "Yes! A war for power!" He was sure now, after ten years of patient waiting; his moment was nearing at last.

That very day, Archbishop Morandi heard the familiar *"Profumi qui"* with which the Pope began the telephone calls he personally made. The rest of what he heard, however, was neither familiar nor very welcome. He listened with growing uneasiness to the Pontiff's instructions.

As head of External Affairs at the Secretariat, Morandi was to brief Pantelleimon Lysenko concerning all he would need to know. Within a year's to eighteen months' time—in two years at the outside—by the grace of God, a new mission would be tested. In addition to "priesting the people," as the Russian still liked to say, Lysenko would be sending back regular and reliable data to Rome on the true condition of churches, priests, nuns, and faithful, as well as political and economic information.

With reliable intelligence available at last, Profumi would be in a position to know where to allocate his resources and how much should be thrown into the Soviet mission effort, where priests were needed most, how many could be safely introduced, what types of literature should be prepared, where diplomatic pressure could and should be applied. Morandi, Profumi's instructions went on, was to see to Lysenko's training by the cryptographers and signals men at the Secretariat. He was to have access to all classified information about the Vatican's very secret listening posts in the Ukraine and Georgia—the "lamplights," as they were known to those who knew of them at all.

"But, Holy Father!" Morandi gripped the white receiver. His expression was shocked, disbelieving. "No one has ever been given such amounts of information! No one but the closest and most trusted of our own people . . ."

Profumi knew there were those who did not like Lysenko, and also those who had never fully trusted him, even after all these years of surveillance and service and study. But the Pope was certain of one thing: the time had come when not to take a chance was too great a chance to take.

"We know, Excellency," Profumi interrupted Morandi's objection. "But never has anyone faced quite the world situation We face now. We are sure We can leave this matter in your good hands. You will keep Us posted as things progress."

"Yes, Holy Father." Morandi put the receiver in place, and sat back in his chair. He felt as though the ground had opened beneath him. The gamble was huge. The Vatican had moved slowly and laboriously to set up those two-way radio stations over there. The lives of hundreds were at stake. Three hundred lives in the Ukraine alone. And decades of work.

In the end, of course, he did as the Pontiff said. He called in his secretary and dictated the orders that would bring the Russian deep into the folds of Vatican secret policy and practice.

Lysenko was right. His moment was almost at hand. Morandi shuddered at the possibilities.

Those and the dozens of other plans and preoccupations and the hundreds of details of his daily duty did not seem to weary the Pontiff. As 1946 progressed, there were perhaps an increasing number who wished he might weary a bit. Some in Washington, for example, who heard what happened to the Honorable William McKay. The senator had come to negotiate a small matter for the President, but he ended up with as brutal a snub as papal protocol allowed.

"All I did, Mr. President," McKay complained, "was to assure the Pope that the Vatican and all free governments could live and flourish beneath the umbrella of our atomic capability, and our bulwark of freedom. He seemed to turn to ice before my eyes, and he simply left the hall; before I could even conclude our business with him. I have no idea what I said. It made no sense!"

Nor was Moscow any more pleased than Washington with Profumi. Few bishops or priests who visited him in his study during those two or three years after the war came away without being warned of the danger of consorting with the Soviets. "We must not take them for granted," was his frequent exhortation. "They must not be treated as though they were normal members in the family of nations. There must be no compromise. The world has paid too high a price for such mistakes to repeat them again so soon."

The Pope underscored his conviction by following his own advice; as when he refused to see Supreme Marshal Mikhail Orgorsky at all. It was smoothly done and very clear. The note signed by a Secretariat underling was polite, simple, direct, and transparent: "The Pontiff regrets that, during your visit to Rome, Vatican City will be closed to outsiders for long-overdue repairs and cleaning."

Moscow thought it best to try another tack. Patriarch Alexis of the Russian Orthodox Church proposed that a well-publicized meeting be arranged between "the two real Bishops of God's Church." It seemed to many a gross move, even for the Soviets; it was widely known that, for all his robes and ceremonious dignity, Alexis was an MGB colonel whose loyalty was not to Christ but to Stalin's Politburo.

Profumi responded with his own very different invitation. Alexis was welcome in the Vatican to render his ecclesiastical submission to the Throne of Peter.

No further word came from the Patriarch.

Not all the grumbling about Profumi came from the secular world. As 1946 progressed, the Jesuits were surprised and critical when, after four hundred years of continuous papal favors and unflagging reliance on them as an elite corps, the Pope suddenly seemed to switch his attention and his increasing interest to an upstart ecclesiastical congregation founded by an obscure Spanish monsignore. Opus Dei was not a welcome subject in Jesuit councils.

At the same time, once Profumi was able to identify the sources of religious heresies that had been springing up in Europe, a whole bevy of previously eminent and comfortable theologians and thinkers were roundly denounced and swiftly launched from their chairs and faculties, to find themselves, like spent missiles, in the outer spaces of Jerusalem or Bombay or Hong Kong or Australia—anywhere far from the Catholic heartland.

Yet, as prolific and as disparate as Papa Profumi's actions appeared to some, there was a unifying theme to it all. His plans to be a shaper of history's broad outlines were plans not for secular power but for solid assurance that secular power would rest always upon the only truly unifying power there had ever been: the power of spirit. The power of Christ. The power of God. Because that was so, he was determined to oppose any tendency of bishops and priests to heresy and faithlessness, including what he characterized as the "wicked movement" of "little unbelieving men" who were already trying "to remove the Tabernacle and turn the Altar of our churches into a dining table" and "have the priest face the people, instead of facing God along with them."

Still, open discontent and grumbling were hardly the hallmarks of those immediate postwar years. As far as the Curia and the wide Church at large could see, Rome was buoyant. Plans were going well. Profumi was firmly seated on the Chair of Peter, governing with a strong and decisive hand. The Maestro was in control of the *impero.* The Church Universal was strong and becoming stronger. God was in his heaven. All seemed right with the Catholic world. The future was secure.

There were moments when Profumi tried hard to see it that way too. But as 1947 dawned, despite all his activity, and even as the first postwar Italian elections approached, there were clear and growing signs of agitation around the world. There were clear signs, too, that as it had been with the forgotten little haberdasher who had told Lansing and Pasquinelli the news of Il Duce's death, the world was no longer fearful or horrified at such things as the brutal Soviet occupation of so many free nations. Nor of Fat Man. Nor of Fat Man's children who had been dropped as devastating visitors on Japan. Rather, the world was tolerant, as of unwelcome boarders who could not be banished, and with whom it might be best anyway to discuss the rent.

No wonder, then, that Profumi's whole life centered increasingly on the new and unwelcome neighbor whose arrival he had tried but failed to block. Banishment of this newly strengthened evil was no longer possible. Profumi could see that. The question now was whether he could keep it at bay long enough, whether he could win enough time to create a counterforce. On that plane of his life and his intent, for all the huzzahs and appearance of success, this Pontiff was not nearly ready to say that the Church was strong and becoming stronger, or that the future was secure.

[14]

The doubts for the future that continued to trouble Papa Profumi and haunt so much of his activity were not shared by Maestro Guido de la Valle. Once he had bested those early scruples about proceeding without the Pontiff's clear agreement, the very success of his careful plans quickly convinced him he had everything under control. The Maestro wasn't a man to look back over his shoulder.

The first footholds of his strength on the mountains of power he was now climbing were the exceptional liquidity of the Vatican Bank, and its already existing foreign branches. Within eighteen months of war's end, the *impero* had gobbled up companies of every size and nature in Italy, widening and deepening its control of everything from telephone communications and railways and shipping interests, to construction and its feeder industries of steel, cement, and real estate development. Whether it was agricultural implements, chemical products, artificial textiles and fibers, or a hundred other interests, there was little that appeared on the horizon of development that he and the *impero* did not enter in an important way.

Always, the method was some imaginative variation of indirect financing. Companies were bought outright by others already owned by the *impero,* or equity control in them was acquired by a company already controlled or owned by the Vatican. Immediately, then, one or two of the *impero*'s trusted men, *uomini di fiducia,* went on the board of directors. Each one of the *impero*'s thirteen associates chose such men with the Maestro's approval. Carlo Profumi, the Pontiff's oldest nephew, became board chairman of a real estate company based in Bari; his interest and that of his brother, Marcantonio, was in buying up land in and around Rome, including real estate known by a few even then to be of interest to certain speculators eyeing the need for a new airport, or to others manipulating already for future, refurbished Olympic Games.

And always, too, as widespread as *impero* activities came to be, discretion was the modus operandi. The Vatican Bank, the *impero,* and Guido himself remained in the background throughout, their anonymity cloaked in layers of financial intricacies.

Predictably, the Maestro's wide-sweeping success brought some changes home to Villa Cerulea. While Agathi would have thought it impossible, Guido's schedule became increasingly demanding; and it often seemed to her that Sagastume, who guarded her brother wherever he went, like some personal treasure of his very own, saw more of the Maestro now than she did. She shouldered ever more responsibility for the house and the estate, as Guido's travels took him farther and farther afield more and more often.

"It's only for now," Guido assured Agathi more than once when she expressed concern for his health under such a strenuous schedule. "Once we have our patterns established, I'll be able to manage it all from here."

What those patterns were and what he would manage Agathi did not know; for it was tacitly agreed, as it always had been between them, that his business life could be shared with no one. "No one except Sagastume," Agathi grumbled to herself from time to time; but she said nothing to Guido, for that strange giant at least took good care of her brother.

The *impero*'s activities changed Helmut's life, as well, and in ways that were not entirely a burden. He had not yet been brought into the deepest folds of *impero* plans and activities—it was certainly not time for that yet. But he was the perfect man to set up new centers of operation outside of Italy. It would be ideal training for him; and who could be trusted, if not Helmut?

The first of those new centers was in Geneva, where Klaus Fabian quickly became Helmut's most trusted man on the spot, as he had been Guido's for years. Fabian in turn was the perfect choice to begin prudent investment of the Swiss Windfall moneys, to see to liquidation at direct auctions of certain collections of art objects, and under Helmut's general supervision to take care of what everyone referred to as "Obligations contracted at the end of the war with certain German associates."

As significant a sum as the Swiss Windfall represented, however, it was only the beginning. The longer-range plans were far grander. Guido set down his reasoning in an early brief to his close *impero* associates; it was as clear and persuasive as his foresight had always proved to be.

"Even when this Europe of ours is rebuilt," he wrote in his memorandum, "it will have nothing but local stockmarkets. We Europeans have always been too hidebound to develop even a truly trans-European market, let alone one of global significance and scope. In time, there may be some possibilities in London, and perhaps in Frankfurt—if and when it is built up. We must not neglect them. But we must look to the Americans and to the Far East; and, as in everything, we must begin now, if we are to have a commanding position among the international power brokers of the coming decades."

Once Geneva was operational, therefore—a matter of mere weeks under Helmut's quick hand—he and a few Swiss citizens founded the Trans-Europa Investment House. Helmut sat on its board as chairman, and Fabian directed its day-to-day operations as a clearing center for certain funds that, by 1946, were already flowing in from all parts of the world, and flowing right out again, destined in large part for reinvestment in the Americas.

Guido's confidence in Helmut's abilities were not misplaced, for simultaneously as he maintained his functions at the Banco, and saw the Geneva operation off to a promising start, he opened an office in Vienna on behalf of the small Italian brokerage house Lombard Land Credit. LLC, as it was inevitably called, was a wholly owned subsidiary of Banco Santo Spirito, in which the *impero* held 48 percent of the company shares.

The purpose of the Vienna operation was quite different from that in Geneva. Despite their differences in outlook, the Maestro and the Holy Father agreed on most practical points concerning the future they expected to unfold. Both, for example, were convinced that the Soviet Union would remain master of a whole series of states it had cleverly and unabashedly ingested. Poland, Czechoslovakia, Hungary, Romania, East Germany, Bulgaria, the Baltic states of Lithuania, Estonia, and Latvia, were, they agreed, areas in which even dreamers did not expect to see any trace of private enterprise or an open market economy for a long time to come. Nevertheless, useful contacts could be made with various ministries as they were set up in those countries, and lines could be developed along which loans, investments, and other funds could flow usefully at the proper times. Helmut's instructions for Vienna were to go slow, but to nourish just such contacts and lines of development.

Once foundations had been set and key personnel put in place, Helmut settled into a routine. Three weeks out of every month, he was generally in Rome. The fourth he spent in the "northern outposts," as he liked to joke about them. And if he looked forward to these trips, it was not because he loved Villa Cerulea or Rome less, but because Vienna was a short enough drive from Waidhofen-an-der-Ybbs, the little Austrian village where he had been born. He loved that place as Guido loved Mount Athos. No longer did he have to wait for vacations, or snatch odd "getaway" weekends to visit there. He occupied a suite of rooms permanently reserved for the de la Valle family at Waidhofen's inn, the Goldner Hirsch. He tried and on rare occasions succeeded in cajoling his aunt Agathi to meet him there.

Once or twice, even Rico was able to get there for a day or two, despite his heavy schedule divided now between the Raphael offices in the Secretariat and his increasing travels to ferret out records in the East European countries that remained his responsibility.

The Vatican "Herr Bischof," as the Waidhofen locals called Rico, and "Herr Direktor" Helmut walked from the Lower Main Square to the Upper Main Square, stopping frequently to chat with the old men sunning themselves on benches. Or they sat in the Café Hartner, where Frau Macher plied them with Sacher torte, marzipan potatoes dusted with cocoa, and coffee. When the weather was fine, Helmut liked to share his favorite walk with Rico: through Schiller Park, past the first ridge of the Buchenberg, all the way up the steep mountain trail to the baroque chapel whose twin towers cradled between them the famous marble relief of the Sorrowing Virgin of Sontagberg.

The first time he had made the climb, though it was Helmut who had talked a blue streak all the way, Rico's breath came in short drafts in the thinner air. He looked up at the incredibly beautiful marble Virgin, and then turned to follow the perpetual gaze of her eyes out over the land.

The Danube was a blue-white thread weaving its patient way along the rolling bulk of the northern Alpine foreland. To the south and east and west, in a *trompe l'oeil* of nature for which the Sontagberg view was famous, the Alps seemed to advance northward like an army of white-scalped mammoths. Helmut drew Rico's attention back to the weather-worn face of the Sorrowing Virgin. "She is gazing down at me as she did twenty years ago." Helmut told him how he had stood there hand-in-hand with his mother, fascinated, as his uncle Guido recited the lines of Margarete's hymn to Mary from Goethe's *Faust.* In his voice was the remembered warmth of his mother's hand, and the echo of Guido's words across the years:

"'Incline, O Maiden,
Thou Sorrow-Laden,
Thy gracious countenance
Upon my pain . . .'"

Before the two friends left the mountain that day, they entered the chapel for a few minutes. Helmut's prayer was deep. Rico, kneeling beside him, asked for its fullest blessing. "Even if this is my friend's only devotion, surely it is a great one; surely it is enough to keep him close to the Virgin's Son." As they left the chapel, they looked for a few moments at the tomb plaques of all the dead and gone de la Valles buried in the walls of the chapel.

"One day, I will be buried here," Helmut said.

Guido was the only one who did not manage to get to Waidhofen. While he obviously loved hearing about the old place, and laughed heartily with Agathi at Helmut's stories of some of the families that never seemed to change from father to son and beyond, the Maestro's time had to be devoted to the investment of funds that were flowing in increasing volume now, and literally from all five continents.

To keep everything manageable, Guido and his *impero* associates had evolved, and were busily putting to work as part and parcel of their burgeoning operations, the concept of an international corps of private Catholic brokers and investment bankers. Eventually this corps would be two or three hundred strong.

Each member was Catholic, male, with an "establishment" family background, already trained in some acceptable institute such as France's École Normale, Bologna's Politecnico, or the Harvard Business School. Each was already qualified by a few years in a respected finance house—the J. P. Morgan Bank, the Banque de Paris et du Pays Bas, the Bank of England, the Deutsche Bank, Credit Suisse, or some such internationally recognized institution. Finally, each new prospect was measured on the basis of achievement, personality, and religious attachment to Catholicism.

Once approved, each became a partner or an executive in Trans-

Europa. While most remained based in their original cities, all were aided in establishing domiciles in two or three additional places where prestige and money were found, places like Gstaad, Rio de Janeiro, Beirut, Hong Kong, New York. From their home base, they proceeded to broker Vatican money into industry all over Europe, Asia, and the Americas.

Out of this plan grew a flexible, skilled, multinational organization with no easily traceable connection to the Vatican Bank. For discretion remained the norm, and most members were aware only of their Geneva-based parent firm, Trans-Europa. The impeccable credentials of these men, their influential friends and contacts, coupled with the ample funds they could bring to new business ventures via Trans-Europa, opened doors everywhere.

The little time Guido spent in Rome during 1946–1947 was taken up in reports—personal and written—to Papa Profumi, in consultations with the Council of State, in conferring with Helmut over matters of the Banco, Trans-Europa, and LLC, and, almost invariably, in planning his next business itinerary.

It was in 1947 that Guido was presented with what seemed to be an unusual opportunity, even by *impero* standards. It came in the form of a report from one of Trans-Europa's new and far-reaching representatives, a Belgian. The report had come first to Klaus Fabian, who read it, immediately marked it "urgent," and forwarded it to Helmut without waiting for his regular visit to Geneva.

The matter concerned extensive and proven reserves of uranium, cobalt, bauxite, and other metals that were important in the areas of atomic research and development. The reserves lay buried in the high ground of the Katanga plateau, near the little village of Kalikawa in the upper Congo. The eventual profits would be considerable, as the detailed estimates in the report made clear. But the expense and the logistics to get to that stage, as Helmut quickly saw, would be far beyond anything Trans-Europa had ever tackled.

For one thing, the local population in and around Kalikawa, the report indicated, was anything but docile and work-prone. The recommendation was to import labor from the nearest source. That would mean from French West Africa. The report became almost personal at this point. The Sarakolle, the Fulani, and the Tukulör tribesmen of West Africa, the report ran, had lived in a state of perpetual and abject slavery to the Moors since the twelfth century. They were kept in conditions that were so abysmally miserable that "it would be a mercy for us to purchase them from their slave-owner masters, transport them to Kalikawa, give them decent work, decent wages, decent housing, and provide them with health care and education for the first time in their existence."

Of course, the transport of a population of some fifteen thousand men, with their women and children, would mean building a two-hundred-mile railroad from the French West African coast inland to Kalikawa. However, the report reasoned, the railroad would be needed, in any case, to bring in supplies of medicine, food, building materials, and to transport the mined uranium and other metals to the coast for shipment.

The sum of it all was that, as high as the start-up efforts and costs would be, the fruits of the project would return the outlay many times over. "In the developing technology of atomic science, those metals are the most precious on the market."

Helmut finished reading and sat back in his chair. If he had been a man to whistle through his teeth, he would have done so then. Instead, he fingered the report. It was certainly clear on one point, he reflected. A project like this would be more costly and more ambitious than anything even he had initiated until now. It seemed obvious that the decision on this one would have to be his uncle's.

Helmut quickly checked the itinerary Guido had left him. Unless he was detained, the Maestro would be back in two days. No point in forwarding the report to him, even by special courier. Best to use the time to develop all the intelligence he could about the situation.

"One thing about the Vatican," he mused aloud as he reached for his phone. "It has at least one expert on everything. Even Fulani tribesmen and Kalikawa village should be no exceptions."

The Maestro had never seen anyone like Father Gustav De Smet. He had to steady himself against the desk in his Vatican office, as he watched this retired missionary of the Holy Ghost Order make his way painfully through the door held open for him by Sagastume, and toward the chair that waited for him.

Father De Smet still stood tall, despite his nearly ninety years. He was cadaverously thin. His skin was blotchy and wizened. In place of a nose, he had what looked like a clumsily sewn seam and two air holes. There was no trace of hair or even slight down on his skull; instead, his scalp was scarred and angry red all over. As he moved angularly and painfully forward, his right hand hung helplessly at his side. In his left, he carried a large envelope.

It had been Cardinal Mangano, head of the Congregation for African Missions, who had led Helmut to his man. And it had been De Smet who had convinced Helmut that, whatever the other merits of the Kalikawa project, anything they might do for the slave tribes of the Fulani, the Sarakolle, and the Tukulör would indeed be a mercy.

"I know you're very busy, Maestro de la Valle." De Smet was used to the unbelieving stare of people who met him for the first time; he had learned that being the first to speak eased the shock of his appearance and made conversation possible. "Your nephew, Signor Helmut de la Valle, suggested . . ."

"Of course, Father." Guido recovered himself more quickly than most. "Forgive my rudeness. Please! Sit down."

"What I have to say will be brief, Signore."

"As long as you like, Father."

"Signor Helmut asked me to gather information from my files for you on certain tribes with whom I have worked." He shoved the envelope across the desk toward Guido. "You will find here reports, affidavits, photographs, maps, drawings, all concerning the inhuman sufferings of the oasis tribesmen in which you are most interested: the Sarakolle and the Fulani and the Tukulör, in French West Africa." His eyes, once brown but now mottled with traces of gray, took on a soft look. "They are a gentle people. There is no word for war in their language. They have never known anything but slavery since the twelfth century. The twelfth century!

"The Moors, who own them—*own* them, if you please, Signore—spend their days sipping mint tea on the verandas of their villas around Nouakchott—that's the capital city—and counting their shekels and their concubines, while the tribesmen work like dogs and are sold as chattel."

Guido listened and understood why Helmut had sent De Smet to him.

"All my efforts on their behalf," the priest went on, "have resulted in what has happened to my body and my spirit. My spirit I need not discuss with anybody. As to my body, I was scalped, castrated, had my nose cut off. All my teeth were lost one by one to a stone hammer." He broke off as Guido winced. "Signore de la Valle, please pardon me. I have got so used to my miseries—my boon companions! I mention them only because, as shocking as my appearance now is, what was done to me is as nothing compared to what has been done to the people of these tribes. What is still being done to them.

"Do you know, Signore, when over thirty thousand were sold to the Belgian Congo cotton growers, barely ten thousand survived! Most of them died from starvation and exposure and overwork. Every tree sheltered starving mothers trying to feed the bloated children stuck to their dry breasts. Some of these sad people actually cooked and ate the flesh of the already dead. Eleven of them, who collapsed on a public highway and were left to die, committed group suicide. The two strongest cut the jugular veins of the other nine, then cut each other's veins. The dogs lapped up the blood and the jackals nosed the corpses, before a move was made to bury them like waste where they lay."

Guido hardly moved as he listened to the litany of horrors that made up the history of the people De Smet had tried so hard to help. Obviously, after so much hell and so much effort had forced the priest into lonely retirement, he thought he had at last been led to the one man who could do the impossible.

"Anything, Maestro de la Valle, would be better than what these people are suffering now. Better than what they have suffered for as long as I have known them, and for centuries before that. I know little of this so-called Kalikawa project. Your nephew explained the outlines to me. He spoke of schools and medicine and regular work hours. What can I tell you, Maestro! Such things would be luxuries to these people, as diamonds and rubies are luxuries here."

Guido was silent. Without bidding from the Maestro, De Smet stood up. There was nothing more to say. Or almost nothing. "I know you are very busy, Signor de la Valle. But whatever you can do for my poor people, please, in the name of the Crucified Lord, do it! Please, Signor de la Valle."

Helmut answered his private phone on the first ring and heard his uncle's firm and unhesitating order.

"Let's get to work on the Kalikawa project."

Guido kept the envelope with its catalogue of horrors that De Smet had left him. It came to symbolize a silent promise he made to himself, and to the old priest.

In addition to frequent meetings when the Maestro was in Rome, Papa Profumi received from Guido through Father Lanser monthly summaries of the *impero*'s activities. They were general reports, of course; not the sort that included every detail, but the kind that showed general developments and highlighted special concerns. The Pope was no financial expert. But in his own clear-headed if simple way he understood the path Guido and the *impero* were following. He read with interest the expanding list of personnel abroad. And he certainly noted the heavy sums that flowed, in one way or another, from the *impero* into the always emptying coffers of the Christian Democratic Party and of Catholic Action, as they prepared for the first elections, which were now fixed for early June 1947.

Profumi even wondered occasionally if he had been correct in opposing Guido and the Council of State. He never doubted the vision granted him at Benediction on that feast of Our Lady of Carmel, the day the sun had been outsunned. But sometimes it almost seemed that Guido, certainly a man of faith if ever there was one, had found one path around the abyss of history's turning. And after all, he was merely exploiting to the fullest degree the potential of the Vatican Bank and the Special Administration as legitimate financial organs of the Church Universal. In addition to every other benefit, by 1947 the Banco could offer, to every diocese and every religious house of the worldwide church, investment rates that were much more favorable than those of any normal bank. The assets of those thousands of dioceses and religious houses were now at the disposal of the Banco for investment and as collateral. The amounts headed for the billions.

Whatever else his detractors might say of him, the Maestro was not imitating that man of Jesus' Gospel parable who buried his master's money in the ground for safety. Guido was certainly no unprofitable servant. Good and wise management of Church moneys, on behalf of the Church. That's what it all looked like.

Well, time would tell. Meanwhile, Papa Profumi had a fight on his hands in Italy. And the Maestro was giving him powerful weapons for victory.

[15]

While Papa Profumi was laboring to influence and mold history's newer outlines, and the Maestro was building one of its future empires, Rico Lansing's life was still devoted to the much humbler destinies of the totally impoverished; for their numbers seemed to increase in the months following the close of the war.

Still, Rico never did have the sense that he was working in a vacuum. For one thing, he gleaned the barest outlines of the Maestro's wide-ranging vision. Agathi, genuinely taken by the young cleric, invited him frequently to Villa Cerulea; and on those occasions when Guido was there, he devoted what time he could to fostering and testing the worth he sensed in his nephew's friend. The time would come, after all, when Lansing would head the powerful Chicago archdiocese; that alone was reason enough to welcome him into the folds of the de la Valle circle. And in the natural course of friendship, Helmut often discussed his personal trials and adventures with Rico.

"Within a few years," Helmut quipped to him over lunch one day, already caught up by the excitement of his new business ventures in the "northern outposts," "within a few years I'll probably be speaking Mandarin Chinese with a Swiss accent and living out of a suitcase!"

Rico's sober reply brought his friend up short for a moment. "Millions haven't even a suitcase to live out of. If you're ever tempted to forget that, come spend time with me at the Raphael!"

There were other and far different occasions that deepened Rico's perception of his own work and his purpose. He did have his private audience with Papa Profumi, as Morandi had told him he would; and because of the Pontiff's very personal interest in the St. Raphael, he had several more as well. Sometimes alone, more frequently with Morandi or with two or three others engaged in that work—Youn or Righi—he had a chance to hear Profumi speak his mind.

If Rico was most surprised the first time he heard the Pontiff joke with his visitors—after all, he had never thought of popes that way—he was most impressed by a wide spectrum of deeper yet equally visible qualities. Profumi's vast knowledge, and his quick reading of any situation presented him, for example. His ability to size up incoming threats in a few words. His constant insistence on the Roman fact. His implacable hostility toward "any social system based on corruption of its privileged members and debasement of its citizens"; Rico inferred a little uncomfortably that the Soviets were not the only targets of that hostility.

Over the months, the young American was deeply struck by the Pope's personal magnetism, his frankness even with such young clerics as himself, his profound and simple piety, his courage in facing down a host of rampant problems. The words "papal mind" and "papal strategy" came to mean something real for him.

In more than one of those meetings with Papa Profumi, Rico thought back to that very first week in Rome, when he and Pasquinelli had watched this Pope stand alone upon his balcony and, without a word from his lips, pull hope down from heaven itself and infuse it into the hearts of his beloved Romans. For Rico, that skillful act became a cameo of what Profumi hoped to do in some measure for the wide world. As time went on, whether in private conversation or public view, this man seemed to him to be the very embodiment of the papacy.

Such heady moments aside, Rico's days were for the most part still sobering ones. The case records that filled his office provided mute testimony to the debasement of human beings Profumi spoke of so frequently. Here, however, Rico himself could do something. With international borders opening again, he began to find it easier to issue passports and arrange for his clients to leave in greater and greater numbers, to regain old homelands or reach new ones.

It was this shift in affairs, actually, that began to change other elements in the character of Rico's Roman stint. As travel restrictions were relaxed, and he was able to relocate larger and larger numbers of his clients, it became normal for him to deal with colleagues he had barely had time to meet, much less get acquainted with, before. His world within the Secretariat had been dominated by perhaps a dozen men—Morandi and Da Brescia, to whom he reported as his direct superiors; the few others with whom he worked closely every day; the brooding Russian monk, Lysenko, who had asked permission of the Pope himself to help in Raphael casework, and who taught Rico his first halting phrases in Russian and Lithuanian.

These men were, nevertheless, only a few in a wider circle of some two hundred and fifty young and youngish clerics, hailing from practically every continent under the sun, who had come to Rome. Most of Lansing's peers had spent the war years there as students. A few were newcomers. Some, like Rico, had come to do their Roman stint. Some had come for a Roman career. Still others had not made up their minds. But all had been weeded out from the common herd of clerical aspirants by their local superiors and by Roman authorities and were destined for high ecclesiastical preferment. Together they represented a future generation of theologians and diplomats, bishops and cardinals. Perhaps there was even a pope or two among them.

If you were one of that group, you gradually got to know most of the others by face, by name, and by reputation. Every large bureaucracy is a whispering gallery and an open stage. The Vatican is no exception. But immediate acquaintances and friendships as well as enmities were formed within whichever group was closest to your own line of work.

In Lansing's case, naturally, that group was the corps of young men in training for the Secretariat of State, and those already launched on that career—men such as Levesque, Demarchelier, Sugnini, Carnatiu, Casaregna, Da Brescia, and Dell'Angelo. Just as naturally, Rico got on better with some than with others. Because they were "career men," and because the prize positions were few and valuable, a certain "rat race mentality" took hold of some. Probably by temperament, and perhaps also because his own assured future as Archbishop of Chicago put him above such a need, Rico didn't care much for the men among his peers who were most obviously dedicated to the rat race.

Peter Servatius was a prime example. The six-foot-eight-inch Bostonian had been sent to Rome in September of 1945 for his doctorate in theology. Rumor was that he, too, had the right of succession in his home diocese, as Rico did in his. That would have meant a sure cardinalate. Rico doubted the story, though, first because Servatius had quickly switched careers and joined the Secretariat of State; and second because no sooner was he in the Secretariat than he began sniffing around for still greener pastures.

Servatius' enormous frame and deliberate movements seemed to create a zone of safety around him; people got out of his way as if by instinct. It was an effect he had already achieved in high school, merely by being what he was. By now it had become part of his expectation, part of his mentality and the reality of his young life, that room would always be made for him. He and Rico circled warily around each other like prize-fighters who expected they would square off one day.

Still, at a pinch, Rico could work with Servatius, joke with him, spend an entire evening with him if need be. Not so with Casaregna's secretary, Monsignore Roman Carnatiu, who never overcame Blackjack Krementz's description of him as a man who didn't "smell quite right, somehow." And not so either with Monsignore Annibale Sugnini. Surely, Sugnini had his friends; no doubt about that. And he was always affable on the surface. It was just that Rico never knew where the man stood on anything that mattered. He once made a bet with O'Mahoney that Sugnini could go for a whole month and never give a direct answer to a direct question. Rico won.

There were others Rico avoided too, as much as his work and his general life at the Secretariat would permit. Archbishop Jean Levesque, who peered through his spectacles the way soldiers peer over battlements, and who clearly had superiors and inferiors but no equals. Levesque was five years Rico's senior and on his way up the ladder of preferment, thanks to his father's millions and his mother's claim to be a descendant of the Bourbon kings of France. Levesque's secretary, Pierre Demarchelier, a North African of French and Berber blood, was a poor imitation of his master. With such men Rico did what business he had to, but no more.

Considerably more to his liking were the moon-faced Korean Simon Youn, Lopez Navarro, Kieran O'Mahoney, and Jaček Righi. Lopez was Colombian, canny, always able to read effortlessly between the lines, especially in complex situations. O'Mahoney was a stocky, balding, laconic, good-humored, no-nonsense character, "a great man to have at your side in a fight," as the Irish compliment went. Youn was a marvelous executive who was noted for his friendly demeanor and his keen judgment in the Raphael work. Righi, a gossamer-thin, lanky Pole, was the realist of the lot. No illusions. No disillusionment. Just hard-core practicality. The

Russian, Lysenko, attracted Rico too, as he did so many, by the force of his very will. It was as if he stood for hordes of invisible supporters who gave him strength.

Taken together, close friends or distant colleagues, good, bad, or indifferent, it was this full gamut of complex men who toiled in the web of Roman activity with Rico in his early days, whose personalities ricocheted off his own, and whose loves and hates and ambitions wheeled and spun slowly into his life. And it was this group of men that was the newest to be drawn close into that exclusive orbit whose center was the gaunt man in the white robes and blood-red slippers, sitting upon Peter's Chair.

One of the brightest and most welcome changes brought into Rico's life by the end of the war was that letters from home began arriving regularly. His father caught him up on all the Chicago political gossip and financial news. Old Blackjack's health was a little better, Basil wrote in an early note, "but he's not the bull he once was." His mother's letters centered more on family news—marriages and new babies and the latest from their old home in Peculiar, Kentucky. She kept telling him to eat well, though with Vittorio Benfatti cooking his meals she needn't have worried. Yet it was Rico's sister Netta who wrote most often and about absolutely everything.

"Dearest Rickey," she would begin, or "My darling Rick." And then she would fill pages with her quick, spidery backhand, painting word pictures of her life, and telling him about their friends who were returning from war at last, or the sad news of some who would never return. Almost always she would enclose family snapshots, "just so you won't forget us little folk, darling, when you get to be an archbishop cooking all that Roman spaghetti!"

Thank God for Netta! Even after a day filled with the most dismal realities of war's aftermath, a glance at some of those photos, or the arrival of a chatty new letter, was happy reminder of the warmth that waited for him a few years down the line.

Meanwhile, there were other things that needed doing.

"My dearest Netta"—Rico scribbled a hasty note in the spring of 1946 —"I won't have time to write for a while. With the borders open and travel easing in Europe, some of us can at last get out of our chairs and do some real digging around the rubble of Europe for the records and information we so desperately need if we're ever to finish our work at the Raphael. Please write all the same. I'll expect stacks of letters when I get back. Tell Dad I pray for Blackjack and all of you. And tell Mom not to worry. I love you all."

The general instructions had come down from Papa Profumi himself. Archbishop Morandi worked out the schedules and filled in the details. The Pope listed seven—Rico, Youn, and Righi among them—who would do the fieldwork. Another batch was stationed as backup in Vienna, Europe's melting pot for displaced persons. The Pope's purpose now was to finish the work well, to satisfy as many queries for lost people as was humanly possible, to relocate, to repatriate.

Lansing, as head of the Passport Section for East Germany, Czechoslovakia, and Poland, was given one of the touchiest assignments. Even Morandi gruffly admitted that. The Soviets were running the show in Eastern Europe, and while Romania, Hungary, and Bulgaria were totally in their embrace, East Germany, Poland, and Czechoslovakia, not yet completely absorbed, were regarded by the Soviets as necessary buffer zones between themselves and the hateful, dangerous, capitalist West.

Lansing's trips into his "territory" were not hazardous, but always laborious. He traveled on Vatican diplomatic passport, generally finding no obstacle placed in his path. One of the first elements of public life restored by the occupying forces was the railroad system. Where there were no trains, trucks or cars or sometimes motorcycles and occasionally military vehicles were at his disposal. Once or twice, in order to reach some remote point, he had to hike a fair distance.

The purpose of each trip was clearly defined. Nearly always it was the verification of interminable lists of men, women, and children. Were they alive? When and where last seen or heard of?

In each of the three countries assigned him there were recognized centers where refugees, displaced persons, ex-prisoners of war gathered. In Poland, there was Poznan, Krakow, Gdansk, and Bialystok. In Czechoslovakia, it was Plzeň, Brno, Karvinà, and Kosice. In East Germany, it was Berlin, Leipzig, Rostock, and Kiel. At each place, he worked with councils made up of one officer from each of the four victorious Allies—Britain, France, the U.S.A., and the U.S.S.R.—and with the international Red Cross. But, as Rico soon noticed, it was usually the Soviet officer who made the decisions.

"Our policy, Monsignor," one red-faced American Army colonel explained, "is not to rile the Soviets. Official orders. They get priority everywhere. Why? Search me!"

Occasionally Rico ran into a stone wall; but in those early days, when nothing had yet been frozen into permanent borders of hate, refusal of his requests or appeals was rare.

Wherever he went in those weeks, Rico saw how deep war had sunk its teeth. There seemed nothing left of that part of the world except ruins, burned-out cities, rubble, makeshift roads and bridges, beggars, pinched faces, worn clothes, interminable food lines, and everywhere the smell of death and decay.

Ecclesiastical property had been similarly devastated. Very few churches, chapels, rectories, convents, monasteries, seminaries, or schools were intact. The few bishops, priests, monks, and nuns who had survived were as hungry, ill-clothed, miserable, as run-down in health, as resourceless, as everyone else. War made no exceptions. It was the great leveler, just as William Blake had said. It was no comfort, but rather a grim embellishment of their suffering, that these people for whose freedom the war had begun, were being dealt into the hands of yet another dictator.

While each trip was quick—a few days, a week at most—there were many of them, and they were frequent. It seemed to Rico that it was his destiny, not Helmut's after all, to live out of a suitcase. His missions were always fruitful, though, and into the bargain he became an expert among Vatican personnel in the delicate art of dealing with Soviet commissars as he traveled in Soviet-dominated territory.

When he did get back to Rome for a week or so, he generally found at least one letter from his family waiting, to keep him in touch with Chicago. As to the Vatican, the marvelous Vittorio Benfatti kept him well abreast of all the news he gathered on his daily rounds. He learned, for example, that "certain friends" of Da Brescia, who had been pressuring to have the archbishop made a cardinal, had been given a flat refusal by Papa Profumi. "A flat refusal, Monsignore!" Benfatti's eyebrows rose significantly as he served the news along with Rico's evening meal. "A very bad sign for the archbishop!" Rico learned more from Benfatti during one dinner at home than most of his colleagues who had stayed on at desk jobs in the Secretariat learned in a month.

With all the activity and the changes in his life, the months of 1946 sped by for Lansing. November's end found him shivering in Poland's winter at Bialystok over near the borders of the U.S.S.R., where conditions were utterly primitive. By the time he was able to finish his work there and then make his way back to the partially restored railway junction at Warsaw to board the train for Vienna, he was frozen through, and it was deep December.

Huddled in his seat in an overcrowded, underheated compartment, attacked by smells and tortured by the discomfort of hard wooden seats, Rico watched the ice-clad forests and mountains rush past until finally the windows frosted over. From sheer misery, hunger, and cold he nodded off to sleep.

He wasn't sure at first if it was the bustle of the detraining passengers or the sharp tapping on the window of his compartment that woke him up with such a start. But it was the tapping that claimed his attention. He glanced blearily toward the sound. Helmut! It was Helmut! Rapping his umbrella on the glass, laughing like a madman, and gesturing for Rico to lower the window.

"Come on, sleepyhead, before we change your name to Rick van Winkle! I've met every train from Warsaw for two days. We were beginning to think you'd defected to the MGB!"

"We?" Rico grabbed his small suitcase. Pushing and shoving, he scrambled out of the compartment. "Who's we? I didn't expect even *you!*"

"Youn is here. And Righi. We decided to spend Christmas at Waidhofen. I've persuaded Aunt Agathi to come too." Helmut took Rico's small bag and led the way out of the Vienna station. "Uncle Guido can't make it. Probably enjoying summer in Australia! I've asked Lysenko to come, also. He's such a solitary character, and he's worked so hard. Youn thought it would be nice. No point in *your* trekking back down through Austria and the whole length of Italy. Waidhofen is a jewel at Christmas. Come on! Hurry up! We've a bit of driving ahead of us."

Waidhofen *was* a jewel that Christmas. Martha Spoeda and her husband, the proprietors of the Goldner Hirsch inn, together with Helmut and Agathi, spun a web of welcome around Rico, Youn, and Righi. Even Lysenko's normally somber eyes reflected a smile or two in those few days.

The de la Valle connection with the little Austrian town was deep and centuries old; there was hardly an acre that didn't bear ancient memories. Agathi, her face flushed and beautiful in the cold air, her blond hair swept back under her fur hat, linked her arm in Helmut's as they showed off to the four young priests all the sights their ancestral home had to offer. Everything of importance there seemed to have been built by one de la Valle or another. They visited the onion-domed church. They climbed the tower that had been built at the top of the Hoher Market to watch for marauding Turks. They meandered through the family castle, complete with moats and spiked walls, still impressive though abandoned now to the government's care. There were a dozen other sights Rico hadn't seen before; and even those he had were still more delightful this time around.

They always went back to the inn for lunch. No one wanted to skip Frau Spoeda's hot soup, fresh trout straight from the Ybbs, the country bread from the Goldner Hirsch ovens, and gallons of steaming hot tea.

Evenings were spent gathered around the ample fireplace in the raftered hall of the inn, talking the peaceful hours away, sometimes with other guests, sometimes just the six of them. Agathi shared family stories she remembered from her own childhood vacations at Waidhofen. Helmut retold legends that were part of the lore and the very air of the town.

It was Agathi who first noticed a young woman, a guest at the inn also, who seemed to be always alone. As her family knew well, Agathi de la Valle had never been one to ignore a stray, and certainly not at Christmastime in Waidhofen.

"Everybody," she announced as she came in to dinner one evening, her new friend in tow, "this is Keti Wilson." And with that the little Christmas group grew to seven.

Keti Wilson, it turned out, was an American. "Of the 'Show Me' Wilsons from Missouri," she said, laughing. Her hometown wasn't so very far from Peculiar, Kentucky, and Rico welcomed her as one of the few people he had ever met in Europe or in Chicago who had heard of his childhood home. Unlike Rico's family, however, Keti's had stayed put in Hartsville, Missouri. Her father was a physician, she told them, content with his work. Keti's mother had received a pleasantly large inheritance, and that had lifted the couple into a position of true comfort and prominence in their hometown community. "There they'll live and die, as happy as any pair of people I know." Keti looked just a bit nostalgic.

She was younger than Rico or Helmut; maybe twenty-three or twenty-four, by the look of her. Her auburn hair and candid blue eyes set off very attractive features. Perhaps she wasn't the beauty Agathi was; few women were. But in this group at least, no one was making comparisons.

"You make home sound very inviting." Lysenko was curious to know more. "What ever made you leave?"

The answer was simple, and led directly to the present. "I wanted to be a journalist. I studied at the university for a year; and then I realized that school isn't where you learn to be a reporter. I worked for a couple of local newspapers for a while. Then I finally landed a job with a syndicate. I'm based in Paris, but I travel any place in Europe where political news is breaking."

"Is political news breaking in Waidhofen?"

Keti took Helmut's joke in good humor. "I'm covering the four-power disarmament conference in Vienna. Someone told me about this place and . . ."

"And you said, 'Show me,' " Rico chimed in.

"Something like that. Anyway, I'm glad I came. I'm glad I've met you all!"

Keti remained a fast part of the group for the time that was left. She walked about the town with Agathi. She was charmed in her turn by the place and fascinated with her new friend's combination of beauty and sophisticated intelligence.

As to Keti herself, there was an intensity about her that turned evening conversation away from family stories and toward the sterner realities of present world conditions. When she learned that Rico, Youn, and Righi had among them been traveling all over Eastern Europe, she was eager for their impressions. She questioned Lysenko about the realities of life in Russia and what exactly it was that had made him leave. She listened so intently to all the answers that Rico finally asked if she was composing a story in her head to run in the States the following week.

"That's not a bad idea!" Keti understood the criticism, so lightly given, and softened both her questioning and her mood.

Christmas Eve descended clear and very cold upon Waidhofen. "This sort of weather is one of our many traditions here!" Frau Spoeda laughed. "It never snows or rains on the birthday of Jesus. It is not the Canary Islands, either! But *achtung!"*

The entire day was filled with customary Christmas celebrations. Mercifully, no Santa Claus or Father Christmas intruded on them; as in most of Europe, gifts were never given here till the "little Christmas" of Epiphany. Instead, there was much visiting back and forth among the hundred townsfolk. Children, all packed up in their bright-colored woolens, caroled in the square that lay between the inn and the village church. The Christmas Child was welcomed at midnight Mass, sung in golden candlelight. Finally there was an uproarious feast at which everyone ate far too much and Frau Spoeda's culinary genius was toasted in mulled wine. All in all, it was a blessed Christmas, and a perfect ending to a brief and peaceful interlude. A time when heaven's smile seemed especially near, and when affections born in the day's sweetness seemed apt to be nourished and grow into a full life.

On the day after Christmas, before he set out with Agathi and Rico and the others for Rome, Helmut drove Keti to the railway junction of Kirchenstadt for her train to Vienna. "If you're still covering the disarmament conference toward the end of January, maybe we'll meet." He swung her bags onto the overhead rack. "I'm generally in Vienna for about one week every month. Most usually, the third week."

"I'll be there." Keti was happy that her time with these special people wasn't ending after all.

[16]

A beehive in swarm. That was the best way to characterize the mood and activity in the Vatican Secretariat of State during the last weeks of April 1947. Some of the older hands had got wind that Papa Profumi was preparing to make wholesale changes in Vatican assignments. The peace accords that had ended the state of war were being implemented; national boundaries and local governments had begun to function; as the flood of refugees reduced to a trickle, even the Raphael's work was fast winding down. The direction to face now was forward.

In the past it had always been Profumi's policy to announce sweeping changes all in one day. "You'll see, my friends, you'll see": Sugnini with his endless garrulousness kept the hive buzzing in speculation until, by April's end, the entire Secretariat was humming in the intensity of expectation.

On May 4, though Rico arrived earlier than usual, a dozen of his colleagues were already clustered around the notice board in the internal lobby of the Secretariat. Simon Youn caught sight of him and beckoned. Rico worked his way through the chattering, black-robed clerics.

"It's here, Rico!" Youn was as excited as everyone else. "The general papal order is posted. Sugnini was right. Word is it's not just the Secretariat. All the departments have new orders."

Rico scanned the paper, from the papal emboss of tiara and crossed keys in the upper-left-hand corner, down through the sectioned lists of names, to the bottom, where the papal seal had been stamped beneath Profumi's regular script: "PP Profumi." A preliminary statement announced that the lists following reflected general assignments of the present Secretariat personnel. Each person listed was to make an appointment with Archbishop Morandi or with Archbishop Da Brescia, whichever was indicated beside his name, in order to receive full details.

At a glance, Rico saw that the changes affected all of his colleagues, including even the newest and youngest *segretariatistas.* Peter Servatius had been assigned, at his own request, to work in the green pastures of the Special Administration under the "Sphinx," Monsignore Di Lorio. The joke quickly surfaced that between them, the very fat Di Lorio and the giant Servatius could carry half the assets of the Special Administration in the folds of their huge cassocks.

The posting that met with the most somber response from everyone was Lysenko's. He was being sent to join the Apostolic Delegation in Rio de Janeiro. His dream of priesting his people in Mother Russia was not to be. Everyone felt his disappointment. Lysenko said nothing.

Annibale Sugnini was to be attached to the Apostolic Delegation in London. Levesque and Demarchelier were both posted to Bombay.

Together with a few others—Simon Youn from Korea, Yves Lacoste of France, Tannio Furla of Sicily, Roman Galinescu of Romania, Leon Thikas of Yugoslavia, Georg Holzmeister of Germany, Jaček Righi of Poland—Richard Lansing was assigned to "special duties" in the Secretariat. Beside each name in this group the letter "M" appeared; they were to report to Morandi for further briefing.

As it turned out, Morandi was only the first of several people to brief the new "special assignment" section of the Secretariat. In his instructions to Rico, as to the others, Morandi was clear and direct as always, but this time he confined himself to the most general outlines.

"I can tell you that you will be part of a team traveling much more extensively than before into all the countries of Eastern Europe. The information we have is that the Vatican must fight even for minimally livable conditions for clergy and lay people alike in that entire area. And we must fight also for survival of our centralized Church structure. Already the Soviets are creating what they call 'national churches.' " Morandi frowned as he sketched the situation for Lansing. "They have bought and coerced and tortured—'persuaded,' as they like to say—a certain number of priests and bishops to declare local churches independent of the Pope. A Polish Catholic Church, a Czechoslovak Catholic Church, and so on for each country. That way, it will be much easier for the Soviets to corrupt and to co-opt, as they have done so successfully in the Soviet Union itself. Already this Soviet trick has caused damage that must be assessed and reversed in every country where you and your colleagues will be traveling.

"In addition, changes in population and even in borders mean huge shifts in dioceses. For example, the shift of what have been German dioceses over to Poland along the Oder-Neisse line will involve entire towns complete with churches, schools, monasteries, convents, bishops, nuns, and priests. Compromises will have to be made between church and political authorities. Agreements will have to be ratified between the Vatican and local government authorities.

"Well, you will learn more details later. But as you can see, your work in Eastern Europe will be far more complex than it has been in merely searching out missing records for the Raphael. You will no longer report to me, in fact. From the time this interview ends, you will be under the direct orders of the papal office. You will report only to Father Lanser, Father Kensich, or the Pontiff himself. When you leave here, you are to go directly to Lanser's office. He will give you instructions from now on concerning this part of your work."

"This part?" It seemed to Rico that what Morandi had set before him, even in general outline, was enough for any one man.

Morandi smiled. "You don't think the Secretariat would let you get away entirely, I hope! A lot of value is put on your service here, my young friend. The Raphael work, or what remains of it, will be done by someone else. But you will remain head of the Passport Section in the Secretariat. You will have a backup staff to do all the preliminary investigations and documentation in Passports while you are away. But I expect we will all welcome you back from each trip, our open arms filled with passports and travel requests awaiting your final approval."

Morandi saw the look of concern on Rico's face and responded to it reassuringly. "It does seem a lot. But there is much to be done. Some of it can only be done by men of trust. Men such as yourself, Monsignore. You will find you have much support. You'll do just fine, Monsignore. Just fine!"

The "team" of clerics Morandi had referred to included Lansing, Youn, Galinescu, Holzmeister, and Thikas. Romanian Galinescu and Yugoslavian Thikas were young men of great verve and stamina who had proved their worth in the Raphael. When they all went to see Father Lanser, the Jesuit had a full dossier ready for each of them concerning what was known in the dioceses of each "territory" to be covered. Each man would work in the countries he had grown familiar with in his work and travels for the Raphael. That meant East Germany, Czechoslovakia, and Poland fell to Rico Lansing. Youn was assigned Hungary. Thikas was given Yugoslavia. Galinescu was assigned to Romania. Holzmeister would deal with Bulgaria.

Each man would also find in his file detailed information on such matters as "sure" and "suspect" clergy, including individual dossiers; the estimated funds at their disposal; proposed mergers and divisions of dioceses; what to expect in the way of surveillance and roadblocks from the Soviet-controlled political authorities in each zone; what changes to make based on current data; what further information to gather.

Before becoming "operational," the entire group would spend a week of intense drilling at the hands of experts from three Vatican ministries: the Congregation for Bishops, the Congregation for Clergy, and the Congregation for Religious. Together, these three departments had more useful and detailed information about Church conditions in Rome and abroad than could be crammed into a hundred briefing dossiers.

Rico and the others would need money, of course. They would have to pay their way, finance new schools, new seminaries, new bishoprics. That might have been a problem, for no one was allowed to take large amounts of currency in or out of Eastern bloc countries, and there was no official exchange.

"Thanks to the foresight of Maestro Guido de la Valle, however"—Lanser smiled—"financing can be handled through Vienna even for such wide-reaching missions as these. Signor Helmut de la Valle will see to it all, as he has for your Raphael travels. Of course, the sums needed will be larger now." Lanser hesitated, obviously not wanting to say more in this delicate area than was absolutely necessary; or perhaps he was not privy to it all himself. Much information in the Vatican is shared only on a need-to-know basis. "But," he finally went on, "between normal banking procedures, couriers, and—er—special arrangements with financial agencies with whom Signor de la Valle has—er—developed a special working relationship, we should be able to manage. He will meet with each of you and explain everything you will need to know."

Finally, they were told, the essentials of all information they would be given were to be committed to memory. "You are to travel light," Lanser emphasized. "Carry nothing in writing."

A matter of weeks later, and only when Father Lanser was satisfied that each man was ready to start his new assignment, did he hand each of them one final list. The "lamplight lists," he called them by their code name: but even by that name, they were not to be mentioned outside this small group.

"Lives depend on that." Lanser's eyes were deadly serious behind the tinted lenses. "A good deal of the information you have been given in the past few weeks has come from clandestine radio positions. 'Lamplights.' We have managed to set up a developing network in countries already locked away by the Soviets from free access by the West, as well as in those that are in the process of being locked away. Each of you has been given the list for your territory only. Memorize it, and then destroy it! Use the 'lamplight' network only if you are in personal and summary danger, or if there is information so urgent that it cannot wait for your return. Discuss your business, and get out. Make it fast. Otherwise, don't go near those addresses.

"I trust there are no questions?"

There were none.

Lansing's final meeting with Father Lanser before becoming operational was private and it was brief.

"The papal office wants you to know, Monsignore, that even though you have been selected for this special assignment, instead of being posted to the Congregation for Bishops, we have not lost sight of the fact that your future lies in Chicago. You have been patient enough not to raise the point, but we thought it best to reassure you. When your work in Eastern Europe is done—in a year or so, most probably—you will be consecrated bishop. Six months or so after that, you will be made auxiliary bishop of the archdiocese of Chicago under Cardinal Krementz. Meanwhile, the expertise you have developed in traveling for the Raphael in your territory, and the fact that you are already known to some degree in your zones, will be of immense help to us."

Rico had handled all the briefings until this one without qualms. This simplest one of all brought him up short. He left Lanser's office in something of a daze. Perhaps it was the intensity of the preparations for his mission; but Chicago had been the furthest thing from his mind.

"A year and a half," he murmured to himself in the familiar corridor. "So soon!"

While Papa Profumi kept abreast of the special missions in preparation, as he did of most things, his attention that June was focused most clearly on the Italian elections. Despite all his plans and work, he realized from the weekly briefings given him by Menda and Della Croce that there were two serious defects in the campaign: a lack of effective coordination between Menda's Catholic Action organization and Della Croce's Election Committee on a national scale; and a shortsighted failure to cultivate the women's vote.

"There are potentially twelve million women voters! Eighty-five percent of them go to Mass and confession regularly," Profumi explained in his effort to counter the overconfidence of his organizers. "Only twenty-five percent of the men practice their religion. That women's vote is the swing vote. You've done nothing to secure it. Unless you do, we are heading for trouble."

The Pontiff's sense of things proved correct, but lamentably, Della Croce and Menda only understood that after it was too late. The Democristiani made a disappointing showing, far short of a controlling parliamentary majority. The Pope knew that not all had been lost. Some of the men who would doubtless now be prominent in Italian government for the next two or three decades had emerged well. Della Croce himself had been a strong vote-getter and was assured of a cabinet post. Nevertheless, the negative side had to be addressed. Real stability and control in Italy had been delayed by the outcome at the polls. That would have to be remedied by the time of the next election. Profumi gave the necessary orders without delay. The entire middle management level of Menda's Catholic Action and the entire Central Committee of the Christian Democratic Party itself were fired, and replaced by more effective people. Perhaps the Pope had not achieved his goal yet, as he told Guido de la Valle, and as he had Father Lanser report to the Council, "but partial victory is better than eclipse of our hopes. We are headed in the right direction."

If Rico Lansing thought, prior to the first trip of his new assignment, that he knew what to expect, he was terribly mistaken. His earlier forays into European countries for the Work of St. Raphael had taken him to this refugee resettlement camp, that war rehabilitation center, such and such a hospital. But that had been way back in 1945 and 1946. Those years were still a time of hope. By June 1947, hope had largely run out for the countries of Eastern Europe.

The official schedules arranged for Rico by Lanser called for him to tackle East Germany first, then Czechoslovakia, and finally Poland. Between each leg of his mission he would return to Rome, be debriefed, convey delicate intelligence matters, and recharge his batteries.

Following instructions, Rico headed for Leipzig to find the ranking

Catholic prelate in East Germany. Ernst Müllerhof. Sixty-one. Archbishop of the Leipzig diocese.

The archbishop was at home, all right, confined by two secret police guards to the cellar of his house. There, with such poor amenities as an army cot, a wooden deal table, a chair, and a sanitary bucket to serve as toilet, the archbishop received Monsignore Lansing. His threadbare robes and gaunt face told only part of his story. He had been tortured, and would be again.

His offense? He would make no deals with the secret police, would not discuss his duties with the Minister of Cults, would not submit the texts of his sermons, and refused to fill out any government forms.

"We will not give in, Monsignore," the prelate said. "We will not compromise." Throughout East Germany, the clergy was in the same miserable condition: the worn clothes; the dank and miserable houses they lived in; their starvation fare; the misery on their faces after one more interrogation session with the local commissar or one more detention in a prison cell; the still courageous, still bright-eyed and loving attitudes these middle-aged and quite old men maintained in what truly was a living hell.

What he found in East Germany he found all over. Everywhere the Soviet Union had military forces and its dreaded secret police, the MGB. They choked and smothered every sector of life like a parasite weed. Soviet army tanks and personnel carriers were at railway stations, street intersections, public squares and parks, bridges, government offices, airports. Everywhere, there were the uniforms of Asiatic Soviet GI's, the slanted eyes watching over mounted guns, the coarse accents of Asiatic dialects, the fearful populations.

The condition of the Church hierarchy was pitiful. Uniformly, the clergy and the Church were in poverty and disarray. Church activities were strictly controlled. Each priest, bishop, and nun had to have a special permit in order merely to function. Every bishop had his own special secret police escort to watch his every move, listen to his every word. And every month, permit or no, some disappeared never to be heard of again. Of course, no Church schools were allowed. There were few religious publications. Public religious activity was being snuffed out.

Rico could not, as an official Vatican emissary, permit himself the luxury of such heroic resistance as Archbishop Müllerhof's. By dint of talking and dealing with the Communist ministries, he had to try to introduce some sanity, some order, into religious diocesan matters.

He reached Prague in the first week of August. His first contact there, Cardinal Jaroslav Tomašek, Archbishop of Prague and Primate of Czechoslovakia, was not at home. His Eminence, clothed in dirty gray-and-black-striped Soviet prison garb, feet bare, was confined in a six-by-nine-foot cell in Prague's central prison. Lansing carried on all his discussions about the reorganization of his diocese with the convict cardinal through steel bars. As with the Archbishop of Leipzig, Tomašek's offense was that he refused to sanction the "national Catholic Church" movement, refused to discuss any Church matters with the Communist overlords, and had instructed his clergy to organize a stiff resistance to the will of the Communist Politburo, even in civil matters.

Though Tomašek knew his conversation was being taped, he gave Lansing what information he could on conditions throughout his country. And he had a message for Rome, as well. "Tell the Holy Father," Tomašek said, "that we will die willingly rather than betray our Church."

Rico wondered where such men as these drew their courage. And that in this part of the world, it seemed almost commonplace. When he said Mass in the half-broken-down churches and ramshackle chapels, there was standing room only; the congregations were people of all ages, and Rico could almost reach out and feel the vibrancy of their faith, the warmth of their devotion.

What an ocean of difference there was between such people and the congregations in Chicago, or even those in Rome. There were no palatial bishops' residences, or substantial bank accounts; no well-heeled parish rectories, or respect-laden social standing for the clerics and religious. There was anything but favorable reception of the clergy by civil and political authorities, or prosperous and democratically free citizens. Yet those were the conditions Richard Lansing had always coupled in his mind with Church life and his own career in his Church. It was like a brand-new revelation for him now to perceive that none of all that had anything to do with Church life, or with the flourishing of belief and religious devotion. It was almost as powerful a lesson for him as if he had been allowed to walk for a time with the martyred Apostles. He felt a greater kinship with each of those harassed priests and bishops than he had ever felt toward his colleagues in the Chicago diocese or his Secretariat colleagues in the Vatican.

Poland was the last leg of Rico's special assignment, and it held him the longest. It was quickly obvious that here, as elsewhere, the Soviet authorities were bent on whittling the Church structure down to mere scrimshaw and useless shavings. But the biggest single matter to deal with was the transfer to Poland of a whole slew of formerly German dioceses that lay along the famous Oder-Neisse line. Cardinal Jan Wallensky's official residence in Warsaw—a large, unheated house in a ruined suburb—was Rico's base of operations for his entire stay in Poland.

Wallensky, Cardinal Primate of Poland, had long since been dubbed "the fox of Europe," and not only because of his large ears and sharp eyes, his long nose and thin mouth. It *was* a foxlike face; but his quick intelligence and wily instincts had earned his reputation. As a young cleric in World War I, he had successfully contended with Russian taskmasters. In World War II, he had frustrated every emissary Hitler had dispatched to tame him. He was now ready to take on the ruthless commissars of the Soviet dictator. Wallensky had two young seminarians, Bogdan Valeska and Adam Lis, living with him.

"I'm the best teacher they can have for the world they face," the cardinal explained blandly. "And besides, if I keep them with me, I can save them from being conscripted into a labor gang by the government."

Both young men were well built, but very lean; in their late twenties by the looks of them; and despite the usual conditions that Rico now expected all over his territory, both were full of good humor and courage.

Rico and Wallensky spent weeks at a time negotiating with government authorities about the transfer of German populations in vast tracts of land that would now become Polish territory according to the terms of the peace treaties.

For Rico it was a maddening frustration to deal for twelve hours at a stretch with petty officials. They obviously hated him and held in contempt everything he stood for. They dealt in lies and deceit and strong-arm tactics. Even with the Vatican at his back, Rico realized more than once, he probably would have accomplished nothing useful in Poland—he might even have got himself arrested—without "the fox of Europe" at his side. As it was, his work there took almost three grueling months.

Those hard-nosed dealings with the Communist bureaucracy afforded Lansing his first real schooling in the art of reasonable and unreasonable compromise. Under Communist totalitarian pressure, only the barest minimum of livable conditions could be extracted from the iron fist of state control—and then only at a cost Rico Lansing would never in his wildest dreams have thought even of considering back in Chicago or in Rome.

Cardinal Wallensky put the case realistically and in a nutshell. "What do you expect, Monsignore? We want to build churches. They want to build factories. Now, you may think that in any normal country the people can have both. But this is not a normal country. And unfortunately, Josef Stalin does not see things our way."

And so it was that he traded the freeing of one key Polish archbishop for the continued banishment of three monks to the Soviet prison village of Boguchany in the Soviet central highlands. To save a convent of nuns from being disbanded, he signed away a church, to be used as an arsenal. He agreed not to press inquiries about a priest whose hands had been cut off, and in return got permits for several priests to function. In order to have a seminary continue, he agreed to allow an MGB officer to reside there. He wrote off whole German villages and towns—henceforth they would be Polish—to save the structure of a diocese. The compromises were many and agonizing. And always it seemed to be the lesser good versus the greater evil.

And yet Wallensky hammered home again and again to Rico that it was not in East Germany or Czechoslovakia, where confrontation and martyrdom were preferred, but here in Poland, where cruel and grueling compromise made them look so bad, that the real battleground lay.

"You do realize that we in the Polish Church have taken on the Communists, don't you, Monsignore?" Wallensky would say after a hard day's dealing. "We're not playing any games. Not even the martyrdom game. Ah! That would be so easy! Resistance unto death and all that!

"Cardinal Tomašek, you told me, will have no truck with the Communists. Yes, and Archbishop Müllerhof too. And your colleagues who deal with Yugoslavia and Hungary have told you of the brave stand that Mindszenty of Budapest and Stepinac of Zagreb have taken.

"We are not taking any such heroic stand. We in Poland don't want to be martyred. We want to live, and to serve Christ by living. We don't intend to be killed off. We intend to survive and to flourish in spite of Stalin's backteeth. To fight, but intelligently, Monsignore. To beat the Communists at their own game. To out-talk them. Out-work them. Out-patient them. Wear them down with their own weapons of harassment. We are Poles. We've been fighting foreign despots since the twelfth century. When they demand that we sign a document, we take the document away; study it; come back with objections, counterproposals, other documents. They want to create what they grandiosely call the 'new man.' We intend also to create a 'new man.' They indoctrinate. We indoctrinate. They abuse us verbally. We abuse them verbally. They call out their bullyboys. We call out our crowds of Catholics. So it goes."

By the time his work in Poland was finished, and Wallensky and Bogdan Valeska put him on his train at Warsaw for the Austrian border, Rico would have said that he understood these people, and loved them, as much as if they were his own. He would never see their faces again in this life, most probably. As his train drew out, he watched the two of them out the window. Wallensky's head was bowed in that way he had, moving just the tiniest bit from side to side as if the cardinal were scenting the air. Valeska stood tall, his head up, his blue eyes lit by that fire of enthusiasm Rico had always seen there.

Lansing learned to thrive on work, with no days off and little rest. On his return from each mission into Eastern Europe, he spent long hours with Kensich or Lanser, filling out in person the full picture he could not put in his on-the-spot written reports.

Papa Profumi called him in for private meetings to satisfy his own mind concerning questions of particular interest. Rico found that the Pope was most concerned with belief and purity of doctrine. His constant question: "Are my bishops falling for the Marxist utopian promise of material welfare?"

And always, as Morandi had promised, there was a pile of passport papers waiting on his desk to be processed. Most were routine and only needed to be given his final *placet*—"it pleases," Vaticanese for "approved"—without much ado. A few exceptions required closer attention: cases that may have come to this or that cardinal, who had been approached by this or that bishop or diplomat, who, in his turn, had been petitioned for any one of a hundred reasons, some valid, some not.

It was one of those cases that caught Rico's attention late one day soon after his return from Poland. Actually, it was not one case, but twelve; and they came, not from this or that cardinal, but from the papal office, in one single envelope bearing Father Lanser's name.

The manifest sheet accompanying the dozen brand-new passports showed that the preliminary work had been done, and that each request had received conditional approval from the usual roster of five names: "p" for *placet* had been scribbled by de la Valle for Finance; Da Brescia and Morandi for State; Lanser for the Pontiff; and Falconieri for the Council. Rank was not the overriding element in these matters, of course. In the workings of the Vatican bureaucracy, Lansing, as head of this Passport Section, had the final say. His scribbled *placet* or *non placet* would be conclusive, and the responsibility for the consequences would rest on his shoulders alone.

Rico placed the manifest sheet aside, and turned to the background memorandum that had been prepared for him. Twelve middle-aged Italian Carmelite priests from the Convent of All Souls at Spartivento in remote Calabria had generously volunteered for pastoral work in Peru and Bolivia, where there was a dire shortage of local clergy.

Well, that seemed simple enough; commendable, even. Rico made the calls to verify in the usual way that each of the five *placets* on the manifest sheet was valid. Satisfied that all was in order, he turned to the final task of validating each of the passports.

It was as he paged through the second passport to be sure all the protocol details were in order that his trouble in the matter began. The name was typically Italian—Corrado Sinigallia. But there was something about the photograph. The monklike haircut and the clothes were normal. But the middle-aged face was odd somehow. Those lines on the cheek: they might have been age lines, but they looked like—of course! That was it! They were *Mensuren!* Rico had seen them many times on German officers who had tried to use the Raphael to escape the long arm of the Allied authorities. He examined the photograph more carefully in order to be absolutely sure; but there could be no doubt. Those hair-thin streaks running from cheekbones to chin were clearly the so-called honorable scars German university students conferred on one another during ritual saber fights.

Quickly, Rico examined the other eleven passports. First the photographs. Yes. The scars were there. More apparent in some than in others; but they were there. Then the signatures. Without exception, they were in a Germanic style of writing. Lansing flung the last passport across his desk in disgust. "Missionaries!" He growled the word contemptuously. "Missionaries for a dead Hitler, maybe; but not for the Risen Christ!"

He grabbed the manifest sheet again and stared at the approving "p" beside each name. Were they blind? Lanser, Falconieri, Guido de la Valle? All of them? Rico shoved his chair back roughly from the desk, and paced his office in rising agitation. He had already spent two full years trying to clean up the mess left by these wholesale butchers, and more months trying to head off still further suffering and human disasters coming from yet another godless dictator and his emissaries. Memories of his interviews with Raphael refugees flooded his mind: their tears, their irreparable losses, their anguish and inconsolable ache of heart at the husband, the son, the wife, the children snatched up and carried away. All this still hurt in his own heart. And now he was being asked to validate passports for twelve stooges of hell itself? Why? In God's holy name, why?

"A reason of state!" Lansing jumped out of his chair, his face flushed with emotion as he leaned over Lanser's desk. He thought he had got his temper under control before he phoned Father Lanser for this urgent conference; but a nonexplanation like that was just a lighted match setting his fuse burning furiously. "What does *that* mean? Something like this is either right or wrong! Truth is simple! You don't bargain about it or split hairs!"

Rico had no idea what sort of bargain he meant; but he did know that was what a "reason of state" came down to: a deal.

Though the Jesuit took the tirade in silence, he was more affected than he cared to show by the depth and openness of this young American's feeling. There was no pretense about it, no toadying, no angling for position or for political advantage. He was outraged, and he wanted someone who could make a difference to know it.

When finally Rico had spent the worst of his anger, Lanser thought he would try to explain. "You live by simple rules, Monsignore. . . ."

Lansing opened his mouth, ready to explode all over again; but Father Lanser stopped him with a gesture. "Monsignore, you have made yourself quite clear."

Rico relented. He would hear the man out, but whatever he said had better be good.

"I know," Lanser went on with equanimity, "many of us know, in fact, how much suffering you have seen and dealt with so conscientiously since you arrived here. It's not easy for you to send wolves back again, free among the sheep. It is not easy for any of us. My father, brother, and sister perished in Ravensbrück camp, because they wouldn't go along with Hitler's propaganda against the Church. I lost hundreds of my beloved Jesuit brothers to that hellhound, as well. Oh, yes, Monsignore! We know. We all know.

"We serve this Vatican, in times that are far from simple. I will not sit here and justify the Pontiff's decisions for you. I will tell you what I can, in total confidence. You must respect that confidence as you do the seal of confession. Is that much agreed?"

Rico nodded his assent.

"I will tell you," the Jesuit went on patiently, "not because it is your due, but because you seem to need it." The rebuke was gentle but clear.

"Over two years ago, in highly complex circumstances generated by the war, the Pontiff gave his reluctant consent to help a German officer named Wolff and eleven others to leave Europe for safe haven abroad when that could be done securely. There were conditions on both sides. The Germans kept their part of the bargain. We have kept most of ours. The moment has come when we must keep the remainder of our undertaking.

"With all due respect, Monsignore, you are no stranger to such dealings. You have bargained only recently in Prague and Berlin and Warsaw with men as bad or worse than those officers; with men who are now far more powerful, in fact."

"It's not the same thing!" Rico was incensed all over again.

"Perhaps not, Monsignore." Lanser appeared calm and even-tempered, though at some cost. "But if there is a difference, I think that it lies only in the fact that you are privy to all the circumstances that make your bargains necessary. For they are necessary, Monsignore Lansing. You have made that clear in your reports.

"Still, suppose for a moment that after giving our backing to those dealings of yours, we turn tail on them. What would happen?"

Rico answered without hesitation. "Innocent people would pay a hefty price; there would be bloodshed and chaos."

"And our guarantees?" Lanser prompted. "Vatican guarantees. What would happen to them?"

"They would be perceived as worthless, I suppose. But there are some things the Vatican should not guarantee!"

"Well, I will not argue that." Lanser nodded as if to underline his agreement with such a broad statement. "But if you think that because we facilitate these twelve in escaping they will finally escape punishment, I can only say that the Holy See never guaranteed that. Only that they get to South America.

"And yet, if it is your judgment that even their passage to South America should not take place, then that is how it will be. For you have the last word. You know the procedure as well as I. You are head of the Passport Section in charge of the matter. Without your *placet* and your validation of the passports, the matter will not go forward. They will not escape.

"In the end, however, it seems to me to be a matter of trust. Our trust in you and your judgment. Yours in the Holy Father and in his judgment. And the trust of the whole world that the Vatican will honor what you have called its bargains. So perhaps it is simple after all. If trust is a simple thing."

Once back in his office, Rico stared at the papers jumbled before him. First at the manifest sheet, marked with the silent approval of responsible men; then at the passports; then at the manifest sheet again. It was evening by the time he knew: at some moment he could not identify, in some cool, rational chamber of his mind, he had decided his only recourse was to ignore the insistent protest that lingered within him; to trust Lanser and Profumi; to go along with this terrible charade.

Slowly, almost mechanically, he stamped and initialed each passport. He had one of his aides photograph each one for Secretariat files. That done, he checked off his own name on the manifest sheet with a simple "p" for *placet,* placed everything back in the envelope, and handed it to an aide to carry to Lanser's office.

It all seemed slow motion to him. His own movements. The aide reaching to take the envelope from his hand. Slow motion, as though he had crossed some boundary into another world. *"Perhaps it is simple after all."* He heard Lanser's words play back in his mind, as if in slow track accompaniment to his movements. *"If trust is a simple thing."*

"Wait!"

Rico's aide turned, alarmed at the monsignore's shout. "Are you all right, Monsignore?" What was the matter with him, anyway?

"Yes—I'm fine. Yes. If trust is a simple thing, Lanser. That's what you said?"

The aide watched uncomprehendingly as Rico came around the desk, almost snatched the envelope, ripped it open, and took the manifest sheet out again.

He would not allow his approval to stand mute and unadorned. He picked up his pen and changed his "p" to "pim." *Placet iuxta modum.* Approved with qualifications. Then in clear, bold hand he stated his qualification: "In preparing these documents, I have trusted that, despite appearances, the love of our Lord Jesus will be served."

It was Papa Profumi's habit to go over his reading material when the day was done. At about nine-thirty or ten o'clock in the evening, Sister Philomena and the two Jesuits said the Rosary with him. The nun then put on some favorite concerto or sonata for the Pope, and all three left him for the night.

This evening, Lanser had placed the materials concerning the German passports as the first item of business in the leather folder by the chair where Profumi often did his evening's work. Profumi sighed as he read Lanser's two-line memorandum saying that the Wolff affair was successfully concluded. The subject was as unwelcome now for the Pontiff as it had been the very day that the Maestro and the Council had opposed him in the whole matter of the Swiss Windfall. Since that time, some useful consequences and some distasteful ones had come of it all. The question of the passports was decidedly among the distasteful.

Normally, Lanser's memorandum would have been the solitary document dealing with the subject. For some reason, though, as the Pope noticed, the Jesuit had attached the full manifest sheet. His interest piqued, Profumi studied the sheet. Every name there stood in his mind for a whole block of names.

"Falconieri," Profumi read aloud. *"Placet."* A not unexpected approval. But when it came down to hard and basic issues of Church governance, was the cardinal really with him? And the other cardinals on the Council for whom that *placet* of Falconieri spoke? And the groupings in the Curia that each of those cardinals represented in turn? Profumi knew unrest was growing under his tightened rule. *Placet* or no, more than a few were going their own way, not Profumi's.

"Da Brescia," he read the next name. *"Placet."* No, my dear Archbishop, Profumi mused to himself. *Placet* is not your state of mind. You are among the ones who wait for me to die. One of the surly ones, biding their time, chafing beneath doctrinal control. And behind you?

Though Profumi had tried to root out from Belgium, Holland, and Germany those who taught false doctrine, he was painfully aware that pockets of abscess still festered beneath the surface of his monolithic Church, ready to burst and seep through the ancient Catholic heartland, corroding and rotting the fibers of faith.

Morandi's *placet* was that of a solid bureaucrat; neither more nor less than that. It was Falconieri who had once remarked that Archbishop Morandi was like most bishops in the Church—a good enough administrator with no special glimmer of light. Maybe, Profumi thought a little wearily; but I wish sometimes there were more like him.

"Guido de la Valle: 'p.' " Profumi read the next to last name. Here at least the Pope knew he had a man who read the contemporary signals as he himself did. But, so faithful in all other things, the Maestro was still so certain he could harvest power for his Church from the green-topped counting tables of the world. Well, perhaps his Pontiff should not be entirely harsh in his judgment, considering how well it had gone so far. The Maestro had said he could keep it all under control, and so far he had been as good as his word.

"Richard Lansing." Papa Profumi came to the last name on the manifest. And then with growing interest he noticed that what at first had been a simple "p" had been changed in great agitation to "pim." The Pontiff read the American's qualifying remark once. Then once again. And yet again. As if to savor and delight in those words that burst like unexpected sunlight into the dark business at hand, an explosion of faith and fervor and conscience. *"I have trusted that . . . the love of our Lord Jesus will be served."*

Profumi thought back over his several meetings with the young cleric from Chicago, and the reports that had come in from him during his long missions in Eastern Europe. Lansing had been nervous in his first few papal audiences. That was not unusual, of course; on the contrary. But even then, he had seemed to understand the deeper import of the questions Profumi put to him; and always the American cut to the heart of the matter without all the flourish and self-serving qualifications that were such a frequent annoyance and a bore in other clerics who served him.

Come to think of it, Profumi reflected, the young man's Roman stint had begun to tell. Rome had emphasized some qualities in him, and put some of his defects into half-shadow. What was buoyant in him, what was childlike and confident, what was enterprising and courageous, had come out in pleasing relief, on the background of a stubborn will. A certain mere casualness had been transformed into the smoothness of *romanità.* The discipline forced on him by the need to speak and think in Italian had begun in him a new subtlety of perception.

And now, in this hasty note scrawled beside the Monsignore's name, there was another quality, one the Pope had not seen in too long a time. All around him there was a monolithic, unquestioning acceptance of the new state of world affairs, of the approaching winter of human dealings, of the scratching of Satan's claws at the very walls of Christendom's city.

Profumi's eyes came back to the manifest sheet. Clearly, Lansing had understood the deepest meaning in this tawdry affair of the passports. "*. . . the love of our Lord Jesus.*" Those words were silent echoes for Profumi of the ancient Christian voice chanting "Holy! Holy! Holy!" over the shrill and mounting scream of the Beast.

Profumi rose from his chair and crossed to the desk. He placed the manifest in front of him and took his own pen. In the margin near Lansing's scrawled words, he placed his own notation: *"Capax potestatis."* Then his signature, "PP Profumi."

In the morning, he would instruct Lanser to route the manifest sheet back again to the Maestro, Falconieri, Da Brescia, and Morandi. With the papal signature affixed, the message to them would be crystal clear. In their Pontiff's eyes, Monsignore Lansing could learn to wield power. Roman power.

[17]

A personal war had begun inside Richard Lansing. Perhaps it was the delayed but inescapable aftereffect of all those months spent dealing with extravagant human suffering in the Raphael. Or, perhaps, the bitter realization, brought home to him by his travels, that Eastern Europe had been dealt by the Allies to the Soviets like a chip in some back-room geopolitical poker game, and that the war fought "for freedom from tyranny" was a macabre, cosmic joke on human decency. Certainly the episode of the German passports was a factor in his inner stress.

All in all, whatever produced it, the effect was as if a series of curtains had been drawn back on Rico's perception of his Church, and on the world it served. He began to perceive that whatever else the Vatican may be—and it is many things—it is indisputably the oldest and most experienced political chancellery in the world. And yet those words he had scrawled on the passport manifest were important for Lansing. He did truly trust that the love of Jesus would somehow always stand behind even the less glorious dimensions of Vatican activity. Otherwise, as far as he could see, everything would crumble: the Vatican, Rome—all of it. Or was he just totally wrong? Was this how the institution of the Church survived? By making deals like everyone else? By knowing when to let go, when to resist? Perhaps Father Lanser had been correct: Rico did live by simple rules. Too simple? That was a possibility.

One result of Lansing's inner turmoil was an unaccustomed personal indecision. It was not a crisis of faith, or a questioning of his priestly calling; those remained the surest underpinnings of his life and being. It seemed more like a hunger let loose in him that nothing could satisfy. When conversation at the Secretariat or at gatherings at Villa Cerulea centered, as it most often did, on Papa Profumi's plans and on Rome, Rico felt a great longing to be back in Chicago—could hardly wait until he would end his exile and be posted in familiar surroundings as auxiliary bishop to his first mentor, Cardinal Krementz. Old Blackjack, too, lived by simple rules.

Yet, as the time drew nearer for Rico to be consecrated bishop, and the reality of his return to Chicago loomed on the horizon beyond that, he experienced what he could only think of as an irrational nostalgia for this Rome, this Vatican that enfolded him at such moments like a well-fitting cloak.

And somehow or other all of his nostalgia, whether for Chicago or for Rome, fused at times with his insuppressible compassion for the people he had come across in those benighted countries of the East. He might be on one of his solitary walks around the Vatican or saying Mass or falling asleep at night, when faces and voices would come back to him, as if crying out from a great distance: "If you can forget us, if you can leave us, then who will remember us in our agonies? Come back. Come back among us."

As if in taunting contrast to Rico's personal mood, the middle of 1948 burst upon Rome with jubilation and triumph at last. The June 2 national elections were like a cannon shot opening the celebrations. Thanks to Vatican financial support and the unswerving political activism of the Pope's refurbished national laymen's organization, Catholic Action, the Christian Democratic Party had, on its second attempt, won the absolute majority it had sought. It held 305 out of 574 seats in Parliament. The Socialists and Communists combined had managed to capture only 30.7 percent of the Italian vote. The mood of optimism that swept the Vatican was extraordinary, and the Maestro was positively expansive.

"Because Italy has won"—Guido raised his glass at a small dinner at Villa Cerulea—"the West will be in the capitalist camp. The Mediterranean will not be a Soviet lake. What the Allied armies could have done three years ago with steel and fire, but refused to do, the Holy See has done without a single shot! We were the only ones with the vision, and with the political wallop!" The green fire shone in his eyes as, one after another, Helmut and Agathi, and Rico too, raised their glasses to join the toast that was resounding again throughout Rome and all of Italy: *"Viva Papa Liberatore!"*

Jubilation or no, the Pontiff—and the Maestro, despite his show of triumph—looked upon the situation with a cool eye. It was clear that the success of Profumi's plans had set the configuration of Italian politics for the next thirty years. Whether future governments would be Christian Democratic, or Socialist Republican, or some centrist compromise, would be less of a worry, because when all the voting was done, the same two hundred names would float at the top of the Italian political pond. Whatever the political stripe of the prime minister, whatever the mind of the president, cabinets would inevitably be composed of various combinations of those same two hundred men. Profumi's will, and Guido's money together with the friendships it generated, had ensured that.

Out of curiosity on the latter point, Rico asked Helmut how much they had really spent on the elections.

"A couple of million, I suppose." Helmut was airily noncommittal.

"A couple, my foot!" Rico would have none of that nonsense. "Must have been at least five; probably twice that or more!"

"Well . . ." Helmut was good-natured, but still not precise. "A Roman couple, you know."

The worrisome side of the situation, however, was not cost. It was that international powers of major importance turned a blind eye to the broad significance of the Italian victory. England and the United States seemed only a notch above total lack of awareness, in fact. And though some of the French, led by Robert Schuman, and some of the Germans, led by Konrad Adenauer, recognized the victory for its worth, far and away the vast majority of Europeans did not or would not see that their impoverished and brutalized continent had just won a short respite; one that might be long enough for their governments to do something about their unity and their future, if they would.

The Italian victory was a good beginning. Nothing more. There was clearly much work yet to be done in the wide arena of pan-European politics and pan-European economics. Still, Guido de la Valle was certain that, with the activities of the *impero* spreading every day, taking hold in ever-higher reaches of the economic and political bastions of the world, he would in time be able to co-opt the major governments, including even the unsophisticated, hard-boiled Americans, into his farthest plans. He would return Italy and Europe to the Faith that had once made them great; and he would mold them into a third, and balancing, force that would hold its own between U.S.S.R. and U.S.A. The heavy-handed Soviets were already making the easygoing Yanks nervous. Guido knew he could manage it all, if anyone could.

It was in the setting of this golden landscape of hope renewed that the preparations for the June 29 consecration of twelve new bishops went forward. Here was the oldest Church consecrating as successors to the Apostles young men drawn from all five continents, and from all races of the world.

In later years, the events of that week remained as a blurred haze of happy moments in Rico Lansing's memory: The anticipation of seeing his family for the first time since he had left Chicago in the chill spring of '45. His first sight of them coming off the plane at Ciampino. His mother's tears on his cheek and her laughter in his ear as she put her arms around him. His father's huge bear hug. His sister's radiance as she flew into his embrace.

It turned out that Netta's radiance was not entirely for Rico. In the midst of the endless catch-up and chatter, at some moment he couldn't exactly remember, she told him she was in love. "William Bradford Brock is his name." Netta showed him the photograph she carried with her. "Congressman for the Eleventh District of Chicago. Isn't he handsome? Mother says he looks a little like you! I wanted to surprise you, to see your face when I told you. So do forgive me for not writing you about him. You will like him, Rick." It seemed as much an order as a wish in the torrent of his twin sister's happy news. "We'll be married by the end of the year! Of course, Brad doesn't know that yet, but he will soon enough. Oh, Richie, I'm so in love and so happy. Tell me you'll come home to marry us! Please!"

Rico remembered trying to take it all in, remembered trying not to be caught up too rashly in the pull of emotions. "Netta, I may not be posted back to Chicago in time. . . ."

"Darling Rico. Isn't that what they call you now? You'll be a bishop by the end of the week! A bishop can do anything! Promise me!"

Rico promised. Sometime during the whirl of preparations, or during the dinner at Villa Cerulea, or the one at the Hassler Hotel, where his family stayed, or during the tours to show "his Rome" to the people he loved, sometime in that week he gave his word to Netta. "You set the date, and I'll be there to marry you and your lucky congressman. I promise."

Of the early-morning ceremony of consecration itself Rico preserved indelible cameo memories: Entering the ornate Basilica of the Twelve Apostles in solemn ritual procession along with Simon Youn, Lopez Navarro, Kieran O'Mahoney, Jaček Righi, Joseph Bugambwa, George Holzmeister, and the others. The sea of guests that filled the nave. The glowing pride of his family as they watched with the Maestro, Agathi, and Helmut. The startling contrast between his valet, Vittorio Benfatti, and Guido's enigmatic man, Franze Sagastume. The look in Cardinal Falconieri's eyes as he placed the bishop's miter on Rico's head and the crozier in his right hand. The cardinal's consecrating phrases. His kiss of peace.

Most clearly of all Rico remembered the moment he turned in that ancient place to give his first blessing as a bishop: He was one more now in a line so long that it reached through ages past to Peter the Apostle, and would reach through ages to come, until the very close of time.

When the day came—too quickly, it seemed—for Rico to see his family off again to Chicago, it was Sagastume who drove them, in Guido's limousine, to the airport. The Maestro and Helmut each sent flowers to the Hassler, and each phoned regrets, sincerely felt and sincerely received, that urgent business required them that day. Agathi had intended to go along with Rico too, but a sudden crisis in the household staff prevented her.

Understandably, there were more tears than laughter this time in the crowded airport. Sagastume saw to the luggage, and secured the seats, while Rico and his family shared all the mixed emotions of such a moment.

"Well, son"—it was Basil who said the last goodbye—"it won't be all that long before we see each other again. You'll be home to marry Netta; she'll have her way, as always, even if Brock doesn't know it yet! And then before we turn around, you'll be home again for good, baptizing all the little Brocks!"

Even though Sagastume tried to fill the silence, Rico's ride back to Rome seemed solitary.

"If I may say so"—the giant glanced at Rico in the rearview mirror—"Your Excellency's Vatican experience has been perfect training for a splendid career in the Church in America."

Rico smiled and nodded his thanks at what he supposed was an encouraging compliment. He wasn't surprised that Sagastume knew something about his "Vatican experience"; all valets knew a great deal, and the Maestro's most of all. Only . . . there seemed a trace of some other note in the chauffeur's voice, as if he looked forward to the end of Lansing's Roman stint. Rico shook off the idea. It was his imagination, surely.

Before he retired for the night, Rico dictated answers to most of the telegrams and letters of congratulation that Vittorio had placed in neat piles on his study desk. Blackjack, fellow clerics, friends—even Big Bill Bailey, mayor of Chicago and head of the powerful political machine that controlled everything but the winds in the Windy City—had all showered congratulations on him and looked to the day when he would be back with them.

Finally, in the small hours, Rico sighed, stretched, and prepared for bed. He found he was distracted from his evening prayers by insistent thoughts that followed the pull of the moment. He did belong back there with them all in Chicago. They were his people. This was his land, his city, his home. Life would soon turn full circle, restoring him to the haunts he knew, the airs he enjoyed. And that was all about it.

The last sounds he heard as he fell asleep were the dimming echoes from the nighttime streets of Rome. In his dreams, he found himself inside the Colosseum, screaming at a stern-faced Sagastume, who had floated the Maestro's limousine in the air very near him, and was insisting he drive the young bishop back to Chicago that very minute. . . .

18

Truth to tell, though the Pontiff and the Maestro were not yet aware, there were certain groups whose interest in the Italian elections of June 1948 stood many notches above lack of awareness. On a mellow September afternoon, representatives of a few of those groups gathered affably together at a place that had always been called the Cottage.

A single-story Elizabethan house some thirty miles outside London, complete with low doorways, creaky floors, and narrow corridors, protected from prying eyes by a green swath of cypresses and gnarled yew trees, the Cottage was the country residence of the Reverend Clifton Ripley-Savage and his able wife, whose given name had long since fallen before her husband's pet name for her. Muffie.

Moneyed and inherently gentle people of intense goodwill, socialist in their politics, polished in their education, steeped in their conviction that peace could always be achieved by "decent compromise," the Ripley-Savages shrank in horror from the idea of religious zealotry or sectarian violence. Rather, their brand of religion was the latest fruit of the English home-grown, hyphenated Christianity: Anglican-Catholic. Like their ancestors of a hundred years before, they had until lately seen the "Anglican-Catholic" and the "Roman-Catholic" as branches of "the one true Church," equal in status with each other and with the Greek and Russian "Eastern Orthodox" branches. But by 1945, along with many Anglican-Catholics, the Ripley-Savages had taken a huge leap into the ecumenical sphere, where Roman-Catholic, Anglican-Catholic, Greek and Russian Orthodox, became as so many components of mankind's thrust toward the genuine unity of "the human family," on a par with such other components as the religion of Islam, of Judaism, of Buddhism, of Hinduism of Bahaism.

As nearly as the Reverend and Muffie could see, the only real need was to rid each of these components of any claim to be "the one true Church" or "the one true religion." Indeed, to rid *all* human society of centralized power blocs. "The parliament of man" was their goal. A loving dialogue of equals. Only so could war and social inequities, poverty and crime—in sum, all human suffering—be eliminated.

The Ripley-Savages were convinced that the natural leaders in this leaderless, collective progress of mankind were to be found in the Anglican-Catholic Church, with its genius for compromise. The Reverend Clifton was presently a mere canon in St. Paul's Cathedral, London. In Muffie's vision, however, and therefore in her husband's, he should one day be Archbishop of Canterbury. Today's meeting was but one early step upon the trail to the ultimate goals.

Of course, given such visions, "the Pope's victory," as Muffie called it, at the Italian polls could only be received as a grave setback. The "Roman fact" that Papa Profumi so ardently represented was bad enough: namely, that the head of Christ's true Church was and would always exclusively be bishop of that one geographical place, Rome. But now this tawdry Italian election had only reinforced Roman exclusivity by putting in Profumi's hands a renewed potential for power in the political and religious arenas at home and abroad.

If that potential was allowed to go unchecked and come to full fruition, it would only be at the expense of "the collective progress of mankind." What Muffie meant, as she emphasized in a rather unfortunate if colorful simile, was that she did not intend to see her husband occupy a castrated archbishopric.

Alone, of course, the Ripley-Savages could not accomplish all that needed to be done in order to maintain the virility of their goal. Indeed, alone they did not even *know* all that needed to be done. But by dint of hard work, willing connections, and a good deal of correspondence around the world in the early postwar years, an ad hoc group of like-minded people, churchmen and lay, was on the brink of formation.

Well, perhaps like-minded was too sweeping a term. All of the six men who gathered with the Reverend and Mrs. Ripley-Savage that day, at the huge refectory table in the dining room of the Cottage, had very different reasons for being there.

Richard Richards, for example: tall and balding, used to command, his aristocratic bearing enhanced by the exquisite cut of his single-breasted suit. Richards was head of the London-based One World Foundation. His interest was in finding a suitable platform from which to implement the ideal of the Grand Lodge of England: to establish "That Religion in which all men agree." Muffie and Clifton surmised that some of the other aims of the Lodge in the religious area did not exactly cohere with their own. But in the circumstances, it was sufficient for their unity with him that there was no room in Richards' ideal for any individual church—and certainly not for one so authoritarian as that which Profumi solemnly professed to head by divine appointment.

Herbert Cale's viewpoint, though very different from Richards', could also be stretched in a crisis; and he did agree this was a crisis. Bishop Cale, secretary-general of the Higher Anglican Council of Canterbury, presided over by His Grace the Archbishop, was firm in the opinion that "the Church Universal has as many branches as there are races and nations and approaches to God." Cale had views on ecclesiastical precedence that clashed with those of Clifton. But in the circumstances, a splinter of common ground with the Reverend and with the others was enough for now: he, too, abhorred the idea of one true Catholic Church.

Muffie considered Monsignore Annibale Sugnini as her personal triumph. Not only was he a real Roman cleric, *and* a member of the powerful Vatican Secretariat of State. He actually worked for the Pope's personal representative in the United Kingdom. Since his arrival in London two years before, Muffie had several times heard him speak before groups of "separated Christian brethren"—that phrase grated badly on her nerves, but she tolerated it, in the circumstances. She adored the way he talked of the hope, nourished by himself and others like him in Rome, for a truly ecumenical movement that would, one day soon, open windows of spirit too long shuttered, and so lead to a great unity among all Christians.

Those were not platitudes for Muffie; they were very agreeable sentiments. It stood to reason that if Sugnini could be persuaded to organize those "others like him in Rome," he could represent a most valuable chink in Papa Profumi's armor.

There was another true ecumenist at the meeting that September day. The white-robed Brother Reginald was in no way linked to the Roman bureaucracy; but he could nevertheless be helpful in destabilizing Profumi's tenacious hold on the European heartland. Reginald was based in the Ecumenical Monastery of Zaite, France. There, twentieth-century French Protestant Reform religion labored hard to recreate the monastic life that the first French Reformers had so zealously uprooted with fire and sword in the sixteenth century. Brother Reginald's dream was of "white-robed millions worshiping beneath safe skies," and of "simple houses cleansed of superstitious statues, furnished instead with plain tables at which the bread of brotherhood would be washed down with the drink of mother nature." His ideas were exercising a strange fascination for an increasing number of Catholics. Muffie thought of him with some distaste as a quiet fanatic whose perpetual smile and burning eyes were unsettling. Sugnini vouched for his dedication, however; and it was said that even such a powerful man as Pro-Secretary of State Da Brescia frequented Reginald's monastery. That was enough, in the circumstances.

If Pantelleimon Lysenko had cut an unmistakable figure during his days in Rome, Metropolitan Nikodim seemed positively ostentatious in this little group. The grinning, voluble Russian Orthodox bishop of Leningrad and Ladoga arrived with black robes flowing about his roly-poly figure, and high, conical *kamilavka* perched on his head. Blue-eyed and blond-haired, barely thirty-seven years of age, Nikodim was not only the second-highest cleric in the Soviet Union, but a ranking colonel in the Soviet MGB. He would attend a meeting of any group that might help dilute the Romanism of the Catholic Church. Socialism in the Soviet Union might have gone to extremes, the Ripley-Savages agreed; but after all, Profumi's policies and his priests were the main cause—and sometimes the only cause—of thorny problems in the Eastern European satellites, and even in parts of the Soviet Union itself.

The final representative in this curious alliance was the only one who did not speak for some North European group. Father Jaime Herreras was a young Colombian Jesuit who had specialized in the theology of social and political life. Liberation Theology, as it was already called. Father Herreras had formed a nucleus of collaborators—priests, nuns, and layfolk—with whom he worked energetically to develop and spread a new Gospel meaning for the oppressed masses of people in Latin America. His first priority was to liberate those masses from all forms of imperialism, including domination by a capitalist-minded hierarchy of Pope and bishops. A "people's church" was the grand aim.

And so each person who sat around the refectory table, which groaned beneath its load of the best of English country fare that day, had widely different reasons to join together, at least temporarily, in the pursuit of one single purpose: the unhinging of Profumi's "Roman fact." The striking political victory of the fragile, armorless, octogenarian sovereign of 108.7 pygmy acres of land on the marshy banks of the Tiber had been nothing less than a call to action for these new associates.

No matter, then, that the goal uniting them was negative. That could not be helped. In the circumstances. And no matter that other underlying purposes entertained by each of the representatives gathered in the Cottage that autumn were at serious odds with those of all the others. The simple fact was, something had to be done about Rome if their visions of the future, however disparate, were to have room to flourish.

Nikodim had surprisingly little to say during the early part of the meeting. He busied himself instead in devouring unbelievable quantities of food. Mrs. Ripley-Savage had spared nothing in her preparations for the afternoon. "An army marches on its stomach," she had said to quiet the Canon's grumbles about the expense. Nikodim obviously agreed. Welsh rarebit, sardines, soft-boiled eggs, Gentleman's Relish sandwiches, hot buttered scones and crumpets, chocolate fudge cake, and Devonshire cream with strawberry jam—all disappeared as if by a miracle into the metropolitan's seemingly insatiable stomach, while the rest of the group chewed over their common problem.

During the first hour or so, ideas for making inroads into Profumi's Vatican, for undermining his policies, for diluting his effectiveness, were explored and dismissed one by one as unworkable. The old Pope's hold was too strong, his reading of events and his moves to deal with them too canny.

It was Sugnini who finally turned the group toward what seemed the only viable path. As long as Profumi was alive, he said, nothing could be done.

Bishop Cale seemed perplexed. "You make it sound, my good Monsignore, as if the Pontiff were about to die. As nearly as we can see, he is as hale and hearty as ever."

"Hale and hearty, no," Sugnini countered. "Profumi has always been frail, has always suffered from a number of ailments. But I do not mean to imply that he will die soon. I submit, in fact, that we should all pray that he survives for a few more years at least. The process of electing popes begins long before the opening of conclave. We need time to find a suitable candidate to succeed Profumi in Peter's chair, and then to manage the difficult task of seeing that the star of *our* chosen candidate rises at the right moment."

Sugnini was admittedly the expert in Vatican politics, but Muffie was not convinced that they could even hope to "beat the Romans at their own game, in their own drawing room." Muffie's similes never seemed grand enough for the scope of her vision.

"Suppose we play this waiting game, as you suggest, Monsignore," she went on. "And suppose another Profumi-like pope is elected. We will have lost precious time: time Papa Profumi will use to his own good advantage, I'm sure."

Sugnini, though always affable, seemed to have learned in London the art of answering direct questions with direct answers. "It is not a waiting game that I am suggesting, Madam. There are people in my Church's hierarchy—some of them highly placed—who are chafing under our present Pope's tightened rule: men who want the same sort of opening up that you and I have spoken of so often. We need time to enlist the help of those we think will agree with our point of view.

"And then, too, we can't just pick a candidate out of thin air. We must compose a careful list. We must narrow that list down to the solidest core of names—a maximum of two. Then we must find a means of transforming our final choice into the most viable candidate in the next papal conclave.

"Money will be needed." He glanced at Richard Richards. "And discreet but constant pressure behind the scenes. Yet, as impossible as the task may seem to you, my dear"—his eyes found Muffie's again—"we must remember that the very mood of success in the Vatican can be one of the most valuable tools in our hands. The Curia is overconfident. I know them. I've lived with them. Like you, they think no one can play what you call the 'Roman game' as well as they."

Reginald and Herreras were at first very unsatisfied with Monsignore Sugnini's plans. Waiting was not the trump suit either of fanatic brother or of activist Jesuit.

"My friends"—Herreras spoke up in deeply accented English—"how can my suffering millions wait on some gamble like the outcome of a papal conclave we cannot control? In my world, it is five minutes past midnight. Today, right now, over two hundred million people go to bed hungry every night, and get up miserable every dawn. Perhaps you can ask them to go on like that for still more decades. But I cannot!"

Sugnini went to great and persuasive lengths to turn the objections around. At length Bishop Cale, together with the Ripley-Savages and Richard Richards, were all convinced of the soundness of Sugnini's strategy. Nikodim and Reginald nodded their agreement. The Colombian was merely silent.

It was Richards who summed things up with a sort of pep talk. "We have friends everywhere," he reminded them all. "We may not have the organized financial resources of the Vatican, but we will not be woebegone paupers, either." Was that a surly glance from Herreras? Did that papist turned anti-papist think such lofty ambitions as they now entertained could be accomplished without money? Perhaps he would bear watching.

Despite his fleeting suspicion, however, Richards continued without missing a beat. "With clear goals, and with coherent plans and strategies, I think the task will not be beyond our means. As you all know, the Grand Lodge here is closely connected with the European brethern. And our Italian associates are not without toeholds in the Church hierarchy." He looked at Sugnini for confirmation, and found it in the Italian's smiling eyes. "What will be done by them on our behalf will be discreetly done, of course; but it should not be difficult to bring important support to our cause almost at once."

The matter was decided in general outline by nightfall. A preliminary list of papal candidates was drawn up on the spot, to be revised and carefully checked before the next meeting of the group. That would be the following June. Meanwhile, they would all stay in close touch through the Ripley-Savages.

Within a year or two, they should settle on a single papal candidate of their own. It would have to be a man who could reasonably be expected to melt the solidly centralized and authoritarian Roman Catholic structure. And it would have to be someone who could do that without setting off any alarm in the consciousness of Catholics that their religious tradition was being transformed.

"Do not think that what you propose will be easy." Nikodim's heavy tones were heard at last. The Americans, whose dislike of Soviet leaders was increasing as their trust in them diminished, had lately become fond of disparaging the Soviets as unable to chew and think at the same time. Today, Metropolitan Nikodim was living proof that the Americans were wrong.

"There are ancient forces in the Vatican, my friends. And the Pope, whoever he may be, possesses immense power. On the practical side of things alone, there are forces arrayed in great profusion against this plan." The blue eyes of the Russian were somber in his rotund face, as he cited examples: cases of deep penetration into the Soviet state apparatus by Vatican emissaries; clandestine surveys of all the Russians by traveling agents of the Vatican; radio listening posts broadcasting regularly to Rome from within the Soviet Union; minute details of "the dangerous intelligence system" of the Vatican.

Sugnini listened in amazement. If there was a moment for him when he doubted the wisdom of his course, it was when it became obvious that even he did not know as much as the Soviets knew about some of the Vatican's inner workings. He felt a kind of icy queasiness. How they must fear Rome, he thought, to spend so much energy in such precise surveillance. But the moment passed. They could manage the situation, he and his allies in Rome. Perhaps, in the circumstances, they would have to lie with Soviet dogs for a time; but no matter. When they got up, they would simply have to deal with the fleas. After all, as Nikodim himself acknowledged, the Pope possesses immense power, whoever he may be.

The meeting ended in relative harmony. Richards thought it well to restate the one common motive of all present. By the time of their June meeting, their labors would be well under way "for the good of the human family, and against the oldest, largest, and most backward Christian denomination that lies as the greatest obstacle in our path toward the union of all men and women under one ethical and religious umbrella."

Just what "good" might come to mean, and under whose umbrella it was to be accomplished, were blanks in the long-range agenda that no one chose to fill in that day. In the circumstances, that was understandable. First things first.

The October wind chilled the Borghese Gardens. Guido de la Valle buttoned his cashmere topcoat, while his athletic-looking companion seemed quite comfortable strolling with his hands joined behind his back underneath the ample folds of his open jacket.

If anyone had cared to rise at such an early hour, it would not have been unusual for him to see the Maestro and Senatore Ectore Pappagallo strolling together among the flower beds and copses and alleyways lined with busts and statues of the national heroes of Italy's Risorgimento. Their "meetings" were always conducted on such solitary early-morning strolls—long or short, as the agenda required—in these gardens.

Pappagallo was a handsome and extraordinarily able Tuscan businessman with diverse financial and political interests at home and abroad. He was, as well, a member of the newly elected national Senate, Secretary of the Bankers' Association of Italy, and very highly placed in the Grand Lodge of Italy. In return for judicious investment services that only Guido could render, Pappagallo was happy to keep the Maestro informed in certain areas to which he would otherwise have had little or no access.

"There was a get-together of some of the brethren in England lately." Pappagallo kept his eyes on the ground in front of him, as was his habit. "The brethren," as Guido understood, meant members of the Lodge.

"Really?" Guido walked erect, swinging his cane in rhythm with his pace.

"Will we be getting this quarter's account of the Lasco FG debentures soon, Maestro?" Pappagallo's question was not as unrelated to the train of conversation as it might have seemed to anyone but Guido.

"Yes, quite soon. My nephew will be phoning."

"Ah!" the banker seemed suddenly to remember something. "A thousand pardons, old friend! I almost forgot." He pulled a bulky envelope from his inner breast pocket and handed it to the Maestro. "That meeting. In London? Names. Plans. Ideas. Connections."

"Grazie, Ectore."

"Prego! Prego! It is nothing." They were nearing the gates again, where their limousines waited side by side. "Until November, eh?"

"Holiness"—Guido brushed the papal ring with his lips—"I'm sorry for intruding on your evening hours."

"Do not apologize, Maestro." Profumi sat down in one of the large chairs in his study and gestured the Maestro into another. "Tell me, what is this disturbing news you spoke of on the phone?"

The Maestro summarized the information Pappagallo had given him, as he handed the Pontiff a full copy of the report that was now labeled "Northern Alliance."

The Pope listened, and read, and remarked to his old friend that "Alliance" seemed an ambitious name for such a potentially explosive group. And yet stranger alliances had proved successful, at least for a while, whatever the problems that came out of them later. "As, for example, the wartime alliance of Soviets and Americans," the Pope mused. The comparison seemed apt.

What Profumi found even more disturbing than the deep connivance of Catholic clerics who had taken solemn oaths of obedience to the Pope was that this small but determined group of highly placed churchmen and influential lay people appeared unaware of the far greater battle to be waged. Unaware or unconcerned. For Papa Profumi was by now convinced that in the arc of human history portrayed in the Apocalypse of John the Apostle, this particular time was the opening of a great apostasy. He had no way of knowing if it would last for centuries or only for brief years. But from atom bomb to Gulag, intelligent evil stared at him with unswerving eyes in the major events of the present age. That was the enemy he fought with the weapons he had, while this so-called Northern Alliance looked for ways to fight against Rome.

The Pontiff scanned the preliminary list of men whom the Alliance considered *papabile.* It was a bizarre array of names. Da Brescia and Levesque were understandable only from the political point of view; they weren't even cardinals, and as long as Profumi lived, they would not be. Others, like Martiri of Genoa, had never been mentioned in Profumi's entire career as *papabile.* They simply had no curial backing.

"This list, Maestro," The Pontiff held up the names. "There is nothing in this report to indicate that these men have an active part in the matter. Martiri, Da Brescia, Levesque, and the others. We must not simply assume they are involved."

Guido agreed that they might be unaware of the dubious distinction of *papabile* conferred upon them by the Alliance. He proposed a quiet surveillance to find out the degree of their cooperation, if any, with the group.

The Pope did not respond at once to the suggestion. He rose from his chair to pace the study in silent thought. He stopped for some moments on the farther side of the room, near the prayer stool and the small statue of the Fatima Virgin. He reflected that there was something else that should be done. Something of a different order. Something he himself, as Christ's Vicar and defender of His Church, had tried to do without success. Still, there might be some compromise possible, some way to knife through the gathering darkness.

"Do you agree, Holiness?"

Profumi roused himself from his thoughts. "Agree, Maestro?"

"The surveillance, Your Holiness. Our clerics in the Northern Alliance. And their list of papal candidates."

"Ah, yes. Of course, Maestro. It would seem most prudent to watch and wait. You will see to it, Maestro."

"Yes, Holiness." Guido rose and prepared to leave.

"One thing more, Maestro. We must pray for them. Da Brescia and Sugnini. And all the others too. Christ has His plans. Even with all their ambitions and inclinations, each of them will fulfill Christ's will. Their very limitations will, in the end, serve some purpose they cannot now see."

[19]

To Rico Lansing, the world of Chicago, Illinois, in the closing weeks of 1948 seemed so far removed from the desolation, deception, and treachery of the Gulag that the Windy City might have been another world. A world where Netta Lansing had her way, just as her father had said she would.

"Bishop Richard Cooper Lansing, meet your brother-in-law-to-be, Congressman William Bradford Brock!" Netta was radiant as she made the mock-formal introduction and watched two of the three men she loved most shake hands for the first time in the drawing room of the Lansing home. "I told you Rico would keep his promise, Brad. He's liberated himself from Rome for two whole weeks, just to come and marry us!"

Brock's smile was open and easy. "From what Netta tells me, Rome had better learn to do without you, Rico. I understand you'll be coming home for good pretty soon."

Rico returned the smile. "Inside a year, I expect." He liked Brad immediately, liked the strong handclasp, the straight look into his eyes, the casual strength of his manner.

That day at the Lansings' was just about the only time the family spent alone. Parties had been planned all over town as a kind of dual celebration, for Rico's first visit home and for the engaged couple. But at least he had those few hours to relax with his father and mother, to enjoy his sister's obvious contentment, and to get to know Brad, this intimate stranger in his family's midst.

The young congressman, he learned, came from Springfield, Illinois, where his parents still lived with his two brothers and one sister. He had served in the Marine Corps and seen action in the Pacific. He finished his law degree at the University of Chicago after the war and immediately entered state government service. He came to the notice of prominent Democrats through his skillful handling of the canneries scandal in 1947. He ran for Congress that same year and won hands down.

There was no doubt that Brad and Netta made a striking couple, as the family group made its way through the merriment that filled the rest of the week before the wedding. At the extravagant party Big Bill Bailey gave for them at the mayor's residence, Rico could see the ease with which the pair fit into the political power groups of Chicago. By the look of things, Brad had a brilliant future in politics ahead of him.

At what seemed an endless round of other parties, Rico saw scores of his own and Netta's friends again; all welcomed him back into their midst as though he had never been away.

What surprised Rico was his own celebrity, even among people he had never met. Word had gotten around, with a little help from Mayor Bailey, that the future religious leader of Chicago was here "on a state visit from the Vatican"—Big Bill, effusive as always, subscribed to the philosophy that a little embellishment never hurt a good cause. When Rico went with Netta and Brad to City Hall to see to the civil details of their marriage, police on duty greeted him with salutes, and officials rushed to shake his hand in the corridors. When he rode up to a busy intersection in the Lansing limousine with his father, the traffic cop gave them both a big smile of recognition and stopped the cross-traffic to let them through.

High-ranking members of the city's clergy, men he knew by name and reputation only, called on the phone or sent messengers with polite letters to say how happy they were that soon he would be back for more than just a few days. Compared to the perpetual subtlety and loaded understatement of Vatican conversation, these priests and diocesan officials were refreshingly blunt, straight-talking, casual. And, Rico remarked, gentle. Even the toughest of them had that live-and-let-live Americanism, that decency in which he had been reared.

All told, it was a heady foretaste of the life that awaited him in what was now the very near future. Of course, it wouldn't be all parties and handshakes. And thank goodness for that; Rico didn't think he could take much more of it. But he could see himself walking handsomely about as Archbishop of Chicago, aloof and safe from all the turmoil on the other side of the world; speaking eloquently from the pulpit; served at every hand's turn; laughing pleasantly, as he did now, at honorific receptions; administering millions of dollars at a level far distant from sweaty struggles and painful confrontations; and finally, on some far distant day, dying in honor, beloved of his people.

In those happy days prior to Netta's marriage, there was no harking back within him to those forlorn but resolute faces in the Gulag. Those pleading voices were mute. His spirit was hermetically sealed from that region of darkness where he had met living saints and smiling martyrs. His inner war seemed to have been decided in favor of his home turf.

The only sadness for Rico during that first week home was for the ill health of Cardinal Krementz. When Basil had written that old Blackjack wasn't the same bull he used to be, he was painting a rosy portrait. Rico was shocked at the sight of the old man, deeply moved by the physical change in him, when he went to pay his respects on his first day in Chicago. The cardinal's big frame was gaunt, his chest sunken, his color bloodless pale.

On doctor's orders, he spent most of his days resting in bed. He was as alert and crusty as ever, though, angry at his physical weakness, eager to welcome his young protégé, and avid to learn all the latest from Rome.

For his part, Rico was just as eager to oblige. He saw the old man every morning. Hectic social schedules and wedding preparations all had to wait each day as he spent at least an hour—more if he could—"talking shop," as Blackjack liked to say, his eyes glinting with obvious pleasure at the transformation he saw in Richard Lansing.

Rico told what he could of his work in Rome; his impressions of men the cardinal had known far longer and better than he; of the de la Valles, his adopted family in Rome; of the Raphael; his travels; the effect on him of the muscular Christianity that seemed to thrive in Eastern Europe despite the threadbare conditions of clergy and laity alike.

"Or perhaps it thrives because of those conditions," Blackjack ventured. "I sometimes think that a good portion of our well-dressed clerics, from seminarians to bishops, for all their expensive regalia and all the blessings and freedoms of this land, haven't half the faith you describe as so commonplace in Poland and Czechoslovakia. When you come home, maybe your best work will be to teach that to us again."

"That's a pleasant thought." Rico smiled. "To think of Cardinal Wallensky reaching out all the way to Chicago through the things I've learned from him!" The idea brought back just a touch of that old nostalgia in him; and fleeting though it was, the shrewd old cardinal caught a glimpse of it in the younger man's eyes.

In the course of their hours together, the two bishops talked of future plans too. "Your father has already had blueprints drawn up for a grand new residence to be built for you. I'm not supposed to tell you." Blackjack assumed an air of conspiracy. "Basil wants to surprise you. So be surprised when he tells you. Or he'll have my head!"

"Don't worry, Your Eminence."

"And if you think Big Bill Bailey's reception was something this time, wait until you come back to take up your post as AB! You'll have every motorbike cop in the city offering to escort you and carry your parcels, and every traffic cop saluting as you go by!"

"Vittorio Benfatti would be proud of me." Rico laughed at the exaggerated picture Blackjack drew, and then was surprised that Benfatti would have come to mind at such a moment.

Cardinal Krementz was too ill to assist at Netta's wedding, but that was the only defect in an otherwise perfect day. Yet even that disappointment was softened a little when, after the reception—the toasts, the gifts, the guests, the laughing and the dancing—Netta and Brad, accompanied by Rico and his parents, stopped at the cardinal's residence to receive his special blessing. The old man was up, fully clothed and robed, sitting in his favorite chair. Rico and his parents waited outside while he talked privately with the newlyweds. When they emerged, Rico could see by the happiness on Netta's face and Brad's solemnity that the cardinal had reached both of them in a very intimate way. A brief embrace then, and they were gone to catch a plane for their honeymoon.

"At least," Margaret said on the quiet ride home, "I may have lost a daughter, but now I shall have my son back again."

It was a sweet moment for Rico. He had not felt such an inner comfort since the morning of his own ordination. This is my family, he said to himself, and this is my city. These buildings and streets and people. Even the winds and the snows. The harshness of its winters and the beauty of its summers on the lakeside. All is mine. And I belong here.

When he walked into the cardinal's bedroom the following morning, he was full of stories of the celebrations to share. But Blackjack didn't acknowledge Rico's cheery "Good morning." He handed him a slip of paper instead.

"A message for you from Rome. Came in a few minutes ago over our Vatican wire." Rico showed no surprise. "You know about the Vatican radio, do you?"

"Yes, Eminence." Rico said no more on the subject, and knew the cardinal did not expect him to.

"I can't make head or tail of the first part. You will, I expect. They seem to want you back in Rome a little sooner than we thought."

Rico read the scant words on the paper. *All lamplights extinguished. Your presence urgently required. Reply. Lanser.*

Every drop of blood drained from Rico's face. It couldn't be true! All the listening posts? All those men and women, isolated in their bravery and their faith? All over Eastern Europe? The Ukraine? Everywhere? The whole system? What had happened to them? Torture, probably. Then death, or prison, or both. But *how?* It couldn't be true!

Rico sat down heavily, unable to speak, almost unable to move. His inner war was on again. He remembered Lopez Navarro telling him how his own life had been saved by one of the "lamplights" in his territory. And then the full chorus of memory was upon him. Strained faces that had appeared in dark doorways on lonely streets in response to a knock and a name. Strong hands shaking his. Saints in patched clothes tapping out messages on clandestine radios. Loving eyes in seas of hate. Walensky's foxlike features and stern mouth. The blue resolve of Valeska's look. The quiet iron in Tomašek's voice in that hateful cell. The reverence and hope of pitiful congregations in broken-down chapels. All of them so important to him, so abiding with him, so isolated now that the "lamplights" had been extinguished. For almost a quarter of an hour he sat there, Lanser's message in his hand, no word passing his lips, a world of emotion in his eyes, as he coped with the sudden shock. He never noticed the old cardinal's fingers moving over his rosary beads, as he prayed to the Virgin.

Blackjack eventually broke the heavy silence. There was nothing grand or eloquent about his words. He merely said what he saw in Lansing's eyes.

"Rome is your world, Richard. Not Chicago. I don't need to know what that message means in detail. I can think of nothing you would ever do here, or find here, or feel here, now or ever in your service to God, that would answer and satisfy your soul."

Rico tried to object, tried to argue and reason. He had promised, he said. The cardinal had planned. His parents had built so many plans around his return home. Scores of clerical colleagues in the diocese were waiting for him. It was all arranged. But all he was doing was clearing away pointless obstacles and useless vanities. He knew Krementz was right. His inner war was over.

Rico's thoughts fell into a new pattern. There were deep contradictions in Vatican service. Works of charity were all mixed up with works of politics. Venal and disobedient men walked the same corridors with living saints. Powerful men like Guido de la Valle raised strange banners beside the gold-and-white flag of Peter's successor. Ambassadors of hell itself, like the Russian Adamshin, attended papal masses. Surely Christ walked with a man like Profumi. But perhaps Satan walked with a Carnatiu or a Demarchelier!

All of that was true. Much of it was contradictory. And none of it was simple. But there was in Rico now a delicate balance of faith and understanding and the deepest need to serve. The fulcrum of that balance was Rome.

There were no more jokes or plans about the Chicago diocese between Richard Lansing and Cardinal Krementz that day. Or ever. There was little conversation at all. Still, in their remaining time together, they shared a world of understanding in faith more deeply than if they had spoken volumes.

"Come now." The old man was ready to see Lansing go. "Let me give you my blessing."

Rico knelt beside the cardinal. He felt the big bony hand on his head, the tracing of the sign of the cross on his forehead, listened to the words of blessing, kissed the bishop's ring.

If Blackjack saw the tears in Rico's eyes when the young bishop rose from his knees, he gave no sign of it. Instead, with as much of the old scrappy vigor as he could still muster, he gave Lansing his marching orders. "You tell those fellows in Rome that I refuse to die until the Holy Father himself appoints my successor. Profumi himself! I won't have the spiritual leader of my beloved Chicago appointed by some dang-fool committee!"

"Yes, Eminence!" Rico had never realized how much he loved this feisty old churchman.

"And one more thing."

"Yes, sir?"

"You teach those galoots to cook *real* Roman spaghetti! Do you get my meaning, lad?"

Rico was certain he did.

It seemed for a while that the cardinal understood his bishop better than the father understood his son. Basil Lansing's eyebrows knit in puzzlement as he stood with his back to the drawing room fireplace and listened to Rico. "What do you mean, you're giving up the Chicago appointment?" It was less a question than a mere repetition of Rico's words that hadn't sunk in, that had no practical meaning yet for Basil.

"Now, Basil . . ." Margaret had sunk back on the sofa at her son's announcement, but was trying to keep things calm in spite of her own shock. "Let Rico explain. I'm sure he only means there will be a delay . . ."

"No, Mother."

Margaret drew her breath in sharply. It was almost too much.

Rico felt as his own the pain and disappointment he was causing these two people he loved as he did his life. That made the words come all the harder. As he returned his father's look with steady eyes, he began to understand with his deepest heart that it was these two, not he, who had to make the greatest sacrifice. Still, he had realized during this little space of time in Chicago what it was to be with these people who cared so much for him. For a few days, while he was with them, he had had that imcomparable luxury of being able to take them and the security of their close-by love for granted again.

He tried very hard now to explain all that, side by side with his decision to leave forever.

"I thought I could do it, Dad. Return here to stay, I mean. I fully intended to. Wanted to. Believe me. The vision of my future back here with you all was what kept me going more than once."

"Well, then?" Basil glowered down at Rico, seated beside his mother on the sofa.

"Well, that was *my* will. *My* dream. It carried your blessing. And Blackjack's. And Papa Profumi's too, ultimately. But it was my will. Today I found out that as much as I love you, and love this city, this is not where Jesus intends me to be. It's *his* will I have to find. And that will is right here." He held up Lanser's message. "That's all I know. But I know it as surely as I know I love you both."

"All because of a scrap of paper with a message from Rome, Richard?" Rico's father had always called him Richard when he was upset.

"Yes, Dad. I guess in a way you could say that."

In the end, Rico was not certain his parents did understand. But he was certain that if they did not, their sacrifice was the greater for that. Without a shred of doubt, it *was* a sacrifice for them. Not of the social acclaim their son would have brought with him as Archbishop of Chicago, or the sheen of glory in the eyes of their friends. "We don't need any of that," Basil said. The grief of this, Rico's closest flesh, was in letting him go.

It was late when Basil finally knew that no amount of talking things out would change the situation. "You're like your sister Netta, Rico." His father could never call him Richard for long. "If your mind is made up, you'll have your way."

"Not this time, Dad. Believe me. It's not my way, but God's way for me, I'm trying to find now. Does that make any sense?"

It did to Margaret. She tried to joke through her tears. "I gave you to Christ on your ordination day, and He has taken me up on that. He always hears a mother's prayers. I should have been more careful!"

A very different thought struck Basil, and he had to laugh too, even in his gloomy mood. "When Big Bill Bailey hears you're not coming back here as AB of Chicago, it'll be as bad for him as having a Republican governor in Illinois!"

Rico packed his suitcase late that same night, and then sat down to write a letter to Netta. He knew his mother and father would explain as best they could; but he wanted her to know something of his mind, even though he still did not understand it very well himself. When he finished, it was nearly light. Time to leave for the airport.

Alone, Basil and Margaret awoke to share their private sorrow. No one, not even Rico, would ever know its measure.

[20]

The Vatican is so structured that, despite its vastness and complexity, the mood and attitude of the man sitting on the throne of Peter colors and even evokes the mood and attitude of everyone else, from the inner circle of his closest aides out to the messengers and clerks who function on the periphery of Vatican life. Before he entered the Secretariat building, Rico Lansing noticed the change since he had left for Chicago. Amadeo Solimando, usually so affable, even effusive, in his greeting, was noticeably solemn now. The little *portiere* was a human barometer of Vatican temperament.

Inside, the Secretariat offices were in a flurry of activity. Yet everything was done quietly, as if people had the sense that too loud a noise might spark some explosion.

Lansing headed for his office. He glanced rapidly through the piles of messages and other papers waiting for him. As he had come straight from the airport, he called home to let Benfatti know he had arrived and ask him to stop by for his luggage; he could tell by the valet's voice that he, too, knew something was up. That done, Rico was just ringing through to Lanser when his assistant poked his head in the door.

"Father Lanser wants you upstairs right away, *Eccellenza!*"

On his way up, Lansing reflected how fast news travels in a highly charged atmosphere; he had not been in the Secretariat for five minutes before word of his return had spread to the fourth floor.

The Jesuit's office, small, uncarpeted, its bare white walls unadorned except for a crucifix, was next to the papal apartment in the Apostolic Palace. Lanser stood up to greet the American. His welcome was brief and unsmiling, but sincere.

"Glad to see you back, Rico. I'm sorry you had to cut short your first visit home."

Rico responded with a nod and came directly to the question that had weighed on him since Cardinal Krementz had given him the coded message. "How, Father Lanser?" As well as any man might come to know the Jesuit, no one ever called him anything but Father Lanser. "How could it have happened?" The "lamplight" system had been so carefully established and was so insulated that no one listening post knew about any of the others. Control was so closely held in Rome itself; and by so few men of such high trust! How could the entire system have been discovered? And not merely discovered, but totally extinguished!

"How indeed!" Lanser opened the folder on his desk and took from it a photograph. "Do you recognize this man?"

Rico took the photo and studied it. There seemed nothing unusual about the man in it. Straight black hair combed back from a serious, clean-shaven face. Conservative dress. A few medals on the lapel of the dark business suit. Everything pegged the man as a functionary of some government or other. Perhaps in Rome. But it could have been any one of thousands of men, in any one of hundreds of cities.

"Look closer, Rico. Look at the eyes."

Lansing wasn't in the mood for guessing games; but Lanser, he knew, didn't play at anything. And it was true; if there was anything unusual about the man in the photograph, it was the eyes. Dark, exceedingly somber, yet burning into the camera that had taken the picture. He had only seen eyes like that in one man.

"Lysenko?" Rico spoke the name as a question; but needed no answer. It was Pantelleimon Lysenko. "But he was posted to Rio! We all saw the orders!"

"No, my friend. You saw orders, all right. But they were a cover. Lysenko was posted to Grotteferrata, one of the papal estates some twenty miles outside Rome. He emerged a week later, transformed as you see him in this picture. Thanks to the Pontiff's cordial personal relations with the ambassador, he was given a new identity as a French diplomat. Third Councillor Couve de Margrethe, if you please! In time, he was forgotten by most of the people who had met him. The few friends he made, such as yourself, assumed he was in Brazil. The plan was to get him back into Russia as part of a French delegation, and then for him to go underground."

"To 'priest his people.' " Rico remembered the phrase the Russian had so often used.

"Yes." Lanser nodded. "But more than that. Much more. The Holy Father intended Lysenko to be the first of many people sent in to penetrate the Soviet Union. For that purpose, we needed accurate guidance under a score of headings. You realize how little anyone knows about the Soviet Union, Rico? Anyway, Lysenko was our man. He had to get around. He had to remain in contact with us. But in order to send back information, he had to know the listening posts. There was no other way."

"All of them?"

"I repeat: he was the only man we had. He was to travel everywhere. That was his plan. And ours. There was no help to be reasonably expected from any other quarter. Nor could there be. The Holy Father has been warning people about the Soviet threat since 1929. Who's listened? Now Stalin has outmaneuvered them all, Europeans and Americans. That doesn't surprise the Pontiff. In fact, it only makes it clearer that the Holy See has to do something. Something independent of all political systems and partisanship. And we thought we had the tool. Lysenko. A willing one. An able one. My God, Rico! He spent the best part of eleven years with us. Was ordained by us. Accepted all the conditions. Passed all the rigors of our system. We really had every reason to trust him."

Rico still couldn't quite believe it. He had spent so much time with the fellow. Months in the Raphael. Hours alone with him, learning languages. Christmas in Waidhofen. He shook his head, trying to square one side of things with the other. "How could a man spend all that time here in Rome, be under the eye of the authorities at the Secretariat and the Russian College, work with us so closely, accept our friendship, and then . . .?" There was no need to finish the sentence.

"If the prize is big enough, some men can do anything." Lanser wasn't even bitter. Just factual.

That Lysenko had turned over the information was obviously not even a question; but Rico clung for as long as he could to the hope that at least it had not been betrayal.

"Perhaps he was caught. Tortured."

"We had one signal before it all went dead. There is no doubt what happened. At least, what happened over there."

That seemed an odd thing for Lanser to say. Was there more to this insanity?

"We don't know." Lanser pulled no punches. "You put your finger on what bothers some of us: He was here for all those years. He was watched closely. The head of the Russian College made a monthly review of all his records. Could he have fooled all the people all of the time? Or did he have help? Was he the only rot? Or does it go deeper? We don't have the answers."

Rico sat back in his chair. It was a lot to take in all at once. That pair of eyes stared up at him from the photograph; he tossed it face down on Lanser's desk in disgust.

In the momentary silence, the white phone on Lanser's desk rang. The Jesuit answered on the first ring.

"*Sì, Santità.* He's here now. Yes, he knows. No, Holiness; I'm about to brief him. In about an hour? Yes, Holiness."

Lanser put the receiver back on its cradle. He rose from his desk and, as though he had borrowed that well-known habit from the Pope he had served for so long, he paced up and down in front of the bookcase. Rico was to see the Pontiff in an hour's time. There was a lot of ground to be covered before then. The Jesuit began from the beginning, obviously moving toward some purpose that involved the American.

The Lysenko plan, Father Lanser explained, had been the first step in Profumi's strategy to ensure survival of his Church in a world he saw becoming increasingly hostile. Profumi had seen it coming for a long time, as everyone knew. In the U.S.S.R., Stalin had been wiping out priests who would not serve as government agents. Now, after Lysenko's betrayal, the situation had obviously worsened. In Eastern Europe, Rico had seen conditions for himself. It was getting as bad elsewhere. In Asia, the conclusion of all papal representatives was unanimous: nothing human could arrest Communism. Not in China, where Mao Tse-tung had already proclaimed the People's Republic in Tienanmen Square. Not in Southeast Asia.

By now, Lanser went on, anyone who cared to face facts could see that within months, a year or two at most, Rome would have none but the sparsest—and certainly not open—official relationship with the Church in Communist-held countries anywhere. The vestiges that might survive in each country would be "nationalized," forced to become "local" churches under close surveillance and control by the state, and—most important of all—cut off from the authority and guidance of Rome, no longer a living part of the church universal. "You can see what that will mean." Lanser glanced at Rico.

The young bishop could indeed see.

"So much for background." Lanser stopped his pacing and sat down again at his desk. "As you can probably imagine, Papa Profumi is furious at the Lysenko betrayal. Have you ever seen the Pope when he is angry, Rico? No? Well, sparks fly, let me tell you. He has no intention of letting the Soviets get away with this treachery, or put an uncontested lock on half the world."

"There is a plan, then, Father Lanser."

"There is half a plan. The Roman half. The other half is to be of your design, if you agree. But agree or not, you have to hold everything we say from this point forward in closest secrecy."

There was little need for Rico to answer. He would do anything needed to repair this damage to papal policy.

"Well, then, do you know anything about the Third Secretariat?"

"A little." Rico searched his memory. "It has something to do with copying papal documents in Latin. It's always sounded boring and obscure."

"And outdated," Lanser added. "All of that makes it perfect for us. Originally, the Third Section of the Secretariat was called the Chancellery of Documents. For centuries, its work was to hand-copy into formal Latin the documents that had been roughly drafted and initialed by the Secretary of State and the Pope."

"A little like lawyers putting in whereases and wherefores?"

"A little like that. In any case, its functions were rendered pointless by the decline of Latin, and by the typewriter and the telephone. So today the Third Secretariat has become a sort of honorary vestige. It will seem unusual to no one—an overdue move, in fact—for the Vatican to bring it up to date by providing it with new personnel and a new mission: the Apostolate for the Devotion to the Hearts of Jesus and Mary.

"As the name indicates, the new work to be done will be pious and devotional. But the work will merely be a cover for a unit in the Vatican engaged in underground penetration of the Soviet empire, so that with time we can establish regular contact with the insides of that entire area. We think the revamped Third Secretariat will serve those two purposes admirably. For you, it will involve well-publicized trips under Vatican aegis into Iron Curtain countries. There will be sermons and lectures and distribution of devotional pamphlets, medals, rosaries. . . . Well, you get the idea.

"The Soviet authorities won't like it. But they can't be totally uncooperative without fostering unrest and distrust they can ill afford, and tarnishing the image they're trying to project of themselves elsewhere as tolerant democrats.

"That, baldly stated, is the Roman half of the plan.

"In addition to the overt visits made for the work of the Apostolate, there will be covert missions. That's why we must have people who know the lay of the land; people who are known and trusted not merely by the Communist officials but by the people themselves. We intend, in sum, to establish a full-blown underground network, with those two purposes I mentioned in mind: the gathering of information about what's going on in the Soviet camp, and the formation of a new mentality in Catholics—really the revival of a very old one, the mentality of the early Christians who had to survive and flourish in spite of the regime around them. That's the sort of world we're dealing with behind the Iron Curtain; and very soon it may be as bad in our so-called free world."

"And you want me to be one of the Apostolate workers." Rico thought he had understood.

"More than that. We want you to be chief of all field operations for the Apostolate. It must be obvious to you that you fit the profile of the man we need. You speak the basic languages. You've traveled pretty widely over there for the Raphael, so the Soviets know you; they probably have a big dossier on you by now, in fact. You've got credibility with them, and with the people they rule. You've shown exceptional judgment." Lanser sat back again in his chair. "And you've shown you can be trusted even in situations that are not personally to your liking." That was an obvious if slightly veiled reference to the incident of the faked passports for the twelve German officers. Lanser did not dwell on it.

"No one will order you—could order you—to take this assignment. You do have your family to consider, besides your own ambitions. But if you agree, then the fieldwork is yours from the ground up. You'll organize the entire operation outside of Rome. Choose the personnel you want, subject to our review and approval. You'll direct all field operations. But it means goodbye to home: to Chicago; to the cardinalate." Lanser gave him a rueful look. "And in the covert work, there will be real danger for you."

Rico knew that there would be no leisure for thinking things over. If the Pope wanted to see him, it was to have his answer, one way or the other. He glanced at his watch. Half of the hour was gone before he was expected in the papal study. He still had important questions.

"Forget my former plans about Chicago, Father Lanser. The moment I got your message, I knew all that was out. So did Krementz. I even told my parents. They're reconciled with my not returning home."

"I see." Lanser was surprised and impressed.

"Tell me, Father Lanser, this 'Roman half' of the Apostolate you mentioned. Who are we talking about?"

"The new secretary-general of the Third Section is Archbishop Giulio Brandolini."

Rico thought he knew the man slightly. Wasn't he the one they called "Sniff-Sniff"? Seemed to have a perpetual cold? Never without a crumpled handkerchief in his hand?

Yes, that was the man. Lanser sketched Brandolini's background. He had passed most of his Vatican service in obscure posts at diplomatic missions in the countries under consideration; he had rarely been seen around the Vatican, had never been photographed or interviewed. His factual knowledge was encyclopedic; and his anonymity and exterior insignificance were such that he could "pass unnoticed in a hall of mirrors," as Lanser put the phrase.

Gian Solaccio had been chosen as chief of base operations under Brandolini. Rico did not know Solaccio at all. That was as it should be. He was the man who had verified Lansing's identity from dental records on his first day in Rome. More significantly, he had come into the Church after ten years in Swiss state counterespionage, and was now the head of all Vatican security. He was an expert in covert activity.

"You'll find him a huge help in planning and execution. There's no better.

"Now, funding for the Third Secretariat will be separate from all other budgets. Maestro Guido de la Valle will take care of that. He will be perfectly acquainted with the mission, of course.

"I will remain deeply involved. Papa Profumi himself will not be bothered with day-to-day operations. Nevertheless, his interest is far deeper even than it was in the Raphael. He will want general reports on a regular basis, and my expectation is that he will want personal briefings from you whenever you are in Rome."

"Is that the lot, then? Solaccio, Brandolini, you, me, the Maestro?" Rico hoped the roster of people acquainted with the mission was not longer. Secrets are not secrets when many share them.

"Well. We have to have someone in the State Council who knows what we're about. The Council can block things, you know. They could truss you up, Rico. Without any difficulty!"

"The Council!" Clearly Rico was not happy. "That means the entire Curia will know! You can kiss secrecy goodbye, Father."

"No, we don't think that will be the case. It will be enough for Cardinal Falconieri as the senior member to be informed in a general sort of way. No one, not even Lisserant, would oppose Falconieri. There is no danger there, I give you my personal assurance. If you can't trust him, you can't trust the Pope!"

Papa Profumi held out his hand, and Rico knelt to kiss the Fisherman's Ring.

"*Bene, Eccellenza.* Father Lanser has explained things?"

Rico rose and nodded.

"Please sit down, then." The Pope's tone was brisk. Rico saw no trace of a smile. Profumi was in high gear. Pleasantry had no place here.

"Two questions to be answered, Excellency. Your Excellency realizes this new mission is not for a month or a year. It's probably for the best years of your life. Perhaps all your life." Profumi's eyes never left the American's face; it was as if he wished to test for the faintest wisp of hesitation. "What is much harder, you must be ready for years of obscurity and misunderstanding. There will be no public honor to compensate for what you are giving up. On the contrary. What we must do must be done without many people knowing it. At best, it will be lonely work. For a long time. At worst, it will be very dangerous. Can you take that sort of life?"

After a short pause Rico answered. "Holy Father, I *think* I can do it, with God's help. I don't know beyond that."

"A fair answer." Profumi smiled. No one could know beyond that. "Now, as regards Chicago. Has the cardinal much time left?"

"No, Holiness." Rico cleared his throat. He had rehearsed this part of the conversation. "His Eminence has requested that Your Holiness decide personally who will succeed him as head of Chicago. Relying on the time-honored Roman custom that enables me to suggest a possible replacement in the see I have renounced, permit me to offer the name of His Excellency Bishop Kieran O'Mahoney as *episcopabile* for Chicago."

"You use the past tense, Excellency. In your mind, you have already renounced your right of succession?"

"Yes, Holiness."

As though Lansing had passed some final test of his will and intention, Profumi rose from his chair, indicating with a little gesture that his visitor was to remain seated.

There was no hesitation in this man, Profumi reflected as he strolled to the study window, his back to the subject of his thoughts; but neither was there any of that fanaticism that had marked Lysenko. Just a good, solid steadiness. Only months ago, the Pope had himself assessed this American: *"capax potestatis."* And yet, as God would have it, he was not only giving up his claim to power, as the world reckons power, before he had even tasted it; he was about to join the ranks of the world's unknown and expendable men. Should he be killed in some "unfortunate accident" on a covert mission, odds were that no one would even know what had become of him.

With a profound sigh, the Pontiff turned back toward Rico, waiting expectantly but patiently for the final word. "Have you any further questions to ask Us, Excellency?"

"None, Holy Father."

The Pope held out his hand. Rico slipped to one knee, kissed the Ring, moved toward the study door, and turned to leave.

"Eccellenza!"

Lansing turned to meet those eyes boring into him again.

"We thank you for your decision."

Though Gian Solaccio had most of the major outline and many of the details for the "Roman half" of the Hearts Apostolate already worked out, he and Rico spent weeks detailing intricate plans for the covert operations, and the dovetailing of Lansing's public and secret work.

Rico's cover would be complete and real; it would, in fact, take up a good deal of his time. The present staff of the Third Secretariat was even now being greatly enlarged—clerks, secretaries, writers, librarians, translators, stenotypists, accountants. They would be housed in offices on the ground floor of the Apostolic Palace.

This part of the work would be energetic and highly publicized. The Hearts Apostolate would, for example, publish a monthly bulletin in twelve languages; establish diocesan and parish branches throughout the Church; organize annual congresses and pilgrimages; assemble lists of contributing members; encourage religious publications; distribute medals, pamphlets, leaflets. It would, in short, be a genuine operating religious apostolate.

Rico, as head of the Hearts Apostolate, would make well-publicized visits to Europe, the U.S.A., Africa, the Middle East. Arrangements had already been made for him to give his first interviews to *Osservatore Romano,* and to several Italian newspapers and international wire services. The Holy Father intended to instruct the Congregation for Bishops to send out a notice in his name to all bishops around the world, putting them on notice about Rico's appointment, and suggesting they give statements to their local news media.

Rico's "second in command" for the Hearts Apostolate would be that long beanpole who had done such good work in the Raphael, Thikas of Yugoslavia. Neither Thikas nor anyone else connected with the public operation, except Rico himself, would have any clue that there was more to the Hearts Apostolate than met the eye.

By far the greatest amount of preparation and planning went into the covert side of the operation, which would be housed on the fourth floor of the Apostolic Palace. Rico's office, and his secretary's, would be there too; but his secretary would be strictly "Hearts Apostolate." Solaccio would have a small office next to Rico's. Brandolini's office would be in the same area. They would have their own radio room, of course. As Lanser had indicated, all additional covert personnel were to be Rico's choice, but Solaccio suggested Jaček Righi to be in charge of radio communications. "He's excellent at languages and codes, and we know he can be trusted."

After some months of very public traveling as the ever-busy, ever-prayerful, piety-inclined director of the Hearts Apostolate, Rico would be ready to begin the formation of the underground operation in the field. Of course, there would be credible stories of his whereabouts for anyone who might want to reach him during those secret missions; officially he would be on retreat, or ministering to the faithful in obscure areas of France or Austria, or shielded by any of dozens of blinds that would be well prepared in advance.

Solaccio was invaluable in helping to select, and in thoroughly checking, support personnel—clerics who would work as radio operators, cipher clerks and cryptographers under Righi, or as stenotypists and chauffeurs. This covert staff would be kept to a minimum. Numbers spelled danger to Rico, and Solaccio agreed. Each staff member was to know his own job only.

In general, the same caution would hold for the covert missions themselves. The complications, however, would be far greater. They would first need to set up information-gathering systems in the Soviet-dominated countries. Brandolini devised a cell system modeled in part after the lamplight system, but with safeguards to help make them "Lysenko-proof." Rather than a single person in each cell, there would be several. Each cell would have a leader, who would be the only cell member known to all the others.

As further protection, every territory would be divided into districts; each district would have a superior. That superior would know and be known by only the cell leaders in his immediate area. The superiors would report only to Rico. The system was cumbersome, but its security blocks were effective. In time—and at Rico's sole discretion—each district superior would have a shortwave radio. Eventually they would penetrate the Soviet Union itself, but that was to be in the future. As each territory was secured by the new network, an individual system of reeducation would be devised, according to the area's needs and its dangers.

While Rico's excursions for the Hearts Apostolate would be as widely trumpeted as possible, even in the Soviet territories, his covert entries and exits were of course another matter. He would travel with assumed identities on those missions, and he would always use "windows"—particular border locations that were safe for covert crossings at particular hours when comparatively poor surveillance was even more relaxed. It was Brandolini, working with a small number of dedicated men and women on both sides of every border, who decided on such "windows." Those helpers made it their business to know all about police patrols, air surveillance, fences, dogs, mines. "Fortunately"—Brandolini explained everything between sneezes and wheezes—"as Lysenko was not expected to come out once he went in, this part of our system was not part of his information." Each "window" had its code name, he went on. "St. Anthony's" stood for a wooded valley running between Austria and Hungary; Brandolini pointed to the place along the border as he blew his nose. "St. Damien's" was a small lake on the western border of Poland. In all, he identified a dozen possible "windows." Use of them would vary, depending on conditions.

After a month of press interviews and of hard, nonstop planning, Rico went on the first of several Hearts Apostolate organizing missions. He preached and lectured, first in the town of Lille, in northern France, then at Mons in Belgium, and Stuttgart in West Germany. He crossed into East Germany to conduct a mission in Leipzig and one in Fürstenberg. Then he swung east into Poland, working in Gdansk, Poznan, and Krakow. After a couple of days' rest in Austria, he went through the same performance in Esztergom and Budapest, and ended his "maiden voyage" with a week's preaching in Belgrade.

Not surprisingly, he had no difficulties with the Soviet puppets. He alerted the local authorities two weeks ahead of time about his travel schedule, stayed in government hostels, was shadowed everywhere, at first covertly, then openly and as a matter of routine. Because he came with known government approval, attendance at his lectures was never full, never enthusiastic. Accompanied by his police escort, he called dutifully on local prelates everywhere he went. These courtesy calls were extremely painful for him, particularly when he met a prelate he had not known before. He could sense the contempt and pain his presence evoked in the men who saw him as a guest of the government that made life a misery. With those he knew—Wallensky and Valeska of Poland, Müllerhof of East Germany, quite a few others—the mood was different. They trusted Rico; and if they didn't understand what he was doing, they knew they would find out in time.

When his first Apostolate tour was over, Rico returned to Vienna to undergo a few weeks' training in what Gian Solaccio called street wisdom, with certain friends of his. "How to save yourself a lot of trouble on the streets, Excellency. Sowing a false trail. The art of anonymity. Knowing when you're being tailed. Elementary cipher work. Use of the newer two-way radios. Parachuting. That sort of thing." Solaccio's smile at the end of the odd litany was as innocent as a babe's.

"You were born for this work, Gian!" Rico returned his smile.

"So it seems. God's spy, eh? Now, another thing, Rico. Even with the most skillfully executed identification papers and a perfect cover, you still will betray yourself unless you learn to think yourself into the part. At times you will have to react to a sudden situation. Your potential pursuers are trained to look for the little things—the wrong gesture, the strange way of walking, the forced tone of voice, the vocabulary that doesn't go with whatever role you're playing, an emotion that doesn't fit your supposed character.

"That's why I say you must think yourself into the part. *Think.* That's the key. Your life depends on it."

To his surprise, Rico found himself for this phase of his training in the hands of two Royal Air Force intelligence officers. He was never told their real names. They were bluff, hearty-voiced, realistic, masters at "thinking" a covert role. Day after day, in the solitude of a safe house outside Vienna, they worked on the American, first with carefully devised formulas, then with mock-real situations. They watched him, criticized him unmercifully, slowly educated him to the difficult role of playacting among enemies. They never gave him full marks. They passed him back to Solaccio with a terse comment. "He may survive."

On a day before dawn at the beginning of March 1949, a small camouflaged monoplane left a private airstrip outside Stockerau, northwest of Vienna. The airstrip belonged to landed relations of Cardinal Ferragamo-Duca; the airplane carried no markings, but belonged to the Royal Air Force.

The craft flew directly eastward until within sight of Czechoslovakia. There, it turned southeast to a course paralleling the border. Near the town of Bruck, it dropped to treetop level and headed directly north, crossing the border at one of Brandolini's "windows," beneath the scope of radar and out of sight of the border guards. It landed like a nervous grasshopper outside Farkašd, precisely long enough to let its passenger disembark.

Rico Lansing spent three days getting from his remote drop to East Slovakia, where the first base of the covert operation was to be laid. And so another form of existence began for Rico, an existence he had read about in spy stories but had never dreamed would be his, or any priest's.

According to his false identification papers, he was a farm laborer. Lodgings had been set up for him with a vegetable farmer in a remote district. Rico now concentrated on two major undertakings: to "think" himself into his new identity as he worked part-time as a laborer, and to choose the initial elements of his first "cells."

After five weeks, he had seven operatives. Though he was reasonably sure of each of them, he took no chances. None of his recruits knew any of the others who had been chosen. Each would be a district superior. In time, and with great care, they would each form a cell.

With that much accomplished as a beginning in East Slovakia, Rico moved clandestinely, mostly by night travel, over to western Czechoslovakia and located in the town of Plzeň. His second false identity was now provided him. He was employed as part of the lowly clean-up crew at the Sumava papermill. Because of the crowds, anonymity was easier in this situation than in East Slovakia; but recruiting was more dangerous. Pilzen, a center for heavy industry, was thoroughly invested by state security.

When he left Pilzen in August and reached West Germany through a "window" in the northern part of the Bohemian Forest, he was exhausted. It wasn't the physical effort; it was the constant strain, the perpetual watchfulness over his every action, over everything around him and the continuous effort at playing the role of a stuttering, slow-witted Czech factory worker. Most of all, though, it was the falseness of his behavior. He was always deceiving. Always creating an illusion.

His two British trainers and Solaccio met him in Munich. To Rico's relief, he found the strain lifted the more he talked about it during the debriefing. Finally, it seemed to evaporate altogether when he and Solaccio arrived back in Rome in September, to find that signals were already coming in from two of the bases in East Slovakia.

[[21]]

"But why *now?*"

Cardinal Giovanni Angelica's face resembled a child's drawing of a summer sun, it was so round and radiant with warmth, even in perplexity. He and his little group moved slowly in the crowd of cardinals and bishops, their backs to Michelangelo's *Last Judgment,* as they worked their way toward the Sistine Chapel door.

"Of *course* we all believe it!" The cardinal gestured with his pudgy hands. "Of *course* we have all told the Pontiff we believe it, and that the great body of the faithful believe it. But to declare as dogma the Assumption of the Blessed Virgin into heaven, uncorrupted in body and soul, at this moment in history! What does he see? Why now?"

Cardinal Angelica was not alone in that perplexity. The year 1950 seemed to many an odd time for Papa Profumi to choose; to some, in fact, it would seem downright inopportune. Surely Papa Profumi realized that as well as any one of these princes of his Church who had gathered in Rome this Easter for the annual consistory.

And yet, for all the wisdom of his eighty-odd years, and in spite of physical frailty, here he had sat in front of them all just moments ago, and announced his intention firmly. Stubbornly, some would soon say. In November, the Pontiff said, he would publicly declare as incontrovertible that the body of the Virgin Mary, Mother of Jesus, had not corrupted in her grave, but that her divine Son had taken it whole and entire into the heaven of God's Glory.

"Well, Giovanni." Bishop McSorley of San Francisco was willing to take the Pontiff's side, though he had no answer to the cardinal's specific question. "It is Easter, after all. What better time to present his intention to make such a declaration? As you say, we all believe it. It is a fact of our faith closely linked to the very meaning of Easter."

"Perhaps." Angelica glanced back through the exiting crowd of high churchmen, toward the throne where Profumi had sat only moments before. He shook his head as his little group reached the door of the chapel. "Perhaps," he repeated himself. "But there have been many Easter seasons in his reign. A dozen, in fact. Why has he chosen this moment?"

As Cardinal Angelica knew it would, news of Papa Profumi's intention to promulgate the Assumption of Mary as official dogma of the Church rolled outward like a wave from Rome upon a world whose leaders, beset by vast troubles, had little of the cardinal's patience and none of his interest in finding the answer to his question "Why now?"

The cold war was intensifying divisions, new and old, among nations. It had already spawned one raging hot war in Korea. The Berlin Wall had been built, and might at any moment cause another war. Mao Tse-tung, a bloody trail behind him, was at his long-sought zenith in China, and Communists were inexorably taking over Southeast Asia as well.

Nor were all the troubles and divisions purely political ones. Despite Papa Profumi's efforts and edicts, the seminaries and Catholic universities in Northern Europe were filled with theologians and thinkers pushing past the traditional limits of permitted Catholic thought. In most of the countries of Western Europe there were tendencies among theologians to question some of the most basic and traditional practices of Catholicism. Throughout Latin America, a strange new breed of nuns, priests, and bishops—even a cardinal or two—fomented the doctrine that Catholicism was "colonialist" and "imperialist" and could not be accepted unless "reformed."

In such a world, and particularly in contrast with Northern Alliance response, the earnestly inquiring "Why now?" of Giovanni Angelica, Cardinal Patriarch of Venice, came to seem a fervent testament of belief and acceptance.

One Worlders, the impeccably tailored Richard Richards vocal among them, heralded the papal intention as "a step backward into medieval superstition."

Bishop Cale echoed even so extreme a sentiment, until an English Jesuit politely asked him to take the trouble of looking at the sculpture over the entrance door of his own Canterbury Cathedral, where he would see depicted the Assumption of the Virgin.

"Still," Cale grumbled to a meeting of the Northern Alliance, "once Profumi has declared the Assumption as dogma, it will be taken as surer than the apparent fact that two plus two equals four; it will be more certain than the next breath I draw, and more valuable to defend than one's own life. For unfortunately, my friends, such still is the authority of this Pope, and the fidelity of believers."

Protestant journals underlined the bishop's dissatisfaction, as they published frequent jeering references to the Pope as "retrograde and out of date" and other such uncharitable assessments of the Pontiff's abilities as theologian.

Metropolitan Nikodim spoke of letters sent to the Pope by Patriarch Pimen of Moscow, who was resolutely opposed to "this foolish proclamation."

Brother Reginald's Ecumenical Monastery sent a delegation to Rome, which, when it was not received by Profumi, delivered its protest with even greater vehemence to a patient Cardinal Falconieri.

That delegation might have saved itself the bother, however; the members of the Vatican Council of State, at least, were pleased with the strength displayed even now by the aging Profumi. In their view, these monkish, white-clad Protestants were not even a pimple to such power.

Monsignore Annibale Sugnini, unwilling to see his own rising star of ecumenical success so quickly dimmed, joined the fray with the publication of a lengthy if somewhat tortured study advising the Pontiff that it was at least unwise, if not perhaps inaccurate, to say that the Assumption of the Virgin had always been believed as an article of faith.

The Colombian Jesuit Father Herreras read the article in disgust;

Sugnini and Profumi had both missed the point: the Mother of God was the mother of the Proletariat.

Archbishop Da Brescia, more restrained in his reaction, and very likely more believing in his way, nevertheless addressed a private memorandum to the Pope stressing that this was the wrong time to start throwing dogmatic statements out upon an already troubled world. Even the majority of the world's bishops, he advised, though surely they found no fault with the substance of belief in the Virgin's Assumption, would criticize the Pontiff for his timing.

It seemed that only the ordinary masses of Catholic believers greeted the news of the coming definition with enthusiasm all over the world.

Papa Profumi could have answered Cardinal Angelica. The Pontiff knew the quiet, persistent dissatisfaction that was spreading among his College of Cardinals and among certain leaders of his bishops worldwide. He was aware of the persistent drumming and beating of expectation for some opening up of his "Profumist rigidity" that was growing in the ranks of latter-day theologians, political activists, and churchmen who saw themselves as the knowing ones, the worldly wise.

And yet, if to all those impatient souls, and to political leaders as well, Papa Profumi's announcement that he would, in eight months' time, proclaim this dogma of the Virgin Mary seemed an ill-timed and belligerent stroke of boldness, the Pope saw it only as a poor and belated compromise. His intention had been bolder still. It had been to fulfill the request made by the Virgin herself when she had appeared at Fatima in October 1917. If the Pope, she had said, acting on the same day and in concert with all the bishops of the world, would consecrate Russia to her, there would be universal peace.

The moment the war was over, at the zenith of his influence, and even in all that unrest and world disarray, Profumi had tried. He had sent out circulars all over the Church, and had addressed inquiries to non-Catholic Christians as well: Is it a belief of your people and a general teaching of your theologians that Christ did perform this miracle for his mother at her death?

The reply was practically unanimous from Catholic sources: This has been and is our belief and our teaching.

And yet, try as he would, Profumi could not get the bishops to join him in the final step of universal consecration at the same moment in time all over the world.

The definition of her Assumption, however, was another matter. Though it was less than had been asked, alone it was the best he could do. He would not be dissuaded from it.

For all the hue and cry they raised against Papa Profumi in this matter, there was not one among his detractors or critics who did not scramble to secure as prominent a seat as possible for the gala day of celebration in St. Peter's. Willingly or not, all were held within the Profumist framework. One way or another, in obedience or rebellion, in agreement or disapproval, all conformed to Profumi's far-seeing analyses; and the cross-purposes they fostered all served to usher in the very circumstances the Pope had long since foreseen and still labored to provide for.

By early morning on that November 21, the unreserved seats in St. Peter's Basilica were crammed with layfolk. The crowd quickly overflowed into the piazza and filled it to its capacity of 250,000. As the hour of celebration approached, the reserved places filled with the men and women whom the little *portiere* Amadeo Solimando thought of as the *pezzi grossi* of the world. The cardinals of Profumi's Church, over 800 bishops, 145 diplomats, splashed the scene with the colors of their finest vestments and sashes. The black garb of 4,500 priests was like a garden's patch of black earth setting off the splendor of colored robes by contrast.

Of course, the two facing balconies, or tribunes, as they are called, that overlooked the High Altar were the most prized of the reserved positions, for the purposes both of seeing everything and of being seen by everybody. In one of those balconies, on the north side of the altar, Guido de la Valle and his party strolled to their chairs in animated conversation. Helmut and Agathi were with him, of course; and Keti Wilson, who, even with her press pass, could not have hoped for such a perfect perch as this. Most of the *impero* were on hand, some with their wives and children, others alone. Richard Lansing, who had delayed a trip to East Germany in order to be here, found it singularly bitter that not a single cardinal or bishop from Eastern Europe had been permitted to come to Rome for this day. Beside him sat Lanser and Father Kensich.

"Well," Guido said, leaning toward Helmut as they settled down, and directing his attention across to the balcony on the south wall. "I see the Workers' Paradise could find nothing better to do today."

As if he could feel the chill of those two pairs of icy blue-green eyes on him, the Soviet ambassador, Anatoly Adamshin, flanked by two aides and their wives, hunched forward uneasily in his corner of space, as though it were suddenly too small for his big frame, or as if he urgently wanted to study the huge *baldacchino* that stood over the High Altar, resting on its bronze pillars filled with the bones of 37,000 martyrs.

Behind the Soviet ambassador, Mr. Richard Richards whispered busily in Bishop Cale's ear, and Monsignore Sugnini held forth to Archbishop Da Brescia and Metropolitan Nikodim, explaining the details of the ceremony to come. The Canon and Mrs. Ripley-Savage used the time to make useful new acquaintances among Archbishop Da Brescia's party, and to cast calculating eyes over the Basilica, as if to count the house.

It occurred to Guido that those two groups facing each other above the altar built over Peter's tomb were face to face in rare confrontation. On one side were gathered the defenders of this traditional Roman Pontiff. On the other were men who were oath-bound to ensure there would be no more like Profumi, once he died.

A sudden flourish of trumpets chased all the hubbub of the vast crowd to silence. A triumphant voice, magnified by an excellent loudspeaker system, began the traditional salutes to the Pope. "The Bishop of Rome . . ."

As the litany of papal titles began, Guido glanced toward the south balcony.

"... Successor of St. Peter, Supreme Pontiff of the Universal Church, Patriarch of the West, Primate of Italy, Sovereign Ruler of the State of Vatican City, Father of Fathers, Servant of the Servants of God, Our Most Reverend and Most Holy Lord, Eugenio Profumi, two hundred sixty-third Vicar of Jesus Christ in the One, Holy Catholic and Apostolic Church."

The Maestro had to give the people in the other balcony their due. That flourish of titles alone, even before the Pope arrived, had probably set their teeth on edge; but not one of them twitched a muscle. In fact, Archbishop Levesque caught Guido's eye from his place behind Da Brescia and smiled—a little acidly, Guido thought with some satisfaction.

The mood of mere expectation in the Basilica was transformed by the first distant sound of choir voices, weaving together in elusive cadences fashioned for just such moments by a long-dead pope named Gregory. Profumi was not the first pontiff who planned to reach from beyond his grave.

Within seconds, the music seemed to take visible form, as down the long central aisle of the Basilica the procession began. Two abreast they came, patriarchs followed by the curial cardinals of Rome, archbishops followed by bishops, heads of religious orders followed by heads of institutes. Each pair was flanked by as many altar boys, carrying lighted candles. From above, the procession looked almost like a steadily flowing stream of purples and crimsons, golds and whites and browns and magentas, its banks all afire with candle flames. The choir itself appeared then, and as a prelude to the finale filled the place with intricate and interweaving chants.

Finally, a detail of Noble Guards appeared, and behind them twelve more men came into view at last, pacing with measured, practiced strides. On their shoulders they bore the famed *sedia gestatoria,* the portable throne upon which Papa Profumi sat, a living icon high above the crowd for all to see. He was clad in white and gold and silver. On his feet, the blood-red slippers. On his head, the triple crown, studded with precious stones, symbol of his divine Master's power in heaven, on earth, over hell. Profumi's hands, encased in gold-embroidered gloves of white, moved eloquently, now in that great Roman gesture of encouragement, now in the triple sign of the cross.

Once the eyes of the crowd fell on that pale, immobile face, uncontrolled pandemonium broke out. Every person was standing. Every hand was reaching, waving. Every mouth was open. Every heart, every mind, willing or no, swelled with the excitement, and the emotion, of the moment. Profumi looked continually from side to side, his eyes seeking out hundreds of other eyes.

Looking down from the south balcony, Sugnini and Da Brescia met those agate eyes of Profumi for an instant in time. Richards and Cale and the Ripley-Savages stared down in disbelief. But Ambassador Adamshin and Metropolitan Nikodim, perhaps more deeply Russian than Soviet after all, felt a momentary pull and a momentary fear. This was impressive beyond words. Unique. And it was happening, not at Lenin's tomb, but at Peter's.

The only sound that could be heard over the joyous shouts and chants was the piercing voices of trumpets. From somewhere above in some shadowed choir loft, they showered down the silvery notes of the papal hymns. Profumi rode forward slowly, blessing, encouraging. His eyes, normally dark, appeared now as luminous as agates—calming, majestic, controlling, all-knowing, looking into faces, meeting other eyes, ranging everywhere over the crowds, again up to the balconies.

The crowd did not pause once in its great continuous roar until the Pope descended from the *sedia* and approached the altar. The trumpets fell silent. The last *"Evviva!"* echoed away. The Solemn High Mass began.

The silence was as profound as the noise had been, when, after the Gospel reading, Profumi sat down on his throne. The Master of Ceremonies brought forward a damask-bound portfolio, opened its cover, and held it for the Pope to read.

All the hard consonants of Cicero's Latin were softened in Renaissance velvet and liquid Italian accents. *"Nos, auctoritate Beatissimi Petri, Principis Apostolorum . . ."* We, by the authority of Blessed Peter, Prince of the Apostles . . .

So it was done. Papa Profumi's will had held, yet one more time.

In the crush of the departing throng, once Mass was over, Guido found himself descending the broad steps of the Basilica side by side with Anatoly Adamshin.

"My dear ambassador." The Maestro milked the moment. "Very impressive, wouldn't you say?"

"A godly thing, if true." The Russian returned Guido's look in the wan November sunlight. "That old Italian, reading his Latin so eloquently . . ."

"I see." De la Valle was willing to complete the trite thought he expected. " 'Opiate of the people,' as Lenin was so fond of saying, eh?"

"Lenin also wrote something else, Maestro. 'If I had ten men as devoted as the Roman missionaries I met, I could take the world in one year!' "

Was it the crowd that separated the two just then? Or Adamshin's unwillingness to speak further at such a moment? Guido neither knew nor cared. As he watched the ambassador make his way with difficulty through the crowd, he realized that he had just been given the briefest glimpse through the tiniest of windows left unguarded for an instant. He had seen a fragment of Adamshin's Russian soul.

In hindsight, there were those around the Pontiff who would later say that he must have known his proclamation of the dogma of the Assumption would be his last great public act. In the years left to him, and for all his strength of will, Eugenio Profumi felt himself growing ever weaker in body and more tired in soul. True, all his life he had acted on two planes. One concerned the practical matters of diplomacy and government. The other was the spiritual level that sometimes bordered on the ethereal. But now, in the early 1950s, he began to withdraw more often to that higher plane of spirit. He held audiences still, but less frequently. He had daily consultations with officials, received diplomats, made hard decisions about concrete problems. He kept himself generally informed, and each day blessed his people from his window. He regularly saw those who were doing work that was most important or most perilous—Guido de la Valle, Rico Lansing, some two dozen or so others.

But the general activity that had marked most of his years was absent now. Profumi often seemed to live and move with an otherworldly landscape in view. Yet it was testimony to his achievement, to the power and ordered quietude of the Profumist Church and to the Pope's own aura of divine authenticity, that even as his health declined, his very presence still lent increasing energy to the vast governing mechanisms of the Vatican.

That ordered quietude was, as well, the most suitable atmosphere for Guido de la Valle's work with the *impero* associates, and for the enormous business ramifications they developed. Within the Church Universal, the Maestro built up closely knit relationships between Vatican financial agencies and the various diocesan chanceries around the world. The Vatican Bank came increasingly to act as broker for the billions in assets engendered by those dioceses. The investment leverage and credit created by access to such enormous funds, together with its already enviable holdings, gradually edged the *impero* group toward the center of international monetary and fiscal activity.

Guido ran the expanding *impero* operations as he might have supervised the construction of a vast pyramid. In doing so, he never lost sight of his primary aim: the Holy See's representatives should take their due place among the major money-managers who were now the real wielders of power over this earth.

The trick, as he knew well, and as Papa Profumi often reminded him, was to keep the increasingly bulky resources of the Vatican under control, and at the same time control the minds and spirits of lesser men exposed to such rapid growth in corporate wealth and corporate ways of thinking.

In the latter regard, it came as a pleasant surprise to the Maestro that Richard Lansing proved to be an interesting foil and sometimes even a corrective. For Rico was drawn inevitably, but not altogether willingly, into some of the workings of the *impero.*

For one thing, of course, the Third Secretariat and all its work in Eastern Europe was funded by the *impero,* just as the early Christian Democratic Party had been. As time went on, a consortium of European banks formed by one of the Maestro's Swiss affiliates had begun experimenting with short-term loans to the Stalinist governments in Poland and

Czechoslovakia. If the results were favorable, the plan was to follow suit in Hungary, East Germany, and perhaps a lengthening list of other Iron Curtain countries.

The need for reliable, on-the-spot economic updates was as obvious as it was difficult to fill. According as Rico's cells started functioning and the information files of the Apostolate began to form, the Maestro came to rely on Rico to include such information in his reports.

The American did what he had to do with good grace, but he seized opportunities to make his misgivings clear. He understood something of the Maestro's intent to make even the Soviets bow a little—more and more, if Guido had his way—to the economic clout of the Keeper, and to the spiritual power of his Pope. But who, Rico wanted to know, would end up bowing to whom?

Guido had no doubt as to his answer. "East or West, my friend, we will be in the thick of it all, able to hold our own, *and* still carrying the banner of the Cross. The Church will be a powerful, unassailable force even in the midst of what Papa Profumi calls the Apostasy."

"It's a fascinating image, Maestro," Rico would remark from a vantage point strikingly similar to Profumi's. "Gold bars in one hand and Christ's banner in the other. I wonder if we might not get cross-eyed or worse, trying to watch both at the same time."

The discussions between Keeper and Bishop were always frank, occasionally heated, but never poisoned with rancor. Nor was it mere politeness, on either side. Just as Rico had told Cardinal Krementz two years before, all three de la Valles had truly become a second family for him. For Guido, Lansing's ability to serve for long periods in the worst situations, and to do so critically rather than slavishly or fearfully, added a sharp dimension of respect to the affection he held for the priest from Peculiar, Kentucky.

As Father Lanser had surmised from the very beginning of the Third Secretariat operations, the Pope wanted to know all the details of Lansing's work. The Lysenko affair had left a deep impression on Profumi, and he pinned many of his hopes for the Church in the Eastern European countries on the success of the Apostolate.

Though his visitors were now fewer than ever in his reign, neither his doctor nor Philomena nor anyone else could dissuade him from spending hours poring over maps with Richard, sending him memoranda, calling him in the late night hours with this question or that suggestion.

"Profumi qui!" Rico became accustomed to those words on the other end of the wire, day or night, whenever he was in Rome. And whatever the hour or circumstance, whatever the subject to be discussed, Profumi was always instructing, advising, enlarging horizons, encouraging, imbuing everything with hope and enlivening it with faith.

Except for Papa Profumi, the Maestro, and a handful of men sworn to secrecy, Bishop Richard Lansing came to be regarded as something of an enigma in Vatican circles. Everyone knew of his friendship with Helmut, of course, and that explained his enviable position with the Maestro. But how did it ever happen that this promoter of a pious Apostolate, this distributor of devotional pamphlets, this fumbling bishop who hadn't even been able to secure the position virtually guaranteed him as "AB" of Chicago, had gained the ear and the confidence of the Pope himself? Perhaps, some surmised, Profumi was on the threshold of dotage!

As if that weren't enough, the Council of State began to ask for Lansing's presence at meetings—actually listened to his views and weighed them carefully when Eastern Europe was the topic!

In such circumstances, it was only natural that the Vatican whispering gallery became a veritable factory of entertaining theories and untrue rumors. In the end, however, even the big Bostonian Peter Servatius had to admit that, bumbling or not, and like it or not, Bishop Lansing was one of the inner circle in the Vatican who knew what was going on. Lansing might even become a force to be reckoned with.

Rico was aware of the rumors. When you came right down to it, in a curious way he had entered the spy business. Of necessity, he developed a quick sense of the mood of things around him. Often he wished he could spike the high-blown gossip and speculation. Was he a force to be reckoned with here? That was debatable at best. Certainly, in Poland, in Czechoslovakia, in Hungary and East Germany, he was, for months on end, nothing more than a faceless nobody burrowing silently underground, leading a life so shrouded and in such ever-present danger that, were he to be done away with, no one would ever know what had become of him.

[22]

While the conclave that would elect Papa Profumi's successor was not a near preoccupation of the Vatican State Council, nevertheless Professore Enrico Matteazi's report on the Pope's health signaled the moment for the leisurely process of pre-conclave politicking to begin.

In late 1953, that report, highly classified and pessimistic, was circulated exclusively to the five Council members. The Pontiff was suffering from acute anemia. His condition was periodically aggravated by attacks of gastritis which, in addition to the usual distressing weakness, also produced in Profumi utterly exhausting crises of hiccups that frequently continued for hours on end. Arthritis was causing severe pain. Considering the sometimes alarming weakness, the pain, the anemia, and the little nourishment the Pope could assimilate, and given the Pontiff's age of eighty-four and his mounting disability, His Holiness' doctor wished to alert the Council that the life of His Holiness must be considered in jeopardy.

The current president of the Council, Cardinal Arnulfo, head of the powerful Holy Office, sent a copy of the medical report at once to Guido de la Valle, along with word that the Council would meet the following day. In this matter, the Maestro would to all intents and purposes be a member of the Council. No one ever mentioned, but neither did anyone ever forget, the de facto veto the Maestro was entitled to exercise at such a meeting as this, where actual papal candidates were to be discussed.

The business at this juncture was not to bemoan the coming loss of the Pope or enter into medical details. Rather, the traditional order of the day in such circumstances was to start looking to that critical period called *sede vacante,* empty throne, when death would claim its present occupant, and a new pope would be elected.

In theory, any man, lay or clerical, could be pope. Legally, however, since about the seventh century, only clerics have been *papabili;* and among clerics, only cardinals; and among cardinals, only a very few.

The process by which those few, the true *papabili,* are chosen varies from age to age; but of that pre-conclave politicking process three things can be said, whatever the age. First, it is never a hurried thing; great bodies take their time. Second, everything about it bears the stamp of *romanità.* Those who understand need no explanation; those who have to ask for explanations haven't grasped the power of Roman understatement. Third, the process is the barometer of conclave itself. If pre-conclave consensus is painlessly achieved, so will conclave be painless; if there is much dispute, however, and consensus is elusive or fails completely, conclave can be difficult.

In the Profumist Church, due to the centralized and authoritarian stamp he had put on his pontificate, the process was orderly and unperturbed. All was done well behind the scenes. In time, and with careful work, outsiders such as the Northern Alliance might peek in the door, as it were, and catch momentary glimpses of the process. But whatever such people might see was certain to be far from the center of things, and masked in charades designed specifically to divert the eye and intrigue the mind of curiosity hound and meddler alike.

The Council meeting was quite informal. The only agenda was, as Cardinal Arnulfo put it, "to examine the cadence and rhythm at which to set the gauges and levers of power that govern our Church."

Guido nodded his agreement.

As oblique as that understatement might have seemed to some, the other four cardinals present, and Kieran O'Mahoney, now Bishop-elect of Chicago in Richard Lansing's place, all understood the decisions to be made.

"Two key questions." Cardinal Hoffeldt of Munich always preferred a tidy approach to matters. "A curial cardinal or a non-curial cardinal? A short reign or a long reign?"

"Good!" Arnulfo agreed, and proceeded to put those two questions to each Council member.

Each answered in his turn and gave a short reason or two for his opinion. There was unanimity on both questions. The Council thought the next Pontiff should be of an age that would preclude a long reign. And preferably he would be chosen from outside the Roman Curia.

The reasoning was not complex. A period of transition would be needed after Papa Profumi's long reign. The man chosen should be tolerant, and not be seen as either activist or authoritarian. No disparagement was even implied in this observation. It was a simple question of suiting the new circumstances of the Church and the world. Both were in a transition of some sort; waiting in an orderly fashion for change to take place was an oft-repeated strategy of Rome.

With those two most basic questions decided, and with a glance in his direction, Arnulfo wondered if the Maestro had anything to say before the cardinal asked for names to be suggested as early potential candidates.

All eyes turned to Guido. His remarks were short and pungent, and concerned two areas mainly.

"Purely from the point of view of business and the financial agencies," he advised, "we are launched on a vast program. We need another seven to ten years' unimpeded progress. Ideally, the next pope will be of that mind. At the very least, the need is for someone who will not interfere with ongoing plans."

The cardinals all indicated understanding and assent. They had not changed their minds on this subject. No more need be said.

The Maestro's second main concern was the Northern Alliance. He distributed folders to all present, asking them to read it at their leisure. To save time, he said, he would summarize briefly what was known about the Alliance, its members, its purposes, their policy and tactics, their weaknesses and strengths, and their more important connections within the Vatican and the Church.

As he listened, Kieran O'Mahoney's eyes showed his surprise at the mention of Sugnini and Levesque, men he thought he knew.

Cardinal Falconieri scanned the report with hard eyes as he listened to Guido's summary. "Clearly, Maestro," he said when Guido had finished, "these upstarts have been hard at work. And they criticize Rome for being Machiavellian! Still, it's surprising that a group so deeply divided in its own makeup could have managed to band together for—what is it?" Falconieri glanced at Guido's report again. "For six years. To me that would indicate serious support behind each one of them."

"A fair conclusion," Guido agreed. "Richard Richards is a One Worlder, as you may know. The Lodge with its long hatred of the Church stands solidly behind them. Behind our old friend Nikodim we can assume that his Soviet masters are lined up in a row all the way to the top. The Ripley-Savages are merely ambitious, my sources tell me. Cale is dangerous; he belongs to that upper echelon of intelligence in England about which no one knows anything precise, except that it is very powerful."

"What about our own people in the Alliance?" Arnulfo had zeroed in on the names of Sugnini and Herreras.

"Well, Herreras has not got the full support of the Jesuit authorities. Signs are that he will, though, in time. And God help the Jesuits when he does; they will be ruined as Pope's men. Meanwhile, he has obtained greater and greater support among the ordinary clergy in Latin America.

"As to Sugnini, you'll see from the report that Monsignore Levesque of the Secretariat of State is solidly with him. Behind those two stand a substantial body of theologians and thinkers persuaded that the Church has to be modernized. Sugnini himself has traveled to Moscow as Nikodim's guest, so we can assume strong support there again."

"That leaves Brother Reginald." O'Mahoney's concern was not shared by the cardinals.

"I think we all understand what ails Brother Reginald." Everyone except O'Mahoney laughed at Falconieri's contemptuous remark.

"Reginald, or rather what he stands for"—the American remained serious—"may yet crucify the Church."

"Meaning?" Cardinal Falconieri remembered Brother Reginald's group and their indignant assault on him for the Pope's decision three years before to define the Assumption as dogma. He had been patient then, and was patient now.

"The 'kiss-and-make-up' attitude to the separation of the Christian churches," O'Mahoney replied, "without addressing anything of spiritual substance and reality—'Reginaldism,' if you'll permit the word to be concocted—can choke Catholicism."

"Well"—Guido frowned—"we must do our best to see that does not happen, mustn't we, Your Excellency?" The Maestro's sharp formality in this informal meeting froze O'Mahoney into silence.

"You use the term 'modernized,' Maestro." Cardinal Ferragamo-Duca broke the icy interlude. He represented the progressive flank of Curia and was hardly opposed to rapid change of a certain order. But such blatant interference by this upstart Alliance was too presumptuous even for him. "What do they mean by 'modern,' Maestro?"

"Ecumenical, Your Eminence. Open doors. Open worship. Open theology."

"I see." Ferragamo-Duca's tone became contemptuous. "The next thing you'll tell us, Maestro, is that they have a candidate of their own!"

"I was just coming to that, Eminence. It seems they expect Archbishop Da Brescia to be made cardinal very soon. He appears to have captured their fancy. That's not surprising, of course. Among other things, he frequently attends meetings at Brother Reginald's Ecumenical Monastery at Zaite. I think we should encourage the Alliance's enchantment with Da Brescia. Papa Profumi will never give the archbishop a red hat, as we all know. He is an ideal diversion for the Alliance, from our point of view. A useful cat's-paw, you might say.

"As to the true *papabili,* we might consider giving the Alliance a little of what they want. Just enough to remove some of their steam, without incurring any real danger."

Everybody except O'Mahoney smiled. Their confidence in the impregnability of the system was absolute. It was important to know of this Northern Alliance, but the Maestro clearly had things under control.

With background and broad profile set, Cardinal Arnulfo suggested it was opportune to begin thinking of actual names. Considering Profumi's advanced age, he assumed correctly that most of the Council members had not waited for a signal to begin thinking about candidates.

Without a great deal of further discussion, three names quickly stood out from twice that number of suggestions.

Cardinal Giorgio Mendalian was put forward by three of the five regular Council members. Should the present Pope die soon, Mendalian's age, seventy-eight, would be perfect. He was presently head of the Congregation for Seminaries. An Italian of Armenian origin, Mendalian was a mild and pious man. True, people were sometimes put off by his bearded, ascetic face, and he had none of that instant charisma that was such a mark of Papa Profumi. But Mendalian had something special: He was reputed to be and, in the opinion of all the Council members, was actually a very holy man.

The Patriarch of Venice, Cardinal Giovanni Angelica, who had so earnestly asked "Why now?" at Profumi's consistory in 1950, was also suggested by three of the Council. At seventy-five, he might be a safer choice than Mendalian in the event that Papa Profumi should live longer than his doctor expected. Angelica had spent his long life as a career diplomat at obscure posts in Eastern European capitals such as Sofia in Bulgaria, Budapest in Hungary, Ankara in Turkey, Bucharest in Romania. After a final stint in De Gaulle's Paris, he had been rewarded by Papa Profumi with the ecclesiastically important see of Venice as a retirement spot. A magnificent trencherman at the table, endowed with the physique of a north-country plowman and the looks of a village elder in a Brueghel painting, Angelica was known for gentle humor, peasant piety, his skill as a raconteur, and, above all, his manifest love for people. Angelica had never made enemies. What few he had were self-appointed.

Arnulfo, the watchdog of faith's purity, did have one scruple about Angelica. "You all realize his theology is weak. He was fired from the Roman University for teaching doctrine that smelled of heresy."

"Your Eminence . . ." O'Mahoney was becoming the habitual contrarian in the State Council. "That must have been a long time ago. He was on the diplomatic circuit for thirty years and more before the Venice appointment."

Arnulfo conceded the point, but not without adding a characteristic remark: "Rarely does heresy, once seriously entertained, ever fully leave a man."

"Tut-tut, Your Eminence!" Only Falconieri could tut-tut Arnulfo in public.

The cardinal chairman nodded smilingly. Rebuff accepted!

The last man to achieve the status of *papabile* at this very early moment in the pre-conclave process was Cardinal Lorenzo Battaglia, Archbishop of Naples. In terms of his age, seventy-six, he was the middle-ground compromise. He was considered to be one of the best administrators in the College of Cardinals. Like all Neapolitans, he was fascinated with politics; and, unlike many, he was an expert at the game. He had an explosive temper, but that seemed to be of a piece with his openness and charisma. Battaglia never bore grudges or prolonged his enmities. His theological prowess was a big factor in his favor, particularly for Cardinal Arnulfo and Cardinal Falconieri.

"So." Arnulfo was obviously satisfied with the matter so far. "It seems prudent to begin consultations."

In practical terms, that meant this Council meeting was at an end. Now the quiet but constant work of establishing consensus—the process of pre-conclave politicking—was to begin well hidden behind the visible activity of the Church. Personalities located at key points in the governing structure of the Church would be visited by the Maestro and the Council members. No one of consequence would be omitted. Professionals shielded from public view in the financial agencies; some of the higher officials in the Secretariat of State and other Vatican ministries; the archbishops and bishops in major dioceses of the Church such as Chicago, Rio de Janeiro, Munich, Paris, Düsseldorf, Madrid, New York—all would be consulted. Soundings would be taken as well at all major Vatican diplomatic missions throughout the world—at the United Nations, in Washington, London, Zurich, Buenos Aires, Bonn, Pretoria. All would be done in confidence, all by word of mouth, all guarded by the strictest confidentiality.

Directly after the meeting, the Maestro stopped by Father Lanser's office. He summarized the Council's discussions for the Jesuit, who, in turn, would keep Papa Profumi discreetly informed. As always, Lanser would know how much to transmit and what to omit. "We need to have some suggestions and comments from His Holiness."

Lanser thought a little. He was no doctor; but he had little trust in the Pope's physician, and not much liking for him, either. "In my view, Maestro," he said, "there will be time for that. Plenty of time."

"I hope you are right, Father."

"His Holiness will have a new itinerary from you soon, Maestro?" Lanser assumed that Guido's travels would increase with the matter in hand.

"Yes, Father. Soon."

Nothing need have disturbed the in-Vatican career of Archbishop Giovanni Da Brescia. In fact, given Guido de la Valle's assessment of his usefulness, nothing short of the most extraordinary blunder on Da Brescia's part could have dislodged him.

The blunder occurred in 1954. It took the form of a detailed report from the archbishop concerning alleged financial misdeeds of two of Papa Profumi's nephews, Carlo and Marcantonio Profumi. And it came just as Profumi was in the grip of what then looked like a lethal attack of gastroenteritis.

"Not wishing to disturb the Pontiff, particularly when he is so ill and confined to his bed," Da Brescia thought it best—or more opportune, it was hard to tell which—to deliver his report, not to the papal office or to the Maestro, but to the Vatican State Council.

As heads of several real estate companies, or so ran the gist of the archbishop's report, the Pontiff's two nephews had traded upon their connection with the Pope to ensconce themselves as *uomini di fiducia,* men of trust, in the *impero*'s activities. The two were accused of using *impero* information to acquire land that would increase enormously in value, and then of clearing such holdings of small dirt farms and other poor tenants by a variety of dishonest means. In addition, there were allegations of kickbacks from the international banana trade, and other less than honest schemes connected with their business methods.

Da Brescia's accusations were damning, if true. The potential for scandal was huge. And the implications of the report were clear: Helmut de la Valle as chief foreign officer of the Vatican Bank, Guido de la Valle as chief financial officer, and ultimately Papa Profumi himself, had been negligent, if not worse, in their supervisory capacities.

Quiet investigation of the basic accusations took several months. The results indicated to the Council that the Profumi nephews had bought wisely and well. They had purchased most of their land for resale in major private and governmental construction deals. No witnesses could be found among former tenants of such land to testify that they had not been fairly and fully paid.

If Carlo and Marcantonio had gained access to certain information not widely available, information that enabled them to buy early and cheap, this was after all in the nature of commercial dealings at a certain level.

By November it seemed abundantly clear to an outraged Council that the great transgression here was not one of land speculation. It was rather in the clumsy, covert attack by a high Vatican official, in a sensitive area and at a critical time, upon the Pontiff himself as the ultimate source of authority, and upon his overall control of the Vatican and the Church.

By December, Papa Profumi's health had improved to a remarkable degree, and he resumed his lightened schedule. The Council deemed it prudent to bring the Da Brescia report to his attention.

Profumi reacted immediately. "We may not have much virtue," Profumi said wrathfully to the Maestro, "but the archbishop should have remembered we still have the power."

And, Guido might have added, His Holiness still had an abiding horror of any truck with Communism. Profumi had learned only earlier this year that Da Brescia had been in secret contact with agents of Josef Stalin in 1942, and with Italian Communist leaders in 1945. Surely, that intelligence weighed heavily in the scales of the Pontiff's anger.

Overnight, Da Brescia was made Archbishop of Milan. Within a week, without even seeing the Pope, he was on a northbound train, accompanied only by his secretary, nursing his deep disappointment. As he kept saying, perhaps he had merely wanted to alert curial officials to a danger. But, sincere in his intention or self-serving in his excuse, Da Brescia was punished.

There were few who knew even the bare facts of the Da Brescia affair. Many indeed saw his departure from Rome as a singular honor. After all, Milan was, financially if not ecclesiastically, one of the most important posts in the Church. But anyone who knew Rome, anyone who understood Papa Profumi's consummate mastery of *romanità,* knew that this was as close to the dregs of papal disapproval as any high-ranking cleric could come; as near to total disgrace as anything short of murder itself could bring a pro-secretary of state. To be dismissed from the Vatican after years near the top, and to be sent to a major diocese without a red hat, or even so much as a papal audience! In Roman terms, this was abject failure.

Despite the December cold, the Maestro kept his early-morning appointment with Ectore Pappagallo in the Borghese Gardens. Perhaps it was the onset of age, but he was beginning to think they should find a more protected place, at least for their meetings during the winter months.

As usual, Pappagallo did not seem to mind the weather. "Our old friends in London and Canterbury and parts unknown"—the senator's jocose way of referring to the Northern Alliance—"seem elated, Maestro. I thought you might like to know. Something to do with your Da Brescia's promotion as Archbishop of Milan. The post always carries a cardinal's red hat, they say."

"Well!" Guido's mood warmed considerably. The Northern Alliance was still enchanted with the cat's-paw. "There's some good in everything, eh, Pappagallo?"

[[23]]

The stubborn knocking at her door pulled Keti Wilson reluctantly from a lovely dream. Still half asleep, she thought she was in her own bed in Paris. She called out sleepily in her flat American accent, pulling on a light robe. *"Qui est-ce?"*

"Fiori per la signorina!" Flowers for the lady!

The velvet Latin accents woke her completely, and she laughed at herself. She was in Rome, of course. The happiest woman in creation was in Rome. In love, and in Rome.

"Grazie!" Keti thanked the patient young porter as he filled her arms with what seemed an entire garden of fresh-cut roses. She laid them on a table by the window, managed to retrieve a fifty-lire piece from her purse, and sent him off with a wonderful smile.

The little white envelope fastened to the flowers was addressed to her in Helmut's familiar hand.

"Darling Keti," said the note inside. "When I told our news, Uncle Guido asked what had taken us so long, and Aunt Agathi cut these roses for you from the garden. One for each decade of our marriage, she told me." Keti laughed again as she looked at the enormous bouquet; she'd have to be Mrs. Methuselah to live that long! "Will you come to Villa Cerulea for dinner this evening? Just the four of us—our private celebration before all the hoopla begins! I'll call at eleven for your answer. Say yes again. It's worth the world to hear you say yes! You are loved, Keti Wilson. I plan to spend my life showing you how much."

When Helmut called, on the dot of eleven, of course Keti said yes again. Just as yesterday in the gardens of Villa Cerulea she had said, "Yes, I love you. Yes, I'll marry you. Yes, I want to be part of your life, part of your world. Yes, I want children. A schoolful of children."

Helmut would pick her up at eight. The day was hers, and she found she was glad to have it to herself. That had always been her way; in the midst of turmoil, even of the happiest kind, she looked for a time of tranquillity to sort things out.

After Helmut's call, and a solitary walk, Keti chose to spend the afternoon in her rooms at the Presidente Hotel. A light northeasterly wind, the *grecale,* dispelled the heat of the day. The bees crowding around the honeysuckle and columbine that garlanded her windows, the towers of Santa Trinità Church across the way, Helmut's roses, all were easy companions to her thoughts. Keti turned again and again to Helmut's note, focusing more than once on that phrase about the Maestro. Uncle Guido had asked what had taken us so long, had he? What indeed!

Keti smiled to think how formidable Guido de la Valle had seemed to her when she first met him with Helmut. He still seemed so in some ways; there was an aura about the man that never quite deserted him. And, at the very first, Helmut had seemed a bit like his uncle. Only slowly had she begun to see beneath the layers of reserve and discover what had attracted her, perhaps from the very beginning, like the bubbling of an underground stream.

It seemed almost strange to her now, looking back from this summit of her happiness, that she had not been in love with Helmut from that first Christmas at Waidhofen. Deep down, she had never felt uncomfortable with him—at their dinners together in Vienna and Paris, their afternoon drives through the countryside, their long evenings of concerts and opera, even during her visits to Villa Cerulea and the dinners with Agathi and Guido.

Her friends who met Helmut saw him primarily as a sophisticated man of wealth and power. A little too "upperclass" in his manner for most of them. But she was taken by the uncommon breadth of his interests and the almost childlike freshness of his perspective on so many things. Their long talks together sharpened her own vision, made it almost easy for her to give a new depth to her work, to her interviews with statesmen and political leaders. He enlarged her world.

Still, there had been nothing in all of that to make it dawn on her that she had fallen in love. Hadn't she always attracted interesting men, after all? Perhaps not many were as bright or as rich as Helmut, but they were no dolts, either. And yet she could not say that she had been the first to understand the closeness that was growing between them.

When finally she did understand, it all happened for her in a moment. It was surprising and natural all at once, as though the simple sunlight of her life had burst into rainbow colors. Thinking about it now, she could almost feel his arms draw around her that first time, could see those blue-green eyes so close, feel the soft beginnings of his first kiss. She closed her own eyes in remembrance of that embrace, searching out her response, the warmth, the reassurance, the discovery, complete and certain in that single instant. All her happiness suddenly lay in the magic that promised to draw her deeply into his most private world, which she could share only with him. She did not want to let that world go by. She did not want that magic to end.

But then what had taken so long? Keti imagined the Maestro asking that question. The tall, bulky frame, the steady hand smoothing one side of his already smooth gray hair in that now familiar gesture, those eyes of his, confident and humorous at the same time. They were always so sure, these de la Valles, as though all of life's complications were under some command to break before their advance, like the Red Sea before Moses, or, as Keti said once to Helmut, "as if you expected angels to level the way for you."

"Why not?" Helmut had seemed delighted at the image. "Stranger things have happened."

Well, maybe so. But even in love Keti was, as she had given fair warning, one of "the 'Show Me' Wilsons from Missouri." The emotional thunder and hurly-burly of love's impatience didn't blind her: Marriage to Helmut would not be all kisses and rainbow colors. There were complications; very real ones.

One of the most obvious was Keti's career. Helmut knew it was important to her. She had always imagined that she would write her way back to the States as a respected reporter—a trailblazer of sorts; for only a handful of women before her had achieved what she had already. She saw no reason why she could not one day rank with any man as a national columnist and news commentator. That career was out of the question now. On the practical level alone, she could not see herself comparing travel schedules, making appointments forever to meet Helmut in this capital or that. That had been fine for them when they were just friends. But that time was over. Nevertheless, such decisions were not to be made in a moment.

Even more worrisome, if a little more subtle, was the whole new way of life she would have to make her own if she married Helmut. Before, if she had ever given a thought to the real world of aristocracy, it was to make very American jokes about it. But that time was over too. She began to realize, even from what she saw of Agathi's life, how different a world this was from anything she knew. Agathi had been born into it; it was second nature to her. Keti couldn't help but wonder how strangers such as she would fare in that world.

What seemed for a while the most serious complication had been the most surprising one for Keti. In all truth, she had never paid much attention to religion. Not nearly as much as her mother would have liked. She was Presbyterian the same way she was blue-eyed: It was a matter of inheritance. The Wilsons were self-admitted "backsliders." Not so with Helmut's family. Not only were they Catholic—the sort she was sure would die for their faith if need be—but they were one of the "papal families" whose every member is drawn into a special and demanding relationship with the Vatican. She had heard of such families—the Chigis, for example, the Colonnas, a few others. But that she would marry into one of them had never even remotely crossed her mind. Much less would she ever have dreamed of marrying into the one that apparently stood at the top of the pyramid.

There was some private humiliation in all this for the hard-minded Keti. It was a shock for her to discover that a subtle but certain anti-Catholic feeling had always been part of her. Never as something in the forefront of her mind, but nonetheless an accepted part of her mentality, a legacy, unacknowledged until now, of her growing-up years. It was the old fear and suspicion bred into the bones of her ancestors. You had to be careful about Catholics and their Church. They would take you over, freedoms and all.

It had only confused things for a while that Helmut's matter-of-fact openness of faith was part and parcel of his appeal for her. How could you say such a man believed in an ugly, distorted, childish superstition? Or that it made a mental idiot of him? Or destroyed his sense of democratic freedom? Nevertheless, such subtle prejudice is not overcome completely in a moment.

Two things finally focused Keti's mind and liquidated all the complications, all her doubts.

The first, the most important, had to do with Helmut himself. Not that he pressured her. That was not his way in intimate matters, was not in his nature. Rather, it was the increasing bleakness of her life in the weeks between their meetings. He sent her little notes and called her from wherever he might be. And that had helped. It helped, too, that she had her work to fill the days between their times together. But as time went on, none of that was enough any longer. Each meeting seemed briefer and each parting more unnatural, as though she were smiling and waving at a part of herself that was being cut away against her will.

Peculiarly enough, the second thing had to do with Helmut's friend, Rico Lansing. Priests, she had always thought, couldn't know the first thing about love; they weren't supposed to. They were so blinded by those silly vows of theirs. Notwithstanding that, priest or no, only yesterday he had sat with her in the sunlight of Villa Cerulea and, like some mind reader, like a Merlin who held the key to her private thoughts, had set her choice out in high relief for her.

They had planned a relaxing afternoon drive together, she, Helmut, and Rico. Agathi was in Rome for the day. But just as they were about to leave, the Maestro's valet, that very odd Sagastume, had caught up with them on the steps: The Maestro was on the phone with His Holiness and requested the presence of Signor Helmut in his study.

Keti had frowned behind Helmut's back, and grumbled under her breath about "papal families."

She and Rico decided to wait down by the pool in the shade of the trees. She couldn't remember now how the conversation had begun; but she had found herself asking for advice. He listened like the friend he had become, as she tried once more to unravel the complicated problems that marriage with Helmut promised. She only succeeded in getting her mind in a tangle all over again, and fell silent in her frustration.

Rico's voice had been gentle in the few minutes more he spent alone with her there; but how stark was the truth he made her see! She could, he told her, spend her whole life sorting out complications into very neat piles. But whatever she did, there would always be more sorting out to do. The world was like that. As many complications as you like! They never ceased. On the other hand, as far as he could see, it was rare to be given the chance to decide about love.

Keti had been unable to respond for the longest time. She had sat there like a prisoner of Rico's words, playing out his warning—for it was a warning—in her imagination. She forced herself to think of leaving the place where Helmut lived, leaving Helmut's world, in fact, never to return. It was an image of the drabbest and most unbearable emptiness.

Rico seemed to know just the moment to break in on her thoughts, to replace that image with its very opposite. "Helmut loves you, Keti. It's your choice. He's strong enough to live without you, if he has to. But he belongs to you, if you want him. Don't let him go."

And then, as if there were nothing more to say, Rico stood up and walked into the house without her. He was not being rude or abrupt. It was rather that he seemed to understand that anything more between them would have invaded some sacred privacy of hers and Helmut's.

Helmut was delayed that day far longer than he wished or she expected. But for the first time since she had loved him, she was at peace, even about his absence. When he was finally free, he had found her waiting for him on the terrace. Everything she felt, her deepest thoughts, were plain for him to see.

"Marry me, Keti." This time it was only a whisper; but before that softest sound, all the complications had finally melted into nothing. As if angels had smoothed the way for her.

That evening, the long ride out to Villa Cerulea close by Helmut's side calmed Keti's nervousness. Agathi, framed in the warm light of the doorway, was waiting to greet the pair. Guido's embrace, somehow both courtly and genuinely welcoming, banished any doubts that might have lingered. All at once, those two made her feel more a part of this place than she had ever felt before.

Barely were they all inside when Agathi shooed her brother and Helmut into the Great Hall. "Mariella will bring you drinks." There was conspiracy in her voice. "I want to take Keti on a little tour before dinner."

Agathi led the way upstairs chatting happily and easily, obviously intending to keep Keti in suspense. Halfway along one of the wide upstairs corridors, she stopped and opened the door to an immense apartment, the south tower suite. Chandeliers and lamps had all been left ablaze.

Keti followed her friend through the sitting room—triple the size of her parents' living room in Missouri, but cozy by Villa Cerulea standards—into a somewhat more private den; then, with Agathi chatting all the while, into the master bedroom, the twin dressing rooms, a sitting room, another, identically furnished bedroom. Then there was what Agathi called a morning room, "because," she said, "it catches the forenoon sun like a crucible." Parquet-floored, with occasional carpets, it was done in bright pastel colors and modern furniture. There was a kitchen, a study, a sewing room, nooks and cozy places everywhere. Altogether, this one little corner of the villa seemed to Keti larger than most entire houses she had ever seen.

"Do you like it?" Agathi finally came to a stop near one of the fireplaces. Was there just a hint of nervousness in her voice now? "Guido and I would like this suite to be yours. We very much want you and Helmut to be part of Villa Cerulea with us. To be happy with us. If this isn't suitable"—she gave a wide glance about her, frowning slightly—"there are half a dozen other suites we can choose from. But this is my favorite for you. We'll do the rooms over, of course, if you want. We'll do that together. . . ."

"Do I *like* it!" Keti was almost in tears for joy—not because of the splendid quarters being offered to her, but at the deep and open sincerity of Agathi's wish to have her here as Helmut's wife. The idea that she would not like the suite! Or that her friend, always so cool, so sane, should be nervous, as clearly she was. "Agathi!" She touched the other woman lightly on the arm. "If you only knew how silly I've been! I know how close you all are. I worried endlessly whether you and Maestro Guido would accept me."

For a few seconds, Agathi thought they would both break into tears. She truly did want Keti and Helmut here. "Your living here, Keti," she said gently, "would mean a great deal. We need you, Guido and I, in our own funny way, as much as Helmut does."

Agathi perched for a few minutes on the edge of one of the chairs. This was a moment of candor too valuable between them to let slip away. "To tell you the truth, there was a little worry at our end of things too, Keti. It wasn't the religious question, or your being an American, or your coming from a different—a different . . ."

“Social stratum?” Keti offered mischievously.

Agathi laughed, but she pursued her point. “The money means so little, Keti. There’s a quality that has nothing to do with wealth. And you have that in your bones.

“No, it is something else. Something harder to explain. All these de la Valle men are Pope’s men. Their first wife is the papacy. She has first and final and decisive call on them. And no one, no matter how close, can know about a great deal that is very important in their lives. Most Italian women leave business to their husbands. But this is something more. Or something different. Guido thought it might be too—too different from what you would expect from an American husband. Do you understand?”

Keti knelt beside Agathi’s chair so that she was able to look straight into the older woman’s eyes. “I know I don’t know, Agathi,” she whispered. “I only know I do want to be his wife.”

Agathi knew Keti was right. There was no way to understand before the fact what it meant to take second place to a pope. She was sure they would talk about it again, sooner or later.

Agathi lifted the mood with that incomparable smile of hers. “Well! That carries its own blessing, *carissima.* Come!” She took Keti’s hand. There were some questions only time could answer, but Agathi would stake her life that this match was a good one. “We have two grumbling males waiting for us. And a lot of planning to do! Put on your best swagger, my girl. And let me tell you one secret: Helmut and Guido may be Pope’s men, but they’re nothing without us!”

Though his back was to the staircase as he sat facing Helmut, and his mind was deep in their discussion of finance and politics, Guido felt the change in his nephew and realized he had lost his audience. Smiling, he got to his feet and turned to watch Keti and Agathi chatting in low voices and laughing, as they descended toward the Great Hall.

How easily the aura that surrounded them and descended to the Great Hall with them dissolved the clear, cold reason of *impero* business.

Both were of medium height, both long-limbed, both dressed elegantly in formal evening clothes, both coiffed beautifully. They seemed to be two reflections of one sheen, and yet to be distinct one from the other. The older woman, her low-cut white crepe gown and turquoise jewelry setting off her blond hair and blue-green eyes, shone with regnancy and steadfastness and mystery. She was a little fuller in face and body, almost severe in her perfection, more sensuous. Keti, with her auburn hair and blue eyes catching the light, mirrored restlessness and playfulness and frankness. She was a trifle leaner, a little tauter, a touch more flamboyant in her decor, more sensual. Both seemed enveloped in an effervescence of contentment.

Guido and Helmut watched the women descending as if on an instant of magic time, in a moment that seemed not to rush along with its fellows, but to wait upon the passage of some delicate miracle of emotion. For Guido, this radiant sister of his was the fruit of the de la Valle past. This newcomer who had enamored his nephew was, he hoped, the womb of the de la Valle future. Helmut, accustomed to his aunt's almost extravagant beauty, had eyes only for Keti. His mind was awash in the freshness and enthusiasm she seemed to bring into his life.

Then, as suddenly as it had been suspended, the magic moment slipped into the affectionate flow of conversation that lasted through the evening.

The wedding day was set for June 15 of the following year. At first, that seemed a long time to wait, but every hour was filled with activity and preparation.

It took Keti a month and more to wind up several assignments for her syndicate that were important to her. If leave her career she must, she intended to do so with bright banners flying.

With that done, and with Agathi's help and a financial boost from her parents, Keti moved into an apartment in Rome. Together then, like two social strategists, the women began the intricate planning for the gala at Villa Cerulea at which the young couple's engagement was announced. It was Keti's first lesson in refined social bravura, and she could not have had a better teacher than Agathi. The evening came off as a bright triumph, rivaling even Guido's famed Ferragosto celebrations.

Soon after, Keti learned that her father had developed a serious heart ailment. It would be impossible for him to come to Rome for his daughter's wedding; it was not even certain he could live until the following June, and in the circumstances her mother would not leave him. Helmut immediately suggested that he and Keti travel to Missouri, at least for a short visit. If he could not eliminate this sadness from Keti's life, he could try to lighten it for her. He cleared a week of his schedule, and they left to spend two or three days in Hartsville, staying in Keti's old home and consoling her parents for losing their daughter to a foreign husband and a foreign land. No real warmth could be born between her parents and Helmut; there wasn't enough time. But as a wise father and a perspicacious mother, the two old people lost whatever misgivings had first troubled them about this marriage. Helmut was a gentleman; he and Keti loved each other. That much was clear and it was enough.

Helmut was tempted to take a day to drive to Peculiar, Kentucky, just so he could boast to Rico that he had finally been even to that little dot of a place where his friend had been born. But he decided instead to spend a day in Chicago, meeting with Cardinal O'Mahoney and attending to a bit of opportune *impero* business. Before he and Keti caught their flight to Rome, he made a point of paying his respects again to Basil Lansing.

Once they were back, the preparations for the wedding began in earnest. With Agathi as her constant guide, Keti became a familiar visitor to Roman boutiques. She found that her mere engagement to Signor de la Valle made her something of a celebrity. She was pampered and deferred to in a way that caused her both embarrassment and laughter. She began receiving invitations from people she would have given an arm and a leg to interview when she was still reporting for the syndicate. The occasional quiet evening in her apartment or at Villa Cerulea was a luxury to her after a time.

The anchor that kept Keti steady in the storm of activity was her religious instruction. She would become a Catholic; but only under Rico Lansing's direction. She knew that Rico traveled constantly for the Hearts Apostolate, whatever that was. But she was adamant. He would simply have to cram her into his schedule.

For his part, Rico enjoyed teaching Keti. During his absence, she did the reading he left for her, and the time he was able to spend with her was never wasted. She was quick-minded and sharply intelligent; she asked tough questions, but never with hardness of heart.

As often as his schedule and the weather would allow, Rico preferred to spend their time together out of doors. If he could manage only half an hour or so, they would meet at St. Peter's and stroll in the piazza while they talked, or take one of his favorite walks down by the Roman Forum and farther on to the Piazza Venezia. When he had enough time free, they might take a taxi out to the Via Appia Antica and walk by the ancient monuments that lined its edges. It was as though Rico needed to breathe the open air of Rome, where religion was free for the taking, before he would have to go back again into the countries where nothing was free and even breathing space seemed a touch of heaven.

Little by little, Keti learned that Rico's faith was as alive as Rome for him; and little by little, he made both come alive for her. He didn't talk of mere rules and ritual, as she had half expected, but of the reality and meaning of faith in all its detail. Whatever point they were discussing—a sacrament, or a heresy, or a dogma of the Church—Rico seemed to have some story that carried home its meaning. As often as not, those stories concerned the people he met and served in the dark countries where his missionary work was done. Keti heard tales of men and women who each day faced armies and governments, starvation and torture, forced labor and cruelest death, rather than give up what Jesus had won for them, and what they could win for him.

There was the seventy-five-year-old pastor in northern Hungary, now a cabdriver, who celebrated Mass alone in his taxi every midnight. There were three young nuns, orderlies on a state farm outside Prague, who still kept their religious vows in spite of their daily slavery and constant degradation by the guards. There were scores in prison or under permanent house arrest because they refused to stop believing in Christ. All these people, Keti came to realize, were living saints for Rico. Through their stories he wanted her to see that for him—and perhaps for her in time—even the saints and the angels of "cock-and-bull superstition," as she had described his Catholicism in one rare moment of insensitivity, were genuine heroes and heroines, people she would be proud to call her people.

"I can't give you faith in these things," Rico told her once. "Only God can do that, subject to your own free choice to accept or reject that faith."

As the year rolled through winter and early spring, Keti's growing understanding of Catholicism entwined itself in the sights and the seasons that were her and Rico's companions. Until finally, on a sunlit day in May, Rico brought his instruction to its end.

Their long walk that afternoon took them past sparkling fountains and clusters of restaurant tables and chairs that had been moved out onto every pavement; past flower vendors and marble statues caressed by the warming new sun.

He focused their talk on marriage; that was, after all, the reason for Keti's interest in Catholicism.

He wasn't talking about love, he told her. Or about attraction or desire. He knew those things were there for her and Helmut. But they were only a means to something more.

"I think you know this, Keti, but let's say it anyway. Marriage is not a human experiment. It is not a human creation, or any sort of fad. It's a sacrament. God's gift, given and accepted on his conditions. Not for as long as love and desire may last, but for as long—"

"For as long as we both shall live," Keti interrupted, smiling her agreement. "Just as the marriage vows say."

"Please God it will be a long and happy time, Keti."

"And if it's not? Happy all the way through, I mean?"

"It won't all be easy. But it will never be impossible . . ."

Before Rico could finish his sentence they were both startled by the cries of a huge flight of swallows, soaring and wheeling and diving on graceful, curved wings, chasing invisible mayflies in seeming celebration of their own return from North Africa to these Roman heavens.

Keti laughed in delight. "A good sign, Rico! A very good sign!"

The nuptial High Mass celebrated for Keti and Helmut by Cardinal Ferragamo-Duca—that ardent Roman of noble family and high curial rank was Guido's choice—and the reception that followed it marked the beginning of a time Keti would always remember more for its blessings than for its disappointments. If she had had her way, her father would have given her away; but as that was not to be, Rico was again her choice. If she had had her way, the honeymoon would have been longer; but the week she and Helmut spent alone was a golden time of love fulfilled for both of them. Their return to Villa Cerulea was not an ending, but the beginning of life in a place that truly became her home. Helmut traveled as frequently as he always had, but his time with her was perhaps sweeter and more passionate for that.

As Keti was drawn more deeply into the life of the de la Valles, she began to feel the special warmth Agathi and Guido had for each other, and to share in it herself. But more than that, she began to see Agathi, especially, with new eyes, and to understand that hiding behind that beautiful appearance and those accomplished manners was a loneliness Keti had never felt. Agathi's closeness to Maestro Guido de la Valle had made her too important, too capital a figure in society, for any member of that society to approach her, to know her, for her own sake. One of her deepest needs was to share simple, unadorned friendship that other women take for granted. No word of this ever passed between the two women, but each of them was happier, day by day, for the presence of the other.

All in all, there was only one shadow during the first year of Keti's life as a de la Valle. But it was a serious one. She conceived a child, but miscarried. She conceived again, but again could not carry to term. The third time, the hemorrhaging was so severe that she spent some days in the hospital to recover. There she was advised by a specialist not to try again. She refused to listen to such advice, and swore the family doctor, Professore Paolo Sepporis, to secrecy. She and Helmut had dreamed of children. "A schoolful of children," they had said. And she knew, too, the importance of an heir for the de la Valles. So adamant was Keti, and so distraught, that Dr. Sepporis, fearful lest she have a relapse, swore that he would say nothing.

It was the only secret Keti had. But it was a terrible one. One that made her feel alone, and gave her more reason than she wanted to think back over some of the things Rico had explained to her during the year before her marriage. "I can't give you faith." She remembered his words. "Only God can do that."

"Well, God . . ." Keti's prayers were never lyrical, but they were sincere, and above all direct. "Here's your chance. Let's talk this over. . . ."

Was it a miracle, then? In Keti's mind, it always seemed so. She conceived again and this time carried her baby to term. And—triumph of triumphs—she gave birth in Waidhofen, as all de la Valle wives before her had done.

She had nearly died, and the child too; Dr. Sepporis, who had accompanied her to Waidhofen, informed her she would never be able to have another.

But the miracle was accomplished. They both had lived, she and her tiny son. She had given Helmut an heir, and by that fact she, too, was now bound by the sinews of life itself to this world that claimed all of her and all she wrought.

A de la Valle baptism in Waidhofen followed tradition.

This tiny being, flesh of her flesh and bone of her bone, who had lived exclusively within Keti and with her alone for nearly nine months, was now placed in Agathi's arms. Led by the mayor of Waidhofen, clad in the regalia of his office—embroidered doublet, black knee breeches, high boots, broad-brimmed hat, the staff of office in his hand—Helmut and Guido following him, Keti and Agathi carrying the child, they all trooped solemnly from the Goldner Hirsch over to the onion-domed church of St. Michael the Archangel, which the de la Valles had built nearly four hundred years before on the banks of the Ybbs River in order to commemorate the defeat of the invading Turkish army nearby. In the presence of the whole village and of about forty close friends from Rome, her child was to be baptized by Rico Lansing in the same baptismal font they had used for Helmut, for Guido, for Guido's father and uncles and aunts, and all the preceding de la Valles of the last four hundred years. His first given name was to be Eugenio in honor of Papa Profumi; his second, Guido. Eugenio Guido de la Valle was Keti's child, but clearly hers only as a de la Valle wife.

They arranged themselves around the font in the baptistery. The Maestro held the baby, with the godfather—the mayor—on his right and the godmother, Agathi, on his left. Helmut and Keti stood beside Rico. The villagers and guests gathered around them. Just before starting the ceremony, Rico, smiling, glanced about the circle of faces and had a fleeting perception of each one. Guido's triumphant happiness. The mayor's stolid solemnity. Keti's face pale with some inner strain. Helmut calm, smiling, proud, his hand on Keti's shoulder. Agathi so radiant with that strange beauty of hers she wore only on special occasions. . . . Hadn't Benfatti told him something about Agathi's early marriage? . . . But his gaze flickered on over the guests and villagers. They were all there and waiting. Time to begin.

"Grüss Gott, Euch Kristen!" The traditional church greeting of priest to people was immediately answered with a chant of *"Grüss Gott, Pater!"*

From then on, Rico was on another plane.

While he put the ritual questions to parents and godparents and received their answers—all was in German—he was talking in his heart with presences none of the bystanders could see. Keti, because she had got to know him over a whole year of religious instructions, knew he lived with these presences—his angel, the Virgin Mary, Christ, the saints—and that in his mind this baptism would make little Eugenio Guido de la Valle as holy and as sinless as the seraphs who worship at God's throne. For Rico, all this was real. Keti knew that.

There was no way she could understand Guido de la Valle at this moment. For the Maestro's consciousness was transfigured with a dimension of power only a de la Valle could understand. Not money power. Not political power. Power of instinct and of origin.

Like him, this baby was heir not merely to the magnificently loyal service the de la Valles had rendered popes and papacy and Church, but to a tradition of power that originated in what was purely German, purely Nordic—race, soil, language, culture; and that had invested itself in what was purely Mediterranean, purely southern—love, faith, Church, civilization. Wisely, his ancestors had lived, worked, and died down south, but insisted all beginnings—births and baptisms—take place in Waidhofen-an-der-Ybbs. No quaint family custom, that. Rather, a reenactment of origins.

When Guido placed Eugenio back in her arms after the ceremony, and she nestled the baby close to herself as they all walked out from the twilight calm of the church into the sunshine where Sagastume awaited them, Keti had tears she knew she had to hide. Quietly and coldly, the thought came to her that she now held this baby in trust. For Guido. For Helmut. For all the de la Valles. For the God they served and she had promised faithfully to worship in their way. Rico, walking beside her and more observant than she credited him to be, noticed her tears.

"Remember, Keti, every good gift is God's. From Him. To take. To give back." She nodded through her tears, persuaded that at least he understood her pain.

She felt better when they all stood outside. It was near midday, with a cloudless sky and a brisk wind blowing from the south. With Helmut and Guido, she passed from the Lower Square to the Upper Square, lined with villagers and guests who strewed their path with wildflowers, as she carried Eugenio so that all could see him. It was the custom. And there was no denying the festive air of communal joy that the entire village shared. It was balm to the air around them. They stopped in the Upper Square as much to enjoy the panorama of the Ybbs and the rolling meadowlands beyond as to say thank you and goodbye to the people.

Gently, Guido took the child from her and raised him up on both his palms for some moments. During the ceremony in the church, Eugenio had struggled and whimpered. But now he lay calm and quiet.

For those short instants, the people around gazed at an unexpected cameo of life and human hope.

This elder de la Valle, whose hands were deep in the stuff and matter of this world, appeared for a few instants to be almost freed from all that held him so tightly to this earth. His white hair ruffled by the wind, the blue-green eyes flashing in the sun, the mouth open in sheer exultation, his body taut and stretched to its limit, he stood foursquare on the ground but reached for the skies through the tiny white-wrapped body of a week-old infant whom he believed to be as pure and holy as God's angels because of that day's holy baptism. Cleanse me, cleanse us all, Lord, his gesture said, because this child has been utterly cleansed by you and is now our offering to your holiness.

At that moment and in one flash of understanding, the meaning of her chosen life came together for Keti. Through her marriage she had entered a life greater than her marriage. She had given birth to her baby, but he and she and the de la Valles and the villagers were bound together in a tradition older than any one of them and a destiny greater than all of them put together. In silent acknowledgment of the step she had taken, Agathi's hand closed over Keti's. The deep pain was gone from her.

And thus she returned to Villa Cerulea with her infant son and her husband, full of a new carefree spirit and trust in life. But her gift to the house, Eugenio Guido, now started to influence all that house's inhabitants, all including Guido—and more than Guido. Villa Cerulea itself suddenly seemed to have shaken itself out of a centuries-old sleep. Keti's inner eye did indeed see those ancient ancestors whose portraits hung on the walls coming to life, watching, approving, praying that this tiniest de la Valle would indeed be the greatest of his line.

The birth and baptism of a new de la Valle had its own special significance for Rico Lansing. A few days after the baptism, Soviet troops and tanks had finally crushed all revolt and dissidence in Hungary. He departed immediately to reassess the underground conditions in that blood-stained country.

The picture was depressing. Something had departed from the underground since the debacle of that unsuccessful revolt against the Soviets. It was not exactly the destruction wrought by 4,000 Soviet tanks and 68,000 Soviet troops. The elite of Rico's underground had died in the streetcars and manholes of Budapest, resisting the Soviets and waiting for help from the American armed forces, help which of course never came. Cardinal Mindszenty was a "prisoner by choice" in the American legation; he would be for fifteen years.

Rico took one long, hard look at the situation, and decided to change the intelligence picture radically. Men (non-Hungarian), matériel, and dollar funds were shifted to other locales. He left the actual network intact. But because he could not assess how far it had been infiltrated and he did not want to arouse suspicions, he put off building a parallel and independent system for ten years. Surveillance was too strict, the spirits of Catholics too low: They felt betrayed by Rome and by the West. The old network he left in place to obsolesce and waste and die.

But the recollection of that baptism and the promise this new baby offered for the future helped in some deep way to mitigate Lansing's disappointment and chagrin. As he remarked to Guido on his return, "Eugenio is a blessing and an encouragement in these dark days of Hungary and these last days of Profumi."

Indeed, Eugenio was a blessing for all of them, particularly Keti. During those quiet years spent within the slowly fading sheen of Papa Profumi's lingering autumn, the landscape of her life remained reassuringly constant. Each season was reliably a tintype of its predecessor, and the landmarks around her seemed unshakable—Helmut and she as much a part of Villa Cerulea as its four-hundred-year-old walls; Guido and Agathi as bright stars in the Roman constellation; Guido and Helmut as Pope's men and Vatican men and Church men; little Eugenio as the ever more promising guarantee for all their future; and, around the five of them, all the orderly and hierarchic world of Vatican Curia, national government, aristocratic circles and upper-class society, and the flourishing business community. The new things that came upon Keti were merely enrichments of that permanent landscape. What deprivations befell her left that richness intact. All in all—this was the blessing—she was allowed the time and the ease she needed in order to become what she had chosen to be: a de la Valle wife, daughter, and mother.

[24]

Although only snatches of news, most of it distorted, reached the general public through the Italian and European media, the upper echelon of government in the Church Universal became increasingly preoccupied by the uncertainty of Papa Profumi's health. Every few months he underwent a new crisis, each one more severe than the last. Professore Matteazi was in such constant attendance after a time that a suite was set aside for him in the Apostolic Palace. The Pontiff's public audiences were cut back further, and his private visits were reserved for the closest circle of intimates—Philomena and Stefanori, of course, who cared for him day and night; the Jesuits Lanser and Kensich; the Maestro; a few of the curial cardinals of Rome; his family; Richard Lansing, whose Apostolate missions continued to be of sharp and immediate interest to him; certain visitors of state; very few others.

Because he loved Castel Gandolfo, and in order to remove himself periodically from the grinding demands of daily decisionmaking, Profumi spent more and more time at the papal villa. Inevitably, then, though it was imperceptible to most, and though no major policy decision was ever taken except by His Holiness, the wheel of Vatican activity began to slow. Any day now, there would be a vacuum, a *sede vacante* situation, in Rome. High winds blew in such circumstances. The wise hastened to secure their positions, leaving the unwary and the unprepared to be swept off their feet, or eliminated from the system.

Archbishop Da Brescia did not leave any of his friends in doubt as to the direction in which he wished to move. He was as aware as any man that there is a crossroads in the life of every highly placed cleric of the Catholic hierarchy, a time when his personal decision, his own determination or lack of it, will advance his career or halt it at its present level. Anything might influence that decision. Health. Family. Politics. Money. Piety. If his decision is to advance, then, to be serious, he must be prepared to cultivate friends at higher levels, and abandon all baggage that will hinder progress—such baggage as useless friendships, damaging enmities, dangerous liaisons, rigidity of opinions, legitimate prejudices, political alliances. And, to be taken seriously, he must project that public persona which seems the most acceptable to those who have it in their power to speed his progress to a higher goal.

Milan was that crossroads for Da Brescia. Given his long apprenticeship in Vatican affairs, and despite Papa Profumi's wrath, he wished not only to return to Rome but to be considered for the highest office in the Church. Until his unexpected and unwilling exile to the north, he reasoned, divine providence had afforded him such privileged tutelage in papal affairs that surely it was meant for him to be so considered. In all good conscience he could come to no other conclusion.

The most important order of business in this affair was for Da Brescia to receive the red hat of cardinal—the *gallero,* as it was called—that Profumi had so resolutely denied him. Of course, he could not petition His Holiness directly. In all likelihood Profumi would still not receive him; but in any case, that was not the way these things were accomplished. Friends must be found and enlisted, sympathetic and highly placed clerics who would be willing to make his case with the Pontiff.

He found one such friend in Cardinal Giovanni Angelica of Venice.

Angelica had good reason to understand Da Brescia's wounded feelings. In his own faithful years of service under Eugenio Profumi, Angelica had never been allowed the Pope's intimacy. That he was awarded Venice and the cardinalate that went with it was no more than a sign of Profumi's sense of justice: Angelica had served the Holy See well; he deserved a reward, and he had got it. But that was as far as he could expect to go. Unlike Da Brescia, Angelica held no grudge; that was not his way. But he could feel a certain sympathy for the archbishop.

Such sympathy aside, Angelica liked Da Brescia. Liked what he stood for—Da Brescia's sympathy with the workingman, his apparent understanding for the discontent in Profumi's Church about the Pontiff's authoritarian manner. And he admired the way Da Brescia administered his diocese of Milan—the sermons Da Brescia himself preached for the poor from the top of a truck; the way the archbishop tried to reach out to Socialist and even Communist enclaves in his city; his championing of better wages for hard-pressed city workers.

The cardinal's benign attitude became clear in meetings with Da Brescia himself; Angelica was nearly besieged by petitions raised in the archbishop's behalf from remarkably diverse quarters. Eastern Orthodox prelates from Bulgaria and Romania and the Ukraine, whom Angelica had known in his day as a diplomat, wondered pointedly why such a brilliant man as Da Brescia was no cardinal. That most affable Metropolitan Nikodim of the U.S.S.R., also a former acquaintance, echoed the same sentiment during more than one visit. There were humble but insistent appeals from Angelica's own private contacts in the Roman Curia—most notably from Archbishop Jean Levesque, Archbishop Dell'Angelo, and Cardinal Lisserant.

Angelica tolerated the barrage with a certain patient forbearance, and an understanding of Da Brescia's plight; but also with a canniness not many gave the jovial cardinal patriarch credit for. He saw the pattern in all these petitions. He knew that the Romanian and the Ukrainian and the Bulgarian were yes-men to the Soviet's Nikodim. Levesque was a political ally of Da Brescia's. Lisserant disliked Profumi intensely.

What really decided Angelica in Da Brescia's favor was not all that intense lobbying, but the fact that he himself could not bear intolerance, injustice, unlovingness. For him, at his advanced age, the key to all the world's difficulties was love.

"His Holiness may not see me, *Eccellenza.*" Angelica was blunt in his telephone conversation with Da Brescia that day. "It is not even certain he will be in Rome; but, as I do have to be there next week attending to some business in the Secretariat, I will do what I can. It might be a good thing if Your Excellency were in Rome at the same time. If I am successful, then you should be on hand, ready to make your apologies and your personal peace with the Holy Father."

"Willingly, Your Eminence. Most willingly." Da Brescia hung up the phone in the spacious study of the bishop's palace in Milan, and at once rang his own secretary. "Monsignore, contact Paolo Lercani for me, will you? Tell him I plan to be in Rome next week. If it is convenient, he should arrange to be there."

Da Brescia hoped Angelica would be successful. But there were other fences to mend, just in case.

It was a fiasco; not the garden variety fiasco, but the kind that is quickly swept into Vatican lore.

Cardinal Angelica himself got only as far as the third floor of the Apostolic Palace.

"A thousand pardons, Your Eminence." The Swiss Guard on duty was abject but unyielding. "Without a special pass, no one ascends to the fourth floor."

"Who gives the passes?" Angelica was agitated.

"Sister Philomena, Your Eminence."

"Call her, please. I want to see her, here. Now!"

When Philomena arrived, all immaculate white starch and black habit, her resolve was more than a match for the cardinal's agitation. The Holy Father was adamant: Not as long as he was Pope would the archbishop be a cardinal. Did it seem she was overstepping her authority? Well, that was unfortunate; but the Pontiff was too ill to receive visitors at this moment.

Angelica was hurt and dumbfounded by such a degrading rebuff from a mere nun, visited on him because of his alliance with Da Brescia. He said nothing further to the steely-eyed Bavarian, but took the elevator back to the ground floor, and went to confer instead with Cardinal Lisserant.

At Angelica's news, that Frenchman's permanent condition of exasperation with Papa Profumi exploded into open anger. By telephone, he quickly assembled a delegation of three younger cardinals, a ritual number for a special representation to the Holy Father. Without pausing to heed or even listen to Angelica's advice to the contrary, Lisserant left him in the wake of his anger, led his little cortege up to the third floor, forced his way past the Swiss Guard, and confronted Philomena at the door to the papal study itself.

Philomena never twitched an eyebrow. There were those who said that Lisserant tried to push his way past her to the Pope's bedroom. And there were even those who said that Philomena not only stood her ground, but that she actually struck the cardinal. Struck him on the cheek!

Whether true in every detail or not, the story was ready made for the Vatican gossip mill. And, true or not, the cardinals did retreat, robes, rings, offended dignity, and all, in total defeat.

When, at dinner that evening, Cardinal Angelica recounted what had happened, Da Brescia apologized for having been the cause of such embarrassment for His Eminence. But already, in his mind, he had switched to the other fence he hoped to mend.

Da Brescia had never understood why Maestro Guido de la Valle, of all people, enjoyed such extravagant favor with Profumi. Oh, he knew he was a valued adviser, but so were many others. The archbishop was not aware of the Bargain, and certainly not of any Keeper other than the Keeper of the Keys. Very few—and almost no one of his rank—were. But no such knowledge was needed. It was enough to know that the Maestro's ear was—or could be—as good as the Pope's own. Enmity with de la Valle was something Da Brescia could no longer afford.

Of course, it would help if he could do more than pay his respects to the Maestro; if he could be of positive service, make his amends tangibly, so to say, his case might be strengthened. In that regard, Paolo Lercani could be useful, as he had been so often during Da Brescia's time in Milan.

Guido received Archbishop Da Brescia's phone call in his Secretariat office with mild surprise. He had heard from Sister Philomena herself of Angelica's and Lisserant's efforts of the day before, and had supposed that Da Brescia would retreat to Milan to bide his time.

"Of course, Excellency," Guido's voice was cordial in a formal sort of way. "Come along now if you like."

The meeting was brief and relatively painless. As he was in Rome, the prelate said, he wanted to take the opportunity to congratulate the Maestro on his becoming a granduncle, and to assure the Maestro of his esteem and his desire to stay in contact.

"Of course, Excellency." The signal was received. "Thank you. Please, sit down."

For five minutes or so there was small talk. The two exchanged views on matters of mutual interest in Rome and Milan. In the natural course of things, Da Brescia suggested that an adviser who had been most serviceable in Milan, a certain layman named Paolo Lercani, had made a connection that might be of interest to the Maestro. "I wonder if you would give him twenty or thirty minutes."

"Lercani?" Guido raised his eyebrows. "The name is familiar, of course. If he could come by this afternoon, I would be delighted to meet him." That was only a quarter true. Guido could and did meet anyone he wanted. He had avoided meeting Lercani until now. His obviously close association with Da Brescia changed his mind; but he did not expect it to be a delight.

Paolo Lercani had two surpassing talents. He could smell money the way animals smell prey. And he could be all things to all men. He had risen like a comet across the skies of Italy's postwar economic miracle. He had come to the *impero*'s attention early in his career, as an established authority on tax laws, currency transactions, and a new genre of international payment just coming into vogue: the Eurodollar. By that time, he already owned outright half a dozen banks, ran several middle-level companies, and sat on the boards of a few dozen more. He was a substantial contributor to the Christian Democratic Party and a cash patron of Menda's Catholic Action organization. He was definitely one of the up-

and-coming financial Turks, looking for new worlds to conquer, when Da Brescia had arrived in Milan in 1954.

Within a week of that arrival, as everyone in Rome's Vatican knew, Lercani had himself introduced to the newcomer by a local auxiliary bishop, discovered that the archbishop needed two million dollars for a charitable project, and returned before that day was out to present exactly that sum to Da Brescia, "with the compliments of the Catholic bankers and businessmen of Milan."

That had been the foundation of an important friendship; Lercani became one of the archbishop's "men," always available for advice; for funds; for whatever service he might render.

But there was an underside to Lercani's dazzling success. It wasn't all financial genius and Lady Luck. From his first business efforts as a teenager peddling vegetables to the occupying U.S. Army in Sicily's Palermo, Lercani had relied on his connections with the mysterious network of killer-protectors, the *mafiosi.* At first, he only dealt with the local *capi di regime* in Sicily's countryside and towns. In time, as more sophisticated but nonetheless corrupt versions of *mafiosi* began to surface all over the Italian economy with large sums of laundered money to invest in legitimate business, Lercani had been perfectly placed. Whatever their level of sophistication or social acceptability, however, these *mafiosi* always backed their investments with the surest threat of bullet or knife for enemies, and with *sasso in boca,* the rock in the mouth, for "friends" who could not hold their tongues.

Lercani's achievement had been to combine the underground strength of these *mafiosi* with his own ability to adapt himself to all circumstances —to be a worshipful parishioner for a gullible Da Brescia, and an icy-blooded colleague of assassins; a patriot, and a friend to those who toppled their own governments and betrayed their countrymen; a husband to his childhood sweetheart, and a patron of the East Mediterranean white slave traffic; father of three beautiful girls, and supplier of narcotics that twisted the children of others into the demonic ways of addiction.

Because Lercani had come to the *impero*'s attention, Guido had a rather full dossier on him. But he had not understood until his meeting with Da Brescia just how much the archbishop seemed to value the financier: enough to make of him a "serviceable" peace offering to the Maestro.

Surely, Da Brescia could not know all that Guido knew. But shouldn't he have taken the trouble to find out something about the man? Or shouldn't his gut feeling, or his instinct as a priest dealing with men, have warned him?

Guido shook his head. Some men, he mused, seem to have congenitally bad judgment. A matter of the genes; it was no exaggeration. Da Brescia must surely be such a man.

Paolo Lercani looked precisely as the Maestro had expected. Nothing about his natural person made him unusual. Roughly medium in height. Spare, but not too slim of build. Triangular face so ordinary as to be difficult to describe. Perhaps the eyes were a little large, a little protuberant, a little too narrowly set, a little dark to see into very clearly. Perhaps his smile was peculiar.

His clothing, however, was perfect. Impeccably correct. Expressed just the right degree of dignity and self-worth.

"Please, Signor Lercani, do me the honor of sitting down."

The walk forward was erect but not swaggering. The handclasp was just right.

"Now, Signor Lercani. What can we do together?"

Signor Lercani would come right to the point. The Maestro *was* the busiest man in the Church, "after His Holiness, of course!"

Those words were more than a correct mixture of greeting and respect. Lercani had done his homework, too. Enough to make the veiled connection between the Maestro and the Pontiff. Or was he fishing? Guido made no response.

The matter, Lercani went on smoothly, concerned the Banco Laziana Privata of Rome. It was up for sale. He would like to form a consortium with the Vatican's Institute for Religious Agencies—say, 45 percent for the IRA and 55 percent for himself—in order to buy the BLP.

Guido did not even blink, but he was surprised. The BLP, family-run, was the largest privately owned bank in Italy. As far as he knew, it was operating at an all-time profit. Why would they sell? He excused himself for a moment and retired to an inner office to phone Di Lorio.

"Che commedia, Maestro!" The Sphinx broke into a rumble of laughter when he heard the news. "The BLP? For sale? Through Lercani? Absurd!"

"Maybe, Monsignore." Guido did not share Di Lorio's high spirits. "But find out. If it is true, there are several reasons why we should not let it go."

"I agree, Maestro. *If* it's true. Why don't you send Lercani over here to me and Servatius? Peter has made quite a study of profitable private banks over the last year or two. We should be ready for your friend when he gets here."

"I'll do that, Monsignore. Tell Servatius to find out not only if the BLP is for sale, but if so, will they invite us to buy it? I doubt they will, but I want to know explicitly. If the BLP's answer is negative, and Lercani is the key, he is proposing 45 percent for the IRA and 55 percent for himself. Reverse those figures, Monsignore. I don't know what his game is. Maybe he's just short of liquid cash, though that's hard to believe. Whatever he may be after, I think it's time we got a little control over this financial wizard. And I think this may be our chance."

"To tell you the truth, Maestro, I didn't think any of it would work out." Monsignore Di Lorio eased his bulk into one of the chairs in the Maestro's office early that evening. "I didn't think the BLP would be for sale. But it was. And *only* through Lercani. Then, I didn't think that fox would relinquish controlling interest to us. But he did. Peter Servatius has it just about locked up by now. You should see them huddled over the figures, that huge Yankee hulk and the dapper little Sicilian! Like the elephant and the flea! It's a funny sight! They get on like a house afire, though.

"Tell me, Maestro." Di Lorio was still curious on one point. "What made you so sure? Why think the BLP would be for sale? And why through Lercani?"

Guido didn't have to explain very much. "In the first place, Lercani is too wily to come to me with a bluff. In the second place, if such a highly profitable operation as the BLP were for sale at all, it would only be to someone like Lercani. . . ."

"Of course!" Di Lorio held up his hand. His and Guido's thoughts were the same now. A banking family unwilling to sell. The midnight telephone call. The threat of acid in the eyes or the rape of a daughter. The soft statement of a felony whose revelation, true or false, could ruin a whole family. At the extreme, a stranger's head delivered by the parcel service at the front door. Whatever the details, the silent, behind-the-scenes threat from the underworld out of which Lercani sucked his power guaranteed his success.

The question Di Lorio didn't raise was the only one Guido still could not answer. What game was Lercani playing? Why come to the Maestro? Was it that the IRA was the only nonpublic agency that could come up with the money for such a major bank acquisition? Was it the prestige of working with the IRA? Was it more than any of that?

Well, whatever the game, Guido would find out in time. Meanwhile, 55 percent gave him control. And, as always, the key was control.

"His Holiness is expecting you, Rico." Father Lanser led the way toward the papal apartments of the summer villa. For the last months of 1957 and well into 1958, Castel Gandolfo was the de facto center of papal administration and of all but very formal audiences. "He was studying your latest briefing again just this morning."

"And his health, Father?"

"Holding his own, I would say." Lanser saw no reason to detail the painful decline in Eugenio Profumi's bodily strength. In fact, the Pontiff had withdrawn to a very large extent from the world of action and dwelt for long periods now on that higher plane of restful contemplation where the focus is on death and what comes after. He read and prayed and spent long hours in silent meditation. At other times, he was plunged into very vivid and exact memories of past incidents, going as far back as his childhood and his early career.

It was at precisely that time that Lansing's work had reached a critical point. Behind the cover of his international organization to promote devotion to the Hearts of Jesus and Mary, he now administered a tightly knit network of "cells" centered in East Slovakia, and covering Czechoslovakia, Poland, East Germany, Lithuania, and a small area—a beginning only—in the Ukraine.

Hungary, however, was temporarily a total loss for him. In the bloody revolt of 1956, most of his recruits had lost their lives. Some had fled to the West. The Soviet military occupation of that country and the virulent efficiency of the KGB made all progress impossible there for the moment.

It was to keep such a calamity from happening ever again that Lansing had devised the plan the Pontiff was now studying. Actually, it was the proposal for a wider application of a strategy Poland's Cardinal Wallensky had designed for his own country. The Polish primate had always been against confrontation as foolhardy and doomed to failure, whatever about the heroics. Hungary had proved him right.

What Wallensky proposed was to appoint as bishops some of the younger priests whom Lansing had co-opted into his network early on. With those young bishops wisely positioned in various cities and towns, a new educational process would begin. Its aim would be to detach the notion of national political identity from the idea of what it means to be a Catholic; to lead the Catholic community to see itself culturally, socially, even in labor relations, as nonpolitical, indifferent to any form of politics —Marxist or capitalist or socialist.

"With such a plan," Wallensky had said to Rico, "we will isolate the Marxists. They are a minority anyway, here and in the rest of Eastern Europe. Leave them their dreadful playthings—the armed forces, the secret police, the Politburo, the Communist Party, their atomic arsenal. But they will not have the people.

"Eventually, we will be able to paralyze government, army, secret police. Eventually, in fact, we will be able to manipulate them."

That was the heart of the plan Lansing and Profumi were to discuss today. Rico had refined the details, even to the point of proposing the men who would be named as bishops in each area. Bogdan Valeska for Krakow. Adam Lis for Lublin. A half-dozen others in Poland, four in Czechoslovakia, eleven in Hungary, two each in Romania and Bulgaria, one in the Ukraine, five in East Germany. Rico knew them all personally, could vouch for their worth. The dossier of each man had been included in the papers Lansing had sent in the papal pouch the week before.

"Ah, Bishop Lansing . . ." Papa Profumi looked up from his desk as Rico was let into his study.

Lansing approached and kissed the Fisherman's Ring. How frail was the hand that wore it now! And how gaunt and ashen was that patrician face.

"Do sit down, Excellency. We have been studying your suggestions for Eastern Europe with considerable interest. We have a few questions, but We are sure you can answer them to Our satisfaction."

In the hour they spent together, the Pontiff displayed an undiminished acuteness of mind. He had discovered weaknesses in the strategy—cities that would be crucial to such a plan as Rico was proposing, but had been left uncovered; faults in the financial underpinnings that must be taken up with the Maestro. But all in all, the Pontiff gave his approval.

Indeed, though he did not say so to Rico, Profumi very much wished that the Colombian Jesuit Father Herreras, who had thrown in his lot with the Northern Alliance, and persisted so virulently in coupling his faith with Marxist politics in Latin America, might have been persuaded to adopt such a strategy as this instead. But that, he knew, was not to be; at least not in the very brief time Profumi had left to him.

The last few minutes of that afternoon's audience were, by the Pope's wish, spent in a more personal examination of Lansing's Apostolate. The Pontiff had not forgotten how lonely a mission his bishop had accepted, or the prestige and career promise Lansing had given up. "You have spent years at this work already," he remarked to Rico. "It seems to Us that it is going well; that it remains of the most serious importance."

Rico was about to supply more details to the Pontiff; his mind was constantly absorbed with his work. But that was not His Holiness' interest just now.

"Can you continue, Excellency? There will be a new Pope soon . . ."

"Holiness . . ." Rico wanted to object, but Profumi raised his hand.

"We are realists, you and I, Monsignore. The next man to ascend the Chair of Peter may or may not give you the support you would like. That will not mean a stop to your work. But it will make it more lonely than it is even now. Should that be the case, can you do it?"

It was an end-time question, almost a deathbed request, and Rico thought carefully before he answered. "I think I can, Your Holiness. With God's help, I think I can."

Profumi smiled. It was the second time this American had given that answer. It reminded the Pontiff of the very words he had used to answer the conclave that had elected him Pope. "With God's help, I think I can."

"Anche Noi, Eccellenza. So do We. Let Us seal that faith with Our papal blessing."

That was, Rico Lansing knew, Papa Profumi's earthly farewell to him.

[25]

In the small morning hours of the last day of September, the white phone by his bed woke Guido out of an exhausted sleep. He switched on the light and tried not to sound bleary as he answered the ring.

"Profumi qui." The Pontiff's voice, though tired, was as unmistakable as the familiar words of his telephone greeting.

"Your Holiness should be resting. . . ."

"So Professore Matteazi keeps saying. There will be time for that soon, Maestro. Soon enough. Tell me, do you remember Kalikawa? Uranium. Cobalt. I believe you told me you saw old Father De Smet."

"Yes, Holiness. It was De Smet's plea for those poor tribes he had tried to care for that convinced me to take the risk."

"Any news lately?"

"Only that it's doing well, *Santità.* The reports from the company we put in charge have been—"

"That was not what I had in mind, Maestro." It became obvious the Pontiff was upset, that he felt the matter to be urgent. Guido listened without interruption. Profumi had received a most pressing report from a source that was usually reliable. As Kalikawa was so remote in its jungle fastness, however, there was room for error; and as there was such rising political agitation in that region, Profumi hoped the matter was untrue, or at least greatly exaggerated.

"If it is true, however, the human disaster is terrible, Maestro. And the disaster for the Church could be as great. Kalikawa may be buried in the jungle, but Africa is changing along with everything else. You are aware of the national plebiscite that took place in Togoland this month, and the mandate it gave to Sylvanus Olympio."

Guido was indeed aware. Olympio was one of the new black African nationalists who had been educated in Moscow's school of economics. He was targeting the Belgian Congo as proof of the white man's corruption and exploitation. But the Kalikawa project was above reproach; Guido's orders had been clear.

"Scandals and muckraking will be the order of the day for some time to come, Maestro," Profumi went on without a pause as Guido's mind raced to assess the possibilities. "We must see that we do not deserve too much of either. If the report is true, we must clean up the mess. But we must be certain. We must send someone whom we can trust. Someone who can get in and out without being discovered as Vatican, and who knows how to get the reliable information we need without stirring up a hornet's nest."

Obviously, Papa Profumi had the man in mind.

"Richard Lansing?" Guido wasn't guessing entirely. The Pope's trust and esteem for the American was clear.

"Is he in Rome just now?"

"I don't know, Holiness. If he is not, we can reach him."

"You will see to it, Maestro." That phrase, like *"Profumi qui,"* was so familiar, even as the voice itself was becoming almost strange in its growing weakness.

"Sì, Santità. This very moment."

While he was still pulling his robe around him, the Maestro picked up his private phone and dialed Rico Lansing's number in Rome. Benfatti answered. No, the valet said in his defferential voice, His Excellency was not there. He was away on a preaching tour in Northern Europe. "The Hearts Apostolate is very exacting. . . ."

Guido didn't wait to hear the rest. He rang Solaccio. How long would it take to find Lansing and get him back here?

Solaccio was silent for a moment, figuring the logistics, no doubt. "I'd say sixty hours, Maestro."

"Do it. Have him come directly to my home."

Guido did not waste any of those sixty hours.

He roused Helmut, explained the crisis, and dispatched him at once, as a point man of sorts, to Geneva and Vienna, to ferret out every scrap of current information about CTIP Suez, the company charged with the running of the Kalikawa project. In addition, Helmut was to prepare to liquidate the three holding companies in Liechtenstein that represented their direct, traceable link with CTIP and Kalikawa Mining and Metallurgy, Inc.

Before Helmut was even out the door, the Maestro set still more wheels turning. He arranged for the first of a series of conference calls to the *impero* members. He called Solaccio again to check progress, and to assure that the necessary travel papers and cover would be ready on Lansing's arrival. He arranged for the needed currency and for air passage. He was in touch with Jan Klaerts, Belgian consul to Elisabethville in the Congo and a longtime friend, to make local arrangements. And, not merely as an afterthought, he retrieved from his Secretariat office the envelope old Father De Smet had left with him ten years before.

By the time Rico arrived, everything was as ready as it could be in such a situation.

In all the years of their association, never had Lansing seen the Maestro so perturbed. His listened as Guido filled in the general background for him. He read De Smet's report and winced, as Guido had, at the horrible photographs. He asked if Helmut's digging in Geneva and Vienna had so far uncovered anything to hint that such a situation had come into being.

On the contrary, Guido told him. All the Kalikawa reports showed profitability and excellent conditions for the miners and their families. "In fact, the accounts show considerable expenditures to maintain those conditions. Nevertheless, Profumi's source is both reliable and alarmed. The Pontiff has picked you personally, Excellency. I think you can see what needs to be done." Guido double-checked the envelope containing passport, airline ticket, and cash, and handed it to Rico. "Find out what's really going on there. Avoid notice of press and officials. Do not be tagged as Vatican. Whatever you find, do nothing about it. Just get back with detailed, firsthand information as quickly as you can manage."

Rico, already on his feet, took the envelope from the Maestro. "Do you have a starting contact for me?"

"You will be met by Father Peter Brentt. A Belgian. Vouched for by the consul there. One of us. He knows the jungles as well as any man." Guido looked at his watch. "You haven't much time. Your plane for Cairo and Elisabethville leaves in a few hours."

Rico glanced at the De Smet photos lying where he had left them on Guido's desk, and shook his head in recurring disbelief. "I hope this turns out to be a wild-goose chase, Maestro."

Guido agreed. "That would be the best news you could bring us."

On the surface, the first eight days of October appeared routine for the Maestro. From early morning to late night his time was filled with *impero* and pre-conclave and State Council matters. He made daily visits to Castel Gandolfo. But beneath his accustomed activity there lay an unaccustomed tension, hidden from others as the sea hides its undercurrents.

Only once in those days of waiting for Rico's return was there a moment when Guido's sense of regret cut so profoundly that, had anyone else been present, he could not have kept it hidden. It was at the end of a long day. He had to pass from the Secretariat of State over to the Belvedere Court for one more private meeting, with Cardinal Lisserant. His way carried him past the Sistine Chapel. The time for tourists was over. All was quiet. On impulse, he stepped inside for a moment.

Truly, Guido thought as he let his eye linger along the Michelangelo frescoes, he did not want to see the last of Papa Profumi. Nevertheless, all too soon he would be listening to the sounds of the conclave that would gather in this room to elect a new pope.

He approached one wall of the chapel. At the slightest pressure on a particular spot, a small door, so cunningly mortised into the decorated surface as to be undetectable, opened just long enough for the Maestro to step through before it closed silently behind him. His hand reached for a switch he knew well; a blue-shaded sconce in the wainscoting above the thickly carpeted floor cast a slightly eerie underlighting and revealed a circular little niche of a place, perhaps twelve feet in diameter. *Il Tempio.* The Temple. Just before he died, in 1484, Pope Sixtus IV had ordered it built behind the chapel that would bear his name. Its curved walls were covered in deep red velvet. The domed ceiling held a fresco scene of Jesus taking a coin from the mouth of a fish to pay his Roman taxes. Below that fresco, around the circumference of the dome, the appropriate legend was chiseled and leafed in gold. "Render unto Caesar what is Caesar's." All the words but one were in Roman letters a foot high. The odd thing was that, for a reason no one knew, one word, *"quod,"* the Latin for "what," had been fashioned in Gothic script.

A winding inner staircase connected the Temple to a Vatican basement corridor, and thence directly to the outer world. There was never more than one key to that exit. Aside from the Keeper himself and the cardinal dean of any conclave, perhaps ten people in all the world at any given time knew about that room, or the key, or who kept it.

By way of furnishings, a red-upholstered Dantesca chair was set adjacent to the locked exit and behind a square ebony table. To its right was a short walnut bench. On the table was a red telephone, a malachite ashtray, and a blue-and-gold toleware tray that held a water carafe and two fluted glasses.

The Maestro leaned for a moment against the back of the chair. Nothing in this room ever changed. In their time, his uncle and his grandfather had sat here to monitor the resonant sounds of conclave deliberations and votes, ready to play the Keeper's part should that need arise. In 1939, Guido had taken his own place here, for the conclave that had chosen Eugenio Profumi as Vicar of Christ. Like his uncle and his grandfather, Guido had sworn to uphold the Pope and the Holy See. Unlike his uncle or his grandfather, Guido was now guilty of negligence. Perhaps that was understandable, given the enormous empire he was constructing; but it was nonetheless a violation of his most sacred oath. He prayed an earnest prayer that Rico would bring better news than he expected from Kalikawa—and that it would come before the time came to enter the Temple again as the unseen and secret monitor of the conclave that would choose Papa Profumi's successor.

Guido drew in his breath, switched off the light, and departed, sadder and more anxious than before.

One after another, several darkened windows of Villa Cerulea blazed into light, as Rico pounded on the heavy doors that had been locked for the night. Sagastume drew the bolts and stood squarely in Lansing's path, ready to stop the disturbance, physically if need be.

"Get out of my way, you hulking giant, or I swear I'll flatten you if I have to. . . ."

"Let him pass, Sagastume." Guido stood in the shadows of the balcony above.

Rico burst past the bodyguard and took the stairs two and three at a time, as wide-eyed house servants in night clothes peered around corners at the astonishing spectacle.

By the look of him—unshaven, still dressed in sweaty, filthy fatigues, eyes red, face strained—Rico hadn't even rested, much less slept, in days. He moved stride for stride with the Maestro through the elegant corridors, making no effort to keep his voice down as they went.

"You're good at reports, Maestro." Rico's words were acid with bitterness. "I've heard you at your best. Well, *I'll* give you a report! I couldn't wait to get back here and give it to you! You've been taken for a ghastly ride, you and your *impero* and the Vatican and those poor slaves back there!" Rico's voice cracked and his mouth twisted in his effort to get control of himself, to sound coherent.

Guido opened the door to his study and both men went inside. The Maestro poured a glass of brandy and Rico took it. His tongue was dry and he needed to calm himself.

There were a few minutes of silence as Rico tried to order his thoughts. His mind was still back in the jungles of Kalikawa. He had no eye for the sheet-white strain on the Maestro's face as he waited with monumental control.

"Porci dannati!" Rico finally spat out a hateful preamble to his report. "Those damned swine! Everything is wrong over there, Maestro! From beginning to end you have filth on your hands. Those photographs you showed me with the De Smet report are like storybook pictures compared to what I saw! We got no sleep. There were eight camps in the area we targeted, and we went to every one of them. Maybe you've been paying for decent schools and clinics and doctors and teachers. But let me tell you what you've got! Every camp is surrounded by barbed wire. The living quarters are nothing more than immense bunkhouses—corrugated tin

roofs and cinder-block walls. Hot as hell in the daytime and freezing at night. No running water. No plumbing."

Rico spared the Maestro nothing; tried in fact to convey the horror just as he had come upon it in every detail. The first house, if he could call it that, had been locked. He had kicked the door in. The tiered bunks were packed everyplace except around the door and one small space where a stove and a large table stood. Everything was in an indescribable condition of filth. Bits of wood and leather that looked as though they had been chewed for food were strewn about. Dead mothers still lay in some of the bunks, their dead children's mouths still at their breasts, just as De Smet had seen them a decade before.

"But even that wasn't the worst of it, Maestro." In disbelieving shock at what he had discovered, Rico had run from that first bunkhouse and was on his way to another in the compound, when the ground had given way under his feet. He fell, or rather sank, into a mass grave that had been barely covered over with leaves and loose dirt. It had all been carelessly done, as if those swine had never thought anyone would come to inspect the place, or care if they did come. Lansing tried to describe the stench. He could still smell it, still feel the insects that were all over him in a second, see the bones, the decaying flesh, the eyes oozing and staring.

He had forced himself to dig part of the grave out, to discover if he could how those pitiable wretches had died. Some, still recognizable as human, had been tied and shot. Probably they were too weak from starvation to work any longer. Others, weaker still, were probably just thrown in with the others to die when they would.

"We went to the other camps too. It was much the same in all of them. The blockhouses. The filth. The stench. Emaciated bodies, bellies swollen from starvation, lying in bunks or buried in mass graves . . ."

Rico sat down, his exhaustion finally draining the strength from his legs. There was no point in continuing the catalogue of horrors. Silence fell like a heavy curtain between the two men, isolating them from one another.

Lansing's imagination was mired in the grotesque scenes he had witnessed; his mind still wandered in the desolation like a soul stumbling through hell. The Maestro tried to hold to the rational, tried to get away from the horror by forming sequential thoughts, logical questions to be answered.

He had thought he had set up the project so well. For the good of the *impero* and the Vatican it served. For the good of De Smet's poor tribesmen. For the good of the companies he had charged with such clear mandates. All those reports for all those years had never led him to doubt that the good was being done. Where had it gone wrong? With greedy managers who thought they would never be found out? With subcontractors, or with overseers, who gulled CTIP Suez and pocketed the money from supplies meant for the workers and their families? Where along the line had control broken down? For that was what had happened. This one time, control of things in the Maestro's charge had failed. And the price that had been paid for that failure was the most blasphemous suffering and murder.

"Tell me." Guido's voice was quiet by comparison to what Rico's had been, but it stabbed the silence. "Did you get near the mining area?"

"No." Rico's forehead was resting on his hands now. His answer was dull, emotionless. "We didn't go near the mining area or the road leading to it. God knows what we would have found. But . . ." He raised his head slowly, eyes ablaze again, as with a fever. "Why do you ask, Maestro? Are you afraid they've killed too many? That there'll be no one left to work the mines?"

"Please, Monsignore!" It was too much. "I was trying to understand what has happened. We have made a very bad investment. Somewhere along the line, arrangements broke down. But I must try to understand! I don't know how long this has been going on. If you saw eight compounds, all abandoned, they must have brought in replacements from the same tribes. They must be platooning thousands. I'm trying to understand how they have done this with no one finding out until now."

Rico stood up again, driven, unable to remain still. "You're trying to *understand!* You don't know! Do you hear what you're saying, Maestro? Let me rephrase your questions for you. How many batches of those poor souls have there been? Because they came in batches, Maestro, like bales of hay! How many times has the worker population been renewed?" Rico's voice rose with each question. He refused to let Guido get hold of any rational support. His questions were like battering rams, and he meant them to be. "How many have been killed? Five thousand? Ten thousand? How many are being starved and beaten and buried right now?"

Every question hammered Guido more heavily than the last and he had to grip his chair, as if to steady himself physically. It was too much! But still Rico did not let up.

"You and I may never speak civilly to each other again, Maestro, and you have the power to break me and my career in two. But someone has to say this out loud in your hearing.

"It wasn't a bad investment, Maestro, do you hear me? You haven't just made a technical error and wasted some money of Christ's Church. This is not a case of arrangements breaking down. No, Maestro! In your calling as master financial agent for the papacy, you served Mammon instead. And Mammon has vomited all over you. You and your associates smell now like any filthy worldling. Did nobody ever say to you, 'Hold, Maestro Guido! Hold it all for one moment. Reflect where it is all going!' Did no one ever warn you, Maestro?"

"Only His Holiness." Guido was not sure he said those words aloud. His head rang, and the pain of Lansing's assault crept through his whole body. He forced himself to his feet. Forced himself to be sure his accuser heard his answer. "Profumi warned me." He glanced toward the white phone; how he wished he could tell the Holy Father; call him, see him, as he had done in so many crises before this one.

“Well”—Lansing’s voice was more controlled—“the dead are dead. But the living, the workers and their families who are still there, we can’t let them suffer and die like the others.”

“We will not, Monsignore. On my personal oath I swear it. I will make the arrangements tonight. I’ll go there if need be. We’ll transport them all back to their homelands. We’ll see to their needs.”

Rico nodded. There was nothing more to be said. Nothing he could do that he hadn’t done here tonight. Wearily, and without acknowledging the pain and sorrow on the older man’s face, he left.

Outside the study, Lansing was startled to see Agathi and Keti huddled in their robes and slippers a short way down the corridor. They seemed so profoundly together, those two, as they watched him in the wedge of light that spilled from the open door of Guido’s study. It was Agathi who stepped forward first, blocking Rico’s way to the stairs.

“Nobody shouts in this house, Rico.” Her whisper was an angry hiss. “Why were you so brutal with him? You can’t leave him like that. . . .”

Rico tried to think of words to say, but Agathi was already past him, inside the study with Keti, both of them comforting the ashen-faced Maestro, their arms around him.

That portrait of their love and caring was a living reproach to Rico. Who did he think he was? Or rather what had he become? Who was *he* to talk of Mammon! He had used every ounce of his strength and passion to wound Guido in his weakest moment. But he had not even made an effort to heal him. The thought hadn’t so much as entered his mind! He was a priest, and he had offered no compassion, no healing, no remedy.

He thought for a moment of going back, but the very tenderness of the scene drove him away. He knew he did not belong here. Guido de la Valle might have sinned grievously, but he would be forgiven and his life would go on here. Rico was different, had become different. He belonged in the state car waiting for him below. He belonged in the Apostolic Palace, or in the underground shadows and byways of the Gulag. He was fit only for the isolation and exile that would never be ended for him in this life.

The white phone rang in the Maestro’s study. Agathi and Keti still close by his side, Guido lifted the receiver, hopeful that just one more time he would hear that voice.

“Lanser qui . . .”

“Rico!”

Lansing, startled to be called, startled that the Maestro, who had never used his first name, did so now, turned on the stairway.

Guido, half in shadow, looked down.

“Profumi is dead.”

Part Three

SUMMER OF THE ANGEL

26

"*E pazz'!* The Pope is mad!"

Only rude shock could have forced such an exclamation from Cardinal Arnulfo; especially in a full-dress papal assembly of high clergy and prominent Catholic and Protestant lay visitors such as this! Though it was no more than a stage whisper, Falconieri to his right and Ferragamo-Duca to his left both heard it. Da Brescia, a cardinal at last, and probably many of the other cardinals heard it. Guido de la Valle, seated with his family and other distinguished guests at the front of the nave of St. Paul's Basilica, may well have heard it too, for it had been the only sound in the stunned silence that followed Papa Giovanni Angelica's bombshell.

"In order, therefore," the Pope had just announced in his rather leisurely fashion, "to knock down ancient walls between the Church and its contemporary world, in order to open the windows and doors of this Holy Church to modern men, and so that the Spirit of Christ's love may once again be poured out over all men in all countries, We have decided to summon an ecumenical council here in Our Vatican, to begin its work not later than 1964. . . . Our aim: a renewal of God's love among his children. . . ."

Very probably the Holy Father himself heard Arnulfo's explosive sentiment; his hearing was sharp, and the distance was narrow between the Pope and the three rows of his cardinals seated in the sanctuary around the altar. But if he heard, he gave no sign. It seemed, rather, that the peace that possessed his soul and the assurance that filled his mind made him immune from self-doubt; and that the love in his heart protected him from hurt.

It was that very cluster of qualities that had won for Cardinal Giovanni Angelica the necessary majority vote in the conclave of November 1958, a mere twenty days after the death of Papa Profumi and barely two months before this Feast of the Epiphany, January 6, 1959.

That had been the most uncomplicated, even the most convivial of conclaves. And, in a true sense, the most controlled. Even before Papa Profumi had drawn his last breath, the near-unanimity that Guido de la Valle and the Council of State had found during the pre-conclave politicking held firm. Among all the cardinal electors, friends and foes of Profumi alike, there was deep uncertainty as to what direction the Church should take now.

By the time Falconieri as cardinal dean of the conclave actually opened the first formal session, therefore, the cardinal electors were as one in their agreement on the "mandate" they must give to the man whom they would choose as Pope. The *impostazione,* as that mandate is called, is the first order of business of every conclave, and is based on the cardinals' informed assessment of the Church's situation and the world's. All saw that a respite was needed. All preferred a short papacy of great tranquillity, a time of easement both from immediate decisions and from ironclad authority. At the same time, all insisted, this should be a papacy marked by no abrupt changes. A delicate balance was required.

When the conclave discussion turned from the mandate to the man, it was Ferragamo-Duca who, in a very private conversation, seemed to sum up the confident opinion of the entire assembly concerning Cardinal Angelica: "He'll create good feelings, and give us the time we need. He's a good infantryman. He'll have power, but not use it."

As Keeper, Guido de la Valle monitored the conclave discussions discreetly from inside *il Tempio* without surprise or worry as Angelica was called upon to express his ideas about the type of papacy needed.

Angelica had only one idea: love. "Human beings," he answered the cardinal dean, "can never be made peaceful and virtuous, individually or collectively, by the use of mere power, but only through the experience of love. . . ." He reminded his eminent brothers that "the first Pentecost was a pouring out of divine light on the Apostles," and suggested that "what the Church needs now is a pouring out of divine love over the successors of those Apostles—you and me, Venerable Brethren, and all the bishops of Christ's Church—as well as on all the people of that Church. . . ."

The Maestro heard Falconieri's careful instructions to the cardinal electors on the procedures of the conclave balloting. He listened as the votes were tallied aloud, keeping his own written count in the dim light that shone on his solitude. And finally, with the satisfaction of a job well managed, he heard the cardinal dean ask for the vote to be made unanimous. The conclave complied willingly.

From the first moment of his papacy, Angelica justified the faith that the State Council and the conclave had placed in him. In all he did, he seemed the right choice for the "steady as you go" mandate that had been decided upon.

Immediately after his election, and his appearance to greet the crowds in St. Peter's Square and give his first papal blessing, Angelica was escorted from the balcony of the Basilica, through the Hall of Lights, crowded with prelates and dignitaries, to the Silver Throne Room. There, only Guido de la Valle waited, as Keeper of the Bargain, to greet his new Pope. That meeting was the ritual moment when the full secret of the Bargain, and the role of its Keeper, was revealed to each succeeding Pope for the first time.

Angelica read the three-page document Guido handed him. It summarized everything—the Bargain itself; the functions, privileges, and obligations of its Keeper; his control of finances; his veto power over conclave choices. It had been signed by every new pope for the past eight decades.

Without hesitation, this Pope added his own name: "Angelica PP." He scrawled his papal signature for the first time, then, his face wreathed in that warm smile of his, Angelica seemed content to leave all else to do with such matters in other hands. "I know little about it all, Maestro, and

I want to know less." He returned the pages to Guido. "You have my blessing on all you do. Come to me whenever you need me. Now"—he heaved his heavy frame from the sofa—"I must be off about the poping of my Church!"

Though Guido never quite made out how much this Pope really knew or wanted to know about the Bargain or the *impero,* he never underestimated Angelica's wily and subtle intelligence, or took his gentleness for weakness, as others had done in the past. Guido and the cardinals who had elected him knew he was nobody's fool. Turkish ministers of state, Bulgarian premiers, Nazi officers, Greek prelates, Romanian military men, Jewish agents, French statesmen, and Angelica's own competitors in the Vatican bureaucracy down the years had all learned that much—some of them the hard way. But for those who gave Angelica his due, there were no surprises in him.

Angelica was no Profumi, of course. His face had none of the hieratic stillness, the untouchable immobility of Profumi's face. He was not a man who seemed hewn in old and sacred ivory, inhabited by the purest of spirits. Instead, Angelica's features had the mobility and openness you expect in a child; the changes shifted with radical swiftness from smiling joy to fatherly seriousness to mischievous fun to enthusiastic appeal to tragic sadness. As if to heighten the contrast with his predecessor, Angelica was anything but regal in bearing. He did not seem to hold himself at an unbridgeable distance from the soiling touch of mortal things and fleshly involvement. A mere five feet five or so in height, he weighed close to two hundred pounds and was built like one of those wide and solid farm doors that kept the cattle inside during the hard winters in his native Domodossola. His head was bald. He had outsize ears, a large hooked nose with wide nostrils, a long, thick mouth, spatulate hands, columnar legs. But nobody who met him ever remarked on his physical traits for long; for over all that, and whether he was smiling or serious, Angelica seemed to wear a cast of lightsome attraction, an invisible but powerful aura that seemed to bring opposites together, and made people smile, and captured their hearts.

If it was true that physically Angelica was no Profumi, it was true in style as well. He was anything but Roman. It was to be expected that any new pope would bring his own team into the Vatican and the papal household, and that the team would bring its associates, friends, and hangers-on. And so it was expected that Angelica's appointments would reflect his own styles and would bring certain manageable changes, mere side effects due to the transition from one pontificate to another.

As expected, this Pope appointed a real secretary of state—something Profumi had never done. His choice, Luigi Picolomini, was a good but malleable man. He had spent twenty-one years as apostolic delegate in Washington, D.C., and was totally fascinated by the character and outlook of the American bishops he had known for so long.

Archbishop Agostino Casaregna, with his years of excellent training by the side of Pro-Secretary of State Da Brescia, seemed to the Pontiff the logical choice for assistant secretary of state. With Casaregna came his own ever-present assistant, Monsignore Roman Carnatiu.

The Pontiff raised to the cardinalate a bevy of men recommended by the bureaucracy. This also was expected, the thing to do. Archbishop Da Brescia became Cardinal Archbishop of Milan; and though he was not returned to the hierarchy in Rome, he was a frequent and now more welcome visitor, with his own rooms in the papal apartment.

Father Lanser, too, joined the ranks of cardinals, along with Archbishop Levesque, who was recalled from exile in Bombay, and Archbishop Dell'Angelo. Archbishop Julio Pirandella, an Argentinian of Italian extraction who had made his way up through the ranks and, like all the others, was clearly due for promotion, received a red hat. Indeed, a whole list of long-neglected *minutanti* or humble secretaries at the Secretariat of State found recognition and status now. Men whose names had rarely been heard outside the Vatican—Adamo Cippi, Davide Silvestrone, Michele Fornacci, a dozen more—were raised to highest ranks in the clergy.

It seemed that no one was overlooked by Papa Angelica. Archbishop Sugnini was recalled from London; and, along with Levesque, Demarchelier was called home from Bombay. Even Gabriele Pasquinelli, the somber-faced little priest who had shepherded Richard Lansing during his first week in Rome nearly fifteen years before, was not forgotten by Angelica. Pasquinelli received his own violet rabat at last; as Monsignore Pasquinelli now, he was made chief aide to the papal master of ceremonies, Monsignore Corrado Amalfeo, whom he would one day succeed. Father Kensich had also been remembered, but he preferred to be posted home to his native Bavaria, and his wish was lovingly granted.

Within a month of his election, Papa Angelica had done all that and more. He charmed the Vatican diplomatic corps. He dissolved solemn meetings into cheerful laughter with his humor—wisecracks, some said. He pulled the leg of prelates in a way that made even the most self-important smile along with him. And always his spirituality, which was of the simplest and most appealing kind, was at the fore. He gave audiences to ordinary people as well as to aristocrats and political leaders. He broke precedent by preaching a short Angelus sermon every Sunday from the central window of his third-floor study for the ordinary people gathered in St. Peter's Piazza. He visited Rome's central prison and chatted with the convicts. He joked in dialect with Carboni, the papal cobbler, and grumbled plaintively when a meal was delayed.

The response to Angelica was as spontaneous and genuine as his own appeal. After the icon-laden years of Eugenio Profumi, people loved the ordinariness, the accessibility of it all.

The most curious thing about Angelica was something only the oldest Vatican hands could notice, something that only became apparent slowly, after the first several weeks of Angelica's reign were behind him, and the tension and dust of reorganization began to settle. And it marked yet another difference between the new Pope and the old. Unlike Profumi, Angelica had no intimates. For all his loving openness, there was no one in whom he seemed to confide. There was no Father Lanser in his household, no Sister Philomena.

It was thought at first that Angelica's private secretary, Monsignore Noris Ducocasa, would emerge as this Pope's intimate adviser, would establish himself as Angelica's Lanser. Ducocasa, a solemn-faced, skinny little man with close-cropped hair and thick-lensed glasses, was always in motion, as though he had been assembled with wire springs. He had been with Angelica in Paris and Venice. And was deeply devoted to him. Like Angelica, Ducocasa was a simple, awkward, loving peasant of a priest. But he was not privy to many of the Pontiff's inner thoughts or his intimate confidences.

Nor did such an adviser emerge from any of those around the Pope. He did see them all, but as a matter of his papal routine. Each month he received his cardinals—Falconieri, Ferragamo-Duca, Arnulfo, and the rest. Each few weeks the Maestro called on him. He seemed interested in Rico Lansing's Hearts Apostolate, but saw him as he saw any other cleric charged with a papal commission. He seemed delighted to discover his old friend Brandolini on the third floor of the Palace, and visited with him in the papal study quite often indeed. And though that raised some questions and some uncertainties, Brandolini kept his own counsel as he always had.

All in all, however, throughout the Vatican the order of the day settled in as quietly as it might in a comfortably moving ocean liner: "As you were; steady as you go."

There was a certain subtle shift only in the highest sectors of Vatican bureaucracy. At that level, it was felt, there was reason for a certain caution, a delicacy of balance, so to say. The return to papal favor of such men as Sugnini, Levesque, and Demarchelier; the frequent visits of Da Brescia; the wide spectrum of Angelica's contacts in the political world, contacts that included not only Christian Democrats, but Socialists, Republicans, Fascists—even Communists—and the absence of any reliable papal confidant as conduit between the State Council and the Pontiff: all of this suggested a policy of guarded discretion.

It was not that unusual. Popes are not told everything. And it was not that the Curia repented of its choice of Pope, or worried overmuch about his papal appointments or his political acquaintances. All of that was just the easing of tension they had hoped for. They were delighted with his response to his few open critics: "They are all my children," Angelica would say; and then he would remind them that his second most ancient title as Pope was *Pater Patruum,* father of fathers, the outstanding father of all: Angelica PP.

Nevertheless, it was a simple, realistic fact that many of the team installed by Papa Angelica were not to be trusted with such information as the State Council, for example, discussed in its daily routine of business. While recent usage seemed to dictate that Cardinal Picolomini, as secretary of state, was entitled to attend State Council meetings, Arnulfo had one of his assistants research the matter in the records. It was determined that the presence of the secretary of state was a matter of courtesy between Curia and Council, not a matter of ex officio right. Picolomini graciously agreed to attend Council meetings on invitation only.

At the same time, perhaps as a sort of balance, because Lanser was now a cardinal, and because of his vast experience in the very heart of papal matters and his understanding of so wide a spectrum of papal concerns, it was decided that he should become a permanent member of the Vatican State Council.

It was decided, too, that in briefing Angelica about the *impero,* the Maestro should be "restrained and brief, sticking to bare essentials." That, in any case, seemed to be the way Angelica preferred it.

In a private meeting, Guido, Lanser, and Falconieri settled upon a policy of discreet silence concerning Rico Lansing's covert work for the Third Secretariat. Better that Angelica not be made an unwitting channel of betrayal. The Lysenko tragedy, with its suggestion that friends of that traitor might still lurk within Vatican walls, was still vivid in their memories.

Rico felt uncomfortable with the secrecy, at first. "We can't maintain these confidences from the Holy Father forever, Maestro": He seemed to direct his comments primarily to Guido, perhaps with the memory of another tragedy, Kalikawa, in mind. "I mean, let's be frank: We do stand in need of reform and renewal of holiness—we, the bureaucrats! If it becomes clear in a reasonable amount of time that Papa Angelica does create a new spirit in the Church, a fresh beginning, then the Pontiff should be fully briefed."

It was not Guido, but Falconieri, so often the peacemaker, who responded to Rico. "There isn't one person here who would not agree with you, Excellency. But, for want of a prudent wait, we would not wish to endanger your associates 'over beyond.' "

"Amen to that!" It was a measure of Lansing's status with these movers and shakers of Vatican and Church that he could have such a blunt and open exchange with them.

Angelica himself made such decisions relatively easy for the Council and the Maestro, and for other elements of the bureaucracy as well. In a manner of speaking, it seemed to be his own will. As far as the new Pope was concerned, each department of his Vatican was to carry on its work and report back to him only when and if necessary. In line with that will, he discontinued many "arrangements" Profumi had set up during his pontificate, including even the time-honored practice of sending his private secretary to the State Council to "present the papal mind" in political-bureaucratic matters, and to monitor important sessions. In every respect, it was as if he intended to leave the smooth running of the vast machinery to the master mechanics, to the Roman Curia and Maestro Guido de la Valle. There were no surprises in Papa Angelica.

As the old year, redolent of Profumi's long reign of influence, drew toward its close, everyone looked forward to a quiet and uneventful time in which a fresh perspective could be formed and solid work could be done without undue interference from the papal office.

And so things might have continued just as everyone expected, had it not been for the private visitor Angelica received three days after his first Christmas as Pope.

Francesco Crasci was the Pontiff's personal physician; the two had known each other since childhood. A week or so before, His Holiness had complained of stomach pains and blood emissions. In the confidentiality of the papal apartment, Crasci had immediately run a battery of tests. Now, one glance at Crasci's face was enough for Angelica. "Operable or inoperable, Francesco?"

Crasci found it hard to look into Angelica's eyes.

"How long have I got, Francesco? Is it months?"

Crasci finally brought himself to say what had to be said. "I don't know, Holy Father. The carcinoma is inoperable. With treatment it may diminish or at least be arrested. Or . . ."

"Or it may not."

Crasci filled his lungs and nodded. "Your Holiness is correct." Tears stood in his eyes.

"Francesco, I must have a few years. There's something I have to do before God calls me home."

"He is calling you home now, Holy Father." The doctor's voice was thick with his emotion. "The cancer . . ."

"Listen, Francesco!" Angelica was a rock of gargantuan staying power, and his piety made him as stubborn as a mule; both of those qualities shone in him now. "You were always the same. Remember when we were children? When we were late for milking the cows in the evening because we'd been up to some devilment? You kept worrying, and blubbering tears as we ran home like two little hares."

Crasci had to smile at the memory.

"And," Angelica went on, "I kept telling you: Stop your blubbering, we have time! Remember?"

"Yes, Holy Father, I remember."

"Well, it's the same now. You're blubbering. And I'm telling you: Stop! We have time!"

"Yes, Holiness."

The Pontiff swore Francesco to secrecy, and had him show him the x-rays, the pictures of the gray slug in his belly that sooner or later was going to kill him.

When the doctor had gone, Angelica peered at those pictures again. "That's how I'm to go, then, Lord." He murmured a little prayer of petition. "Your will be done. But let me do what must be done here. Please, Lord."

From that moment, everything changed for Papa Giovanni Angelica. The one thing the conclave had asked him for was time. And time was the one thing he no longer had to give.

This Pontiff didn't pace the floor as Profumi had so often done, or lean on the sill of the window overlooking the piazza when he had great problems to work through. Instead, he sat in one of the big chairs in the study that had been redecorated in a comfortable style more to his liking. But his mind encompassed the problems of the same Church and the same world as Profumi's had.

In fact, the biggest error of judgment his contemporaries made about Papa Angelica was to confuse his piety with his mind; to assume that the way he thought was of a piece with the childlike simplicity they saw in his sermons and prayers and in his uncomplicated relationships with anybody and everybody he met on life's path. He had, after all, never been earmarked as an intellectual or as a scholar. As Ferragamo-Duca had said, from the time he became a seminarian at the age of twelve until he became Pope at eighty-two, Giovanni Angelica had been "a solid infantryman."

Nevertheless, the reality was that Angelica had a larger mind than most of his Roman contemporaries. It was not simple and childlike. It was highly complex and even ruseful. But it worked in categories that weren't drawn from a bookish education, a cultural heritage, or a scientific training of any sort. He had spent the best part of fifty years sharpening that mind as a Vatican diplomat in Europe, from Calais to the Bosporus, before, during, and after two world wars. He, like the race from which he sprang, had learned how to remain human while contending with nonhuman, even inhuman, forces. Like the cattle herders and dirt farmers of Domodossola, who evoked harvest promise from the sometimes bountiful, sometimes cruelly exacting nature around them, he had an immediate understanding of trust and hope tempered by self-reliance and wile. And like them, in life as well as in the presence of death, Angelica went forward with unshakable dignity.

The difference between Giovanni Angelica and his forebears was one of dimension. Life and divine providence had not confined him to the farmland of northwestern Italy. He had been exposed to the wide world. Unfailingly, he interpreted the men in that world, and the small and great events of their lives, with the same fundamental and somehow articulate power of intuition that allowed his seven brothers and his scores of cousins to read the skies and the earth.

Angelica's prime perception of his world at that moment was of a society of men and women in deep distress of spirit, simply because love lacked to them. Every decade that passed seemed to increase that lack. Their fears, their rages, their vicious little wars and sudden revolutions, their eternal divisiveness, were as much caused by that lack as they were the cause of it. The intellectuals had failed them, as had the aristocrats, the politicians, and the scientists.

"If I could create one moment," Angelica had said to Ducocasa only a day or two before, "in which all of them experienced lovingness, everything else would fall away like a leper's scales and scabs."

He had planned to spend his pontificate in the search for such a moment. That was his work as Pope, he felt; leave the other work to the Vatican bureaucrats. But even when he had thought to have some little time, he knew the odds he faced. The stark fact was that he was a religious leader. And the stark fact was that, in the modern world, institutional religion had no say at all in the ongoing life of nations.

His own Church, all the other churches—Judaism and its rabbinates, Islam and its holy places and its Muslim brotherhoods—all of them had been wrapped up in the cocoon of "optional matters," of things the great world could safely bypass, of essentially irrelevant things. In the councils of the world's greats, membership in a religion was as unimportant and by-the-way as the French prime minister's mistress, or a preference for the Surrealist school of painting.

Even as things had been before Crasci's bad news, Angelica expected to make only a bare beginning in his work, if even that. But now?

He looked toward the desk he used as Pope. It was a simpler one than Profumi had used. The x-ray still lay there, a dark blotch in the lamplight. He let his mind wander back over his conversation with Ducocasa. *"If I could create one moment in which all of them experienced lovingness . . ."*

"Well, Holiness"—he recalled the seemingly thoughtless answer Ducocasa gave as he bobbed about the study (he was rarely able to stay still for long)—"what we need, then, is for the good God in heaven to send his Spirit of love and show his face once more. Because what Your Holiness is talking about is a new Pentecost."

Of course! Angelica jumped up as quickly as his bulk would allow and stamped one elephantine foot in his excitement. That was it! A new Pentecost! God must show his face! And Angelica must create the opportunity!

"E pazz'!"

Not a single cardinal so much as turned a hair. For one thing, they knew their beloved Arnulfo; you can't expect a Neapolitan to suppress his emotions when a bombshell like Angelica's explodes without warning. And for another thing, all the cardinals were seated directly in front of the Holy Father.

Among the spectators at the right side of the main aisle, discipline held. Rico, seated with some of the Secretariat of State personnel—Youn, Thikas, Righi, Galinescu—felt that fresh shimmer of hope that Angelica had sparked in him before. Perhaps, as he had said so hopefully to Falconieri and Lanser and the Maestro, this Pope could resurrect holiness in the ancient Christian heartland. But he remained as still as everyone around him.

It was among the important non-Roman visitors to the left of the aisle that a little rustle of open excitement could be detected. Even the self-consciously solemn Mr. Richard Richards broke his grave demeanor and turned his head gracefully in order to exchange glances with Bishop Herbert Cale, the Ripley-Savages, and the others. Only Metropolitan Nikodim didn't budge. For the Alliance, the news could not be better. They hardly bothered to listen to the overall directive with which Angelica continued his bombshell announcement:

"All the ancient truths, in their truly Catholic and pristine integrity, are to be explained and reaffirmed by Our Council. . . ."

The Alliance had its own plans to make.

What Cardinal Arnulfo really thought about the condition of the Catholic Church was quite stark; and his thoughts were those of many of his equally well-informed colleagues: the structure of their Church was undergoing some profound and frightening strains. Like Angelica, they all had detected that drumming, beating impatience with the status quo in Latin America; they heard the ill-suppressed clamor of appeals for change, for adaptation, for reorganization, in the heartland of Europe. Angelica had translated all that unrest as a feeling of lovelessness.

Arnulfo, however, saw something else. As head of the Vatican's Holy Office, he was the official charged by oath to watch over the purity of belief and the observance of morality in the Church. Over the past ten years, his files had grown higher and thicker with dossiers chronicling the extraordinary increase of theological speculation and fresh interpretations of traditional morality. In Arnulfo's view, the Church in Europe was like a forest of bone-dry trees. The first touch of a hot spark could turn it into a conflagration. So perturbed was Arnulfo, in fact, that he said those very words to Angelica.

"Sì! Sí! Fa be'," Angelica had responded quietly. *"Ci vedremo noi, Eminenza."* That phrase was to become famous as Angelica's way of putting things off—or of laying them aside. "We'll look after it, Excellency. Don't worry."

For most of the rest of January, Arnulfo and the Vatican State Council stewed and fretted a good deal. To announce a general ecumenical council! To give every episcopal Tom, Dick, and Harry license to spout his distorted doctrines and give vent to his dissatisfaction with the Pope's Curia! In the Vatican and in public! Truly, it was madness! Surely, Papa Angelica was mad!

Some of the State Council, Arnulfo among them, calmed down considerably in late January when Papa Angelica actually formed a commission to prepare for the Ecumenical Council. Wily Angelica named Arnulfo to head the Preparatory Commission. And almost to a man, the Pontiff packed that commission with Arnulfo's men—the majority traditionalist and Roman—and an acceptable smattering of Roman conservatives. There were a few foreign cardinals, but all very traditionalist, and all close friends of Arnulfo. There were a few newcomers, such as Da Brescia; but in the total scheme of the commission, nothing to worry about.

Arnulfo felt suddenly less queasy. In fact, considering the uproar the papal announcement had caused, and considering the tacit mandate the Pontiff had given Arnulfo in the makeup of the commission, it might just be that Angelica would be willing to put the council off *sine die;* perhaps even forever. Of course, it would have to be done with care. With *romanità.*

Arnulfo called the Preparatory Commission together for its first meeting. Considering the vast amounts of work to be done, the materials to be assembled and distributed to all the bishops worldwide, collected again, collated and digested, 1966 was the absolutely earliest possible opening date for Angelica's Council. A complete report of that meeting was sent to Angelica. Roman republicanism was at work.

About three weeks later, when Arnulfo had begun to conclude that perhaps the Pope had renounced the idea of a Council, a sweetly worded message came down from the papal office.

The Holy Father had decided that, in view of the pressing problems facing the Church, the Ecumenical Council would begin on October 11, 1962. That was the feast day of the Virgin Mary's Motherhood. She would help His Eminence Cardinal Arnulfo, and all their other eminences, to make all necessary preparations in time for that date. "God made the world in six days," Angelica quipped in reverent Latin, "but the Preparatory Commission has over three years for their creation. Let there be light!"

The monarchic absolutism of the papacy was at work. And the stubborn will of Giovanni Angelica.

[27]

It must be admitted that for most of 1959 Papa Angelica's announcement of an Ecumenical Council evoked nothing better than pious and dutiful "amens" from the generality of the clergy, and nothing worse than private groans from a definite minority who complained about the "mind control" that would be exercised by the Roman Curia, and then rubber-stamped by the bishops in council. And, it must be admitted too, that very reaction was one of the things that helped to ease Cardinal Arnulfo's fears; that, and the overall papal directive, which the Northern Alliance had chosen to ignore: *"All the ancient truths, in their truly Catholic and pristine integrity, are to be explained and reaffirmed by Our Council."*

"In this climate," Arnulfo suggested to the co-chairmen of the Preparatory Commission, "which I must admit is much calmer than I expected; and with the backing of the Holy Father's overall directive to reaffirm all the ancient truths of our faith, this Council could be just what we have needed. If we are to reaffirm our beliefs, then by definition we must address and condemn the doubters, the tinkerers of our faith, the experimenters, and the theologasters!" Arnulfo's expansiveness was a measure of his newfound enthusiasm for Angelica's plan.

His three co-chairmen had other views. Cardinals Mangano, Lanser, and Cardinal Corelli had come to this early-morning meeting out of obedience and out of duty. Out of that same obedience and duty they would carry forward the enormous labor of preparing and managing the Council. But they could muster none of Arnulfo's optimism. Their view was one of simple realism: Papa Angelica was firm, and so there was no way out of the problem, as far as they could see. Lanser, always the supreme realist, said as much.

"Better wait until the soufflé rises, Eminence. Too many variables are involved."

"You're such a worrier, Cardinal Lanser! You should be a Neapolitan!" Arnulfo stuck to his guns. "We and the Preparatory Commission have all the means at our disposal to control the situation, and to carry out the Pontiff's wishes at the same time. The bishops of the Church are the most invariable of invariables. They won't gang up on the Pope's Curia any more than they will have a new idea! In fact, whatever ideas they have will be thoroughly incorporated beforehand into the daily Council agenda. When they see that, we will have a stampede of *placets* for our traditional beliefs."

Arnulfo was not being simplistic; Lanser and the others understood that. His obedience to Papa Angelica stemmed from his belief in the sacrosanct character of papal authority. His concern for control of the Council, if Council there must be, stemmed from his sincere concern for integrity of Church doctrine. Without those two things, the Church would cease to be its true self. With that wily instinct of his, Angelica had chosen well in appointing Arnulfo. He was the perfect man to create the occasion of spiritual renewal the Pontiff hoped for, and at the same time to protect doctrinal purity.

That meeting of the four cardinal co-chairmen of the Preparatory Commission of the Second Ecumenical Vatican Council marked the start of two and a half years of the most complex and rigorous labor the Vatican had seen since the establishment of the Work of St. Raphael during World War II.

The belief, the hope, and the dream of Papa Angelica was that through his Council a fresh Pentecost would be realized; that it would attract the special blessing of God and become the occasion of an outpouring of light and love and unity and peace and strength so great as to penetrate the hard rind of bitterness and hatred that divided the world—religious and secular—into warring camps. He wanted his Council to speak to the entire universe of men and women the world over—Catholics and non-Catholics, Christians and non-Christians, believers and atheists—so that they would pause to look on the transfigured face of the Catholic Church with a newly inspired realization that hers was the open visage of Christ's salvation.

Accordingly, His Holiness laid down several conditions for Cardinal Arnulfo and the Preparatory Commission.

His Council, he said, was to be plenary. It must be composed of a majority—and if possible, of all—of the 2,500 bishops resident in dioceses throughout the world. All would sit together as one great body in St. Peter's Basilica and carry on their divinely inspired discussion, face to face with each other and the world. And, Angelica said, the bishops were not only to participate in the Council by their very physical presences and cooperation in Rome; he insisted that they were, every one of them, to participate as well in preparing the *Schemata* that would be promulgated by the Council as the expression of the ancient doctrine of the Church, cast in shining terms that the modern world would understand.

Furthermore, Angelica directed, each one of the *Schema* was to express Church doctrine vis-à-vis the world at large. All the *Schemata,* together and individually, were to open the Church—its beliefs and practices and its relation to society and individuals—so that the world itself could understand it freshly and in terms that would be meaningful and transforming.

Finally, and the Pontiff was firm, if the full realization of his dream was to flower, every effort must be made to have at his Council observers from every religion. Not only Orthodox and Protestant Christians but Jews, Muslims, Buddhists—the full religious panoply of the world; and observers from the secular governments of the world, as well.

The first order of business for Cardinal Arnulfo and the twenty-four cardinals who made up the Pope's Preparatory Commission, then, was to produce that series of texts, officially called *Schemata,* each one of which would deal with a particular aspect of Catholicism in the contemporary world of the midcentury.

There would be one *Schema,* for example, on the papacy—"the Pope and the World," it was to be called—which would reaffirm the position of the Pope in relation to the world, and open that position out so that all could understand it. The *Schema* entitled "The Church and the World" would explain the Church's attitude to the society of men and women: what claims the Church made on them, and the confines of those claims; what help and cooperation the Church had to offer its contemporaries; and what the Church feared in the world of today. "Christianity and the World" would open for general understanding the meaning of the practices of faith—prayer, the Mass, fasting, and liturgy. "Christians and the World" would deal with social questions. And so on, for "Mary and the World," "Christianity and Other Religions of the World," and *Schemata* dealing with the priestly role, the role of religious orders of men and women, marriage and human sexuality, and the other main aspects of Catholic theology and moral teaching.

Once the general subjects were set, the Preparatory Commission divided each one into themes, and divided itself into committees. "The Church and the World," for example, was divided into twenty-four themes. Each theme was given to the care of a commission cardinal, who, with his own committee of theologians—Roman and non-Roman—would draw up a basic text about that theme. If necessary, as it often was, the committees would form subcommittees to take on separate parts of the themes.

Of course, this entire process had at its disposal the resources of universities, monasteries, scholars, students, and researchers situated in Rome. In addition, Rome could always dispose of enough secretarial manpower to establish, if necessary, twenty-four hour shifts every day and every night of each week for the full two and a half years of work.

All the partial texts of each theme of each *Schema* thus prepared and produced by this multilayered system would finally be assembled by the commission cardinals, always aided by their theological experts, into one whole text. The full text of each *Schema* was then to be read, discussed, and voted on by the full Preparatory Commission.

In any "normal" council, that would have been all the preparation needed. But because of Papa Angelica's directives, a copy of the completed text of each *Schema,* once approved by Angelica himself, was then mailed out to each one of the 2,500 bishops for comment. Each of those bishops would assemble his own committee of theological experts and, with their advice and counsel, return his copy of each *Schema* annotated with suggested changes and modifications. All of those annotated copies would then have to be collated by another cardinalitial committee, working again through the same layered system.

The end result of this remarkably complex and efficient labor would be the quasi-definitive text of each *Schema,* incorporating the main changes and views of the majority of bishops worldwide, and carrying as footnotes the more important of the suggestions that had not been adopted as part of the text.

It was by this paper-strewn path, peopled with an army of cardinals, bishops, theologians, librarians, archivists, historians, stenographers, typists, helpers, and printers, that each of the *Schemata* made its way into final form to be ready for presentation to the Council when it opened on October 11, 1962.

Because the system was so entirely accessible to the bishops of the Church, and because they would all and each have such an important input into the text of the *Schemata,* it was envisioned that the Council, once in actual session in Rome, would progress quickly and without strife to its desired end. In Angelica's vision, his bishops, when gathered together in the sight of the world, would receive the necessary light from on high; they would develop among them a scintillating expression of Christ's loving salvation that would once more tell the world that victory over sin, over poverty, over discord, over death, was won by the Cross and the death and the resurrection of Jesus. All—the bishops and observers—would take that light back home with them, where it would pulsate outward ever farther in new waves of divinely inspired love. A worldwide Pentecost!

In that vision, that dream and hope, Angelica trusted everybody—people, bishops, cardinals, the Holy Spirit, Christ, God the Father.

By 1961, the Preparatory Commission was well into its work of sustained communication with bishops and institutions in every corner of the world. The cardinal co-chairmen as well as the committee heads were traveling widely to conduct interviews; they were receiving endless streams of visiting bishops; they were corresponding constantly, sending questionnaires and *Schema* drafts for comment. They were weighing all the feedback carefully with their staffs of theologians and their cardinal peers.

Under the commission's unflagging and able effort, the *Schemata* were taking shape, and the Council agenda was beginning to look manageable.

In all the hubbub of the preparatory process—the only process in his Vatican that Papa Angelica monitored on a daily basis—it was Cardinal Joachim Lanser who seemed to stand out for the Pontiff. In the cardinal's reports as well as in private meetings with the Pope, Lanser seemed to wear his learning and experience as well as his cardinalate and his personal prestige lightly. His judgment seemed unfailing. He showed a mind that was cool, widely informed, passionless yet compassionate, subtle and perceptive, yet reliant on simple, honest faith. His humor was often as earthy as Angelica's and never scurrilous.

It was not surprising, then, that the moment Papa Angelica decided that he would have to take extraordinary steps to involve non-Catholics in his Council in a serious way, he called for Cardinal Lanser's dossier. One reading of it confirmed the Pope in his opinion.

Joachim Lanser had come from a family of peasants in the village of Grindlsbach on the edge of the Black Forest in Bavaria. Before he was forty, he had made his name as a biblical scholar and theologian in Germany. He had been in the service of Eugenio Profumi since 1929 and, in the Roman expression, wore more coats that any other single living cleric, high or low. He was an important member of every Vatican congregation, tribunal, and committee that mattered. Except for Arnulfo, he was the ultimate recourse in matters of doctrine. He was a mine of information about everything going on in Rome and the Church. He had had the ear of Profumi whenever he liked—"and no wonder," Angelica murmured to himself as he read on through the pages of the dossier. In Roman parlance, the cardinal was *venerandus*—a man revered by his colleagues, friend and foe.

There was one important bit of information revealed in the dossier that Angelica had never known. Few people did. When Profumi had been secretary of state, he had sent Father Lanser on a secret assignment, traveling the Soviet Union from its borders with Poland over to Vladivostok on the Sea of Japan, and from Archangel to the Dardanelles. After thirty-two months with no outside communication, Lanser had somehow emerged in Hong Kong and had returned via Singapore, India, and the Suez Canal. If Roman Catholic bishops functioned through the long night of Stalin's hell in the thirties, forties, and fifties, it was largely due to Lanser's discreet and effective implementation of Profumi's commission to him.

"Perfect!" Angelica sealed the decision aloud to himself, snapping the dossier closed. "He's above reproach as far as the Curial traditionalists are concerned. He's sound in every respect. He has languages and presence. He knows the Vatican and the Church. Perfect!"

As in everything to do with his Council, once Papa Angelica's mind was set, he moved ahead as though he were in some sort of race. No one could understand it; but there it was. Within a half hour of his reading of Lanser's dossier, he had the cardinal in his study.

The Pope's commission was typically simple and brief. The Pontiff had ideas, but he had little detailed notion of how they were to be implemented; that was for others.

"Your Eminence." Angelica leaned forward in his favorite chair. "I want my council to be a new beginning of love among Christians. All Christians. How, I have asked myself, are we going to love each other if we do not even see each other, much less speak to each other? Shall I tell you, *figluolo?*" Angelica generally used each visitor's proper title once, but after that single gesture to protocol, everyone from cardinal to cobbler was "little son."

"Sì, Santità." Lanser did not expect to be happy with what was coming.

"You will go out and build bridges to our separated brethren. You will create a climate in which we do see each other and speak to each other. They must have some participation in Our Council, or we will all remain congealed in the ice of our separation.

"Now you'd best be off. You have little time to effect all that."

As Lanser kissed the Fisherman's Ring and left the papal study, Angelica was not quite smiling, except with his eyes.

"Little time" was the mildest of papal understatements. The Council was to open in scarcely more than a year. Building those bridges would mean adding a superhuman load to the heavy work Lanser already carried. But that was the least of the matter. What bothered the cardinal far more was a suddenly insistent memory. More than a year ago, the Maestro had somehow got hold of a tape of one private meeting of the Northern Alliance. He had played that tape for the full State Council, and Lanser had asked him for a written transcript.

He headed immediately for his own offices. As cardinal, he had moved to the Belvedere Court, near the Maestro's office and across from the Apostolic Palace. Though larger, his quarters were still as bare as any Jesuit's cell.

As soon as he entered, he sent his assistant scurrying through the files for that old transcript.

Lanser was never impatient with weakness of the flesh or honest errors of judgment. But the foolishness of stupid people made him angry. As he paged with mounting temper through the Alliance transcript, he was reminded that their entire meeting had been nothing better than mindless blather, revealing only that the Alliance members had no clear idea of how to turn Papa Angelica's plans for a new openness in his Church to their own advantage. Yet one statement made by Annibale Sugnini had stuck in Lanser's mind like a poisoned barb. Ah! Yes! There it was: ". . . and we must create such a wave of intra-Catholic interest in ecumenism that the Pope must accept it, must incorporate it into his council plans. That's the fatal wedge in the door. . . ."

Had they done it, then? Lanser wondered. He had warned the State Council at the time that this Northern Alliance might yet force Angelica's hand. But the Maestro and the others had disagreed. The Alliance was nothing more than a tasteless joke, they had said; pygmies attacking with bows and arrows. The Church had survived far worse in every one of its nearly twenty centuries of existence. By comparison, the Northern Alliance wasn't even a pinprick.

Lanser hadn't been so sure then, and he felt he had reason to be more worried now. He decided to discuss the matter at once with Cardinal Arnulfo as head of the Preparatory Commission.

Arnulfo listened gravely as Lanser recounted Angelica's commission to him. He reread the Alliance transcript, and remembered well hearing the tape. "And you think they've somehow got to Papa Angelica?" Arnulfo made the point for Lanser. "But how? And who?"

"I don't know." Lanser was frank. "Sugnini wouldn't be the man to have done it. It may be Angelica's own idea. He's so obviously genuine in his concern. And he is right about the distance between the Christian churches; he's right about the suffering it causes. I've seen for myself how the churches in Eastern countries have been forced by their suffering to draw together in a way we've never achieved in the West. It's true it's not produced heresy there. But this isn't the East. . . ."

Arnulfo was confident Lanser was worrying needlessly. The *Schemata* would be all-encompassing and soundly based on doctrine. The very machinery the Holy Father had required for the Ecumenical Council would be its greatest protection from heretical influences. "There will be no opening for wedges"—the cardinal smiled—"whatever Sugnini might think.

"Besides, look at it realistically. We've all learned to our surprise that this Pope, who continually charms so many with his openness, has turned out to be far more monarchic, absolutist, and stubborn than Papa Profumi ever thought of being."

That was true, Lanser agreed. "Especially when it comes to his Council."

"Precisely." Arnulfo pursued his point. "So if Papa Angelica has decided to . . . what was that phrase?"

" 'Build bridges to our separated brethren,' Eminence."

"Yes. If he's decided to build bridges, we know from experience that nothing is going to stop him from doing just that. It seems best, then, to have it done by one of our own. Someone who can keep things under control."

The members and associates of the Northern Alliance reacted to Papa Angelica's announcement of an Ecumenical Council like men waking up from sleep, rubbing their eyes, unable to believe what they saw.

All they had originally hoped to do was help make a liberal-minded cardinal pope, in the vague expectation that such a change might possibly lead them to some way of getting at the very fountainhead of Romanism. As it had turned out, they hadn't helped make Angelica pope at all. He was a gift! He was liberal. And, to boot, he had declared what amounted in their eyes to open season on the exclusive privilege and absolute authority of the Roman papacy.

At first, of course, they had little idea of how to proceed, how to take advantage of this miraculous opportunity. Except for one or two visits to Rome, and what they thought were discreet meetings with Sugnini and Da Brescia, their activity in 1959 had been chiefly focused on certain Catholic centers in France, Holland, Germany, and the United States. Uninformed observers noticed, but could not interpret properly, a sudden wave of interest and enthusiasm for ecumenism—a swelling in the numbers of magazine articles, news reports, books, conventions, congresses, conversations, and public discussions, all centered on the getting together of formerly warring sects of Christians. Ever so slowly, the terms "ecumenism" and "ecumenical" became prime buzz words that elevated their users and practitioners to the ranks of the truly forward-looking men and women of the world.

Though the Alliance's effort was somewhat helter-skelter, the objective was not. They aimed to secure papal interest in ecumenism. But that was a tall order, and by and large, both the word and the fact remained alien to most Catholics, who had always thought of it as a Protestant gambit to corrupt the One, True Church.

Nevertheless, because Angelica was so open and unprejudiced, and because he genuinely expected his Council to be the occasion of an event of supernatural origin and importance that would touch everyone, the Northern Alliance was convinced that, with diligence, they would find an opening. They would not be excluded from the vast welcome Angelica had announced at St. Paul's Basilica in Rome. Surely, then, it would at last be possible to accomplish a voluntary liquidation of what Profumi had called his "Roman fact." At last, it would be possible to de-Catholicize the Catholic Church in the name of a universalism as ancient as Gautama Buddha and as new as Maharishi Mahesh Yogi, but alien to what Papa Angelica had inherited from the 263 popes who had preceded him. That very hope had a near magical effect in redoubling and galvanizing the determination of the Alliance.

It was only in 1961, however, after two years of searching and effort, that Mr. Richard Richards realized that they had all been going about it the wrong way.

"It's totally backwards," he announced at a key Alliance planning meeting early that year. "We have been going about this whole affair as though we want and expect another Reformation in the style of Luther."

"Yes, indeed!" Canon Ripley-Savage would stand for no backsliding. "That is exactly what we want. Another Reformation. And a successful one, too!"

Richards calmed the Canon, and explained his view of the way Luther and the other reformers had revolted. "They left the Church." He underlined the point. "But with all the damage done to it, that Church went ahead, more centralized, more Romanized, more deeply rooted in the Roman fact than ever. And over a period of four hundred years, it beat us at our own game.

"No, my friends. There isn't going to be another Reformation. I want you to listen to me carefully, all of you." Richards proceeded to explain in great detail what the new game was to be.

As they all knew, through the kindness of Archbishop Levesque, the Alliance regularly received copies from the first printings of the *Schemata* that would form the basis and the machinery for Angelica's Council. Until now, Richards had not seen clearly how to use them.

"You can't use them." Ripley-Savage interrupted Richards. "It will be a rubber-stamp operation all the way. The bishops are practically supine. There's no way to change that."

"And anyway"—Muffie offered one of her incomparable images—"those *Schemata* are as dry as bones marinated in Romanism. Who can even get through them all?"

On the contrary, Richards suggested in a tone that was a shade more superior than usual; their job now was to study the *Schemata,* "dry and rigid as they are." He nodded toward Muffie. They would discuss them privately with as many Catholic theologians and bishops as were friendly enough. Right through those discussions, they would sow only one seed: fear. Fear that such rigid traditionalism in the Catholic Church's bishops would merely repel their non-Catholic brethren; would not serve the good Papa Angelica's loving purpose of reunion with all the separated brethren; would, finally, not be intelligible for the billions of non-Christians. For wasn't that the Pontiff's very aim: to open doors and windows, not install a new set of impenetrable shutters?

"Remember." Richards was practically issuing instructions now. "Each bishop coming to the Council will bring at least one personal theologian, his *peritus,* his expert. We must have as many bishops and *periti* as possible in our pocket.

"If we work well with our friends inside the Roman Church, this Council can be a gigantic fulcrum with which we can hoist Romanism and its *romanità* out of the womb of Christ's Church and leave it behind us at last."

Bishop Cale and Metropolitan Nikodim were dubious. Nikodim spoke from experience: "I agree that to change Rome, we have to work from within the Roman Church. Otherwise, as you say, we will end up with a repeat of the Reformation. But the number of friends we have, the number who will help us to the degree you describe, is not enough to serve as a fulcrum in a Council of 2,500 bishops!"

"True," Richards admitted. But he had saved the best news until last—the very news that had made this plan click into place in his mind. "The good Papa Angelica has appointed a cardinal to talk ecumenically and officially to non-Catholics. Joachim Cardinal Lanser, by name. The doors to Rome are about to open wider, my friends!"

It took a moment for this information to sink in around the table. But as it did, smiles appeared and heads nodded in a predawn of understanding. The fulcrum! The thing might just be possible after all!

Cardinal Lanser's impact was immeasurable. He was the perfect emissary of ecumenism for the papacy. By the autumn of 1961, he had papal approval for a new Vatican secretariat—the Secretariat for Christian Unity—and was already launched on a series of wide-ranging travels across Western Europe, the United States, and Canada, parleying with churchmen of the major Christian denominations, presiding over ecumenical gatherings where Catholics and Protestants discussed their mutual differences. In whatever free time he had, he was constantly dictating articles, letters, and a whole series of pamphlets. His basic message was clear and impressive. "I am neither an optimist nor a pessimist in this matter of our lost unity as Christians," he said many times, in one way or another. "I am a realist. And the first step into reality, for me, is for all of us to learn once more how to love each other. Already, we all know about mutual hate and discrimination. Let us turn now to love and to justice."

Wherever he went, a certain comity and civility entered relations between Catholic and Protestant bishops and theologians. Behind him, of course, there stood a force of tremendous support: Papa Angelica and the official Roman Church. But Lanser himself—like so many of the Curia, largely unknown to the world until now—revealed a remarkable force of personality; like a butterfly suddenly come out of its cocoon. He found himself invited as honored speaker even to major universities that normally would have shunned a papal emissary. Doors opened for him everywhere, as if by magic.

Gradually the *Schemata,* arriving everywhere regularly from Rome, came to be read by the Catholic bishops in the light of this new element. And gradually, too, in that heady atmosphere, there began to appear important articles and books by internationally established Catholic theologians—a Hans Kleiser in Tübingen, Germany; a Jean Ormais in France; a James Courtland Molloy in the United States. All of them stressed the need for Catholic bishops to act as genuine apostles and co-workers of Peter the Apostle, to be active and articulate participants in Vatican life.

Lanser read as much of this new material as he could. Some of it aroused his suspicions, but he could find no heresy in what he read. And after all, he, too, had sometimes thought it would be a good idea for some of the bishops to get out of their chairs or off the golf course and start being real bishops.

Nevertheless, the cardinal was not altogether relaxed about things. He relied on Guido to provide him with whatever continuing information he could concerning the Alliance. The result was that Lanser began to learn, sometimes well beforehand, what would take place at this meeting or that conference, or what advice a particular *peritus* was giving his bishop. In those situations—there were rather more than he expected—he applied himself with some success to "correcting a certain pattern of erroneous expectations" that seemed to be recurring around the world.

But despite his efforts, and according as the ecumenical helter-skelter increased among the bishops, clergy, and nuns of the free world, Lanser expressed his continuing apprehension more often to the Council of State. "Too many people I meet seem to expect unity of all the churches to pop out of the Pope's Council like a cup of espresso from a machine! Some even talk of the Holy Father surrendering large areas of his papal authority. I tell you, there are dangerous illusions and impossible expectations seeping in, not only among Protestants but among our own people!"

In time, the other members of the State Council were forced to agree. The constant burrowing into the hinterland of Catholicism by the efforts of the Alliance was having its effect; was creating "dangerous illusions and impossible expectations," as Lanser put it.

"But, Your Eminence," Arnulfo would respond, "we have firm control of the actual Vatican Council itself. Nothing can happen that we do not want to happen."

"Magari!" Lanser sighed more than once, responding in street Italian that made the others laugh. "Would to God! But . . ."

There were yet other bridges that Papa Angelica was intent on building; and his time was growing shorter. In truly papal fashion, he set more and more builders to work. The brief summer of this angel had begun at precisely the chilling height of the cold war. Not only were Catholics and the approximately 2,500 warring Christian sects frozen in their distance from each other—and each of them from Jew, Muslim, Hindu, Buddhist, Marxist, and atheist—but the political superpowers were equally frozen in a stance that could tear the world in two.

Angelica's intuition told him that far beneath all that fixedness, that black-and-white monotony of discord, there was an ever-beating and growingly insistent desire to be free of it all, to see "a new Heaven and a new Earth." His hope was to fling open that very vista for everyone. Not only for the avowedly and truly religious, but for everyone.

"Ah, Excellency!" Papa Angelica welcomed Rico Lansing with the naturalness and warmth that had long since won the American to him. "Please, please, *figluolo."* The Pontiff waved Rico to a chair, and sat down himself with a wince. *"Santa Maria,* but my feet hurt! Carboni made me a wide ten, and it still hurts!"

Rico had to smile; Telesforo Carboni, the papal cobbler, was notorious for scrimping on shoe leather. He made a mental note to ask Benfatti to solve that little problem for the Pope.

"Well." The Pontiff settled forward in his chair as he so often did. "I didn't call you here to discuss my shoes!"

"No, Holiness."

"Most of my beloved flock still think that my Council is just another intra-Catholic event. But it is not, little son. We are aiming at a human event." Angelica inclined his head, as if listening for an accustomed sound he knew would be there. "If you cock an ear in the right direction, you will hear the voice of all poor humanity. Listen to it! They want relief. They want peace. Salvation. Hope. At least, hope!

"So." He pushed himself back onto his pained feet and waddled to his desk. He brought back two sealed envelopes and sat down, this time beside Lansing. "So," he said again, "we need Russians and Greeks.

"There is a letter for Patriarch Pimen of Moscow"—he handed one envelope to Rico—"and here is one for my good friend Athenagoras, Patriarch of Constantinople. Have you ever met Athenagoras, *figlio?* No? Well, you are going to meet a great man! And you will know it!"

The papal commission to Lansing was typically straightforward. Both Pimen and Athenagoras had already communicated their wish to send observers to Angelica's Council. The Pontiff had not thought it possible to get the Russians, until Cardinal Da Brescia had taken a hand in the matter. Rico was to go and see each man, Pimen and Athenagoras, privately and alone if possible. He was to deliver each letter personally, without making any commentary or suggestion to either of them. He was a messenger. He should expect to bring back official confirmation that both had secured assurance from their governments that observers would be allowed out of their respective countries. "And that is all, Monsignore."

Angelica sat back a little awkwardly. Like a man in some pain, Rico thought fleetingly; and not just from shoes that pinch. But he said nothing.

"I am told you deal well with foreign clergy, *figlio,* even in unfriendly places."

"I do what I can, Holy Father." Like Guido de la Valle, Rico Lansing was never certain how much Papa Angelica knew. There was no way to tell if that was an open reference to his Hearts Apostolate travels, or a veiled reference to his covert work.

"That is all anyone can do, little son. Have a safe journey."

28

Guido de la Valle felt a hand slipping quietly beneath his pillow and toward his neck. He tensed his muscles and the hand withdrew. He opened his eyes. The sun was just up, streaming at a slant through his northeast window. Nothing in the room was disturbed, but the door was slightly ajar. He sat up quietly, still on the alert, certain that he was not alone.

"Happy birthday, Nanno!" A shrill little voice rang out from beneath his bed. "Happy birthday!" Eugenio popped his head up, joyful, mischievous and totally triumphant. "You were asleep, Nanno! You didn't see me!" Without giving his granduncle time to catch his breath, he flung himself into Guido's arms and threw the pillow aside to reveal his surprise: a little box lay there in its gilt wrapping paper. "It's special, Nanno!"

Guido laughed in simple delight. "I know it is!"

"Really! Mama and I bought it for you at Gianfranco's. I paid for it from my box."

By that time, Guido was holding up a truly handsome linen kerchief with one hand, and hugging Eugenio with the other. "It's the best present I can ever remember!" He meant every word. This child was the heart of the Maestro's life; and the feeling was mutual.

Through the open door, the two heard the boy's name being called in an early-morning stage whisper.

"Eugenio! Come here immediately!"

It was Keti, not wanting to wake the whole house, but still trying her best to sound imperious and annoyed.

"Shsh!" Guido hushed the boy. He slipped on bathrobe and slippers. Eugenio looked a little apprehensive at his mother's stern half-whisper.

"Chin up, de la Valle," Guido encouraged him. "Let's face this together."

Eugenio took his granduncle's hand in brave and total trust, and marched by his side through the door to confront this summary danger.

"Eugenio!" Keti was striding down the corridor, her eyes sternly on her son. "I told you never to enter Uncle Guido's rooms unless he invited you!"

"Madame!" Guido seemed about to make a most serious speech. "These two de la Valle men want you to know that if they decide to have an early-morning conference, they expect their women to understand!"

Keti looked at the Maestro with his ruffled gray hair and total seriousness of expression, and then down at Eugenio's unflinching but apprehensive gaze. It was too much. She couldn't keep a straight face, much less be angry. She and Guido broke into laughter; and Eugenio, relieved that he would not get a spanking, rushed into his mother's arms and began telling all about how he had surprised his uncle Guido.

"He loved his handkerchief, Mama!"

Keti beamed at Guido and kissed him. "Happy birthday! I hope you didn't intend to sleep later than usual! I'm sure with all this ruckus Helmut must be awake. I know Agathi is up already. Suppose I ask Mariella to prepare a birthday celebration breakfast."

"Right!" Guido agreed. "I'll dress and be ready in half an hour! I plan to wear my new kerchief today, right in my breast pocket."

Eugenio was obviously proud. "Uncle Guido?"

The Maestro turned back from his door.

"Are you very old?"

"Sometimes." Guido nodded in all seriousness. "Sometimes I am."

"Then I'm going to be old too!" The lad was all determination. "I'll be five this year. Is that old?"

"Very old," Keti said with a swat to his small behind. "Now off with you!"

Eugenio Guido de la Valle was by natural disposition a happy and confident child. He seemed to love everyone in the household at Villa Cerulea—except Sagastume, who still frightened him—and it was impossible not to love the boy in return. He adored his mother and father; Agathi was wonderful with him, almost like a second mother. But the bond between Guido and Eugenio had always been special. There seemed to be some current that flowed between the two of them.

When Guido was not traveling, he spent time with his grandnephew every day, walking with him in the gardens, contriving ever-new stories to tell and games to play. When the Maestro had to be away, as was so frequently the case, Eugenio counted the days until he would come home again. He would listen for the special signal Guido would have Sagastume make on the car horn as they rode up the long curved drive to Villa Cerulea; and when at last he heard it, he would run to welcome his granduncle back, those incomparable de la Valle eyes that he had inherited sparkling with a child's open excitement and delight.

As he grew, Eugenio became interested in everything. Following Guido's lead, he began to make up his own games with numbers or letters or words, and invent his own stories to tell. To his wonderment, Sphinx Di Lorio showed him how to do some magic tricks. Regice Bernardo brought him records of children's music. His uncle Rico was a special favorite; he was an American like his mother, and knew all about cowboys and Indians.

Helmut and Keti took their son to a soccer game in Rome once, and he instantly decided he wanted to be a soccer champion. Nothing would do but for Helmut to buy him a soccer ball. Eugenio practiced with it for hours at a time, careening it off his little legs, up to his head, and into Agathi's rose garden more often than not, until he could make it do almost anything. Of course, he also wanted to be a pilot and a train engineer and a fireman. He told Rico, though, that it wasn't practical to want to be a cowboy. He went with his mother and father, Guido and Agathi for a private audience with Papa Angelica; like everyone else, Eugenio fell in love with the loving, comical old man, and for a while he wanted to be pope, until he found out that he wouldn't be able to live with his parents and his Nanno and Nanna at Villa Cerulea.

This year he had started classes at the *scuola* in Rome, where he was taught by the very efficient Sisters of Don Bosco. Helmut would usually drive his son to school in the morning. Sometimes, though, Guido would ride him to the city. Eugenio would ignore Sagastume at the wheel, comfortable in his granduncle Guido's protection, chatting away during the ride, and feeling very much the important man as he clambered out of the limousine in front of the *scuola.* Keti and Agathi would pick him up in the afternoon and hear all his latest tales and adventures with his new friends in the new world that school was for him.

The "birthday breakfast" that day was a special treat. It wasn't often that the whole family gathered for the morning meal. The conversation was mostly about the little informal dinner party Agathi and Keti had arranged for that evening. The Sphinx would be there, they told him, along with Cardinals Ferragamo-Duca and Falconieri. Regice Bernardo was a little under the weather, Agathi said, but Luigi Garganelli and Cardinal Lanser would be coming.

"I hope you've kept it small." Guido patted the kerchief folded nattily into the breast pocket of his dark suit, and winked at a very pleased Eugenio.

"Very small, darling." Agathi knew her brother was not fond of birthdays. "Only a dozen, including ourselves."

"Will Uncle Rico be here, Nanna?" Eugenio had his own ideas about parties and guest lists. "He promised we'll play Indians next time he comes!"

"No." Helmut ruffled his son's hair affectionately. "Uncle Rico has gone to Russia for the Holy Father."

Eugenio considered that for a minute, not sure just where Russia might be. "Do they have Indians there?"

Grigori Golovin, publicly known as His All-Holiness Pimen, was Patriarch of All the Russias, claimant titular Head of all Eastern Orthodox Churches, Metropolitan of Moscow, ex officio paid employee of the government of the U.S.S.R., ex officio colonel in the Soviet State Security Police, the KGB. His patriarchate was not tucked away in some onion-domed basilica, but was one among thousands of identical offices in the Moscow complex of government buildings.

He was seventy-three years old, bespectacled, gray-bearded, bald. He sat at his desk, reading Papa Angelica's letter for the third time, as though Rico Lansing were not even there.

Slowly and at last, as if he were meditating deeply upon holy matters, Pimen folded the letter and looked over the steel rims of his spectacles at the young bishop. Still he said nothing.

Finally, his beard bobbing against his black robes in a way Rico found comical, he spoke.

"Do you realize, Excellency, where you have now penetrated? This is the Patriarchate of All the Russias."

Rico couldn't make out the reason for such a remark. He was, however, only a messenger on this trip, and waited in silence for Pimen to go on.

"Now, my answer to Papa Angelica: Yes. We will participate in his Council by sending two observers. Clerics of high rank. But on two conditions.

"First, that His Holiness the Patriarch of Constantinople will not attend himself or send observers."

Immediately, Rico understood the meaning of Pimen's opening remark. He was after ecclesiastical primacy; tacit but public recognition by Rome that he, Pimen, was sole head of Eastern Christian Orthodoxy. He would not share his triumph, or have it clouded, by the presence of Athenagoras or his minions.

"Second," Pimen continued without pause, "Papa Angelica must undertake solemnly that his Council will issue no attack or condemnation against Soviet Marxism, or Marxism in general."

Rico's mind was spinning. The first condition was bad enough; the second leg of his journey, after all, was precisely to see Athenagoras. But this last condition would mean that Angelica would have to break with every pope since the middle of the last century, each of whom had specifically and unswervingly condemned Marxism. Angelica could never agree.

"That is all, Excellency." Pimen pressed a button on his desk; a security guard, automatic weapon strapped to his side, immediately entered from the outer office. Pimen exchanged a few words in Russian with the guard, who then escorted Lansing out.

In one of the downstairs corridors, Rico heard his name called, and turned to see the full, round blue eyes and cherubic face of Metropolitan Nikodim.

"So, my dear Bishop." Butter would not melt in the Russian's mouth. "You have finally made it all the way to Moscow, have you?" He smiled beneath his conical hat; but now, as on the few previous occasions when they had met in Rome, he reminded Rico of a bloodhound sniffing the air.

"Just leaving, in fact." Rico turned and left the building.

When Lansing arrived in Constantinople two days later, he went straight to the Apostolic Delegation to speak with Monsignore Rafael Sanzio. He needed to send an urgent radio message to Rome. He had to let Papa Angelica know Pimen's message. Should he see the Greek patriarch, or come back to base?

Rico waited four tedious days for Rome's reply. He was certain Angelica would not capitulate. Obviously, Pimen had been told what to say. The Soviets brooked no rivals even in the skeletal religion they tolerated. They considered Moscow as the Third Rome. But it was all too transparent, too cynical.

Finally, when the reply came through, Rico had to read it twice to believe it. He was to destroy the envelope originally destined for the Greek patriarch. He was still to see Athenagoras, however, and explain as best he could that the Holy Father had no choice in the circumstances except to withdraw his invitation to the Patriarch of Constantinople. Lansing was also to give a short verbal message from Papa Angelica to his Greek brother.

"Cold comfort, that!" Rico was furious. For the first time in the nearly three years since the conclave had made Angelica its choice, he began to examine the wisdom of papal policy. Openness was fine; but this was unjust. And it was Pandora's box the Pontiff was tinkering with.

Still, Lansing knew he had no choice. This was not a Hearts Apostolate mission; he was not the decisionmaker in this situation. He was a messenger for his Pope.

The dingy office of the Greek Orthodox Patriarchate at Phanar in the suburbs of Constantinople was a shanty. The worn carpet, the cheap furniture, the bare walls, the surly guards, all bespoke penury and isolation enforced by the hostile Turkish government. But neither the drabness of the hovel that was his prison, nor even the splendors of the nearby Golden Horn, diminished the princely grandeur of Athenagoras. Angelica had said Lansing would know he had met greatness when he laid eyes on this man; it was true.

At eighty-two, this highest of Greek prelates was fully a head taller than the American bishop. His large black eyes were penetrating, but gracious in aspect beneath long lashes. His nose was aquiline, with delicate nostrils above a full-lipped mouth. His hands were as expressive as his speech.

"Monsignore, welcome!" He spoke French with the unmistakable accent of the Mediterranean lingua franca. "Please do us the honor of sitting down."

He turned with such unquestionable imperiousness and command to the two Turkish guards who had insisted on accompanying Rico that, though no word was spoken, they backed out of the room under his stare, suspicion in their own eyes.

Never had Rico met a man so physically impressive, but in whom spirit so clearly invested his whole body. He felt a marvelous ease with this man, imposing though he was. It became less difficult than he had expected to find the right words to explain Angelica's dilemma: Moscow and the Soviet Union had been so totally impenetrable until now. Shouldn't they seize this chance to have even two of their number come to fraternize with other Christians?

"Is that all, Excellency?" It was not a challenge; more an expectation that Angelica, whom he had known so well and for so long, would not send him so stark a communication in so barren a manner.

"No, Holiness." Rico apologized for his stupidity in not thinking to give the Father's personal greeting sooner in the interview.

Athenagoras waved his hand gracefully, as if to banish any need for apology, and Lansing went on.

"Papa Angelica asked me to say this: 'No amount of evil will among men can destroy the love that Our Lord Jesus has given me for Your Holiness. We will meet in another world.' Those were exactly his words. . . ."

His voice faded into a silence that seemed to last for moments. Yet those dark eyes were so filled with expression that Rico could almost read the emotion, the disappointment, the understanding.

When Athenagoras finally spoke, his words were measured, full. "If our brother in Moscow can send two observers on the condition that we do not participate in the Council, then we understand.

"This we say to our brother, Angelica, in Rome: 'We send you our affectionate embrace.' "

There was no more to be said. Athenagoras stood outside the door and watched Rico walk down the little dirt path between the beds of vegetables. The two Turkish guards, carbines at the ready, followed behind him; Rico almost felt their hatred of Christian clergymen as a physical thing.

He turned to look once more at the giant patriarch still standing at the door of the shack that was so grudgingly allowed him. In the bright midday sun, Rico thought he saw the glint of tears on the old man's face.

"If we hadn't Angelica as Pope," Rico whispered to himself, ignoring the guards, "we should have you, Athenagoras. God's presence is with you."

It was Angelica's habit to listen in silence as personal reports were made to him by his emissaries; only at the end did he ask a few simple-sounding questions that might bring to light whole new possibilities in a situation.

When Rico had made his report and answered the Pontiff's queries, he had one question of his own.

"I understand, Holiness, the importance of a breakthrough with Soviet Moscow and the Sovietized Orthodox Church of the U.S.S.R. But surely an iron-fisted order from the Politburo delivered through Pimen will not stop the Council from dealing forcefully with the most important and threatening factor of our time—with Marxism in general and Stalinist Marxism in particular."

It was also Angelica's habit to draw such objections out, to have them stated as concretely and succinctly as possible. "What do you mean, little son?"

"I mean, Holiness, that the Council will surely repeat the condemnations of Marxism that popes since 1870 have issued."

Angelica's answer was quiet and firm. "You've seen the *Schemata,* little son, that give the subject matter of the Council's discussions?"

"Yes, Holiness."

"Does any one of them deal with Marxism or Communism?"

"No, Holiness. But I thought the condemnation of Marxism would be dealt with in a separate *Schema,* as a special issue."

"There will be no condemnation of Marxism, nor any attack on Communism, nor any critique, direct or indirect, of the Soviet Union.

"Now"—Angelica stood up, indicating that the conversation was over—"I am most grateful for the way in which you accomplished this mission. I thank you, little son." The Pontiff's face broke into a sun-ray smile. "Whenever you want, please come and see me. Just phone Ducocasa."

As Rico made his way to the elevator on the fourth floor, his mind was awash in troubled disappointment over Papa Angelica's twin decisions to exclude the Greek Orthodox observers and to satisfy Soviet chauvinism.

Under Profumi, Lansing's spirit had sometimes been galled by the recurrent compromise with the Mammon of power and money. Angelica's papacy had promised at the outset to leave all that behind. When Rico had set off on this papal mission, his heart had been singing. The fullness and the openheartedness of the Pope's move had buoyed him with a great hope that finally Rome would go on the offensive, reaching out officially to the Eastern Orthodox churches, and even to the Gulag. Yet now what difference was there essentially between the two papacies? Rico had seen the dreadful havoc wrought by Soviet Marxists and their iron-fisted atheism. To go along with their nefarious conditions now was to compromise again with summary evil. And it was to abandon the millions of Christians caught in the Soviet net. That, at least, Profumi had never done.

So immersed was he in his somber thoughts that Rico didn't at first realize that the elevator doors had opened and that two people had stepped out.

"Ah, Excellency . . ."

It was Cardinal Da Brescia, standing beside a dapper little layman. "Let me introduce Signor Paolo Lercani."

Almost absently, Rico held out his hand to shake Lercani's. He would hardly even have remembered the encounter except for the man's peculiar expression—not so much a smile of greeting as a raising of his upper lip, a baring of his teeth.

Richard Lansing's bitter reflections only deepened as he immersed himself again in his lone travels through Poland, Hungary, East Germany, Czechoslovakia. The bishops and priests and people of these lands had held on through the lengthening night of Stalinist persecution. In large part, their strength had come from the sure knowledge that in Pope and Church they had an ultimate basis of hope, a support, and a divinely sanctioned stimulus to keep holding on to the faith they had received. As he carried the news of Angelica's twin decisions to men such as Wallensky in Warsaw and Valeska in Krakow; to Cardinal Mindszenty of Hungary; to the bishop and priests of East Slovakia, the East German bishops, and to Bishop Alexander Chira of the Ukrainian Catholic Church, Rico's chagrin and disappointment became a personal torture.

It was the Jesuit Father Provincial of Hungary who came to symbolize for Rico the disbelief and pain of all the others at Angelica's portentous decisions.

By order of the Communist government in Hungary, Father Partos had been forced to take up an occupation "useful to the Socialist economy." He had been made a pig buyer for the local sausage factory.

In his basement lodgings one night, dressed in his worn overalls and hobnailed boots, his battered hat hanging on a nail by the door, he sat with Rico and listened to the evening government broadcast—the only news there was, officially. The state radio announcer sounded almost gleeful as he described the gratitude with which the Vatican had accepted the generous Soviet offer to send two Soviet delegates to Papa Angelica's Ecumenical Council. The announcer read a public statement, put out, he said, by Cardinal Secretary of State Picolomini at Papa Angelica's own insistance: "His Holiness of Rome has no intention of slandering the Socialist Internationale, or the Soviet homeland of Marxism-Leninism, but rather intends to cultivate fraternal relations."

Father Partos snapped the radio off with one chilblained hand. "Of course"—he turned his gaunt face and joyless eyes to Rico—"most of this is lies. Or so I would have thought. But you tell me it is at least partly true.

"Can you imagine what this is going to do to us? Not simply to our morale, but to our perseverance in belief? Why, millions are going to give up! To lose faith—faith in the Church, and faith in Christ. Can you blame them, Monsignore?"

The smelly clothes, the querulous words, the bedraggled aspect of this once refined man, all came together as a living accusation of personal betrayal for Rico. He had no answer except, "Hold on, Father. Hold on to your faith in Christ."

Partos looked at Lansing as if to ask if the American could begin to know what he was asking, or even knew what faith was. "Have our enemies penetrated the Church?" He put the question in its hardest terms. "We know our tyrants. Does Rome? Does Angelica? Here, they make their way past the door, up the aisle, into the sacristy and around the altar itself. Have we all been taken from behind?"

There seemed no respite for Rico, or for anyone. The Soviets continued to make the most of their triumph in the controlled press, until finally, in December of 1961, they were able to cap their euphoria by splashing photographs in all their newspapers of a smiling Papa Angelica receiving Nikita Khrushchev's son-in-law, Alexei Adzhubei, editor of the U.S.S.R.'s *Izvestia,* and his wife, Nina.

For Rico, the Communist message to all oppressed Catholics and other Christians was a fulfillment of Papa Profumi's forevision: Along with the rest of the world, the Vatican was agreeing to cohabit with evil.

Only Cardinal Wallensky and Bishops Valeska and Lis showed even a glimmer of hope. But even they were dour. "The Vatican is using us as pawns in a power game," Wallensky grumbled. "Angelica calls this love? Well, I call it tomfoolery. We will have to be independent of it, and of its betrayals of its own; yet at the same time we will have to be more Catholic than ever. That is a big problem, Rico. But it is the problem we are faced with."

"Perhaps," Valeska added with a forevision of his own, "it is Poland's destiny to be the catalyst in this whole sad situation, not merely for the satellite countries but for modern Europe and for all of Catholicism."

"And it is just possible," Wallensky took up again, "that this cell system we have been helping you with in Poland will prove more useful than even Papa Profumi envisioned."

Such rare encouragement for his work, however, was too thin to support much optimism in Rico's heart. The constant labor of preaching and traveling in relative hardship conditions, and the ever-present stress of his double identity and his covert work, began to take their toll of him. Wherever he went, he seemed to see Father Partos' joyless eyes, and to think constantly of that priest's questions to him: *"We know our tyrants. Does Rome? Does Angelica?"*

In a world where Jesuits were forced to become pig buyers, while commissars parleyed with the Holy Father, who could answer?

Not Rico Lansing.

"Do you know the real question we face, Eminence?" There was no stray lock of hair on Cardinal Falconieri's forehead today; he was anything but pleased or relaxed as he strolled with Joachim Lanser to a meeting of the full Preparatory Commission of cardinals for a discussion of a *Schema* text.

"It's not what Angelica will do next, though he's unpredictable enough. It's not even how far he might go. It's how far beyond the pale of reality he is going to lead expectations."

Lanser listened quietly as the two walked slowly across the Belvedere Court. The November mists of Rome had passed, and the December chill had not yet taken hold.

"I mean," Falconieri went on, "in some places it is as if open season on basic doctrine had been declared. In France, for example—or Belgium, or Holland; take your choice!—ordinary people are being led into the most outlandish array of speculation. And the bishops are doing nothing to stop it. Some are even getting caught up themselves. We've had bishops in here babbling that Angelica will single-handedly make peace between the superpowers; and that he will abolish the Holy Office and allow theologians complete freedom to explore 'new ways of faith,' whatever that may mean! The view among such people is that Angelica dislikes Vatican bureaucracy and intends to 'give the Church back to the people.' That's a direct quote from one of the questionnaires from Holland! Some say he intends to allow divorce, and that he intends to unite Protestants and Catholics in a 'new Church'!"

Lanser had heard such talk on his own travels, but by and large he had been able to correct the thinking in his endless dialogues, speeches, and informal talks. "Surely," he said, "you and the other cardinals of the commission can do the same."

"Can we, my friend?" Falconieri was very close to open anger. "I thought we could. I still hope we can. But now the Holy Father has actually named his infernal commission to 'study,' as he says, the question of contraception. It's simply an impossible situation!"

Lanser tried to temporize. The demands on Angelica had been huge on that question. He had been pressured incessantly by a highly organized and unyielding army of ecumenists, and had finally capitulated to a long petition signed by hundreds of European and North American theologians; and he had established a commission of seventy men and women, mostly lay people, to investigate the question.

"You must examine," the Pontiff had written in his Letter of Constitution for the new commission, "the age-old doctrine of the Church concerning the act of procreation in the light of modern science and the developing culture of our fellowmen, so as to assuage the anguish of many and enable the Church to preach the gospel of love unhindered by prejudice and aided by the findings of dedicated men. . . ."

"There has always been pressure." Falconieri was not appeased. "Popes and the Church have been assailed with far more powerful means to change our teachings of the positive law of God and the laws of nature that stem from it. Not even a pope can set up a commission to tamper with such laws. Angelica already had one brush with the modernist heresy. It was decades ago, I admit. But can't he see the fundamental fallacy in setting up such a commission?

"And just look at the commission itself! At least a third of the lay people on it are non-Catholics. We know that seven of the ten priests and three of the five nuns already teach that contraception is acceptable. I promise you, Eminence, if the full commission doesn't put out a report recommending contraception, we'll be getting off lightly. But in any case, the least we can expect from this is a minority report recommending it. And believe me, there are millions and millions of Catholics out there just waiting for even that much of an excuse to practice contraception.

"You're a better theologian than I am, my dear Lanser; but no matter how you look at this commission, it has a very un-Catholic purpose. And the expectations it raises will be inescapable."

They were halfway across St. Peter's Square by now. Falconieri shot a disconsolate glance up toward the papal windows of the Apostolic Palace. He wasn't finished with his tirade yet.

"And then there's this question he's put in your lap, Eminence. The Jewish Document. That's another can of worms we'll have to deal with, mark my words."

Lanser had already been working for some months on the Jewish Document, discussing the issues with prominent Jews and Catholics in order to prepare a text that would be acceptable to all. Angelica's bold plan was to travel to Jerusalem, if possible before the opening of the Council the following autumn, to announce this stunning breakthrough. Though Lanser had at first thought success would be highly unlikely, and though again he had begun his labors out of obedience merely, one incident had changed his mind.

Late one evening, a group of American Jewish leaders, all rabbis, who had come to thrash the matter out with him—and thrash was the word—had expressed an interest in seeing the inside of St. Peter's Basilica privately. Lanser had awakened the *portiere,* Amadeo Solimando, and the group had begun its little tour. Despite the hour, he had also sent word to Angelica. The Pontiff, already retired for the night, had got out of bed and joined the group as it made its tour of St. Peter's splendors and art treasures.

The effect of Angelica's presence had been transforming, stunning. For that little time, suddenly they were no longer merely a number of Jews and Catholics walking and talking there. The Catholics, all clergy, seemed to forget what they were. The Jewish visitors seemed to have forgotten what they were. Grouped around Angelica, listening to him and each other talking animatedly, the hardened divisions had melted. All were truly walking and talking in some special penumbra of unifying light. Once Papa Angelica left them, they reverted to their usual roles. The experience was both exhilarating and frightening.

Lanser had told Falconieri and the other cardinals about that experience, and he repeated it now. "Until that night," he concluded the retelling, "I thought, as you do, that this time Angelica had bitten off far more than he could chew, that he would be forced to see that. But I wonder now if that was not a little foretaste of the Pentecost Angelica is always talking about."

Falconieri shook his head vehemently. "When this Pope speaks about his ideas, they not only seem attainable, but above all desirable—even inspiring. But that's exactly what I'm talking about, Eminence. That's the disturbing thing about Angelica—he raises impossible expectations to a fever pitch. He's an angel by name, and an angel by nature. But should he die too soon—should his reign be as short as we envisioned in conclave, or even shorter—who will be able to harness what this angel has begun? I don't like to think what might happen! Oh, no, I don't!"

As the cardinals neared the Holy Office, Lanser reflected, as he had several times in latter days, that many years ago, when Papa Profumi had waited for his sign, the Curia had not judged it prudent to pause in their rush to action. Privately, it seemed to him that the scales were now tipped the other way. Papa Angelica awaited his new Pentecost. Perhaps he would get it, as Profumi had got his sign. In any case, the Pontiff would not pause in his efforts; of that much Lanser was certain.

"Let's have faith," was all he expressed of that thought now, "that what Christ has started through Papa Angelica, Christ will finish in a Christ-like manner."

With that, the two cardinals disappeared into the Holy Office building together, to work on the machinery that would define the boundaries and the realities of Papa Angelica's Ecumenical Council.

[29]

At the beginning of 1962, barely more than three years after the start of his papacy, Papa Angelica sat calmly and ever-benignly at the center of a sea of interests that swirled about his person and the forthcoming Council that would open on October 11. It was said without exaggeration that the entire world of Christianity was in motion due to his initiatives. Who could have guessed that he was not yet satisfied?

The Pope had made a visible beginning at knocking down the walls—as he had said in announcing his Council—of religious intolerance. However, the walls between religion and the contemporary sociopolitical world where men and women fashioned their daily lives stood as firmly in place as ever. As things were, Angelica's Council would come and go, and religion would remain wrapped in its cocoon with all the other unimportant, optional matters. The great world of power would go on with its strife and its wars and divisions as if nothing of importance had happened.

Angelica understood the problem; he was a remarkably good historian. As far as his Catholic Church was concerned, the unimportance of religion and its formal institutions in that great world of power was, in the Pontiff's perspective, an artificial thing, the residue from the time when the Church had stooped once too often to take sides in the political—mainly imperial—squabbles of the European powers.

Taking sides had been the great mistake, to Angelica's mind. The muck of politicking had disfigured the Church's face; and the secular powers had decided Catholicism was too explosive an element to retain in their geopolitical arrangements.

Angelica's last major move before his Council opened would be an attempt to tear that artificiality away. He would begin with Italy; and he would begin by correcting the fatal error of taking sides. Was he not, as he so often reminded his supporters and his critics, the father of all? Was it not wisest to demonstrate that simple truth by removing the favoritism of the Church for one single party, and for one political system—to stop "taking sides," in other words? Only then, he reasoned, could Catholicism seep into all of the sociopolitical arteries of Europe.

What with the increasing river of visitors that flooded into the papal study as Angelica opened the windows and doors of his Church ever wider, it was not much remarked by anybody when the general secretaries of all the political parties of Italy began to appear. Picolomini as Vatican secretary of state, and Ducocasa as the Pope's loving but undiscerning secretary, always assumed that such politicians were simply a few more among the hundreds of *"visite d'amicizia,"* visits of friendship, that would have been considered odd in other days.

And so January 6, 1962, dawned quietly enough. It was the third anniversary of the day that Papa Angelica had announced his Ecumenical Council. Today's papal activities would be less grand than other days; the Pope would merely hold a semiprivate audience in the Sala Aurea of the Apostolic Palace. Some but not all of his Cardinals were invited, together with some but not all important Vatican officials, some privileged lay people, and a large contingent of the media representatives at the Vatican.

Helmut and Rico entered side by side through the Bronze Doors and fell in with the trickle of visitors heading up the broad staircase leading into the bowels of the Apostolic Palace.

"Any word about why Angelica has called this gathering?" Rico had returned only a few days before from Poland. Vittorio Benfatti had made sure the invitation was the first thing his master saw among all the matters that awaited his attention; but even that most informed of Roman valets had not been able to get a line on any special reason for the papal audience.

"Probably just to mark the anniversary of the announcement of his Council," Helmut speculated now. "To keep the pot boiling, you know."

"It's boiling enough for me already." Rico's laugh blunted the edge of cynicism and disappointment in his remark.

As they reached the top of the stairs and turned into the cavernous, decorated world of the popes, they lowered their voices; as usual, countless other meetings were taking place in any number of the rooms and halls along the route of the Sala Aurea.

Passing through the complicated arrangement of passageways and galleries, bypassing other halls nestling in the mazes of further corridors, Rico remarked how strange this world often seemed to him these days.

"After seventeen years," Helmut replied, "it's more your home than anywhere else. You've been spending too much time away, that's all." In truth, Helmut had noticed a change in his friend—more than just the loss of weight that worried Keti and Agathi.

"I suppose so." Rico nodded. Still, the array of uniforms, dresses, robes, and decorations all worked together to place him at a curious distance from the activity around them. There were Swiss Guards at this door, Palatine Guards in the next chamber, some *minutanti* and *bussolanti* in another, Knights of the Holy Sepulcher, Knights of Malta, chamberlains in ruffs and breeches that had not changed since El Greco had painted his Spanish hidalgos. The bright-colored sashes of diplomats and the red robes of cardinals contrasted with the severe black of secret service guards.

"Take my word for it." Helmut read the thoughts of his companion, knew his mind was on the Gulag. "You've become too accustomed to the drab gray of Eastern Europe. You need a change. Maybe we should all spend a few days up at Waidhofen."

That attractive thought had to remain unanswered for now, because the pair had reached the Sala Aurea. They were far from the first to arrive. As they surveyed the long room from the doorway at one end, the mixtum-gatherum of people who had already been escorted to their places by the papal chamberlains struck them both as a little odd.

There was a small group of nuns huddled in one corner like obedient penguins, their faces alight with expectation. In one gathering of about six couples—men in dress suits and women decked out in high mantillas—Rico recognized the nonsmile of Paolo Lercani. The Italian politicians and lawmakers, who had been placed apart, made an odd picture; it wasn't the usual group of Christian Democrats but a mixture of Socialists, Republicans, and Communists as well.

Helmut and Rico caught sight of Guido and some half-dozen of his *impero* associates. The Sphinx and Peter Servatius towered behind them like men on stilts.

A papal chamberlain came over and led the two friends to their reserved places behind the *impero* group and the cardinals of the State Council.

"Well," Lansing said, noting the heavy press turnout, "if what the Holy Father wants is to keep the pot boiling, he'll get his wish."

A stirring of the crowds near the doorway was a signal for all heads to turn that way. As this was merely a semiprivate audience, there were no trumpet flourishes or elaborate processions. Merely two Noble Guards—helmeted, cuirassed, booted, long tasseled cavalry sabers swinging from their silver-studded belts—followed by six jowled and slightly pompous-looking clerics in lace-trimmed purple robes.

After the slightest of pauses, the short, block-shouldered, white-clad figure of the Pope appeared in the doorway. The Pontiff waddled half the length of the room toward the papal throne placed against the long wall. Over his white robe he wore the ermine-trimmed scarlet mozzetta around his shoulders as if he wished it weren't there. He mounted the little platform on which the throne was placed, turned to face the room, and before sitting down, held out his arms in an all-inclusive embrace, smiling broadly, his eyes traveling over every group there.

"Sons and daughters! Welcome! Welcome!"

The words were not unusual, but with them, somehow, this Pope drew the innermost attention of each person there; each felt the words were addressed to him or to her personally.

While Angelica settled into his throne, a fussy chamberlain tried to place a red cushion under his feet; the Pontiff's legs were a bit short. But obviously it was too awkward; the Pope kicked it aside with one of those almost comic expressions that had endeared him to so many.

As the Pontiff began to speak, Rico relaxed a little. Helmut had been right; there would be nothing new today. He watched the changing emotions on the Pontiff's face—that smile, so like a flowering garden at morning time; the overwhelming seriousness that now and again replaced it; the hundred outward reflections of the inner lodestone of this man; the light from the Pope's eyes, large and brown, that diminished every other trait. The appeal of this Pope, Rico reflected, was not simply to surface emotions of loyalty and reverence, but to some deeper pool of humanness. It was as though Angelica, saying nothing very different, could speak to the heart of the poet in you, the soul of the saint in you, the hope of the sinner in you, the desperation of the merely mortal in you, the belly of the peasant in you.

Even at odd moments, when he might fumble for a word or glance at his notes, or when the spell broke and you noticed the ordinary look of the man, even then you could not help but see that he had an expression and a demeanor corrected by patience and molded by love. And if you looked closely, you would see all the little wearings and tearings that love and patience work in a man when he submits to those twin taskmasters.

After Papa Angelica had bathed his listeners in a salve of spiritual feeling for some fifteen minutes, and though most wished he would go on all day, it was clear he was coming to the end of his address.

"Now, we have been desirous of creating a new hope, of kindling a fresh light in our beloved Italy and in our common heartland, Europe. And, in all humility, we wish to say that the good Lord and God of this world has given us a veritable inspiration."

Rico glanced at Helmut. It was to be more than a routine address.

The Pope's voice became deeper, more resonant. "Holy Mother Church up to now has given its tacit blessing and support to those political parties She thought would best serve the banner of Christ which She carries on high."

The members of the Christian Democratic Party, unaware of what was coming, straightened their shoulders and lifted their heads a little higher.

"She has resolutely opposed the entry into national government of those She assessed as dangerous to the spiritual and moral health of the country."

The Socialists and Communists looked straight ahead, their faces like stone.

"For Holy Mother Church is a prudent mother.

"But"—Angelica now raised his eyes with a reassuring glance at the mixed group of politicians—"She is also a wise mother. And She knows that times change, as the Latin poet said, and we change with them.

"We are now convinced that for the unity of our lovely Italy and the harmony of our people, the Church should not give its preference to any one political party."

At papal audiences, no one speaks while the Holy Father speaks; but this was another bombshell, and there was an audible rustle throughout the entire room. Angelica made no pause, however.

"Hence, with welcoming eyes we will see various combinations of political skill welded together in a national government devoted to the civil order and economic well-being of Italy."

Had Angelica announced his intention to become the next Dalai Lama of Tibet, he could not have stunned his audience more completely. There was no rustle in the Sala now; no sound at all. No applause; no cries of *Viva il Papa!* A dead silence followed, as if people were afraid of what they might say. Angelica, with that calm assurance that never seemed to leave him, handed his notes to an attendant, gave his papal blessing to all, stood, and followed the tiny procession of guards and clerics out of the Sala Aurea.

The moment the papal cortege was outside the double doors, some wise functionary had the impulse to shut them, and immediately pandemonium broke loose. Everyone began talking at once. Politicians, lawmakers, cardinals, distinguished visitors, formed into groups, gesturing, shouting to be heard over the din. Reporters weighed in everywhere, some trying to figure out why all the fuss, others, who were more acute, trying to get the best interviews for their newspapers.

Rico let the crowd swirl around him. His face was sheet white. "This means he's opened up the national government to the Left. Tomorrow, or next month or next year, we could have Socialists and Communists in the government, in major cabinet posts."

Helmut had not lost his color, but he was as surprised as Lansing. "He's set the cat among the pigeons again. He has a knack for it. It's a far-reaching policy change."

That remark seemed to force a terrible little laugh from Lansing. His mind flashed over the weeks he had just spent in Poland and Hungary, and over the reactions he could expect to this latest papal bombshell when he went back there again. "It's more than that, my friend. It's a revolution. And I could give you a long list of people who may well call it a betrayal."

"I tell you, Gian, I fear for His Holiness' life." Guido de la Valle's judgment of the reaction in some quarters to Papa Angelica's explosive announcement was remarkably similar to Richard Lansing's; but he expected danger to come from closer quarters than Poland or Hungary. And he thought it might be lethal.

As soon as he could manage it, the Maestro had slipped out of the noisy Sala Aurea and had gone at once to make the situation clear to Gian Solaccio, still head of Vatican security, and to Giulio Brandolini.

Neither of the two had been at the papal audience; and Brandolini, for all his frequent visits with the Pontiff, had known nothing of the Pope's planned announcement. Both were stunned by Guido's quick summary. And both quickly understood the danger to the Pope's life.

"He's too vulnerable." Guido underlined his fear. "He's jumped into the middle of a political snake pit. He's no Julius II or Gregory the Great. He hasn't the statecraft or the political skill or the ruthlessness necessary for the plane of politics he entered with that speech today. This Pope believes in love as the most potent force in human affairs. He couldn't kill—not in any sense of that word; not even for the sake of this Church he loves so much."

The Maestro was too agitated to remain seated; he began to pace the floor of Brandolini's inner office. "Why, Angelica wouldn't even understand or imagine someone plotting against him, setting a trap for his feet, killing him off."

Brandolini thought that a little too much to say. After a loud sneeze, he reminded Guido that the wily Angelica had dealt with many a trap on his way up in the ranks of the Church.

"Granted, Monsignore. But it's not ecclesiastical promotion we're talking about now. He knows nothing about the detailed processes of secular political power. He's just burst right into the middle of a shooting gallery."

Solaccio spoke up for the first time. After his ten years in Swiss counterespionage and twice that in Vatican security, his mind fixed at once on the practical aspects of the situation. "Maestro, in the few minutes you've been here today, you've mentioned killing and snake pits and shooting galleries. But *who,* Maestro? Where do we search for the snakes? Or for the gun? We can't cover all of Rome. And you know Angelica as well as I; he already complains about too much security."

Guido was painfully aware that Solaccio was right. They couldn't cover all of Rome. And the danger now would be everywhere.

When Angelica was elected Pope, Italy was in a political straitjacket. The government, legally and freely elected by the people, had been formed by the Democristiani since 1948. It stood to reason, just for openers, that some of their numbers would be unhappy with Angelica's announcement.

Then there was what the Italians called the *sottogoverno,* the underground government. The *sottogoverno* was a potent combination of big moneyed interests, mainly in the industrial north; of vital public services such as the armed forces, the police, the judiciary, the state security organizations; of the half-dozen former *mafiosi* who had successfully "laundered" their dirty money and gone into legitimate business, though they kept up their financial ties with run-of-the-mill underworld crime syndicates; of the Italian Lodge, which, under its ancient Bargain with the Vatican, made sure that the principal industrial capital and activity of the nation backed the status quo; of the Vatican financial agencies that, in the heel of the hunt, were clearinghouses for funds from every quarter. The people knew that what mattered really for jobs, privileges, and advancement was the *sottogoverno.* That whole tangled mass of interests was now threatened by Angelica's simple call for openness.

But even that wasn't all. The Socialists and Communists couldn't be ruled out, either. Though they appeared to be the beneficiaries of the day's bombshell, Guido knew that the Democristiani had maintained their sturdy control of the government only with the willing cooperation of the left-wing parties, which were happy to accept handsome monthly sums of money to ensure that they would not join together to form one political force. If they did align with each other, as everyone knew, they could transform Italy, in the wink of an eye, into the world's first fully elected Marxist state.

Guido did not expect the under-the-table payments to these parties to stop, and perhaps Angelica understood that too; counted on it, in fact, in making his decision. But that didn't alter the fact that there were individuals in the left-wing parties who would be very nervous by now.

It was in fact the whole Italian *commedia politica* that Papa Angelica had so blithely disrupted, as with a clap of his hands. Until today, all who had a part in it understood their roles and played them according to the script. Disrupting that process of power was like reaching into a nest of bees; you were bound to get stung.

"We're both right, Gian." Guido's frown made clear how worried he was. Angelica might not be what the conclave had wanted, or what anyone of them had expected; but he was the Vicar of Christ. Guido and Solaccio and Brandolini would all three give their lives, if they had to, in order to defend him. "There's bound to be real danger, at least until things cool down a little. But we have to sort it out. Not everyone who will feel threatened by this new policy will go on the offensive. Among those who may want to, only a few would have the means to get at him."

"True enough." Solaccio knew where Guido's mind was going. Like most security problems, this one would be a matter of pinpointing the people with enough power and enough connections to pose a real threat, and then to keep up a nonstop surveillance of every one of those "targets."

"Anything unusual, Gian"—Guido summed up all they could do for now—"even a blip in a phone conversation, must be picked up and followed to its source.

"Giulio." He turned to Brandolini. "You see Angelica more often than any of us. It's a plus that your offices are on the third floor of the palace now. Try to be with him even more often. And tell that fool Ducocasa to be careful."

"We'll do everything we can, Maestro." Brandolini wheezed his answer. "I just hope you're wrong about the danger."

Guido opened the door to leave. "The best thing we can all do for Papa Angelica now, Giulio, is to assume I'm right. At a conservative estimate, there are a hundred interests who will see themselves at risk. And I can think of fifty men in Rome alone who could pull off the death of the Pope, if they used all their resources."

Six men of substance gathered that evening in a secluded villa on the Via Appia Antica, south of the city. Three were Italians; three were foreigners; all were close associates in business, and still closer as members of an exclusive club of their own. They had one thing on their minds: Angelica's *apertura a sinistra,* his opening to the Left. In their outlook, it was a political abomination.

"He won't stop there." The speaker carried an American passport, but spoke with a heavy German accent. "He has been sucked into the process."

"We really have no alternative," another agreed. "This Pope moves very fast when he makes up his mind. The time is short."

"Then we are all agreed the order should be given?"

Quiet, serious nods from everybody. Once the major decision was reached, the rest of the conversation went as though this were nothing other than an efficient business conference.

"Just quiet disposal, or do we make an example?"

"Quiet disposal."

"It should be from outside the house; but, of course, we will need the help of an insider. Have we a trustworthy associate?"

"As a matter of fact, we have."

"Let it be done, then."

Cardinal Lanser was not a sentimental man; but he was acute and he was compassionate. Like Helmut, he had noticed the change in Richard Lansing since the Pimen-Athenagoras affair. And he had seen the pale shock on Rico's face at the papal audience that afternoon. He glanced at his watch; it was late, but he decided to ring Lansing's office anyway.

"Ah, Excellency," he said, as Rico answered on the first ring. "Catching up on some paperwork, eh? I wonder if you'd care to drop by my office."

The call came at the right time for Lansing. There was almost no one left he could take counsel with. He had long since made his peace again with the Maestro; but while their broad loyalties were identical, their detailed views often differed. Helmut remained as close a friend as he ever hoped to have, but on many things he shared the mind of his uncle. All in all, among the hundreds of people he dealt with in his Hearts Apostolate and covert work, Rico was isolated, in Rome and abroad.

He found the cardinal's door open. Lanser was seated in one of the more comfortable chairs in his spare inner office, reading what looked like a huge brief.

"One of the *Schema* texts." The cardinal took off his tinted glasses and rubbed his eyes. "Have you eaten?"

Rico shook his head and dropped into a chair. "Benfatti would have me as fat as Sphinx Di Lorio if he had his way."

The cardinal left the small talk behind quickly. "I noticed your reaction today at the audience."

"Did Your Eminence know beforehand what Angelica was going to do?"

"I guessed there was something afoot. But not many know beforehand what Angelica is going to do, or when he will do it. That's not really the question, though, is it? The thing is done."

True enough, Rico agreed. "It's done, and it's a clear message. It's only been a few hours since his audience, and the place is already abuzz with Angelica's opening to the Left! But that's not the only thing that bothers me. He's cut the Church's mooring lines to the secular world. The Church has always needed allies. I give the Maestro his due on that point. We can't just float free on a sea of politics."

Lanser was coolly rational. "Let people buzz all they want to. It's not because of what Angelica said that things are going to change. The whole world is already in flux in a very fundamental way. Profumi saw the signs of it. So does Angelica. So will you, if you look around you."

Rico wouldn't give the point away. "Profumi would have fought tooth and nail. He wouldn't have just let it happen."

"I know. But now we have Papa Angelica." The Jesuit cardinal paused, knitting his brow. There was so much faith, so much potential in this American. He had come so far since his days in the Raphael. *"Capax potestatis,"* Profumi had said; it would be a pity to see him lose that capacity, to see him derailed by events, as so many men were.

"Look, Rico, you've spent years now educating whole populations of the faithful to go on in spite of the regimes that enslave them. If you're successful, thousands, maybe millions, who may be prisoners in body all their lives will never be slaves in spirit. They'll suffer, and I'm not making light of that. I've seen some of what you've seen. It's horrible. But, in ways that really matter, those people will be freer than their jailers.

"Well, this Pope is going you one better. No—don't interrupt just yet. You're educating the faithful. He's trying to pour out light on the unfaithful as well. He's gambling that he can open it all up, the ungodly as well as the godly, to religion, to light, to love. To Christ's love, finally.

"That's what he means by a new Pentecost. He's gambling that he can open up even the world where wars and killings and thievery are the order of daily life, to a real event of the spirit."

Rico conceded that Angelica's purpose was as bright as his name. "But you admit yourself that it's a gamble, Eminence. And I say it's a dangerous one. The commissars are betting they can beat him at his own game."

"Of course it's a gamble. And do you know why? Profumi could have told you. Everywhere people are trying to make Angelica's initiatives—that hope of his for a Pentecost—serve their own interests. The Soviets aren't the only ones in that game." Cardinal Lanser reached over to a nearby bookshelf for one of the Maestro's recent surveillance reports on the Northern Alliance's activities. He tossed it over to Rico. "Here. Read this when you have a moment. And figure the Americans in the game, and the French, and—well, everyone has an ax to grind, a cause to push. And most of them for selfish ends. So, yes, it's a gamble."

"And if Angelica loses the gamble?"

Cardinal Lanser looked long and hard at Rico. Without his tinted glasses, the Bavarian's faded blue eyes were remarkably intense. "Remember one thing, Rico, for as long as you live. We have good popes and bad popes. Like all of us, they do their best. Like all of us, some succeed and some fail. Like all of us, most do a little of both. But we go on. All of us. We are a republic within a monarchy. Like Christ, we are crucified, and we rise again. It's too easy to think everything depends on one pope. It doesn't. When popes fail, it doesn't mean they stop being popes. And it doesn't stop the work of salvation. Christ works His will ultimately."

Rico thought all that over in silence for some time. For the moment, he decided, he had only one more question. "Tell me, Eminence. Do you think Angelica can succeed?"

Lanser gave the younger man a half-smile; Rico had always been one to come to the nub of things. "I don't know. The odds he faces are obviously great. But if he fails, I don't want it to be in any part because I stood by wringing my hands."

[30]

Metropolitan Nikodim looked anything but beatifically happy. He fell into bed bone weary. The voyage on the S.S. *Adriatica* from Syria to the Italian port of Bari, however, and everything that had preceded it, had left him too exhausted to sleep, and too troubled.

Nikodim was forty-eight years old. Over the span of his meteoric career, he had now been arrested and interrogated eleven times. Each time, until this one, he had managed to come out of it with an official rating as loyal and trustworthy, and a less official reminder that his family—his mother and sister—stood hostage for his continuing faithful service to the KGB. But this last session in the interrogation room of the Damascus embassy had been almost too much.

Paid hireling of the Soviet secret service though he was, Nikodim had not entirely lost his faith. "Control" had grilled him relentlessly on that very point, those black eyes blazing as if to burn the truth from him.

"We have pictures, Nikodim! Look at them! Here you are kneeling in front of the Madonna's statue in Fatima! Here you kiss Papa Angelica's ring! Here, rosary in hand, you are beaming up at the *Pietà!* Beaming, Nikodim!"

The metropolitan had never seen such hatred of faith in general, and Catholic faith in particular, as Control showed in that week of interrogation. And never had he seen such intensity of purpose as in those eyes.

Nikodim's background didn't seem to have any importance for this man. No matter that his father before him had been NKVD, and his mother a card-carrying Party member. No matter his own obedience to the Party—as theology graduate at seventeen, monk at eighteen, parish priest and newly accepted member of the NKVD at twenty-one, master of theology and dean of Yaroslavl Cathedral at twenty-five, head of the Russian Orthodox mission to Jerusalem at twenty-eight, chairman of the Department of Foreign Relations of the Moscow Patriarchate and already colonel in the MGB at thirty-two, Bishop of Leningrad and Ladoga at thirty-four. His invaluable service to the Soviets in each post had always been enough to convince every normal authority of his loyalty, whatever his sexual proclivities or religious indiscretions. But this was a new Control, and a different breed.

Nikodim had played for time. That had lengthened the interrogation, but at last he had managed to worm his way out of the net. He couldn't remember everything he had said. He had tried to appear quiet and confident, but words had poured from him in his inner desperation—until finally he struck the right chord. "I had to put on a show," he said, "for the jackasses in Rome."

Control's black eyes had lit up at that image, and Nikodim had embroidered it for all he was worth. Control relented. Nikodim was acquitted. He was free to go. But one more occasion like this and it was all over for him; it would be back to Mother Russia for perpetual "rehabilitation."

Siberia, Nikodim reckoned. Or someplace just as bad. He would have to be much more careful. Much more discreet. A pity, with Easter just two weeks away. But Control could smell the slightest trace of piety from a thousand miles away.

It seemed to Nikodim that he had barely closed his eyes to fall asleep in his bedroom at the Orthodox Seminary in Bari, when an insistent tapping at the door wakened him. He looked at his watch and groaned. Five forty-five. He stumbled from bed, pulled his black robe around him in the morning chill, and opened the door. There was no mistaking the huge bulk of Anatoly Adamshin from the embassy in Rome.

"Crisis." Adamshin pushed the door fully open and came into the room. "Couldn't talk on the phone. We have to act quickly. And very discreetly. Dress while I explain. The car is waiting. We're heading back to Rome."

While Nikodim splashed some water on his face and scrambled into his clothes, Adamshin filled him in. The embassy intelligence unit had uncovered information about a plan "to send the angel to heaven," as the ambassador put it dryly.

"The Americans?"

"No. Not this time. In fact, our unit does not know the master planners. But they have identified the in-Vatican contact and the method to be used."

"Who?"

"A Romanian. Carnatiu. Know him?"

"I've met him a few times. An anti-Soviet jackal. How do they plan to do it?"

"A masterpiece of simplicity. Gas. Tetracyclophenol. Odorless. Lethal. Beneath a thin film on the surface of a light bulb. The one on his bed lamp. This coming night."

"Gospodi! Have you alerted the Vatican?"

"We can't risk compromising our sources. Control says you're to do it any way you can that will leave us out of it. And you're to make sure they know Carnatiu is the inside man. Can you do it? What's the quickest way?"

They were out the door by then; Nikodim's mind raced through possibilities. He wondered for a minute if Control had been tempted by his hatred not to interfere in the plot.

"Can you do it?" Adamshin pressed for an answer as they clambered into the car.

"Yes. Sugnini can handle it."

"Be discreet, Nikodim. But make sure. Control wants no foul-ups."

The warning was unnecessary; Nikodim couldn't afford another clash with Control.

Rico Lansing had dodged meeting John Liebermann for as long as he could, but finally the U.S. Embassy official had trapped him.

"Tomorrow, Mr. Liebermann? I'm afraid I have to be in Verona."

"What a fortunate coincidence, Excellency." Liebermann had been most agreeable on the phone. "I promised to take my wife to buy a Verona fur. Tomorrow is as good a day as any."

Liebermann had been posted to the American Embassy shortly after the turn of the year as "officer in charge of labor relations." The fact of the matter was that Papa Angelica's overt opening to the Left had ensured that among the secular world powers, at least the United States would now take notice of what was happening in the Vatican. As long as the Pope had dealt in spiritual matters such as his Ecumenical Council, he cut a clean enough profile to ignore. But of late, planners in the State Department and the National Security Agency had begun to feel he had more than a tendency to ignore the realities of the cold war. His policies might run counter to United States policy. Precise information about his intentions was needed. John Liebermann, a first-rate operative and a Catholic, was the perfect man for the job.

It had taken Liebermann a little time to fix on Lansing. But the word was that, in addition to being an American himself, the bishop moved within higher Vatican circles. And although his primary occupation was strictly pious and devotional—Liebermann had read some of the Hearts Apostolate pamphlets—he was reputed to be one of the *cognoscenti.* Besides, more than one voice suggested, was it possible for His Excellency *not* to be engaged in a bit more than pious preaching?

Rico had the advantage on Liebermann that April day, and he intended to keep it. He had gotten a full dossier on the man, and had discussed the coming luncheon meeting with Solaccio and Brandolini. He knew Liebermann was CIA. He expected to be questioned on the Holy Father's policy for the Communist East—his *Ostpolitik,* as the media were now calling it. He didn't enjoy the prospect of being pumped for information, and he intended to make the meeting as short as possible.

To that end, he arrived a little early at the Dodici Apostoli restaurant on the Viale Corticella San Marco. He ordered the meal in advance; he told the maître d' to begin serving as soon as he and his companion were seated, and to allow no time at all between courses.

"Sì, sì, Eccellenza!" The captain took the thousand-lire note from the American bishop. "Leave it to me."

Liebermann arrived late, and full of apologies. "You know what the Via Mazzini is like at this hour, Excellency."

"The name is Rico." Lansing stood, offered his hand and a chair, and glanced at the maître d' to begin. "Please don't apologize."

When the Bardolino 1959 was poured, and the first course of fettuccini cooked in a stock of chicken livers was served—both without question or pause—Liebermann got the message. With all the finesse of *romanità,* he was getting the bum's rush. It was a smooth performance. He decided he'd better come right to the point.

"We were very struck at the embassy by that papal audience last January."

"Were you in Rome then, John?"

Score one for Rico. The Pope's policy change announced at that meeting was the reason for Liebermann's assignment to Rome, and the bishop knew it.

"No, no. But I heard about it. . . . Tell me, Rico. One Yankee to another. Do you think there's even the remotest idea of a deal with Moscow on the Holy Father's part?"

That was to be the approach, then. Yankee patriotism. "I really wouldn't know about that, John. But tell me, doesn't the U.S. already have several deals with Moscow?"

Liebermann had to laugh. At himself, really. He had been outclassed in the opening gambit; he had underestimated this Lansing fellow, and had not expected him to be so direct. "Look, let me put my cards face up. We'd like to know anything you can tell us about this *Ostpolitik* business because we think it may be a complete switch on the part of the Holy See. It affects us, for one thing. And for another, any move toward an accord with the Soviets would surely bring some fanatic wierdos screaming out of their holes."

"True enough as far as it goes." Rico acknowledged the last remark. "But I wouldn't fear the fanatics; at least they're aboveboard, out where you can see them. I'd fear the vested interests who would stand to lose by such a papal move."

Liebermann noted the point in silence as the main course of *peperata* was efficiently served and his wineglass refilled. "Well"—the American agent drew his own conclusions—"I would say the Pope is going to hew his own path, whatever about the fields of cooperation between the U.S.A. and the U.S.S.R. and whatever about the cold war."

Lansing didn't avoid the implied question, but he didn't give the answer Liebermann hoped for. "John, you and I and the Pope and every one of you in the service knows it's all a very unfine joke. You raise a big anti-Communist banner. You've expanded the number of your intelligence operatives by three hundred percent. You have clandestine operations going in all five continents. For what?

"You know, if the American government were serious about all this, you'd have a half-dozen governments-in-exile in Washington—for Lithuania, Estonia, Latvia, Poland, Hungary, East Germany. Shall I name more?

"Instead, you sniff about for policy changes among your friends, and at the same time you talk to us all about peaceful coexistence. I think your people have the idea that if they can get the Soviets to clean their fingernails, and get the Chinese to put creases in their baggy trousers, they will have solved all the problems.

"The fact is, both of them hate us. They won't be placated. They both run dark empires of blood and oppression; and you deal in fairy tales.

"The real fight, John, is between the Church and Communism. We know each other for what we are. And we know there can't be a compromise. Your people always hope for one."

Lansing started to pay the check, but Liebermann took it from him. "You're probably right, Rico. But it looks to me, and to a lot of others, as if Papa Angelica wants a compromise too. That's the impression he gives, anyway. That could mean a big shift in the cold war balance."

They walked from the restaurant toward the taxi rank. The river glistened under the Ponte Novi. Liebermann felt a little weary. He wasn't coming away with much news; the disappointment could be anticipated in pretty high echelons in Washington. Well, there was always a chance down the line.

"Rico, think about some cooperation between our two services, will you?"

Lansing tried to think of a clever answer to a clever question. A yes would confirm that the Vatican had services to offer, and that he knew of them, might even be a part of them. A no could mean the same thing. He signaled for the first cab in the line.

"We already help each other here and there in tight diplomatic situations. Our two diplomatic corps render mutually useful advantages. Let it continue. But make no mistake in that other question, John. Rome doesn't envisage compromise with Communism."

Liebermann smiled a little dubiously as the two shook hands. "Like the fellow said, 'We'll bury them!' Eh, Rico?"

"Something like that."

"Goodbye, Excellency. Let's stay in touch."

In his report to Washington, Liebermann wrote about Lansing: "Probably engaged in a two-track assignment."

In his report to Solaccio and the State Council, Lansing wrote about Liebermann: "Wants closer ties, and is willing to share information and favors."

With the edge of his mind, Helmut de la Valle thought he recognized something about the voice, muffled and disguised though it was, that rasped through his office telephone. But the information was so stunning and rapid that identity was not the urgent matter. He listened without interruption. Then there was a click as the caller hung up, and the line cleared.

Immediately he rang through to Gian Solaccio, and repeated the message almost verbatim. A specially treated bulb had been placed in Papa Angelica's bed lamp. Carnatiu had been the contact for passes and other details. "Get in there and get that bulb, Gian! We'll deal with Carnatiu later."

On his way out of his office, Helmut paused only long enough to tell his assistant to put two calls through urgently. The first was to the Maestro. "He's at the banking conference in Milan. Get a message through to him to come back to Rome at once."

The second was to Paolo Lercani. If there was anyone who had the connections to trace something like this to its source, it had to be the ambitious Sicilian. "When you get him, put the call through to me at Vatican Security."

Monsignore Annibale Sugnini removed the handkerchief from the mouthpiece of the receiver and hung up the phone in the public booth. Too bad he wasn't able to get the Maestro. Still, Vatican Security would move just as fast on Helmut's word. Maybe it was best this way. Even less chance of his call being recorded. Like Nikodim, he didn't want any lines traced to him in this mess. The fewer questions about his private connections the better.

As his chauffeur drove out of Rome past the various seminaries and convents on the Via Aurelia and toward the suburb of Urbicino, Paolo Lercani had the look of a man who has things under control. And why not? The Maestro's own nephew had turned to him for help in a situation of summary importance. Perhaps the plot had been broken; but the pieces were falling into his hands, and he could still make excellent use of them.

His car swung into a tree-lined driveway. Two men approached in the early-evening darkness, flashed a light on Lercani's face and on the driver. One man led him into the house. The other stayed with the chauffeur.

Inside, Gennar Schiavone had been waiting for him. "Paolo. You made excellent time." Schiavone was the Capo dei Capi, the boss of bosses in the families that governed organized crime in the district south of Rome down as far as Bari. He was one of Lercani's oldest business associates. When it came to following a trail, Lercani would bet any money on Schiavone.

"The trail followed me, this time." Schiavone's voice was gravelly. "My son Cici, he visits this prostitute over on the Via Giorgio by the Tre Fontane. She is drunk already and boasts she's just laid the Pope's assassin. Can you beat that? We got people all over Italy following your leads, and Cici pops into bed with this piece of filth and pops out with the goods! Finding the man was easy after that." The Capo had a good laugh.

"Who paid him?" Lercani seemed a little nervous. "Who is he?"

"Corsican, he says. Calls himself Lugo Corsini. Haven't got anything else out of him. He's no more Corsican than I'm St. Bartholomew. Speaks Italian."

"Where is he?"

"See for yourself."

The Capo led the way down stairs that wound beneath the house to a maze of cellars. On the lowest level, in the farthest corner of a long low-ceilinged room, a couple more of the Capo's associates stood under the twin bare light bulbs. A man was lashed with wire to the wall, his armpits resting on two pegs, his hands stretched out from his shoulders, his feet off the ground. He was a mess already—an ear gone, the nails on his toes and fingers pulled out, his mouth bleeding. He looked to be about twenty-five. He was blond. His naked body was brawny. Lercani pulled the head up by the hair. Blue eyes. Gennar was right. The man wasn't Corsican; and probably not Italian. Whoever he was, he had been careless, and he was paying for it.

It was hard to believe anyone could have gone through as much torture as this fellow and still not have broken down and told anything. Lercani had to be sure. "Was there anything on him when you took him?"

"Yes." Schiavone pawed through a pile of Corsini's belongings. "Some special Vatican passes, the yellow and blue ones with numbers and photographs. Here they are." He handed them over to Lercani.

"If he knows anything more, we'll find out. Why don't you wait upstairs, Paolo. I won't be long."

As Lercani left, he heard Schiavone resume his interrogation. "Now, you and I are going to have a conversation, my friend. You're going to tell me your life story. . . ."

Twenty minutes later, Gennar joined Lercani upstairs. "No use. He was paid ten thousand dollars front money, with five thousand to come when the job was done. Some priest named Carnatiu was his inside contact, gave him those passes you got downstairs. Lives at 149 Via Rizzoli. Corsini, or whatever his name was, kept repeating some Jewish broad's name. Hannah—that's it. He's dead. I don't think he knew any more than that, anyway.

"But at least we got the little bastard! Imagine taking a contract on the Pope! You can bet he wasn't one of ours."

"I know he wasn't, Gennar."

"Sorry I couldn't get more for you, Paolo."

"It couldn't be helped." Lercani raised his upper lip. "I won't forget the favor."

They came for Carnatiu after he had gone to bed and was already in a deep sleep. The Romanian never knew how many there were. He woke to a blinding light in his eyes. His arms and legs were pinioned. Someone plastered tape across his mouth. Brawny hands lifted him off the bed and laid him on the carpet. He saw the shadowed outline of the automatic and the long nose of the silencer.

"Say your prayers, Padre. This is for the Holy Father. . . ."

Carnatiu couldn't think of any prayers. He tried. He tried very hard. Suddenly he remembered. His home. His mother. At evening. "Our Father. Who art in Heaven. Hallowed be . . ."

The *chuck-chuck* of the silencer disturbed the cat. She hissed, and streaked from beneath the bureau to the safety of the kitchen.

Downstairs, the *portiere* opened the door for the men carrying the rolled-up carpet on their shoulders. "Working pretty late."

"You never saw us, *bruto.*" The big fellow who seemed to be in charge stuffed some lire notes into the doorman's open shirt.

They loaded the carpet into a van. The big one waved the others off, and walked down a deserted Via Rizzoli to a telephone booth.

Despite the early hour—barely five in the morning—Helmut and the Maestro were already up and dressed. Or perhaps they hadn't been to bed; Paolo Lercani couldn't tell as he sat with them in the Maestro's study at Villa Cerulea and recounted the events of the night.

The Maestro sat quietly at the desk in his study; it was a time to listen.

Helmut was still examining the photos on the yellow and blue passes Lercani had handed over. "He said nothing of value, Signor Lercani? Nothing we might trace?"

"My associates took great pains to persuade him, Signor Helmut. He was very stubborn, I am told."

"These passes. They're used only for special workmen who have to enter the Apostolic Palace. They're controlled by the office of security under Casaregna's division. That squares with our information that Carnatiu was the inside link."

"Yes." Lercani nodded from his chair. "We traced them to Father Carnatiu too. But he seems to have vanished."

"Vanished?" Helmut glanced at his uncle.

"Without a trace. Unfortunate, but there it is."

The Maestro heaved a deep sigh and rose from his place. The plot against Angelica had been scotched. The assassin had been dealt with. Carnatiu too, probably. Perhaps that was all they could reasonably hope for.

"You have been a great help to us, Signor Lercani. Surely this will be a signal to anyone else who might have similar plans."

Lercani got up from his chair, aware that the Maestro was ready to end the interview, but hopeful to extend his new advantage still further if he could. "I hope so, Maestro. It is always my privilege to serve. You might advise His Holiness to take heightened precautions. He has stirred interest in many new quarters."

Guido understood the implication. "We have thought it best not to trouble His Holiness with yet another worry, Signor Lercani. He will not know about this attempt on his life. But we have already taken measures to increase security. And though the Pontiff will not personally know of your service to us in this affair, you may rest assured that we will not forget the favor."

Lercani showed his teeth and extended his hand. To have the Maestro's gratitude, he reflected, was a considerably better position than he had enjoyed twenty-four hours before. "It's nothing, Maestro. Nothing at all."

After a phone call to Brandolini, and another to Falconieri, to fill them in on Lercani's information, Guido joined Helmut downstairs for an early breakfast. Conversation between them was intense and hushed. The Maestro felt his nephew had handled the crisis well. Quick decisions had to be made and every resource tapped.

"What do you make of Lercani, Uncle? The only two leads we might have had are gone. What do you think of his story?"

"The whole affair carries an eerie thumbprint." The Maestro sipped the strong coffee Mariella served. "I don't mean what happened to this Corsini fellow, or the 'disappearance' of Carnatiu. That's typical *mafioso* style. The question is, are they covering their own tracks, or someone else's?

"Tell me." Guido's thoughts changed abruptly. "Did you read Rico's report I gave you? The Liebermann meeting he had yesterday?"

Helmut looked confused. "Yes. But you don't think the Americans . . ."

"No. I didn't mean that." Guido was remembering the conclave that had elected Angelica as a quiet interim pope who would set an example of piety, and provide a few years of quiet breathing room for his troubled Church. "I just meant that in a single day Papa Angelica survived a plot that was probably political in nature, with lines reaching who knows how far; and he attracted an open overture from a major world power. He and his Council have leaped with a vengeance over that wall he talks about and landed right in the middle of world affairs."

"That seems to be what he wants."

"Yes," Guido agreed. "And there'll be no going back from it."

Eugenio's high voice piping up in the distance, as he chattered with Keti and Agathi, signaled that a normal day was about to begin at Villa Cerulea. It was good to be reminded of normal things, to be surrounded by them at least part of the time. It was the welcome irruption of innocence into the somber matters of the day.

[31]

In May of 1962 the semiannual meeting of Guido de la Valley's *impero* associates opened on a high note. Only twelve of the usual group gathered with the Maestro and Sphinx Di Lorio at Villa Cerulea. Regice Bernardo, in his eighties now, was struggling with a crippling arthritis.

Each of the group had been sent copies of the financial reports in advance. Sphinx elaborated on them now in his usual competent manner. Profits were up enormously. Even their recent acquisition of SII, one of Italy's biggest construction companies, showed a gross of slightly over $50 million, with net earnings of $3.5 million. Their whole spectrum of activity showed similar healthy profiles of rising earnings, with very few disappointments.

In less than an hour, the group went on to the next order of business, and that, too, was a routine matter. Expansion required new talent, and Di Lorio had prepared dossiers of half a dozen men who seemed ready for more important posts in the banks and companies controlled by the IRA. Most of the names were familiar—Capodanno, Digiacomo, Barsiglia, Figliacci had all been associated with IRA and *impero* work at lower levels and had proved their worth. One name, however, Roberto Gonella, was new to some of the *impero* members. His bio sheet showed that he was an ex-cavalry officer, held a master's degree in business administration from the Politecnico of Bologna. Peter Servatius' report indicated that Gonella had turned in a promising performance as assistant manager of gold stocks in the Banco Commerciale di Torino.

"It's Servatius who's recommending him as assistant director of our Banco Agostiniano in Milan." Di Lorio made the point.

The bankers in the group—Frank Kelly of the Boston Immigrant Savings Bank, Philippe Dominique of the Banque Commerciale de Dijon, and Carlo Benelli of the Banco di Venezia—all studied Servatius' report with considerable care. Benelli, the only one who had met Gonella, had no reservations in giving his stamp of approval. Dominique finished reading the report and nodded his agreement. "Seems solid to me too." Kelly turned to the head of the table. "Maestro?"

Guido nodded his approval. The man would either produce or not; and Di Lorio would, as always, keep an eagle eye on all the new appointments.

Attention turned then to the financing of Angelica's coming Council. It was still mostly a matter of question marks and estimates, Di Lorio explained a little defensively; he didn't like to be inexact, but such events were hardly routine.

There were smiles around the table at that understatement.

The big-boned Michael Manley spoke up with his Australian accent, his attention focused on the only piece of financial information that was definite; three million dollars had been received as a gift to the Holy Father from one Paolo Lercani to help offset the Council costs. "A very generous gift, I'd say. Who is this fellow?"

"You've heard his name, Michael." Luigi Garganelli, a Sicilian like Lercani, reminded Manley of the donor's impressive career as entrepreneur supporter of Church activities.

"Just a hometown boy made good, eh, Garganelli?" Daniel Loredan couldn't resist the barb, but it was good-natured enough.

"I've done some personal business with him." Luigi failed to notice Guido's surprise at that bit of information. "He's ambitious and he's got a nose for success."

Di Lorio pointed out that the matter wasn't a point of discussion in any case. "The gift is made, and it's directly to the Pontiff, who has accepted it. Anyway, as far as I can see, why not use Lercani's money instead of our own?"

"Do you think that will cover the cost, Di Lorio?" The question came from "the Turk," Count Adolfo Sarimati di Sarimate.

The Sphinx screwed his eyes into gimlet-sized points as he tried to reckon the imponderables. "Well, the State Council and the Preparatory Commission estimate Papa Angelica's Council should last about two months overall. We haven't got the final figures from the Vatican architects yet—the construction for seating in the nave of St. Peter's and all. They figure on lodging and food from October to December for 2,500 bishops, and at least half again as many *periti.* We can't handle them all in our colleges and monasteries, so there will be some outside costs for all that. And we'll have to lay on transportation. . . ."

"In other words," Manley interrupted the survey, "three million dollars is a nice contribution, but we'd better figure on a bigger outlay."

Di Lorio nodded, his pince-nez bobbing on his nose. "The Council will be over in December. Our January figures will tell the tale. But Lercani's three million is substantial."

"In any case"—Guido seemed a bit impatient—"this is another point where discussion is fruitless. The Council will cost what it costs. The Holy Father has accepted Lercani's contribution and we will make up whatever difference there may be."

Franco Graziani, aristocratic head of the state-owned Industrial Reconstruction Institute, the IRI, agreed. "That's what we're here for. To finance the needs of the Holy See. In that regard, we have a more important issue to decide." Graziani glanced at Guido, as if to see whether the Maestro preferred to present this order of business himself. Guido nodded slightly, a signal for Franco to proceed. "And it seems to involve your friend Lercani again." Graziani looked across the table at Luigi Garganelli. "As you all will see from the report in your folders, on behalf of the IRA, Monsignore Di Lorio is very far along in discussions with the finance ministry of the national government for a twenty-to-thirty-year development plan for the *mezzogiorno.*"

"We've reached a tentative verbal agreement, in fact," Di Lorio corrected the IRI head. "Some initial plans have already been drawn up, just to indicate the possibilities."

For the benefit of the American, the Australian, and the three Latin

Americans, Di Lorio had included a map and some statistics with his report. The *mezzogiorno,* as the map showed, was spread out over 41 percent of the land of Italy, and encompassed eight southern regions—Sardinia, Sicily, Calabria, Basilicata, Apulia, Abruzzi, Molise, and Campania. The accompanying statistics made clear that the available labor force of the region was about four million, while the median income was less than 40 percent of the national average. Housing and urban facilities were woeful. Unemployment was endemic, double the national rate in some places. Each year, hundreds of thousands emigrated to the north. All in all, the area was not merely ripe for development, but, as Di Lorio underlined to the *impero* associates now, "a bleeding ulcer in Italy's belly that must be cured."

Kelly was quick to agree. "That kind of endemic poverty and hopelessness are exactly the conditions that provide a breeding ground for Communism."

"Excellent point," Garganelli chimed in with some enthusiasm. "The Socialists and Communists both made hay in that whole region last time around. And besides that, the whole *mezzogiorno* is overripe, ready for development. There are huge profits to be made. But, Luigi, you said this involves Paolo Lercani. What has he to do with all this?"

It was the Maestro who took up the point. "Signor Lercani has done a little speculating in the region already. And he has a very long nose, it seems, when it comes to plans of the magnitude we are discussing. He got wind of Di Lorio's negotiations with the finance ministry, and he approached Peter Servatius."

The count let a little laugh escape him, and the others shifted their attention. "That explains it." The Turk let the others in on the joke. "I've seen Servatius and Lercani together on the golf course at the Olgiata Club. They made a comical pair. That giant, Servatius, is a passionate golfer. Lercani always looks like a struggling little ferret next to him; he's terrible at the game!"

"Terrible at that game or not," the Maestro went on, "Signor Lercani wishes to be a co-investor with us."

"As long as we have the control"—Julio Montt shrugged—"why not? As Monsignore Di Lorio said about his contribution of three million dollars to the Holy Father, why not use his money to expand our aim?"

"That is exactly the point I want to discuss." Guido took Montt's question as a serious one. "There are two problems, as I see it. Both have to do with the source of his funds."

Garganelli guessed what was coming. "You mean laundered money, Guido. *Sottogoverno* money. 'Dirty money,' if you will." He showed the palms of his hands and pursed his lips. "A fact of life, my friends. We all use it, trade with it, exchange it. Sometimes we know. Sometimes we suspect. Sometimes we don't know, or don't want to know. There is no edict of church or state that says 'Thou shalt not!' We all know that floating around on the public stock market and in some of the largest and most legitimate industrial concerns in this country there are vast funds that originated as *sottogoverno* money. Fifteen billion would be a conservative estimate. Even banks and governments have to deal in such moneys. It's the same question we faced when Profumi wanted us to go slow, back in 1945. If we rule out this kind of money, then we can't go forward. We make a decision to rein in our activity. Those are the only two choices.

"If Lercani has the means to join us in this *mezzogiorno* deal, I say we regard his money as second-generation legitimate. A little like the children of the Albanian killers who settled in Milan. Your son or daughter wants to marry one of those children? Why not? I ask you. Surely we're not going to say that because the fathers ate sour grapes, the children's teeth are blunt."

Daniel Loredan wasn't sure it was so easily decided as all that. "Since you bring up Papa Profumi, Luigi, it's worth mentioning that he was a different sort of pope from Angelica. He dealt in politics, but Angelica has jumped into these matters with both feet. If we go even farther, who is there to hold the whole thing in bounds?"

"We will." Kelly jumped into the fray. "We keep control in this deal. And we cover ourselves all along the way. If we and the IRI together keep, say, 55 percent or 60 percent control; and if we go into the *mezzogiorno* deal in a third- or fourth-hand relationship through subsidiary banks and companies that are all several times removed from us and from the IRA, we'll keep Lercani at a comfortable distance from the real control. We can leave ourselves an out, in case it all becomes too—shall we say, unwieldy. We can provide an option for Lercani to sell to us outright within five years, or be bought out within ten years. It seems to me we're covered all the way around, if we structure a deal along such lines."

Guido agreed. "In fact, we had just such an arrangement when Lercani approached us the first time over the BLP, a few years back. The value shot up by 66 percent and he offered to buy us out even at that level. It was a considerable profit for us, as I'm sure you all remember.

"Just shortly after that, he bought two German banks. Lerstadt of Hamburg and the Friedensbank of Stuttgart. The sums involved came to some two billion."

"Guido, I don't follow you." The Colombian, Trujillo, wasn't the only one at the table who seemed confused. "You're the one raising doubts, but you make this fellow sound like the perfect partner."

Guido clarified his concern. "I just wonder where all his money comes from. It's like a bottomless well. How can he have two billion to spend like that, on top of the money he paid us for our controlling interest in BLP?"

Benelli, who sat on most fences for as long as he could before making up his mind, sensed a similar and very uncharacteristic indecision in the Maestro. "Guido, if I understand you so far, you're concerned that the real contamination of the source of Lercani's money is *sottogoverno,* as it surely is. I get that part of it—but based on that, I don't get your question about where his money comes from. Leave that aside, though. My question is more simple. You've agreed to consider his proposition or we wouldn't be sitting here discussing it. What's on the plus side for Lercani in your mind?"

"A fair question." Guido had not told even his *impero* associates of the plot on Angelica's life. Lercani was owed a favor for his attempt to help in that matter, and the Maestro understood without words being needed that he was calling that favor in. "Signor Lercani performed a singular service for the papal office shortly before Easter. He has a certain expectation that we will regard him favorably when possible in financial deals."

"Well, then?" That seemed the clincher for Garganelli.

"Di Lorio, why don't you tell us about those initial plans you mentioned for the *mezzogiorno* project."

The Sphinx was prepared as always. They were talking about financing to the tune of about thirty billion dollars, he said. Naturally, with the collaboration of the IRI, and the IRA and the *impero* holdings, he would expect private investment to come in too. It had been proposed that they set up Romasider Sud as a branch of their Milan Romasider, and specialize in high-quality welded pipe. There were plans already for three hotels, at Taranto, Naples, and Costa Smeralda.

As Di Lorio droned on, and questions were asked and answered, Guido listened with only half an ear. He thought about Garganelli's arguments. It was true that the *impero*'s aim remained one of securing the Holy See's vantage in the international money markets. If they did not involve themselves in *mezzogiorno* in a major way, they would seriously jeopardize everything they had built; they would be left behind. And it was also true that, with an investment of this size, Lercani's infusion of money would allow them some important breathing room. The start-up would be costly. And returns would not be immediate.

The Maestro sighed deeply. It was time to face facts; the old strict rules that had governed most of his actions and decisions in years past had been rendered obsolete by the hard realities of financial life in 1962. Just as Garganelli had said, *sottogoverno* money was so pervasive, no one could hope to sort it out anymore. Perhaps there was a tinge of regret in Guido de la Valle's mind that things had changed so, and that the *impero* perhaps had a hand in that change. But he hardly seemed to notice himself that his indecision about the use of Lercani's money had more to do with the safety of employing such funds than with the legitimacy of their sources. Frank Kelly's proposal had solved that problem. They would have control—that was always important. And they would stand well behind the cover of their subsidiaries in the actual dealings.

"*Bene,* Maestro." Benelli's voice roused Guido from his thoughts; even the handsome, cautious Venetian banker seemed convinced, provided, as he said now, that they could rely on Lercani's personal reliability.

Di Lorio was willing to vouch for Lercani on that score. "He's always come through with his word, whether in our BLP affair or in Cardinal Da Brescia's affairs in Milan."

The advice of the group was summed up by Philippe Dominique. "If we were proposing that this Monsieur Lercani join our group, that he share what we share or even know of the existence of the *impero,* I would say no, absolutely not. But that is not the case. Lercani is outside. He stays outside. This is merely a question of how best to approach a profitable deal."

The consensus was clear, then. Nevertheless, Guido preferred to err on the side of caution. He did not want another Kalikawa. Kelly and Garganelli were to ride herd on Lercani's funds, reporting back monthly on their quantity and, insofar as possible, their origin. "Let's keep our records straight and respectable. You can never tell when we may have to hang it up in the public marketplace for the wide world to see and examine."

The Sicilian and the American agreed to be the watchdogs, though both seemed to think Guido was being remarkably cautious—a measure perhaps of their being farther down Mammon's road than they realized.

Guido's final instructions were pointed: "I think all of us should stay at arm's length. Luigi"—he turned to Garganelli again—"I'd advise you to get out of those personal dealings you mentioned with Lercani. Monsignore Di Lorio, I suggest you have Peter Servatius act as go-between for us with Lercani. The association between them is already made. Let him use it to maintain our own distance. Have him break the good news to Lercani."

Paolo Lercani was in Milan when Servatius came through on the telephone announcing the IRA decision: It was a go on the *mezzogiorno* proposal. They could discuss the details in Rome at Lercani's early convenience. "And then a round of golf," Servatius said brightly. He loved winning.

The financier's voice never changed as he thanked Servatius, and through him, Di Lorio, "for your kind offices on my behalf."

Another miserable round of golf was not too high a price to pay for this coup, Lercani reflected as he hung up the phone in his tenth-floor office. He allowed himself a moment of personal satisfaction. Hands joined on the desktop, he surveyed the perfect view of Milan's Piazza del Duomo and the Gothic Cathedral of St. Ambrose, whose spires reached toward the heaven of the God of Catholics.

In all truth, Lercani mused, he preferred St. Peter's in Rome. That hooded dome seemed to block the superstitious leaping of the imagination away from this earth, to clamp the mind to the here and now, to the only reality there was. For nearly twenty years his nose had been pointed in the direction of that domed storehouse of power. Whatever Guido de la Valle and anyone else thought of his powers in matters of money and finances, the riches of Rome were merely the sauce on the meat of that power. Each move he had made—his proper Catholic marriage, the public identity he had cultivated, the friendship with Da Brescia, the gift of millions to Angelica—had taken him another step closer to his goal. He had moved from penny-ante trucking in Sicily to major banking in "the neighborhood of St. Ambrose." With this decision of the IRA, he was within sight of his next ambition: to become the banker of St. Peter.

After some time, Lercani lifted the phone and dialed Senatore Pappagallo's private number at his villa at Arezzo.

"The *mezzogiorno* proposal is going through, Senatore."

"Bene." The Maestro's walking companion in the Borghese Gardens was pleased and relieved. "Now, no more pressure for a while. Consolidate your position, make yourself invaluable in the *mezzogiorno* project."

"Sì, Signore."

The *sottogoverno* of Italy, with its diversities of purposes and its tangled interconnections that reached now even into the *impero,* and so into the Church in Rome, was not unique in the wide world. Even the countries of the Gulag had their shadow organizations, their underground networks that, like the disparate elements of the *sottogoverno,* could and did interconnect for diverse purposes of their own.

It was through such a complex and hidden network that Rico Lansing's covert cell in Gdansk, Poland, was provided with hard data, and with photographs to back it up, that Nikita Khrushchev had five shipments of missiles, armed with atomic warheads, being loaded in the north, at the Latvian port of Riga on the Baltic Sea. The information was that the shipment was bound for Cuba. Probably in the fall of the year, though the timing was considered the "softest" part of the data. At an emergency coded signal from the captain of that cell, Rico made an unscheduled covert trip into Poland. He emerged again, photos and data in hand, perplexed as to what to do with such unprecedented information, so far out of his or anyone else's experience. Once back in Rome, he decided to head straight for Brandolini's office, picking Solaccio up on the way.

Amid sniffles and monumental sneezes, Giulio Brandolini studied the intelligence with a practiced eye before dialing Cardinals Falconieri and Lanser and Guido de la Valle for an urgent conference. Having such data was one thing; what to do with it in the practical order was beyond his authority to decide.

Brandolini had two questions for the cardinals and the Maestro. Should they tell the Holy Father? And should the Holy Father be advised to alert the Americans? "My own answer," he said, unfolding a fresh handkerchief, "is yes to both questions, provided Monsignore Lansing as the source is kept out of it. His covert status is at stake."

Whatever they decided, Falconieri pointed out, the full Council of State would have to be informed. Again without naming Lansing as the pipeline.

As to Papa Angelica, Falconieri and the Maestro were both afraid that the Pontiff's first instinct would be to appeal to the Soviets.

"He is keen to win them around." Brandolini granted the point. "It wouldn't be hard for them to make a crooked deal with him and then double-cross both the Pope and the Americans. They would be alerted that their plans were known. They might or might not stop the operation."

Guido's was the suggestion finally adopted. John Liebermann had indicated the Americans wanted closer ties. The situation was different in nature from anything that had preceded it in the cold war; that alone made it important and urgent enough to have Lansing contact Liebermann and convey the essentials of the Soviet move. "Supply no evidence." The Maestro turned to Lansing. "As far as he's concerned, this is no more than a rumor you picked up on your devotional travels. They have the means to check it out, if not at Riga, then on the high seas. Leave the matter in his hands.

"Simultaneously," and Guido turned back to Brandolini, "I agree that you should advise Papa Angelica; and tell him the Americans are receiving the information."

"That might hold him back." Lanser sounded as dubious as he was. "Or it may not. This Pope does as he thinks fit, as we all know."

"Still . . ." Brandolini threw in with Guido's strategy as the only viable one. "I think if I emphasize the delicacy of the situation, His Holiness will not insist on contacting the Soviets."

May of that year seemed to be a time for initiating changes of the sort the Council of State would have to be apprised of. The beginning of the *mezzogiorno* project was one such matter. This unprecedented and unexpected Soviet gambit was a second. And Guido had yet a third and more personal change to bring up. In fact, as he had been planning to chat with Falconieri before the next Council meeting in any case, he left Brandolini's office in the cardinal's company.

On the fifteenth of the following month, Guido reminded his old friend, he would have his sixty-fourth birthday. In the custom book of the Keeper, it was time to start grooming his successor. He had no immediate plans to retire, but it was a part of his trust to make certain that the man who would come after him would be inducted without reservation into the Bargain—would be able to step fully into his place, should the need arise. It would be a private but formal act—an induction of his nephew. The Council of State must be aware to the degree that was proper and needful.

Like the other State Council members, Cardinal Falconieri knew the essence of the Bargain, but not all of its details. And like the other Council members, he knew that the Maestro was not merely another valued papal and Vatican adviser, but the Keeper of the Bargain and of some special oath that was associated with it. He would do as the Maestro asked, of course, and place the matter of Helmut de la Valle's induction on the agenda of the next Council meeting. He questioned Guido closely, however, with obvious concern, only on one point; and he was clearly relieved to have the Maestro assure him that he was not planning to retire anytime soon.

"Not that Signor Helmut would be an unworthy successor," the cardinal was quick to add. "In fact, he has the full confidence of the Council. I myself am sure he could take over tomorrow if necessary. But you will understand if I say that I hope such a day is yet far off."

As close as Helmut was to many of his uncle's affairs and the Vatican financial agencies, he, like the young Guido before him, took for granted the power and status of the de la Valle name. And, like the young Guido before him, he was unaware of the very formalized and official status his uncle possessed within the Vatican system. He was attuned to the hierarchy-within-hierarchy, circle-within-circle character of Vatican government. He realized there were layers of confidentiality and levels of power, all the way up to the real movers and shakers of the Vatican world, that lay far beyond his own ken and privilege to know. But more than that he had no way of knowing, until it was time for his own induction into the Bargain.

Guido's induction as Keeper of the Bargain some forty years before had been abrupt because of his own uncle's discovery of the cancer that killed him in half a year; and it had been a shock because it had pulled the Maestro so unexpectedly from the totally different life of spirit he had discovered on Mount Athos. Sudden pangs of regret still stabbed at Guido now and again when he compared his life as Keeper to the one he had been so ready to follow on those barren heights.

He consoled himself that it would be different for Helmut. His nephew had led a life of considerable involvement with the financial world; he was extraordinarily talented at his work, and had never for a moment been tempted, as the Maestro had, to step aside from the family calling. It would be a matter of explanation—nothing abrupt or rushed about it. Then in December the formal oath ceremony itself. And, finally, Helmut would begin to share some of the burdens and decisions the Maestro had carried alone for so many decades.

If there was any worry at all in the Maestro's heart, it was not for Helmut but for Keti. Until now, there had been little his nephew could not discuss with his wife, if he wanted. True, she had taken his frequent absences from home like a trouper, just as she had told Agathi she would try to do. But the secrecy—the separation of silence even from partners of one's heart—that the Bargain demanded was different from mere physical separation. It lasted far longer, and with time became only harder to endure.

[32]

"I wish Nanno could have a birthday every day!" Eugenio shared this sudden confidence with Keti as she tried to keep her excited six-year-old still just long enough to smooth his hair and get his jacket on him.

"Stand still a minute"—Keti laughed—"or you won't be ready when the guests come." She tugged the boy back within easier reach and fussed over him a little more.

This June 15 had become a rite of passage for Eugenio as much as for his granduncle. Normally, at this hour, he would be in the care of his nanny, Regina, and dressed in his pajamas. But tonight, for the first time, he would be allowed to be with the dinner guests, sit at table with them, be one of the grownups, instead of sneaking out of bed to spy what he could from the top of the stairs.

"I'm going to sit between Papa and Uncle Rico." Eugenio was full of plans for the evening. "Uncle Alberto and I will do magic tricks for Nanno." Di Lorio was an honorary uncle, like Rico. Cardinal Falconieri could help too, if he wanted, Eugenio said generously.

Keti cautioned him not to climb all over Uncle Regice Bernardo. "He's better now, but remember he was very sick. You mustn't tire him too much."

Eugenio promised, and chattered on. Keti listened and mused to herself how like Helmut and Guido her child was already. He had the same bright luminosity in those eyes. His blond hair was still not darkening to the auburn of his father's. The lithe freeness in his movements, the zest for all the new things in life, were strong de la Valle traits. There was still an unspoiled freshness in the boy that seemed to invest everything else about him with newness.

Keti knew her son was that—the embodiment of newness—for Guido, and for Helmut too. For all their love, and all their delight in Eugenio, they saw in him as well the visible link between the past and the future of the ancient de la Valle line.

"There now!" Keti buttoned her son's dark-blue jacket and smoothed his hair for the last time. "You run and knock on Nanno's door. Tell him it's almost the time that our guests arrive."

In her own rooms, as Keti finished dressing, she gave a glance at the half-packed suitcases. She and Helmut would be off tomorrow with Eugenio for six weeks in Waidhofen. Guido and Agathi were leaving for a few weeks in South America. It was all Guido's idea, almost as though he suddenly wanted Keti to have some time alone with her husband and son. She was happy at the prospect, but mystified at the sudden and special concern he had seemed to show for her as his sixty-fourth birthday drew closer.

"Ready, *cara?*" Helmut came up behind her, fastened the clasp in the diamond necklace she was struggling to close, and kissed the top of her head. "Agathi is downstairs already."

The party was small and intimate, the first respite in the recent storm of Vatican activity, and a prelude to a summer away from Rome. Rico seemed in good spirits, though Agathi and Keti both remarked again that he was too thin and needed a rest. Regice Bernardo looked better than he had in months, and despite the cane he had to use, was obviously happy "to be back in circulation."

After dinner, for Eugenio's benefit, they all played a game of charades; everyone laughed long and hard at Di Lorio's antics as he prompted his team to guess he was "taming the shrew."

Eugenio wasn't able to last through the whole evening, of course. He began to droop around nine-thirty, and was put in Regina's charge to be trundled happily off to bed.

The group gathered after that in one of the cozier rooms of Villa Cerulea for quiet conversation about the great events that filled the dailiness of their lives. Sometime near eleven o'clock, Mariella came with a tray of vintage brandy.

The Sphinx was the first to raise his glass, glancing mischievously at Falconieri: *"Cardinales amici inutiles sed inimici terribiles."*

"Cardinals make useless friends but terrible enemies," Helmut translated, laughing, for Keti. It's an old saying in the Roman Curia.

Falconieri took the jibe well, and gave back as good as he got.

The brandy glasses emptied slowly with lighthearted toasts and laughter all around. The last toast of the evening was offered by the cardinal, who, mindful of the Maestro's plans to prepare his nephew fully for succession, turned his eyes, warm with affection, toward Guido.

"You could have done so many things with your life, but you accepted this demanding service to the Holy See. I'm sure you realize the merit of all that in God's sight."

Falconieri's genuine feeling and graciousness filled Agathi's eyes to brimming and touched Guido deeply. It was a special blessing to end a special day.

By the time the summer heats assaulted Rome, Papa Angelica was at the papal villa in Castel Gandolfo, Guido and Agathi were in South America, and Helmut was with Keti and Eugenio in Waidhofen.

Rico intended to spend the summer preaching a series of Hearts Apostolate sermons, and then visit his parents for a week or so, if he could, just before the Council opened. His plans changed abruptly, however, when he returned from one leg of his journey and Benfatti handed him a letter from Basil. "This arrived a week after your father phoned, Monsignore. He said it was not necessary to call you while you were away, and that a letter would follow."

Rico read his father's short note as he listened to the valet.

"Your mother is ill," Basil had written. "Cancer is suspected. There will be an operation. Call as soon as you can. We all embrace you."

The date of the letter showed it was almost two weeks old. Rico glanced at his watch. With the time difference, it would still be late morning in Chicago. He put a call through to his father's office.

The old boisterousness was gone from Basil's voice. "If you can come home for a few weeks, son, it will be a blessing for your mother. And for me, as well."

Rico was not prepared for the change in Margaret Lansing, or for anything else that awaited him in Chicago that summer.

The exploratory operation had revealed a cancer in his mother's liver. It was a matter of time—six or eight months was the estimate. Her illness, however, had been painfully complicated by a careless nurse who had driven a needle into Margaret's sciatic nerve. Her physical suffering since then had been constant, and sometimes overwhelming. To get around, Margaret had to use a leg brace and a crutch.

It numbed Rico to see the slight, almost girl-sized figure of his once beautiful mother making her way jerkily about the house. Only her courage and her smile reminded him of all those years, once upon a time, when she had been the perpetual morning star on the horizon of his life.

There was no mistaking Margaret's courage and faith. Rico spent hours with her every day, had long talks with her, and found again and again that in the growing twilight of her dying, and in all her sea of pain, his mother had a depth of wisdom he had never suspected.

Basil came home from the office early each day. Often, Rico would leave his parents alone together then. The partner of his father's life was fading slowly out of his existence, and with her, a part of Basil was disappearing too. Some of their time together now should be only theirs.

Aside from his mother's condition, the thing that shocked Rico most was the change in his sister. Netta and Brad had returned from Washington at about the time Rico had arrived from Rome. But even though her own children—two boys, twins like Rico and Netta—were away at camp, Netta spent almost no time with her parents. Either she was too immature to realize her mother's suffering, or she wanted to escape from the truth. Either way, she was not the same person Rico had known in his younger years.

The excuse she gave when Rico spoke up on the subject had mostly to do with what she saw as her responsibilities in Brad's career. "He's a senator now, after all, darling. We have so much entertaining to do. And there are all those committees! I honestly think senators' wives are busier than their husbands. Anyway, Mother knows I love her."

"Netta," Rico pressed in one such conversation, "Mother is dying! It's not a matter of things going on as usual." But his sister had simply turned away, as she might dismiss a bad dream at waking.

There were other changes in both Brad and Netta that troubled Rico. Deep changes in matters of their faith and their general outlook on life. Though he had never asked, Rico had always assumed that, like their mother, and like Keti de la Valle, Netta was not able to have more children after the twins. A chance remark from Brad at the only full family dinner of Rico's stay revealed otherwise.

"It's about time the Church began to understand married people." Brad beamed approvingly at his brother-in-law. "Everybody talks about 'the good Papa Angelica,' and I'll tell you, his commission on contraception is the best reason why. Netta and I had real problems about that at first. But not anymore. Even our priest in D.C. has told us it's just a matter of settling our consciences with God."

As her husband talked, Netta could see the change on her brother's face. She shot a glance at Brad, a signal to be quiet. He had already said too much.

Brad only pooh-poohed her openly, however. "Come on, sweetheart.

Rick knows it's ridiculous to go around dropping babies like dogs and cats. We've got a pope now who's willing to open things up to reality at last. That's what his commission on contraception is all about. And that's what the coming Ecumenical Council is all about. And high time, I say!"

"I don't think you understand." Rico tried to be calm, to keep his voice even. He could see the strain on his mother's face; perhaps she hadn't realized, either, that Netta had avoided having children. He didn't want to make a scene, but he had to say something.

"Don't understand what, Rico?" Brad seemed truly surprised to be contradicted. "Papa Angelica is the first pope who understands the newer generation and the fresh outlook of the sixties. We have a young President in the White House with a beautiful young wife. And we have a pope who is young in heart. Change is everywhere. What is there to understand?"

"There's Papa Angelica, for one thing." Rico's face was tight with the anger he was suppressing. "He has a fresh outlook, all right. But it has nothing to do with the surface kinds of changes you're talking about. Nothing to do with fads and customs. He is not putting our religion on a tray like a Swedish smorgasbord and issuing an invitation to pick what you like and leave the rest! His idea is obviously much more profound than your political mind can assimilate."

Brad winced in anger at the barb, but said nothing as Rico went on.

"Papa Angelica is looking for a renewal of faith, not a change of beliefs. He hopes his Council will be the beginning of a greater and deeper living of Christianity. You're talking about the dilution of Christian ideas by the ideas of the world around us. He's talking about waves of Christian love that will break outward from his Council and reach over the whole world. His idea is to bring us back again in an overall renewal of our ancient faith."

"Come now, Rico!" Netta was disbelieving.

"Netta, if you knew this Pope, you would understand. I know you would. His Catholicism is the straight, tough variety that permeates everything. You can't be with him without feeling it. And that's what he expects—an infusion into the world of a Catholicism renewed by love. He is definitely not looking for an infusion of the world into Catholic faith!" He looked pointedly at Brad again.

There was silence around the table for a few moments. It was Basil who seemed to understand the immensity of what his son was saying. "Do you think one pope, by himself—or even with a Vatican Council—can do so much?"

"No, Dad. Neither does he. That's why he talks about a new Pentecost. And about his Council being an occasion for the Spirit to move people in the same way Christ moved the Apostles. Those aren't just words and images for the Holy Father. You should see his face when he talks about it."

"Well," Brad chimed back in, "we have dreamers in the Senate too. Wait till you're in Chicago a few more days, Rick. The people here expect something else. They want a Church they find modern enough for them. There is talk everywhere of abolishing Latin so that we can all know what's going on at Mass. There's talk about modernizing those outdated clothes the nuns wear. There's talk of the Pope limiting the authority of parish priests and bishops, and curbing all the old autocratic rule of pastors. And there are a lot of people fed to the teeth with the comfortable Irish-German-Polack-Mafia that runs the Church, and ties it up with money and business. Wait till you're here a few more days. You'll get an eyeful to take back to Rome with you!"

Rico ended the conversation as quickly as he could; Brad was obviously angry. The whole conversation was becoming too bitter a family scene for his mother to have to put up with. Anyway, he guessed there was probably more temper than truth in what Brad said.

That guess, however, quickly proved wrong. If anything, Brad had understated the climate of expectation. At the end of the first week of his visit, Rico attended two meetings of the diocesan clergy where the Pope's coming Council was the topic of discussion. The speaker at both meetings was the well-known Charles McMurren, professor of moral theology at the Catholic University of America. The good father's message was a repetition and a confirmation of all Brad had said. Everything in the Church was going to be updated. The old was going to be out. The new would replace it. From now on, things would center around the need for greater personal liberty, the liberalizing of Church laws, the loosening of the overpaternalistic hold of the Roman bureaucrats.

In the informal discussions after Father McMurren's lecture, the younger priests did most of the talking; the men over fifty seemed more like fish out of water than clerics welcome in the midst of their brothers. What amazed Rico was the romantic lyricism with which the younger men told each other all about what the "good Papa Angelica" was going to do, and what rivers of spiritual renewal would come from freedom.

At the end of the second meeting—a virtual tintype of the first—a young priest with a banjo strapped around his shoulder strummed out a new hit song. "I have dreamt our troubles are over,'" he began. Before he had even got through the title phrase, nearly everybody had joined in. Rico left.

It was only at the beginning of his second week home that Lansing stopped by to see his friend Kieran O'Mahoney, now Cardinal Archbishop of the Windy City. Rico had never expected Kieran to be another Blackjack Krementz, but over the years an unbecoming and too-worldly coarseness had taken over in him. None of the compassionate toughness that had leavened Blackjack's humor had rubbed off on the old cardinal's successor, and none of his broadness of mind, either. O'Mahoney's interests had steadily narrowed, until now he seemed to talk volubly on only two subjects—money and politics. In spite of himself, Rico was forced to recall Brad's remarks at dinner about tying the Church up with just those things that interested Kieran most.

O'Mahoney had become enormously fat. He treated Rico as an old buddy, and somehow Lansing found that humiliating. He spoke of Rome and the Vatican and his old friends there the way other men talk of Fortune 500 corporations.

"What's Peter Servatius doing these days?" he wanted to know. "There's a guy who's going to go far." And: "That IRA is a moneymaker!" And: "How much longer do you think old Di Lorio will last?"

As far as the Council was concerned, the American cardinal had long since decided it was "Papa Angelica's plaything," as he put it with a big belly laugh. "It's a rubber-stamp affair that's going to bring a huge leap in tourist dollars over there."

"But, Kieran." Rico was trying to find something of the friend he had known in his early days in Rome. "There are serious issues at stake! Have you heard what your own priests are saying right in this diocese?"

"Now, Rico! You were always a sucker for all the trappings and lingo they use in the Vatican. Old Papa Angelica! He knows how to keep the politicians fat and happy. And so do I!"

Was that all Papa Angelica's Council meant over here in the States, then? For the priests, not a serious step forward in the religious history of the world; but a romantic vehicle for dreams of personal freedom? And for their cardinals, not an event that would have a deep bearing on the fortunes and policies of the Church, probably for centuries to come; but a business venture run by hard-nosed money changers and callous politicians, all led by a pope who outclassed them at their own game?

"You happy with all this devotional stuff they've shoved at you, Rico?" The two were walking toward the chancery door by then, Kieran's hand resting on his old buddy's shoulder. "You can always come back home, you know. I've a place in the diocese for you anytime."

Rico thanked him, said he was all right. He couldn't get away quickly enough. He decided to walk back to his parents' house, to give himself some quiet time to sort things out, make some sense of all the changes he found here. Maybe it was just that he had spent so much time in the past few years in Eastern Europe that made things so confusing. There, people fought and died rather than let anyone tamper with the truths of their faith. Here, they strummed banjos to celebrate heresy.

Rico thought for a minute about the Northern Alliance material Cardinal Lanser had given him to read back in January. A lot of what Father McMurren and the younger priests had been spouting sounded like quotes right out of those reports.

On the other hand, he argued with himself, if the roof in the house of Catholicism was leaking, maybe the timbers were simply rotten. Papa Profumi would probably have chopped the rot out, one way or another. "But"—he sighed and quoted Lanser to himself—"now we have Papa Angelica."

It was amazing, Rico mused, how the spirit of this Pope had spread so quickly, and so silently. Like the all-embracing glow of a golden summer—warming hearts, melting age-old barriers, evoking an almost universally shared yearning for peace and unity and human goodness. But raising curious expectations too. What could explain his sudden ascendancy in men's minds? Angelica was seen on television newscasts only rarely. Few of his words were broadcast. He gave an occasional radio talk, but never a press interview. And yet everywhere people now talked, as McMurren had, as Brad and O'Mahoney had, about the "good Papa Angelica." And for most of them—O'Mahoney was an exception, and perhaps McMurren was too—but for most of them Angelica did appear to signify the one element that increasingly seemed to be lacking everywhere: love. He had come upon the world like an angel in sudden flight from heaven to grace a winter waste with warmth and light.

It was evening by the time Rico turned up the walkway to the Lansing home. He paused a moment as he approached the door, as if to finish a conversation.

"Never was a man's love so angelic as Angelica's." He said the words aloud, but softly. "And never was an angel's love so sorely misunderstood as here. Lord Jesus, help your Vicar. Help our Pope. Your will be done!"

In the peaceful hours Rico spent with his mother in those weeks, they talked with each other about everything. Margaret understood that Netta had let go of some of her lines of faith, or had traded them for what she saw as personal advantage. "The trouble is," Margaret confided with more than physical pain in her eyes, "when you start picking at the fabric of faith, it begins to unravel. I know you're angry with her, Rico. But the time will come when she needs you. Or, anyway, I pray so. Take care of her."

With very few words, Rico's mother understood, too, how out-of-date and out-of-place her son was feeling just now. Everyone here seemed to be changing, and not for the better, as far as he could see. Yet there was no reason, she insisted, that Richard Cooper Lansing had to be one of the crowd. "As far as I know, your father and I taught you to make up your own mind, to follow your judgment. If we didn't teach you that, but reared you as a little collaborationist with every flick of fashion, then we failed. I don't think that's the case."

Sometimes in the evening, through the open door, Rico might see his father kneeling by Margaret's bedside, both her hands in his, the two absorbed in each other as if they were teenage lovers. On his mother's face at such moments there was a little sunset trace of the beauty she had brought to all their lives.

"I was blessed," Rico would tell his intimate friends for years afterward. "I had parents who were truly married."

[[33]]

The din in the Secretariat lobby was overwhelming. It was still only September, yet fully half the 2,500 bishops who would participate in the Council were already in Rome.

"Monsignore!" Amadeo Solimando caught sight of Rico as he entered the crowd on his first day back. *"Siamo stufati di vescovi!* We're choking on bishops!"

"Brace yourself." Rico smiled down at the little *portiere.* "This is only the beginning."

Lansing was right. Tourism of an extraordinary and sustained kind was about to swell the coffers of the Eternal City and those of many of its inhabitants. All of the bishops brought with them at least one theological expert or *peritus*—some brought two or three. Many brought their own secretaries and the coadjutor bishops of their dioceses. In their wake would flow endless pilgrimages of every possible human coloring, speaking a babel of languages.

That, as Lansing said, was only the beginning. Governments that had come to expect Angelica's Council to have some bearing on their fortunes and policies increased their accredited personnel with special envoys, observers, agents, emissaries, and specialists. Not to be forgotten, either, were the representatives of non-Catholic religious bodies that were, for the first time ever, taking the deliberations of the Catholic Church in Council as a serious step forward in the religious history of their world.

Rome loved it. The sheer numbers of them all! They moved about in droves, dined in herds, and like late-coming scholars, were ferried about the city in hired buses. The restaurateurs, the hoteliers, the *pensione* owners, the espresso-bar keepers, the sidewalk-café waiters, the cabbies, the policemen, the city fathers, the city pickpockets—all had more to do than they could handle. Even seminaries and convents were awash with bishops waiting in line to say Mass every morning.

The variety in race and language, and the already impressive number of foreign journalists, and the activities of television and radio teams come to stay for the duration, all reminded the Romans that in not too distant days their city had been the hub of the civilized world, and was still of considerable importance. *"Noi Romani"*—we Romans—became a fresh cry on the lips of street vendors and tour guides.

The excitement of it all infected even the normally sedate Vittorio Benfatti, whose response was to replenish every area of Bishop Lansing's wardrobe, and to advise his master, in the sternest terms he could permit himself, to wear his most proper clerical garb every day of the week.

After all these years, Rico knew it was best to heed such advice from his valet. But he had precious little time to concern himself with niceties. It fell to him to make all the arrangements for the Eastern European residential bishops—those who actually administered dioceses—to get to Rome for the Council. That meant endless wrangling with every Soviet puppet regime, ensuring that visas were issued, supplying money and means of travel, making sure there would be adequate living quarters in overcrowded Rome, and transportation once they all arrived. Had it not been for the help he continually needed to ask from Helmut and the Maestro in the transfer of extraordinary funds to so many places at the same time, he might not have had an occasion of seeing the de la Valles for weeks.

By mid-September, a continuous series of cocktail parties and receptions had begun, given by cardinals, bishops, special news reporters, and some of Rome's best families. Rico had to attend some of those parties, and found at them the same heady brew of buzz words and slogans that he had found in Chicago. "Democratization." "Rehabilitation of Martin Luther." "Humanization of religion." "Updating our outmoded morality." "Rights of the community." "The people of God versus the hierarchic Church."

If Papa Angelica sensed the mood growing around him in Rome and in his Church, those such as Lansing who saw him fairly frequently knew he read it all as a movement of the Spirit. The same Spirit, the Pontiff said again and again, who had infused the twelve obscure Galileans over nineteen hundred years before this September of 1962 would remain with their successors.

Some of the Curia, members of the "Old Guard" and defenders of Romanism—certainly most of the cardinals of the Preparatory Commission and the Vatican State Council—regarded the onslaught of undisciplined and unrealistic romanticism as just one more battle to be fought, one more difficult passage along the eternal road traveled by the battered caravanserai that the Vatican always would be. As the Church had left behind it in successive heaps the bleaching bones of those in every age who dreamed they could destroy the hated thing perched on Vatican Hill in the crook of the Tiber River, so it would discard the unruly elements of the coming Council. After all, they reassured themselves, papal absolutism had in the end always overruled bureaucratic republicanism. The very presence and most amazing influence of Papa Angelica was a major factor in their confidence. That, and their own control of the *Schemata.* "We have it in hand," was their continuing watchword. "It can't go very far."

Cardinal Wallensky was one who made no secret of the fact that he disagreed. Rico spent as many evenings as he could with the cardinal and Bishop Bogdan Valeska. They would dine sometimes at the Polish Convent on the Via Sistina, where Rico still said morning Mass when he was in Rome, and where the nuns were delighted to have the Polish prelate and his entourage in residence. Or they might gather instead at Rico's apartment. Wherever they were, Wallensky left no doubt as to his opinions.

He was appalled at what he saw and heard. For the first time he was able to move freely among his clerical equals from France, Germany, Belgium, Holland. He was able to listen to the "Anglo-Saxon"—the English,

Americans, Australians, Canadians. He had talked face to face with Papa Angelica. He even spent time with some of the continuous streams of Protestant observers, consultants, analysts, and enthusiasts who were frequenting many of the meetings and informal gatherings.

As far as he could see, he declared unrelentingly, there was a runaway intellectual Church in Northern Europe. There was an intellectually backward Church in North America. And there was a capitalist Church in Latin America.

"Over all that," he observed at an otherwise quiet dinner with Rico and Valeska, "sits our Pope, who takes a strong stand against nothing, and in favor only of what he calls love. He is advised and ordered by a Roman bureaucracy whose complacency is exceeded only by its ignorance of the forces arrayed against us."

Bogdan Valeska felt his old mentor and friend was being too pessimistic by far. "I cannot believe that the bishops in Council will be led so far astray as you think, Eminence. I must believe that Papa Angelica is right. Something can be done here. A Council is guided by the Holy Spirit. This is not the first that has seemed to be off the track, at the start. Other troublesome councils have worked well in the end."

Wallensky's foxlike features were the picture of skepticism. "And I remind you, Bogdan, that there have been other councils that have done harm in the end, as well!

"I grant you, Papa Angelica's intentions are holy. But look around you. It's not merely this fuzzy, romantic ecumenical zeal. That's bad enough, of course. It's not Roman. It's not Catholic. It's not even specifically Christian. To listen to some of these people, you would think that salvation began in the Garden of Paradise, and not in the bloodied body of a God-man on an executioner's gibbet. That's too rigid, prosaic, stodgy—too old-hat—for these romanticists. They don't care about the shadow of the Cross, or the light from the empty tomb on the first Easter Day! All they want is something they call freedom for something they call humanness; and they want it cut off from everything they see as old or autocratic.

"That Papa Angelica puts up with it is already a warning. But on top of that, he also turns a smiling face to the Soviets; and he ignores the places where Catholicism is strongest—Ireland, Portugal, and our own Poland are just three good examples. If the Pontiff does not defend us and bolster us, then what can we expect?

"You are right that Papa Angelica is a good man, Bogdan. But he is in the wrong place. And unless I read all the signals upside down, he is about to throw open the walls of the Church to a genuine flood of secular religion. Dogma is about to be ground into some meaningless mixture of poetic doggerel by this Council, unless Angelica shows something he's kept hidden until now.

"And except for your work, Excellency"—he turned his gimlet eyes on Rico—"and our own wiles, we—the Poles, the Czechs, the whole lot of us in the East—will be left to the tender mercies of that same Soviet Marxism which Angelica has declared a nonenemy."

Rico knew there was no point in rehearsing for Wallensky, as he had for Netta and Brad, what Papa Angelica hoped for his Council. The Polish cardinal understood all that. The disquieting thing for Rico was that everything he saw in Rome, everything that pointed to disaster for Wallensky, was merely a heightened picture of what he had seen in Chicago. If the cardinal was accurate in his portrait of the calamity to come, it applied by extrapolation and with full force to the Church in America.

Wallensky ended that evening on what seemed a portentous note. "I'd love to find a way," he confided in a conspiratorial tone, "to dramatize for Papa Angelica what the Soviet nonenemy has already done to millions of us. To the Hungarians, for example." The cardinal seemed to be forming a plan. "They've been so trampled and compromised since the Soviet invasion of fifty-six that none of us can even talk with them in confidence any longer. The best who are left there have been devastated by the Pontiff's glad hand to Moscow. All they can ask is 'Why?'

"And I'll tell you this, Rico—though you've seen it for yourself: There are a lot more of us who want to force an answer to that same question from Angelica. *Why?*"

The farthest person from Rico Lansing's thoughts in the midst of all the excitement, preparations, and heated discussions was John Liebermann. His late-night call at the end of September found Rico at home, and still at work in his study.

That same night, in the security of Lansing's apartment, Liebermann explained that American intelligence had taken very seriously the "rumor" Rico had passed along. They now had the Soviet missile-carrying freighters under observation en route toward Cuba. He was here to ask if the Holy Father would do the United States a favor. Would he transmit a discreet message to Moscow for them?

He pulled a single sheet of paper from an inner pocket as he spoke, and handed it to Rico. Two series of disconnected words and phrases were neatly typed in Italian.

"The day after tomorrow," Liebermann went on, "the President is going to go public with the news about the oncoming Soviet missiles. On that same day, but before the President's speech, we need His Holiness to make a short plea for peace over Vatican Radio, intermingling with his own words the ones on that sheet of paper."

Rico studied the paper briefly. The words were ordinary: "Danger." "God's mercy." "Please." "Women and children and men." He recognized the cipher system being used, but wasn't enough of an expert in code to make anything of the message. That didn't bother him; Giulio Brandolini or one of their cipher specialists would make short work of the problem.

"Why should His Holiness do this, John?" Behind Rico's question was his feeling that the Pontiff was taking enough heat already, without stooping to intervene in a completely political, totally secular squabble.

"Because peace depends on it," Liebermann replied without a second's hesitation.

Rico said nothing, simply sat looking at his midnight visitor. He'd have to have more than that.

Liebermann shook his head in frustration, much as he had after their lunch in Verona. "The plain truth is this, Rico. The Soviets have bluffed and tricked us in the past, and we've done the same to them. But this is no joke. Papa Angelica is the only one who can give us the credibility we need to convince the other side that we're not bluffing. If they think we are, it could mean war."

Rico folded the paper. "I'll see what I can do, John."

The meeting in Sniff-Sniff Brandolini's office was brief. Cardinal Falconieri was the only one who wasn't available on such short notice.

Brandolini needed no cipher clerk to understand the substance of the coded message. The Americans were signaling that they had accurate and highly detailed data about the Soviet missile cargo, data the President would doubtless omit from his public speech, but that showed the convoy was a row of sitting ducks.

Gian Solaccio, hard-nosed and experienced at intelligence, was impatient with "all this nonsense." He threw up his hands. "We gave them the information, and that should be that! It's up to them. Why don't they just blow the ships out of the water? They don't have to leave their open signature on the act. Believe me, that will be enough to convince the Soviets they're not bluffing."

"Maybe they are doing just that, Gian." The Maestro seemed almost amused at Solaccio's armchair strategy. "Bluffing, I mean."

As far as Cardinal Lanser was concerned, bluff or no bluff, the Holy See did not belong in this matter at all. "You've been the contact for all this, Excellency." Brandolini turned to Rico last. "Any opinion?"

"Yes. I agree with Cardinal Lanser. But I think Papa Angelica will make the broadcast. He's told every one of us here that he is the father of all his children. And he is the Pope of peace and love. He may not enjoy this part of it; but I think he'll do it."

Lanser looked at Rico in some surprise. He was becoming a realists' realist, this American.

Two days later, at eleven o'clock, Vatican Radio announced that the Holy Father was about to speak on the subject of peace. After the briefest of pauses, Angelica's unmistakable voice was heard. He sounded strained and very serious; he spoke for twelve minutes, and faster than normal for him.

The minority of officials in Rome who understood how unusual it was for Angelica to speak directly over any of the public media—even Vatican Radio—was mystified. "If His Holiness finds it necessary to broadcast a sudden plea for peace," the comment ran, "when there is no real sign of war—and when he speaks so vaguely—then there must be real trouble."

Within hours, that observation was confirmed. The American President went on the air, and the missile crisis was public. In hindsight, it was obvious to the *cognoscenti* that the Pope had involved himself in the affair; that he had, as his critics complained, dipped the papacy once again into the muck of international politics. And so, as Lansing had feared, yet a new debate began to swirl about "good Papa Angelica."

Most of Rome, however, remained blithely unaware, wrapped ever more deeply in the cocoon of rising expectation and romantic hopes. Even before the missile crisis was resolved, the world of the Council continued on its merry way.

As a titular bishop—a bishop without a diocese—Richard Lansing would not take part in the daily proceedings of the Ecumenical Council. That was reserved for the residential bishops who presided over the thousands of actual dioceses around the world. While most bishops, along with everyone else in Rome, did want to attend the all-important ceremony of October 11, when Papa Angelica would formally "receive the world at St. Peter's," as Benfatti put it expansively; and while Monsignore Corrado Amalfeo as master of ceremonies would certainly have assigned him a place, Rico had long since decided not even to join the Maestro and his family in the balcony overlooking the High Altar. He was still wholly occupied with taking care of his prelates from the satellite countries, he rationalized; and he had the Hearts Apostolate to run, besides.

If that was the case, Helmut suggested over one of their quick lunches in the Vatican commissary, perhaps Rico would do a favor for him. "We all want Eugenio to see something of the opening. The magnificent panoply and ceremonial will be like a glimpse of God's wonderland for him. But Keti is worried that two and a half hours will be too long for him to sit still in the loggia with us. Maybe you could find some little cranny where the three of you can sneak in for part of the time. If Eugenio gets cranky or restless, Keti can take him home, and you can stay on if you like."

"Splendid!" Rico was delighted. The only thing he had to do was find "some little cranny."

Of course, the person who had the solution to such a problem was Lansing's valet. Benfatti had close personal friendships with the Vatican firemen, particularly Captain Adagio Berulli. They, in turn, inspected every inch of the Vatican every day and so knew all the little crannies that existed in the Vatican, as well as they knew the buttons they polished on their uniforms each morning before roll call.

With hands folded one palm on the other, Benfatti worked the whole thing out aloud. "I myself, and His Eminence Cardinal Lisserant's man, were going to use the St. Cecilia. But you and Signora Keti and Master

Eugenio should have that. The St. Augustine will do very well for me and my guest."

Rico was fascinated. "The St. Cecilia? The St. Augustine? Vittorio, you might as well be talking about the St. Ambrose and . . ."

"Ah, no, Excellency." Benfatti wanted no confusion on such matters. "The St. Ambrose is for the lesser fry. I do believe His Eminence Cardinal Da Brescia's man will use that."

And it turned out the four monster piers upon which floated the great dome of St. Peter's itself were not entirely what they appeared to be. In each of those piers, huge niches held enormous statues of the saints in question. Behind each figure, an openwork of vines had been carved. And behind the vines, rooms big enough to hold a small contingent of papal guards had been built into the pillars. The original idea, as Vittorio explained, had been to have a vantage point from which to protect the pope, without being too obvious about crossbows and such warlike obstructions to prayer.

"The view from those rooms is excellent, Monsignore." Benfatti beamed in satisfaction. "Like the vigilant soldiers for whom they were built, you and your guests will be at eye level with His Holiness, with a perfect view of the Pontiff and the entire nave where the bishops will be seated. You will not miss a single detail.

"With Your Excellency's permission, I shall have a word with Captain Berulli. He will conduct you personally to the St. Cecilia, I'm sure."

On the morning of October 11, Papa Angelica was borne with full panoply into St. Peter's Basilica on the *sedia gestatoria.* He celebrated a pontifical High Mass for the 2,500 mitered, white-robed bishops who sat together in tiered rows of seats on either side of the principal aisles. Thousands of privileged visitors were packed into the remaining areas of the Basilica. Tens of thousands more in the piazza outside listened to the loudspeakers. Millions throughout the world were connected through radio and television.

Rico had gotten the morning's schedule from the meticulous Monsignore Amalfeo, papal master of ceremonies, and so was able to time things almost perfectly. Captain Berulli led him, Keti, and Eugenio through a narrow iron door into the huge wall of the Basilica. As the foursome climbed a set of steep, winding stairs, the sounds of the Mass just ending boomed louder and louder in their ears.

For Eugenio, the day was already a wonderful success. He had seen the firehouse; he had made friends with the captain himself; and now he was sneaking about in secret passageways.

With Berulli as their guide, the little group soon found itself in a narrow, boxlike room with decorated walls and ceiling. It was large enough to hold some half-dozen adults. The fire captain entered first and switched on a light just long enough to show his charges to three cushioned chairs. Once they were seated, he turned the light off again, and slid back a decorated panel about two feet high. Two lateral openings were uncovered that gave directly onto the innards of the Basilica. The trio saw that they were a few degrees higher than Angelica's throne placed below the steps of the High Altar, facing the bishops. St. Peter's main doors had been thrown open, and the sun from the east fingered the nave with brilliant rays. As Benfatti had said, they could see everything.

Captain Berulli whispered that he would come back for them, reminded his new little friend and admirer, Eugenio, to be very quiet, and was gone.

Eugenio clambered into his mother's lap to get a better view. To the chanting of the Sistine Choir, Monsignore Amalfeo was just leading His Holiness in solemn procession from the High Altar, where Mass had been sung, to the throne below the altar steps. Two papal chamberlains, each carrying an ostrich-feather fan, took up places on either side of the throne. The main officials of the papal court, Picolomini, Arnulfo, Lanser, and some dozen more, reached their chairs. Last of all came Papa Angelica, in full regalia and wearing his triple tiara, to sit upon the throne.

In accordance with custom, Amalfeo approached the Pope, opened the red damask folder that held the Pope's prepared allocution, and pointed at the first word of the opening line. Angelica put on his spectacles. He did not begin at once, however. He looked over the top of his reading glasses, as if to absorb the entire scene—his bishops bathed in the morning light, visitors crowding all the balconies, television cameras trained from their strategic positions, paparazzi whose flashbulbs flicked like constant daystars. At length, however, he glanced down where Amalfeo's finger still pointed.

"Grazie!" he whispered under his breath to his master of ceremonies for his patience, and to his God for having brought his Council thus far on its unknown road.

Then, in a very loud voice:

"My dearest brothers and sisters!" Angelica was improvising, as usual; all here were his brothers and sisters. But Amalfeo would have none of it. The Pope must not improvise at such ceremonies as this.

Angelica blinked at that imperious, bony index finger pointing insistently at the first printed word of the prepared speech. *"Fa be'!"* he relented, and began reading.

"Most Eminent Lord Cardinals! Most Venerable Lord Patriarchs! Reverend Fathers! Most distinguished Ladies and Gentlemen of the Diplomatic Corps! Beloved Sons and Daughters everywhere! This is the day the Lord has made! And this is the hour that God has appointed! We have invoked the blessing of Christ on the forthcoming labors of our Council, and now We wish to share Our joy and Our hopes with you. . . ."

To Keti's surprise and relief, Eugenio remained fascinated and quite still, even through the Pontiff's speech. Rico had explained the importance of it all to him, and he knew, too, that the processions were still to come.

". . . and because We desire that the first fruits of Our Council will be peace and loving harmony of all Our beloved sons and daughters throughout all the nations in God's world, We now impart to each of you here and to each human being Our Apostolic Blessing as the Successor of Blessed Peter and as Vicar on this earth of our most adorable Lord and Savior, Jesus Christ."

Monsignore Amalfeo closed the damask folder and moved to his place in the papal entourage. The Sistine Choir raised again the sounds of chants and hymns; and, exactly as the master of ceremonies had arranged, the procession of bishops to the papal throne began. Four abreast they came, filling the central aisle, each new row now kneeling in its turn in obeisance to the Pontiff, and then retiring again in quick succession.

Immediately the bishops were all back in their places flanking the aisles from the throne to the open doors, all eyes turned to the east.

"Now, Uncle Rico?" Eugenio whispered expectantly.

"Yes, now." It was the turn of all the delegations of pilgrims from every part of the world who had massed outside in St. Peter's Square to salute and bring greetings to the Pontiff. This was the "parade" that Eugenio had looked forward to, and he was not disappointed.

Rapidly, the broad center aisle became a moving sea of every brilliant color as group followed upon group, each stopping for its moment of special greeting by the Pope and for his blessing. Each delegation displayed a large banner proclaiming its identity. Each was filled with smiling faces.

Flags waved in hands. There were national costumes from every European country, from Africa, from Asia and Latin America. There was a mélange of ankle-length robes, knee-length dresses, bonnets, caps, hats, Arab kuffiehs and Turkish fezzes, uniforms of two dozen national armies, choirs of chanting children, bands of musicians playing melodies of their homelands, the deep bass drums of Africa following the piping bouzoukis of the Middle East and preceding the reedlike flutes of the Assamese and the Indian harps.

Papa Angelica on his throne seemed as delighted with it all as Eugenio was. The Pope received each delegation with that great smile of his that seemed to warm the world. He gave each his blessing, and as each one wheeled off to the left, to exit by a side door, he received the next, and then the next, until the last scheduled delegation appeared at the great double doors.

It was the one from Ireland, and it was led by a six-man bagpipe band. The gentle keening and caroling of those pipes echoing in the huge Basilica seemed the perfect climax; it quickly took the fancy of bishops and Pope alike. Angelica stamped one big foot in time with the cadence. Some of the bishops stood; others, finding their view blocked, stood as well. Angelica began to clap his hands in rhythm; a few of the bishops took it up, and then more, until all were standing and all were clapping time, and a moment of joyous freedom seemed to bind all as one.

The pipes were silent for just a moment while the Irish delegation knelt before the papal throne and received Angelica's blessing. Then, their pipes keening anew in a goodbye strain, Ireland's sons marched to the left and out of sight, leaving the center aisle emptied at last. Most of the bishops remained standing, expecting His Holiness to rise. But Amalfeo was whispering in the Pontiff's ear. The word passed down the aisle that there was one more delegation to come. Heads began to turn back toward the doors.

Sure enough, a very curious delegation was just starting up the aisle, throwing its shadow before it, its silence contrasting darkly with the echoes of the Irish pipes. No one in this final group spoke. No one sang. Perhaps forty-five men and women shuffled forward. Their costumes were the strangest of the day—the dirty blue and gray stripes worn by Soviet prisoners. Their faces were raised. Their eyes were fixed on Papa Angelica. They carried more than one banner, each with a different name on it. Poland. East Germany. Czechoslovakia. Lithuania. Latvia. Hungary. All the names of all the Soviet slave states, down to the Ukraine. At the very front, held higher than all the banners, the starkest symbol came before: a large wooden cross, wound round at its center with coils of barbed wire. At the top of the cross, a white placard. In tradition, the message written on it would have been INRI, as the inscription on Christ's cross had read. But here one word only had been printed, in blood-red paint. PERCHÉ? *Why?*

A whispered buzzing of questions trailed the grim procession toward the papal throne, as bishops turned to one another in puzzlement.

"They're asking why." One explained the placard to another, who couldn't read Italian.

"Why what?"

"I don't know."

"They're from the Soviet satellites."

"Haven't you heard that His Holiness has had interviews with some of the Soviets? These people obviously feel he's betrayed them."

Papa Angelica needed no explanation. He watched the delegation approach at its funereal pace. His face flushed, and he continually clasped and unclasped his hands in his distress at the sharp public rebuke implied in the symbolism. In spite of his emotion, His Holiness stood to receive the representatives of the Gulag. He raised his arms, and in a voice that was near to breaking, pronounced the triple papal blessing. It was the only sound; it faded slowly as though the sad-faced group bore it away with the cross.

Immediately, the Sistine Choir filled the air with lovely music; but the zest and joy could not be restored.

Rico was sure he knew what had happened. Mindless for that moment of Keti and Eugenio, he leaned forward to catch a glimpse of Cardinal Wallensky. The old man was seated quietly, looking straight ahead, amid a crowd of bishops chattering in whispers around him. How very sad he looked, Lansing thought. There could be no doubt! The Pole had found a way to make his statement.

Throughout Rome that evening, at all the official receptions, the conversation centered on the magnificent success of the opening ceremonies for the Ecumenical Council. The main subject on everyone's mind, of course, was that final demonstration and its obvious effect on Papa Angelica, but only those unacquainted with the way of Roman affairs brought it up at all. Those few who were foolish enough to mention it seemed unable to make themselves understood. It was an unwritten rule strictly observed in the part of Roman society that interfaced closely with Vatican life: No topic touching on the Holy Father and his interests was a matter for such public comment.

The gathering at Villa Cerulea was small, and the conversation more candid for that. Wallensky and Valeska, along with Rico Lansing, were the only guests. After dinner, they retired for a while to the library with the Maestro and Helmut for brandy and cigars.

The contrast between "the fox of Europe" and the Maestro was striking for Rico. Both had a remarkable bigness and quickness of mind. Both had vision and foresight that were as far-reaching as any man's who lived. And yet, except on fundamentals, those two giants would probably never be in accord.

"Perhaps, Maestro"—the cardinal mused over that very point while he enjoyed the rare pleasure of an excellent cigar and vintage brandy—"perhaps it is simply that I come to your Western world from a place so different. I seem to see everything here in outline, without the clutter of details that entrance those of you who live here. I do not offend you, Maestro? I would not . . ."

"There is no question of that, Eminence." Guido was sincere; here was one man with huge capabilities who would speak his mind.

"Well." The Pole fixed his eyes on his host. "I know little of your work for the Holy Father except that it is mainly financial. My own work is different, of course. Still, we are both open ultimately, I think, to whatever will promote the Church's mission. But I cannot see the point in securing a place of honor and might for the Holy See in the great capitalist power circles of the Western world. That is a repetition of past history."

"Not entirely, Eminence." Guido pointed out that classic capitalism, under which the Church had lately looked to bolster its spiritual authority "with a goodly dollop of temporal power," was dead. The arena had changed.

"It has," Wallensky agreed. "And I am not the expert you are, Maestro. But this newly emergent system of international, capital-based power brokers that we seem to be witnessing shows all the signs of being as inhuman and certainly as anti-Christian as Marxism. The Marxists cut our jugular veins; this new system injects a poison that invades the body. It is more subtle. It takes longer. But in the end?"

Guido did not deny the possibilities or the dangers. It was simply that he hoped to achieve in terms of money and power what Angelica was trying to achieve in terms of Spirit. "It is either that, Your Eminence, or divest the Holy See and the Church of its material independence. That is a grave step to contemplate."

"Agreed." Wallensky accepted a second brandy. "But it seems to me that a spiritual Pentecost such as His Holiness dreams of, and, if I may draw upon your comparison with Papa Angelica, a financial pentecost, share the same danger. You both hope to influence the world for the better. He with Spirit. You with brokerage that will bring the Church back into the world's power centers. I fear Papa Angelica leans the Church so far toward our enemies that we may topple right into their midst; become just like them, in other words.

"Could that not happen, too, in finance? Indeed, as the means are temporal, is it not even more likely?"

Listening to the two older men seemed only to sharpen a growing puzzlement in Rico. Both were important to him. More to the point, both were important to the Church. Yet each had grown deeply into the grooves of his own convictions, and those grooves could never run together.

Lansing tried to balance his sympathy for Guido, and the fact that his own important work in the East depended on the financing the Maestro provided, with the fact that he agreed in substance with Wallensky. And all the while, at the back of his mind was the memory of the Polish cardinal's sad face at the Basilica that morning, contrasted with Angelica's expression of pain and puzzlement at the Gulag demonstration.

Angelica, so open and unprejudiced, shedding warmth and light with the ease of a summer sky above upland meadows, seemed now to be hemmed in on every side.

On no lips but Angelica's, Rico reflected, did he hear the word "Pentecost." Is such a thing possible? he wondered. In a world where two such good men as these were divided, were things so out of kilter, so off balance, that the real Pentecost needed would be too fearful to contemplate?

"We have them nicely off balance, my dear." Canon Ripley-Savage took Muffie aside for a quiet moment. It was, in effect, a perfect evening as far as he was concerned. A buffet dinner in the Roman suburb of Ostia, in full view of the Tyrrhenian Sea. He and Bishop Cale and the others mingling actually with the likes of Cardinal Jan Svensens of Belgium, and the French Cardinal Paul-Marie Grandville, Archbishop of Dijon.

"Cardinals are nice," Muffie granted the point. "But I place greater store by the theologians and *periti* we attracted. They're the ones who will be in the trenches for us. The German Hans Kleiser over there. Charles McMurren and Harry Corcoran of Catholic University in Washington are somewhere in this mob. I even saw the famous Jesuit James Courtland Molloy of New York chatting with our Richard Richards! Christian unity is a wonderful thing, don't you agree, darling?"

The bell-like clang of a spoon rapped on crystal hushed the din of conversation and brought all eyes to Metropolitan Nikodim. He was standing happily in the company of Annibale Sugnini and Archbishop Levesque, and very near the buffet table laden with stuffed clams and swordfish and carafes of dry Polichella.

"Where else would he be?" Muffie whispered under her breath to the Canon.

"I propose a toast." Nikodim raised his glass to all. "This is an auspicious day, the eve of a joyful reunion. Let us drink to success and to God's blessing on all our labors during the Council. For if we are successful, we shall make history."

Muffie raised her glass, and whispered to her husband. "The only history I'm interested in is yours, dearest. I drink to your becoming Archbishop of Canterbury. And to my having four o'clock tea at Buckingham Palace. And to our shares in the Bank of Kuwait. Otherwise, to quote Matthew Arnold, 'History . . .' "

"I know, my dear." The Canon led his wife back into the evening crowd. " 'History is bunkum!' "

In festive Rome that night, it seemed that only the good Papa Angelica was alone. None of those who talked and argued and celebrated even guessed at the agony of his self-doubt and the physical pain that gripped him as he tried to rest. What troubled him was far different from the insidious preoccupations of the Alliance, or the Maestro's concerns in his dedicated rush to serve the Holy See's material welfare. His was not Wallensky's troubled realism, nor Richard Lansing's maturing view of the grave issues at stake. Even the divisions of the State Council and the Curia were not troublesome for him. All those things, Angelica knew, belong to the human scene. All could be transfused and transformed by Spirit. He concentrated his papacy with all his energy and all his heart on achieving the big event that would transform the issues, liquefy the frozen divisions—even for those more intent on wreaking their own will than the Catholic will in his Council. His great gamble was that the new Pentecost he spoke of so continually would change everything—even the bleak world of those sad-faced ones who had reproached him that morning for abandoning them to their crucifixion behind the barbed-wire fences of the Gulag.

What preyed on his mind and wakened him time and again on many nights was his cancer. Not the physical pain of it; but the fact that it, too, was the creation of his loving God, the obvious way his papacy would end. Should it cut off his life before his Council could succeed, would that also signal God's will? God's judgment against his entire venture?

There lay the question for Angelica. Not possible failure, nor bitter memories of Gulag faces, nor the pain that brought the sweat to his face. But only his will to do the will of God.

And so only the prayer of request for forgiveness, and the prayer of hope in Christ, who had made of this peasant a Vicar for His people, calmed Angelica, and allowed sleep to fall on him.

[[34]]

Only the God Angelica worshiped and Christ in whom he hoped as Savior could know the expectancy that illuminated this Pope's soul as the daily sessions of his Council began. It was not the same expectancy the curial cardinals entertained—or, at least, it was not entirely on the same plane.

On the ordinary level, the Roman hierarchy knew rather well how the Council should progress. The bishops would meet in formal session for five hours every morning. The supervision and control of each day's session would be in the hands of the rotating Council presidents. There would be three such presidents sitting each day, chosen from the cardinals of the Preparatory Commission headed by His Eminence Cardinal Arnulfo, head of the all-powerful Holy Office and protector of doctrinal purity.

The Council presidents would introduce the *Schema* to be discussed in each Council session. They would approve the application of any bishop who wished to speak on any *Schema.* They would decide the composition of committees of bishops that would be entrusted with the task of taking all the views and suggestions made on the Council floor during each morning session, and remaking the original text of the *Schema* so as to reflect those views and suggestions. The bishops on the committees depended on the help of their theological experts. Those committees—as well as more informal study groups—would meet in the afternoons and evenings, after each day's session was over.

Though the years of preparation of the *Schemata* had been arduous, to say the least, the fact that each had been so thoroughly circulated in advance of the Council, and that so much of the bishops' own comments had already been incorporated in the texts, should mean that the daily sessions themselves would move along swiftly. It was reliably felt by nearly everybody in the preparatory mechanism of the Council that, on an average, two *Schemata* could be completed each week; and that by early December, therefore, all of them would be in form, voted upon by the bishops, and ready for a final summary vote, and for approval and promulgation by the Holy Father.

The curial cardinals' expectation was that the Council deliberations and finally official texts would lay to rest much of the discordant waves of doctrine, of theory, and of ideas that had been buffeting the Church for quite a while now. The demonstration to the world by the Council would be a display of unity in Church government and attractiveness of teaching enshrined in a freshly hewn format. The old, old wine of Catholicism in attractive new bottles!

Angelica shared this expectation; but more important, in his eyes, was his hope and trust that, as the Council progressed, a new charisma would appear in the dry and musty bones of theological teaching, filling bishops and observers alike with a fresh Pentecostal wisdom. In the light of that wisdom, differences and hatreds and opposition would melt, according as more and more people shook themselves out of age-old grooves, stood up, and said to each other: Let us, under God, remake our unity as his children in his Church. It was a vision of the Pentecost of latter days! The prelude to Christ's final appearance among the men and women he saved!

From October onward, Papa Angelica faithfully watched the proceedings of his Council on one of the two closed-circuit television sets he had installed in the papal apartments. Most often, he would sit at his oaken desk or in one of the more comfortable chairs in his study. If his pain was overwhelming, he would sometimes watch from his bed. But never did he neglect a moment of any session. Now and again, he would telephone the cardinal presidents, or call on one of the bishops for a consultation about a particular point. But he had a "hands-off" attitude. Was not the Holy Spirit active down there? And could he not rely on that Spirit finally to evoke the best from his bishops?

"You see only what you know," an ancient Greek philosopher once remarked when discussing the ability of man to read into events what he thought he knew those events signified. For the first two or three weeks, Papa Angelica read the daily happenings on the Council floor—the instructions given by the presiding cardinals, the stream of speeches made by the individual bishops, the special interventions, the occasional ad hoc voice votes, the reports of consultative committees, the occasional acrimonious exchange between bishop and bishop or bishop and presiding cardinal. All of it was read by him as a necessary and due preparation for the time when the real momentum of his Council would become apparent, and the very atmosphere on the Council floor would be transmuted into a living, quickening dialogue. That vivifying dialogue of apostles was what Angelica *knew* his Council signified.

Therefore, that is what he *saw* in preparation.

The reality was a good deal different. Among the bishops, there was a new and growing consciousness of themselves as a group, and as quite distinct from the Roman bureaucracy of the Holy Father. Emphasized in their mind was the fact guaranteed by their faith: Each bishop was ecclesiastically regarded as a successor to the Twelve Apostles, with a mandate from Christ himself, whereas the curial bureaucracy was a collection of appointed functionaries with no divine mandate. Rubbing shoulders with those functionaries—most of them were Italian, most had never put their nose outside Italy—showed the bishops that the Romans had no idea of the changes and evolution in progress among the peoples of the Church's provinces.

The catalytic factor that precipitated these elements in the makeup of the bishops as a group—prior to the actual Council, intensely so during the Council—was the highly organized and carefully focused activity of the Northern Alliance and of the friends it had cultivated and the converts it had made among Catholic theologians and *periti,* as well as among a small, restricted number of bishops.

Papa Angelica knew nothing of all that; and, to adapt the Italian proverb, he was deaf in one ear to the siren song of Modernism. He was no theologian in the first place. His personal piety would always have preserved him from gross error; but he was inclined to favor modernization. If he were dealing only with machines, it would have been feasible. But at stake was the immutable teaching of the Catholic Church. To set out to modernize it usually—perhaps inevitably—ends up in Modernism, jettisoning an ancient doctrine and replacing it with some modern theory.

Nor could Papa Angelica guess at the constant activity of Sugnini and his friends, always making sure that the theologians and *periti* thought along two lines: a mildly anti-Roman line; and a line of generality rather than specificity in doctrine. The generality carved huge holes of ambiguity in the phrasing of doctrines and rules. Through these holes, individual bishops would be able "to drive a coach-and-four," as Arnulfo remarked after the Council was over and done with.

One of the more spectacular successes of the Northern Alliance was to lead theologians and bishops to draw on contemporary psychology, anthropology, sociology, politics, even Far Eastern mysticism, rather than on the gargantuan and overflowingly rich treasury accumulated by the Church since the time of Peter the Apostle. But success here was made possible by a weakening of faith among the bishops as well as by their general ignorance of their own sacred tradition.

In these circumstances, and under the impulse of such forces, Papa Angelica's perception started to focus more accurately on the reality before him.

Each day, the Vatican printing press spewed out a small river of the Council's speeches, commentaries, recommendations, theological essays, opinion sheets, emendations, notices, directives, summaries. The Pope's table began to fill up with it all. There seemed to be no end to the flood. And it was in November that Papa Angelica started to know something else, and therefore to see it. Seated between his desk, laden with documentation, and the television set whose screen always seemed to show yet another bishop producing yet further ideas, the Pope recognized the process that had actually taken over his Council.

There was no sign of a break or change or elevation in the daily round of exchanges of opinion; not even a remote sign that the bishops would accept the *Schema* under discussion and hurry on to the next *Schema.* There was no gathering pool of divine light down there on the Council floor. Rather, that floor had now become a theologizing cockpit in which the mind of the bishops contended with the minutest details of each *Schema* according to the advisement of the theologians and *periti.*

It got so that each morning Papa Angelica could scan the list of scheduled speakers, and not only calculate the diminishing scope of work that would be accomplished that day, but guess at the uneven struggle being waged behind the scenes between those who shared his views and the vast majority of bishops in the Council who had the bit between their teeth.

One scene around mid-November drove the full truth about his Council home to Angelica. Cardinal Arnulfo, formidable head of the Holy Office, claimed the right to speak at the podium, and in no uncertain terms took the bishops of the Council to task for the "flippant way," as he put it, they were demanding "a total revision" of the *Schema* on the nature and role of the Church in the modern world. "We, here at the center of the Church, have a view of the Church which is universal," he asserted.

To Angelica's surprise and Arnulfo's personal chagrin, heckling shouts came from the floor. The mildest were very strong. The strongest were nearly offensive.

"We are the bishops of the Church. You are a functionary, Your Eminence. . . ."

"Your Eminence is violating the rules of procedure. Either talk to the topic in hand, or surrender the microphone. . . ."

"Abolish the Inquisition!"

There was more along those lines. Arnulfo realized he was beaten. He looked out over the assembly with a semi-smile:

"And I suppose you are going to reject our *Schema,* anyway, no matter how strongly I object or how long I speak."

There was a wave of gentle—not mocking—laughter at the apparently good-natured way the once-feared guardian of doctrinal purity was taking his defeat. Arnulfo ceded the microphone. The *Schema* was rejected by a large margin, and sent back into committee for a total rewriting.

For Angelica, the scene was a revelation. When Arnulfo, in high dudgeon, came to see him that evening, he found the Pope quiet and resigned.

"The bishops of Christ's Church are now in Council, Excellency." He waved aside Arnulfo's indignation. "I understand your distress. But we must believe the Holy Spirit is with them. The Council was never *my* Council. It was and is Christ's. Let us be patient, and see where the will of God takes us all."

Arnulfo departed to lick his wounds, and to discuss the whole affair with his collaborators. But without a papal intervention, there was little he could do.

The underlying fact for Angelica's mind was a poignantly true one: His Roman bureaucracy over the years had created the impression of being a collection of cynical autocrats applying the laws of God and of the Church with much exactitude but with little love and, sometimes, with an unfeeling rigidity that bordered on heartless cruelty. The resentments, the fears, the hurts, the broken hopes, had all gathered into a hard lump. Now, given the unique opportunity of facing their oppressors—but en masse, as the bishops of Christ's Church—the bishops had thrown that hard lump back in the face of the bureaucracy. Angelica had no means of knowing the orchestrated way in which the Northern Alliance and its friends had played upon that resentment. In any case, he could have done nothing to offset the bishops' headlong course.

But, at least, Angelica now knew and saw the reality. "We will not live to see the end of this Council," he remarked to Ducocasa one evening. "The Lord has given. The Lord has taken away. Blessed be the name of the Lord."

Papa Angelica never put in words, even to Ducocasa, his deepest disappointment. He was too humble for that, and too dependent on Christ's will. But he had his little late-night solitary regrets, and his early-morning bitter reflections that perhaps his whole idea of a new Council and a modern Pentecost had been a delusion of the Devil himself.

With his dawning realization, Angelica slowly reviewed all the happenings leading up to his Council. What galled him in particular was the cost of his mistake, if mistake he had made. Of course, he knew that his Catholic subjects in the terrible darkness of the empire of the Soviets were suffering martyrdom. Precisely, he had planned his new Pentecost to shed a brilliant light over it all, penetrating even the hardened hearts of the Gulag's oligarchs. He had sacrificed the Greek Orthodox observers for this reason. He had even promised not to attack the Soviet Union or to condemn Marxism. That was why he could give no answer to that blood-red PERCHÉ, that soul-disturbing *Why,* daubed at the top of that barbed-wire-entwined cross. The Council was to have been his answer why.

Now? The Council would be no answer. The whole effort had been useless. Perhaps worse than useless.

He remembered the anguish on the face of that American monsignore —the one who knew the Gulag so well—when Angelica had told him of his policy not to condemn Marxism. Now, without any special light, the American's work was going to be trebly difficult, more lonely than ever, even more despair-ridden. He must see that young man. He surely had God's blessing. He must tell Ducocasa to give him an appointment soon. Brandolini spoke about that American with a special respect. And Brandolini rarely made a mistake.

Rico had nothing in particular to discuss with Papa Angelica; but neither was a call from the papal secretary to be shunted off.

The fact that the Ecumenical Council had taken on its own life and was being slowly but surely molded to the mind of Rome's enemies, and the fact that he could not discuss his own covert work with Papa Angelica, both came to weigh heavily on Rico Lansing.

In his purely rational mind, Rico had to agree with the Maestro and with Cardinals Lanser and Falconieri that silence about his network of cells in Eastern Europe was the prudent course to follow. The unprecedented fruits for the Soviets of his mission to Moscow and Constantinople had made that plain enough. But now that the Council itself was turning into a long-drawn-out struggle between those who intended to make the Roman Church over to their wishful image of it, and those who were fighting for their very existence as Catholics, Lansing wished at times that he could openly plead with Angelica for the support so needed by the religious underground that was forming slowly, laboriously, and at great personal risk on the part of so many in the empire of the Gulag. He wished he could tell his Pope the daily torture priests and nuns in the East were willingly undergoing, while these bishops in Rome were picking away at theological niceties like so many roosters picking at worms in a barnyard. At times, he almost had to bite his tongue to keep from pleading with Angelica to get back to the things that mattered.

When Ducocasa showed him into Papa Angelica's private study, the Pope was at his desk, reading by the light of a table lamp. His feet were resting on a hassock. The moment Rico laid eyes on him, he was shocked by the change that had come over Angelica in a few short months. Deep ravages had swept over the flesh of Angelica's face, leaving intact only the strong features—the deeper age lines, the huge ears, the solid bone of the nose, the firm-lipped mouth and solid chin—but sweeping away all else that bespoke ease and joy in living or any felt boundlessness of mortal hopes.

"Come, Monsignore Rico." The Pope smiled in welcome. "Come! Have a seat."

It was Angelica's habit rarely to attack a delicate subject directly. He preferred to get at it in his own roundabout way. The lines on the American's face told of strain and aloneness and, also, that peculiar vulnerability of the man who has plunged trustfully into a mystery, not knowing where his path would lead him. Lansing obviously was at grips much more poignantly than most of Angelica's curial bureaucracy and most of his bishops with the grandiose and overarching mystery of the Church.

Angelica heaved himself out of his chair and made his way over to a window. "Come with me, Monsignore. Come over here and see where Christ has placed me." He swept the scene with a pudgy hand.

It was close to dusk; the sun was setting in a reddened glory that peered dubiously between the rain clouds. Over the whole scene there was a lightsomeness only found in this southern part of Europe—what the ancient Romans used to call "the veil of the evening star goddess."

Immediately below, on the square, there was little activity—some people clustered around the obelisk at the center of the piazza, a taxicab making its way diagonally across the square toward the city of Rome.

"This is my view on the whole world," the Pope said quietly. "Look! I can see all: Old Rome near me, New Rome near me. The brown Tiber near me. Those eternal hills, the countryside, the world. You can even imagine that from here you could touch it all with the tips of your fingers.

"And yet, how do you think a peasant such as I can live here, my little son? I was born into a big family with brothers, a sister, cousins, grandparents on both sides, and a multitude of neighbors—all of us bound together by our labor on the land and by our belief in our common destiny.

"And now since they made me Pope, I am alone. I lost every one of those beloved intimates. I live with strangers who feed me, put me to bed, get me up on time, dress me, shave me, instruct me, guard me, lead me out and lead me in, tell me what I must say and what I must not say, whom I must meet and whom I must not meet, when to sit, when to stand, when to walk, when to bless, when to turn away. They watch over my breathing and my writing and my talking. They are waiting for me to die, and then they will bury me and put another prisoner in my place, and start the whole carousel all over again. They are already picking that successor of mine! They started the day they elected me. So!

"What have I now?" He gestured out the window. "I have the wide world. And all my sons and daughters in that world. I cannot take one side or the other when they fight among themselves. I cannot walk away from any of them when they fail according to my book. I cannot leave them in their pain. I must labor to reach them, even if I think and even know they are in error. God will find it hard to forgive us, if we treat them with coldness and condemnation.

"And, *figluolo*"—Angelica turned back to go to his desk—"one thing I cannot do is correct an error of practical judgment that has imposed a process on the subjects in the Church. The way the Church works, to stop a process, once it is begun, requires much time; much, much time. And I have not much time, *figluolo.* Not much at all."

Whatever mistakes this Pope had made, Rico felt, surely the love radiant and alive in him would be his passport to forgiveness by a very exacting Christ.

"Now, Monsignore, you labor in the darkness. In obscurity. You labor well, so they tell me."

"It's nothing, Holy Father. I just—"

"Monsignore, it matters greatly what you do." For the first time in this interview, Angelica's tone became pontifical. "The Council has happened. The Church will never be the same again. There will be much confusion, possibly erroneous ideas and even erroneous practices. What you are doing, what you labor to create, I feel it is going to be of prime importance in the Church that will emerge from all this brouhaha and hubbub of theologian and bishop. Prime importance, Monsignore!"

He struggled to his feet again, and held out his Fisherman's Ring. When Rico had kissed it, Angelica stayed him one moment longer. "Monsignore," he said softly and pleadingly, "tell them all I love them. Tell them I will be of better use to them in the next world. And, Monsignore, bind up the wounds that I may have inflicted unknowingly."

Rico walked home slowly, across the piazza and down the Via della Conciliazione, passing five or six groups of bishops on their way to and from meetings or meals. In a sense, he now realized, they did not matter anymore. The Council as an event had hit the Church broadside. The rest would be an amalgam of individual choice and group tendency. But the Church, the mystical body of Christ, had already absorbed the shock. In all its sanctity. In all its weakest members. He was both troubled and at peace about Papa Angelica. Troubled for his near-future death and for his disappointment. At peace because of the grandeur of the man's humility and the rocklike persistence of his love.

Cardinal Ferragamo-Duca chaired the stormiest and gloomiest State Council in memory. That ardent Roman had been infuriated by Angelica's Council of bishops, and he showed it this morning as he fixed Cardinal Arnulfo in a vicious stare.

"Somebody told me a few years ago that this Council would be over and done with in one autumn session. All finished and done, with control in our hands!"

Falconieri, Hoffeldt, and O'Mahoney winced as they, too, looked at Arnulfo. It seemed to the first two, at least, that the head of the Holy Office had taken enough of a beating at the hands of the bishops.

Lanser and the Maestro looked at one another. The fact that the Maestro had been asked to attend this morning signaled the unusual nature of the agenda.

"Well"—Ferragamo-Duca didn't pause in his bitter preamble—"Papa Angelica will end the session, all right. Next week, with the celebration of the Feast Day of the Immaculate Conception. But there is no hope of finishing even a respectable fraction of the essential Council business in these final days. All the key committees are still occupied in their so-called redrafting of the *Schemata.* The way this circus is going, it will be dumb luck if it's finished in anything less than two or three additional sessions."

Cardinal O'Mahoney, who now represented American interests in the State Council, had little patience for the niceties of protocol. He spoke up without waiting for the chair to open the floor to general discussion. "Your Eminence paints too black a picture." He smiled confidently above his double chin. "You'll see how fast the bishops forget this little jaunt to Rome when they get back to reality. It's a passing bit of trouble you're talking about. It is going to make precious little difference when it comes to the real business of raising money and running our dioceses."

In this gathering of realists, O'Mahoney was a dreamer; and his dreams were not very grand.

"Kieran." Arnulfo spelled the situation out for the American cardinal with a display of almost saintly patience and restraint. "The reality, to use your term, is that—thanks to the Northern Alliance strategy and the zeal of the Catholic ecumenists—we have a runaway Council on our hands. Its obvious goal seems to be to override every directive of the Holy See, and to replace all the *Schemata* with air-filled and meaningless documents on the most basic and vital subjects of faith and morals. If you ask yourself why this is so, the answer can only be that those same strategists and zealots will do all they can to use the new documents to tear the fabric of the Church to pieces!"

O'Mahoney only blinked in silence. These Roman prelates were always worrying about something.

"That's a fair summary of the problem," Ferragamo-Duca took up again. "However, the question of Papa Angelica's health may place the problem on, let us say, a more manageable level. You have all had a chance to read Dr. Mazzoni's summary of the Pontiff's condition?"

All heads nodded, but only Falconieri spoke. "Poor old Giovanni. He deserved better than cancer ravaging his body and the bishops ravaging his Council."

"What he deserves is not for us to say." Ferragamo-Duca preferred not to speak his full mind on that issue. There was a revolt in process against the Roman government of the Church, and the Pope who had let that happen was dying. Those were the facts. "Papa Angelica has not more than half a year to live, if his doctor is correct. Most of us have seen Angelica in recent days. The deterioration and the pain are palpable. I'm sure we all pray for him." A glance at Falconieri. "But we must turn our practical attention to the next conclave; to the choice of the next pope. Everything depends on Papa Angelica's successor."

It was Lanser who understood first what Ferragamo-Duca probably had in mind. "I think we all realize that Papa Angelica intended another type of Council. And a shorter one. You're suggesting, Eminence, that we may not be able to restore the Pontiff's high aims for his Council; but that by the choice of his successor, we can ensure its end."

"Exactly!" Ferragamo-Duca could not have been more emphatic. "The optimum choice is a man whose first act as Pontiff will be to adjourn the Council *sine die.*"

"Or"—Arnulfo brightened at the prospect—"a man who is strong enough to dragoon the bishops in Council back into line in one more session, and then end it by papal order."

"A Pius IX, in other words." Hans Hoffeldt of Munich, though a radical in Church politics, had little stomach for Angelica's Council. But neither was he prepared to see so authoritarian a solution. "I think we will all agree, Eminences, that among the true *papabile,* there is no such man. And I for one would not propose such a response to our problem."

To everyone's surprise, Cardinal Lanser agreed at least in part with Hoffeldt. Not because Lanser was a radical, but because he did not agree that the real problem they faced was the Ecumenical Council.

"What then?" Ferragamo-Duca was impatient.

"The problem"—Lanser explained his mind smoothly and lucidly—"is what has *allowed* the Council to get out of hand, and allowed the Northern Alliance its foothold. If the Council is in revolt—and I obviously agree with Cardinal Arnulfo that it is—then that revolt is fed from a deeper source within the Church itself. The Alliance has merely taken advantage of that source, utilized it for its own ends. The Council is merely a stage on which that deeper source has found its chance to play a leading part."

Lanser turned to Cardinal Arnulfo. "You spoke a moment ago, Your Eminence, of a pope in the mold of Pius IX. He and his successor both condemned a grave heresy according to which Church doctrine and practice should teach in one age what it condemned in prior ages, in order to evolve and adapt itself to modern times. That heresy was called Modernism.

"Well, I submit that Modernism is the source of our problem now. The fact that it was condemned and proscribed by two popes did not kill it, but merely drove it underground, where it festered and spread its poison, until now it has infected bishops and theologians, seminaries and university faculties. Indeed, Angelica's very Council is infected with it. It has emerged, in other words, stronger than ever.

"Now, how are we going to deal with *that* enemy? Suppress it again?

We are now observing what happens in the long run when we do that."

Falconieri saw the logical conclusion, but it seemed far too much of a risk. "You cannot give heresy free reign, Joachim! It will destroy the whole institution of the Church!"

Never had Lanser appeared so coldly rational, so far removed from the personable aspect he normally displayed. "The only way," he insisted quietly, "in which the hidden abscess that is affecting the very nerve centers of the Church can be cured is to draw its pus to the surface so that the sores that appear can be lanced. We have to draw out the Modernist-minded among Catholics with total openness, so that they can be seen for what they are and rejected. That can only be done if they think they have complete freedom and approval, even from the Pope himself."

No one had been prepared for such a radical and dangerous suggestion. Falconieri repeated his earlier objection. "The damage to the Church, Your Eminence. What about that?"

Lanser remained almost detached in his logic. "What about the damage being done as things are? Arnulfo said just moments ago that the fabric of the Church may be torn to pieces as we're going.

"Your Eminences, Maestro, the fact is that Modernism is making headway now. If we force it to the surface, it may make still more headway at the beginning. But the tide will change.

"Will it destroy the Church? The answer to that question may be chilling to some. But it should not be for us. If this Church is the Church of Christ, then the Spirit, working through believers, will surmount the evil. But not if we sequester the evil in dark recesses.

"If this is *not* the Church of Christ, then . . ." He left the sentence unfinished.

Arnulfo had no fear that ultimately the Church would not survive even such a daring flirtation with doctrinal heresy as Lanser was proposing. "But," he countered, "purity of doctrine is the guidepost for souls. It is truth. And truth is a practical thing, Eminence. Will souls not be lost on such a course?"

"Are just as many souls not going to be lost if we let the poison gather in the very arteries of the Church, mingling with the blood of Christ? The Modernist predilection today is for a naturalist religion, and for salvation won by the natural genius of a few men of our own time. How long can we hold out against this poison? For a few decades more?" Lanser truly could see no solution other than the one he proposed. "Whatever we do, Eminences, the time has again come when each person, like Daniel of the Old Testament, will have to decide if he will acknowledge God himself, or men who put themselves and their fabricated, latter-day godlets in his place. I believe we must do all we can to make that time as short as we can. I believe the peril will be no greater. But I acknowledge that it will be no less."

The Maestro had been silent until now. He was no theologian, as Arnulfo and Lanser were. But he understood the force of Lanser's argument in the light of one very practical fact. He reminded the State Council members that Angelica had been elected in the last conclave as an interim pope. That meant that even as conclave ended, the cardinal electors were already thinking about the next pope. "And Giovanni Da Brescia is the cardinal the key electors speak of most often. He has been restored to papal favor by Angelica. He has over thirty years of deep Vatican experience. He has been an obedient and successful primate of one of the most important dioceses in the universal Church. And the fact of the matter is that he is the one *papabile* whom the Modernists would consider to be their man."

Ferragamo-Duca looked in some surprise at his old friend and ally. "Then you agree with Cardinal Lanser, Maestro?"

"It's not as simple as that." Guido shook his head. "There is no optimum solution, Your Eminence. But the evil is upon us, as Papa Profumi said some years ago. Angelica's attempted solution has failed in one sense. But it has at least revealed the depth and extent of the problem, brought it out where we can identify it and begin to deal with it. I do agree that we cannot drive the rot underground and expect it to disappear as if by magic."

"Who would have thought it?" Falconieri's smile was not a pretty one. "Our prime *papabile* is Da Brescia, whom none of us like. And the mandate of the conclave will be to bring this Council we abhor to a successful conclusion."

It wasn't quite that cut-and-dried. Guido pointed out that there was still some pre-conclave work to do in order to achieve consensus. "Notably among the South Americans. But I think they will come around, especially as they have no one to offer in place of Da Brescia. In fact"—he scanned a small piece of paper in front of him—"the few names other than Milan are too weak to achieve any consensus."

"Da Brescia appears to be the man, then," Ferragamo-Duca acquiesced with a wan smile.

"God help His Eminence." Lanser's sincere prayer ended the State Council meeting.

[35]

Rome at Christmas Eve is like a festive, unruly concerto for a thousand voices. Street fiddlers are all about. Groups of songsters wend their way in and out of noisy traffic. The shepherds from Abruzzi are in the city—you know them by their Robin Hood hats and their rust-colored coats, and the coarse leggings held together by cross-stripes. This time of year, the lonely keening of their bagpipes rises above the streets and squares around the Piazza Venezia and the Via Imperiale, and up the Corso as far as the Piazza del Popolo, a wild, gentle stream of notes and chords seeming to be without beginning or end, never descending to a low note, balancing and teetering along every narrow edge of breeze, threatening to die away, but then rising again to cascade its questing lament in plangent carols like a passing summer shower. And over all the city, bells in ancient towers chime incidental accompaniment from dawn to midnight.

It was less design than happy remembrance that normally brought Rico Lansing and the de la Valle family together on Christmas Eve. With that Roman concerto as backdrop, they would retell the story of Agathi's discovery of Keti at Waidhofen; and they would make more memories to recall in future years.

This year was an exception for everyone. The day was cast in a more somber mold, as if in counterpoint to the accustomed celebrations.

Rico left Rome on a hurried flight to Chicago in response to a phone call from his father. Margaret Lansing died on the evening of Christmas Day. Her son was not prepared for his sensation of numb helplessness at the immobility and silence shrouding that beloved face, nor for the cold and unresponsive hardness of her forehead when he kissed it before they closed the coffin. As he sang the Requiem Mass and officiated at the funeral rites, he understood the parting of death in a new way that only doubled his sense of loss.

His father, Basil, bore up reasonably well. But to Rico, he seemed to have got old and weary overnight. Netta saw it too, and drew closer for a time to her father and brother. The twins, Brad and Basil, were home for Christmas recess; and once the stream of condolence calls ebbed, the whole family decided to spend some days in the snowy silence of their cabin on the shores of Lake Michigan. In that tranquillity, they rediscovered many of the old bonds that had made them a family. And yet each of them listened at unguarded moments for the accustomed sound of Margaret's voice; and each had to make an effort to remember they would not hear it again on this earth.

Just after ten in the evening, Monsignore Di Lorio and Guido emerged from the Maestro's study. Helmut was already waiting for them by the main door, and Sagastume had the limousine waiting outside.

"Don't wait up for us." Guido kissed Agathi, and then Keti, on the cheek.

Helmut knew Keti was disappointed to be left behind tonight, and perturbed that she and Agathi couldn't know what took the men away on Christmas Eve. He would make it up to her. He kissed her lightly, and followed his uncle and the Sphinx to the car.

"Never mind, Keti, darling." Agathi closed the door on December's chill and listened to the limousine purr away. "Tomorrow morning we'll all go to Mass together and things will be back to normal."

"This is normal." Keti smiled ruefully as the two walked through the semi-deserted villa. "Since we came back from Waidhofen last summer, Helmut has spent so much time with Guido, in addition to his usual work, that we have precious little time together. And he talks less and less about what he's doing."

They stopped by Eugenio's bedroom. He was fast asleep. Keti smoothed the covers up around him and kissed him. Then she and Agathi settled down in the older woman's sitting room, as they often did these days, for a quiet evening together.

They always had a great deal to talk about. Keti had become invaluable in the managing of Villa Cerulea. And now, in addition to the usual day-to-day responsibilities, Helmut had asked her to remodel their suite. The time had come when he needed to have a private study, much like the Maestro's, he said. And Eugenio's rooms, which had not been extensively redone since he was a baby, needed to be remodeled to a young boy's needs.

The women occupied themselves deeply for an hour or so in studying the architect's drawings, suggesting changes to one another; and planning ahead for colors and fabrics, cabinets and furniture. After a time, though, it was clear to Agathi that her companion did not really have her mind on the matter.

"Why don't we fix ourselves a cup of tea," she suggested. "It's a good night to put our feet up, and let our hair down."

There is something intimate about sitting at kitchen tables in late-night hours. Perhaps Agathi counted on that to draw Keti out. She did not want to ask prying questions; yet she knew the time had come to talk again, as they had before Keti's marriage—but more deeply now—about what it means to take second place to popes.

"Where do you suppose they've gone?" Keti let the strong Indian tea cool in her cup.

"To Rome. To some meeting. Or to see the Pope. Like you, I can only surmise."

"To Rome." Keti echoed. "I'm losing Helmut to that lady, Agathi."

"She's demanding, I'll say that," Agathi concurred. "But in a way, we probably have the better of the men. Sometimes when I feel abandoned, the way you do now, I remind myself of everything Guido gave up when the time came for him to take on the de la Valle responsibilities."

Keti had heard bits and pieces of Guido's early life; but she had never thought in terms of the rich and powerful Maestro as having given up anything, ever.

"He did, though." Agathi told in deep detail, now, how her brother had been given a present of a summer vacation in the Greek islands. "Our own Uncle Guido had promised him a special gift when he graduated at seventeen with honors from Basel University. I was only five then. Our parents had both died. And the sun rose and set for me in my brother. He was tall and muscular. He had the strength of an ox and the tenderness that always gave me confidence. I remember watching the coach that took him down the drive until I couldn't see it any longer. It was the first time I lost him."

"But he came back." Keti wasn't talking about a summer's vacation.

"It didn't turn out to be a summer vacation," Agathi countered. "And he came back only because he gave up forever what he wanted more than anything else."

Guido had got as far as Patmos on that island tour. The stark simplicity he discovered at the monastery of St. John held him there for the high summer months of July and August. Beneath the blue sky that did not host even one fleck of cloud, and within the unbroken heat of the Aegean, he sensed a gentle preamble to the dawn of ever-bright eternity.

After some weeks, he went for advice to the abbot of the monastery. Yes, the abbot had told him: Patmos was the place of Revelation. But it was not the place to start a life of contemplation. The very starkness that attracted the young man was for later stages of spiritual advancement and monastic commitment. He must begin at Mount Athos. There he would find his vocation, if he had one.

Guido went to Athos that same day. There he remained for eight years, and desired to remain for all his life, courting the Angel of Revelation.

"If it was what he truly wanted, then why did he come back at all?" Keti remained the practical American in many of her attitudes.

"Because that is the de la Valle code." The question brought Agathi to the point she hoped to make. "You do your job. He loved his life of devotion; the little chapel and the hermitage he built on Athos were all he wanted. It went against every grain in his being to give it up.

"But when our uncle knew he was dying, he called in the promise he had asked from my brother at the very start: to come back when the moment required.

"Now, I don't mean to compare you with Guido, Keti. For one thing, you're not being asked to give up what you want most, as he had to. Only some of the joys you've had in such profusion. That's not much, considering the harsh code we live by. Still, it is a sacrifice. I know that. But it works out. It even brings its own happiness in time."

Keti smiled a little wanly. "I'm sure you're right, Agathi."

"You're not so sure right now, my love. I can see that in your eyes. In your whole expression. But remember, though: Marriage, like life itself, is an enterprise. It's not a state or condition of happiness."

That triggered something in Keti's memory. Something to do with Rico. He had said something just like that when he was instructing her in the Catholic faith the better part of a decade before. It was something about marriage not being a human experiment, but God's gift granted on God's conditions. And about its not being easy, but not impossible, either.

"But do you know something, Agathi? There's just enough of the American in me to think that God leaves some things up to us. Some things God wills, and that's that; you can't change them. About other things he is just willing—leaving it up to us to decide a lot."

"Yes," Agathi said slowly. "Yes. That's so. But look, sweetheart, Helmut belongs to an iron tradition out of which he does not wish to step. None of the de la Valle men do. I can't explain it. I understand it, though. And it's not just family tradition and not just in the blood, as the saying goes. It's something else, lovely Keti. They're not priests, but no priest is more consecrated to his priesthood than these de la Valle men are to their papal service."

"Eugenio too, then." Keti said aloud for the first time what she had always understood. "He is going to grow up and . . ."

"Now, now." Agathi stood up in mock reproach. "He's our child of grace, isn't he?"

As she settled down in bed that Christmas Eve, she reflected how different the de la Valles were from that picture of worldly sophistication any casual stranger must have of them.

At about the same time Keti was cooling her first cup of tea, Sagastume guided the limousine slowly through the heavy city traffic. The Maestro and Helmut were quiet in the rear seat. Monsignore Di Lorio talked in a low voice to Helmut, instructing him in what they were going to do. These three men were about to enact a ceremony as old as Christianity and steeped in the original meaning Christianity held for its adherents.

Guido listened; but his mind was partly occupied in memory, as Agathi's was that evening. Though he was aware of Rome's December streets, he walked again, in recollection, in the blinding light of that far-off Aegean summer. He saw the face of the old abbot of St. John's Monastery on Patmos, heard again the words that sent him to Mount Athos, saw the hermitage and the chapel he had built for himself, felt the grace, warming and more blinding than the sun itself, that sometimes touched his spirit as he advanced toward perfect contemplation in those eight years he spent as a hermit. He could almost sense again the enveloping sound he had constantly heard in his days and nights, much as he imagined the rush of angel's wings would be when the Revelation was brought to him.

The angel had never arrived, however. His dying uncle had come instead, calling him down from those heights of prayer and promise.

Guido hadn't yet known of the Bargain when his uncle came to fetch him from Athos; only that the de la Valle service to the Holy See was a family affair, and that he had given his oath to do his duty as a de la Valle. At least, Helmut was not being asked to give up so much. His life with Keti and his son would change—had changed already in these past months—but it would not end. Besides, Helmut's life had been a preparation for his work to come; his past had been of a piece with his future. Until his return with Keti and Eugenio from Waidhofen this past summer, Helmut hadn't been aware of the depth of commitment he would be required to make. But there had been time to prepare him in a manner far less abrupt than had been the case for the Maestro; and there would be still more time for that.

It was an added help, in fact, that Helmut need not be thrust into the burdens of the Keeper all at once. The formal oath he would take this Christmas Eve—his consecration, in a manner of speaking—was preparatory. The Maestro was still as hale and fit as most men half his age. It was unlikely, therefore, that Helmut would have to bear the title "Maestro" or discharge all the heavy responsibilities of the Keeper until many more years had passed. As was required, Guido had explained the Bargain to his nephew, and had begun to include him much more intimately in his work. After tonight, Helmut's full apprenticeship as Keeper-designate would begin. The continuation of the family line would be guaranteed.

As Helmut surveyed the Christmas crowds strolling about the sidewalks, his thoughts were less somber than his uncle's. He had been fascinated over the past five months or so, as Guido had begun to include him in the *impero* activity. Once he had actually learned of the Bargain, the true de la Valle mission, he had looked forward to this night's formal ceremony almost as a priest looks forward to his ordination.

The Maestro glanced at his nephew's face in the flickering lights of the holiday streets. No; there was no question of this being as brutal a sacrifice for Helmut as his own renunciation of Mount Athos had been. None of that awful anguish and yearning he had been pained with for years would be Helmut's. It would be easier for him.

Sagastume pulled the limousine to the curb in front of a building abutting but separate from the Basilica of St. John Lateran, where midnight Mass was being prepared.

"Wait for us here, Sagastume."

"Sì, Maestro."

Di Lorio led the way to a door in that building now called the Church of the Savior, whose inner walls and parts predate any other church or ecclesiastical building in Rome. Once the trio was inside, and the Sphinx locked the doors behind them, the noise of traffic and festive music and bells was closed out. Everything from that moment was a re-creation of ancient ceremony.

With Di Lorio and the Maestro on either side, Helmut walked forward to the base of twenty-eight marble steps. Each step was protected by a plank of walnut wood. This was the famed Scala Sancta, the Holy Stairs, brought from Jerusalem sixteen centuries before by Constantine's mother, and traditionally held to be the steps Christ climbed to face his trial and condemnation by Pontius Pilate.

As Simon Peter had felt he was not worthy to be crucified like Christ, and so requested to be fastened to his own cross head downward, so pilgrims who came to the Scala Sancta have always felt they must not walk upon these stairs, but make their way on their knees instead.

The Maestro, his nephew, and the aging Di Lorio did that now. Side by side, each in silent prayer, they knelt on the first step and began. Only some fifteen minutes later, at the top of the stairs, did the three men rise from their knees. Then, still in silence, uncle and nephew followed Di Lorio into the oldest and holiest chapel in Rome, the Sancta Sanctorum. Its high frescoed vault, its gilded pillars and Cosmato-work pavement, dated from the fourth century, when Pope Sylvester I had accepted an earlier bargain between papacy and temporal power. He took from Emperor Constantine the Lateran Palace, of which now only this Sancta Sanctorum exists in modern times; and also money, jurisdiction, and authority throughout the Roman Empire.

The Maestro and Helmut knelt in the chapel while Di Lorio donned cloth-of-gold vestments. Before he began Mass, however, he went by himself to the room adjoining the Sancta Sanctorum. Like everything in this building, that room, too, was steeped in the history of the Church and the State and the bargains those two had always contracted with one another. Here the passing keepers of those bargains had all been at one time or another—Roman nobles, German emperors, Crusaders, Knights Templar. Here Pope Leo III had crowned Charlemagne Emperor of the West on Christmas Day in A.D. 800. Here, scant decades before this modern day, Mussolini had signed the Lateran Pacts, and a Vatican wit had remarked that the ghost of Charlemagne must have laughed at this goose-stepping pretender to his title—Emperor of the West.

Di Lorio had none of that at the forefront of his mind. From one shelf of a small glass case, he removed a velvet-covered plaque with a long nail fastened to it. From a lower shelf, he removed two small red-leather notebooks, identical to the one the Maestro carried, and to those painted in the hands of several de la Valle ancestors whose portraits hung in the library of Villa Cerulea.

Di Lorio returned to the Sacred Chapel and placed plaque and notebooks on the altar. With the Maestro as altar server, Di Lorio intoned the Latin Mass of the Vigil of Christmas. As the moment approached for him to receive Holy Communion, Helmut knelt alone at a table set before the altar rail. The Maestro took the plaque and one notebook from the altar and placed them on the table before his nephew. The second notebook he opened to a certain page, put it in Di Lorio's hands, and stepped back a pace.

"Helmut de la Valle"—Di Lorio began the consecration in solemn tones—"do you understand the decision you have made, and the office you will accept on a day that God shall appoint?"

"I do," Helmut answered clearly.

"Have you made your decision freely, and unto death?"

"I have."

"Do you believe that the nail lying in front of you did pierce the hand of our Lord Jesus Christ and fixed it to his Cross?"

"I believe that."

"Then place your own hand upon it now and read the Oath in the book that lies beside it."

Though the light was dim, Helmut had no difficulty reading the Oath. " 'I, Helmut de la Valle, Keeper-elect of the Bargain, do swear to uphold the pact according to all the rules of the Bargain, to observe all the guidelines laid down for the Keeper of the Bargain and in all things, and thus to uphold the Keeper of the Keys, the lawful successor to Blessed Peter the Apostle, and Holy Mother Church in all her integrity.' "

Guido took Di Lorio's book from him, and placed it beside Helmut's copy. Then Di Lorio brought the consecrated Host forward from the altar. Helmut waited to hear the next question in the ceremony.

"By what do you swear this Sacred Oath?" Di Lorio asked.

"By the Sacred Body and Blood of my Lord and Savior, Whom I am about to receive in the Sacrament."

He received the Host from Di Lorio's hand, and lowered his head to recite a post-Communion prayer. When he finished, he looked up again, ready for the final pledge he must make.

Di Lorio read from the notebook. "And now, as consecrated successor to the Keeper of the Bargain, do you swear that you will do all in your power to protect the next successor, Eugenio Guido de la Valle, from all spiritual and physical harm, and that you will prepare him at the proper time for the vocation you now share with Maestro Guido de la Valle and the forefathers of your line?"

Helmut looked into his uncle's eyes. "I do swear, upon my life and the Sacrament I have received."

When Di Lorio had finished Mass, he removed his vestments, and knelt down with the other two. Embedded in each was the deeply rooted belief that by observing this ritual, at this time, in this place, they had done much more than perform a ceremony or commemorate past and dead men and their works on this earth. A real change had taken place. Something real had happened. But only Spirit could perceive it.

This ritual—their words and their actions—had centered around the living, physical presence of Jesus of Nazereth under the sacramental guise of the consecrated Bread and Wine. Jesus was God, now as always; nothing was past for him, nor was anything in the future. God's eternal now was the ambient of Jesus. This midnight celebration was assumed into that eternal now; and it was united with the ritual whenever and wherever it had ever been performed before this particular Christmas Eve. That was the intangible reality behind the tangible words and actions of Helmut as devotee and Di Lorio as celebrant and Guido as witness.

There was another dimension to that reality. There had been a time at the beginning of Christianity's rise, and for the thousand years of its heyday, when it was not unusual for its members solemnly to commit themselves in the presence of the Sacred Host—as Helmut de la Valle had just done—to fight and to shed their blood for the Church of Christ and for his vicar, the Bishop of Rome. Such consecration had lost all meaning for the mentality of the twentieth century. It had even disappeared from many Catholic religious orders. But the de la Valle tradition was one of those in which commitment by solemn consecration persisted as a living reality to be handed on from generation to generation as part and parcel of their very identities.

When Helmut left the Sancta Sanctorum with his two companions, he had changed, was another kind of man. Nor could he, of his own accord, ever divest himself of this new dimension in his spirit.

[[36]]

Rome in winter was left to the Romans. The oceans of bishops, theologians, observers, pilgrims, and press washed back into the rest of the world like a receding tidal wave. Within the walls of the now rather peaceful Vatican buildings, even the preparations for the second session of Papa Angelica's Ecumenical Council ceased to be in the forefront of people's minds. They were replaced by the seeping realization that a pre-conclave process had begun.

Guido and Helmut de la Valle traveled in tandem for many of those wintry weeks, as did others, testing the validity of the Maestro's sense of cardinalitial support for Giovanni Da Brescia.

As always, the cardinal electors in each country had underlying concerns of their own—their relationship with their governments, the social problems peculiar to their populations, the pockets of some peculiar unrest that were suddenly appearing randomly. Still, by May it was clear to all that the Maestro's early assessment was accurate. Even the Latin American prelates, who ran the gamut from far left to far right, and among whom Guido had expected the most serious pre-conclave dissension and division, were ready to fall in line. Only the Chilean cardinal, Pedro Arrabaza, voiced articulate warnings. The first concerned the terrible poverty of most of the three hundred million Catholics in Latin America; they were a naked target for Communism, Arrabaza pointed out. The second had to do with all the faithful everywhere. "Carry my best wishes to Angelica," he said to the Maestro and Helmut, in parting. "Surely he must realize with his peasant's judgment that the Church has a crisis of belief on its hands. But, I fear, not so Da Brescia."

Guido did not make light of the Chilean's worries. "We must count on the grace of God and the Holy Spirit, Your Eminence, as we bring everything out into the open."

Within days of the Maestro's and Helmut's return from South America in early May, the Italian government lobbed a political bombshell into the Vatican. During that fiscal year, a new tax, the *cedolare,* had been levied on all stockholders in the Italian markets, with the intent of raising new revenues quickly. Prime Minister Fanfani, a lifelong and loyal Democristiano, fought against the Socialists in his cabinet, and in a divided parliament, to keep the Holy See exempt from the new tax, in accordance with the provisions of the Lateran Pacts of 1929. All postwar governments had honored those pacts, he argued. Although the Vatican was geographically in Italy, he went on, juridically it was not Italian soil. But it was no use.

Normally, the Pope, as head of the State of the Vatican, would have struck an immediate offensive against such a serious incursion into his sovereign domain. He would have initiated talks with the Treasury, called on those he could count as allies in the government, enlisted the active help of others powerful and sympathetic enough to be pressed into service. But by the first week in May, it was clear to Guido that such a course was far beyond Angelica's strength. The Pontiff was confined to his bed, suffering more than ordinary attacks of pain, and often laboring even to breathe. "At times," he would say to his few intimate visitors, "I hear in my soul the voices of my father and mother. They tell me I am to come home soon. I tell them my bags are packed."

Until a new pope could be elected, it fell to the two de la Valles and to the State Council and to the Banco to head off a confrontation with the government. Not many helpful suggestions came from the State Council, however.

"I told you all Angelica's opening to the Left would come home to roost." In Ferragamo-Duca's bitter assessment, there would have been no Socialists in the cabinet in the first place, and no *cedolare* tax crisis now, had it not been for the *apertura a sinistra.* "Wait until the other wild chickens he's let loose come home into the coop. His Commission on Contraception, his Jewish Document, his cavalier attitude to the enslavement of the Church in Eastern Europe, his agreement with Moscow." The cardinal didn't even bother to mention the Ecumenical Council any longer.

Whether or not all that was true, Guido kept to the point: Recriminations were no aid in heading off the *cedolare.* The only suggestion from the Banco was Peter Servatius' invention. "Dump all our shares on the market," he stormed, "and bring the government down!"

To that, Guido's response—which he shared only with Helmut—was a fervent hope that the aging Di Lorio would have many more years to live and thus be able to curb such rash judgments by his heir apparent. Such a move would be worse than pointless; given the huge sums the Holy See had invested in Italy, the losses incurred in such a step would exceed the *cedolare* taxes by far.

With his remarkable patience and force of will, the Maestro finally brought the Council members, together with Di Lorio and Servatius, into something like an effective phalanx of resistance. His own information was that Fanfani's government was about to fall. The most likely successor as prime minister was said to be Aldo Moro; and though he, like Fanfani, was a Democristiano, he too would head a divided government that would surely refuse to ratify the Holy See's tax-exempt status. In view of that complex tangle of changing powers on both sides, Guido decided to pay the *cedolare* tax on certain dividends only, provided the shaky government would in return give the Vatican time to rethink its position and formulate an acceptable solution for both the Holy See and the Italian government. That much achieved by way of bargaining, they were in a position to wait until Da Brescia would be in place as pope. Only then could they formulate a proper strategy to avoid *cedolare* and the enormous loss it would mean in revenues for the Holy See.

During those weeks of May, word of Papa Angelica's imminent death filtered through Rome and all the countryside, drawing little crowds to stand and pray beneath the papal window. A few hundred came. A thousand. Two. A hundred motives and emotions held them there. Sorrow.

Love. Reverence. A secret hope that a miracle would make Angelica whole again. A wish to pray with him. A wish to share his pain. Pain that a special measure of radiant love the world had barely had time to glimpse was about to pass from sight.

The police cordoned off the square to all vehicular traffic. Crowds, great or small, in this piazza were usually boisterous and noisy. But among those who gathered now, the sound of voices was muted, and all eyes were fixed on that window behind which Angelica lay in his agony, its blinds drawn by day, the light just visible when darkness fell.

For those who had not properly appraised the nature of Christianity or understood what it would cost a man really to follow Christ, the dying and death of Papa Angelica—or indeed of any close follower of Christ—must have seemed so incongruous as to lead one to the conclusion that the whole Christian thing was a vast and bad joke. Here was a pope, claimant vicar of God and of Christ, now dying in his eighties after a life of nearly seventy-five years devoted directly to that Christ. And yet his dying was one drawn-out process of dreadful pain. Why so punish such a faithful, such an exalted, servitor?

It was a sentiment that surfaced in more than one form at the press conferences Rico Lansing was asked by Cardinal Secretary Picolomini to conduct during that last illness of Angelica. When Rico did reveal, in response to a question, that Angelica's dying pain was horrendous, he could almost hear a sigh of pity from the scores of journalists crowded into the narrow press room.

"Why, according to your Church," the Swedish correspondent asked in all honesty, "does an all-loving God make his pope suffer so much?

"In order to make him more like Christ, who died in unspeakable sufferings," Rico answered. He could see incomprehension on some faces, immediate understanding on others.

While he battled with the pulsating waves of pain that rippled through his body as the cancer literally ate him alive, Angelica saw nothing incongruous in it all. It had been precisely by means of the unmitigated death throes of God Himself made man that Angelica's Church had been founded, and salvation won for all men and women. His very agony was congruous with his faith.

Where he lay, in the human twilight between the folds of his dying flesh and the portals of eternity, Angelica hoped that all those who came to say goodbye to him and, while he could still give it, to get his papal blessing would be able to look past the frightening dislocation that death was operating on him, the unmanning and dehumanizing of his body. Look past all that, and be with his spirit as it struggled to be free and depart out of the cosmos of man.

After a time, even when his brothers came to see him, the Pope could not easily lift his eyelids. His cheeks were sunken; and his whole face, with a stubble of beard and little glistening spots of sweat, was marked by the hours of physical agony he had already lived through for days.

His breathing came in long, laborious, irregular drafts, as if he were continually testing his lungs to see if they could manage another breath, and another. . . . His relatives could, he realized, get past the physical horror of it. And so also could the Maestro and Signor Helmut de la Valle when they came for a final visit. But many of his papal entourage could not. Whatever compassion they may have had was drowned in the peculiar panic the sight of the dying Pope aroused in them.

When they erected an oxygen tent permanently around his bed in the last ten days of May, he breathed more easily. And his thinking became easier; it was transfused by an understanding he never had possessed before. As he lay in bed on the fourth floor of the Apostolic Palace, it seemed to him that his feeling and perception enveloped the entire cluster of the Vatican buildings, all its hallowed walls and corridors and chapels. In great calm of spirit, he perceived a certain fringe of darkness, as if a black fire were simmering around the edges of it all.

He saw all his beloved bishops now as unknowing survivors of a disaster they did not seem to recognize—some dazed at what was happening to them, others full of illusion; some just serving time, others still holding on to their faith. But now no sheen of the Spirit's unique glory surrounded them; and he could hear no heralding announcement of a new summer season, either for the Church or for the peoples of the earth. He could still hear that insistent, drumming message from those peoples. He had formerly interpreted it as yearning hunger for love. It was, he saw, only partly that. But also it was partly the spirit of revolt, the primordial cry of rebellion echoing the first and most ancient "I will not serve!" hurled at the face of the Most High and Eternal God.

And that was why Papa Angelica was heard murmuring intermittently through his painful waking hours: "May the mystery of Christ's love cover us all and all our sins. May the mystery of Christ's love . . ."

In the last few days of life, his eyes closed more often and for longer periods of time. As he slipped into fitful sleep, he often prayed aloud that Christ would not hold him too long more in his body. He would drowse and sleep, thinking and dreaming of all the faces he wished to see again—his father and mother at his first Mass; Papa Profumi conferring the cardinal's red hat on him; the Jews he had put aboard trains with false baptismal certificates in order to get them out of wartime Hungary and Romania; the large-eyed Raoul Wallenberg in Angelica's house on the Golden Horn overlooking the Bosporus, asking him for another million dollars. All of them—all would be waiting to usher him into the presence of his Christ.

Papa Angelica came in and out of coma several times before he died at 6:27 in the evening on the last day of May.

Rico's thoughts all that day were prayer. By the time he left the Apostolic Palace, everything had come to a standstill. He glanced into the press office as he passed by. The camera crews and radio announcers, the newspaper reporters and columnists and commentators, had all packed up and left once death had sprinkled the first dust of eternal sleep over the Pontiff in his agony. The floor and tables were strewn with outdated bulletins and discarded newspapers. One Italian correspondent remained, droning his last dispatch into the transatlantic telephone. "The Holy Father has breathed his last, and the See of Peter lacks a pope. His Holiness' heartbeat ceased at . . ." Rico turned away.

In the empty lobby of the Secretariat, only the marble busts of former popes saw him pass. Even the papal messengers were gone. Probably they were in the square with all the others.

Outside, the sunlight that had gilded every stone and wall that day had faded. Standing in the silent crowd of ordinary people, Rico knew and shared their mood. He looked up at that fourth-floor window. They had unshuttered it now. A strong lamp threw a stream of white light out into the gathering dusk. All the other windows were dark. From below, that light looked festive. It was an illusion. The summer of the angel was over.

Part Four

THE SECOND SPRING

[37]

HISTORY IS WITNESS that some popes take years to settle into the exacting job of running the vast and complex machinery of the Church and of the Vatican State. Some popes, indeed, never succeed, but only give their blessing, as it were, in passing. Others, at first sanguine in their plans, find they can change a washer, turn a knob here and there, even budge a minor lever, but that the great machine keeps grinding and roaring on its ponderous way. A very few men of whiplash willpower roll up their sleeves and set about running the entire works. When they succeed, they create an era. When they fail, the legacy they leave behind is darkness and the scream of clashing gears.

Just after eleven o'clock in the morning on the twenty-first day of June 1963, the cardinal dean of conclave raised his voice and announced the vote.

Cardinal Lisserant, one of the seventy-two who had cast their ballots in the Sistine Chapel, leaned to the man next to him, Tran Anh Ngoc of Hanoi. His whisper was a hiss. "At last! A francophile!"

"Hopefully more than that, Your Eminence," the Vietnamese cardinal hissed back. The French battalions so recently in his country were still a vivid memory.

Within moments, the white smoke appeared above the Sistine, and the cry went up from a thousand throats: "We have a Pope!"

His Holiness Papa Giovanni Da Brescia spent the first two months of his pontificate wisely and well. Within a week he had moved out to the summer villa. He spent in the gardens of Castel Gandolfo long and satisfying hours that were for him the essence and image of contentment and happiness. Sometimes alone, sometimes with his secretary, Monsignore Delucchi, sometimes with favored visitors, he walked and thought and planned the lines of his pontificate.

"Papa Da Brescia has an excellent head for organization." Delucchi kneaded his hands in nervous habit as he walked Cardinal Levesque to his limousine one summer's eve. "And he knows where the power levers are."

"Indeed, Monsignore." Levesque had been singled out on the very day of the Pope's election to be secretary of state, and was now a daily visitor to Castel Gandolfo. He had every reason to agree. But Levesque, however frequent a visitor and however intimate an adviser, had little understanding of the complexity of Papa Da Brescia's makeup, or of the motives that drove him now as Pope. Little understanding, and no interest at all.

From the start of his life in northern Italy, Giovanni Da Brescia had been poor in health and small in build. His mother, Beatrice, the daughter of a French aristocrat, was a doting mother to all three of her children; but Giovanni was her favorite. How often had she smiled at him and said in one of a hundred different ways: Do not worry, child! Christ loves the small and the weak. He will make you a great man, and you will protect all the weak and the small.

Giovanni loved his father too, of course. But in his youngest years he remembered him as a shadowy and authoritarian figure. Arnulfo Da Brescia—journalist, parliamentarian, Catholic activist, internationally known expert on Church property—was away more than at home. "Mr. Coattails," Beatrice sometimes called him affectionately; for they seemed always to be seeing his coattails disappearing out the front door as he hurried off on yet another mission.

The first pang of sorrow Giovanni Da Brescia could remember in his life came when he saw some locks of hair thrown into the fire by one of the housemaids. It didn't matter that they were the residue of the barber's visit, and it didn't matter whose hair it was. In his child's mind, it was human, and it was being destroyed forever.

Beatrice calmed his tears and his fears. No beauty, she told him, and nothing humanly valuable, was lost forever. It lived on in God's beauty. And though he didn't understand it at the time, she taught him some lines from her favorite poet, the Frenchman Baudelaire.

> Be wise, O my pain, and be more peaceful.
> You cried out for repose. Look! It is here!

How often he had said those lines to himself since his childhood. And, with his mother as his early guide, how deeply he had come to value the clarity of French intellect and reason.

His personal tenderness and compassion never afterward left him; nor did the formalism of French thinking and logic that was clamped onto his Italian background and heredity.

With such a background, Rome had been a revelation for the young Father Da Brescia. If his career was as a cleric, his father had decided, then it wasn't going to be as a mere parish priest up north. With Arnulfo's connections, it was a simple matter to obtain preferment for his son in the diplomatic section of the Vatican. And so the young priest had entered the place that had been little more than a distant Mecca for him; the place where all clerics were dignitaries who spoke quick, hard Italian in voices that were always too loud, and where logic—French or otherwise—seemed forever subordinate to passion and feeling.

Over the years of his diplomatic service he learned to develop a hard-rind exterior for his "official" world. Whether in the Vatican itself or during his brief time in the "outpost" of Warsaw, he found it necessary to shield his innate kindness and gentleness behind a mask of authority. He must survive, after all, in a world where he was constantly at someone's beck and call, always a *secondo* to hard-nosed officials shielded in their Vatican awesomeness and buried in their Roman interests. In time, his public composure and gravity became such that it seemed to many that Da Brescia was eavesdropping on celestial conversations while talking with mortals. Those who found the commanding look and the authority in the voice a bit much began to call him *il gufo,* the owl.

And yet, hard-rind exterior or no, during those years as second fiddle to higher-ups on the Vatican ladder of power, Da Brescia became a sort of magnet for a never-ending stream of "outsiders." It was as though they knew him as one of their own, and having found him, were touched by the personal kindness. That was still accessible in him. As to the fifteen children of his two brothers, and to his three grandnephews, he was thought of by many not as *il gufo,* but as *zio,* uncle.

Greek emissary of the Patriarch of Constantinople, Belgian bishop, Dutch theologian, German philosopher, French intellectual, American prelate, Protestant biblical scholar, English ecumenist, ordinary men and women, anyone oppressed by the *romanità* of Vatican officials, found they could approach him, talk to him, even if they had been rebuffed by Papa Profumi.

Were they not also the Church? Shouldn't the church universal be bigger and broader in its scope than Romanism allowed? Wasn't the Pope supposed to be Pope for all human beings? Even his official stint as representative of the Holy See in the Lodge revealed to Da Brescia the innate goodness of the universalists, who, after all, desired only peace and harmony and plenty in the world. As his Lodge associates had said to him more than once, what was valuable in Rome, and what was eternal there, must surely be the heritage of the whole human race; perhaps it was entrusted to the care of the Romans, but no one had made it their exclusive possession.

Da Brescia had once stood talking in St. Peter's Square with a Brazilian bishop who had just been banished from his diocese by Papa Profumi for his involvement in politics. True it was revolutionary politics, but still and all . . . From where they stood, they could see the statues of St. Peter and St. Paul that flanked the entrance of the Basilica, St. Peter's hand pointed toward the Basilica, St. Paul's to the horizon.

"Do you know what they are saying, Monsignore?" The Brazilian made a bitter joke. "St. Peter says: Here they make the laws. St. Paul says: But only out there in the Church Universal must they be observed."

Da Brescia, the little Vatican functionary, could only stand and watch the bishop walk away, to disappear into exile in some monastery for the rest of his life. It was like those locks of hair tossed into the fire, he thought; a waste of human goodness.

Now, however, it would all be different. Da Brescia could do more than stand and watch. He was Pope. It was his right now, enforced by the weight of 264 predecessors over a period of nineteen hundred years, to mold his Church. Now he could give control, under his papal jurisdiction, guidance, and leadership, back into the hands of the local bishops throughout the world. Now he could end the bureaucratic imperialism, the thoroughly Roman choke-hold on the Curia, that had for too long made the Church an abhorrence to non-Catholics, and a source of suffering, doubt, irritation, sometimes loss of faith, even for Catholics.

"Integrated humanism," he told a delighted Cardinal Levesque, borrowing both thought and phrase from another French writer he admired, Jacques Maritain. "Not theological preciousness, but integrated humanness is to be the rule of Our government of the Church. We, as Pontiff, will act directly with Our bishops, not through a phalanx of cardinals who know nothing beyond the Vatican walls. Everything about Our Church must be liberated, so that it can truly be the Church of all men and women. Its morality and its politics must be integrated with the ordinary humanism prevalent in our times. For this We and Our bishops must reach out directly to the people." The meek *would* inherit the earth.

At long last, it was his turn to say, "Christ loves the small and the weak." It was his moment to reach out to them. It was time to lead all those "strangers" outside Rome to come take possession of it with him.

Of course, that meant war. Not war on a battlefield, with sledgehammers or spears. Roman war now was waged more coldly and carefully than that. Now that he was Pope, his battlefield was the structure of the Church. And his weapon was his power as pontiff to appoint his own people at every level, from clerk to cardinal.

Of course, war meant strategy. He must target the near and farther goals he intended to reach. The most important and sweeping of those goals—and the one without which nothing of his own vision could be implemented—was displacement of Papa Profumi's central policy.

Unlike Profumi, Papa Da Brescia did not believe that the Vatican should or could be centered around "the Christian heartland"—Italy, Spain, Belgium, and France, backed up by Austria, Germany, and Holland. From Warsaw and from Poland, Da Brescia had learned a more accurate lesson. In his mind, the mistake of Profumi's policy was parallel to the horrendous mistake made by Benito Mussolini; it was to allow Rome and the Vatican to be dominated by the Germanic mind, and to neglect, even alienate, the Slavs.

That must end. For Da Brescia, the true identity of Europe encompassed everything from the Urals to Calais and Calabria. Indeed, the true identity of the Church went farther still; even as far as the populist movements of little people in the forgotten Third World.

It was with that mind and that aim that Papa Da Brescia named Cardinal Levesque as secretary of state, and Monsignore Pierre Demarchelier as Levesque's second in command. It was with that mind that he indicated publicly that major roles were to be played by Cardinal Dell 'Angelo and Monsignore Casaregna, who would work with Demarchelier to aid the new secretary of state. It was with that mind that he did everything in those summer days. Others who had been closely associated with Papa Da Brescia in his Roman or Milanese past were named to head each section of the Secretariat. He made new diplomatic appointments for such all-important posts as Paris, London, Washington, Beirut, Hong Kong, Bombay, Rio de Janeiro, Bonn. For Washington he chose Belgium's Archbishop Jobert, who, like himself, had once been exiled as "dangerously doubtful about the prerogatives of the Roman Pontiff." His aim was to end the lockstep alignment of Profumist policies that had coincided so perfectly with the stupid cold war the Americans were waging all over the West. Papa Angelica had not been able to change that alignment. Da Brescia intended to fare better.

Of course, key men had to be placed at the head of the all-powerful Roman congregations as well, and Da Brescia had the ideal men.

First, he dealt with the Congregation for Bishops, the all-important ministry for appointing bishops throughout the Church. The Pontiff had every intention of appointing his type of bishop everywhere—young so as to have impact over time, populist in outlook, free of attachment to Profumist traditions. As head of the Congregation for Bishops, therefore, he named Julio Pirandella, an Argentinian who, though born of Italian parents, was an "outsider" in Rome and disliked the traditional alliance between the Church hierarchy and the landed proprietors, industrial giants and agribusiness men, in his country.

The Congregation for Missions, meanwhile, which made universal policies regarding the conversion of non-Catholics to Catholicism, was vital if Papa Da Brescia was to make Catholic rites palatable for other Christians; and if he was to make any headway in the hard task of changing the Catholic attitude to non-Catholics. He intended to do both. Cardinal Benigno Fustami was his choice there. Like Pirandella, he was a disaffected Latin American of Italian parentage. The only difference between the two, in fact, was that Fustami had been born in Nicaragua.

Finally, there was the second-ripest plum. The Congregation of Rites regulated the way Catholics prayed and worshiped. Not only had Archbishop Annibale Sugnini been regarded as an expert in such matters since his early days in the Secretariat, but he, like the Pontiff himself, had learned a great deal from such interested friends as Bishop Cale and Brother Reginald and the good Canon Ripley-Savage. Unfortunately, Sugnini could for now only be named secretary-general of the Congregation of Rites, second to the enfeebled Cardinal Casimir Stephanicius. Roman custom forbade removing the old man. But no matter. The cardinal could no longer work, and Sugnini would have a free and unfettered hand.

There was a fourth Congregation, the ripest plum of all, the Holy Office, charged with watching over purity of doctrine and observance of morals in the Church. It had been harshly run, Da Brescia reasoned, and he had little liking for Cardinal Arnulfo. Da Brescia knew he could not remove that Roman watchdog without causing an earthquake. But he could and did attach to Arnulfo's side an assistant. Monsignore Gianpietro Pavagna of Milan shared none of Arnulfo's views, and would doubtless hamper the cardinal's plans at every turn.

Yet even all that was only the beginning. In about five hundred key posts up and down the Vatican bureaucracy, Da Brescia's appointees formed an interlocking grid of one tendency and one mind: his own. Once everyone was installed, and the stream of instructions and directives from his papal office began to percolate through that grid to be transformed into practical terms for the regimen of the far-flung Catholic Church, the change would be total.

It was true, Papa Da Brescia realized, that he could not do only or entirely his own will.

There was, for one thing, the mandate given by the conclave that had elected him: Bring the Ecumenical Vatican Council—Vatican II, as the press had long since dubbed it—which Papa Angelica had begun, to a speedy and worthy end. In conclave, Da Brescia had been able to agree without hesitation to that mandate.

Not that he intended to rely on anything so humanly unpredictable as a new Pentecost. Papa Angelica had been a holy but impractical man.

Papa Da Brescia hoped he was as holy; but he knew he was more realistic. Vatican II was an ideal resource placed in his hands at a truly providential moment. Without it, his reforms might take a lifetime to filter out around the world. By his skillful use of its complex structure—and he was nothing if not the consummate structuralist—Papa Da Brescia was sure he could speed his reforms by decades. The very momentum would itself make those reforms hard to reverse, once truly begun. The primacy, privilege, and infallibility of the Pope would be asserted. No bureaucracy would stand any longer between the supreme pastor and his people. The character of Church hierarchy would be changed, so that he and his brother bishops and his people would stand with each other to face the future.

There were three other areas, however, where Papa Da Brescia's will did not fit so neatly as it did with Vatican II.

The Holy Office under Cardinal Arnulfo was one. Pavagna as assistant was only a stopgap measure. Papa Da Brescia calculated that the aging Arnulfo could take just a certain amount of opposition in his own office. But it could turn into a long fight, if the Pope was not careful. It would bear further thought. Control was essential if he and his new breed were not to be open to the Office's fearful censures.

The Council of State was an element that he did not dare touch directly at this stage. His cardinal secretary of state, like Angelica's, would probably be blocked from attending meetings except by invitation. Even Levesque with his brass neck would have a hard time getting in that door. Eventually, though, Da Brescia knew he had to control that State Council.

The most immediate problem, and the one that he had not for a moment expected, was the problem concerning control of Vatican finances.

When on the day of his election Amalfeo as master of ceremonies had opened the door to the Silver Throne Room and gestured for the newly elected Pontiff to enter, Papa Da Brescia had still been under the intoxicating effect of his loggia reception by the crowds in St. Peter's Square. He had stepped inside, and the door had closed behind him, before he realized he was in the presence of Maestro Guido de la Valle. Well, he had supposed the de la Valles had their precious little hereditary job for the papacy, like the hereditary papal cobbler, the hereditary supplier of Easter palms, the hereditary *portiere* at the Secretariat. A pope must observe all the little in-house traditions.

It was only when he read the three ancient, handwritten pages that the Maestro placed before him in a red leather folder that he understood at last the curious power that people always saw or sensed in that man. He now saw the explanation for a thousand puzzles, for incident after incident that even he, with all his thirty-two years in the Vatican, had never understood. Never had he heard of the Keeper or known of the Bargain or realized the hand that secretly moved so many levers of power in this Vatican. The privileges of the Keeper appalled him as he read: power over finances, automatic acceptance in the State Council, liaison with the Lodge, veto on all *papabili.* . . . Truly, the Maestro.

Never again would he look on Guido de la Valle, as he had for almost forty years, as a faithful, slightly pompous, but apparently useful confidant of popes. Nor could he tell anyone or consult anyone about him; or reject him; or ignore him. Six popes, since the 1880s, had signed that paper before Da Brescia. Keeper, Bargain, de la Valle predominance—these were all as much a part of the papacy as anything he knew.

Though neither man would willingly have chosen to be associated with the other, they were held by the sacred oath of office and by duty. Neither would allow himself to be hindered in his aims by the other. If necessary for the purposes they held sacred, each would obstruct the other. Of all that Papa Da Brescia was certain. He had seen it in the Maestro's face, in those hard de la Valle eyes. And surely the Maestro had seen as much in his.

He was not sure yet how to get around the Maestro's control of finance. Perhaps Paolo Lercani would be able to help. Lercani was always able to help in such matters.

Nevertheless, and even taking into account those problems he had not yet unraveled, Papa Da Brescia was reasonably certain that the scope of the changes he mapped out by his new appointments, and by the cardinals he would soon create, placed the traditional republicanism of the curial bureaucracy under a sentence of death. It was the first time in a very long time that a band of outsiders had swept into commanding positions within the Vatican. It was to be their great enterprise, their *avventura del secolo,* their chance to make history by changing the source of history's logic.

They weren't anti-Roman, this Da Brescia band. They simply weren't Roman. As their head and symbol, Papa Da Brescia, wasn't Roman. But the stage was theirs: the Vatican, with the long, yawning shadows of its epochal history as backdrop and scenery.

The autumnal color of Profumi's reign was a dimming memory. The winsome light of Papa Angelica's brief summer was extinguished forever. The new mood was as enterprising, as energetic, as brash and untried as that of any fresh spring.

Indeed, that was almost exactly how Papa Da Brescia put it as he added the last names to the last list of appointments and directives and handed them to his harried but patient and loyal secretary.

"When the early Christians were freed from the catacombs, Monsignore Delucchi, they poured out all over the world in a first spring of conquest. Now, in God's providence, Christians may expect a Second Spring."

Once the papal appointments began to be posted and new directives were distributed, nobody occupying a position of power in Papa Da Brescia's Vatican—and least of all the Maestro and the members of the State Council—had any doubt about His Holiness' policy.

"He has declared war!" Cardinal Ferragamo-Duca thumped the folder bulging with his copies of Da Brescia's lists and memoranda that flowed from Castel Gandolfo as waters flow from a ruined dike. "He has declared war on *us!* On Rome!"

Everyone at the Council meeting that August morning had received and read those documents. All understood them. But it took the outraged Ferragamo-Duca, that Roman of Romans, to put the case so baldly. "I tell you, he's in over his head. Just look at the names! Sugnini for the Congregation of Rites! That's practically blasphemy in itself! This upstart Pavagna appointed as your assistant, Arnulfo! And that quartet he's appointed to the top of the Secretariat. Levesque is bad enough; but to back him up with the likes of Demarchelier, Dell'Angelo, and Casaregna is a triumph of bad judgment!"

Guido, sitting calmly through his good friend's tirade, thought back to that moment when Da Brescia, as archbishop in pursuit of a cardinal's hat, had brought Paolo Lercani as a peace offering. Bad judgment. Ferragamo-Duca was probably right—that was the flaw. "But," he finally broke in on the cardinal, "let's remember that we now have the Pope we all decided would be needed at the present juncture of the Church. The Holy Spirit has confirmed him in his post. That we must and do believe. He is Peter's successor.

"And let's remember, too, the reason for our own judgment: to bring the rot into the open, where it can be seen in the light of day."

"Rot is the word, Maestro." Ferragamo-Duca sat back in his chair in disgust. "If we want it in the open, we have a good start, just with the Pontiff's first rack of appointments. I hate to think what he might do next!"

"Well, Eminence"—Guido jumped on that point—"whether we hate to think of it or not, that is what we must do. Whatever the details to come, it is clear that Papa Da Brescia plans to be authoritarian with the Curia and the Roman offices of the Church. That, my friends, means you and me. So we have to be clear on our own positions without delay under two major headings: this State Council, and the financial agencies."

The first order of business, then, as Papa Da Brescia had anticipated, concerned how to block Levesque from assuming the traditional place of secretary of state in the Council. Papa Angelica's secretary of state, Picolomini, had at least been benign, and he went along with the Council's suggestion to come on invitation only.

"But he was a decent little gentleman," Cardinal Falconieri reminded the group. "In Levesque we're dealing with a hostile megalomaniac. He'll want to know the color of our underpants!"

It was agreed that if Cardinal Levesque were a permanent fixture, privy to all Council affairs, then Papa Da Brescia would automatically share full information about the *impero*'s exact achievements: about the full resources the financial agencies of the Vatican commanded as a result of the *impero*'s work, for example; about the *impero*'s banking enterprises in Eastern Europe; about the system of international Vatican brokers and banking associates.

And it was agreed that, given not only Levesque himself but the others who would be Da Brescia's intimates, and given further what that said about the Pope's own intentions, Levesque must be blocked from as many State Council meetings as possible, by whatever means could be devised.

"We'll have to make do and hope for the best," Falconieri summed up. "And if there are meetings at which the cardinal is present, I suggest that Maestro Guido and Signor Helmut will have business elsewhere that prevents them from attending."

"I hate two-track systems." Cardinal Hoffeldt put in a weary two cents. "We've done this now for five years. How long is it going to go on?"

"For as long as it takes, Eminence." Arnulfo was firm. "And one more thing. As Cardinal Ferragamo-Duca pointed out, Annibale Sugnini is not the man to head up the Congregation for Rites. Nor is that Milanese, Monsignore Pavagna, suitable for my own Holy Office. Neither man must become a cardinal. Pavagna is no problem, as I think you will all agree. But Papa Da Brescia has virtually promised the red hat to Sugnini. He even publicly presented his own cardinal's biretta and skullcap as pledge of that intention."

Falconieri took on that task willingly. "I give you my pledge, Eminences. Sugnini will not become a cardinal. Not this time around, anyway. He can keep Da Brescia's biretta and skullcap as mementos of what might have been."

No one doubted that Falconieri could use his position and his authority to prevent at least that promise to Sugnini. Even as stubborn a pope as Da Brescia promised to be would have to bend in some things. That was the way with Roman war.

The Maestro and Cardinals Lanser and Falconieri had one more hatch to batten down. The entire covert operation run by Bishop Richard Lansing must be protected. Like the State Council, Lansing and all his associates were to operate under the same orders as when Papa Angelica was alive. That much was quickly settled on in their meeting with Giulio Brandolini and Gian Solaccio. But Brandolini was not certain Lansing himself would agree. They all remembered his objection to keeping secrets from the Pontiff when Angelica was alive.

Cardinal Lanser felt differently about Rico. "Don't underestimate his attachment and devotion to the course of the Church behind the Iron Curtain. Bishop Lansing may not yet understand all the complexities of how Rome governs and is governed. But he has learned that popes come and go. He will not jeopardize all that he and the others have built up. I will speak with him. I don't think there will be any difficulty."

In the midnight silence of his study at Villa Cerulea, Guido could not shake the alien feeling that had taken hold of him. He tried to take refuge in memories of Eugenio's curious and excited questions about the new Pontiff: "Does Papa Da Brescia talk to you like Papa Angelica did, Nanno?" Or: "Has Papa Da Brescia a private study like you and Papa do, Nanno?" Or: "Will Uncle Rico come to see Papa Da Brescia with us?"

It was no use, though. The innocence of his little Eugenio only deepened his troubled thoughts. He wished he could have such childlike hope as his grandnephew. Guido was accustomed to fighting for his pope, not against him. His every instinct was formed to protect the Pontiff, not make war with him.

When he and the Council had settled on Da Brescia as prime *papabile,* they expected that many in the Church would feel free to reveal their true colors—to "come to the surface," as the Council had said so often. That aim was risky, but it was a risk that needed to be taken. The imponderable thing now was that danger seemed not merely to be *around* this newly consecrated Pope, but seemed to be his very person. And that danger, if the Maestro read the signs correctly, was to the very primacy and power of the Pontiff that Guido and his family had sworn to uphold.

He was certain that Da Brescia could not see that, and that no amount of talk could make him see. He had tried, in fact, on his own few visits to Castel Gandolfo that summer, to focus the Pope's attention less on the structure and more on the type of men he was placing at its controls. But His Holiness would have none of it.

So, Guido sighed deeply, Ferragamo-Duca was right. It would be war —but war in the Roman sense of the word. An internal struggle for bureaucratic power and dominance. A war that could not be decided overnight or by any sudden coup d'état. Like all things Roman, it would take time. It would be the Curia with Guido and his *impero* associates drawn up to face a Pope who seemed intent on sweeping away the underpinnings of the papacy.

In that regard, they could expect the mind of the Northern Alliance would be pushed more strongly now through Sugnini. As to Vatican II, at least there Da Brescia had vowed to the conclave his intention of ending it with the session that would open on October 1. That in itself would be a welcome blessing. Perhaps the curial cardinals of the Preparatory Commission might even work a miracle: Perhaps they could regain some semblance of control over the bishops in Council. Just to bring them back within sight of legitimacy and responsibility would do. But, Guido conceded to himself, that would indeed be a miracle. They could not count on it.

The Maestro rose wearily from his chair to prepare for bed. What a strange war this would be, he thought. Never had he expected that his role as Keeper would oblige him to fight his pope in order to protect the papacy.

[38]

Papa Da Brescia returned from Castel Gandolfo in the last week of August. Almost immediately, an unaccustomed assortment of visitors began to flow past Amadeo the *portiere* and into the papal study.

Milanese politicians and university professors, middle-of-the-road Socialists and Christian Democrat deputies from the national assembly, French philosophers and writers, were but some of the bevy of "outsiders" who finally were welcome at the highest level of the Vatican.

One of the few clerics who was a regular among the visitors was the pious parish priest of Avellino, a village south of Rome. Da Brescia had known Don Guglielmo since his own student days, and had always taken a deep interest in him. Now, late every Thursday afternoon, the priest drove his one-horse trap the seventeen miles from Avellino to the outskirts of Rome. From there he took a streetcar to St. Peter's, where he would have a quiet dinner alone with the Pontiff.

Don Guglielmo had been in a cassock since he was eleven years old. He still spoke only in dialect, and his conversation always was about his little village—his parishioners, the cows calving, the caterpillar blight on the vines, the village whore. He kept Da Brescia in touch in a special way with the little people, and with the important things in their lives. And in any case, the Pope loved those visits; he looked forward to them and needed no excuse or justification for them.

There were other meetings too. As sweeping as his early appointments of new officials throughout Vatican and Church seemed to many, Da Brescia had only begun his structural shifts and adjustments of the great machinery. The Pontiff's practical decisions were taken in consultation chiefly with two men, Cardinal Secretary Levesque and Monsignore Annibale Sugnini. Frequently, Levesque was accompanied by his three top aides, Demarchelier, Dell'Angelo, and Casaregna.

Because the Roman Congregations were so important, Cardinal Pirandella, Cardinal Fustami, and Monsignore Pavagna also had the ear of the Pope. There were other favorites as well, and notable among them, to no one's surprise, was the very serviceable Paolo Lercani. By and large, meanwhile, many of the old guard, the former "insiders," were now among those who found it necessary, sometimes difficult, to make formal appointments to see the Pope, unless His Holiness summoned them for his own reasons.

In the second week of September, Curial Cardinals Arnulfo and Lanser each received just such a summons. Papa Da Brescia's secretary, Delucchi, phoned to say they were both to come to the Pontiff's fourth-floor quarters for an early-morning consultation.

They arrived at the appointed time on the dot, and were met at the elevator by His Holiness' valet, Commendatore Geraldo Marsala, who ushered them into one of the papal parlors. The Pontiff was still in conference with Cardinal Levesque, Cardinal Pirandella, and Monsignore Sugnini, the valet explained in an apologetic semi-whisper. He was certain that Monsignore Delucchi would have met them, but he, too, was with the Pope. No affront was intended, he meant to say. The wait would not be long.

Sister Benedetta entered without a sound, bearing a tray of light wine suitable to the hour, and some sweet biscuits. The Franciscan nun, who, with five of her sisters, maintained His Holiness' living quarters, smiled gravely as she served the two cardinals, but did not raise her eyes to look at them.

Lanser and Arnulfo were too experienced not to understand what was going on. In Da Brescia's version of *romanità,* the two curial cardinals were getting the back of the papal hand.

During the twenty minutes they were kept waiting, Lanser and Arnulfo commented on the silence of the staff. "Everyone speaks in whispers." Arnulfo's face was bleak. "I pity anyone hard of hearing who comes here."

"And I pity anyone who isn't wearing tinted glasses," Lanser said, adjusting his own to get a better look at the newly refurbished surroundings in which the pair waited.

There had been much gossip in the Vatican about Da Brescia's wholesale redecoration of the Apostolic Palace. It had become one of the latest topics of conversation among the network of valets, in fact. The Pope had engaged Ectore Danieli, his favorite decorator in Milan, to take charge of the entire project. They had all seen the changes in the lobby. They had all heard about the "terrace house" the Pontiff had ordered constructed on the roof of his palace. But for the most part, the changes in the papal apartment were the stuff of rumor and hearsay.

Speculation had it that ancient walls were now covered with fine, gaily colored Milanese fabrics. The living room, it was said with raised eyebrows, was all pastels now. For the study, Danieli had decided on forest green and baby pink, and for His Holiness' bath, mirrors surrounded by rose tiles.

"Perhaps it is all good Milanese taste," one valet would comment to another while purchasing food in the Vatican store or over coffee in the firemen's commissary, "but it is not Roman."

The Jesuit Cardinal Lanser, who lived as simply as he always had and without a valet, was less prepared by the gossip than Arnulfo for his first glimpse of Danieli's handiwork. "I only hope this is not a visible sign of the Pontiff's intentions for refurbishment of the Church!" Lanser meant the remark as a joke; but neither he nor Arnulfo could summon much of a laugh.

Finally, Monsignore Delucchi arrived, all whispered apologies and kneading hands. His Holiness was just ending his meeting. He would be here any minute now. Lanser and Arnulfo exchanged a glance. Their meeting would be here, not in the papal study. They had not expected intimacy; but apparently there would not even be a bending of formality.

The two cardinals stood up to wait with Delucchi in awkward silence. But when the door opened, it was not the Pontiff who entered. Pirandella and Sugnini, both in excellent humor after their own meeting with His Holiness, wanted to stop on their way out to pay their respects to Lanser and Arnulfo. They were followed almost at once by Cardinal Secretary Levesque, who was almost boisterously patronizing, his eyes glinting behind those rimless "battlements" of his. Unlike Pirandella and Sugnini, Levesque did not leave, but stayed with the little group waiting for the Pope.

At last, Commendatore Geraldo entered. "Your Eminences and Monsignore," the valet announced grandly, "His Holiness is arriving."

It was all very grand for such a meeting as this; for a moment Lanser thought Arnulfo was going to choke—whether from amusement, shock, or both, he could not make out. There were no more formalities. The Pope launched directly into the business for which he had summoned the two Roman cardinals, and he went methodically through it all. It was not a discussion. It was a series of orders.

The business at hand concerned Vatican II. Papa Da Brescia had decided to change the membership of the Standing Committee of Presiding Cardinals. Of course, His Holiness knew Their Eminences understood how important that committee was, with its control over the speakers and the agenda of the daily sessions. Of course, both Lanser and Arnulfo would remain members. "But, as We feel it most prudent to internationalize the committee and Vatican II itself, all of the other members will be replaced."

Da Brescia did not have to consult notes to recite the names of the new members of the Standing Committee: Svensens of Belgium; Arrabaza of Chile; Azande of Nigeria; O'Mahoney of Chicago; Pirandella of the Argentine; Tillman of New York; Grosjean of Paris.

"That makes nine, including Your Eminences," Da Brescia summed up. "Cardinal Secretary Levesque here will be an ex-officio member. Each cardinal will name two theological experts of his own. And We, as Pontiff, have decided to name Our own personal theological expert, Monsignore Annibale Sugnini."

Da Brescia paused to ask if there were any questions. Because Lanser and Arnulfo either understood the situation perfectly or because they were too stunned to speak, both remained silent.

"Bene!" His Holiness went on to the next change, in preparation for

the coming and final session of Vatican II. He had decided to establish a completely new group. The Procedural Committee, as he had aptly decided to call it, would be charged with setting the broader agenda of Vatican II. It would be composed of a president—Cardinal Svensens—and seven bishops.

Arnulfo sat and listened in stoniest silence as Da Brescia read off the names. Except for one obscure and retired French missionary, Archbishop Edouard Lasuisse, he knew these bishops of the Procedural Committee as young, progressivist, and radical. To his mind, they were all anti-Roman, anti-tradition, and, though he doubted Papa Da Brescia would agree, fundamentally anti-papist. He doubted if any one of them except Lasuisse and Svensens believed any longer one scrap of Catholic teaching. As for Svensens, that man was a Fleming with a French education; anyone who knew Arnulfo knew he saw that as a "bad mix."

The choice of these men in particular could not have been done without Pirandella, Da Brescia's new head of the Congregation for Bishops. That was obvious. But Arnulfo knew that the Argentinian was a lightweight in this affair; a willing tool. The source of the strategy, he was sure, was Levesque, seated now so smugly beside His Holiness. Levesque probably enjoyed an able assistance from Sugnini. The Pontiff's habit was to meet with both of them first thing every morning, and they had obviously learned well how to capitalize on Da Brescia's thought and outlook.

"Your Holiness," Arnulfo ventured, when Da Brescia finally paused again. "Are we to understand that these two lists—the Presiding Cardinals and the Procedural Committee—are established and final?"

"Not only that," Papa Da Brescia confirmed. "The members are being notified as quickly as they can be reached. We desire that both committees meet as soon as possible so that all will be in order when Our session of Vatican II opens on October 1. That is barely six weeks from now, Eminence."

Arnulfo sat back as though he had been struck a physical blow. Da Brescia seemed not to notice.

"Now," he went on, "We have directed Cardinal Svensens, as president of the Procedural Committee, to ensure that the first *Schema* to be discussed and affirmed is the one concerning 'The Pope and the World.' Your Eminences"—the Pontiff smiled first at Arnulfo and then at Lanser—"will convey our wish to your own Committee of Presiding Cardinals as well.

"Once the bishops in council have reaffirmed Our primacy and jurisdiction in a manner that the people can understand in today's context, their attention will be turned to the *Schema* on 'The Church and the World.' . . ."

As Papa Da Brescia explained his intent on *Schema* after *Schema,* it became clear that the basis of his ideas and reforms were almost exclusively juridical and bureaucratic. The fresh concept—the Pope avoided the word "new"—to be put forward was that of "the people of God" led by their Pope and their bishops. Again, Sugnini's hand could be seen.

But His Holiness' repeated use of that term "the people of God," one of the most important elements of Liberation Theology, suggested strongly that Father Herreras, political champion of the oppressed Latin American peoples, had drilled Sugnini well.

Cardinal Lanser, while very much a part of the instructions so far, was given his own special and very clear directives by the Pope.

"We want you, Eminence, to become even more prominent in ecumenism than you are. So prominent—preeminent, We might say—that whoever hears your name will think of Church unity."

As the Pontiff detailed his wishes, Lanser understood not only that he would have to undertake still more travel and lecturing, but that he must bring non-Catholics into the work of Vatican II in an advisory capacity, even attaching some of them to the various committees of Catholic theologians who advised the bishops.

"Protestants must be made to feel at home in Our Church," Da Brescia emphasized. "They, too, are a part of 'the people of God.' It could be the beginning of Christian unity."

On the other hand—the Pontiff continued his litany of orders and reforms—there was to be no special treatment of anti-Semitism by Vatican II. Instead, the bishops would issue a statement championing religious liberty in general; Judaism and its enemy, anti-Semitism, would be included but not singled out.

Monsignore Delucchi, still standing unobtrusively by, stopped kneading his hands long enough to look rather obviously at his watch and make a little sign to the Pope. It was time for another meeting in his busy day.

"If there are no questions, Your Eminences?" The Pontiff stood up, and so everyone else did too.

Lanser and Arnulfo each kissed the papal ring. There were a thousand questions, but nothing would be accomplished by asking any of them. They watched their Pope, followed by Levesque, disappear through the door.

Richard Lansing barely had time to take in the effect of the forest greens and pinks of the papal study before the door was opened and Papa Da Brescia, fresh from his meeting with Lanser and Arnulfo, was announced rather grandly by Commendatore Marsala.

It was no surprise for Rico to see Cardinal Secretary Levesque and Monsignore Sugnini enter on the Pope's coattails; that, he knew, had become their accustomed position.

Levesque hadn't changed his opinion of Lansing since 1945. For him, the American was a big, decent, honest, and rather simple man. Rico's abdication of the powerful Chicago diocese in favor of a purely devotional career as head of the Hearts Apostolate had confirmed the Frenchman in his opinion. Sugnini had no particular opinion about the American. He was never at ease with him; but Sugnini himself put his reaction down to some basic difference in personality.

Papa Da Brescia was extremely complimentary about Rico's Apostolate. As he and Rico spoke for a few moments about the devotion to the Hearts of Jesus and Mary, Lansing was surprised to detect a childlike element in the Pope that reminded him of Papa Angelica. All that, however, was merely agreeable preamble. Da Brescia's assignment to Rico was to collaborate with him and with Cardinal Jean Levesque in promoting diplomatic relations with each of the Soviet satellite governments, and eventually with Moscow itself.

"The time for hostility and stand-off politics is past, Excellency," the Pontiff explained in the quiet tones that he preferred everyone around him to use. "The Soviets and their puppets are paranoid with fear that We are plotting their ruination. The Holy See desires peace and harmonious relations. Differences can be ironed out by goodwill on both sides. But We must make the first move. Now, some of Our highest churchmen in the most sensitive areas have only made things worse, Your Excellency. Cardinal Wallensky, for example, with his continual yapping at the heels of the Communist watchdogs.

"Cardinal Levesque here has rightly pointed out that you are excellently positioned for our purposes. Not only have you come to know the Polish cardinal well, but you are known by the governments of at least five East European countries. You speak their language, in both senses of that phrase. We think it will be a simple matter for you to take preliminary soundings with as many governments as possible, and report back directly to Us from time to time. The long-range goal will be to sign formal diplomatic protocols with our Eastern European brothers."

Cardinal Levesque had become just a little fidgety, a sign that perhaps there was a point that needed clarification. The Pontiff asked him to speak his mind.

"Being a nonpolitical man, Holiness"—the cardinal's tone was more understanding than critical of Rico—"concerned entirely with spiritual things, Bishop Lansing cannot be expected to initiate serious discussions on the governmental level about protocol arrangements."

Levesque shifted his attention fully to the American. "We professionals can do that, Excellency. But you can open doors for us. And"—a smile of special appreciation—"Your Excellency can remember us in your prayers."

By late September, Guido de la Valle's tenuous hope that the Curia might regain some control of Vatican II vanished entirely. Arnulfo and Lanser met privately with the Maestro, Falconieri, and Ferragamo-Duca to summarize for them in candid detail how the meeting of the new Committee of Presiding Cardinals named by Da Brescia had gone.

"It was a disaster!" Arnulfo began his remarks with that conclusion. The Presiding Cardinals had met under his chairmanship. He had opened the meeting with a routine summary of the membership of the bishops' committees set in the previous session of Vatican II; and a summary of the Pope's wishes for the order in which the *Schemata* should be discussed in the coming session.

He had thought that much at least would be simple. But he had not even finished his run-through when Cardinal Arrabaza of Chile had interrupted him.

"Point of order, Your Eminence!"

Arnulfo had looked up from his notes and, as graciously as he could, asked the Chilean to wait until the opening summary was complete.

"Point of order, Your Eminence!" Arrabaza insisted.

Arnulfo had looked up again at the gaunt face and the unsmiling eyes. "Yes, Eminence?"

"We have all read and studied the lists of bishops' consultative committees. We need a vote. Procedurally, it is necessary."

Arnulfo was puzzled. "A vote, Eminence? On what?"

"A vote to accept or reject those lists, Eminence. It's in the council procedural rules."

Arnulfo had been blindsided. The point of order took precedence. He had to allow the vote. In any case, deferring it would make little difference.

"I presume a voice vote will satisfy Your Eminence?" Arnulfo glared at Arrabaza, who nodded his assent.

Tillman, Lanser, and Azande voted with Arnulfo to accept the bishops' committees as they stood. Svensens, Arrabaza, Pirandella, and Grosjean voted to scrap them. O'Mahoney was the tie-breaker. He voted with the opposition. In Arnulfo's opinion, he did so because he knew the new Presiding Cardinals were the Pope's personal appointments, and because he felt his own interests lay on the side of papal favor.

Falconieri interrupted Arnulfo's retelling of the meeting. "Isn't he aware of Papa Da Brescia's feeling about the Americans?"

"Perhaps." Arnulfo shrugged. "But I believe he intends to be on the winning side, however it may shift, when it comes to matters that influence funds for his diocese.

"In any case, whatever his reasons, the vote went against us. And no sooner was that done than Arrabaza was on his feet again proposing that we choose a subcommittee entrusted with the job of establishing new lists of bishops for the consultative committees.

"Svensens seconded, and the vote broke on the same lines." With a rapidity that was almost dizzying, five of Their Eminences—Azande, Svensens, Arrabaza, Grosjean, and Pirandella—were selected by voice vote.

Arnulfo had then tried to maneuver a vote on the order and division of *Schemata.* After all, as he made clear to the Presiding Cardinals, that was the Pontiff's own proposal. But Arrabaza had intervened for a third time.

"That is not to be decided in this committee," he said. "That is a question of the general procedure of Vatican II. Papa Da Brescia has named a Procedural Committee to handle such decisions. The order and division in which the *Schemata* are to be discussed by the bishops in Council is their responsibility, not ours.

"Am I right, Your Eminence?" Arrabaza directed the question to

Svensens, the president of the Procedural Committee.

"Entirely right," Svensens agreed.

There had seemed no more reason to continue the meeting of the Committee of Presiding Cardinals, and so Arnulfo, gathering his papers and controlling his temper, had moved to adjourn, rising from his chair as he did so. But Arrabaza had one final point to make.

"Eminence, once Vatican II is in session again, each day three of us must preside at the formal sessions in St. Peter's."

At least that much, Arnulfo had thought, was decided. "The Holy Father has already drawn up the groups of three for each day of the first month." He looked down at the still seated Chilean cardinal.

"Yes, Eminence." Arrabaza conceded the point and then proceeded to brush it aside. "But that is invalid. According to procedural rules, we have to do it. And we have to do it in an open and plenary meeting such as this one."

Arnulfo had not been able to go on with the farce. He had left the meeting in charge of Lanser, with instructions to cast his vote with his own. When it was all over, Arnulfo's name appeared twice in the October roster, once in the November roster, and nowhere in the December roster. Lanser's appeared for one session each month.

As chairman, Arnulfo had dutifully reported the results of the meeting to Papa Da Brescia. Obviously, Pirandella or one of the others had already made a full report. "In any case," Arnulfo concluded his story, "the Pontiff's reaction was one of joy rather than surprise. 'At last,' he told me, 'We are seeing the first sign of Our bishops' awakening.' "

Cardinal Ferragamo-Duca had listened in total silence until Arnulfo had finished his account. Now, as he said in no uncertain terms, he agreed that the whole thing was a disaster. "Da Brescia has obviated any real influence of the Roman Curia on Vatican II. And he has done it by the simplest of means. By naming new and mainly foreign cardinals to the Committee of Presiding Cardinals. And by creating his new Procedural Committee, and staffing it with even more extreme bishops."

Lanser agreed that the Pontiff had used the structure of the Church very well, from his own point of view. "But"—the Jesuit frowned as he analyzed the signs and possibilities that faced them now—"the men he has been persuaded to place in positions to do what was done by the Presiding Cardinals Committee could well impose a totally new theology on the Church. A theology that no past Ecumenical Council and no past pope has ever proposed.

"We've commented before on Papa Da Brescia's increasing use of Herreras' phrase 'the people of God.' We know Sugnini has been a member of the Northern Alliance for fifteen years now.

"My greatest worry is that the Pope, led by his attentive and doting advisers, has unwittingly taken a first step toward destroying the central government of the Church. I believe the Pope is to be isolated and then faced with these bishops of the 'people.' "

Arnulfo was chilled by the cool, logical progression Lanser set out. "If that's true, Eminence, then we've stepped right into the bear trap. You'll remember that our strategy was your idea. To let it all spill out. Now we face a worse catastrophe than Martin Luther's Reformation! At least *he* had the decency and honesty to quit the Church! Svensens and Sugnini and Pirandella and their like are going to stay in and corrode the whole House of Catholicism from cellar to roof timbers!"

Arnulfo's attack on Lanser provoked a rare angry response from the Jesuit. "We foresaw all of that, Your Eminence," he said with icy vehemence. "Have you been head of the Holy Office for so long that you think the Church depends on you for its existence? Well, it doesn't, Your Eminence. You are neither Keeper of the Keys nor Keeper of our eternal salvation. One is: Christ. And we are all unprofitable servants."

The Maestro had never seen such cold anger erupt in Lanser, during all their years of service. He intervened to keep things from getting out of hand. "I think, Eminences, we had all better watch our mouths and our hearts. We agreed on a policy. We agreed on the risks. This is not some street fight with bishops and theologians. Our struggle is from the broad heights, from the perspective of history. We must see this entire attack on Roman authority as merely a repetition of what it has undergone several times in the past. The attack mustn't drive us into panic, mustn't let us drop our sights from the main target. What matters is the Roman fact and its supporting structure. As long as that structure of the Church remains intact, the rot can be cleared out once it's identified, and the membership can be renewed." A somewhat chastened Arnulfo apologized for his outburst. Until the day either Pope or bishops started to advocate heresy, he would do his part and, as he put it pathetically, "even take all the kicks in the face that 2,500 pairs of episcopal feet" would administer in Vatican II.

Lanser, too, apologized. He could not let his sharp reprimand to Arnulfo stand. He, too, was miserable, impaled on the Pope's commissions to him. "Many will say that I've become a Protestant, and that I've fallen into the hands of the so-called Judeo-Masonic plot to destroy the Church. No matter what I do, no one will be satisfied—not Catholics, not Protestants, not Jews. And no matter what happens, I will be crucified."

"Your Eminences." The Maestro broke in again. "We all know the road we have chosen will not be an easy one. I suggest we keep two things in mind. First, we are only accelerating what was a slow but certain process. The rot was already there, seeping into every area of our Church. To let it continue secretly, so to say, would have brought us to the crisis later, perhaps; but by then it would have been even harder and more painful to deal with.

"And second, we must prepare our minds and our souls. Cardinals Lanser and Arnulfo will not be the only ones to suffer. This is just the beginning. The worst is yet to come."

Paolo Lercani listened, fascinated by the possibilities, as His Holiness explained the Holy See's difficulty with the *cedolare* tax.

On the Maestro's advice—De Brescia explained the full situation—they were paying taxes on some dividends. The Maestro and others were talking with people from the Treasury. But eventually, when push came to shove, the Pope's view was that the Holy See had only two choices. They would have to give in like any other shareholder in the Italian markets. Or they would have to fight.

When he was certain the Pontiff had finished his explanation, the financier's own comments were quiet and professional. "When I have faced two horns of a dilemma, Holiness, I have generally avoided them altogether by finding a third way."

"In this case?" Papa Da Brescia was interested.

"In this case, the two horns Your Holiness faces are payment versus litigation. But the dilemma has only arisen in the first place because the Holy See is such a heavy investor in our domestic markets. I have thought for a long time that was unwise of the Holy See. There are simple mechanisms by which the major portions of the Holy See's investments can be reinvested outside Italy, and even in tax-free havens.

"Of course, Holiness, that would be a major decision." Lercani raised his upper lip in a smile. "Fortunately, Your Holiness is the sole person who can legally dispose of the Church's goods as Your Holiness sees fit."

To the sharp-eyed Lercani, Papa Da Brescia seemed for some reason to break away from him at that point. He couldn't tell why. But he knew. Suddenly, the Pope lowered his eyes, refused to meet his visitor's gaze, began to fiddle with a letter opener on his desk.

"We thank you, Signor Lercani." Da Brescia knew such a transfer of assets could be effected only over the signature of the Keeper. The Maestro would never agree. Only if the Maestro ceased to be Keeper, and if someone with Lercani's skill in manipulating money in the network of international currency laws was given the task, only then could such a plan be implemented. But Papa Da Brescia's lips were sealed about the Keeper. He would have to devise that part of the plan without Lercani. "We will think more and talk further with you about this plan." The Pontiff raised his eyes again. "Fortunately, Signor Lercani, the full crisis is not upon Us yet.

"Meanwhile, a few practical problems. We need to establish a new fund to provide shelters for the homeless in Rome."

Lercani listened patiently. He always listened patiently to Da Brescia. His instinct—that unfailing nose of his that could catch the first scent of a new kill—told him he was within a stone's throw of his highest ambition. He might yet become the Pope's banker, and broker for the Universal Church to boot. In fact, it might even be the time to raise his sights higher still.

[39]

Bishop Richard Lansing had not the slightest intention of furthering Papa Da Brescia's plans for protocol arrangements between the Holy See and the Soviet satellite governments. He reckoned he would have to make a good show of it; that much would be necessary for his papal office reports and personal debriefings. But that should present little difficulty. By now he had the better part of twenty years' good experience dealing with Communist authorities. He could, when he chose, be as expert as they at dancing about an issue without making undesired headway toward its substance.

"How heartening to welcome you again, Excellency." The Polish consul in Rome granted Rico's latest visa with a smile. "You are becoming an old friend of Poland's Socialist experiment."

Rico smiled his thanks. Like all "old friends," he knew he was under constant surveillance on all his overt trips to the East. He had become expert in picking that up, as well.

Aside from the time he would have to devote to the Pontiff's specific assignment, Rico's primary purpose on this trip was to finalize long-nurtured plans with Cardinal Wallensky and Archbishop Valeska.

Lansing had long since explained to the clerics the true nature of his work. He had judged it impractical to keep it from them in the circumstances. As it turned out, neither of them had been very surprised at the revelation. And not only had the friendship among the three warmed and deepened in the intervening years, but Rico found both men an invaluable help in developing the underground network at which he had been laboring now for a decade and a half.

While that underground was more thinly spread than Rico would have liked, it was secure—"Lysenko-proof," as Rico still sometimes put it—and it was firmly rooted. It had already proved itself extremely effective as a funnel of detailed and accurate information of exactly the nature Papa Profumi had envisioned. Now it was time for a new development; time to take the next step of mental and spiritual training so that the underground network would become the moral and spiritual spearhead for the people within the social and political realities enforced by Marxist Communism.

Cardinal Wallensky had never wavered from his own conviction that the two most obvious options available to the Church under the strictures of the Stalinist and post-Stalinist regimes both spelled death.

"To become a church of silence," Wallensky often repeated, "holding on to our faith as best we can, and suffering the totalitarian hardships of Fascism with a Marxist face, is really to yield in the long run.

"On the other hand, even though we Christians are fighters, to join the ever-multiplying anti-regime movements is to force our struggle into the social and political arena. It is to say, 'May the best man win.' And in *that* arena, the Communist is the best man. He has no scruples; we have."

Over the years, Rico had seen firsthand how accurate that analysis was. Hungary, Czechoslovakia, Lithuania, East Germany, and, increasingly now, Cuba showed the inadequacy of both options.

The ideal hammered out among Rico, Wallensky, and Valeska enshrined a third way for believers to conduct themselves under hostile regimes. In this third way, the areas of public life specifically claimed by totalitarian Communism as vital for its existence were to be shunned in writing, in speaking, and in all public activity. They were not, then, to choose as their own arena anything having to do with political activity, whether parliamentary or municipal; or anything touching the Polish Politburo, the military, police or security forces, or questions of foreign policy.

In every other arena, however—ecclesiastical, religious, cultural, academic, artistic, and in the field of labor relations—the aim was to enable Catholics to insist on a regime compatible with their beliefs. In borderline cases, where one of the "off-limits" areas was touched, direct clashes with the political government were to be avoided.

"This new approach," as Wallensky summarized the topic of the strategy, "this third way, is the fruit of years of painful learning. The Moscow Politburo and our own masters, here in Warsaw and elsewhere in this suffering Soviet empire, have learned two very bitter lessons: Communism does not provide enough bread. And Communism cannot destroy religious faith. Of necessity, they have now developed a degree of tolerance. We are going to capitalize on that tolerance."

The task Lansing, Wallensky, and Valeska set themselves in those six weeks before the opening of the second session of Vatican II was to draw up instruction manuals covering all the areas in which they could and could not act, and the kinds of actions to be tested and refined. Once those manuals were put together, the educational process could begin in earnest with night classes, lectures, training sessions, and publications.

The work was arduous and very carefully done. "If we make one mistake"—Valeska emphasized the danger—"if we take one step into their sacred areas, they will cut us down like so many useless weeds."

Life was anything but easeful during those weeks. Lansing, like Valeska and Wallensky, rose at four-thirty each morning. After prayers, Mass, and breakfast, work began. The morning hours were consumed with discussions, not only among the three clergymen, but with the leading members of the underground network. Afternoons were often spent visiting various parts of Warsaw and nearby towns and cities. Evenings were devoted to more discussions, reading, and writing. If they got to bed before midnight, or slept more than four or five hours, it was a luxury. There were few diversions. Food was very scarce and unavoidably bland and monotonous. No coffee ever. Sometimes weak tea. Plenty of milk, bread, and potatoes. Meat once every two weeks or so. Enormous supplies of warm vegetable soup, morning, noon, and night.

For Rico, all of this seemed a change for the better. As always, he found in Eastern Europe a special peace of mind and a certain welcome consistency in his life.

Rico did make one pilgrimage with his two friends to the shrine of the Virgin of Jasna Gora at Czestochowa. And Valeska found time to give him a guided tour of Wawel Castle, a magnificent Renaissance palace built on top of a Romanesque palace dating from the eleventh century. "Poland started here," Valeska told him, "and its faith was planted here at the same time. Poland and its faith are one."

This was a peculiarity of Polish Catholicism that Lansing could not parallel in his experience in the U.S.A. or in Italy. Valeska's attitude to Wawel Castle was as religious as it was patriotic, and as patriotic as it was religious.

"A far cry from your separation of church and state, eh?" Valeska knew Rico's mind well enough to read his unspoken reaction. "Well, that is how it is here, my friend, and that is how it should be. The secular state, whether it is Marxist Communism or what you call democracy, is ultimately incompatible with Christianity. Poland learned that lesson long ago. And that is the only reason there is still a Poland."

Rico chose not to argue the point. It was clear enough to him that Valeska and Wallensky, with nothing but token support since Profumi's death, and surrounded, in a manner of speaking, by the barbed-wire restrictions of a hatefully atheistic and hating Communist regime, had never ceased to seek fresh avenues to get around the obstacles in their path. At every turn and corner, the iron-clad fist was there to hinder, to bother, to threaten, to frighten, to discourage, to subdue. But the cardinal and his archbishop never stopped their solitary fight. Surely they were among "the lonely and the brave" of history.

One of the most important lessons in this for Rico was a personal one. Ever since he had agreed, in Papa Angelica's time as Pope, to continue his already difficult work without the open blessing and advice of his Pontiff, he had felt uncomfortable. Even if Lanser hadn't told him he would have to continue that policy at least for a time under Papa Da Brescia, Da Brescia's own instructions to Rico made that necessity clear. But he could not forget the halcyon days with Papa Profumi, hard and all as they had been. Before Profumi, he had been able to look to the cardinal in Chicago for direction. And before that, he had been under his own father. Always there had been someone over him, some authority he could look to. But no longer. Was this really the life he was supposed to lead? God's will for him?

He found the beginnings of an answer to those questions as he came to see that Cardinal Wallensky and Archbishop Valeska could love their Pope—love in the sense of veneration and respect for the Vicar of Christ. First of all they loved and looked to Christ, and then to whatever valid authority there was between them and Christ.

Toward the end of that six-week stint of unrelenting labors, Rico began for the first time to talk out some of his problems in the area of ecclesiastical authority—or the lack of it—in his life.

"We've been in that same boat these last few years." Wallensky had no difficulty in understanding Rico. "The late beloved Papa Angelica and his secretary of state, Picolomini, were always on my back about the way I treated the Communist authorities, always wanted me to be more conciliatory.

"True, the Pope is infallible in certain special circumstances, and in ordinary circumstances concerning faith and morals. But in practical judgments about practical things, the Pope can err like any man.

"I have never seen the justification for larding such practical mistakes onto Christ, and thus excusing myself from the obligation of taking my own responsibilities.

"Now, Papa Da Brescia has placed you in the same position. You have received the sacrament of holy orders. You are a valid bishop, an apostle in the line reaching back to the Twelve, and to Christ Himself. It is time for you to grow up!"

Rico's objection was immediate. "Isn't that just what the bishops said in the first session of Vatican II? They went so far as to act as if the Pope wasn't Pope at all!"

Wallensky conceded only part of Rico's point. "If and when a bishop does that," he countered, "he is excusing himself from another and more important responsibility. I have never acted as if the Pope were not Pope. I have acted in practical circumstances with which His Holiness was not acquainted. And I have acted to maintain the Church and the papacy. We have been around for a long time, Rico. We've seen popes come and go. We have made it clear that they can rely on us for fidelity to the Holy See as the See of the Blessed Peter.

"The bishops in Council, on the contrary, were trying, for whatever reasons they may have had, to democratize everything about the Church, and to de-pope the Pope in the process."

Only on the last point did Bogdan Valeska disagree. He put great store in Vatican II, the full body of bishops getting together for the first time, all acting together as apostles.

"It can't go wrong," he insisted. "We are the bishops of Christ's Church. The Holy Spirit will guide us all."

It was the only point of deep disagreement between Valeska and Wallensky.

The moments for such discussions were few and rather brief. By the time they had to prepare to leave for Rome—the Poles were to travel with Rico to attend the Council—the three friends had completed their plans for the next stage of the underground educational process. Rico would review it all with Solaccio and Brandolini, and then arrange with Helmut de la Valle for the safe transfer of the additional funds needed to launch the project.

In Rome, everybody from Papa Da Brescia down to the most insignificant Vatican *minutante* was caught up again in the excitement, interviewing, listening, talking, arranging of meetings and accommodations, dinners and luncheons, working feverishly toward the October 1 opening of Vatican II.

Keti de la Valle had long since become as accustomed as Agathi to throngs of visitors and the babel of languages at Villa Cerulea. Nevertheless, by the week before the second Council session, she began to witness with a mounting puzzlement the comings and goings of Vatican officials, foreign bishops, and other visitors through the Great Hall and the upper-floor studies of Guido and Helmut.

It wasn't just that there were far more visitors than usual—almost every night there were at least thirty for dinner, and dinner was inevitably followed by private meetings upstairs. And it wasn't just the crisis atmosphere she detected. After all, crises of one sort and another seemed endemic to the life Helmut and his uncle led. If it wasn't that some government was falling, it was the vagaries of the stock market or the Somalia banana trade or the price of platinum.

This was different. It seemed to concern the Ecumenical Council, and that itself was puzzling. Everywhere but here, including from her friends in Rome and from the newspapers, Keti had got the impression that positive changes were in the offing: changes favoring peace, mutual trust, mutual love. Catholics and Protestants were actually talking and making plans together for long-range cooperation that was exciting for her. Even the Soviet representatives from the Russian Orthodox Church had returned to participate in Vatican II as observers. It all seemed so good a prospect.

And yet, at dinner after formal dinner, conversation was not animated as it generally was during such affairs at Villa Cerulea. Instead of lively talk punctuated with toasts, loud exclamations, jokes and laughter, the tones were subdued, and Keti was constantly hearing references to "bishops" and "they." Apparently, she gathered, "they" were interfering with the "bishops."

"We'll end up just as splintered as they are . . ." she might hear. Or: "They surely have done their work well. . . ."

Agathi was not bothered by the mystery of who "they" might be. It had never been her habit, nor was it in her makeup, to enter into Guido's or Helmut's affairs outside of the running and well-being of Villa Cerulea.

Keti, however, was not merely curious; she was concerned for Helmut. She knew his moods now better than anyone. Rarely did he laugh during those weeks, or show signs of that witty humor she loved in him. Worse still, the two had not had what she thought of as "a cuddling conversation" for a long time. She knew in her heart he was still hers. But there was a distance growing between them that she couldn't bridge. He would come to bed late. He might talk with her a little, about his latest trip perhaps, or about some political happening. Most of all he wanted her to tell him about Eugenio. He missed the time he usually spent with his son. He would hold Keti while she told him about the boy's latest antics, about his growing friendship with Donatello Graziani, about his wanting a bicycle like Donatello's, about how he liked to accompany her on her visits around Guido's estate. But as much as he wanted to hear her news, in moments Helmut would fall into an exhausted sleep.

Keti thought of talking things over with Rico. Perhaps he could explain this crisis that was affecting Helmut, taking him farther and farther away from her and Eugenio. But even Rico, who always seemed so sure and strong, appeared caught up in this contagious pre-Council fever.

Well, at least he promised to have a good conversation with her "as soon as things quiet down."

Keti both smiled and frowned at that. The way things looked to her, that could be a long time from now. "What's going on, Rico? I thought Vatican II was supposed to be going so well."

"Not so well, Keti. But it can't be helped." He smiled reassuringly. "It's not the end of the world. It may be the end of an era."

Sometimes Keti, in bed but still awake and reading, would wait for Helmut to come in after those long after-dinner meetings that lasted frequently until midnight or one in the morning.

"Is it over for the evening?" she would ask.

More often than not, he would brandish a sheaf of papers. "Well, they've all left, but I still have a couple of hours' work." He would bend down and kiss her. "Try and get some sleep. Be sure and have me up by seven-thirty, no matter how I grumble."

Keti still didn't know who "they" were, or what they were doing to the "bishops." But she knew she didn't like the effect they were having on Helmut.

His Holiness' joy at the "awakening" of his bishops was rudely disarmed by the first meeting of the Procedural Committee, whose job it now was, under the chairmanship of Cardinal Svensens, to regulate the subject matter to be discussed by the bishops in formal Council session. The meeting lasted five hours and was excessively stormy.

Just as he had told Lanser and Arnulfo, Papa Da Brescia had let Svensens know that he wanted the bishops to discuss, amend, modify, and finally approve some acceptable version of the *Schema* on "The Pope and the World" before they tackled any other theme. The primacy and the jurisdiction of the Pope must be the first order of Vatican II business.

However, only one bishop on the committee, France's Édouard Lasuisse, wanted what Papa Da Brescia wanted. All seven others, including Svensens himself, wanted none of "The Pope and the World." Not at the beginning of the Council, or at the end, or anywhere in between.

"We know all about the primacy and jurisdiction of the Holy Father," shouted Bishop Halliday of Birmingham, England. "What about *our* jurisdiction?"

"Are we running dogs in the Church?" Bishop Vernij of Maastricht, Holland, was less loud but more sarcastic. "Are we just here at the beck and call of a Roman emperor? Or are we the successors of the Apostles?"

At the end of five hours of turbulence, a perspiring and scarlet-faced

Svensens, who had done his share and more of shouting and table thumping, put a motion to the committee. "We must reach *some* conclusion! How should we decide the subject matter of the formal Council sessions? And especially of the first session? It is only days away."

Again, Lasuisse cast the lone vote in favor of following His Holiness' plan. All seven of the others voted to throw the agenda open on the floor of the Council.

Everywhere in Rome and the Vatican, in all the seminaries and colleges where the bishops of the Council were housed, out in the dozen villas where whole blocs of them—from the U.S.A., Canada, Germany, Australia, England—were installed for the next two months, one subject only was on everybody's lips: Finally, the Council was out of the hands of the Pope and the Curia.

The excitement and enthusiasm caused by this realization was infectious. Delegations of bishops and bevies of theologians scurried from seminary to seminary, from villa to villa, discussing strategy, planning first moves once the Council was formally convened on the first day of October. Smaller groups of cardinals met separately, some accompanied by a theologian or an auxiliary bishop. Out in Cardinal Lanser's rooms on the Via Aurelia, or at Cardinal Arnulfo's home in the Parioli suburb, or in a suite at La Presidente Hotel, where higher churchmen usually stayed if they had no apartment at their disposal in the Vatican, or at Villa Cerulea, the conversation, as Keti had seen, was far more subdued and filled with worried speculation.

Papa Da Brescia held an emergency meeting with Levesque, Sugnini, and Pirandella. He had wanted from the bishops a strong affirmation of the privileges and power of the Pope. That was the basis of his entire policy and of his vision. Was this undisciplined rout of his Procedural Committee a taste of things to come? Had his entire calculation been inaccurate?

It seemed to the Pontiff's three close advisers that he was teetering on the edge of decision. It was not the first time they had seen that tendency in him.

"They are Your Holiness' bishops." Sugnini soothed the troubled air.

Levesque was well acquainted with Svensens; and Grosjean of Paris, together with a few others in the Procedural Committee, he knew as friends. "They know what they are doing, Holy Father. It is for the good of the Church."

Pirandella's advice was on the cautionary side. "Holy Father, you have put certain powers in the hands of your bishops. You cannot retract them now. Otherwise there might be a massive walkout. All that has been accomplished with the Protestants and others would be wiped out."

Still, long after Levesque and the others had left him, Da Brescia wrestled with his problem.

On impulse, and despite the hour, he dialed Cardinal Lanser at home. "I do not agree with Sugnini or Levesque, Holy Father." Lanser was brief. "Pirandella has made the only valid point. A massive walkout—whatever its effect on the Protestants—could lead to de facto schism within the Church. The wine is poured, as they say in Sicily, Your Holiness. We have to drink it."

On October 1, Papa Da Brescia opened "his session" of Vatican II. After a High Mass celebrated in St. Peter's Basilica for all his bishops, he delivered an impressive address with the verve and solemnity befitting the occasion. He reminded the bishops of the grave importance of their coming labors in the Council. He exhorted them for an hour and a half to perform those labors in such a way as to vindicate the primary and jurisdiction of the Roman Pontiff, to promote the good of the people of God, and to exalt the Church before the eyes of all the world.

The bishops rewarded him with gentle flows of applause. The choir raised its voice in the traditional hymn "Thou Art Peter." The Pontiff gave his bishops his papal blessing and was carried on the *sedia gestatoria* down the transept, between the sloping tiers of white-robed bishops, each one wearing his miter, the symbol of his apostleship.

"As president of the Procedural Committee"—Cardinal Svensens' voice was wonderfully amplified by the new loudspeaker system Papa Da Brescia had installed—"I have two announcements to make.

"First, you will now receive lists of the bishops proposed to sit on the fifteen consultative committees. Those lists were drawn up by a special group chosen by the new Standing Committee of Presiding Cardinals. The full Council must vote on those lists.

"Second, you, my brothers, all of us together, must decide what *Schema* we will discuss first. His Holiness has proposed the *Schema* concerning 'The Pope and the World.' "

A few disgruntled shouts were raised, but they did not perturb Cardinal Svensens. "You will all have your chance to register your opinions.

"Now, in order to expedite these two important matters, and because it is now moving toward midday, I propose we adjourn. That will give you all time to study the lists, and to discuss them, as well as the matter of which *Schema* you wish to take up first.

"Tomorrow, the first item of business will be to vote on the bishops who will make up the consultative committees. The second will be the subject matter with which this Council chooses to open its deliberations."

A murmur of approval. A smile from the presiding cardinal.

"Finally, before we adjourn for the day, my brothers," Svensens went on, "as one further means of expediting our opening deliberations tomorrow, I ask each of you to prepare in advance two written ballots. Again, the first will be your vote to accept or reject the lists of bishops for the consultative committees. The second will be on what *Schema* this Council will take up first.

"When we convene tomorrow morning at eight o'clock, boxes will be provided, in which you may deposit your ballots. If you will all kindly follow this simple procedure, we will very quickly have the Council's decisions on these two important matters, and then get down to our real business.

"Remember also that if you wish to address the Council, you must submit your name and the subject on which you will speak by five o'clock on the day before you would like to come to the podium."

Arnulfo and Lanser walked out of the Basilica together.

"A very businesslike performance by our Belgian brother," Arnulfo observed acidly.

"And"—Lanser glanced cursorily through the fifteen lists of bishops—"a very businesslike job of packing the consultative committees. I see our Belgian and French, Dutch and German brothers are well represented."

"And our Latin American brothers as well." Arnulfo had already glanced at his copy of the lists.

"Are you heading for your office?"

"Yes."

"Tomorrow, then."

"Yes, tomorrow."

In their private, after-dinner meeting that night at Villa Cerulea, the lists of bishops and their theological experts, their *periti,* were the only topic of discussion between the Maestro and Helmut.

There had never been any doubt, even in Papa Angelica's mind, of the importance of the consultative committees. It was their function to take the suggestions for revision of each *Schema* made in the full Council, and to "harmonize" those changes with the original prepared text. But neither had Papa Angelica or anyone else foreseen the manner in which those committees would exercise their function. In the first session of Vatican II, it was precisely those committees that had refused to move on any of the prepared *Schema,* no matter how carefully all the bishops had been polled and consulted beforehand. And it was precisely that refusal, that revolt of the committees, that had forced a second session.

With the Vatican's official list and dossiers of Catholic bishops, and with full dossiers as well of the theological experts whose advice was so pivotal, Guido and Helmut made a thorough analysis of the committees. The results were clear and stark.

Nine bishops sat on each committee. That gave huge power to 129 out of 2,500 bishops. Of the 135, there were 42 Frenchmen, 37 Germans, 4 Austrians, 18 Dutchmen, 11 Englishmen, 4 North Americans, 13 Latin Americans. No bishop had been selected from Italy or Portugal or Ireland. There were no Africans, no Asiatics, no Middle Easterners.

As to the *periti,* names such as Hans Kleiser of Tübingen, Jaime Herreras of Colombia, Charles McMurren of Washington, and other associates of the Northern Alliance were noted down as theological experts to more than one bishop and more than one committee.

The Maestro already knew, from the Nigerian Cardinal Azande, that Svensens and Pirandella had presented the group named to select the bishops for the consultative committees with those selections already neatly drawn up. Azande's was the only vote against their acceptance as drawn, from start to finish.

"And tomorrow?" Helmut sat back in his chair and looked at his uncle.

"Tomorrow?" The Maestro put all the folders aside. "Well, the Northern Alliance has the whip hand in the consultative committees, as we've seen. Probably, too, they have already canvassed a large minority, or even a small majority, of the 2,500 bishops. So tomorrow the bishops in Council will approve of these lists." He laid a hand on the stack of folders. "And they will reject Papa Da Brescia's proposal to discuss first 'The Pope and the World.' God alone knows what they will decide to discuss. Or what sort of hash the consultative committees will make of what they discuss. It's the committees' Council now, not the bishops' Council."

[40]

Cardinal Secretary Jean Levesque was enjoying himself. In the war for control of the Church, he counted his forces well ahead so far. But some skirmishes gave him greater personal satisfaction than others.

He had requested and been granted a rare invitation to be present at this morning's meeting of the stiff-necked State Council. His only disappointment was that other business had kept the Maestro and Helmut de la Valle from attending. It was a pity they would miss this performance.

As he sat through such droning business as the State Council's deliberations on new plumbing for the sacristies in St. Peter's and repairs to the roof of the governor's residence in Vatican City, Levesque counted himself fortunate not to have to attend such boring meetings on a regular basis, and settled back to savor the anticipation of catching the curial cardinals off balance yet again. He particularly looked forward to watching the reactions of Arnulfo and Falconieri and that so-called noble cardinal Ferragamo-Duca. The others—Lanser, Hoffeldt, O'Mahoney—didn't matter so much.

Finally, when the Council's regular agenda had been covered, it was Levesque's turn.

"Your Eminences"—he milked the moment—"I have a small piece of news to communicate to you." He took a sheet of paper from his pocket and unfolded it. "On December 8, His Holiness will confer the office of cardinal on thirty-seven prelates. I will leave the list with you."

Nobody stirred. All eyes were on that sheet of paper Levesque held in his hands, unwilling to relinquish it quite yet. In the silence, the sound of a pin dropping would have been a loud interruption.

The cardinal secretary smiled as he peered over the rim of his "battlements." "You will note the multinational character His Holiness' choices will give to the Sacred College. As the Pontiff has said so frequently, the Church is the people's, and the people are the Church."

Cardinal Arnulfo suddenly got a frog in his throat. Levesque waited contentedly for the coughing and wheezing to subside, and then continued. "Of course, the Holy Father desires that all the bishops of Vatican II assist at the ceremonies. It will be a great day for the Church, as I'm sure Your Eminences will agree."

The moment was all Levesque had hoped. His only regret, aside from the absence of the Maestro and his nephew, was that he could not yet reveal to these self-important guardians of the Church more of the papal intentions that lay behind these thirty-seven appointments. For this was only the beginning in a long-range plan. As Papa Da Brescia himself had said to Levesque, "Our College of Cardinals is rightly called Sacred; but it is also gerontological! We need young men, not old, to elect popes and govern the Church. How do we eliminate the old from voting? From holding vital positions in the Curia? From sealing off even the State Council from Us? Or, for that matter, from holding the various dioceses of the Church Universal in their hands?"

The Pontiff and his cardinal secretary had made considerable progress in mapping out a long-range reform of the Sacred College. But Da Brescia had warned Levesque to say nothing of that at this morning's State Council meeting, and the Frenchman knew it was not the moment to tip their full hand. For now, he must be content with the opening gambit.

"Ah!" Cardinal Levesque suddenly seemed to realize that he still held the list of new cardinals. "How careless of me!" He rose from his chair, all six feet two inches of him towering over the others, who remained seated. Instead of handing the list to the presiding cardinal, as was protocol, he laid it on the table in front of him. Certain that he had demonstrated their helplessness, he bade Their Eminences a good morning, "God bless you all!"

With Levesque gone, Arnulfo reached for the paper and read out the names of the thirty-seven cardinals-to-be. The Italians, French, Irish, Dutch, English, Spanish, most of the North Americans, and two of the Germans were due appointments, replacing cardinals who had died or retired in important dioceses of countries that traditionally had cardinals. That accounted only for nineteen of the number. The remaining eighteen included thirteen brand-new cardinal posts in Latin America, three in India, one in Oceania, one in Vietnam, and two more in Germany. Sugnini's name was absent, but there was little else to be pleased about.

"They're all half-baked theologians." Arnulfo passed the list to Falconieri. "Every one of the Latin Americans is well known for extreme progressionist views on social questions and political matters. Even the due appointments are of the same stripe. Lionel Buff of England, for example. He's as bad as Svensens. The Belgian lacks an ounce of real religious faith, as far as I've been able to see."

"And so it goes, my friends." Ferragamo-Duca had scratched the names on a pad as Arnulfo read them out. "Papa Da Brescia is packing the Sacred College. It's a mirror image of what's been done with the consultative committees of bishops in Vatican II. This list of thirty-seven brings the number of cardinals in the Church to 109. But you can bet he isn't finished. The next conclave is a long way off, but my guess is that the Pope intends to do all he can to control it from the grave by his appointment of such cardinals as these."

That, however, as Cardinal Levesque could have told them, was only a part of Papa Da Brescia's long-range strategy.

Papa Da Brescia was angry and disappointed, and he let Levesque and Sugnini know it.

"We are quite content"—the Pontiff's owlish eyes were blazing—"to see the consultative committees of Our bishops staffed by non-Roman, non-Italian, and mainly non-Mediterranean bishops. And We are content to see them aided by nontraditional theologians. That is a good trend. It means the people are finally going to repossess the Church.

"We are not content, however, that 2,247 out of 2,500 of Our bishops attending Vatican II have rejected Our expressed wish that their first order of business be the *Schema* asserting the primacy and jurisdiction of the Roman Pontiff!

"It is the people of the Church in conjunction with Us, the Supreme Pastor, that constitute the earthly institution of Christ! Why do Our bishops refuse to go along with Our wish? Did you two not reveal Our wish to them?"

Levesque and Sugnini had known this moment would come, and they were well prepared for it.

The cardinal secretary was deferential. Yes, he said, he had communicated the Pontiff's wish. But from his careful consultation with key bishops, he had learned they thought this would give the wrong impression to the "separated brothers"—Protestants, as well as Russian and Greek Orthodox.

What wrong impression might that be? His Holiness pressed.

That the Council was merely convened to put a stamp on Vatican imperialism and "Caesaropapism," the Frenchman countered smoothly.

As Levesque knew he would, Da Brescia recoiled from those terms as from an evil poison, or a pair of vipers. For nearly two hundred years, Protestants had hurled toward Rome such epithets as "this little red-robed Caesar, the Pope."

If it did nothing else, Da Brescia was determined that Vatican II must end all that.

It was Sugnini's turn in this well-prepared duet. "Holy Father, there are other and even better ways for Your Holiness to assert and make clear the importance of the Roman Pontiff." Sugnini did not use the words "primacy" and "jurisdiction," but surely he meant to include them in the meaning of "importance."

"Action, Holy Father." Sugnini's voice was colored with excitement. "Bold action, not mere words from men gathered together in a basilica in Rome. 'Words create no reality,' Gabriel Marcel said. 'Human action evokes reality.' "

Marcel was one of Da Brescia's favorites, as Sugnini realized. The

Pope's interest was roused, but his anger was not dispelled.

"What reality, Monsignore? We are talking about the fatherhood of the papacy for all men!"

"Yes, Holiness. But how better to assert that than to act like that? Would not the reality become clear to all if, for example, Your Holiness were to meet with the other great churchmen of our day in the very place where the Lord Jesus died and rose from the dead? In Jerusalem? Would not the whole world, and certainly our separated brothers, be impressed to see you, the Vicar of Christ, traveling as a pilgrim to give the kiss of peace to, say, Patriarch Athenagoras?"

Sugnini smiled at Da Brescia. "*That,* Holy Father, is to create reality! No imperialism there! No 'Caesaropapism'! All that would be replaced by brotherly love, fatherly care."

"Just imagine, Holiness!" Cardinal Levesque rejoined the duet on cue. "And that could be only the beginning. After Your Holiness embraces the Eastern Church in the person of Athenagoras, would it not be possible to assert the reality we speak of even in the very center of the non-Christian world? In the poorest part of that world? In India, for example?

"And to be certain that the message—the reality—is clear, there is even a way Your Holiness can visit all nations at once. Poor and rich. Christian and non-Christian. Catholic and Protestant. Capitalist and Marxist. We are suggesting, Holy Father, a formal state visit to the United Nations headquarters in New York!"

Papa Da Brescia saw the possibilities. He stood up in his excitement. The impact of such a triad of pilgrimages would be worldwide. He, the Pope, the greater of the two churchmen, would make a voyage to reconcile Athenagoras, the lesser of the two. Then he would enlarge his embrace to include the poverty-stricken Third World. And then the world itself. The Protestant churches and sects would be galvanized; but the potential was far greater still.

As if he could read Da Brescia's very thoughts, Cardinal Levesque spoke the papal mind. The new reality would be much more than the so-called Roman fact. That was sufficient for a Papa Profumi. But in the new reality, the Pontiff would no longer be called a little Caesar. No longer a minor emperor holding onto a shrunken enclave on the edge of the Italian peninsula. The new "fact" would be His Holiness as universal father of all men!

Sugnini rounded off the plan. "The beauty and the godliness of it all will be that, while Your Holiness is creating this new international fact, this reality, Your Holiness' Council will be producing historic statements for all men concerning the Church's salvation, human hope, and world peace.

"When it is all over, Council and pilgrimages, there before the whole world will be this universal father surrounded by his international gathering of bishops, inviting all Christians—all the world!—to partake at the same table of divine bounty!"

Sugnini's face was flushed as he concluded his performance. Even Mr.

Richard Richards himself could not have done better. Papa Da Brescia knew in his very soul that Levesque and Sugnini were right. "Very good," he said at last. "Let Us put Our shoulder to this work. But you are to say nothing. The papal pilgrimages are to be kept secret until We Ourself announce them."

"Yes, Holy Father." Sugnini and Levesque chorused the final notes of their duet. Once more the Holy Father had teetered on the edge of a dangerous decision. And once more he had been persuaded to remain firm.

"Surely," the Pontiff said quietly, looking at his two closest aides, "We are approaching the day of the Lord, and a turning point in history."

At the beginning of 1964, Helmut de la Valle's responsibilities increased a hundredfold. The Vatican State Council, worried by the ever-threatening *cedolare* tax, on the one hand, and by Papa Da Brescia's increasing reliance on Paolo Lercani on the other, gave instructions for Guido to take all possible steps to protect Holy See funds from both the government and the Sicilian financier. The Maestro summarized the situation in its simplest terms at a special meeting of the *impero* associates.

First, all conversations with Government officials had made it clear that there was no escape from the *cedolare* tax if the funds they managed for the Holy See remained on the Italian stock markets.

Second, Papa Da Brescia was determined not to pay the *cedolare* tax. It appeared that he would choose flight of funds abroad. The Maestro therefore expected the Pontiff to demand a full accounting and to pressure for the end of the Holy See's present arrangements in the financial agencies.

"That I would not mind," Guido explained. "But Monsignore Di Lorio and I are convinced that the Pontiff will put most of the assets of the Holy See in the hands of Lercani."

Di Lorio, retired now from Vatican service, but still a valued aide to the *impero,* adjusted his pince-nez and cleared his throat. "That is not our judgment alone. Each member of the State Council is deathly afraid that Lercani—a crook and a scoundrel, gentlemen—is going to become literally the Pope's banker." The Sphinx shook his spectacles from his nose in his outrage at the very thought. "Before that can happen, we propose shifting a major block of funds abroad, out of reach, as the Maestro has so wisely said, of both the *cedolare* and Lercani.

"Naturally, most of the funds to be transferred will be those that ostensibly have nothing to do with the Holy See. All anonymously held companies and stock will be sold or bartered. We will include as much of our identifiable assets as will seem normal."

The only questions from the associates were practical ones. The assets involved were enormous, and each one of them would have to lend an able hand. Helmut would be in charge of the vast shift. The Maestro did not need to point out that his nephew knew the foreign markets extremely well by now.

"We'll head for American and Far Eastern markets in the main." Helmut picked up at this point. "The boom is coming in those areas. Europe may not be a very safe place for the big investor in the next ten to fifteen years."

By February, Helmut was deep into the work of the transfer of sums so huge as to affect the mission of the Church and the lives of millions. His new assignment meant not only more frequent trips abroad, but prolonged absences that kept him away from Keti and Eugenio for five and six weeks at a time. Indeed, that was the only painful thing for him.

Helmut had never regretted his marriage to Keti Wilson. Being married to her had introduced a sweet equilibrium into his life, and quieted a gentle unrest he had felt before he had known her. Everything about Keti—her intelligence, her smile, her beauty, her very being—was lightsome and radiant. From the first, she had brought a sense of delight and joyfulness into his already exciting existence. Loving her was in itself a dimension of meaning he could never have known or guessed at without her.

Even before this increase in his work and travel, Helmut had felt guilty when he thought about Keti. He knew that some of the physical tenderness had disappeared from their life together. And some of the closeness of their quiet conversations had disappeared too. The oath he had taken as Keeper-designate meant there were things he could not share even with her. And always the demons of work to be done and decisions to be made accompanied him, wagging invisible fingers at him, dragging him away from the folds of intimacy.

He told himself, too, that Eugenio was another reason his relationship with Keti had changed. She was, after all, not merely his lover now, but the mother of his child.

And yet, true as they might be, these were only stopgap explanations. What Helmut could not yet articulate, even for his own understanding, was the curious and deep effect on him of the vow he had taken from Monsignore Di Lorio in the presence of the Sacred Host. In effect, that vow had been a religious consecration, and it had worked a change in him, as such things often do. Even his sensuality was affected, and with it the desire to celebrate love in the unbridled outpouring of himself without restraint.

He sometimes thought—almost absently, and without connecting the thought with Keti—that he understood a little better now why his uncle Guido had chosen to maintain the vow of celibacy he had taken on Mount Athos.

Without question, Helmut still loved Keti. It was harder to show it now, and it was harder still for her to understand the change in him. His long absences from Villa Cerulea did not help, he knew. Perhaps if he had been aware earlier in his life of the Bargain, had known his fate as its Keeper, he might have done things differently. But that was vain speculation.

"Soon," he said to himself often as he crisscrossed the world, "soon I will find the time and the way, and Keti will know I love and cherish her. Soon."

By the spring of 1964, Rico Lansing's network had been thrown as far east as Bialystok near the Polish–U.S.S.R. border, and as far north as the Latvian port of Riga. Latvia was less than a quarter Catholic; but moving by boat from there to Leningrad and to within the U.S.S.R. itself would be easier than any overland route. In any case, he never forgot that the first information about the Soviet missiles being loaded for Cuba had come from Riga.

Rico's chief of operations in Riga was a man named Karlis Pelse, a colonel in the Soviet army, a member of the two-hundred-man Supreme Soviet that governed Latvia for Moscow, and military governor of Riga port.

Pelse, whose mother was Russian, had successfully passed himself off as a Communist after a brilliant war record against the Germans. Neither his wife nor his children knew of his charade; he loved them too much to expose them to danger.

Fortunately for Rico, Pelse was one of those men who can plot and plan painstakingly, patiently, for years without any reward. As a crypto-Christian, he had formed a small group of similar-minded Letts, years before. Rico heard of him through people in Bialystok, where over fifteen thousand Letts had fled and settled in the latter stages of World War II.

Learning that there was a Pelse, and capitalizing on that knowledge, were two different things, however. Lansing had thought that he was well versed and experienced in covert movement; but the subtlety of Pelse and his group was amazing. Only those who lived and sometimes worked with the KGB, Rico reflected, would be driven to such lengths of caution and secrecy. It took the best part of a year to make contact, much longer for Solaccio and Brandolini to find a secure "window" for Rico's entry and exit, and a very long time before Pelse really trusted him.

Once trust was finally established between the colonel and the bishop, the Lett's value to Rico's network was immense. Because he had access to military and political circles in Moscow, a steady flow of unprecedentedly valuable information came through him and back to Rome. With typical caution, however, the method of communication Pelse nearly always used was impersonal. Rico or his "guide" would deliver a package at a certain address, pick one up from another. Occasionally the two would meet; but only after a long time did Rico even know Pelse's home, Varangia, was in Akshile suburb.

On this trip, Rico had simply picked up a package from Pelse at a drop, and left one in return. It was not until he was safely back in Bialystok and waiting for his "guide" to convey him west to Plzeň, his jumping-off stage into West Germany, that he had time and ease of mind to examine Pelse's latest batch of documents.

On the cover sheet of one sheaf of papers, Pelse had written a terse and intriguing reference to their developing underground education effort: "Others have a different educational process in mind for Catholics."

Leafing rapidly through the papers, Rico found a whole series of memos written in Spanish, some addressed by "General Control" to "Father Centro," and others from "Father Centro" back to "General Control."

At the bottom of the first of these memoranda, Pelse had written, "'Father Centro' = 'Jaime Herreras.'" The name meant nothing to Rico. Through earlier information from Pelse, he already knew that "General Control" was the office in the Moscow Ministry of Cults that dealt with Catholic affairs. Who ran that office, Pelse did not know.

The memos dated back to a 1949 meeting in Cuernavaca, Mexico, between General Control, Father Centro, and three other "brothers."

At that meeting, General Control had given Father Centro and the others a Moscow-conceived plan for "penetration of the masses in Latin America." Rico became almost hypnotized by the elements of that plan.

There was no way, Moscow laid down, that the people could be turned in large numbers against their Catholic faith. The words and acts of worship, and the basic tenets of that faith, were unshakably fixed in the popular mind. What was needed was an elaborate plan by which those very words and acts of worship, together with the concepts behind them, could be given a Marxist meaning. "The words and actions themselves, and even to a degree the tenets, must all remain the same," Rico read in the memorandum of instructions. "The masses remember these, and they respond to them in a most useful way. It is the content of all three that must be subtly altered."

The memorandum went on to give random examples of how this alteration was to proceed. It began with the basic Christian idea that Christ liberated men and women from the oppression of Satan and sin. The words "liberation," "sin," and "Satan"—*Liberación, pecado, Satanàs*—were to be retained. But over time, Satan was to be portrayed to the faithful as Yankee imperialism. Sin was to be understood as the poverty and misery created by that Satan. Liberation was to be seen as armed revolution against that Satan.

Rico's eye traveled down an entire glossary of the most basic Christian ideas, terms, and actions that were to be transformed in this manner, over time, and with great patience, so that little outside attention would be attracted until the re-education process was well along.

"Christ" as savior was to become in the new litany an armed revolutionary saving the people from capitalism. "The Church" was, of course, the mass of the oppressed people as distinct from the capitalist class. "The Bread of life" would no longer be the Eucharist, but the goods manufactured by the people in "liberated" industries. "Mary the Virgin" was the prototype of every Latin American mother of a revolutionary. "The Kingdom of Christ" was to be seen as the dictatorship of the proletariat; and its leaders were "the successors to Christ's Apostles."

The plans went on for pages to show how, by careful planning, study, and preaching, the new "Church"—the Marxist—could be re-educated, and the Marxist interpretation of ordinary Catholic piety, worship, and belief could be thorough and convincing, rooted as it would be "in the most common and general elements of life in that backward region."

What sort of mind was it, Rico asked himself, that had devised this plan? Surely, it was somebody who was well acquainted with Catholicism. And somebody who hated it with an almost religious passion.

The memoranda down the years since that first meeting in 1949 gave a grim outline of the progress of this educational plan. There were detailed requests for liquid funds. For supplies of arms. For contacts among the clergy in both Latin America and the United States. There were accounts of study centers established in at least half a dozen Latin American countries, and instructions for the routing of funds to Cuba in order to pay for supplies. Identities of people mentioned in the memoranda were impossible to tie down because code names were used throughout. The arms quartermaster was somebody in Fidel Castro's government. Rico would be able to check on this Jamie Herreras, if the name wasn't an alias. But for the rest, he needed more to go on.

The latest memorandom from Father Centro to General Control was dated just a few months before, December 1963. It concerned the Ecumenical Council, and mentioned among other things "our success in reaching the papal office and implanting the idea of the people of God as preferable to the idea of a hierarchic Church."

When he had finished reading, Rico sat for a long time, stunned. The layers of the plan were intricate and diabolical. This "liberation" had been devised by an expert and single-minded theologian for the purpose of making the simple Catholicism of Latin American masses into a totally different faith—if you could call something so entirely materialistic faith at all.

That was one thing. But then there was the armaments aspect. He could only imagine one use to which all those arms were going to be put. If you tied both levels of the plan together, and if it was successful, then within a short generation a fair number of Latin America's Catholics could become willing allies for the Soviets. With this new "religion" to fire their souls, and with its new "successors to the Apostles" to lead it, the new "Church" would bring the armed "Salvation" of Marxism to half a hemisphere. Worse still, it would bring the end of Catholicism as the faith of over three hundred million individual men, women, and children.

Rico reread the December 1963 memo, and shivered to think of the number of times he had heard Papa Da Brescia talk of "the people of God." Hastily, then, he made a complete list of all the coded names in the memoranda. Before he left for West Germany, he dispatched it back through the underground to reach Pelse in Riga, along with an urgent request. He must know, he said, the identities behind all those code names. Most important, who was General Control?

With luck, he hoped to have Pelse's answer within a month or six weeks.

As he packed his belongings and got ready for his midnight trip across the border, he decided to try to catch Helmut in Vienna and give him the memoranda to carry down to Rome, while he entered Czechoslovakia for a tour of his operations there. With luck, he himself would be back in Rome by the middle of May.

Helmut always stayed at the Friedrichshalle Hotel when he was in Vienna, mainly because it was owned by one of the *impero*'s Austrian companies. He was not altogether surprised that Rico had been able to find him; he and the Maestro both regularly gave him their rough itineraries in case emergency contact might be necessary. But he was stunned by Pelse's intelligence when Rico summarized it for him.

As the two close friends talked on until the early hours of the morning, poring over the Latin American memoranda together, something kept gnawing at the edge of Helmut's memory. Something to do with his own banking arrangements in that region. But he couldn't quite nudge it into his mind.

"It's the damnedest thing, though, Rico." Helmut laid the sheaf of papers on a table in his suite. "I'm beginning to believe that our old friend Paolo Lercani is the kingpin in a vaster organization than we thought. Do you know what the governor of the Banco Central of Panama told me? Lercani has had an account with them for the last three years. In the millions! It's a sort of revolving account. It fills up. It empties. It fills up again. God knows what he's up to! But the wierdest thing is that the characters who do the withdrawals are mainly clerics, and that one of them regularly has large sums transferred from Lercani's account to an account in Havana. Castro's Havana! Can you beat that, Rico!"

Lansing whistled through his teeth. "Not only can I beat it, Helmut. I'm almost tempted to tie it into this Pelse information. Into the routing of funds to Cuba to pay for arms and supplies."

"But it's insane! What would Lercani, the consummate and greedy capitalist kingpin, have to do with a Soviet plan to dump capitalism in Latin America?"

The very insanity of the thought made Rico decide he was punchy with fatigue. He thought the best thing he could do was to go back to his own suite and get a few hours' sleep.

It was still dark when the phone rang by his bedside.

"Rico!" Helmut's voice brought him full awake. "You remember something kept jogging at my memory when we were going over those memos? Well, it finally hit me. The name of one of those clerics I told you about. It's Herreras. Jaime Herreras. It's a pretty common name, I'll grant you. But it is the same name your man put in the memos. Just to be sure, I checked my own notes. There's another name there too. Filipe Lobano. But it doesn't mesh with your material."

By the time Rico managed to get back to Rome, Pelse's memoranda had been thoroughly analyzed by Solaccio and Brandolini, working closely with the Maestro, to whom Helmut had also given copies. There was no doubt, they told Lansing, that the Jamie Herreras who withdrew funds from Lercani's account in Panama was the same Jaime Herreras who was Father Centro, General Control's center for the plan to co-opt the masses in Latin America.

In fact, he was the same Jesuit Father Jaime Herreras who was theologian to Chilean Cardinal Arrabaza and several other bishops in Vatican II, and close associate of the Northern Alliance.

"Wheels within wheels!" Rico was almost dizzied by the myriad implications when they gave him the news. "What about the other man in Helmut's notes? Filipe Lobano."

"Also a Jesuit." Brandolini got the information out just before a mighty sneeze, and passed the Lobano dossier to Lansing.

Lobano was a close associate of Jaime Herreras in the Center for Catholic Action, established and run by Herreras in the capital of El Salvador. Like Herreras, Lobano held extreme leftist views, and for some time had been associated with Socialist and Communist politicians and writers.

"Any more information from your contact?" Even Guido did not know how or from whom Rico had managed to get that stunning batch of memoranda. But he did know the American had asked for further intelligence.

"A blank." Rico handed the Lobano dossier back to Brandolini. "No one knows who General Control is. We may get some other names in time. But it's going to be a slow process."

Disappointed, Guido dealt with what they had. "At least we know why half the bishops and His Holiness keep talking about what you and I call the Church of God as 'the people of God.' But we still have more questions than answers."

Why, for example—Guido ticked the items off on his fingers—would Lercani fund the likes of Herreras and Lobano? How far had Herreras carried Moscow's plans for the new theology? Did Herreras' and Lobano's Jesuit superiors know of their activities? Had the contacts requested by Moscow been made in the United States? Closer to home—and considering the Pontiff's own use, which they had all noted, of some of the terms in Moscow's directives—did Herreras have a mole in the papal office itself?

"We are still in the dark about all this." The Maestro could have added still more questions. "What seems clear is that Moscow controls Herreras, and that Herreras has used both the Northern Alliance and Vatican II very skillfully."

"Whatever about the Northern Alliance," Solaccio put in, "one man working alone could not have derailed the whole Ecumenical Council."

"True enough." The Maestro had already thought that through as far as he could with the scant details they had. "But Herreras has been working at this since 1949, according to Rico's memoranda. And the way Vatican II is structured, the real work on the *Schemata* is done by the consultative committees. One hundred and thirty-five men isn't so many. Herreras himself is theologian for a number of them. And I expect we'll find that some of the other *periti* are his cronies.

"The interesting thing is the membership of those committees. The Bishops themselves, I mean. The question there is whether Cardinal Pirandella, as head of the Congregation for Bishops now, had more of a controlling hand in that than we thought. He's an Argentinian. Has he been co-opted by Herreras into this Latin American re-education plan?"

As Guido had said, they still had more questions than answers. For the time being, they could do nothing more than increase surveillance, be more careful than ever before about their own movements, watch for every hint of information that would help them to find all the pieces of a growing puzzle, and then put them together.

Until they could do that, the only thing that was clear was that they were dealing with something far different from what they had thought when the State Council voted to follow Cardinal Lanser's plan to "let the rot surface in the Church."

The imperturbably haughty and self-confident Cardinal Levesque was pleased to drop the other papal slipper in a second State Council meeting. His announcement this time did not concern new cardinals. However, it was one of the most important skirmishes of His Holiness' endless war to wrest control of the central structures of the Church from the Curia.

The Pontiff, as Levesque was pleased to remind the Council cardinals, had suggested several times that this very body, the Council of the State of Vatican City, be expanded by three members. Indeed, His Holiness had long since named those new members: Cardinal Pirandella, Cardinal Dell'Angelo, and Cardinal Fustami. As Their Eminences would surely admit, Papa Da Brescia had shown remarkable patience. Now, however, His Holiness desired an answer. "Before he leaves for his summer vacation at Castel Gandolfo, Eminences!"

Once the cardinal secretary had left, the Maestro was summoned and briefed. This latest papal demand was a threat of disaster, and not a matter for debate or division. It wasn't only that the addition of Pirandella, Dell'Angelo, and Fustami would destroy the State Council's balance between the conservative, traditionalist, and progressive elements of the Curia, though that was serious in itself. And it wasn't that none of these three proposed new members could be trusted, though that, too, was serious, most especially considering the questions that had now arisen about a possible connection between Cardinal Pirandella and Father Herreras.

The deepest threat this time was that the autonomy of the State Council from the papacy, which was the only guarantee of republicanism in the Vatican and in Church affairs, would be destroyed.

"You have certain powers, Maestro." A hesitant Cardinal Falconieri spoke for the rest of the Council. "Certain recourses that cannot be ignored even by a pope as stubborn and determined as Papa Da Brescia has proved to be."

Guido paled just a little. He knew what was being suggested. In a situation where the Holy Father himself was the cause of a crisis that threatened the Church and the papacy, the Keeper, acting with the State Council, could apply the "supreme sanction." But that was an action of the most extreme kind, and one to which Guido himself had never had to resort.

The Maestro considered the matter in silence for some moments. Once Da Brescia's men were on the Council, it would be only a question of time until the full scope of the *impero* was known to the entire papal office. Rico Lansing's covert work would become an open book, not only to His Holiness but to his entourage—Levesque, Sugnini, Lercani, Pirandella. There was no need to go on with a full inventory of the damage that would be done, or how far it would reach. Nor was there any question or hope that Da Brescia would listen to mere argument.

"It's a pity." Guido gave his answer to the Council. "But His Holiness has backed us into a corner."

The Maestro lifted the phone in the meeting room then and there, and dialed.

"De la Valle here. His Holiness, please."

Whoever answered at the other end said something that made the blood race to the Maestro's face; and even the casual O'Mahoney stiffened at the whiplash tone of Guido's reply. "This is Maestro Guido de la Valle calling His Holiness on a matter of urgent business. Put me through at once."

Despite Papa Da Brescia's invitation to be seated, the Maestro chose to remain on his feet. The meeting would be brief and formal.

"Holiness." He came to the point immediately. "The Council of State has discussed Your Holiness' proposal to increase its membership, and has rejected that proposal. Its ground for rejection is that the proposal itself is a violation of a vital rule of tradition: Only the State Council itself decides who shall belong to it as cardinal members."

The Pope was about to respond—angrily, if his eyes gave any clue—but the Maestro showed not even that much deference in this situation. Everything in him was geared to fight *for* his Pope against his Pope's enemies. That was as integral to his character as the marrow to his bones. His oath and role as Keeper were to support the papacy. If he had to confront a particular pope in order to do that, so be it. But he did not enjoy the confrontation, and had no intention either of prolonging it or of allowing it to degenerate into an undignified argument.

"If Your Holiness were to insist on violating this rule that no Pontiff has broken since the Council came into existence over two hundred years ago, then the Council and I will apply the supreme sanction."

Papa Da Brescia had been looking down at his desk with a show of patience, but at that threat, he jerked his head up, his large eyes filled with a sudden passion. He opened his mouth to speak, then thought better of what he wanted to say and remained silent.

He knew as well as Guido what the supreme sanction meant. It was the ultimate weapon of the Keeper, and it depended on his power. It would mean no further cooperation between the papal office and several offices of the Curia Romana. It could mean investigation and charges by the Holy Office against the Pontiff himself concerning doctrine and moral practice. It would paralyze even the most routine operations in the Holy See. Mail would be interrupted somewhere along the way, in and out. Telephone communications would be hampered. Bills would not be paid for various departments. Salaries would be delayed. Visitors would be turned away at the doors of the Vatican. Coded radio instructions would not be sent out regularly. Documents that shuttled routinely through the Vatican offices, dealing with normal everyday matters in the Vatican and all over the Church, would be stopped somewhere along the lines of transmission. Diplomatic missions abroad would be isolated. Indeed, the Pope himself would be isolated.

"It could"—Guido put it very succinctly—"mean a hammerlock on Your Holiness' papacy, until God calls Your Holiness to judgment."

It could, indeed. Papa Da Brescia stood up slowly and let out a great sigh. Charges concerning doctrine and moral practice would involve a judicial process. That alone would consume time, energy, and patience, and perhaps even uncover irregularities somewhere in his own entourage. Even without such charges, the rest of it would stop expansion and implementation of Church reform dead in its tracks. And, though the Maestro hadn't chosen to point it up, the supreme sanction would obviously mean putting off the autumn session of Vatican II *sine die.* That would cause huge damage, in Da Brescia's judgment. Perhaps even schism, as Levesque and Sugnini had warned.

"Maestro, We never wanted it to come to this between Us and you."

"It is unfortunate, Holiness." He would not bend.

"Very well, Maestro." Da Brescia's voice was brittle and cold. "We will observe the rule."

The Keeper of the Keys turned away. The Keeper of the Bargain bowed deeply and left the room.

[41]

In all his forty-one years of papal service, Guido de la Valle had neither seen nor imagined a situation such as this. There was a war, certainly. But it was not merely the one declared by Papa Da Brescia and the entire club of his collaborators and intimates against the Curia for control and change of the present structures of the Catholic Church. The evidence Richard Lansing had brought back from Eastern Europe made it clear that they were fighting much more than heretical clerics and theologians who favored Modernism.

And, while Lansing's evidence seemed to point straight at Moscow and the enigmatic General Control, the piece that did not fit into that puzzle was Paolo Lercani. Yet there he was. His connection with Herreras through the financier's Panama bank account was irrefutable. Of course, the greedy Sicilian would do anything to increase his fortune and his power; Guido had no doubts on that score. But that was the only cause Lercani served. Nothing—neither political ideals nor religious conviction—lay beneath the surface there. The Moscow-Lercani link was, in the long run, sheer insanity, just as Rico had said several times. Whatever game Lercani was playing, the Maestro could not convince himself it was Moscow's. But whose, then? His own? Or were there strings to some third element—one more compatible with Lercani's ambitions—that was still hidden?

Whatever the answers, the Maestro was convinced by the pattern he could see so far that there were people in the Church, and deep within the Vatican itself, who were using Papa Da Brescia, his administration, and his Ecumenical Council in ways far cleverer than the Northern Alliance, and for purposes so alien to the Church as to damage it irreparably.

The acute problem was that until he knew who the collaborators and sympathizers were, there was not yet any practical way to go on the offensive. If he forced Papa Da Brescia to halt Vatican II, there would be an immediate revolt among some of the bishops, and the resulting split would leave the Church even more open to the pernicious work of its enemies. And in any case, it had become obvious now that Vatican II was only one tool being refashioned for the purposes of others. Calling a halt to it would not call a halt to the wider war, and would probably only make it more difficult.

The Maestro called a meeting with Falconieri, Lanser, Helmut, Rico, Solaccio, and Brandolini to consider the possibility of laying the whole situation out for Papa Da Brescia's consideration. The two cardinals and Brandolini declared themselves dead against that idea, however. At the very least, they argued, confirming Guido's own fear, the Pontiff would share the confidence with Levesque and Sugnini—"Tweedledum and Tweedledee," as Falconieri called them. And that would be like making an announcement over a loudspeaker in St. Peter's Square.

"Well, then," Guido said, "given the state of things, we need a new and extraordinary security group. We need to know the alien collaborators and sympathizers who are pulling strings in the Vatican. Whether they're bishops or theologians or secretaries, we have to get at them. Whoever they are, they have the upper hand as long as we're blind.

"And at the same time, blind or not, we must do all we can to block any irreparable damage to the structure of the Church. As long as we protect the structure, the membership can be renewed."

That seemed to Rico a rather cold-blooded view. The faith and salvation of millions could be affected. But he had no other practical solution to offer.

It was decided, then, that the new security group would be called Security Two, to distinguish it from the existing security office, which was manned by the fire department, some salaried laymen, and the Italian police.

The core of Security Two would be the seven men present at this meeting, who already functioned to protect and further Rico Lansing's covert work. They would now meet on a more regular basis to share and analyze all pertinent information. A meeting once a month would be the goal. Even with Helmut's, Rico's, and Lanser's travel schedules, that should be possible. And at least one member of Security Two must know the whereabouts of the others at all times. Given Rico's situation, Brandolini was selected.

Eventually they would require help from others, the Maestro acknowledged. But in securing that help, they would not reveal either the existence of Security Two itself or any part of its purpose.

"The broad ironies of this situation are terrible." The Maestro made the observation as the meeting drew to a somber close. "The white-hot interest of foreign governments in Vatican II has died away. Some of them are still monitoring the sessions, but on a purely informational level. The American ambassador in Rome told me he had reported home that our bishops have stopped looking outward; that they're just exchanging reflections on what they think about the outside world. As far as foreign governments are concerned now, all of them, the Council that Papa Angelica initiated as a history-making event to invade all areas of government and political life has not come off."

Guido smiled as he might at a sad joke. "The 'reality,' as our friend Levesque would say, would probably astound them. And poor holy Papa Angelica most of all!"

"I love the smell of the earth when it's planted with vegetables." Cardinal Lanser appeared to relax from the pressures on him as he strolled with Rico between the beds of the kitchen garden, and out toward the orchard. "Takes me back to Grindelsbach."

For Rico, too, these serene gardens behind the Brazilian College, out on the farther end of the Via Aurelia, where Lanser had his apartments, held something of the peace he found in the bleak and aseptic austerity of Eastern Europe. What with Lansing's travels for the Apostolate, and the cardinal's travels as the Pope's "summit spokesman" for ecumenism, the two weren't often able to spend quiet afternoons such as this together.

Not that it was all relaxation. Rather, it was a chance to catch up with one another's work, and to compare notes, in a manner of speaking, without the usual interruptions.

Lanser wondered how Rico's work for His Holiness' *Ostpolitik* was coming along. Slowly or not at all, he presumed.

"Not at all, for the moment, Your Eminence. I've been able to temporize whenever the Holy Father has asked for a report. Up until now, Vatican II and the Pope's trip to Jerusalem have preoccupied him. One of these days, though, he'll put the pressure on."

"And then?"

"And then we'll see, Your Eminence."

"Yes," Lanser agreed. "Sufficient unto the day . . ."

Speaking of Papa Da Brescia's trip to Jerusalem prompted Lanser to ask if Cardinal Wallensky had talked to Rico about it.

The Polish cardinal had been honored by the Pontiff with a place in the papal entourage during that pilgrimage. There had been a lot of buzzing around the Vatican since then that Wallensky would not attend the third session of Vatican II this coming autumn. In fact, the rumor was that he had had a head-on confrontation with His Holiness on the papal plane while journeying back to Rome.

It was true, Lansing confirmed. Wallensky had expected nothing from the Jerusalem escapade, as he called it, and nothing was the sum of it, in the Pole's opinion. It was a media triumph. He had conceded that much. After all, it had been a thousand years since a Roman pope had met a Greek Orthodox patriarch, and over six hundred since one had spoken civilly to the other. It was ready-made for flashbulbs and television cameras. But as far as Wallensky was concerned, it was all window dressing and no substance.

"I agree with that." Cardinal Lanser turned a bit of warm earth under one of the apple trees with the toe of his shoe. "But what has it to do with returning to the Council of bishops?"

"The way he explained it to me when I was in Warsaw, Wallensky sees both the ecumenical pilgrimage and the Ecumenical Council as what he calls 'magical operations in a dream world.' For him, the Council has become an undisciplined free-for-all, where bishops he sees as remarkably untutored in their faith grapple over a bunch of documents drawn up, in turn, by committees who want to make us all acceptable to something they see as 'the modern world.'

"You should hear him talk about those committees and about the documents, Eminence. 'A bunch of architects tearing down the two-thousand-year-old treasure house of the Catholic faith,' he says, 'and replacing it with the jerry-built shanties of psychology, anthropology, and sociology.' "

"Is that what he said to the Pope?" Lanser asked in surprise.

"He said that and more. One by one, he tore apart the documents the bishops have voted on so far. He'll talk about them to anyone who gives him half a chance.

"The *Schema* called 'Light for the Nations,' for example. He told Papa Da Brescia that he would be content if there were even one mention of the light of Christ's salvation; or the light of divine grace; or the light of the Holy Spirit; or of the Church's teaching as a means of illuminating our nighttime journey through mortal existence to the day of eternal life.

"But he could not see any point in voting on such a *Schema* when all it talked about is an arc lamp of psychological and sociocultural excuses for Catholics to tinker with political conditions in the workshop of creation.

"The rest of the *Schemata* are just as bad, in his view. After their mention of some 'acceptable Christian truths,' as he phrased it, the bishops are stringing together a farrago of statements of intentions, condemnations of cruelty and poverty, appeals to world opinion, propaganda for peace and world government, and insistence on the nobility and the rights of mankind. But they obviously wish to avoid specifically Christian strictures concerning even such basic matters as sexual misconduct, marriage, family duties, Christian penance."

"Poor Papa Da Brescia!" Lanser had to laugh in spite of the seriousness of the matter. "But it's a good thing for the Pontiff to hear and he certainly won't listen to us. Wallensky is right, you know. The *Schemata* this Council has produced in draft so far adds up to fine sociology. But it's not theology. It's not necessarily even religious. It's secular. It's humanistic. And it probably will end up being totally pagan.

"What about Valeska?" The sudden turn in Lanser's questioning took Rico by surprise.

"Valeska?"

"Yes. Does he share Wallensky's opinions?"

"Some of them, yes. But he still thinks the Council will turn out to be a good thing. With the guidance and grace of the Holy Spirit, he doesn't think it can end up badly. He's decided to come back for the next session, without Wallensky."

"And what about you, Rico? I know that as a titular bishop without a diocese, you've chosen not to attend the sessions. Your Apostolate schedule wouldn't leave you time, anyway. But I presume you read the draft *Schemata."*

"Yes, Eminence, I've read most of them. Like most of the bishops who are in the Council. I'm not the theological expert you are. But if anybody had presented most of that blather to me as a boy, I would never have become a priest. I probably wouldn't even have remained a practicing Catholic. I'd probably have run for Congress instead, like my brother-in-law, and done my bit for the national economy, instead of for Christ's economy of salvation."

"It's interesting you should say that, Rico. That you wouldn't have become a priest or remained a Catholic, I mean. Once the Vatican II committees and their busy-bee theologians are through, I think the Church may well face just such a problem. It's a democratic-sounding thing to say that everyone is free to believe anything he chooses. But according to Catholic doctrine, you are never free to choose error, and certainly not to teach it, no matter how much you pant after acceptance. The Sacraments of our faith and our faith itself are, in our belief, channels of real, honest-to-goodness grace. And grace is a real thing. A real connection between God and ourselves. A direct avenue between us and Him. If you choose error, you opt away from grace. And without grace, the validity of the Sacraments and the attraction of faith itself disappears.

"To the degree that happens, I think men will not feel the pull to the priesthood exerted by the Holy Spirit that you and I did, and still do. And I think the ordinary people will see little reason to come to a Church that turns away from grace, that is not a source of grace."

Lanser stopped as they were nearing the vegetable garden again, and squinted at the now lowering afternoon sky. "Our enemies have done their work well, Rico. I think you will agree, we have to give them high marks.

"The bishops in Council see themselves as Catholics surely. But now that they're all been drawn together in one deliberative body in one place, they have come to see themselves with a will distinct and apart from the papacy and the Curia.

"It's that new sense of their own will, their 'identity,' as the psychologists like to say, that has been played upon as though it were a musical instrument. As Wallensky has observed, most of those bishops are not deeply trained theologians, to put it mildly. A lot of them have probably forgotten what they did learn. They have every reason to depend on and trust the Council theologians. As nearly as they can see, this rush to be accepted on terms that please the world around them probably seems a most charitable attitude on their part. Especially when the *periti* couch it all so agreeably in the *Schemata.*"

Lanser sighed deeply, as though he suddenly felt tired after their long stroll in the dappled sunlight. Rico thought back to the Security Two meeting, and the Maestro's insistence that if they could only maintain the structure of the Church, the membership could be renewed. It had seemed a harsh thing at the time. Now, in the light of Cardinal Lanser's analysis, it began to seem like a beautiful and unattainable dream.

"No." Lanser's answer shone with that muscular faith that had never dimmed in any trial or crisis. "It is still Christ's Church we serve, Rico. And if it is, we have His guarantee that it will go on. It has survived attacks from within and from without many times before. Perhaps this is the most diabolical attack by infiltration we've sustained. But the crucifixion of His Church, like the crucifixion of Christ Himself, will serve His purpose in the end. Should we ask to be spared, when He did not spare Himself? Or, like Peter, who felt unworthy to be crucified as his Lord was, and like the Christians we are, should we not offer our work and our sufferings to be made a part of his?"

"Tell me, Eminence." Rico needed to change the subject. "What about your own special work for His Holiness? The Jewish Document and the report of the Commission on Contraception, and all the rest. Is some of all that going better than the rest of this mess?"

Lanser looked at the American bishop for a long minute, and then turned back toward the house. "In fact, Rico"—the old man spoke as calmly as if he were discussing Euclid's work on geometry—"I expect those papal commissions will be my own personal crucifixion. But that is something we may talk about another day."

"Your father called from Chicago, Excellency." The patient and loyal Vittorio Benfatti had kept dinner waiting for Rico, but he was sure that word of Basil's call would be even more welcome than the well-prepared meal.

If Helmut felt guilty about his neglect of Keti, Rico matched him in his own feeling about his father. They wrote to each other, of course, as they always had; but Rico was away so often, and for such long periods, that Basil wrote ten letters to Rico's one. Basil understood; he'd been as busy as that himself for most of his life. At least, that's what he said.

Rico didn't always believe him, though. Even after all these years, Basil had never adjusted to life without Margaret. Netta and Brad were in Washington most of the time. The old man was too much alone.

When Basil answered the phone, he sounded tired but very happy to hear his son's voice. He hadn't called for anything special, he said. No. He'd just been thinking about the walks they used to take together down by the lakeside. Rico remembered those walks, and the way he and his father had enjoyed each other's company. Their "man-to-man" talks, as Rico had called them when he was fifteen or so, had made all the difference in the world to him.

"When you come home next time, son, you and I are going to do that again. We'll walk and talk things over the way we used to. Is it a deal?"

"It's a deal, Dad."

"Make it soon, son."

"I will. I promise. Dad?"

"Yes, Rick?"

"Dad. I love you."

There was a pause on the wire. A cough. When he did manage to speak, Basil's voice sounded a little foggy. "Well, of all the fool things! Don't you think I know that?" That was the old Basil, the father who loved his son enough to give him up. "Don't forget, Rick. We have a deal. I expect you here. And soon."

"Soon, Dad."

[[42]]

The day Rico had spoken of with Cardinal Lanser as they strolled by the kitchen garden—the day the Pope would pressure him for progress toward formal protocols with the Soviet satellite governments—did not come for two years. In all that time, Papa Da Brescia gave no outward sign to anyone but the Maestro of having lost his battle for the State Council. After all, he reasoned, as Pope he had the whole vast bureaucracy at his disposal. There were many fronts on which to wage his campaigns, and many weapons at his command. He used them well, and he made steady progress. Vatican II had run its course, and the *Schemata* had been voted on and approved by the Council of Bishops, then promulgated by His Holiness. Back in the home dioceses of the Church, the bishops proceeded to ensure that the *Schemata* were published and brought to the notice of their priests and people. Immediately, the inevitable happened. Almost everywhere, the vague and ambiguous language of the *Schemata* was interpreted to mean sometimes the most outlandish things, sometimes things directly contrary to what the framers of the *Schemata* intended, sometimes in a sense that contradicted the actual dogma and truth of Catholicism. A wave of innovation swept the different dioceses, always accompanied by wholesale change and sometimes destruction of age-old traditions and practices. The gamble and calculation of the Northern Alliance paid off.

Papa Da Brescia had made two more of his papal pilgrimages; they had gone brilliantly before the whole world, and he was already planning more of them. His special missions confided to Lanser, Sugnini, and others were progressing. Indeed, change was coming almost too rapidly, causing a bit of nervousness among some of the bishops; he would have to have a word with the cardinal secretary about that. The only area, in fact, where no visible progress had been made was in Eastern Europe.

"When can we expect results, Excellency?" The Pontiff had summoned Bishop Lansing to his study, and confronted the American in the presence of Cardinal Levesque, Cardinal Fustami, and Monsignore Casaregna.

"We are all impressed, Excellency"—Levesque felt it a good idea to throw Lansing a bone or two—"with your reports, and with your knowledge of government members in the East. It is merely that your pious work in Poland and Czechoslovakia and the other countries in the area appears to have impeded Your Excellency's progress for His Holiness."

It was the wrong thing to say. Rico had lost none of his tendency to speak his mind when provoked, and he did so now.

"Your Eminence." He fixed Levesque in a cold, steady stare. "I would have thought that assuring this hierarchic structure of the Church in Eastern Europe *is* making progress for His Holiness."

Levesque hit the ceiling. "You, Excellency, have been too busy traveling to realize that the Second Vatican Council instructed us to think of the Church as 'the people of God.' We have a new ecclesiology. You should bone up on it!"

"Perhaps so, Eminence." Rico kept his voice even. "But with all the Council did, it also confirmed and professed the same beliefs as the First Vatican Council and the Council of Trent. Or has Your Eminence not read that in the various *Schemata?* Both the First Vatican Council and Trent describe the Church as essentially hierarchic. In case *doctrine* has changed, Eminence, you owe it to me to tell me."

Levesque's long neck was beet red. Who did this American think he was, anyway, instructing a cardinal on Church doctrine!

"Your Eminence! Your Excellency!" The noise level was uncomfortable for Papa Da Brescia. "No more wrangling, please!" He turned to Bishop Lansing. "Your Excellency, in two weeks We will convene the cardinals of Our Church in a secret consistory. That will be followed shortly afterward by a public gathering. One of the things We intend to announce in both is that We expect the first results soon in Our plan to end the negative and hostile attitudes of Our Church to the governments of Eastern Europe. By the time the first consistory meets, We will expect Your Excellency to be traveling in that area, fulfilling Our instructions to the degree possible. That will be September 8, Excellency."

Da Brescia extended his hand. Lansing kissed the papal ring.
"Yes, Your Holiness."

Cardinal Levesque had a problem concerning Bishop Richard Lansing. True, he was the Pontiff's leading expert in matters concerning Eastern Europe. But he seemed to stand outside full papal control. His outburst concerning Church hierarchy had been only one example. And now the itinerary Lansing had obediently drawn up for the Holy Father showed that he would end his coming trip with a vacation in the United States! In the light of Papa Da Brescia's request for early results, that seemed nothing less than an affront!

Yet Da Brescia appeared to regard Lansing as special, and for no obvious reason. It was not logical, and to Levesque's bureaucratic mind it was dangerous. In his strategy for the Pope, control was essential. And for the bureaucrat, knowledge is the handmaid of control. In any case, Levesque plainly disliked the upstart American.

"Doesn't it strike you as curious, Monsignore?" The cardinal confided his mind to his closest and most confidential aide, Pierre Demarchelier. "This Bishop Lansing is rather regularly unreachable when he is traveling. Oh, he always has a provable reason. But I just wonder. What is he doing when no one can find him? Does he have a woman somewhere, this pious little saint? Or is he doing financial work for the Maestro? Perhaps, Monsignore, you could just check up on him at some point along the way." Levesque handed over a copy of Lansing's itinerary. "Discreetly, of course."

Demarchelier took the bishop's travel schedule from the cardinal. "But of course, Eminence."

When Demarchelier met his Soviet contact at Monte Mario in Rome that afternoon, they remained together only for as long as it took them to climb a flight of eleven steps in the midst of a bunch of chattering French tourists. But it was enough time for Demarchelier to explain what Levesque needed.

It would be done; the Soviet connection saw no problem. "We will put out a general alert, so that wherever he shows up he will be spotted."

"Be in touch." Demarchelier broke off from the group of tourists, and descended the stairs by himself.

Rico's trip would be a long one this time; and because it would be a combination of open and covert travel, it was more complex to set up than most of his schedules. He would have contact with "lamplights" only in case of extreme need, as usual. Mail drops would be set up in certain places by his organization. He would go first to Bulgaria, Hungary, and Romania. After that, he would proceed to Poland, Czechoslovakia, and East Germany.

Finally, around December, he would return to Poland, but that visit would be underground. His itinerary showed him on vacation in the States for that month, returning to Rome from New York on TWA flight

241 on December 29. To cover the time spent on that part of his trip, he took the normal precautions. Postdated letters were dispatched to New York by Solaccio, to be mailed back at the proper time to Youn, Benfatti, Levesque, Casaregna, and one or two others. Other covers were put neatly in place in the normal manner. All the same, Lansing was dogged by an uneasiness, a vague sense of anxiety, a rousing of that now finely honed instinct that caught the faintest whiff of being "tracked." In his mind, he went over his Vienna training in "street smarts."

As he would be gone for nearly four months, Rico decided to take a drive out to Villa Cerulea before he left. Keti and Agathi had Mariella prepare a special lunch for the three of them. They had finished eating and were relaxing over coffee in the morning room when Eugenio came home from school. By prearrangement, the Maestro's close associate and friend Franco Graziani had picked him up along with Franco's own son, Donatello.

"Can Doni stay the afternoon, Mamma?" Eugenio never failed to bring an air of freshness and excitement, like sunlight, into a room.

"Is that the way you say hello?" Keti found it hard to discipline her son when he was so happy, but Eugenio took his mother's meaning at once and in good humor. He ran to kiss her and Agathi hello, and then his Uncle Rico.

"Can he, Mamma? Uncle Franco is in a rush. He's waiting in the car with Doni for your answer."

"Yes, *carino.* He can stay overnight too, if Uncle Franco says it's all right."

In a twinkling, Eugenio was back, Doni Graziani at his side to say hello in his turn. The Graziani boy was Eugenio's closest friend of his own age. He had his father's *occhi di ghiaccio*—eyes of ice—but his open smile and ebullient character were his mother's.

"Uncle Rico!" Eugenio pulled at Lansing's hand. "We're going to race up to the pine forest at the back of the property. Come with us! I'll beat both of you!"

"Why not!" Rico was always infected with Eugenio's innocence and verve. He loved strolling and running with him, and listening to his variations on the stories Guido had spun for him about the "magic isles of Greece," and the giants who strode from one island to the next in steps that covered a thousand kilometers at once.

"Be back in time to clean up for dinner, the three of you!" Agathi called out after them. "Guido and Helmut will be home early!"

It was a perfect afternoon. Rico raced with the two boys down the gardens, out the postern gate, across the road, and up to the pine forest. Eugenio was like a gazelle, all litheness and speed, and Rico—a little out of shape, anyway—didn't have to let him win. He laughed as he watched Eugenio and Doni roll down the bank to the river and then hitch up the legs of their trousers to wade near the shore. He lay on his back, looking up at the sky through the green lace of the trees, listening to the sounds of the river and to the young voices.

He and Eugenio had come here together many times before. It was one of the boy's favorite spots. He had told Rico that sometimes, when he came here alone, the wind sang a special song to him. It rose and rose and rose, Eugenio said; then it fell a little, and rose again, and almost went away. And when it was very far away, up near the top of the sky, he imagined it was the voice of Holy God and the Holy Angels saying precious things to him.

Rico listened for the soughing of that wind, for the sound of Holy God and the Holy Angels.

"Uncle Rico!" Eugenio was the angel who called. "Uncle Rico! Take off your shoes and come wading!"

Rico sat up and reached to untie his laces. "I'll be right there!"

On September 8, 1966, the feast day when Catholics celebrate the birthday of the Blessed Virgin, Papa Da Brescia held the first of the two special meetings he had mentioned to Richard Lansing. This one, the secret consistory, met in the Sistine Chapel. Except for the Maestro, who monitored from *il Tempio,* only cardinals were present.

Papa Da Brescia appeared both authoritative and jaunty as he sat on a special throne. He had in mind several important matters regarding the future of the Church, he told his cardinals, that he wished to communicate to them. He would make these announcements again—"along with a few others we will reserve for that occasion," he said mysteriously—at the public consistory to be held in two weeks' time in St. Peter's Basilica.

The greatest lesson of the Ecumenical Council for him as Pope, Da Brescia proceeded to confide to his cardinals, was that the present governing structure of the Church was so cumbersome that it had almost reached the point of immobility and uselessness. He included the Vatican as well as the dioceses around the world in his sweeping criticism.

"The watchword, Venerable Brothers, is 'the people of God.' They are the Church. They are the faith. They are the mystical body of Christ. They, in all their classes and categories—poor as well as rich; women as well as men; black and yellow as well as white—must participate at every level." His Holiness peered owlishly over the rims of his reading glasses. "We are nothing if we are not the people of God."

Arnulfo looked at Lanser and put his face in his hands.

In order for the people of God to assume their rightful position with the Vicar of Christ, Da Brescia continued, it must be admitted that the method of electing the Supreme Pontiff by a closed conclave was rapidly drawing to the same point of zero usefulness as the rest of the outmoded structures and procedures of Church government.

A dozen cardinals seemed to stiffen and freeze at that pronouncement. But His Holiness had lowered his eyes, to read on imperturbably.

He had resolved to begin now the planning and construction of a new People's Audience Hall, the main portion of which would hold seven or eight thousand of the faithful sitting, and twice that number standing. In the upper story, there would be a conference amphitheater capable of holding the cardinals in conclave, or a conference of bishops. The Pontiff referred to the planned amphitheater as the "Upper Room," reminding his listeners of the upper room where the Twelve Apostles received the Holy Spirit before going down to "the people."

"We envision the day, Venerable Brothers, when you and your successors will meet in that Upper Room, and then, with your candidate for pontiff proposed, proceed to the Hall of the People of God on the ground floor to have his election made by the voice of the people, which is the voice of God."

The same dozen cardinals squirmed, or sought each other's eyes. A few who were seated close to one another whispered brief remarks.

Da Brescia ignored the stirring as he went on. The matter of papal elections was for the future. There were means nearer at hand by which the expression of the will of the people of God would be heard.

In the ceremonies of the public consistory, for example, the Pope would elevate twenty-six more bishops to the rank of cardinal, again broadening the international character of the Sacred College, and bringing its membership to 135. Yet a further expression of the people of God was Cardinal Lanser's work among "the separated brothers of Anglicanism, Protestantism, and Eastern Orthodoxy." Vatican II had approved the special Document on Religious Liberty. In accordance with that document, His Eminence Cardinal Lanser had now been instructed to make sure that all non-Catholics knew that the Church defended their right to belong to any religion that private conscience dictated to them.

Of course, that Document on Religious Liberty now included the Jewish Document, as Their Eminences were aware. Because the vast majority of Catholics in the Middle East lived in Arab countries, the Church had to be careful about the use it made of what was now the Jewish section of the Religious Liberty document. There would, however, be no doubt that anti-Semitism was condemned, and that "not all Jews participated in the killing of Christ."

The Pontiff glanced in Lanser's general direction. The cardinal bowed his head as though in prayer and he closed his fingers around the small crucifix he held in one hand.

Papa Da Brescia touched then briefly on the Church of Middle and Eastern Europe. He had commissioned His Excellency Bishop Richard Lansing to probe those governments, seeking to establish cordial and eventually even formal diplomatic relations between them and the Holy See. There had been no concrete results so far, but there would be in time to come.

The last major theme of the secret consistory, and the only one that would not be repeated again in the public consistory, was "the faulty structure of the Holy See's financial agencies, consigned to some whose hands have not been consecrated with the sacred oils of ordination, and who do not wield the pastoral crosier of a consecrated bishop." His Holiness was aware of the Maestro's presence in *il Tempio.* His message was clear.

With a few final expressions of gratitude for their cooperation, the Holy Father gave his cardinals the papal blessing and departed.

By its very nature, the public consistory was far grander than the secret one, from the solemn entry of the Pontiff on the *sedia gestatoria* amid the sounds of trumpets and the music of the Sistine Choir, on through the High Pontifical Mass and the conferring of the red hat on the twenty-six bishops who were called forward in sonorous tones by Monsignore Pasquinelli, who was now the fully fledged papal master of ceremonies. He had practiced the more difficult names aloud for hours. "Most Reverend Lord Joseph Cardinal Bugwamba of Lagos . . ." "Most Reverend Lord Peter Cardinal Tran Anh Ngoc Hue of Hanoi . . ." "Most Reverend Lord Harold Cardinal O'Reilly of Melbourne . . ." "Most Reverend Lord Joseph Cardinal Lazifimamahatra of Sri Lanka . . ." That one had kept poor Pasquinelli up late for three nights. "Most Reverend Lord Corrado Cardinal Amalfeo of Santa Sabina . . ."

When the roll call was finally finished and the newest cardinals were once more seated, but this time among the other cardinals, Guido seemed more intent on the people present than on the Holy Father's address. Helmut, seated beside him, understood why. In the first place, of course, both of them had already seen a copy of the Pope's prepared speech. But more than that, the officials and the invited guests in the Basilica were like a miniature portrait of Papa Da Brescia's idea of the people of God. The Sacred College, now with a complement of 135 cardinals, was studded with enemies and opportunists—in any case, with men who owed their allegiance to Da Brescia. The Maestro's allies, meanwhile—Lanser, Arnulfo, Ferragamo-Duca, and the others—looked tired and old as they sat in their dwindling numbers, flanked by Levesque, Fustami, Pirandella, Svensens, Dell'Angelo, Buff, Grosjean, and Arrabaza.

Over among the high Church officials who were not cardinals, Sugnini, Demarchelier, and a whole set of new faces confronted him, all probably hand-picked creatures of Sugnini and Levesque.

Among the distinguished visitors, Canon Ripley-Savage, Metropolitan Nikodim, Brother Reginald, Father Hans Kleiser, Father Jaime Herreras, Richard Richards, Father Charles McMurren, Bishop Cale, were all sitting back comfortably in their places with the air of men who have done their work well. Very near the front of that section, Guido caught sight of the ubiquitous Paolo Lercani, with two aging gentlemen dressed in black clothes, one on either side of him. "Lord knows who they are!" the Maestro said under his breath.

Three balconies had been reserved for less distinguished, non-Catholic observers. They were crammed with Protestants, Greek Orthodox, Russian Orthodox, Jews, Muslims, Copts, Buddhists, Armenians—who could name them all by now?

Papa Da Brescia's words were well chosen that day. And they were congratulatory. He lauded the "glorious assemblies of the Ecumenical Council," which, in the four sessions over the years 1962 to 1965, had produced a plethora of major documents, mostly pastoral in character, one of them "dogmatic," and none anathematizing anybody, as past councils had. Deep bonds of friendship with the "separated brothers" had been formed—the Pontiff raised his right hand in their direction in a kind of papal salute. In this regard, he had special praise for "Our Venerable Brother Joachim Cardinal Lanser," whose untiring work would continue in order to strengthen those bonds still further—another wave of the papal hand.

Rather quickly, the Holy Father came to those announcements he had so mysteriously reserved for the occasion of this public consistory. As Guido had read the prepared speech, he recognized the words of preamble to the text that set out six new papal reforms.

"We have taken some special steps"—the Pontiff read the passage—"in order to implement the will of Our Ecumenical Council."

"One," Guido whispered under his breath, and listened to Da Brescia announce that he had created a new Roman ministry, the Congregation for Justice and Peace, which was to be largely staffed with lay men and women. Its task was to deal with matters vaguely referred to as "human rights and world harmony."

"Two," the Maestro whispered. And Da Brescia announced that he had established a special Commission for the Reform of the Liturgy, to be directed by his beloved son and faithful servant of the Church, His Excellency Monsignore Annibale Sugnini—a wave of his hand in Sugnini's direction.

"Three." The Maestro had his eyes closed now. As if on cue, the Pontiff made his third announcement. Within a year he would publish the report of the Commission on Contraception, and with it, a special letter of his own on the subject of human sexuality.

"Four." Da Brescia had particularly warm words for the bishops, "Our fellow apostles," whom he had now directed to hold periodic regional conferences on themes important to "the people of God." Once every two or three years, each regional conference would send delegates to a general Synod of Bishops to be held in Rome for the purpose of "helping Us in the renewal of faith and practice among the people of God."

In time, the Congregation for Justice and Peace would join with the Synod of Bishops to form "a consultative assembly for the Roman Pontiff." What was not in the speech, what even Guido could not guess, and what the Pontiff could not yet announce without causing unmanageable turmoil, was his intention that just such a "consultative assembly" of bishops and lay commission members would participate with the cardinals in the election of popes. All in good time.

"Five." Guido opened his eyes again and looked down at Cardinal Arnulfo. The Maestro had warned him this would be coming, and saw that he had his arms crossed and his head lowered.

"In order"—Da Brescia moved quickly on—"to ensure that Our separated brothers retain no idea that We condemn and excommunicate them, We are renewing the true spirit of the Holy Office by changing its name." Everyone, he said, could recall that its full name was the Supreme Holy

Congregation of the Holy Office of the Universal Inquisition. All thought of the Inquisition must be a thing of the past. Henceforth, it would be known as the Congregation for the Doctrine of the Faith. "There are no longer heretics and schismatics. There are only separated brothers."

Cardinal Arnulfo looked up and met Guido's eyes for a moment, then lowered his head again.

"Six."

All should note with gratitude, Papa Da Brescia observed, that the first fruits of the Ecumenical Council had been tasted. Papa Angelica, of happy and holy memory, had intended the Council to open the Church and the world; and "had even told Us of his hope for an outflowing of the Holy Spirit, a new Pentecost."

Now he, the humble and unworthy successor of Papa Angelica and Blessed Peter, had already witnessed the first glimmers of that Pentecost. He was certain it had not escaped his pious sons and daughters in the Church that he had been to Jerusalem, where Jesus preached and died; to Bombay, where, in the midst of human misery, he had witnessed the new desire of many peoples for the truth of the Gospels; to the United Nations, where the Secretary-General had welcomed him on his visit to all the nations at their permanent meeting place.

These great events had received worldwide attention in the media. The Pontiff was sure they were signs of things to come. "In God's good time" —he neared the end of his prepared speech—"all the nations of the earth will lay eyes upon Christ's Vicar, hear his voice in their own native airs, and come to see him as the successor to Blessed Peter and the sign of salvation that he should be to all."

When the Pope had been borne from the Basilica, to the accompaniment of applause and choral music, Guido took Agathi's arm and guided her through the crowd behind Helmut, Keti, and Eugenio.

The Maestro turned the Pope's words over in his mind again and again. For some reason, his own mood brought to mind some frescoes of martyrdom that Fra Angelico had done in a little-known Vatican chapel. He thought of the faces of St. Stephen's executioners, and St. Lawrence's tormentors; Fra Angelico had made their dominant expression not hate, but bewilderment and hesitation. Angelico had portrayed the same emotions on the faces of the Doctors of the Church, as they symbolically contemplated and puzzled over the twin martyrdom, their brows furrowed, their mouths questioning. Even the four Evangelists on painted clouds floating in radiant blue skies seemed, under Angelico's brush, to display the same melancholy hesitation, mystified by the persistent faith of the dying saints in the face of their agonies.

That is the key, Guido reflected. Whether you were a man of exalted reason like the Evangelists; or of scientific certitude like the Doctors; or of cruel zeal like the executioners; or sworn to duty to God and Church like himself; or, he concluded with a wry smile, of ecclesiastical power and intent like Papa Da Brescia, finally it was all a matter of fundamental faith. A matter of men's puny minds coming up against the inexplicable strength of belief.

If he believed, then he could only go on with his duty, whether or not he could understand how Papa Da Brescia's brand of faith had led him, and all of them, into this strange battlefield.

"Gesù." Guido moved his lips in quiet prayer. "Sweet Lord, I believe. Help my unbelief."

Agathi gently took his hand.

"Did you notice one small thing about the papal speech?" Arnulfo caught up with Falconieri on the way out.

"I noticed many things, Eminence, including the serious attack on you and your Holy Office—or rather, what is it now? Your Congregation for the Doctrine of the Faith."

"Yes. There is trouble in the heavens, as our Chinese friends say. But did you notice that the Pontiff never once mentioned the Blessed Mother, the Angels, or the Saints—aside from Peter, of course, whose power he wishes to be his own."

"Perhaps that's his way of not offending the 'separated brothers.' "

"What about not offending the Virgin and the Angels and the Saints? They're real too."

[[43]]

Rico Lansing began his official trip in Bulgaria, talking with some low-ranking members of the Ministry of Cults in Sofia. He made no headway there at all on religious matters. However, he did get several discreet offers of money under the table, if he could arrange for accounts to be opened in the Vatican Bank. It seemed that certain ministry officials, along with others of the Bulgarian *nomenklatura,* were engaged in making capitalistic profits abroad in the gold and drug trades and other such ventures forbidden to the "paradise of the workers," and they needed access to secret banking havens.

Rico made a mental note to discuss with Security Two whether, by accommodating one or two of these requests, he might "turn around" some official and have him work for the organization.

Other than that, he picked up some mail at the designated drop and moved on.

In his next stop, Hungary, there were lamplights but no organization, so he had no mail pickup. He was lucky, in fact, to have listening posts. Hungary was a painful place for Rico, and for all Catholics. Joszef Mindszenty, the irreducible and irascible Cardinal Primate of that country, was now in his tenth year of refuge in the American Embassy. Seminaries were allowed a grand total of four new candidates for the priesthood per year; and even at that, the KGB and the Hungarian secret police had to pass on each one. Moreover, inside the door of every bishop's house and every seminary there sat a member of state security.

All in all, Hungary was so locked up that even Romania and Bulgaria were freer.

Lansing interviewed János Kádár on behalf of the Pope's mission. That Communist leader, who had been jailed and castrated on an earlier day by his Soviet puppet masters, ruled Hungary for them with a tough but clever hand. Kádár was a roughneck, and made no bones about it. "The day your Pope removes that cancer Mindszenty from this workers' Socialist Republic," he told Rico flatly, "that day we can begin talking diplomatic turkey. We will have no active Hungarian cardinal, and no talk of protocols, as long as that foolish old man cowers in his American rathole!"

Rico did persuade Kádár to arrange for him to visit Bishop Sekai in Esztergom. Sekai was the ranking prelate in Hungary until such time as a new cardinal primate could be named.

"See him, Monsignore!" Kádár spat. "And then tell your Pope that Sekai is our next cardinal!"

Shades of past emperors in Marxist garb, Rico thought.

As Lansing walked with Bishop Sekai up and down the driveway of Sekai's residence in Esztergom, nature itself suited the mood of Hungary in its painful autumn decadence. Leaves were yellowing on trembling branches. The freshly turned earth, brown and rich-looking, was cleared of the early year's flowers. The bishop prattled on about how conciliatory Kádár was prepared to be, if only the old troublemaker Mindszenty could be removed.

"He has outlived his usefulness here, Excellency." As he walked, only half listening to Sekai at times, Rico measured the depth of Hungary's sadness, tasting the edge of its pain and regrets. His thoughts traveled back over the years to that sad demonstration in St. Peter's Basilica, the cross wrapped in barbed wire; to Papa Angelica's pained expression as he gave his blessing.

If ever he had been tempted to abandon his work, the conditions of this martyred country dispelled any such inclination.

As usual, Papa Da Brescia began his day of work with an early-morning meeting with Cardinal Secretary Levesque. Sugnini, who as a perennial rule was part of these sessions, was for once absent. Da Brescia began with Bishop Lansing's first reports. "Have you read them, Eminence?"

"Yes, Holiness."

"We think We may as well forget about the Bulgarians for the moment. But the situation in Hungary seems more promising. We intend to send Lansing back to talk with Kádár again early next year. The premier is right. It's about time We got Mindszenty out of there."

"Very well, Holiness. I will see to the matter personally."

The Pope laid aside Lansing's reports and folded his hands on his desk. "We are aware, Eminence"—he launched into the next problem on his mind—"that some of the changes We propose will come as a shock to many of our faithful. But to have to face problems over changes We have not yet made, and at such an early date, is borrowing unnecessary trouble. And yet We Ourselves have had reports of gross irregularities at the Masses being said in some dioceses."

The Pontiff had in mind particularly the complaints from German Cardinal Hoffeldt, who had told His Holiness there were three new kinds of Mass ritual being used in Germany alone. And he had heard of at least eighteen other variations being used in France and Belgium.

"Just the initial confusion, Holiness." Levesque would have to manage this little papal wavering without Sugnini's help. "All will settle down finally."

"But Your Eminence doesn't understand." Da Brescia was not so easily mollified this morning. "The Council absolutely forbade Us to abolish Latin in the Mass. It forbade nuns and priests to abandon their distinctive clerical garb. It . . .

"Well, Eminence, We could go on. The point is that all these things are occurring. And they are causing unrest. What does Sugnini think he's doing? He and his central planning committee for the liturgy?"

Cardinal Levesque adjusted the "battlements" on his nose. "Holiness, believe me, I do understand. We have to expect excesses in the beginning. I will have a personal word with Monsignore Sugnini about Your Holiness' concern.

"Meanwhile"—Levesque gave Da Brescia his most reassuring smile—"Your Holiness will be pleased to know the reason Monsignore Sugnini is not present with us himself this morning. He is anxious to finish the draft of Your Holiness' letter on human sexuality. I think, when Your Holiness reads it, you will find that it will go a long way toward allaying the fears of those who believe we are going too far with change and reform in the Church."

The cardinal secretary stood up, looking at his watch. "With Your Holiness' permission. I have a meeting scheduled this morning with the ambassador of Cuba."

Papa Da Brescia's thoughts followed Levesque's bait. "Good. Excellent. Tell me, how are things with Our delegate there? Does he get on well with Premier Castro?"

"Excellent personal relations, Holiness. It bodes well for the Church."

"We are glad to hear it." Da Brescia was content to have the meeting end. "Instruct Sugnini that We await the draft of Our letter on human sexuality at the earliest moment."

Once back in his own office, Levesque rang Sugnini and filled him in on the latest papal teeterings at the edge of dangerous decisions—mainly about the Latin Mass. "That text you're working on about human sexuality had better be good, Monsignore."

"Don't fret about it, Eminence. I'll steer the old man in the right direction. When I'm finished with this letter, it will take the minority report of the commission in favor of the old ways, and canonize it. It will reiterate all the traditional teaching on marital and sexual matters. The text is so clear, unequivocal, and theologically sound that Torquemada and Thomas Aquinas would approve of it. It's compassionate of weakness, yet firm on dogma. His Holiness will be so pleased—and the furor he will cause by taking such a backward-looking position will be so great—that we should have little difficulty, due to the resultant confusion, in moving forward for acceptance of a new form for the Mass.

"I tell you, Eminence, this letter may be the masterpiece of my entire clerical career."

"Fine, Monsignore. Just be sure you get the masterpiece to His Holiness in a hurry."

When Lansing finished his official conversations at the Ministry of Cults in Warsaw on November 20, he took an afternoon plane directly to Vienna. There he stayed overnight in one of the organization's safe houses. From that point on, he would be covert.

On the following evening, he was taken by car to his "window" on the Czechoslovak border. He made his way into East Slovakia, where one of his district supervisors was forming a new cell for the purpose of infiltrating the educational board of a whole region. The man who had been proposed as cell leader—one Milan Palkovič—was ready to begin, but Rico's personal and on-the-spot approval was needed.

Lansing would not meet the man, of course. He never met the heads of single cells. That was an essential rule of security. In this case, as the record and character of the new candidate became clear to him, he was truly sorry not to have that opportunity.

He reviewed Palkovič's dossier and talked to subordinates who had known the man since childhood. A canon of the Church, he had an impeccable war record. He had in fact been tortured by the Nazis but had not broken. He had never been in trouble with the Communist authorities. Besides being a zealous priest, he was a poet of some renown, and enjoyed great status among the literati and academicians of his area.

"Our kind of man." Rico had no qualms as he gave his approval.

He crossed the rest of Czechoslovakia in two stages, and passed back into Poland on the thirtieth. He arrived in Bialystok without mishap on December 2, to wait for clearance to travel north to Riga.

During covert trips, Rico never stayed at the same place twice. This time, he was directed to a little tailor's shop. The hand-painted sign over the door of the small basement apartment on Senkiwicza, just off the main square and around the corner from the chapel of Swienty Roch, announced simply: TADEUSZ JAROSZEWICZ—KRAWIEC. Thaddeus Jaroszewicz—Tailor.

Rico opened the door and was greeted by an old man seated at a vintage sewing machine. His full head of white hair framed a smooth face, with steel-rimmed spectacles perched halfway down the nose. His humped shoulders were testimony to the long years during which he had plied his trade from six in the morning to ten at night. He seemed from the very first moment Rico saw him to be shrouded in a vast peacefulness and tranquillity. He spoke with authority, but with no trace of arrogance or common superiority. Rico had rarely encountered such a rich combination of traits in one man.

"His Excellency Archbishop Bogdan Valeska sends you his best welcome," the old tailor said, once Rico had identified himself and settled in.

"Thank you, Panie Jaroszewicz."

"Your Reverence remains here for one week. Possibly two. It depends on communications with Riga. Then you go on to Krakow. There are important things to discuss. Bogdan said to tell you that."

"Am I not to go to Riga?"

"No, Reverend Monsignor. Security."

The old tailor did not mind in the least sharing with Rico what little he had. They both slept, cooked, and ate in the back room of the two-room shop. There was no bath, and no running water. The lavatory—not a flush toilet but the sink-hole variety—was an ancient outdoor installation in the small yard at the back of the house. Rico went outside only to go there.

During the day and well into the nighttime hours, Jaroszewicz sat on a little stool in the front room. Sometimes he would go out to deliver mended clothes, or to bring food supplies. Five or six times a day he would pause in his work to pray or to read for a few minutes.

When he was not chatting with his new friend, Rico spent his time in the back room. For there, in these unlikely surroundings, was a unique library of well-worn, dog-eared copies of many of the major classical works on religious mysticism, most of them in their original languages. John of the Cross was there, and Ruysbroeck; Adam Sapieha and Bernard of Clairvaux and Teresa of Avila; the Jewish Kabala, Maimonides' *Guide for the Perplexed,* St. John Climacus. They were all there.

What made the library unique, however, was that the flyleaves of all the volumes were covered with signatures. And among the names in nearly every one of them was that of Bogdan Valeska.

As Rico drew the old fellow out about those signatures, he began to realize that, in all his personal humility and physical poverty, and in the midst of the so-called religious desolation that Communism endeavors to create, his benefactor at this safe house was one of those rare individuals endowed with the special gift for directing the deepest spiritual life of others. Valeska was but one of scores who had come to him over the years. Rico began to understand Bogdan Valeska better now.

"You see, Monsignore"—the tailor didn't look up from his flashing needle as he spoke about the archbishop—"he has the gift of higher prayer. Even back when he worked in the German underground, and when he earned all those honors at the university, and then taught there and published his books—even with all the activity, he progressed. He had the Gift of the Spirit.

"Then, just when he had reached the point where further progress depended on his entering what John of the Cross calls 'the Dark Night of the Soul,' they made him an archbishop!" The tailor threw up his hands.

"What's so bad about that, Panie?" Rico asked. "He's doing fine work as archbishop."

"I know, Monsignor. But it's all the color and sound and detail. Episcopacy is rife with passion. Passion can deflect one from Spirit. It gets in the way. I told him so, too. I told him it was better to be a tailor."

"What did he say?"

"That it is only another difficulty along the way. That the humanity of Christ suffices to divinize all our passions.

"That's true, of course." Jaroszewicz picked up his needle again. "But when Bogdan came home from Vatican II, he came to see me. He asked me if I thought Christ was present among the bishops in Council. I knew then that he was having trouble getting back to that higher level of prayer."

Rico understood. "Whatever happened in that Council, Christ is the Keeper of all salvation."

Without raising his head, the tailor smiled back at him over the rims of his spectacles, but he said nothing in reply.

At the end of Rico's first week in Bialystok, Pelse's packages came through from Riga. In the first envelope was a note of specific warning for him not to come to Riga again until he had direct word to the contrary. Soviet security had been tightened. Until further notice, information from Riga station would come either through Bialystok or through an agent whose code name was "the Driver."

As to Rico's question concerning General Control, Pelse was only able to confirm that all of General Control's operations and those of the ministry in Moscow were KGB-sponsored; but the identity of the man or men in charge of General Control was still unknown.

Across the top sheet in the second package Pelse had scrawled a short message: "Better try to get to Herreras before he goes much further." A swift reading of the documents, most of which related to Father Jaime Herreras, revealed a set of scheduled plans coordinating the activities of certain sympathizing clergy and nuns in Latin America with the "slash-and-burn" tactics of guerrilla terrorists, the whole to be armed by Moscow and funded through Havana. It was a blueprint for the marriage of political dynamite with ecclesiastical arson.

Rico was tempted to cut short his covert trip and take this latest Pelse intelligence back to Rome at once. But Valeska's message, through the tailor, that he had urgent business to discuss persuaded Rico to follow his planned schedule.

As nightfall approached, Jaroszewicz had Rico change into overalls, high boots, and a brownish fur hat. He brought around his big wheelbarrow, placed Lansing's things at the bottom, piled several packages of mended clothing on top in the usual way, locked the shop, and set out with the disguised bishop to make his deliveries, chatting all the while in his usual manner, as they gradually moved toward the edge of town.

The last stop they made was a small cottage at the edge of what appeared to be oblivion. "You rest here until midnight. Then they come for you, Monsignor."

Inside, a tall fellow barely twenty years of age waited for them. He exchanged clothes with Rico, and left with the stooped old man.

On the evening of December 8, Bogdan Valeska welcomed Rico Lansing to Krakow. The enormous seven-story structure that served as the official residence of the archbishop, stripped though it had been of everything but essential furniture, was worlds apart from the cramped tailor's shop in Bialystok. There was no central heating, of course, and the place resounded with echoes of the slightest sound. But it always reminded Lansing of a Roman palazzo.

When he found Cardinal Wallensky waiting for them in Valeska's study, Rico knew Valeska's business was as urgent as his message had indicated. Their first news for him was that Papa Da Brescia had just published his encyclical letter on contraception and other sexual matters. They had heard it earlier in the day over Vatican Radio. First-class traditional doctrine, they told him. Hard-hitting and quite unequivocal.

"And"—Wallensky ran a hand over his foxlike face—"there'll be the devil to pay when some of the bishops get over their shock." Sugnini would have been delighted had he heard the Polish cardinal's opinion.

Rico brought the two Poles up to date on his own situation in Rome—on the Pope's insistence that he show some progress on the diplomatic front; on his own blowup with Levesque.

Very soon, Valeska was ready to get down to brass tacks, as he said. All of Rico's news only made it clearer that Poland might well be sold down the river again, as it had been by Roman popes and Roman emissaries quite a number of times.

"We are sure of you, though, Rico." Cardinal Wallensky made no apology for the implication that they might once have mistrusted him. "We are convinced that you and the people you work with make common front with us against people in the Vatican who would destroy not merely Catholic Poland but the Vatican itself and the Church."

It was time, the cardinal went on, for Rico to learn that his was not the only peaceful underground organization in Eastern Europe. Since the death of Stalin in the fifties, when it became clear that the Soviet maniac's removal from the human scene would not dislodge the cancer of Marxism from their lives, a sort of movement or network had begun. It had started in the U.S.S.R. But as it became ever clearer that the capitalist powers were too weak, too decadent, and too "moled" by their enemies to be of any help, the organization had spread.

"The Soviets nearly died laughing at your so-called cold war," Valeska confirmed. "Operation Focus! Operation Veto. Radio Free Europe! I remember when the Americans once sent fourteen million balloons a month floating over East Europe, all of them carrying propaganda pamphlets. The Soviets' answer was to stop shipping toilet paper to those areas blanketed by the balloons!

"And when things got deadly over here, Poles and Germans and Hungarians and Ukrainians and Lithuanians died in explosive situations the United States created. But then suddenly it was all peaceful coexistence: mutual trade, bilateral agreements, dollar loans, cultural exchanges, scientific cooperation. Useless tommyrot!" Valeska was the picture of that episcopal passion Jaroszewicz had worried about in Bialystok.

"In any case"—Cardinal Wallensky's voice calmed the atmosphere—"this organization I speak of has no name. It's generally referred to as "blue card," merely because its first members used blue cards for messages. It has no political aims. It has no connection with Western powers. It does not garner or barter intelligence. It's mainly been a morale-building organization, with more hopes than actual plans for any practical way to be effective.

"Now, quite independently, we find that you developed a very similar idea for a very similar organization."

Correction, Rico interrupted. The idea was not his, but Papa Profumi's. And it had a very definite purpose.

"Corrections willingly taken." The cardinal nodded. "But you have been able to carry it forward without allowing it to become polluted with politics and finance; and while it is a papal commission, you have also been able to carry it forward without the help of two popes who have followed Profumi."

"So?" Rico preferred not to confirm or deny his special status, at least in so many words, even with such close friends as these.

"So," Bogdan imitated Rico, "we propose a merger of the two organizations to speed the creation and activation of a living current of culture and religion that will wash into all the corners of the immovable political and military machine the Soviets have locked onto their so-called satellite countries."

In the new plan, both organizations would remain covert. But with their combined resources, they could start "surface" organizations of a religious and cultural kind. They could polycopy novels, plays, and poetry for distribution on the vast black market. They could organize music recitals, literary contests, lectures, conferences. Valeska and Wallensky had even thought of ways to operate universities out of private apartments—"flying" universities, Wallensky called them.

The participants in all these activities would be "aboveground," though they would not seek publicity. Indeed, they would avoid it. The organizers and the brains behind it all would remain covert.

The side-by-side culture that would be fostered in this way would in time move into every level of ordinary society. If they were successful, they would literally honeycomb the world beneath the Soviet grid system, with whole populations totally separate from the Marxist whip masters in culture, moral outlook, and aspirations.

That could not happen overnight; no one expected such a miracle. It would take years. But it would be a worthy investment for the future, Wallensky said. "We will not die. Our various cultures will not die. Our religion will not die."

When Wallensky talked about the plan, he made it sound much like the "catacomb culture" Papa Profumi had sometimes used as a comparison for his darker visions of the future. But when Bogdan spoke, Rico had the clear sense that the younger Pole had an eye on subversion in the political arena, and even among the armed forces and the security forces in satellite countries.

"For the love of Heaven, Bogdan"—Wallensky was sharp in his criticism of any such idea—"be wise! That could be your death. It could be the death of all our plans!"

In the days of discussion that followed between the three prelates, that point rose again and again. It made Rico nervous for the safety of the people in his organization, and because it could mean pollution of the purely religious intent of his educational unit.

The plan and their sometimes heated discussions remained foremost in Lansing's mind as he left Krakow to make visits to his stations in various sectors of Poland. There were advantages and dangers in the proposal; in fact, probably there were more of both than he could think out on a trip as long and difficult as this one. But when he got back to Krakow near Christmas, he promised Valeska he would discuss the plan with his own group of trusted people.

"And with no one else!" Valeska's caution was unnecessary but understandable.

Rico was packed and waiting for his "guide" when a new message from Pelse arrived through Bialystok. A special bulletin from the Soviet station in Rome had been flashed through security wires everywhere: to be on the watch for an American cleric who was supposed to have arrived in New York or Chicago by now, but had not turned up in either place. Pelse didn't interpret the message, but his concern was obvious in the very fact that he had relayed it.

Rico signaled Solaccio through a lamplight that he had to change travel plans. He would have to go underground all the way to the States somehow, turn up in New York, and be seen returning to Rome from there.

His new route was arranged in record time. Getting to East Berlin and to the safe house assigned to him was no great difficulty. But he couldn't dare move from there without checking for clearance with a local agent whose code name was Gregory. That meant two visits a day to a street phone near a certain newspaper kiosk. It was the longest wait of Rico's life.

When finally the call came, and the lengthy identifying codes were exchanged, "Gregory," still speaking in code, supplied the time and the place for Rico to meet his next guide, a man called Albert.

"Are you going back to Uncle?" Gregory asked.

"Yes. Immediately."

"You cannot go south. You must use the ticket Uncle has arranged for you. Mona has it."

Mona was the code name for Scandinavia.

"I've never met Mona."

"Albert will help you." The phone line went dead.

It took five days for Rico to get to Sweden and from there to New York, and they were the most harrowing of his life.

When he disembarked at Kennedy Airport in New York, he was approached at once in the main concourse by two nuns, rattling a collection box for their foundling home. He slipped one of his last single dollar bills into the slot. The younger of the nuns handed him a devotional pamphlet on the miracle of Lourdes. Inside he found his one-way ticket—New York to Rome, on TWA flight 241. Rico looked at his watch. He had thirty-five minutes to catch his plane. The two sisters smiled at him, nodding as pious nuns do, and rattled their way through the terminal building, accepting little donations as they went.

"How nice to see you back, Monsignore." Demarchelier flashed a smile at Rico as they crossed paths on the second-floor corridor of the Apostolic Palace. "How was your vacation? Did you visit your family in Chicago?"

Rico put on the perfect act. "You know how it is, Monsignore. You arrive in New York. You find a lovely friend. They ask you to stay for a week. Time flies, and you find four weeks have passed. You know how it is."

When Demarchelier dropped a word in Levesque's ear, suggesting even a possible clandestine love affair, the cardinal was disgusted. "It all smells to high heaven! He must be a Jesuit in disguise!"

After sleeping once around the clock, and catching up on all the gossip of Rome while Vittorio Benfatti served him a huge breakfast, Rico had dropped off his report and Pelse's intelligence with Solaccio and Brandolini. He heartily thanked both of them—and Youn and Righi too, who had been on signals—for saving his neck in a tight spot. He suggested a Security Two meeting for very early in the new year. Brandolini said he would see to it.

All of that and a bit of small talk taken care of, he asked Youn for a ride out to Villa Cerulea. He had already called Agathi, who had told him to come right that moment, and to spend the last days of 1966 with them. "Eugenio has a very big surprise for you. We'll all be waiting, darling!" Only Agathi could call bishops "darling" and get away with it, Lansing mused happily.

Youn pulled the car to a halt outside the gates at the main road. He honked the horn once. "Signor Manesco is getting a bit on in years, and a little deaf too." Rico laughed at Youn's impatience. The Korean honked again. Manesco peered between the curtains and then came running out, all apologies and greetings for the two visitors.

Villa Cerulea had never looked more majestic or more welcoming than that late morning as it came into view. Suddenly, two figures appeared in front of the slow-moving car, pedaling furiously toward it on bicycles. They were a blur as they whizzed past the limousine. Rico stuck his head out the window and cried out. *"Eugenio! Doni!"* And then, to Youn, "Hold it! Stop a minute!"

The boys, having made their dramatic entrance, curved their bikes around in tire-scraping skids and raced back to the car.

"That was my surprise for you, Uncle Rico!" Eugenio was breathless as much from excitement as from pedaling. "My new bicycle! It's my very own. Nanno bought it for me for Christmas! I don't have to borrow Doni's now, or the gardener's! Look! It's got three speeds! I can go as fast as the wind. Will you race with me, Uncle Rico?"

Rico's joy to be back was clear in his eyes. He reached out the window and rumpled Eugenio's hair. He said hello to Doni when he was finally able to get a word in. "It wouldn't be a fair race between an auto and a bicycle," he said, "even if it does have three speeds."

Doni was quick to solve that problem. "I'll lend you my bicycle, Monsignore! And I'll be the starter. I'll count to three."

Rico glanced at Youn. "There's no way out of this one, my friend."

He got out of the car and swung a leg over Doni's bicycle. At the count of three, he and Eugenio rode off. The boy and the bishop tore up the drive, neck and neck, Doni running and shouting and cheering behind, and Youn bringing up the rear, sounding the horn in encouragement all the way. By the time they all pulled up in front of Villa Cerulea, the commotion had brought Keti and Agathi to the door.

"It's a tie!" Keti ran down the front steps, Agathi close behind her, and both of them spontaneously flung their arms around Rico in welcome. In a sudden rush, Lansing felt all the coldness and aloneness and danger and stress of the past few months gather together and melt in the warmth and the softness of their embrace.

44

It was warm for late December, and Guido felt an unaccustomed desire to be out of doors. The winter chill would settle on Rome all too soon. Ah, well. The business of this year-end *impero* meeting—particularly Helmut's report concerning the transfer of assets from Italy to foreign locations—was too important. The Maestro cast a longing eye over his sunlit gardens, and turned his attention back to his associates.

Helmut, who spoke from typewritten notes, was the star performer of the meeting in Guido's large study. The vast transfer operation was his to direct, with advice from his uncle, and with extensive cooperation from the others wherever they could smooth his path—Francis Xavier Kelly and Jean-Pierre Duchesne in North America; Julio Montt, Ari Potamianos, and Claro Trujillo in Latin America; Michael Manley of Australia in Asia.

"I cannot stress too much," Helmut was saying, "that now more than ever we will all have to make treble use of our already hard-working and efficient team of international brokers. We now have some $180 billion abroad. The balance at home in Italy is $17 billion in round figures. Of that sum, at least $9 billion is anonymously held. You will find details in the usual reports in your folders.

"Now, some of you are centrally located in areas where we are heavily invested. Most of us have considerable business interests, both personal and corporate, in those areas and in others we are now entering. Again, details of our near-future plans are in your folders. The point I want to make now is that we will need much closer intercommunication than ever before, particularly in Latin America.

"Let me give you an example. . . ." The door of the study opened and Sagastume caught the Maestro's eye. Guido rose from his chair and stepped out for a moment. Monsignore Lansing had arrived. Guido told the chauffeur that the meeting would not be finished until quite late. Let the good monsignore have a leisurely day and make an early night of it. They would see each other in the morning.

When he returned to his place at the head of the conference table, his nephew was answering questions about the *cedolare* tax, and what they now called their "Italian exposure."

"No one," Helmut pointed out, "can have any factual foundation for saying we have not allowed the government a solid basis on which the *cedolare* can surely be levied.

"For example, SII assets alone are over $300 million as of this month, and its profits are up to $8.2 million. It has a controlling interest in over seventy companies. Eleven of those companies specialize in investment and property holdings. The others are spread out over insurance, agricultural projects, general service companies, technical services, industry and manufacturing.

"Or take another example. Through RIS, in Rome alone, we own nine apartment complexes, five office buildings with commercial parking facilities and shopping arcades, and fourteen garden-villa developments."

He flicked over a few pages. "You are all acquainted with what RIS has accomplished in Geneva, Milan, Bari, and Turin. . . ."

Guido followed his nephew's presentation, turning the pages of his copies of the various reports. He glanced down the summary of RIS projects and let his eye stop at the item detailing a shopping mall and a housing complex of seven buildings and 196 units built on the Piazza Loreto in Milan. The Maestro's memory was tugged back for a moment to the horrid death scene he had witnessed in that piazza—of the partisans hanging the bodies of Mussolini and Clara Petacci and the others by their feet, to the hate-filled chanting of the crowds. . . . "Thus are Italy's sins finally hidden." He formed the words in his mind, and quickly forced his attention back to Helmut's summary.

". . . The merger of the Montecatini and Edison companies . . . real estate value over $3 billion . . . profits nearly $1 billion . . . our RCO and ITS company in West Virginia . . . Holland . . . Spain . . . Italy . . . Brazil . . ."

Guido leaned back. This Helmut he was listening to now was so different, so much more developed than the Helmut who had begun working with him in 1944. More developed even than the Helmut of five years before.

He had often heard that heredity leaped a generation. Perhaps it was true; at times, in a little gesture of the hand or an expression that shadowed his face briefly, Helmut reminded Guido of his own uncle, the Keeper before him. That man had been outstanding. If Helmut took after him, Guido reflected, there was not much danger for the Keeper's custodianship, at least in the next generation, even given the turmoil they were now going through in Italy. And then, after Helmut, blessing of blessings, there was Eugenio.

Of course—Guido returned to his thoughts about heredity—there was that old tendency of de la Valle men so often repeated in their family history. They chose their women carefully, wed them sumptuously, housed them royally, bedded them—and no other—faithfully. All with great love. But often it had happened that as they became busy in great affairs, they took home and family for granted, and etched love into a bronze distance at the end of the mind. Their great love became a gorgeous gold-feathered bird on a stylized palm, singing a song without feeling, without the meaning of caress, embrace, or kiss, without the stuff and matter of human meaning. To hold a de la Valle close, a woman had to spin a song as soft as the murmur of doves at evening time in order to offset the cold metal of her man's acumen in business. She had to offer him the wild flowers of a lover's imaginings, with scents as strange as sorcerers' eyes, in order to distract him from the everyday glazed look on the poker face required at the negotiating table.

". . . Romacementi is up to $7.2 million." Helmut's voice forced itself back into the forefront of his uncle's attention. "Romaceramica's assets over $17 million . . . Profits from Hungary and Tunisia, $3.8 million . . ." The list went on through mining, pasta, steel, automobiles, passenger ships, telephone and telegraph, credit institutions, motion pictures, insurance, reinsurance, banking.

A movement out in the gardens caught Guido's eye, and he turned his head. Was that Rico Lansing and Keti? Yes, he could see them now, walking at a slow pace, stopping now and again to face one another, after a while continuing on their way along the Family Path. Keti took Rico's arm. They stopped again. It looked almost as though they were arguing, engrossed as they were in their conversation. But then they laughed and moved on together.

". . . Romagas capital was $12.8 million for 1966, with a net profit of $1.24 million—an increase of $226,000 over 1965. . . ."

Guido watched Rico and Keti as he listened to his nephew. A European woman knew all about murmuring doves at evening time. American women were so different. . . .

"You must see me as a terrible old female grampus, Rico." Keti took Rico's arm and looked up at him with an easy smile. "But I'm always worried about Eugenio. It's irrational, I know. But sometimes at the dead of night when I can't sleep, I creep into his room. He sleeps so peacefully I can't even hear him breathing. I sometimes get a sudden fear he's stopped breathing, and I bend my ear down until I can be sure, until I can hear his breath. I know it sounds mad, but that's the sort of mother I've become!"

"It's not mad, Keti." Rico stopped and put his hands on her shoulders like an old-fashioned schoolmaster about to discipline a pupil. "Don't think such black thoughts. It's just that he's growing up now; and like any mother who loves her son, you don't want to lose him."

"That's true enough, I suppose." Keti took Rico's arm again and they strolled slowly on through the gardens toward the back postern gate. "Someday soon we will look at Eugenio and find he's a young man. I just hope he never loses the sense of completeness he has now. I sometimes think he didn't even have to be born to have that inner sense of knowing that's such a special quality in him. It came with him, already full blown from the womb, from the first moment of love that gave him life. That's why he was able to believe the truth at the back of all those tales Guido used to tell him about angels and giants, about Good and Bad. He hadn't to search for that completeness. For that sense of knowing. It was just there."

"That won't change, Keti. He's growing out of his child self. But he has a pristine faith that I almost envy in him."

"His child self." Keti repeated Rico's phrase. It seemed a moment ago, she said, that her son had confided, with the seriousness only a child can summon, that he had always been a child. Forever. And his parents and Nanno and Nanna had always been grownups. And that was how he reckoned it would always be. The present was the future and the past. They would live at Villa Cerulea always. Years did not measure rushing time for him, but framed his space in eternity.

"He used to go with me sometimes, on my rounds of the estate. To check on the plantings and harvest in the pine forest, and out to the sheep pastures. Often we would take a picnic luncheon and sit in his favorite place by the river. On the way home, he would watch the colors of the sunset and make up stories about the faraway Islands of the Blessed, where the sun never set." Keti stopped again, her face radiant with the memories. "He has a lot of his granduncle's imagination in him."

"He's older now, Keti. That's all. But he's never lost that freshness."

"No, never. But he doesn't need as much care as before. In fact, he's beginning to take on a caring role himself. Now, when he goes with me to see about the dairy farm or the lumber or whatever I may have on my schedule—less often now, what with school and all—he takes a real interest in the details of the estate. He understands it's going to be his responsibility someday. And that, like his father and Guido, he'll hold it in trust for those who come after. That's a big change, Rico. I don't know if I'm happy about it or not. They grow away from you. Until one day, like an arrow fired from your bow, they're gone. And you cannot recall them.

That's where the pain is for me. A gentle pain. But a pain."

Keti held Rico's arm a little tighter and pulled herself a little closer. And Rico understood then that on her lips, "they" didn't only mean Eugenio.

"Helmut?"

Keti jerked her head up, startled that Rico had so easily read her thoughts. But then—she glanced into his eyes—he and Agathi always seemed to have that sixth sense about other people. And who knew her better than those two?

"He doesn't need me as much anymore, either." Keti finally answered Rico's question. "It's the emptiness that gets to me. I know you can't know much about"—she paused for an uncertain second, then decided to go on—"about this side of a woman's life; but if you love Helmut as much as I do, and you can't have him in the way you want and need to, then a woman—a wife—has to close off a very deep and intimate part of her very soul. She can do that. But it never stops hurting."

Rico said nothing, knowing that she was right, that he didn't know much about that side of a woman's life; but knowing that by their walking gently in step, and by the current of sympathy and understanding between them, some secret balm was being poured on her inner hurt.

Palermo is lovely in December. Lovelier by far than the gathering of men in the fourth-floor suite at the back of the Hotel Las Palmas. Paolo Lercani had been summoned by the members of what he jokingly—and with an affable raising of his upper lip—referred to in accented English as "the U.N." The Underworld Nobility.

They were all there. Jimmy "Fingers" Benevuti, prince of the Sicilian Honored Society. Busto Salvucci, boss of the Lombardy syndicates. Paolo Barazini of Naples. Carmine Pezzullo had flown in from Detroit. Giuseppe "Stonebottom" Scozzofaza had come all the way from Los Angeles. Giulio "Gesumaria" Jacopazzi was there from Marseilles. All the leaders. All flanked by their top lieutenants.

These far-seeing businessmen perceived a terrible threat looming on the horizon. A very important part of their revenues depended on the "supplies of poppy" from the Golden Triangle, that invaluable piece of real estate formed by the convergence of Thailand, Burma, and Laos. Those supplies would obviously be endangered by an American military victory in the gradually escalating war between North and South Vietnam. Already there were more than 75,000 United States troops over there, together with a whole array of sophisticated ground, air, and sea support. And more was sure to come. The Americans were definitely on the way to total victory.

The danger was that, with North Vietnam defeated, American influence would extend over Laos and Cambodia and all the way to the borderlands of Burma. Hanoi would be ruled by American-picked leaders. And, altogether, that would mean a severe setback for their share in the opium trade.

"Look, Paolo." Benevuti rasped out some facts and figures for the dapper Lercani. "Our position is weak enough as it is. We get maybe ten percent of the Thailand harvest, tops. We can't touch Burma. We have good friends in the governor's mansion in Chiang Mai as well as in Lampang. That helps a little. But we're a long way from having the solid contacts we need in the 273 northern villages where the best crop comes from. So when the plants are a foot tall in late October and early November, only one out of ten is cut for us. A lot depends on our building up that percentage. And we sure can't afford to lose what we've got!

"Now, Paolo." Benevuti knew he could speak with total confidence. He had known Lercani since his earliest days in Sicily. "You've come a long way. And we've stood by you on various occasions—y'know—some unwelcome competitor here, some nosey government investigation there—y'know what I mean, Paolo, eh? Now, from where you sit in Milano, you know Europe. You know how things work. I mean, how things really work. What we need is advice. Give us some idea of how to go about this thing. How the hell do we save our ten percent?"

"First," Lercani obliged, "you can't go off half-cocked."

"Meaning?" Salvucci didn't need a big meeting to tell him to do nothing.

"Meaning it isn't clear that the Americans will win. If and when that seems more likely than it does now, then you find some indirect way to twist the arm of the American commander in chief."

"You mean General Whatever-his-name-is?"

"I mean the American President."

"Gesumaria!" Jacopazzi used that expression that gave him his nickname. "How do we do *that*!"

Lercani's face was a mask of inscrutable triumph. "Through the Holy Father."

Not even Jacopazzi had a big enough exclamation for that.

"It's simple enough." Lercani's lids dropped part of the way over his eyes. "You mentioned Hanoi, Fingers. The Pope has a cardinal in Hanoi. A troublesome, American-hating cardinal." Lercani reached a hand to the table and walked his index finger and his forefinger along its edge in three strides. "From the cardinal to the Pope. Step one. From the Pope to the President. Step two. From the President to your General Whatever-his-name-is. Step three. Simple!"

That was a fine plan, Scozzofava said; except for the fact that Paolo moved in circles of government, Church, and business that were out of even their reach on anything like a "regular basis." Scozzofava was always clear-headed.

"Paolo, we—*and you!*—will watch the situation. If it gets as bad as we think, then you come back in the picture. *D'accordo?*"

"*D'accordo,* Giuseppe."

[45]

As intelligence control for Rico's covert work, and now as well for Security Two, Archbishop Giulio Brandolini had prepared well for the January 1967 meeting, with the able assistance of Monsignore Gian Solaccio. With the Maestro, Helmut, Cardinals Lanser and Falconieri, and Rico Lansing all giving full attention, Brandolini laid out his assessment of where they stood.

First, as to the matter of the leak that had put Rico in such danger on the covert leg of his recent trip, Brandolini and Solaccio pointed the finger at Demarchelier. One product of their increased surveillance had been the report of a brief meeting at Monte Mario between the good Demarchelier and a Soviet Embassy official. In hindsight, the timing of that meeting just as Rico's trip was beginning was too much to lay to coincidence.

Because Demarchelier was suspect, Brandolini ticked off the important points, and because Demarchelier was Levesque's close aide, and finally because Rico had given his itinerary to Levesque for the Pontiff, the cardinal secretary himself was under suspicion as well.

"What about Sugnini?" It was Rico's question. "He's practically glued to Levesque."

"True." Brandolini nodded. "But the lines don't lead in the same direction. Sugnini's only tie seems to be with the Northern Alliance. Levesque and Demarchelier are not a part of that. Sugnini probably thinks he's using Levesque. But who is really using whom is the question."

"In any case"—the Maestro summed up the point, anxious for Brandolini to go on—"we'll have to be more careful about Rico's underground work. No more linking his covert trips with his official travels, for one thing. The official itineraries make him too vulnerable. Agreed?"

There were no objections or comments, and Brandolini went on, without further interruption, to amplify his own question: Who was using whom?

"The thing I look for is a leak in all the confusion; some common thread running through the little we do know so far, that will begin to give us a grip on what we're dealing with, and how to get it under control.

"I've come to the conclusion that the link is the confusion itself. Let me start where we are and work backward to make my point clear.

"Right now, we're dealing with a tidal wave of unplanned and unauthorized change in the Church. It's barely a year since Vatican II ended, and already there is a plague of experimentation, rebellion, and outlandish practices sweeping and swilling everywhere. As Cardinals Lanser and Falconieri here can attest, the Mass is under attack everywhere. Bishops and priests are making their own translations, inventing new words for the most sacred and essential moment of the Mass, the consecration of bread and wine. Cardinal Arnulfo has pointed out publicly that transubstantiation itself is in question there—in other words, that the bread and wine do not become the Body and Blood of Christ in such circumstances—and that the adoration of mere bread and wine is material idolatry.

"Less important, perhaps, but a part of the picture, are the new rituals springing up out of whole cloth everywhere; the discarding of religious vestments; the use of cookies and ordinary baker's bread for the Host instead of the unleavened bread prescribed by the Church.

"Add to that a loss of over fifteen hundred priests to date. Half of them have left with permission; the rest simply walked off their posts as curates and pastors. The fallout in nuns is just beginning, but it's likely to continue. Among the priests who haven't left, there are terrible irregularities. Several in Holland and France, for example, have married but continue to function as priests.

"One of the most alarming and significant symptoms of this confusion is the overall rejection and revolt against Papa De Brescia's own encyclical letter about contraception and human sexuality. Except for the bishops in Portugal and the Iron Curtain countries, all other national groups of bishops have either soft-pedaled the strict prohibition against contraception that Da Brescia laid down, or have followed the lead set by Catholic University's Charles McMurren, who wrote an article declaring that contraception could be used when it was necessary for something he called . . ." Brandolini shuffled through some papers and came up with McMurren's piece and read from it: "growth toward creative integration,' whatever that means.

"The point I make, however, is that altogether this is a portrait of a wholesale breakdown in Church discipline and in papal authority."

"Granted." The Maestro spoke up again. "But where does that lead?"

"It leads," Brandolini went on, "at least in the first instance, to the Northern Alliance. But in a strange way. Look at the makeup of that group. Sugnini is in it. So is Nikodim. Go down the whole list. Richard Richards. Cale. Ripley-Savage. Herreras. They have almost nothing in common except a negative goal. Each one, for totally different reasons, is a willing participant in a campaign to open Rome up to whatever use can be made of it. It's a kind of controlled free-for-all, whose only aim is what I have just described: a wholesale breakdown in Church discipline and papal authority.

"The trouble is, there is no other side to the coin in the Northern Alliance. There is no cohesive, agreed-upon, positive plan to replace what they want to destroy with anything else, except a vague 'brotherhood.'

"What that leaves is a dangerous vacuum in which any insanity might be born.

"Now, let's look for a second at our friend Father Jaime Herreras. As you all know, he began his career as a theologian and sociologist. He is a member of the Northern Alliance. He was one of the most influential *periti* at Vatican II. And, as we now know from Rico's Riga intelligence, he has a direct link with Moscow, with General Control, and with the only cohesive and positive plan to make use of this breakdown of Church discipline and papal authority. That breakdown is, in fact, a potent and essential tool in General Control's plan for a wholesale change in the meaning of basic theology into a purely social and political message.

"Together, General Control and Herreras have come up with the insanity to inject into the vacuum. As far as they're concerned, the Northern Alliance is probably just another one of the tools that happened along to help them to that end.

"I still don't get the Lercani connection, beyond the fact that it indicates, to me at least, that Herreras and his group will link up with anyone who can be useful, whether in destabilizing Vatican authority, as in the case of the Northern Alliance, or in supplying funds, as in the case of Lercani.

"In that sense, Herreras is like everyone else we've named so far. He's an opportunist. Like Lercani, like Richards, like all of them, he thinks he's using everybody else for his own ends. As I said, it's a free-for-all."

The Maestro got up to stretch his legs for a few minutes, and to try to get some practical direction from Brandolini's analysis. As nearly as he could see, at this juncture there were only two positive steps that they could take into this minefield of confusion.

"First," he said, pacing about Brandolini's office, "Cardinal Walensky's proposal to strengthen Rico's organization seems extremely desirable in this climate. As you pointed out, Giulio, and as ironic as it may be, the active clergy in Iron Curtain satellites do remain stalwart in their support of Church and papacy, and the people are and intend to remain stalwart in their faith.

"From Rico's report—correct me if I misremember, Excellency"—he looked down at the American—"an increase in our funding over there will be needed."

"Not all that much." Rico had done some rough figures with Walensky and Valeska. "Our yearly budget runs now to about three-quarters of a million. We're not looking for opulence, as you know. And it's going to be a long-term process of development. But a fifty percent increase should do it for now."

A quick nod between Helmut and the Maestro. "That's hardly a problem, Rico." Helmut made the reply.

"And the second step, Maestro?" Brandolini and Solaccio both spoke up at once.

"The second step has to do with Herreras and the latest report from Riga indicating that he is to begin a 'slash-and-burn' campaign of terror in Latin America."

Brandolini interrupted with a piece of information "from another quarter." On Brandolini's lips, that expression generally meant some very confidential source of his own. There had been a top-level meeting in Panama last November. "Herreras was there, together with people from Mexico, Cuba, El Salvador, Nicaragua, Guatemala, Chile, and the Argentine. We weren't able to get any details of the discussion, except that in general it concerned destabilization of present political structures in as much of the area as possible. It fits with the latest Riga intelligence."

The Maestro ran a hand along one side of his hair. "The ubiquitous Herreras! I agree with Riga that we should try to divert him. I imagine we all agree. The question is how?"

Rico characteristically supported a direct approach. "He may be a revolutionary, but he's still a priest. Maybe he's still a man of faith. Maybe he can even be 'turned around.' I say I try to arrange a meeting with him."

"If you can find him!" Solaccio snorted. "The fellow's a will-o'-the-wisp! Except for that meeting in November, no one's seen him since the public consistory in September of last year."

"Well"—Rico frowned at the problem—"he's not only a priest; he's a Jesuit. The general of his order might be able to help."

It was decided that it was worth a try. If Rico could talk with Herreras—all pretense down, and one on one—even if he couldn't turn the man around, at least they might have a better idea of the only person who had so far emerged as one of their most significant and powerful adversaries. "The only one, in any case," as the Maestro said, "who has *both* a clear identity and a clear objective in his own mind."

Jesuit General Evaristo Corda was stocky, bald-headed, pious, and stubborn. He had been born in Brazil of Hungarian émigré parents. He had spent years as a young Jesuit working the shanty slums, the *favelas,* of Rio de Janeiro. Burned into his soul were the memories of the teeming populations of poor, not only in Rio but in all of Latin America; and of the hordes of Cadillacs and Rolls-Royces—the price of any one of which exceeded the lifetime earnings of whole villages—that streamed past the misery each day on the way to and from sumptuous villas and high-rise office buildings.

Those memories made Corda, even as Jesuit general, a quietly angry man. Some of the Americans among his 37,000-man order said that a Yankee-born motto described his outlook: "Don't get mad. Get even."

Corda would do his best to get even. For the love of God.

"What can I do for you, Excellency?" He received Lansing with all due decorum, and listened attentively.

The monsignore wished to meet with Father Jaime Herreras, but it had been impossible to locate him. But of course, Father General would help; he personally would make sure Father Herreras would be available. Perhaps the week after Easter? Very good. In the meantime, could he himself, Father Corda, be of help? No? Well, God's blessing on the monsignore, then. Corda would be in touch as to the exact date and the place of the meeting with Father Herreras.

Rico thanked the Jesuit general for his help and for his valuable time, and departed with a new appreciation of the term "jesuitical."

On Easter Monday, Rico and Helmut rode out to Rome's international airport together, Helmut to catch an early-morning flight to Panama on *impero* business, and Rico to board a plane for Mexico City. At the last possible moment, Father Corda had supplied the time and the exact location of the Herreras meeting. It was to be that afternoon at the Cuernavaca residence of a gentleman named Otto Domenici.

Even Brandolini had not been able to check on Domenici in the few hours between Corda's call to Rico the evening before and this morning's flight. Lansing would have to go to the meeting "blind," while Brandolini did his digging for information. As a precaution, Rico was to call Helmut in Panama before the meeting, and again as soon as it was over. The assumption was that these were not "friendlies," as Helmut put it; if there was no second call by early evening, Helmut would make a call from Panama that would "bring hell itself down on Domenici's house."

Rico's plane landed in Mexico City in the early afternoon, local time. He hired a car and driver for the short ride south to Cuernavaca. After checking in to the Hostería Las Quintas, and making the prearranged call to Helmut in Panama, he followed his usual "street" instincts and set forth on foot to smell out his surroundings.

Promptly at four forty-five he rang the bell at Domenici's house. From the moment the servant led him through the ample rooms of the lower floor and out into the high-walled garden at the rear, Rico knew he was in alien territory.

One of four men seated around a shaded table got up to greet him. Otto Domenici was a tall, heavyset man who spoke a guttural Spanish. Rico apologized that he was not fluent in the language, and Domenici switched to English. He introduced Enrico Martola and Juan Cepeda, who were both over sixty, conservatively dressed, and carried themselves more stiffly than the usual Latin.

The fourth and youngest man at the table, as Rico had guessed when he laid eyes on him, was the elusive Father Jaime Herreras. He was slight of build, not tall, dressed in gray flannels and a white shirt with a black sweater over it. He wore spectacles. In spite of that, his hollow cheeks and pale skin emphasized his large and intensely serious brown eyes.

Rico took the chair that was offered him.

"Will you drink something?" Domenici held the servant with a gesture.

"If you have a lemonade?"

Domenici waved his hand. The servant disappeared, quickly returned with a tall icy glass for the new visitor, and disappeared again.

Small talk was almost impossible. Rico did his best at it for about a half hour, mostly with Domenici. Herreras said nothing after the introduction, but neither did he take his eyes off the American.

Lansing was uncomfortable. Every instinct told him to get out of there as quickly as he could. In any case, to have the talk he intended with Herreras, he had to get him alone. Again, he decided on the direct approach. He had to make a private phone call soon, he said. Cepeda and Martola exchanged a look. Rico shifted his own eyes to the Jesuit. He would consider it a favor if Father Herreras would walk him back to his hotel.

"Como quiere, Monseñor." Herreras spoke for the first time since his brief greeting. "As you wish."

"Señor Domenici." Rico got up, and the others followed suit. "Thank you for your gracious hospitality."

Stiff bows all around.

"My house is yours." Domenici gave the time-honored Mexican reply, but without its usual warmth.

When they were on the street, Rico spoke his mind frankly, and asked Herreras to do the same. "Roman authorities are aware of your involvement with revolutionary and terrorist groups, Father."

Herreras spoke English with a gentle and agreeable accent. His voice was firm, but not strident. "A Jesuit is a man of obedience. What I do, I do with the blessing of Holy Obedience, and the approval of Father General."

"Do you think, Father, that you can really help the poor people of this continent with guns and dynamite?"

Herreras gave a little laugh, the kind that said he had heard that spiel before. "Let me answer with a question, Monseñor. Or with a puzzle. If you can solve it for me, I'm yours.

"Suppose you are a young man of, say, twenty-five. You are permanently out of work and so is everyone you know. You have a wife you love and six children you adore. You had three others, but they died of starvation and disease. You scavenge in the trash left at the city dump for scraps of food and anything else of use discarded from the houses of the rich. Sometimes you find an hour's work at the central market, where you pack two-hundred-pound sacks on your back like a mule and get pennies for the labor. You live in a six-by-nine-foot shanty made of flattened tar barrels and cardboard boxes. If you're lucky, you've scavenged a bit of tarpaulin to help keep the wind and water out. The sewer waste runs openly down the street outside. If you and your wife can scrape five dollars together in a month, you're luckier than most of the people you know. There's no hope you can buy a dress for your wife. Or shoes for your children. No hope. Not now. Not tomorrow. Not next week. Not next year. Not ever.

"Now, one day a priest comes, and he tells you Christ is the Savior.

" 'At last!' you say to him. Because the first thing you think is that this Christ he wants to tell you about will save your family from filth and sores and hunger and all the hopeless tomorrows. But the tomorrows just keep coming, and they are like all the yesterdays.

"Then another priest comes. He puts a gun in your hands and tactics in your head and courage in your heart to blast away the rich and the fat and the comfortable few who live in the villas and chalets and bungalows that cast their long shadows over your hovel. And all that, the priest offers you in the name of Christ the Savior.

"What would you say to him, Monseñor?" Herreras stopped and made

Rico look him in the eyes. "What would you say to him, standing in the doorway of your stinking hovel with the stinking sewer water running down the street outside and not enough stinking food inside to keep body and soul together? What would you do? Ask for the first priest to come back?"

Rico stared back at Herreras. What could he say? In the terms the Jesuit chose, any counterargument would sound inhuman, criminal. "I have no solution," Rico admitted. "But I won't take Marxism as a refuge. And I tell you to your face, you're a fool if you do. I can match every horrible story you want to tell me of the misery here with stories of my own from the Gulag."

Herreras resumed walking, and Rico fell in beside him.

"I don't think you understand the little human puzzle I put to you, Monseñor. The first offer to my starving peasant was from a priest too, remember. It was from me, in fact. Back then, I was as wrapped up in Romanism as you are. But then I discovered that Romanism is all wrapped up in capitalism. And capitalism isn't salvation. It's starvation —at least for my peasants.

"I've run out of options, Monseñor."

The two walked in silence for a while, the scudding clouds forming spectacular shapes overhead.

"The thing is, Father"–Rico broke the silence—"your solution must be wrong, because it's totally in disagreement with what Christ taught."

"Did he teach starvation, then, Monseñor? Is that what you're telling me and my starving peasant in the doorway?"

"Did he teach killing, then, Herreras?" Rico raised his voice for a minute, but then caught himself. "Forget your peasant for a minute, Father. Let's talk about you. Why is it you have nothing but a gun to offer? Nothing but war and killing and death? You're a priest! Have you lost everything the Church has been given? Have you lost all but the words that you now empty of their substance and grace, and then twist into some gargoyle shape?

"And you're also a Jesuit! Have you learned nothing from St. Ignatius of the power of moral strength? Are you so poverty stricken yourself that you have only political and military power to offer? Even if it means clamping the burden of Marxism on top of all those other burdens your peasant in the doorway already carries? Even if it means you'll come up empty, with no solution and no salvation to offer anybody?"

It was Herreras' turn to ponder in silence; but just for a little while. "I'm sorry, Monseñor." He was sincere. "I cannot do as you ask. I cannot forget my starving peasant in the doorway. Even for a minute.

"I say I've tried your way. I say I've run out of options. I say that if the salvation we preach is not primarily a social and political salvation, then we will be whistling in the dark when we speak of supernatural salvation. And I say that as long as Rome is wrapped up in capitalism, it, too, is encased in political and military power, just as I am. It's the pot calling the kettle black.

"You say there must be another way. When you find it, Monseñor, perhaps we will talk again."

Lansing's mind was so deeply wrapped in the enigma Jaime Herreras had laid at his doorstep, he almost forgot to call Helmut. When he did call, his friend suggested Rico join him in Panama. He had some information from Brandolini, he said, and thought it would be very wise for Rico to get the next plane out of Mexico. "Anyway, Rico, danger aside, you could use a couple of days' rest."

It was nearly dawn when Rico checked into Helmut's hotel. He showered, and then went along to Helmut's suite for breakfast.

The information Helmut had from Brandolini concerned Otto Domenici. "His real name is Schwängler." Helmut read from his hasty notes. "Adolf Schwängler. Turned up in Buenos Aires toward the end of 1950, according to the Inter-American police files. Ample funds. Plenty of friends. Moved to Peru the following year. Lima. Bought his winter residence in Cuernavaca three years later. Heavy investor in real estate. Regularly receives money gifts from his European relations."

Nothing sounded unusual in all that, as far as Rico could tell. But the "kicker," as Helmut said, was still to come. "The whole thing rang a warning bell in Uncle Guido's memory. On a hunch he had Brandolini check your old Raphael files. Something about twelve passports you arranged as part of the old Swiss Windfall arrangement."

Rico sat back in his chair in disbelief. A dark tunnel opened in his memory and led him back nearly twenty years. With a clammy feeling, he saw the shadow of himself confronting Father Lanser, returning to his own office, giving his own *"placet,"* and then amending it: "I have trusted that . . . the love of our Lord Jesus will be served." He shuddered.

Finally, he collected himself. "Domenici is one of the twelve, then?"

"It appears that way. Brandolini has some then-and-now pictures for you to look at when you get back."

"But what on earth is Herreras doing in such company? If Guido's hunch proves out, Domenici's not a Marxist, he's a Nazi!"

"We don't have the answer. In fact, it gets even more confusing. Schwängler, a.k.a. Domenici, has a villa in Lima, as I mentioned. On the Avenue Oaxa. It turns out that the villa two doors down from his belongs to the illustrious Senatore Ectore Pappagallo. You've heard of him, I know. Used to be very highly placed in the Italian government. Lodge. Connections everywhere. Knows everybody. It was from him that Guido first learned that there was such a group as the Northern Alliance.

"Now, what do you suppose the odds are against it being sheer, innocent coincidence that Schwängler and Pappagallo are neighbors?

"The only connection that makes sense in all this is that 'common thread' Brandolini talked about at our Security Two meeting in January. Confusion. Destabilization of the status quo. And everybody using everybody else. The Reds using Herreras and the Northern Alliance. Herreras using Lercani's money. If he uses Lercani's, why not Domenici's?"

"And Pappagallo's?" Rico shook his head. "It doesn't make sense, Helmut. I can see Herreras using their money. He's so single-minded, you'd have to call him a fanatic. He'll use whatever he can from wherever he can get it. I'm sure of that. But why would the likes of a Domenici or a Pappagallo finance the likes of a Herreras? It's insanity!"

Helmut nodded in agreement. "Just as Brandolini said." He poured another cup of coffee for himself and filled Rico's cup too. "Speaking of Herreras, how did your meeting go? Did you get him alone?"

"Yes," Rico answered. "I got him alone. I'm too pooped to tell you about it right now. He's a formidable character, though. Maybe we can have dinner tonight, and talk more?"

"Sure. Ari Potamianos and I have a round of meetings this afternoon on *impero* business. I should be free by about eight."

As Rico lay down, bone tired, in his own suite to get a couple of hours' rest, his weary mind began to make odd associations. Here was Helmut going off to talk about millions of dollars, probably, with Ari Potamianos. And up north in Cuernavaca, there was Herreras, talking about more millions with Domenici. What made Herreras think he was doing anything different? How did guns and dynamite make him think he was doing anything better? Was it the "pot and the kettle" as Herreras himself had said? Or wasn't it, as far as the Jesuit revolutionary was concerned, the frying pan and the fire?

Helmut and Rico talked late into the night. After dinner they sat out on the veranda in the sultry night air, each man a shadowy outline limned in the glow from the rooms behind them.

Rico told his friend about the Herreras meeting. Helmut outlined his *impero* progress in the area; they now had equity control in ten Panamanian money houses, and in four others in Latin America, including one in Lima.

As the hours drew on, Rico's thoughts turned to Chicago. He would be going home for a couple of weeks in June, he told Helmut. "I got back there last year. It was a promise I'd made to my dad. But I had to cut the trip short. This year, nothing's going to get in the way. We're going to go up to the cabin. I've told Dad to see that the phone is shut off." They would walk and talk and do a little fishing, he said, with remembrance and anticipation clear in his voice.

Helmut had never known what it was to love his father the way Rico loved Basil. His were a child's memories, held fast in the amber of his adult idealizing of a now distant past. Such a love as Rico and Basil had seemed to Helmut like a log fire they kept burning night and day in a cozy family room. Only they belonged there. Everyone else was a visitor.

His own thoughts turned to Keti. That was where the fire lay for him. He began to talk about her to Rico. About how hard it was to husband a woman, really husband her, unless she was more important than everything else in life put together. "Even you, Rico, couldn't be as dedicated as you are, if you had a wife."

Rico turned toward Helmut, but couldn't make out the expression on his face. "I swear to you on the Sacrament," he said, his voice low and vibrant, "if I were married to the woman I loved, there would be no other action in my normal life—short of dying for my faith—that would be such a profound expression of love for God as loving her."

In the early hours of the morning Helmut still lay awake, Rico's words still in his head: "on the Sacrament." He had taken such an oath as Keeper in the Sancta Sanctorum that Christmas Eve. But if he really believed that he had sworn it in the presence of Christ's sacred humanity —"on the Sacrament"—then it should only draw him closer to Keti. He had also sworn an oath to her, on the Sacrament. It should all work together. But it hadn't. His lovely, faithful Keti had paid a price for his failure to make it work together. He wondered if there would come a time, too late, when unbidden memories would rush upon him: Keti's face in the gentle moonlight. The lovers' connivance between them. The earth-free ecstasy in which they orbited together. The first rush of his sensuality. The sweetness. Keti's cry and the windswept look on her face.

He jumped out of bed, a surge of emotion and resolve with the truth of what Rico had said, and with his own prayer. "Please God it is not too late." He picked up the phone, dialed the operator, and gave her the number at Villa Cerulea.

Sagastume answered. Blast him! Helmut thought. I don't want to hear him. I want to hear Keti. I want to tell her I love her. I want to . . .

"Signora Keti has just gone into Rome, Signor Helmut. She left about ten minutes ago. She isn't expected home until quite late."

Helmut hung up. Overwhelmed by his disappointment, he didn't move until the jangling of the phone under his hand startled him. He lifted the receiver again. Maybe it was Keti! Maybe she had forgotten something, come back for it, heard that he had called. "Hello?"

"Helmut." The Maestro's voice came through on a clear connection. "Is Rico with you?"

"He's in his rooms, Uncle." Helmut steadied his own voice. "Asleep, probably. He's fagged out."

"You'd better wake him, *caro.* Benfatti just phoned. Basil Lansing had a stroke two hours ago."

[46]

"But, Your Eminence! My dear Monsignore! It is insanity!" Angrily, Papa Da Brescia brandished the thick report in his hand, and splayed across his desk the photos that Cardinal Arnulfo had sent along with it. "Even granted that Cardinal Arnulfo is a prejudiced party, as are his confederates in the State Council and those who remain loyal to him in our Congregation for the Doctrine of the Faith, nevertheless this documentation is irrefutable!

"I am told here"—the Pontiff flourished the forty-four-page report anew—"that Latin has been dropped from the Mass altogether in *more* areas than before, *not* in fewer! And that the sacred words of consecration are unrecognizable! Arnulfo speaks of material idolatry!"

The Pontiff picked up a handful of photographs. "See for yourself, Monsignore! No tabernacle on the altar in this picture. In this one, the altar itself looks like a dining table decked out with the family linen! In these, no statues of Christ or the Virgin! No crucifix!"

The Pope laid a half-dozen photos aside roughly, and took up a few more at random. "When did we ever dream that nuns would wear makeup and jewelry!" He tossed one photograph down. "Or that women would don priests' stoles and distribute Holy Communion!" Three or four more photos left his hand and fluttered to the floor by his desk. "Or that priests saying Mass would wear dungarees and T-shirts!" A few more pictures were thrown down. "Or that a whole group of priests in Chicago would sit in a hotel bar with 'dates'!

"Monsignore, We repeat! This is insanity, running through the Church like mercury. We appointed you to the Liturgical Commission to monitor such things; to curb them. You assured Us last year that you understood that lesser things than these were excesses. You assured Us that steps would be taken. Now We find . . ." The Pontiff seemed suddenly at a loss for words. "Look at these!" He threw down the last of the photographic documentation that had come with Arnulfo's report. "Disgraceful! What are Our bishops doing?"

As the papal tirade cascaded over him, Sugnini looked at Cardinal Levesque. They had seen Arnulfo's report, of course; even before Papa Da Brescia had. Arnulfo had delivered it through Levesque, in fact, in the normal way. By good fortune, Arnulfo made his move just during the time that Bishop Cale was in Rome for a private conference with his Roman brothers. He had been of help in developing the hefty arguments they knew they would need to head off the "papal teetering" this time. But they honestly had not counted on so forceful a show of temper.

"Holiness." Sugnini ventured a toe into the hot water as he bent down to retrieve the photographs. "For all the deficiencies in the performance of my duties, I do apologize and beg Your Holiness' pardon. The abuses have to go. No doubt about it.

"There is, however, this to be said about some of these changes. Your Holiness has made such headway, created such an expectation of change everywhere, especially among our Protestant brothers of High Church. If we disappoint that expectation now, it would be very counterproductive, Holiness."

"But they cannot expect Us to renounce Our own ways—the Mass itself!—to please them, Monsignore."

"If I may, Holiness." Levesque felt he might be of some help in this impasse. "Of course, Your Holiness cannot change the *essential* things. But the exterior trappings—the Latin, the—"

"Eminence, We remind you again that the Council declared that Latin should be preserved. It ensures that the Mass is universal in both practice and meaning. The bishops said as much. And it is traditional. Latin has been the language of the Church from the very beginning."

"Just the point I was going to make, Holiness." Sugnini saw an opportunity here. "For it is precisely because Latin has been the language of the Church that we face a very delicate problem. Many of our Protestant brothers believe as we believe, in the main. But who in the modern world understands a blood sacrifice? *We* do, of course, Holy Father. But my point is that we can *accommodate* our belief, our meaning, in different words. Words not so tinged with Romanism. We can believe, if you will pardon the expression, Holiness, without shoving it down the throats, as the Americans say, of those who are interested in drawing closer to us.

"Now, Your Holiness and His Eminence have both mentioned Latin. And I have just mentioned 'sacrifice.' Both of those things are redolent of times past. If we can make certain alterations, then Cardinal Levesque and I have reason to believe that the Anglican bishops will see reunion with Rome within finger's-length!"

It was true; anyway, it might be. In any case, Bishop Cale had come to Rome to negotiate that very possibility, and to make a considerable donation to the poor, when Arnulfo's report was delivered to Levesque. Cale had confided to the cardinal secretary and to Sugnini that the confidential consensus of all Anglican bishops participating in the Lambeth Conference was now optimistic about reunion with Rome. That, in fact, the miracle would ensue if the Holy Father adapted the Mass so that any well-meaning Protestant could sincerely accept and participate in it.

What was needed was a ceremonial that had room in it for Catholics and Protestants, each to believe and worship as they wished, at one and the same celebration.

"For instance, Eminence . . ." Cale had obliged with some examples. "Instead of 'sacrifice,' you might use that very good word 'celebration.' Or perhaps 'spiritual sacrifice.' You might speak of 'the bread of life' and not 'the body of Christ'! Perhaps 'spiritual drink' would be appropriate for 'the blood of Christ.' "

It was that very litany of suggestions that Monsignore Sugnini laid before His Holiness now. "It can be clear what the Church teaches, Holy Father. But can we not see ourselves as 'ministers of the Word'—the Word made flesh, of course—as easily as we see ourselves as 'priests of sacrifice'?"

The very fact that Papa Da Brescia was silent, was listening, meant that Sugnini was making headway. The Pontiff was firming up again on the right side of the question of the Mass. The monsignore felt it was time for a little more help from Levesque, and told His Eminence so with a look.

The cardinal obliged. "We are so close to achieving Your Holiness' vision of integral humanism, so close to speaking with the accents of men of our age, so close to showing all men we are human in the very same way they are, Holiness, that it would be a tragedy to tremble and pause now!"

How clever of Levesque, Sugnini thought. An element of counterpoint. A warning.

"A tragedy, Holiness." The monsignore took it up. "And one by which we might incur certain ill will. Your Holiness knows, for example, that with permission of the Holy See, I with one other was dispensed from Church Law which forbids Catholics to join the Lodge. Our Protestant friends know this, of course. Now, the brethern would not break their oath of silence, but if we anger them, there is more than one way to skin a cat. I don't mind for myself, of course! But Your Holiness, in another time, fulfilled the same useful role for Holy Mother Church."

Da Brescia paled before their eyes. Even Levesque was afraid Sugnini had gone too far this time, papal favorite or no.

"Holy Father," he intervened as soothingly as he could. "Let us not disturb Your Holiness any further. It is just that we—the monsignore here and I—know how important true ecumenism is. We all remember the outcry when Your Holiness tried to satisfy such opinions as are held by Cardinal Arnulfo by promulgating Your Holiness' letter on contraception. Your Holiness relies on us as advisers. We would be doing Your Holiness no service if we did not mention our concern that any sudden reversal in what Cardinal Arnulfo chooses to call the 'new Masses' might have a similar effect."

"We will consider all you both have said, Eminence. Now We would like a little time before Our next appointment." Papa Da Brescia's old friend Don Guglielmo, the parish priest from Avellino, was coming for his weekly dinner. That, at least, would be enjoyable.

Senatore Ectore Pappagallo was less in Rome now since his retirement from public life. But when business or family affairs, or just nostalgia, brought him home, he still found his walks in the Borghese Gardens with the Maestro productive.

This particular walk, at least from Guido's point of view, was a fishing expedition. Too many familiar names had suddenly cropped up in Latin America, and all of them seemed to be linked, at least tenuously, to the religious revolutionary Father Jaime Herreras. That made sense from Herreras' point of view. But not from anyone else's. Pappagallo himself was not a man to do favors for nothing. If he was a source of aid in that quarter, what could Herreras possibly give him in return? And then there was the Lercani puzzle. And now Schwängler. The Maestro's hunch had paid off there. Rico had seen the photos. Domenici was the old Nazi in new surroundings.

Maybe the Maestro was jumping to conclusions, thinking there might be a link between such disparate characters and a man like Herreras, who stood foursquare against everything they lived for. Nevertheless, he reasoned again as he and the senator strolled the deserted paths, why not see what he could see?

"I do miss our walks here, Maestro." Pappagallo inhaled deeply the fragrances of summer in the Borghese.

"Indeed, Senatore. It is worth rising at such an early hour, is it not? Oh, and speaking of worth, I think you will be pleased at the AMB reports this quarter." The *impero* exercised a monopoly in the banana trade through the AMB, the government-backed regulatory board originally established by Mussolini with forty-eight concessions. It had been deftly changed from a regulatory body to a profit-making organization; and its concessions had been increased to eighty.

"How welcome that news is, Maestro." The senatore had the payment in advance. Now he would wait for the goods paid for to be named.

"Some friends of mine caught sight of Paolo Lercani in Panama. Perhaps you know Lercani, Senatore? He's made a name for himself in high-yield investments, and may have caught your eye. My nephew feels that area of the world is very fertile just now. I have been skeptical myself. That is, until I heard of Signor Lercani's interest. Tell me, Senatore. What is your opinion?"

The senatore was suspicious. Guido de la Valle needed his financial advice about as much as a dog needs fleas! So what was he asking? Latin America. Lercani. Investments. Those were the elements in Guido's question. Had he guessed at the connection, then? Pappagallo's tan paled visibly for a moment. But he recovered himself in a second; after all, he and the Maestro had shared many secrets in perfect trust over the years. There was even that time when Pappagallo had invited Guido himself into the group. . . . Of course! That was it! What couldn't they do with the Maestro as one of them!

Guido saw the subtle changes on the senator's face as he considered the question. He saw him pale a little. And he knew the very second the bait was taken.

"You remember, Maestro"—Pappagallo was once again as offhand as ever—"I once asked you if you were disposed to form closer bonds of association with some friends of mine. You had to refuse then. You haven't changed your mind, have you? Or developed a new interest in discussions?"

Bull's-eye! "Interest is certainly the word, Senatore. But there is still a difficulty in my joining."

"The Sacristy again?" Pappagallo always used that word to describe the Church.

"The Sacristy, Senatore. Some of us still regard it as necessary."

"Oh, mind you, Maestro, we understand that. We did, too, once upon a time. She was our mistress, indeed. We were her first protection against the night. We defended her. We only asked that this mistress keep us in her wonderful eyes. But she has forgotten the old times when she was alone and terrified on the darkling plain."

Guido followed every word, tucking each one into his mind. "Quite so, Senatore."

The senator's limousine was already idling as the pair reached the end of their walk. "Maestro, it is always a pleasure. Perhaps we will continue this particular conversation again."

"I will try, Ectore. You have my word. *Arrivederci!*"

When Papa Da Brescia joined Don Guglielmo in the papal dining room, he was still pensive.

"Holy Father." The old man looked at him with great concern. "There are difficulties?"

" "Yes, Don Guglielmo. Difficulties. I am now starting down a road that may lead to my Calvary."

The little parish priest was not much good at the great affairs of the papacy, but there was one sign of progress dear to Da Brescia's heart that even he could see. He went over to the window from where cranes and trucks could be clearly seen across St. Peter's Square. "Holiness, I see that the workmen are well along with the job of clearing the site for your Hall of the People. Each week I come here, they are farther along."

"Yes, yes, Don Guglielmo. It will be a masterpiece of modern architecture. A humble building. A symbol representing a fish, the *ichthus* of the catacombs."

Don Guglielmo had heard it all before; on each weekly visit, the Pontiff led him to the window and detailed the progress of the new building, and spoke with enthusiasm as he imagined in words the scenes of a whole new way of electing successors to the throne of Peter.

This evening, however, Papa Da Brescia did not approach the window at all. And his words of praise for the building were flat. There must be difficulties, indeed!

"Holy Father, let us chat about the various Calvaries on which my poor parishioners suffer.

"Now, take Signora Cuccia, for instance. She lost her three sons and her husband in the war. She lives in a miserable shanty on about a thousand lire a month. . . ."

At first, Papa Da Brescia only half listened as he toyed with his spoon and watched Don Guglielmo break crackers into his soup. Little by little, though, the priest's simple stories cooled the Pontiff's mind from the worries of schism and the new Masses, from the dangers in ecumenism and the threat from the Lodge.

In between loud and luscious sucking of soup and bread from his spoon, and echoing gurgles as he swallowed, the parish priest regaled the Pontiff with Signora Cuccia's miseries; and with the strange fate of a three-legged calf born to Achille Bustamente's only cow; and with the tale of the village blacksmith, whose wife ran away with a soldier who was now posted to Sardinia. . . .

Soon, Don Guglielmo had the Pope's full attention, and was answering his compassionate questions about this one's needs, that one's sufferings.

For Da Brescia, it was all like the peaceful music of the simple life; its cadences soothed his own pastor's soul, in a brief respite from the clashing war that engaged him.

[47]

Once every autumn, according to an ancient Roman legend, at a certain midnight when all the city was abed, the gods sent Hermes to swoop down in swift and soundless flight over the very rooftops, to scatter strange and troubling dreams of the future into the heads of the slumbering populace. Nobody ever remembered those dreams in details, the ancient Romans said; but when they awoke, many were filled with foreboding and "Hermes has visited you!" was the reproach to anyone in a black mood.

In the Roman autumn of 1967, the Vatican of Papa Da Brescia seemed to many to be just coming into its own, accelerating its activity that promised such tremendous changes in organization, and a long and glorious future for the renewed Church. But there were an increasing number, in places high and low in the Eternal City, who felt they had had troubling and unremembered dreams about the future. Though they didn't speak, people became apprehensive and jittery. They sensed they were in a lull before a storm. No one could pinpoint what general calamity he feared, or what might bring it on. And yet the strange mood began to spread, to permeate the social life of Rome, and to color the political scene.

Immediately after his "fishing expedition" with Senatore Pappagallo in the Borghese Gardens, the Maestro prepared a detailed—indeed, a very nearly verbatim—summary of the conversation for analysis by Brandolini and Security Two. Guido was still looking for the elusive link that would make some sense of the association that now seemed certain between such disparate interests as were represented by Herreras, Lercani, Schwängler, and the senatore.

It took some weeks, but not surprisingly, it was Brandolini who came up with a working theory. "Everything in God's world has an orderly explanation," he was fond of saying. His theories—even his most outlandish ones—very often led to just such explanations, at least in intelligence matters affecting the Holy See.

"The trouble is," Brandolini said to this July meeting of Security Two, "every theory in this case leads to more questions than explanations."

"Why don't you give us what you have, Giulio?" Cardinal Falconieri's suggestion was seconded by the Maestro, Helmut, and Rico.

"Gian." Brandolini turned to Monsignore Solaccio, who was standing behind him. "Is Cardinal Lanser coming along?"

"No, Excellency. He is not feeling well, and the Pontiff is pressuring him to finish some writing he is doing."

Guido looked a bit dismayed, but Rico was concerned. Lanser seemed to be faltering lately, seemed less sure in his judgments and reluctant to supply that touch of competent analysis that had always been so characteristic of him.

"This matter is too important to wait until His Eminence feels better," the Maestro directed. "We can fill him in later, if need be."

"Bene!" Brandolini rose from his desk and went to the blackboard that hung on the long wall of his office. "Let's begin with what we know." He drew a large tracing—a sort of Gothic arch—with a squeaky piece of chalk that set everyone's teeth on edge. "Rico's information from Riga led us to the one name—Herreras—that has so far tied together several more: Lercani, Pappagallo, and Schwängler."

He scratched the names of all four men near the base of the arch.

"Now, we've agreed that these men, though associated with one another, cannot have the same ultimate aims or goals. Nothing logical binds them together on any long-range basis.

"Nevertheless, we have reasonable evidence—and it should now be a simple matter to get more—that the association exists.

"We have all read the Maestro's summary of his recent conversation with Senatore Pappagallo. One of the most interesting things about it is the senatore's immediate association between the Maestro's question concerning Lercani and Latin American investments, and what he called his "friends," some organized group with which he has ties. His closest known ties are to high levels in the Italian government and to the Lodge. But whatever the exact nature of the group he referred to, the important point for the moment is that his name here"—Brandolini pointed to the senatore's name chalked at the base of the arch—"is linked to a group." He drew a line upward to connect Pappagallo's name to a square he traced at the middle of the arch.

"In my theory," he went on, "I have taken what we can see by the evidence one step further; and the implications are extraordinary.

"Suppose *each* name we know down here at the base of the arch stands for some organized group of related interests, just as the senatore's does.

"Let's begin with Lercani. That name logically links up with capitalist interests—both underworld and legitimate—in Italy, Europe, and Latin America." Brandolini drew a second line, and linked it to a square representing Lercani's "business" interests.

"The name Herreras links up with anti-capitalist interests—with Moscow and the fascism of the Left." Again, Brandolini drew a line and a square, above Herreras' name.

"The name Schwängler, or Domenici, as he calls himself now, links up with the Nazis and fascism of the Right." A fourth line, to a fourth square. "In fact, we now know that the two men you saw with Schwängler and Herreras in Cuernavaca, Rico—the ones who call themselves Martola and Juan Cepeda—are two more of the twelve Nazis who were given passage to Latin America when you were at the Raphael. The others are probably somewhere in Schwängler's square of interests too.

"Indeed, it's probable that there are interests we can't yet identify who belong at this middle level of the arch. Other 'associates,' in other words, who are also involved in this insanity of destabilization."

Brandolini turned from the blackboard. "What I am suggesting, my friends, is the existence of some large special organization of interest groups"—Brandolini turned back and traced a sweeping oval to encompass all four squares at the middle of the arch—"that spans at least two continents: Europe, including Italy; and Latin America. It may reach further, of course. We all remember, I'm sure, that directive from General Control for Herreras to penetrate the clergy and religious in the United States. Has he done so? Perhaps. If he has, does that spread this network of interest groups into a third continent: North America? Again, perhaps.

"One problem for us is that we can't yet identify the undivided members of these middle-level interest groups, and we can't assume what I call 'wholesale membership.' We can't assume, for example, that *all* high-level members of the Italian government, or *all* members of the Italian Lodge, would be part of Pappagallo's interest group.

"The same goes for Lercani. We can't assume that every major business interest or every crime boss is involved.

"And so, too, for Herreras. His name, in fact, has a greater number of contradictory links than the other three. In fact, as I've said, it was the emergence of his name in Rico's intelligence from Riga that led us to Lercani and Schwängler; and, through Schwängler, to Pappagallo. But we can't assume, to take another of his obvious links, that every Jesuit is involved. Or the Northern Alliance."

Brandolini paused in his explanations. "Is everyone with me to this point?" He looked at each man in the room.

"It seems a little—er—extraordinary, to use your word, Giulio." Helmut's criticism was polite. "But it's simple enough. Your little diagram of squares encompassed by a circle essentially represents an international network of influential and highly placed people. But that leaves your first question. What could possibly hold such disparate groups together for any length of time; or even make them cooperate at all?"

"Precisely, Signor Helmut!" Brandolini nearly pounced. "That is what I have been asking myself ever since the Maestro's recent conversation with Pappagallo started my mind working on this theory. In fact, I have been asking myself two related questions.

"First, what could hold such disparate groups together? The answer, obviously, is a common goal.

"Now, the only common *effect* of all the groups that we've observed so far—the only pattern—is that common threat of insanity, of breakdown in authority. In the Church, which is primarily why we are concerned. And through Herreras, who is a priest of the Church, in governments in Latin America.

"But, as we said before, that pattern is a negative thing. It's not a positive goal in itself. It implies the sweeping away of some obstacle, of something that stands in the way. In other words, it is only an interim goal, if you will; a means of reaching a farther goal."

"Herreras has a goal," Rico reminded them all. "Could that be it?"

"No." Brandolini was emphatic. "The Nazis wouldn't back that line, for itself, on a long-term basis. Neither would the Lodge or the capitalists. No, Herreras is a user, like Lercani. He sees himself as using the others for his own ends. Just as they see themselves as using him."

"What then?" The Maestro leaned forward, studying Brandolini's chalked sketch of the arch on the blackboard.

"Suppose for a minute"—Brandolini turned back to the board—"that there is yet another group." He traced a final square, placing it at the apex of the arch. "The keystone of the arch, if you will. And suppose that it has superior lines of influence that reach to all the other squares of interest." He drew four lines downward from the keystone to the squares at the center of the arch.

"Once those superior lines are in place, linking all the disparate groups to one source of influence, order can be maintained. Strings can be pulled." He retraced the lines from the keystone square to emphasize the point graphically. "Whatever is the aim of that keystone interest, that is the aim all the others serve, whether they know it or not.

"But if you remove that keystone, the arch itself collapses, and all the other interests are buried in the rubble.

"There *must* be a keystone, in other words. Some sort of higher group with an aim that is—or will be—served by sweeping away the present systems of authority that are under attack everywhere. Otherwise nothing could maintain any sort of order or cohesive activity among these disparate middle-level interests."

"*What* aim, Giulio?" Helmut was still highly doubtful. "And what group? Who would be so powerful as to have what you call 'superior lines of influence' to all the others?"

Brandolini pondered the arch for a time before he replied. In all candor, he could not answer Helmut's question. "I have not yet been able to dig out information pointing to any known group whose interests would be served across the board by the activities we have been observing.

"And yet, not only do I agree, Signor Helmut, that identifying such a group is a problem. Because that group, if it exists, is the keystone that supports the elements in a cohesive whole, it is *the* problem of first importance. P–1, I call it, for Problem Number One." Brandolini scrawled a large "P–1" inside the keystone square.

"It may be that if we can identify more members of the middle-level interest groups"—Brandolini turned his attention back to the squares at the middle of the arch—"we will find more leads to P–1.

"In any case, the identities of the members of this middle-level group are obviously of great practical importance to us in themselves. As I have called the identity of the keystone Problem One, or P–1 for short, I have in my own mind dubbed this middle level as Problem Number Two. P–2." He scrawled the shorthand identification in the circle that bound all the middle-level elements together.

The Maestro, who had been unusually quiet through Brandolini's explanation of his theory, now had a few suggestions to make. "About P–2 in particular, Giulio."

Helmut looked at his uncle, obviously surprised that he was taking this sweeping P–1/P–2 theory so seriously.

Guido seemed not to notice, at least for the moment. "If your theory holds up, Giulio, our special concern has to be how far P–2 has penetrated the Church. We already know about Herreras in Latin America. And we know, as you say, that he had instructions from General Control to make contact with North American clergy and religious.

"My guess would be that the inner structures of the Vatican itself are 'moled' directly. In anything as sweeping as this, we would be a central target. It's a hard thing to pin down, though, just as you pointed out in your explanation. Take Demarchelier. We know he was the leak who caused Rico such trouble. But that doesn't automatically mean he's P–2. He might unwittingly be playing into someone else's hand, the way the Northern Alliance has played into Herreras' hand."

"Members or not"—Solaccio spoke as security chief of the group—"the used can be as damaging as the users. That's the most diabolical thing about this P–1/P–2 theory. It is a planned system of users and used. Every resource of Security Two must be utilized by us to track down much more closely the hidden identities involved here."

Rico shook his head and stood up, his face a picture of confusion and near-revolt. "It's too complicated and diabolical even for me, and I deal in terrible and clandestine things all the time! Are we all going to have to walk around wondering whom we can trust, even in the Vatican!"

Cardinal Falconieri looked up in some surprise at Rico's outburst. "What would be so unusual about that, my friend? We're already walking on eggs when we talk to half the papal office."

The remark was like the cold water of realization. It left everyone speechless.

Helmut followed the Maestro to his office. How, he wanted to know, could his uncle take Brandolini's theories so seriously?

"P–2, maybe!" Helmut walked up and down in front of Guido's desk. "At least we know there *are* the Lercanis and the Herrerases of this world. And Pappagallo pretty well established his tie to Lercani in your meeting with him. But P–1? That seems a little farfetched to me. And I noticed you only commented on P–2. So you don't buy P–1, either, am I right?"

Guido seemed not to want to answer Helmut's question, because he replied to it with an apparently unrelated request. "I want you to do something you've probably done several times since you took your Oath as Keeper-designate. Reread that part of your red notebook that shows the signers and the guarantor witnesses of the Bargain. Not our side. The other side."

Puzzled, and feeling a little put off by his uncle, Helmut nevertheless took his red book from an inner pocket of his jacket. He opened it to the proper page. His eye fell first on the huge sweep of his great-grandfather's signature; but his uncle had said, "Not our side."

The second signature, then: Minister Cesare Sella's, written in a tidy little stylized hand, all the Gothic-script letters in a neat row like monitors of a meticulous but rather unadorned mind. Below the minister's name, in the lower-left-hand corner of the page there were four sets of hand-printed initials, bracketed together beside a legend in Latin. Those were the initials of the guarantor witnesses for the "other side," as Guido had said.

"Beside those initials?" the Maestro prompted as he watched his nephew study each element of the page. "Read the legend there."

" 'For the Universal Assembly.' " Helmut read it aloud. It seemed clear. The Bargain was witnessed on behalf of, and guaranteed by, all of the Italian branches of the Lodge.

Guido shook his head gently. "Not quite. No assembly of Italian brethren alone, however many branches they might represent, could authorize or guarantee a bargain that enabled us to operate and cooperate worldwide. The word 'Universal' in that legend means just that: the guarantee of the Bargain on a worldwide basis. Almost since the time the money and trade systems of Europe extended to cover America and Asia as well, there has in fact been a universal assembly of sorts."

"And the Bargain—our Bargain—is with them?"

"Yes."

Helmut wasn't certain if he was surprised or not. Perhaps he had half guessed. Hadn't doors opened for him more easily than he might have expected—particularly these last few years as he transferred such vast funds with so little difficulty? "But, Uncle, why was it a secret—from me, I mean? I've taken the Oath!"

"It wasn't a secret from you. But neither was there any reason to lay it out to you in detail just yet. None of us ever knows the full truth beforehand, at the beginning."

"But suppose something had happened to you, Uncle? Who would have told me?"

"There is a cipher message among the papers that will be yours on my death. And if something should happen to you, those same papers and that same message will be given to Eugenio."

Helmut let his mind take it all in for a while in silence. Finally, as piece after piece fell into place for him, he had a dawning understanding of his uncle's interest in the P–1/P–2 theory.

"Does Brandolini know? The full truth about the Bargain, I mean?"

"No. His analysis is all the more intelligent for that. He hovers near the truth. His theory may turn out to be right or wrong. But if there is a P–1, the other side in our Bargain is one group—the only one I am aware of—that can field enough power on a worldwide scope to exercise the kind of control Brandolini was talking about."

Helmut still wasn't satisfied. In Brandolini's theory, the Church and the Vatican itself figured as important targets for what he called the "insanity of destabilization." But didn't the Bargain preclude that, by establishing cooperation between the Church, in the person of the Keeper, and the Universal Assembly? "My Oath, in fact," Helmut argued, "binds me to the Bargain, as it does you, only 'for the exaltation of Holy Mother

Church, the defense of the papacy, and the salvation of all men and women.' Those are the very words I swore before the Sacrament."

"Let's see." Guido reached into one of the drawers of his desk and pulled out a folder containing the summary he had prepared after his conversation with Pappagallo. "What I began to think about, as Brandolini was positing the existence of a P–1 group, was the little speech the senatore made about 'the Sacristy'—the Church, in other words." He found the passage in the transcript. "He said that his group had been the Church's 'first protection against the night.' That they only asked that the Church keep them 'in her wonderful eyes.' That's their language for conferring a special status on someone. 'But she has forgotten the old times.' The times, in other words, when his group came to our assistance, to the Church's assistance in the past. I wonder was he thinking of where Church and business and Mafia and Lodge all joined together at some juncture in past history—as they did in Sicily after World War II? The implication, however, is negative. That *we* have *forgotten*—the cooperative trust. 'We defended her,' Pappagallo said. Past tense.

"All that could be a reflection on those 'superior lines of influence' Brandolini traced from the keystone of his arch, P–1, down to Pappagallo's interest group, which presumably includes some members of the Italian Lodge.

"If that's the case, and if our partner in the Bargain turns out to be Brandolini's P–1, then that means the Universal Assembly has begun to push its advantage. Nothing in the Bargain precludes that."

"Does it have meetings, this Assembly, Uncle? Can you get to them and ask some questions?"

Guido nodded pensively. "It meets. Once every twenty-eight years. The next meeting isn't until 1978. A lot of water will flow under the bridge before then. As Brandolini and Solaccio said, we will have to concentrate for now on P–2."

When Rico reached the Brazilian College out on Via Aurelia, he found Cardinal Lanser in his rooms, making the final revisions in the book he was writing on the subject of ecumenism. "It will please nobody, Rico." Lanser left his desk and moved to a more comfortable chair to visit awhile with the American. "Arnulfo has already read the manuscript and told me it is 'the finest bit of ecclesiastical waffling in modern time.'

"Of course, I sometimes think that Arnulfo considers himself the only appointed residue of the true faith! Nevertheless, he is not alone in his criticism, and he's more charitable than some.

"A lot of others think I've gone too far down the road of cooperation with Papa Da Brescia's ecumenists. Even the State Council is divided now.

"But you can be sure that when the rabid ecumenists read this book, they will say I have betrayed them because I will not relent on the questions of primacy and absolute authority for the Roman Pontiff."

The Jesuit cardinal looked very old and very tired. "No matter what I say or do," he sighed, "neither extreme will be happy."

Rico knew Lanser had already suffered bitter attacks over the Document on Religious Liberty. He had not been able to reconcile accepted Church doctrine with the idea of complete freedom of choice in religion. There was no way to say everyone is right—Jew, Muslim, Catholic, Episcopalian, Anglican—without implying that everyone is wrong; that no one has the truth; that Catholicism itself is false and should be shucked off.

In the same vein, the Jewish section of that Religious Liberty document had brought special brickbats flying at Cardinal Lanser's head. The traditionalists regarded it as another piece of blasphemy flowing from his pen. Many prominent Jews spat upon it. One Jewish world leader had gone so far as to say, "I stamp upon this piece of nonsense." Others—Catholics, Protestants, and Jews—exaggerated its meaning.

"This book on ecumenism will be no different," Lanser said without bitterness, looking over at the pile of finished pages on his desk.

But why do it, then? Why go on with it? Rico was almost tempted to ask those questions; but he didn't. For one thing, he knew they would only cause more pain to this man who was already suffering so much. And for another, he knew the answer: Cardinal Lanser was doing the will of his Pope to the farthest degree he could without betraying the essential teachings of the Church.

Rico remembered Father Jaime Herreras' remark that a Jesuit is a man of obedience. He should know, this Jesuit cardinal, Rico thought to himself.

"But forgive me, Rico!" Lanser brought himself around from his dour anticipation of more criticism of his work. "I haven't seen you since I heard of your father's death in the spring. I have said several Masses for him. I wanted you to know. I realize how close you and he were. A son's love for his father is irreplaceable."

The recent memories flooded back upon Lansing. The news of Basil's stroke; the scramble for the flight from Panama to Chicago; the vigil by his father's bed as the old man lay in coma. Even at his mother's death, Rico had not suffered as much. Somehow, looking at his father's still form, he had the sense that Basil had lost a struggle. He could never again square with him, shoulder to shoulder, into the harsh winds that shrieked around the Loop where they used to walk. His father's last battle had been nobly fought. But it had been lost. Never again would Rico know that unbroken and innocent love, taken from him now by the crude intrusion of alien Death.

"You know, Rico," Lanser said after the younger man had shared some of those thoughts with him, "only Christ consoles. I often think back to what Papa Angelica used to say about Vatican II when he saw it was all going wrong. Remember? 'It was never mine,' he said. 'It always belonged to Christ, and he will use it in the end for his own purpose.'

"That's true of everything, Rico. Your suffering, and your father's, and mine, and the suffering of the whole Church and of the whole world.

And the joys and the triumphs too. Though we haven't seen much of either in latter days."

Lanser's little added complaint brought a smile to Rico's face; but then it made him think of that morning's meeting and Archbishop Brandolini's worrisome speculations. He brought Lanser up to date, laying out the P–1/P–2 theory for him briefly.

The cardinal shook his head in wonderment. But even that, he said, even such a diabolical plan as Brandolini suggested, would serve Christ's purpose in the end. "He uses everything, Rico."

"Yes. But he also judges, Eminence."

[48]

When Cardinal Secretary Jean Levesque read the confidential October report from Papa Da Brescia's representative in Washington, Archbishop Marcel Jobert, he drew his breath in sharply.

The subject was the undeclared war in Vietnam between the armed forces of the United States and the invading North Vietnamese.

> One more mighty punch from the Americans, and Hanoi is finished. Roads, harbors, railways, energy, food supplies—all vital areas in North Vietnam—are almost paralyzed. The Americans have succeeded in interdicting all movement. The guerrillas in the south are helpless.
>
> It is from the highest source that we learn the following: The U.S. Military High Command based in Cam Ranh Bay, South Vietnam, have sent to the American President their plans for that one final and mighty punch. They hope to get his approval very quickly, and to deliver the knockout blow before the end of this year.
>
> Obviously, as Your Eminence will see, the spiritual mission of the Holy Father is involved in this situation, since His Holiness' foreign policy is hinged on the cessation of all economic imperialism by capitalist countries and the independence of small struggling countries like Vietnam.
>
> Your Eminence will do what is necessary. . . .

Levesque's hand went to the buzzer. Immediately Demarchelier came in.

"Ask the Holy Father if I may see him immediately. Make two copies of this report first. Put one copy into an unmarked envelope. Call Signor Lercani and ask him to send a messenger over here—someone he trusts—to pick up that envelope. Hurry, now!"

By comparison with the mood around Rome that fall of 1967, Rico Lansing expected Warsaw—or at least his time there with Cardinal Wallensky and Archbishop Valeska—to be a relative sea of harmony. The expectation was not fulfilled. Hermes had been there too.

The work of merging his network with the "blue card" organization was progressing quite well. But when Rico briefed his two friends under the seal of secrecy about Brandolini's theory of P–1 and P–2, Cardinal Wallensky matched it with a bit of news of his own.

"Rico." The cardinal's gimlet eyes bored into him. "Do you remember Pelse's note to you some time back that 'others' were going to establish a different sort of educational system than the one you are setting up here?"

Rico remembered, of course.

"Well," Wallensky continued, "a new organization has very recently come to light in Poland. KOR, it's called. The initials stand for *Komitet Obrany Robotnikow*—Committee for the Defense of the Workers. Its principal leaders are Viktor Adamchik and Jaček Kuron, two ardent and well-known Trotskyites. Communists, in other words. This KOR of theirs has begun holding lectures, seminars, poetry readings. They even hold exams and publish underground literature. In other words, they've begun doing exactly what you're doing. And they've attracted some of the younger clergy.

"I think they're trouble. They certainly bear careful watching, and our people should be warned against cooperating with them, or revealing anything of our organizations to them."

Valeska disagreed. In fact, he said, he was impressed with KOR. He openly embraced Jaček Kuron and Viktor Adamchik. "They're Poles before they're Communists—Catholic Poles!" Bogdan was emphatic in his defense. "The Trotskyites hate Moscow as much as we do."

"They don't just hate Moscow, Bogdan." Wallensky was just as emphatic. "They hate government. Period. Any government."

"Not Kuron and Adamchik. Anyway, they can serve our cause. We can keep them in line."

"What you're saying, Bogdan," Wallensky countered, "is that any stick is good enough to beat a dog with, if you want to beat him?"

"No." Valeska didn't want to be that blunt. "It's just that you think KOR is a Trojan horse, Eminence. I think it's in the spirit of Vatican II to embrace old enemies." The archbishop wasn't rationalizing. He had great trust in men, and he was sincere in his argument.

But that was the clincher for Wallensky. "I will be moldering in dust the day you find out how wrong you are, Bogdan. And as for your Vatican II, it sounded the death knell for the Church of Gregory the Great and Pius X." Both of these popes stood out as heroes for Wallensky.

When Rico was finally able to wedge his way into the hot discussion, it was to ask a question. He knew from experience that it cost money to develop an organization such as KOR. And from the sound of things, they were going faster than Rico had. Surely Moscow wasn't funding them. But who, then?

Wallensky and Valeska thought the KOR backing came from the West. From Europe. But more than that they had no way of knowing. "Your people are better positioned to find that out than we are," Bogdan pointed out.

It was a question Rico would bring up with Helmut. And with Security Two. Meanwhile, for his part, he said, he wanted nothing to do with KOR. "Count me out of any cooperative effort with them, Bogdan." He spoke brusquely. "I'm not going to risk the lives of my people, and all the years of work they've done, on some romantic theory that Trotskyites are more lovable than Stalinists!"

Reflecting later on the sharp difference between Valeska's attitude to KOR compared with Wallensky's and his own, Rico couldn't help but feel a shadow had fallen between them. They were still warm friends; but their almost perfect unanimity had broken. Another pillar of support was knocked away from his life.

The slow process by which the fascination and problems of power take possession of the soul seem as innocent as, say, a neighbor riding by to report a fallen boundary marker in the woods. But soon the visitor is in the best guest room, clamoring loudly for service; and within a few years' time, the interloper has become the proprietor and master of the house.

Once the heat and resolve of Helmut's emotions had died down in the disappointment that followed his useless call from Panama to Villa Cerulea, the metallic grid of his ordinary life descended again on his days.

It was not that his desire to bridge the distance that had grown between himself and Keti evaporated altogether. In fact, it was he who suggested they join Ari Potamianos on his yacht for a six-week cruise of the Greek islands. But when the day came to board the flight for Candia, the main port of Crete, and to board the yacht that lay waiting at anchor for them between the tall cliffs of Suda Bay, Helmut was caught up again in Vatican affairs.

"Why don't you take Eugenio, *carissima,*" he suggested to a deeply disappointed Keti, "and go on ahead? It will be a wonderful vacation for both of you, and I'll join you as soon as I can."

When he did join them at last, five of the six weeks had already flown by, and still another level of secrecy had been dropped over his life by his conversation with Guido after the Security Two meeting.

In many ways, however, that sixth week was an idyll for Keti. Helmut was warmer in his manner than he had been in a long while, and freer in some way too—very much with her and Eugenio. Yet she knew something else had happened to him. He smothered her with attention, and wanted to know everything that had happened since the vacation began. But there was not the slightest crack in the invisible shell that encased the inner man. Only through the wordless language of touch—when he held her hand or caressed her hair, when he curved his arm about her waist as they strolled on deck or lay beside her at night—did she know the one most important thing: she was still his precious and cherished wife. Nevertheless, there was always a second thread in that wordless conversation. Bear with me as I am, that voiceless message from Helmut ran. Nothing will ever separate us. This is the only way I can cope.

If that week was an idyll for Keti, for Eugenio it was a little visit to heaven's gate. He was together with the two people he loved most in the world, and with them he was actually seeing all the islands, from Athens to Crete, along which the great giant in Uncle Guido's stories had jumped so easily.

Excitedly he told his father about all the places he had seen already. About Patmos with its monastery of St. John, "and the grotto, Papa"—his eyes were alight with that blue de la Valle fire—"where the Apostle actually sat and wrote the book of Revelations!" He told about the old man on the island of Zákinthos who tried to teach him the bouzouki, and regaled Helmut with interminable descriptions of bathing off the island of Sífnos, diving for seashells, and climbing up the mountain at early dawn in order to visit the Chapel of St. Nicholas. He knew the names of all the islands by heart, and wanted Helmut to build him a small flat-roofed, whitewashed house by the sea "where we can fish for ever and ever."

In earlier years, when Eugenio was seven or eight, he would have spun reams of imaginary tales of a life for all of them here in these islands that floated like magic mounds of earth between blue sky and blue sea. But now, Helmut saw, at the age of eleven, Eugenio was almost ready to leave that special world he had always been able to create for himself, and re-created for anyone who would listen to the lightsome weaving of his child's imagination. And yet that grace and innocence that seemed his special treasures remained pristine in the boy.

What would it be like, Helmut wondered, that day when he would have to tell his son about the Bargain; would have to go with him to the Sancta Sanctorum one Christmas Eve and administer the Oath that would drop its veil of secrecy so lightly but so finally around his inner world?

Cardinal Secretary Levesque could hear the shouting the moment he stepped out of the palace elevator the morning of that first Monday in November. He followed the sound to Monsignore Demarchelier's office.

"I must see the Holy Father!" someone was railing at poor Demarchelier. "Right away! I must have action at the highest level! There is no time to be lost!"

Levesque stepped into his aide's office to find a weary-faced Demarchelier trying to placate the Cardinal Archbishop of Hanoi. Cardinal Tran Anh Ngoc was in high dudgeon and, the moment he caught sight of Levesque, turned his full energies loose on the secretary of state.

"Eminence, I have flown directly from Hanoi to Rome on the most urgent business! This minion"—he turned his back on Demarchelier—"has kept me waiting too long already!" The Vietnamese cardinal had long since found that the best way to get through the layers of protection that surrounded the Pope was to scream his way past them, one by one.

"But of course, Your Eminence." Levesque gave a reassuring nod to Demarchelier and led the Vietnamese prelate into his own office. At once, he called Papa Da Brescia's secretary.

"*Dica,* Giorgio," Levesque said familiarly. "I am sitting here with His Eminence the Cardinal Archibishop of Hanoi."

"*Sì, sì,* Eminence. I know all about it. Demarchelier called earlier. Have you got earplugs?"

They gathered in the papal study to wait for His Holiness. The Cardinal Archbishop of Hanoi had brought his coadjutor bishop, Trinh Quoc Nga. Levesque was there, of course; and, pro forma, he had summoned three members of the Council of State—Falconieri, Ferragamo-Duca, and Lanser.

When the Pope arrived, announced grandly by Delucchi, he was all smiles and graciousness.

"We are honored to see Your Eminence's face," he told the Vietnamese cardinal. And to the others, "Let us all sit down and talk these matters over quietly with our Venerable Brother from Hanoi."

The Venerable Brother turned out to be a veritable spigot of details. He seemed to know the exact number of shells that had ever been lobbed so murderously into Hanoi, Haiphong, and other North Vietnamese cities. The exact number of air raids that had ever taken place. The exact number of dead and wounded; of houses destroyed; of starving women and old men and children; of the extent of malaria, dysentery, and various other plagues; of what essential foodstuffs were lacking; the number of orphans. On and on went the cardinal's litany of pain.

"The leaders of our people have made mistakes, Your Holiness." He granted the point at what seemed the right moment. "But they now realize that. And they are at this very moment in the process of drawing up concrete proposals for a just and lasting peace."

Papa Da Brescia had listened to Tran Anh Ngoc somberly, obviously deeply affected by the portrait of wholesale suffering. But when he heard that Hanoi was prepared to negotiate peace, he brightened visibly. "This, Venerable Brother, is a great and welcome piece of news!" The Pontiff spoke warmly.

"Yes, Holy Father," the Vietnamese cardinal acknowledged. "But there is another great piece of news that is not so welcome." He explained to His Holiness that the American high command in Southeast Asia had prepared their own plans—for one last, all-out blow at North Vietnam. At this very hour, in fact, those plans were on their way to Washington for approval by the American Chief Executive, the President. "This miraculous chance for negotiated peace will be lost, Holiness. If the Americans deliver that blow, thousands of women and children and old people will be burned in their beds. And to what purpose, I ask Your Holiness, when peace can be had by peaceful means?"

Papa Da Brescia had been moved almost to tears. "What can We do, Venerable Brother?"

"Holy Father, the President of the United States will listen to Your Holiness. Ask him to postpone this last offensive. Give my people a chance to live, and their leaders a chance to complete their peace plans."

The Pontiff looked at his secretary of state. "How do you rate the situation, Your Eminence?"

"Just as our Venerable Brother describes it," Levesque responded. "The situation is lost for the North. There is no reason for the Americans to deliver their graceless coup de grace."

"So the war is won?"

"Without a doubt, Holy Father."

"There is therefore no possibility the North Vietnamese could recover in a period of peace and thus continue the carnage of war?"

"None, Holiness," Levesque and Tran Anh Ngoc answered almost in unison.

Papa Da Brescia turned to the three State Council members. "What do Your Eminences think?"

It was clear from their faces that, despite the growing divisions within the Council of State, on this issue all three members present, Falconieri, Ferragamo-Duca, and Lanser, were opposed to any papal intervention.

Ferragamo-Duca spoke for them. "This has been an American war from the beginning, Holy Father. With respect, Your Holiness' queries about the possible recovery of Hanoi, and about the American victory, are both pointless from the Holy See's vantage. Rome's interests are not affected one way or the other by this war. We do not belong in it."

It was also clear from their faces that the Council members knew, when it came down to a choice between their view and Levesque's, Papa Da Brescia would rely more heavily on Levesque.

"Your Eminence." The Pontiff turned his attention to the cardinal from Hanoi. "We think, in spite of these negative opinions, that Your Eminence should have your wish."

Turning to Levesque, then: "Your Eminence, you will draft a cable for Our approval to be sent to Our Apostolic Delegation on Pennsylvania Avenue. You will say that We ask the President to give the North Vietnamese a breathing space of, say, two months, during which We are sure that the North Vietnamese will sue for peace.

"Will that be satisfactory, in Your Eminence's opinion?" De Brescia turned back to the Vietnamese.

"Satisfactory, Holiness," he confirmed.

After Monsignore Delucchi had ushered the rest of the visitors from the papal study, Papa Da Brescia had but one further question to ask Cardinal Levesque.

"How, Eminence, do you suppose the North Vietnamese knew the American plans? We knew from Pennsylvania Avenue. But how did they?"

"North Vietnamese intelligence must have penetrated the GHQ at Cam Ranh Bay, Holiness."

"Yes. It's the only answer."

After Christmas Mass at midnight in the village chapel, the de la Valles and Rico Lansing returned to Villa Cerulea. It was the first Christmas Eugenio had been allowed to stay up with all the others, and it was he who decided they should all open their gifts before their late-night supper. He knew his Nanno had something special for him, he whispered to Keti; he didn't think he could wait through a whole long dinner to find out what it was.

So they all gathered around the crêche in the Great Hall while a log fire crackled in the fireplace. They laughed and chattered and ooohed and aaahed as boxes were opened and surprises revealed. A pair of coral earrings set in gold for Keti. A ruby brooch for Agathi. A suede leather tie case for Helmut. A golden chalice was a special surprise for Rico from them all. There were books and games and clothes for Eugenio, but . . .

There was a blank look on the boy's face for a moment when he realized there was no gift from Nanno after all, and that his granduncle had disappeared in all the hubbub.

Manfully, he swallowed his disappointment and squatted down on the floor by Keti to help her open the rest of her gifts. "Eugenio," she whispered, "where do you suppose Nanno went?"

He turned an embarrassed face to her and was about to whisper back when he realized she was looking over his head to the stairway.

He turned to follow her glance, and saw his Nanno just coming to the last steps, the most beautiful smile on his face, his eyes beckoning. He had a cushion crooked in one arm, and at first that was all Eugenio could see. The boy got up from his mother's side, all curiosity now; and that was when he caught first sight of her.

Nestled at the center of the cushion under Nanno's free hand was a wheat-colored bundle of a puppy, with little black ears and a black tail. It was no bigger than Guido's hand, and couldn't have weighed much more than two pounds.

"Nanno!" Eugenio was so surprised he could say nothing more.

Guido came forward, lowering the cushion to the boy's level. "Eugenio, this is Tatiana. Tati, she's called. She's a little girl."

Eugenio had never seen anything so minutely and adorably alive. The tiny dog, her head resting on her forepaws, trembled under Guido's gentle hand, and didn't budge until her two black eyes fastened on Eugenio. She raised her head off the cushion then and gave a tentative wag or two of her tail.

"Take her in your hand, Eugenio. She wants to go to you." Guido held the cushion while Eugenio cupped one hand carefully around Tati's bottom and slid the other beneath her head and forepaws. He drew her gently against his chest. It was all a new wonder for him—the heat of her tiny body, the feel of her soft coat, the little sounds she made in her throat, the clean smell of her.

He felt her straining to push herself higher up, and helped her until her nose was up against his neck and she was licking him and making herself quite at home.

Agathi and Keti and Helmut and Rico all crowded round, touching Tatiana lightly, getting their fingers licked as they did, wishing Eugenio happiest Christmas, kissing him. The helpless little creature nestled against her new master made them all want to protect and soothe and cherish her, make her feel safe and at home.

"Tati has come over ninety miles by car to be with us, Eugenio." The Maestro felt the puppy's pink tongue flick against his finger. "She's a pedigreed cairn terrier. She'll run like the wind with you. They're great hunters too. They were bred to ferret out weasels and such from the cairns of Scotland. That's where they get their name."

"Nanno!" Eugenio finally found his voice again. "I love her! She'll be yours and mine! She'll be our dog! And when you have to be away, she'll go with Mama and me to see about the sheep. And we'll chase squirrels together in the pine forest. She'll come with Doni and me when we ride our bikes, and . . ."

"Not too fast, now, *carito!*" Helmut was happy and excited for his son. "Tomorrow Nanno will tell you how to take care of Tati. She has to grow up a little before she can do all that!"

Danni Mastrangelo, the head gardener, was just carrying in a small sleeping box. He put it down by the fire and unfolded a tiny blanket that went with it. "A little gift from the wife and me, Maestro." Danni had been in on the Christmas conspiracy to fetch Tati and keep her as a special surprise for Master Eugenio.

"It's a wonderful surprise, Danni," Agathi thanked him.

"And at just the right moment too, Danni," Guido agreed. "It's been a long day for Tati, Eugenio. Why don't you put her to bed in her new sleeping box. We'll all have supper, and then you can take her to your room to sleep with you."

The Maestro fitted into the sleeping box the cushion he still held. Reluctantly, Eugenio laid Tati down and covered her with her blanket. Tati licked his hand one more time, and was fast asleep.

No sooner was everyone seated at table for the late Christmas supper and all the plates were filled with Mariella's superbly prepared feast, than Eugenio asked permission to take his heaping plate and sit by the fire beside Tati while he ate. He wanted to be sure it was all true, that Tati was really there, really his.

It was nearly two in the morning when supper was done. The grownups found Eugenio curled up by the box, as fast asleep as Tati was, his hand resting lightly on one of her paws, while the flames danced and waved at them both from the grate behind.

"May the whole world love as simply and innocently as Eugenio and Tati." Rico's voice was rich with his own affection.

"Amen," Helmut answered his friend. That hour of peace was part of their blessing from the Christmas Child. "Amen."

[49]

There were those in the Vatican during the turbulent years of Papa Da Brescia's reign who thought then and said later that, in his own soul, the Pontiff must frequently have asked himself if his papal policies were really furthering the Kingdom of Christ.

If they were right, Guido de la Valle saw no sign of it. There seemed no outward clue that the Pontiff had any sense or feeling that his Church was being impoverished or damaged; that he shared any part of Papa Profumi's outlook on good and evil in the world; or that he empathized with the simple piety of Papa Angelica.

As nearly as the Maestro could see, Papa Da Brescia's viewpoint was altogether different. Whatever it cost, however many Catholics were scandalized, no matter what disruptions it caused to traditional ways of thinking about Christ and worshiping God, the change in the Church had to be total. Its pope, its priests, its Mass, its morality, its politics, had to be integrated with the ordinary humanism current in the last third of the twentieth century. Papa Da Brescia was a structuralist through and through, and his means of effecting that change were structural.

As the Pontiff's plans matured, and as he drew still more, for the reform and remodeling of his Curia, the one area he had still not been able to touch by late February 1968 was finance. "And yet," as he said to some of his close aides from time to time, "this is the Patrimony of St. Peter; and We, to all intents and purposes, are today St. Peter."

His disastrous confrontation with the Maestro five years before over the papal effort to pack the Council of State had been a caution to him, but only that. Da Brescia had been too abrupt in his action, too direct in his approach. He would not make that mistake again.

The Maestro, for his part, was sufficiently wise and experienced to realize that Papa Da Brescia would set his sights on control of financial domains of the Vatican. It was, he knew, only a matter of time.

He was not surprised, therefore, when the Holy Father summoned him on the last day of February for a "consultation and discussion."

Guido entered the papal study prepared for what he expected would be a tough negotiating session. The Pope began with some specifics. He needed, he explained, an increment of about $1.5 million for special projects. "For Our Justice and Peace commission, for example, Maestro, and for some special missions We have in mind for later this spring."

"Yes, Holy Father." The Maestro settled back comfortably in the chair opposite His Holiness. "That will be no problem."

"Excellent." The Pontiff also appeared relaxed. "Now, as We have been reviewing Our needs, it has seemed to Us that certain reforms in the structural setup of Our financial agencies would make things less cumbersome for Us."

The Holy See, the Pope knew, had five principal financial agencies. He felt that one of the five—the one that handled such routine matters as the

Vatican payroll, Vatican police and security, sanitation, medical care, utilities, the Vatican newspaper and radio station, and sundry things of that nature—might remain untouched.

He proposed that the other four agencies, however, would operate with far greater efficiency if they were combined under a single umbrella—a kind of prefecture or administration of cardinals that would oversee economic affairs of the Holy See. "In fact, Maestro, that is the exact name We propose for the new administration: the Prefecture for Economic Affairs, or PECA, as We have begun to think of it already."

Guido saw clearly the aim of His Holiness' plan. The four agencies involved were the Office for the Special Administration of the Holy See, which administered the indemnity moneys paid by Mussolini in 1929; the Office for the Administration of the Goods of the Holy See, which administered the Holy See's normal revenues; the Institute for Religious Agencies, the IRA established by Papa Profumi in 1942—the all-important Banco, in other words; and the Administration of Vatican City State, which administered Vatican extraterritorial property, and real estate in the Vatican itself, and under whose aegis fell the funding of the Third Secretariat. Here the entire Hearts Apostolate staff, including Rico Lansing, Brandolini, Solaccio, and the signals operations, were at risk.

It seemed obvious that once the Pontiff succeeded in establishing a single group of supervisory cardinals with power over all these agencies, it would be a simple matter indeed for Papa Da Brescia to name his own cardinals to the new body. Levesque would no doubt be the first one named, Guido surmised, though not out loud. The point, however, was that the Maestro's own function in such a structure would be eliminated—probably sooner rather than later—and that the Bargain could no longer be kept.

Guido realized, of course, that the Pontiff had no very detailed understanding of which agencies were most important to the Bargain or why. Papa Da Brescia had no more idea than any normal Vatican outsider, for example, what went on in the IRA, much less that it was the Keeper's principal banking arm. The Pope was throwing a wide net into unknown waters and would likely regard whatever he came up with as a good first catch.

"Your Holiness must remember"—the Maestro was calm but categoric—"that all financial agencies as well as the organs of papal government depend ultimately on my use of the IRA. And it would be most unwise, if Your Holiness will allow me to venture a second criticism, to remove the Administration of Vatican City State from my control, close as it is to the Council of State."

Da Brescia took the point of the last remark to heart; he wanted no more direct confrontations involving the State Council. That would only be a setback. He would deal with that problem in a different manner.

The Pontiff eyed his silver-haired adversary while he considered what compromise position he might take. "Very well, Maestro," he said at length. "But We do think We should co-nominate the head of the IRA."

That papal ploy brought an interesting counterpossibility to Guido's mind. "I think we could agree on that, Holiness, provided I reserve the right of veto over the cardinals who will head PECA, Your Holiness' proposed Prefecture for Economic Affairs." He was bartering, in effect, for the right to appoint those cardinals.

Papa Da Brescia stared at the hard fire in those blue granite eyes. Why did this man always seem so unyielding, so sure, so difficult to understand?

Had Papa Da Brescia chosen to ask that question aloud, the Maestro would not have hesitated in his answer. As Keeper, Guido de la Valle already looked beyond the present wearer of the white robes and the Fisherman's Ring, whose vision was so personal and so idiosyncratic as to endanger the very office he held. The Keeper's Oath was to Christ, and to Peter's line. It was not a pope he served, but the papacy itself—the Rock upon which Jesus built his Church. Nothing would divert the Maestro from discharging that Oath. And nothing would wrest from his hands the only means he had—money and the power it brings—to defend that Rock and to strengthen it.

"Very well, Maestro." Papa Da Brescia finally lowered his eyes. "Have it as you will. Which are the cardinals you choose for PECA?"

"Arnulfo, Ferragamo-Duca, and Falconieri, Your Holiness."

"But . . ." The owlish stare clamped on Guido again, but fell away. It was useless.

"And Your Holiness' nominee for the Banco?"

"Monsignore Peter Servatius."

Guido smiled. Papa Da Brescia's liking for the giant American was well known. He was impressed by everything about the burly prelate—Servatius' girth and obvious strength, his genuine and protective affection for the diminutive Da Brescia, his never-failing and buoyant good humor, his organizational ability, and, to cap it all, his apparently genuine contempt for personal wealth or monetary gain.

The Maestro was fairly certain that it was Servatius' value as general organization man, personal bodyguard, and general adviser that led Da Brescia to nominate him as Di Lorio's replacement as head of the IRA. In any case, the American had not a fraction of Di Lorio's genius. He was a financial simpleton by comparison. Guido saw no difficulty in managing things "around" him, so to speak.

"Of course, Holy Father. Servatius will be acceptable. I presume Your Holiness will make him an archbishop?"

Da Brescia confirmed that he would.

"May I suggest, Holiness, that Monsignore Di Lorio has given lengthy and laborious service to the Holy See? Though he will be retiring from his post, he does merit the cardinalate."

"We had already decided on that, Maestro, before you spoke." The Pontiff rose and held out his hand for the obeisance of Guido's kiss on the Ring.

Guido complied and, with a deep bow, retired to let the Pontiff examine as best he could the catch in his net.

"Rico, there's a Franciscan monastery out on the old Appian Way, just past the Metella tomb. Know it?"

Rico frowned as he listened to John Liebermann's voice on the phone. He knew the place. What he didn't know was why the American intelligence operative was being so careful. The two didn't meet often, but when they did, it was generally for a meal and another good-natured try on Liebermann's part to enlist Lansing's trust and cooperation.

"What about five o'clock this afternoon?"

"Okay, John. See you there."

He found Liebermann waiting for him. The sky had been clear of clouds all afternoon and the lowering sun cast a yellow-bronze hue over the earth around them.

"You're growing backwards, John." Rico held out his hand. "You look younger!"

"It's the good life spent in labor relations." Liebermann laughed the compliment away and they set out for a stroll along the polygonal blocks of basalt laid down by the ancient Romans.

"A few things of mutual interest have come across my desk," Liebermann ventured as they rounded the end of the monastery wall and faced south.

Rico leaned back to rest against one of the motionless cedars by the side of the road. He said nothing.

It was always the same! This American-turned-Roman was always inscrutable, and Liebermann always ended up nowhere in his attempts to form a link with him. Well, this time it had to be different.

"Look, Rico. I'm going to level with you." He was, he said bluntly, Rome station officer for one branch of U.S. Intelligence. He didn't specify which branch, but only that it was engaged specifically in counter-espionage. He realized the Vatican did not have any parallel organization, but he was sure that an association of some trust and strict confidentiality between him and Rico Lansing would be beneficial for both sides.

"We know, Rico. We know you enjoy the confidence of some very highly placed circles in the Vatican. Also, we have kept you under a certain degree of surveillance. You give us the impression that you are two-track. We can only find one track—your priestly activity. But we still have the other impression."

Rico jumped as a group of starlings suddenly began a loud chatter and squabble among themselves in a clump of bushes nearby. He left the cedar and began strolling again, but still made no comment to his frustrated companion.

"We're not alone in our impression, Rico." Liebermann fell into step beside him. "We know Moscow has organized one whole section of its KGB specifically to deal with Catholicism. It's run by someone they call General Control. Your name figures on General Control's list as a suspected counterspy for the Vatican.

"You're good, Rico. A professional. We've been bamboozled by you, if you are double-track. Apparently, you've bamboozled them too.

"Now, I'm going to give you a piece of information. Call it a good-faith effort on my part to convince you we're on the same side, and can help each other in situations that might get out of hand otherwise.

"We think that some in Papa Da Brescia's entourage, if not the Pontiff himself, are working for the other side."

That brought Rico up short. Da Brescia might be a lot of things, but an intimation such as Liebermann's was the blue limit. "This had better be good, John." He gave his companion a hard look.

"It's bad, Rico. Very bad." In curt terms he explained how, the previous November, his government had suddenly received an undeniable request. It had come from Papa Da Brescia, through his delegate in Washington, to the President. It had contained papal assurance that the North Vietnamese were preparing peace proposals, and a strong request that an American plan to deliver a final coup de grace be postponed on that account. The President had compiled with that request.

"Instead, Rico, you and the whole world know what happened: the Tet offensive of the last few weeks. They never meant to make peace. The whole thing was a deception. A ploy to give the North Vietnamese at least two months to resupply and regroup.

"Now, your Pope and his entourage were part and parcel of that deception. Someone leaked that top-secret plan of ours to the North Vietnamese. Someone told the Cardinal of Hanoi to go to Papa Da Brescia. We know all that. Result? We've lost the initiative. For all we can tell, it looks like we've lost the war, as well. It will take time, but you don't get a chance like that twice in this life!"

Rico was thunderstruck.

"You see . . ." Liebermann pressed his point with great intensity. "The foreign policy of Papa Da Brescia, the overtures you're making for him with the governments of satellite countries, that's one thing. But we have to think now that there's more to it than that."

"But the Pope himself, John! That's going too far."

"I agree with you, Rico. But not all of my associates do."

It had to be Levesque's office, Rico thought to himself. He knew the Secretariat structure and functioning as well as anyone in the Vatican. It had to be someone very close to the secretary of state. Someone who could get at the huge traffic of messages and documents that flowed through that office. And someone who had sway over the Pope. But who? Levesque himself? Sugnini? Demarchelier? Casaregna?

"You see," Liebermann went on, "we are all in danger. And if you're two-track, as we think you are, whoever you're working with, and whatever you're doing, that's all in danger too."

The specter of Lysenko's betrayal rose yet one more time in Rico's mind.

"What in particular are you asking me for, John?"

Finally! Liebermann thought. A glimmer of some headway. "We know that whatever you're doing is centered mainly in Eastern Europe. Primarily, we need information. From time to time, the transference of funds. Rarely—very rarely—the accommodation of one of ours who may need to get out in a hurry."

By this time they had retraced their steps and were standing again by the Metella tomb. Rico stopped still, deep in thought, for some time. Here he was, a priest of God, sworn and deeply dedicated to the service of Christ, and yet caught in the middle of intricate spyworks. His name was even on a special list of General Control. And hundreds, literally hundreds of men and women, in a dozen countries, depended for their very lives on how he fared.

His eye fell on the tomb nearest to where he stood, and he noticed the single word the Romans used to inscribe on the stones that covered the remains of their loved ones. *"Vale."*

"Do you know what that word means, John? It means 'goodbye.' It was the only word the Romans of that day had to deal with death."

He turned, then, and looked toward the northwest, toward the hundred domes of Rome glinting under the last rays of the setting sun. "*That* is my Rome, John. The Rome I serve means life. Not an eternal goodbye to loved ones; not a parting. Eternal life after death. An eternal holiday within the beauty and fullness of God's very being.

"What I do, I do for that Rome. In Christ's Church." He turned back to a puzzled Liebermann. "I'll help you, John. But I will not be your agent. I will not serve some shortsighted political aim. And I'll only help if all requests are directly from you to me. I decide what I can and can't —will or won't—do. All results go back from me directly to you. No one else knows where you get what I give you. No third parties. Ever."

Liebermann laughed out of sheer relief. "Agreed!"

Once his negotiations with the Maestro were completed, it took Papa Da Brescia no time at all to produce his document entitled "Reform of the Roman Curia." When it was published in March of 1968, it presented the image of a Pope who was endeavoring to streamline an ancient and cumbersome clerical bureaucracy.

It revealed the formation of the new Prefecture for Economic Affairs. It named the appointees the Maestro had selected. It detailed several other revampings throughout the ministries of the Holy See. And it included the revolutionary ruling that henceforth every bishop, including the Pope himself, who was Bishop of Rome, would be expected to offer his resignation voluntarily upon reaching his seventy-fifth birthday. The Pontiff alone would decide which resignations would be accepted, and which would be deferred or denied.

It seemed obvious to many that Papa Da Brescia had finally found a way to begin to dislodge the old guard, including, at long last, the cardinals of the Vatican State Council, and to replace them with newer, fresher blood.

Almost simultaneously, the Pontiff published another special papal document, this one concerning the method of electing popes. In it, he gave greater precision to the balloting system with conclave; forbade all photographic and recording apparatus within the entire conclave environs; prescribed rigorous surveillance of the conclave area for the duration; and in addition, he laid down that only cardinals under the age of eighty could henceforth participate in conclave.

Again, the world at large, and much of the world of Catholicism in particular, saw these as further signs of the rejuvenation Papa Da Brescia had promised for his pontificate—as nearer signs of the long-awaited Second Spring.

There were still more elevations of archbishops to the College of Cardinals; but they, at least, raised no eyebrows in the Curia this time around. Lamennais of Paris, Tillman of New York, Da Fonseco of Bombay, and Muldoun of Sydney had all died the previous autumn. For their replacements, and for eleven totally new cardinals, Papa Da Brescia had carefully solicited the opinions of the curial leaders and, in the main, followed their suggestions. As he explained to Levesque, he had enough surprises in store for them in the near future.

Bogdan Valeska's elevation to the cardinalate was recommended both by Richard Lansing and by Cardinal Wallensky. The old cardinal came down to Rome with his archbishop for the ceremony of consecration, but declined Papa Da Brescia's invitation for a private audience in the papal apartments. He had no further desire, he told Rico, "to watch the slow demolishing of the Curia, and the secularization of the Church." That Valeska was now a cardinal was some assurance of Poland's future religious health; and that was as much as Wallensky could hope for. He left Rome, taking Valeska with him, after barely thirty-six hours, and did not expect ever to return.

After the full rush of such events, Papa Da Brescia took a week's vacation out at Castel Gandolfo. He needed the peace and quiet and beauty of those gardens to set his thoughts in order, and to prepare himself for the next phase of his plans.

Late that same spring, Paolo Lercani also had an elevation conferred upon him, in a manner of speaking. Over the years he had provided ever more valuable services to Senatore Ectore Pappagallo, and had placed the facilities of more than one of his banking institutions at the senator's disposal, no questions asked, for the purpose of easing the international transfer of funds. And over the years, as Pappagallo's interest in the matter seemed to sharpen, Lercani had taken care to let him know how frequently Papa Da Brescia called upon him for advice about the papal privy purse. Indeed, the Holy Father had now asked him to assess the net value of the Holy See's assets.

The senatore had also been informed, but by other sources, of Lercani's recent and lamentable demarche in favor of Hanoi. However, one had to weigh these things in a careful balance. Lercani's growing closeness to His Holiness, and to the Vatican's billions, had to count most heavily in the senatore's scales at the moment.

The dapper little Sicilian financier allowed himself to be blindfolded by two silent individuals, who then led him from his car on the outskirts of Florence to a waiting limousine, and drove him to a country villa.

When his blindfold was removed, Lercani was shown from a spacious courtyard into an inner room whose only light played directly on him, nearly blinding him at first, as he stood alone in what he presumed was the center of the floor. Even when his eyes adjusted, he could only see vague outlines and confused splotches of the faces of the men seated all around him.

Only one of those men spoke to him. Pappagallo did not disguise his voice.

"When we meet here, you will know me only as Naja Hanna," Pappagallo's voice said.

Lercani nodded his agreement. "Naja Hanna." Where had he heard that name before?

"Authority is in my hands."

Another nod. "Yes, Naja Hanna."

"We have no oath of membership. In order to belong to our group and participate in our plans, all you have to do is agree with us. But once you say, 'I agree,' you must know you can never again withdraw. And you must know we are a secret organization. We punish betrayal, or even the smell of betrayal, with death. We regard failure as betrayal; death is the penalty, but self-imposed and according to our ritual. Is all that understood?"

"Yes, Naja Hanna."

"If you agree, you will be assigned a number. That will mark your point of no return." There was a pause. Then: "Do you agree with us?"

"Yes, Naja Hanna. I agree with you." Lercani wished he could remember where he had heard that name.

Another pause, shorter this time. "We assign you," Pappagallo's voice said, "number 1555."

One of the silent men who had blindfolded him came forward from the shadows then, and took Lercani's arm to lead him away into a large and comfortable sitting room.

He barely had time to pour himself a tall drink at the open bar and take a welcome sip before Senatore Pappagallo joined him, followed by a dozen others whose identities and ranks almost made Lercani drop his glass. It was a miniature Who's Who of Italian political, military, and professional life.

"Paolo"—the senatore made the introductions all around—"you should know Air Force Commander Mozzani. Carlo Andreali of the Treasury Ministry. General Dibello of Special Forces. Giovanni Legame of the Petroleum Institute. Professore Emilio Cardogna of the Atomic Research Laboratory of Fiesole. General Tomaso Bellucini, head of Italian counterintelligence . . ."

When he had finished the introductions and hands had been shaken, drinks were poured for everyone.

"Well"—Pappagallo turned a satisfied face toward Paolo Lercani—

"there are 1555 of us now. I don't suppose, Paolo, that you'll meet all of us. But shortly, when we've finished our drinks, we'll join the others who are waiting inside. We still have a business meeting to conduct."

"But . . ." Paolo was still dazed by the importance of the people Pappagallo had attracted. "I mean, security . . . How do you . . . ?"

"How do we remain secret?" The senatore laughed. "We have the ultimate security. Total revelation of ourselves within the organization and total silence for the outside world. We all agree in purpose, and we all know the sanctions."

After a quarter of an hour, Lercani followed the others back into the room where he had given his agreement. It was fully alight now, and he calculated there were another forty-five men, all of similar high standing in the Italian world, seated at tables that formed a huge square. He was assigned a place at one of the tables, and took his seat with the rest.

Naja Hanna stood at his own place. "Now"—he began the business meeting—"you will all be pleased to learn that the first stages of the new operations plan will be implemented in the autumn. The violence that will now be involved is regrettable, but necessary, as we have already discussed. The question of funding that has delayed us is solved for the moment. Because of our latest member, number 1555, we can expect to have at our disposal the largest single assemblage of assets in the world.

"Your assignment, 1555, is to secure entrée into those assets. We will need heavy financing for a period of anywhere from five to ten years, depending on how quickly things progress, beginning in about two years' time. About 1970 . . ."

Pappagallo did Lercani the courtesy of driving him back to his car on the outskirts of Florence, and of explaining a little more of what was afoot. He kept referring to some organization that seemed distinct and separate from the one Lercani had just joined. That organization, the senatore said, had embarked on a program of destabilization of certain existing governments. Italy was one. Pappagallo named Chile and Argentina as two more. Why? "Because," the senatore answered his own question, "more countries have also been targeted for takeover by a Communist popular front. We plan to beat them at their own game. To make the existing weak governments totter and fall, then put our own people in. Now, it is unfortunate that strong-arm tactics have to be used to destabilize governments. But how else are we going to get there before the Communists? We must keep the larger aim in mind. The West is not going to be lost to Marxism."

Violence was not a problem for Lercani. Like money and banks, it was a tool to be used when it served the purpose at hand. Whole vistas of possibilities began to open like verdant pastures in the Sicilian's quick mind. He had always known that, on a high enough level, finance would lead to power. But this was a grander panorama than he had hoped. There was only one immediate question he wanted to ask. American interests would be touched deeply by these plans. What about them?

Pappagallo's answer was reassuring. "The Americans are with us.

Why do you think there's a junta of generals in charge of Greece today? The same danger. And the same solution!"

"Now." Pappagallo had given as much explanation as he intended, and was ready to move on. "Your accounts, Paolo, at the Vatican Bank and your own banks in Italy and abroad will be of great importance in the funneling of capital to our destabilizing forces. Of course, you must not ask questions about the destinations of those funds. The organization knows what it is doing."

The "organization" again, Paolo thought, and filed it away with the unanswered mystery of where he had heard the name Naja Hanna before.

"Tell me, now," the senatore continued. "How do you get access to Vatican funds?"

"Two ways." Lercani was confident. "His Holiness will give me one road of access—and soon, I expect, now that Servatius is to head up the IRA."

"And the second way?"

"I've always followed my nose in these matters, Senatore. For years my nose has pointed to Guido de la Valle as an avenue all on his own to Vatican money. Why or how, I don't know. But two of his close associates may be ripe for the picking. In over their heads in their personal finances, or so some rather intensive inquiries I initiated seem to show. They may be my second means of access."

Pappagallo mulled that over. He knew Guido managed funds for the Pope. But he also knew from his many years of conversations and exchanges with the Maestro in the Borghese Gardens, and from all he had ever heard of him from others, that he was more than a match for most men. "Well," he said finally as he pulled his car up to the curb behind Lercani's, "whatever happens, Paolo, do not fail. Remember. Failure is betrayal. But if we succeed, you will be asked to blueprint a new monetary system for the whole of the Western World. Do you realize what that means?"

The answer to that question was obvious. And for Lercani it brought a moment of anticipation that had all the glow of power itself. Immense power. All the trappings of the superman were going to be his. "Yes, Naja Hanna."

If Archbishop Giulio Brandolini could have been a flea on the head of Paolo Lercani that day, he would have known how close to the truth he had come, with his theories and speculations about what had to lie at the bottom of what he had called the negative insanity of destabilization. Lercani raised his upper lip and waved at the senatore's receding car. He was member number 1555 in what Brandolini had dubbed Problem Number Two. P-2.

Close friends though they were, both in and out of the *impero,* Franco Graziani and Luigi Garganelli were surprised to the point of horror to meet face to face in one of the sumptuous anterooms of Paolo Lercani's Milan office. Nor was either of them happy that they were rushed so quickly, and together, into Lercani's private domain.

Each took a chair, eyeing the other, and the Rembrandts and Picassos that hung on the walls, in evident discomfort as they waited for the financier to finish his phone conversation.

"Sì. Sì." Paolo raised his upper lip at both of his visitors while he listened intently to the voice on the phone. It was Jimmy "Fingers" Benevuti of the Sicilian Honored Society, telling him how well the whole "Hanoi gambit" was paying off. "Not only that, Paolo!" he was saying. "On top of the Southeast Asian source, we're onto a new one. In the Middle East. Did you know that the upper Beqa'a Valley in Lebanon has an ideal morning dew with just the right chemical mix for producing the best hashish?"

"Isn't it amazing, the details one gathers in business?" Paolo replied, nodding again to Graziani, who eyed him back with those *occhi di ghiaccio.*

"Listen, Paolo," his Sicilian crime brother went on. "We project our annual crop yield in the new area will be maybe two thousand tons! That's a lot of profit. We're going to have to launder a lot of cash."

"We can handle it, my friend." Lercani had let his visitors stew just about long enough. "Let's talk later in the week. I'm glad it's worked out so well. *Ciao,* Jimmy. Be in touch."

"*Ciao,* Paolo."

From the moment Lercani hung up the phone, it was a one-sided game of cat and mouse, with Lercani as the cat. After a few pleasantries, he came directly to the first point. He told both men that intensive inquiries about their personal assets had revealed they were both heavily in debt, and spending enormous sums of money that couldn't be backed by their decreasing capital assets. Not only were they dangerously near financial disaster, but they were flirting with desertion of public confidence in their judgment should this predicament become a matter of common knowledge.

Franco and Luigi looked at one another in surprise, less at Lercani's detailed knowledge of their personal affairs—there were always ways to get such information—than at the discovery by each that the other was in the same boat of near financial ruin.

"I do not wish in any way"—Lercani continued to paw the mice—"to violate your individual privacy or your consciences. Only, the few words we have exchanged in the past have led me to believe that, far from being unworthy of confidence, both of you are men of a certain daring. The type of men I consort with." He smiled deprecatingly. "The type of men with whom I have built my own little empire." A wave of the hand to dismiss all that as next to nothing.

"Now, I have a proposition for quick investment with"—he lowered his voice slightly, as if in reverence—"over two hundred percent return."

Graziani and Garganelli looked at one another again. They knew that only one kind of investment paid like that. Lercani was talking about some intricate way of laundering moneys derived from the drug trade.

It was a measure of Franco Graziani's financial panic that he turned to Lercani to ask how safe from scrutiny the whole operation would be. And it was a measure of Luigi Garganelli's that he made no objection or protest.

"Absolutely one hundred percent safe," Lercani assured them both. "You deposit your money with my close colleague Roberto Gonella, at the Agostiniano Bank here in Milano, and Roberto takes it from there, investing the money in Liechtenstein trust funds."

At Lercani's mention of the name Roberto Gonella as his "close colleague," another look passed between Graziani and Garganella. They both remembered clearly the *impero* meeting in the Maestro's study at which Gonella had been proposed and approved as central director of the Agostiniano Bank, in which the Holy See had a major equity interest. This dapper little weasel of a man had his fingers everywhere!

"You see, gentlemen," Lercani went on smoothly, taking it for granted that his mice were sophisticated enough to understand that they were talking about laundering money for the drug trade, "you will not be investing in the trade itself. We can leave that to the scum who enjoy it. Your investment will be engaged in assuring the market viability of funds derived from the trade. At a two hundred percent return on investment, as I said, and"—he drove home the final and irresistible clincher—"within sixty days!"

Graziani and Garganelli said they needed some time to talk the matter over privately.

"Of course," Lercani agreed. There was a fine restaurant just down the street. Perhaps they would lunch together, and they could all meet again in the afternoon.

The lunch was somber and all business. The two friends understood that they had been brought together in Lercani's office as witness of each other's decisions. They understood as well that Lercani was not making this offer to them out of the goodness of his heart. They knew all about cat-and-mouse games. He wanted something from them. Perhaps that part of it had to do with Graziani's position as regional head of the Italian Industrial Reconstruction Institute, and with Garganelli's publishing empire. More likely, though, they decided, what Lercani wanted had to do in some way with Guido de la Valle and the *impero.*

In the end, they decided they had no choice but to make the "investments" Lercani was offering. The two-hundred-percent, sixty-day return could stave off ruin, giving them time to climb out of the hole they had spent themselves into. But they could play cat and mouse too.

"Let's work the situation for all it's worth." Graziani paid the check for lunch, and the pair walked out into the noisy street. "But we keep our oath with Guido. Whatever Lercani wants, and whatever happens, we don't betray the Maestro."

"But we can't tell him, either." Garganelli pointed out the dilemma they were entering. "We can't even warn him about Roberto Gonella and the Agostiniano Bank without getting into a lot of questions we can't answer, if we go ahead with this dirty business."

"It's just for a while, Luigi," Franco Graziani reasoned. "All we're doing is playing for time, and the money we have to get our hands on. It's that or ruin for us."

"I suppose you're right, Franco. But it's going to be like shaking hands with the Devil."

The two entered Lercani's office building again and let the heavy glass doors close out the sound of the world behind them.

Cardinal Joachim Lanser could fight no more. He was tired. All his expectations of abuse from every quarter for the work he tried to do for the Holy Father had been fulfilled a hundredfold. He was lambasted by the ecumenists for being too reactionary. He was crucified by the conservatives for betrayal of the Church. Catholics, Protestants, and Jews all had at him endlessly for the Document on Religious Liberty. The Pope himself had called Lanser on the carpet for the book on ecumenism he had published the previous fall—the very book he had been working on when Richard Lansing visited him in his rooms.

The Holy Father had reproached him paternally but firmly. "Your Eminence has reiterated old theological clichés about hierarchic privilege and jurisdiction, as well as about the weaknesses of humanism."

Lanser had taken it humbly. "Holiness, Christ will, it is hoped, purge me and all of his servants of our sins before he calls us to final judgment." But he had left that papal dressing-down feeling in his bones that he had only a short distance more to travel on what he now chose to call by its classical Catholic name—the "earthly pilgrimage."

Rico Lansing was saddened by that same premonition as he sat one Friday in June, sipping tea with the cardinal. He had come for a brief visit before leaving on another of his Apostolate trips. He had intended to keep the conversation light, knowing as he did that Lanser had been in some pain for months. Not localized pain, but a general aching all over his body.

Today, though, he was feeling better than he had in weeks. He wanted to talk. In the tense and explosive atmosphere of the Vatican these days, Rico was one of the few people left he could talk frankly to and get a rational, unemotional response.

Lanser had been doing a lot of thinking, he told the American. And he had come up against a fearful problem. It concerned Papa Da Brescia, he said; and it concerned heresy, and schism in the Church.

Lanser was an intellectual, a theologian, and a Jesuit. For him to mention the Pope, heresy, and schism all in one sentence was not a light matter.

"As far as I can see, Rico, Papa Da Brescia has already committed *material* heresy. That is, he has rejected dogma either unknowingly or for reasons he has somehow justified. If he had done so in full knowledge and without even an erroneous reason, that would be *formal* heresy."

For Rico, it was a fine point. Heresy was heresy; and he hadn't thought he would ever hear such a direct denunciation of the Pope, above all from Joachim Lanser.

"Look at it calmly, Rico. That's hard when you're talking about the Holy Father and heresy in the same breath. No one knows better than I how hard! But bear with me.

"If a bishop, or, in this case, a whole bloc of bishops, refuse to obey the clear commands of the Holy See, and those commands directly concern faith and morals, then they reject the teaching of the Roman Pontiff about faith and morals. Point number one. And that's heresy.

"Point number two is that they also reject the jurisdiction of the Roman Pontiff. That places them in schism."

"Even granting that, Eminence," Rico countered, "it's the bishops you're talking about. Not the Pope."

"So far, yes," Lanser conceded. "But if the Pope then praises the bishops when they reject the jurisdiction of the papacy—as Papa Da Brescia has done on the issue of contraception, to name just one—he not only shares their guilt; he compounds it."

Lanser pushed himself out of his chair wearily, to look at the pleasant and rather pastoral view from his study window. "I've thought it through again and again these past few weeks, Rico. I've tried to find a way to justify the Holy Father. But I can't find the way. Not anymore. All I can do now is to look for some occasion to warn him. Some moment when I think he will listen—really listen—to what I have to say on this matter."

Rico put his cup down on the table beside him, but remained seated. "That's not going to be easy, Eminence. Papa Da Brescia won't take lightly to talk of heresy, even from you."

He saw Lanser nod. "True enough. But if someone doesn't speak up, aren't we all in it with him? Arnulfo has tried, of course. But he's so prickly lately, Da Brescia will barely even see him anymore."

Lanser heaved a weary sigh and turned from the window. "The day is so beautiful. Isn't it good of God to give me such a day. . . ."

There was the merest tensing of Lanser's shoulders, the upward movement of a hand toward his chest, an intense staring of his blue eyes.

"Eminence!" Rico was across the room in a split second, just in time to break the cardinal's fall as he collapsed. Lansing got him into a chair and headed for the phone.

"No!" Lanser's voice was breathy and weak, but urgent. He seemed to know exactly what was happening to him, and precisely what he wanted done. "Go to my private chapel in the next room. . . ." He had to pause frequently as he spoke. His breath came short and he was in obvious pain. "Get the Blessed Sacrament. . . . The Holy Oils. . . . Anoint me. . . . Then call the Holy Father. . . . Tell him I am dying. After that, you can call the doctor. But no ambulance. . . . I will die here. . . . At home."

For the first time in Roman memory, a pope left his palace to visit a dying man. Within an hour, after all had been done according to Lanser's instructions, the papal limousine arrived. Rico and the doctor waited with Monsignore Delucchi and Cardinal Secretary Levesque while Papa Da

Brescia went alone into the bedroom. In a quarter of an hour, he came out again, slowly.

From all he could see, Rico judged that Cardinal Lanser had found the moment when the Pope would "listen"—really listen—to warnings of heresy and schism. Papa Da Brescia kept his head lowered, looking to neither right nor left. He walked haltingly, with an almost shuffling gait.

Delucchi, worse in his own way, didn't move. Levesque, however, stepped forward and took the Pontiff's arm.

"Lascia me!" His Holiness recoiled from the Cardinal Secretary as he hurled those sharp words, which had a proper place only on the lips of a tormented person against his tormentor.

A shadow of black anger passed for a second over Levesque's face before he regained his usual composure. He stepped back from the Pontiff, fell in beside a forlorn Delucchi, and followed Da Brescia out the door of Cardinal Lanser's rooms.

It was a matter of a few peaceful hours after that. And when Rico Lansing left that place for the last time, the only comfort in his own heart was the certainty that Joachim Lanser's soul had gone arrow-straight to the Lord he had served for over seventy years.

[50]

As though Joachim Lanser had taken with him to his quiet grave in the little village of Grindelsbach the sweet secrets of reason and innocence, his death seemed a signal for the violent explosion of insanity. All the rotting parts of Italy finally began to give way—the rickety financial structure, the unquenchable avarice of politicians, the laissez-faire attitude of the higher clergy, the secret connivances and universal ramifications of a distorted state depending ultimately on the *sottogoverno.* A civilization that had cannibalized its own flesh too fecklessly, too godlessly, for too long, now began the awful vomitings and defecations induced by the virulent force of its own poisoning.

It began with the devastating and seemingly senseless explosion in a crowded Bologna supermarket of the first bomb planted by a totally strange organization calling itself the Red Brigades. Naja Hanna, reading the first reports of the casualties, once again regretted the need for violence. But not for a moment did he doubt or flinch from that need.

Rico decided to put off his trip to Poland and East Germany. To the delight of the de la Valles, he spent two quiet weeks of summer with them at Villa Cerulea.

Young Eugenio was the happiest of all to have him there. For some reason no one could understand, his best friend, Doni Graziani, wasn't able to spend as much time with Eugenio now, and the boy reveled in his Uncle Rico's company.

Lansing quickly fell into an easygoing schedule. The joke in the family was that he went to bed as early as Eugenio and Tati, and got up as early as the birds.

Every morning began at about five-thirty, when he heard gentle whimpering and the scratching of little claws on the coverlet of his bed. It was Tati, who had nosed the door open and wanted to be lifted up beside him. She was about three-quarters grown now, and except for the black ears and tail, was ten pounds of wheat-colored energy. Once she was lifted onto his bed, Tati rumpled out a place for herself beside Rico until his alarm went off at six. Then, while Rico bathed and dressed and went off to say Mass at the village chapel, she would scamper back to Eugenio's room, barking and growling him out of bed, as if she had a special mission to have him ready for breakfast when Rico got back.

Houseguests were nothing new for Mariella, who ran her kitchen according to the needs of each day. By seven-thirty, she had fed Eugenio, Rico, and Tati too; as often as not, she had packed a basket lunch and watched them all set off on a hike to some remote part of the estate, Tati happily racing ahead, then doubling back to run playful circles around them as they made their meandering way to the stream one day, the woods the next.

There was many a bicycle race in the late afternoons. Frequently Helmut and the Maestro would find them waiting at the gatehouse when Sagastume turned their limousine in from the main road. Eugenio, on his beloved three-speed bike; Rico, perched on the rather dilapidated workhorse affair that Danni, the head gardener, sometimes used; and Tati, jumping and romping between them, would all set off at top speed to lead the way like a playful cortege to the door of Villa Cerulea. Those were happy homecomings for Helmut and Guido. Only Sagastume seemed untouched by them; that stern-faced giant was not a man who liked whimsy.

While Rico was with them, the days took on a gentler pace for Agathi and Keti too. They spent sunlit hours on the terrace behind the house, chatting with Rico, listening to Eugenio's stories of where they had been the day before, or watching him show off the new tricks he and Rico had taught Tati. Sometimes they would all make the rounds of the estate together, to see the dairy farm or inspect the chicken coops.

Even dinners were quieter and pleasanter during those two weeks. There were rarely other guests, and Guido and Helmut fell willingly into the relaxed mood of the house. By now Eugenio was a lively part of mealtime discussions, even though the men talked a lot about people he didn't know and events he had never heard of. Sometimes he sensed they veered away from certain topics because he was present. But he accepted all that. He loved being with them, enjoyed their presence as a guarantee of his world. He felt so secure, sure that they knew all about the world outside and that their love and protection would be always around him. His only disappointment would come on those evenings when his father and Nanno would retire after coffee to the Maestro's or Helmut's study, unable to ignore altogether the never-ending pull of their concerns.

On the last Friday of Rico's vacation, he and Keti, together with Eugenio and Tati, made a morning trip up to Guido's timberlands, which Keti managed totally for the Maestro now. The foreman picked them all up in his jeep and drove them along the narrow dirt road that wound in curving laps up the side of the mountain overlooking Villa Cerulea's gardens and the back wall of the estate. They stopped at a clearing halfway up, and while Keti discussed such things with the foreman as the number of trees felled and the number of new plantings, the condition of the silver birch and the elms, Rico and Eugenio wandered off toward the river that wound like a ribbon around the estate.

It was a couple of hours before Keti finished her business with the foreman. Instead of honking the horn of the jeep to call Eugenio and Rico back, she sat for a while on one of the wooden benches beneath a giant sycamore. Eugenio often came with her on these little surveys; they would sit here together sometimes and eat lunch from the basket Mariella would prepare. Now, during this short time of Rico's visit, Eugenio preferred to be with him.

It was a clear day. Keti followed the winding course of the river with her eye until she caught sight of her son lying flat on his back on a grassy slope by the bank, his arms outstretched in a T-shape. Rico lay beside him, looking straight at the sky. They must be talking, Keti said to herself, telling one another about the wonders of the world. Tati lay on her back between the two, her paws in the air, and just within reach of Eugenio's fingers, which lazily scratched her belly. Were there ever, Keti wondered, three more contented-looking creatures in all God's world?

Except for the occasional cry of one workman to another coming muffled through the woods, there was no sound but the almost imperceptible chorus of nature—soft rustlings from grass and trees, the sporadic clickety-click of a cicada—to bustle over the threshold of her consciousness.

Soon, she reflected, her eye on those three figures in the distance, Eugenio would be as tall as Rico or Helmut. Would he grow as tall as Guido? she wondered. He would be a man before long, attend university, bring girlfriends home, start working. Would he drift away from her, as children do? Insist on leaving home, as she had done, in that rush for unthinking independence that she herself had yielded to? Only now did she begin to realize how lonely her own parents must have been the day they knew she would never again live at home with them.

No, she thought then; Eugenio was different. This home of his was different. He was a de la Valle. He would follow in his father's footsteps. He would live at Villa Cerulea, marry from it, return with his bride to it, and remain here always, as she and Helmut had done.

Were all de la Valle brides like Keti, making this home their world, creating vast significances in a series of concrete chores, supervising harvests and house accounts as she did? Were all de la Valle husbands like Helmut, pouring out all their energy and interest and cleverness and effort into the creation of empires, little and big?

Sometimes she was convinced that marriage was really a sacrament only for the woman; for the man, it was one more contract, agreed upon and signed, and then taken for granted.

For Keti, her marriage still remained a sacrament. The tangible elements of that sacrament were her body and Helmut's. The intangible element was love—and that was the one thing that made their bodies more than animal, more than aging flesh, mortal cages of lush desires. She did not want love to flee away up some mountain and hide its face in the stars. Did Helmut know that? she wondered. Did he feel it too? The love and the desire she still felt for him? She could not always tell.

"Is the signora ready to return now?"

Keti was startled at the sound of the foreman's voice. "Yes, Baffi. I'm ready." She got up from the bench and sounded the horn of the jeep. She saw her son jump to his feet when he heard it, and lope easily back toward the clearing, Rico not far behind. Tati was the first one in the seat, yapping and wagging her tail for the others to hurry, ready for the next adventure of her careless, happy life.

Lying in his bed, the easeful days of this stay almost all behind him, Rico was perfectly at peace. The night was tranquil. The whole earth seemed to be breathing calmly after the oppressive heats of midday. A fresh breeze began to cascade through the open window. Far away somewhere was Rome and its Vatican; farther away still was Eastern Europe and its closeted millions. The great, noisy, disturbed world was part of a distant planet.

His thoughts centered on young Eugenio. He tried to remember back to his own early-teen age; not for sounds, but for memories of that indefinable freshness and virginity of feeling and perception that Keti's and Helmut's son carried so lightly with him. Rico had been like that once. There was the memory of a memory. The delight he had felt at the family cabin on the shores of Lake Michigan, or during the long fishing holidays with his father in western Canada. Long years when the anticipation of adulthood did not hint or imply willfulness and egotism and raging passions. When did he lose that freshness?

The quiet of Villa Cerulea slowly crept around him, engulfing his senses and his memories in some timeless dimension of its own.

Rico closed his eyes. Life, he thought dreamily, should always be like this.

Down the corridor in Eugenio's room, Tati stood up on her master's bed and growled.

"Shush, Tati! Shush!" Eugenio pulled her down beside him, cuddling her into the crook of his neck. She licked his chin, growled once more, and settled down, letting out a sigh as she always did before they both went to sleep.

Archbishop Édouard Lasuisse descended upon Rome in November of 1968 like a modern Savonarola, defying the Pope, denouncing the Pope's entourage and sympathizers, galvanizing the State Council and the Black

Nobility, setting universities and seminaries at hot war with one another, carving a swath through the Vatican as though he were a human sword of division.

Lasuisse was an unlikely man for the part. Thin and spare, of medium height, he belonged to a missionary order called the Society of the Holy Spirit. He had spent most of his life, in fact, as a missionary in West Africa. He had become an archbishop at the age of fifty-one, and was recalled to France three years later when his health broke down. When he recovered, he was made superior general of his Society, and in that capacity had attended the Ecumenical Council, where he had been outvoted on committees and ignored when he spoke to the full assembly. Soon after Vatican II had ended, he resigned his post and devoted his time to private study, conducting conferences, and giving sermons. He had since proved himself to be an alert mind, a sharp debater, a very expert and very conservative theologian, fearless and as stubborn as a mule. Yes was yes. No was no. Gray areas existed only to be swept away. Always, his message was as clear as it was simple: There was a danger that the power and privilege of the Roman Pontiff would be destroyed by the enemies of the Church.

The occasion for his swoop upon the Vatican that November was the publication of Papa Da Brescia's new Mass—the *Novus Ordo,* or New Arrangement, of the Mass ceremonial.

The Pontiff presented the *Novus Ordo* as a fait accompli, and as in complete cohesion with "the Holy Spirit of our Second Vatican Ecumenical Council," and as drawn for "the greater spiritual benefit of the People of God" and "the renewal of faith in the Church."

Archbishop Lasuisse denounced the *Novus Ordo* as an aberration of the evil spirit embraced by Archbishop Annibale Sugnini together with his Liturgical Commission; and as a betrayal of the entire Catholic tradition.

In fact, for Lasuisse, Sugnini's Commission was itself the Devil's own joke. It was composed of nine members. Six of them were Protestants, including, as the Archbishop was not too reticent to observe, "the likes of Brother Reginald, Canon Ripley-Savage, and Bishop Cale." The only three Catholics were Father Hans Kleiser of Tübingen, Father Charles McMurren of Catholic University, Washington, and Archbishop Sugnini himself—"who are hardly even Christian any longer, if you ask me!"

"With such a group assigned by Papa Da Brescia to 'renew' the Mass," Lasuisse proclaimed vehemently to an informal meeting with Cardinal Arnulfo and several other members of the State Council, "what did the Pontiff expect? Nowhere does the nonsense of this text refer to Jesus' Sacrifice on Calvary! Or to his Resurrection! Or to the Bread and Wine becoming the Body and Blood of Jesus! What we have now, Your Eminences, is a specially blessed meal eaten to help men and women 'to praise the Lord and love their fellowmen.'

"In fact"—the French archbishop thumbed back and forth through the pages of the New Arrangement as he went on—"the tabernacle holding the Blessed Eucharist is to be removed from the altar to 'a suitable place.' That 'place,' as nearly as I can make out, can be in the sacristy of the church or in a separate building or, presumably, somewhere down the street. Perhaps in the local YMCA! There is not even supposed to be a crucifix on the altar. The altar is supposed to be a table. The priest is to be something called a 'minister of the Word.' The 'Word' is to be said out loud in its entirety, in any language except Latin. And everyone is supposed to be so happy about this blasphemy that when they're not speaking the Word, they're to sing hymns! In the vernacular, of course."

Cardinal Arnulfo replied that he and many of the State Council agreed in the main with Lasuisse's passionate criticisms of the new Mass.

"Well, then!" Lasuisse plunked his already much read and worn copy of the *Novus Ordo* noisily on the table. "What have you *done* about it!"

"We have tried," Arnulfo explained, "to reason with His Holiness. Cardinal Hoffeldt here has detailed for Papa Da Brescia some of the experimental excesses that have already been going on in Germany. I myself delivered to him an enormous forty-four-page report, complete with photographs of nuns in jewelry and priest in jeans, altars that look like party tables—all of it! It does no good! He wavers for a moment; teeters toward some step in the direction of sanity and order. But in a day or a week or a month, it's as though he's heard nothing except the chorus of praise from his entourage, and has read nothing but the encouragement and gratitude printed in so many of the diocesan newspapers."

"One truly odd thing," Cardinal Ferragamo-Duca interjected, "at least to my mind, is that Papa Da Brescia sees everything he has done, and is doing, as an exercise in absolute papal power. He insists over and over on the primacy and jurisdiction of himself, Giovanni Da Brescia, as Pope, as Bishop of Rome, and as Successor to Peter. But he does not seem to see—refuses to see, perhaps—that Peter's very throne is being pulled out from under him."

Lasuisse not only saw what Ferragamo-Duca was saying. He had said as much to the Pontiff himself. "There is going to be a veritable pogrom against the old man, Your Eminences. Whatever the Holy Father's perception of his power and jurisdiction, he has betrayed them both. He is in heresy, and he's not only allowing but forcing a schism in the Church!"

Arnulfo was taken by surprise at that. Since Cardinal Lanser's death the previous summer, he had heard little open talk of heresy and schism. And Lasuisse was no Lanser; he was far more conservative, far more outspoken, and had far less regard for papal obedience than Lanser had. With this firebrand on the loose, Da Brescia would have his hands full.

For an entire week, Lasuisse was seen and heard everywhere in Rome. He lectured at seminaries and universities—the Lateran University shouted in approval; the Gregorian University closed its doors to him—not only denouncing Sugnini, blasting the Liturgical Commission, and excoriating the *Novus Ordo,* but tearing to pieces as well the Pope's Justice and Peace commission, formed by the Pontiff after Vatican II, and charged with promoting the rights of man everywhere. He had no good words, either, for the Secretariat for Christian Unity, flooded more than ever, now that Lanser had died, with men Lasuisse characterized as "bright-eyed, poorly trained optimists, each one with a fresh idea of how the Catholic modes of worship can be changed so the Protestants will buy it."

Arnulfo, Hoffeldt, and Ferragamo-Duca had been sufficiently electrified by their own visit with Lasuisse to make yet another try at Papa Da Brescia. His Holiness put the trio off for as long as protocol allowed. When at last he had to receive them, he listened stonily.

"Holiness."Arnulfo was the spokesman. "My Eminent Brothers and I have come representing the Council of State and the remainder of the cardinals in Curia; and indeed, we believe, the principal members of the Sacred College in Europe and the Americas."

"Yes, Eminence." The Holy Father's voice was testy.

Arnulfo spoke as plainly as he knew how, in stern terms but without the inflammatory rhetoric of Édouard Lasuisse. The sum of his message was that the New Arrangement for the Mass was so deficient and irregular in doctrine as to be heretical. And that the Document on Contraception was no better. He would allow no excuses and no scapegoats. No underling was responsible. No final editor had twisted the intended truth of the texts. The documents had been printed from His Holiness' own manuscripts. Arnulfo knew that. His Venerable Brothers knew that. The world need not know. But His Holiness was not to take his cardinals for fools.

Papa Da Brescia's face flushed as he listened, but whether from anger or from some other powerful emotion, it was impossible to tell. "What the Church believes is important, Your Eminence." The Pontiff's voice shook. "We all *know* what the Church believes."

Arnulfo's voice was firm as ever. "What the Church *believes* must be expressed in what the Church *says,* Holiness! This new text does not say what the Church teaches. In some instances, it says the opposite." He had to bite his tongue to keep from repeating, "It is heresy." But he did say that he, and those represented by this delegation of three, were prepared to take drastic measures unless His Holiness gave assurances that His Holiness would take speedy corrective steps, at least with regard to the Mass.

Papa Da Brescia sat silent, calculating the odds, wishing that this meddlesome old man were seventy-five years old, so he could be retired out of the State Council. As it was, Arnulfo still had the power to take the "drastic measures" he threatened. For the second time in his pontificate, Da Brescia was in danger of being paralyzed by the imposition of supreme sanctions. He did not doubt that the Maestro would back the cardinals if it came to full confrontation.

"Your Eminences." The Pontiff was no longer flushed. He seemed pale, in fact. "We will comply with your wishes. We need your continued support and inspiration. The Holy See needs the benefit of your faithful services and your concern for the purity of its faith. We assure you"—he was speaking now directly to Arnulfo, countering the cardinal's argument that there could be no excuses—"that We cannot explain the apparent inaccuracies in Our text, except that the final editors mistook Our intentions. We will issue a corrective in the next issue of Our bulletin. We thank Your Eminences."

By the time Cardinal Secretary Levesque and Monsignore Annibale Sugnini arrived, having been summoned and forewarned by Monsignore Delucchi that there was trouble afoot over the new Mass, the Holy Father was pacing the study in undisguised agitation. Try as they would, the two prelates could not entirely calm His Holiness. This time, it would be best to compromise, relent a little.

"We agree that one or two phrases will have to be inserted into the text of the New Arrangement, Holiness." Sugnini made the suggestion. "It should be sufficient to add the statement that the Bread and Wine become the Body and Blood of Christ."

Da Brescia agreed, and his two close aides left him as quickly as possible for fear he might insist on still further compromises.

When he was alone, Papa Da Brescia sank back into his chair, put his head in his hands, and wept. He was overcome with frustration and with pain; with his inability to get things done; with the way everything he set his hand to seemed to go awry; with the accusations against him. Arnulfo and the others were bad enough. But even the obedient and truly venerable Cardinal Lanser had not understood Da Brescia's vision. On his very deathbed he had whispered of heresy and schism.

Da Brescia's tears flowed through his fingers. "I believe in the Holy Catholic Church . . ." He began to say the words aloud, his hands still covering his face. "I believe in the Holy Catholic Church . . . I believe . . ."

Monsignore Delucchi opened the door to the study to see if His Holiness might want him. At the sight of Papa Da Brescia, weeping in his chair and mumbling to himself, he quickly retired to his own office, shaken and saddened for his Pope. What demon was His Holiness struggling with, and to whom could he have recourse in his battle? To what higher authority could a pope appeal? To whom could he run in his hour of doubt or helplessness?

Delucchi had no answers.

Through Cardinals Arnulfo and Ferragamo-Duca, Édouard Lasuisse found his way to Guido de la Valle. The fiery archbishop was somewhat more subdued in tone with the Maestro, but not one whit less adamant. He seemed determined, in fact, to do more than rail in the halls of the Vatican. He had formed a plan of organized opposition.

"I am only a humble archbishop"—he explained his mind to the Maestro—"but Papa Da Brescia himself has forced me into this position. He has not suppressed the old Mass. He couldn't do that. It is forbidden to do so by papal tradition and canonical practice. Nor has he forbidden Catholic priests to say it. He cannot do that, either. What he has done is to make every attempt to substitute his New Arrangement for the old Mass. He has the power to do that; but he does not have the right!"

Lasuisse had decided, he said, to found a special institute. He had even decided on a name for it. The Pius X Institute, he would call it, after the pope who had stood as the greatest, most voluble, and most fearless enemy of the heresy of Modernism. "There, Maestro, I will train priests in solid theology, and I will preserve the old Mass. And from there I will launch a worldwide movement. In my calculations, fully thirty percent of Catholics abhor the New Arrangement already. Many more will come to abhor it, when they begin to see its full effect."

For the Maestro, there were two immediate and practical results of his meeting with Archbishop Lasuisse. The first was his decision to become a private contributor. Using only his personal funds, he would provide the grateful Frenchman with sufficient capital to start his institute, and he would ask his associates to make similar contributions.

The second decision was a private one. The de la Valle family had been given the perpetual right to have its own resident chaplain. They had never exercised that right; but now, as far as the Maestro could see, it would soon come to the point where they would find the Mass said by an Episcopal or Anglican priest at least more dignified and probably as reliably valid as the new hodgepodge they were faced with.

Guido started a search, and found Don Filippo, a very old, retired priest, whose only function at that stage in his life was to say his morning Mass.

With the permission of his bishop, who was glad to be rid of the obligation to pay for the old man's upkeep, Don Filippo arrived at Villa Cerulea early in 1969. Agathi refurbished a small suite of rooms for him at the rear of the house. Guido lined the walls of one room with collections of Church historians and writers. Mariella assigned one of the house servants to take care of the priest's meals and his housekeeping.

Don Filippo, an extremely simple man—pious and a bookworm—felt he had been installed in an anteroom of heaven. He lived contentedly at Villa Cerulea, saying his Roman Mass for the family every morning, and spending his days and long happy evenings reading all the books he had yearned for but never had at his disposal.

Inevitably Eugenio and Tati made their way to Don Filippo's rooms. "He is very gentle, Nanna," he told Agathi, "and he understands everything!"

Inevitably, as well, the statistics of dropouts from the clergy and observant faithful continued to climb, and aberrations continued to increase. Cardinal Arnulfo, poring over his monthly reports, began to be dizzied by the numbers, and by the multiple variations in ceremonial and words that sprang up like mushrooms in Masses throughout the Church. Even when Papa Da Brescia published the promised "corrections" to his first version of the new Mass, it served little purpose.

"What does he think we are? Children?" Cardinal Wallensky raged at the hapless Rico Lansing in Warsaw.

Guido never regretted his decision to welcome Don Filippo under his roof. In their home life and in their worship, at least, he would protect his family from the insanity that was besetting the world.

[51]

The first day of May, 1969, was one of rare anticipation for Papa Da Brescia. Before another dawn, by a bold stroke of the papal pen he would accomplish two cherished goals. He would end the deepening threat of the *cedolare* tax by removing the bulk of the Holy See's assets from the grasping hands of the Italian government; and he would end the Maestro's exclusive hold on the assets of the Holy See, as well.

Of course, he could tell no one about it beforehand. Like his replacement of the Roman Mass with the New Arrangement, this too would have to be presented as a fait accompli. The new Mass had caused uproar in certain quarters. But no one had been able to undo what he as Pope had done. And so it would be now. Not even the Keeper had the power to erase the papal signature.

The Pontiff put in a very heavy day of public audiences, and consultations with the people from the Secretariat of State. In the early evening, he had a quiet supper with his old friend Don Guglielmo, the good pastor from Avellino. His Holiness listened with full affection but only half an ear to the priest's latest bulletins about Signora Cuccia, who had broken her hip and needed hospital care. He heard about the latest outrages of the local Communist labor leader—"a real thug, Holy Father"; and about the baby born two days before to the village prostitute—"truly an angel of God, Holy Father." The shrine of Saint Cecilia in Orte parish was being restored. The generator in Don Guglielmo's rectory had broken down.

At about seven-thirty, Don Guglielmo departed with some extra lire notes in his pocket to pay for a new generator, and a letter authorizing the Santa Susanna clinic to treat Signora Cuccia's broken hip and send the bill to the Holy Father's secretary.

Monsignore Delucchi came in at about ten-thirty and found His Holiness still bent over his desk.

"Better you go off to bed, Monsignore," Papa Da Brescia said.

When his secretary had left, the Pope picked up his phone and dialed the number for the Vatican security chief.

"Michele Storza here."

Papa Da Brescia's instructions to him were precise. "We want you to send one of Our cars to pick up a single passenger at the Excelsior Hotel. He will be waiting at the entrance at eleven forty-five. The gentleman in question will ask the driver if he is returning to the Vatican slowly. He must use that formula. Arrange for him to enter and leave by the Michelangelo tunnel. Escort him to Our door, if you will, Signor Capitano Storza. Wait for him to come out, and escort him back to the car when We have finished Our meeting with him."

"Of course, Holy Father."

Ever since the aborted plan to assassinate Papa Angelica, a strict security drill had been in place; and recently Archbishop Brandolini had increased the precautions still further. Without thinking twice about it, Storza dialed Brandolini.

Papa Da Brescia was waiting in the little sitting room when Paolo Lercani stepped through the door some minutes after midnight. The Pope acknowledged his greeting with a nod, led him into the private study, and took his seat at the desk, whose solitary lamp cast the only light in the room. He motioned Lercani to the chair on the opposite side of the desk, where the financier found a pen and two copies of a document waiting for him.

"It's the agreement you drafted at Our instructions, Signor Lercani. We have made certain changes throughout. Initial them if you agree, and then sign on the back page of each copy."

Lercani took up the top copy of the contract, and began to read. The lamp threw its light eerily upward, bathing his face in distorted shadows, so that his chin and mouth, cheekbones and brow, seemed almost like features of the bodiless head of some specter, floating above the white pages before it.

The contract essentially and in effect confided into Paolo Lercani's hands the international brokerage of Holy See funds. It enabled him, by written papal order, to extract slightly in excess of $1 billion from the IRA, and to parlay that sum into greater ones on the foreign business and investment markets.

Papa Da Brescia had given a lot of thought to the matter. He had listened to Lercani's explanation of his methods. He didn't understand them very well, but the man's expertise was clear, and that was what the Pope needed.

Strictly speaking, he knew that the Maestro should have the final say in financial deals of this sort. But the Maestro's heyday was over. It had peaked in Papa Profumi's time—and what had that pair ever done? Profumi had always talked about change, but he had never really understood what was going on in the outside world. And neither did Guido de la Valle.

Furthermore, the Pope knew that the exemption of the Holy See from the *cedolare* tax would end this very year. The Socialist-dominated coalition that now held power in the Italian government would not be put off any longer. The Socialist deputy from Bologna had been screaming in parliament about "the $2.5 billion that the Holy See should have paid since 1962"; and the New Year headline of the *Giornale,* Rome's Socialist

Party newspaper, had demanded, "When Will the Clerics Pay Their Lawful Debts?" The Italian prime minister had finally stated over national radio that "The Holy See will not have to pay tax on sums earned on the Italian market since 1962; but as of 1969, the Holy See will pay the *cedolare* tax."

Through this contract that he would sign tonight, Papa Da Brescia would be out from under that burdensome threat of the *cedolare* at last; and he would no longer have to connive and beg the Maestro for the funds needed for the future changes he planned. Within ten years, if all went well . . .

"It would seem, Your Holiness," Lercani interrupted the Pontiff's thoughts, "that all is in order." He spoke in a deep, calm, and satisfied voice as he took up the pen, initialed the dozen or so places where changes had been made in the Pope's hand, and quickly affixed his signature on the last page of each copy of the contract. Papa Da Brescia then did the same, and handed one copy to his midnight guest, who folded it away in his inner breast pocket.

At long last, Paolo Lercani was the Pope's international banker and broker. And this was just the beginning.

Giulio Brandolini phoned the Maestro at once with Michele Storza's information that there would be a secret late-night visitor arriving to see the Pope. Guido said he would wait up for further news. When Brandolini reported back, after midnight, that the visitor had been none other than the Sicilian financier, Guido was confident that he would soon know what had taken place at the clandestine meeting. If Lercani was involved, then money was involved, he reasoned. And nothing touching Vatican finances remained hidden from the Maestro for long.

It was the bulky American archbishop, Peter Servatius, who had replaced Sphinx Di Lorio officially as head of the IRA, who brought the matter to light.

As Guido had always known, Servatius was not a genuine expert in banking. He did not have all the Banco data at his disposal, and seemed either not to realize that fact or not to care. Nothing of significance could be done at the Banco without the Maestro's or Helmut's specific approval, and each week, Servatius received from the de la Valle Vatican office a sheet of instructions, which he carried out to the letter.

When Paolo Lercani presented the papal contract to Servatius, asking for immediate access to the IRA books of account, and indicating that he would be withdrawing the sum of over $1 billion as stipulated over the Holy Father's own signature, Servatius knew enough, out of his sheer instinct for self-preservation, to make a photocopy of the agreement and forward it by messenger to the Maestro.

Guido and Helmut examined the copy of Lercani's papal contract together. Lercani had full power of attorney to dispose of Holy See assets in the value of something over $1 billion, with the option to return for additional sums after the initial capital had been successfully invested out of reach of the *cedolare.* Archbishop Servatius was to be kept *au courant* with the financial operations.

What disturbed the Maestro and his nephew was not so much the money that the Pontiff had placed in jeopardy. They themselves had long since removed the bulk of the Holy See's assets out of reach of the *cedolare* tax. By the same token, those assets were also out of Lercani's reach.

The truly unsettling thing was the flawed nature of Papa Da Brescia's judgment in trusting the patrimony of Peter to the likes of Paolo Lercani.

"The Holy Father simply doesn't know the nature of the man he is dealing with, Uncle."

"Doesn't he?" Guido responded to Helmut's rather weak defense of the Pope in this matter. "It seems to me that after all these years he *should* know. Even if his instincts didn't warn him, it would be a matter of simple prudence to have him and his empire fully investigated before even thinking about entering into such an agreement as this one.

"No, Helmut. It is stubborn and congenital bad judgment. He seems always to fix his eye on some vague goal; and then, to help him reach it, he unfailingly chooses self-interested users as his advisers and aides. Then he compounds his bad judgment by refusing to see anything but the goal he has set for himself. He seems to blind himself, or allow himself to be blinded, to all the signs that would—if he would only look at them—warn him how far off course he is being led.

"This time, though, he has stepped into the wrong field of expertise. We have no power to abrogate this agreement. He has the right to sign it, and he has done so. We have no spiritual weapons and few spiritual sanctions on a dangerous pope. If we had not removed most of the assets already, the supreme sanction would be in order, even with all the damage it would do. But as it is, we do have financial weapons with which to defend the Church—even from a pope, if he endangers her welfare.

"If I know Lercani, he will make some smart investments, all right. But it will only be a matter of time before he commits his first provable malfeasance. Then we cut him off, and we use his wrongdoing to put hobbles on Papa Da Brescia—to keep him from galloping full tilt on this path toward deformation of the Church and destruction of the papacy."

It was not a gentle plan. But as nearly as the Maestro and Helmut could see, the alternative was to have the wily fox Lercani running hither and thither in the vineyard of the Lord, mashing and destroying the precious vines of the Church's wealth. The Pope himself had made Lercani the "Vatican connection" with organized evil; yet, in doing so, he had now introduced him into the domain of the Church where the Keeper ruled.

Perhaps Peter Servatius did not well understand the intricate books of the IRA; but to Paolo Lercani, even the partial records to which he now had access were a revelation. And what they revealed left him reeling in shock and paralyzed with fury.

When Ectore Pappagallo joined Lercani in the intimacy of the Isola di Capri restaurant in Rome's Trastevere district, he found the financier boiling with rage.

"Paolo! *Pianissimo!* Calm yourself! What has gone wrong? Has the pact with His Holiness gone sour?"

"No, no. Of course not! But I've been deceived! I exercised the first right conceded to me by the contract. I went and asked that big, stupid ox, Servatius, for the IRA books. I've examined them—such as they are. There's only a miserable $2.5 or, maximum, $3 billion available! *Cristo!*" He banged the table so hard the flatware jumped. "Who did that?"

"Did what?"

"Look, Ectore, there's twenty, thirty, maybe even forty times that amount in the assets of the Holy See."

Pappagallo's mouth fell open.

"And," Lercani raged on, "that castrated oaf Servatius knows nothing. He just does what he's told. The only time he gets into trouble, I'll bet, is if he tries to think for himself!"

The senatore listened patiently through lunch to the bitter and sometimes blasphemous anger of his associate. Who did that crowd of louts in the Vatican think they were dealing with? Did they think they could match his brain? He would let them see what a superman does to pygmy enemies!

Pappagallo's contribution was briefer and more pointed; it came late in the meal. "Your undertaking for us, Paolo," he said in icy calm, "is to provide the financing for our operation. I don't know why you come here to tell me your sources have unforeseen limits. That's not my problem. It's yours. If there is more money in that quarter, you're going to find it for us. Aren't you, Paolo?"

"I'll do my best, of course!"

"You will, Paolo." The senatore downed the last of his wine and rose from his place. He did not need to remind Lercani that in their group failure was betrayal, and betrayal was death; the tone of his voice said that. "You will do your best. I bid you a very fine day."

The pre-summer meetings of Security Two were catch-up affairs. So much had been happening so fast that the Maestro, Brandolini, and Solaccio thought it wise to spend a few hours running through the state of affairs in as many areas as possible, always looking for patterns, as Brandolini had done when he came up with his P-1/P-2 theory.

Rico Lansing's report on the Apostolate for the Devotion to the Hearts of Jesus and Mary was largely a long list of cancellations, as far as Western Europe and the Americas were concerned. In diocese after diocese, the bishops had withdrawn patronage from the various sodalities of pious men and women that Rico's associates had built up. The vogue now ran instead to ecumenical groups, social-enrichment groups, experimental liturgy groups—a whole new tribe and breed of activities.

The demise of Rico's Apostolate was, as Cardinal Falconieri was quick to add, only one casualty of post–Vatican II "renewal," as it was called in the latest catchphrase. In most dioceses, the bishops had taken the bit between their teeth and had contracted what Falconieri called the "disease of democratization." They wanted to run the Church like a multiple-party system, he said, where God and the Sacraments and devotions could be voted on. They had all but given up the weekly public recitation of the Rosary; Benediction of the Blessed Sacrament was becoming a thing of rarity; membership in the traditional confraternities that focused on specifically Catholic devotions, such as the Holy Souls in Purgatory, St. Michael the Archangel, and the like, was being discouraged.

"Maybe they like to call it renewal," Rico commented acidly. "I call it decadence and death. We'll have to fall back with the Apostolate in the West for a while, and regroup.

"Thank God, though, that it's all going far better in the Soviet satellite countries."

Rico's glowing report of both the overt and covert work of the Apostolate in Eastern Europe led to a much briefer report by Brandolini.

"You remember you asked us to look into the source of financing for KOR, Rico? The *Komitet Obrany Robotnikow,* set up by our Trotskyite friends Viktor Adamchik and Jaček Kuron?"

"The Committee for the Defense of the Workers." Rico nodded his head. "Of course I remember. Did you find the source of their money?"

"Wallensky and Valeska were right in thinking the funds come from the West," Brandolini confirmed. "The setup is an account maintained by several New York–based companies in a Liechtenstein bank."

"And guess who owns the bank, Rico," Helmut put in. "Paolo Lercani."

"That guy's a jack-in-the-box!" Rico almost laughed in his surprise. "Every time I turn around, he pops up again! Jaime Herreras gets huge amounts out of an account he maintains in Panama; and that links him with Moscow. KOR gets funded by some big corporate account in a bank he owns in Liechtenstein; and that links him with the Trotskyites, who hate Moscow and every other government besides. Maybe you can figure it out, but I can't!"

The Maestro had a couple of additional Lercani links to tell about. He filled Rico and Falconieri in on the contract the Sicilian had inveigled Papa Da Brescia to sign. "And," he added, "surveillance has reported some recent meetings between Lercani and Senatore Pappagallo."

Rico shook his head in helpless bewilderment.

"Speaking of Herreras"—Solaccio spoke up for the first time—"Rico's meeting with him apparently had no effect. There are reports of a number of guerrilla bands operating under his direction, mainly in the southern part of Latin America.

"Closer to home," Solaccio went on, glancing down at a dossier he held, "since that Red Brigades bombing a year ago in Bologna, those savages have been having a field day. Since the beginning of this year alone, they have pulled nine armed robberies of major banks, bombed seventeen public buildings, had forty or fifty shootouts with security forces, and kidnapped eight people. Each of the kidnappings has been for heavy ransom. Everything they do is like a public manifesto. They always make sure everyone knows it's the Red Brigades who've done it. There's even been a rash of gangland-style executions, from the tip of Italy all the way up to the Alps. And every time, they leave their signature: 'Red Brigades.' Talk about insanity!"

Rico, like everyone there—everyone in the world, probably—had read about most of the Red Brigades' atrocities in the newspapers. But why was Solaccio bringing it up in connection with Herreras' guerrillas in South America? "Gian," he asked, "are you suggesting some connection between Herreras and the Red Brigades? That would be too much even for me to believe!"

"I'm not suggesting anything, Rico," Solaccio countered. "My job is to collect information. What we manage to make of it once we have it is something else."

Cardinal Falconieri, who generally sat silent in these meetings as the formal "presence," so to speak, of the State Council, did have something to say this time. "I think there is some connection, Rico. Oh, not the kind you're talking about, maybe—funding and priests-turned-guerrilla-leaders and all. But a very real connection, nevertheless. We used to have good solid names for it: Evil. Satan.

"People don't like those names anymore. But like it or not, some evil is let loose among Italians. And the picture Gian, here, paints in South America, and even our own reports about the decline in specifically Catholic activities in the Church in North America, in favor of what amount to no more than social get-togethers—all that suggests to me that the same evil that is afflicting the Church is let loose everywhere.

"Monsignore Brandolini has called it the 'insanity of destabilization.' But I call it an increasing lack of grace. In the world, and in the Church itself. I'm not the expert the rest of you are on the world, perhaps. But the Church is something I do know. It's plain to me that increasingly our officials lack grace. Hence we're losing priests and nuns. Hence we have a Pope who is at sixes and sevens. Hence we are watching the corruption of the very Sacrifice of the Mass itself. Hence we are discouraged. Hence, in fact, all our misery, all our doubt, all our fear.

"What we too often fail to remind ourselves is that grace isn't some airy-fairy word, a synonym for 'happy' or 'beautiful.' The word means 'gift.' And that's what it is. A real gift won for us by Jesus on the Cross, and transmitted anew to us every day in the Sacraments. That and only that is what the Sacraments are for. Baptism, Marriage, Absolution, Holy Orders, all the rest—they were all set up by Jesus himself as the real means by which he transmits his real gifts to his people forever. When Sacraments are corrupted, so is grace. And so is belief that only grace fosters and deepens. The more that corruption takes place, the freer Satan is to sow his seeds of harm. And we, my friends, appear to be reaping the first harvest of his biggest planting in a long, long time."

Cardinal Falconieri's voice trailed off into silence. So at odds was the theology of grace and Sacraments and sin, which he spoke of, with the normal stuff of Security Two's practical, this-worldly deliberations about surveillance and plots and the like, that every man there, each one a believer, was caught up for a moment in what was, after all, the only reason for their common and sometimes unpleasant work.

The cardinal's words brought home a new thought to Rico Lansing with sudden force. Oh, he had heard Cardinal Wallensky and the Maestro, too, talk often enough about serving the papacy rather than a single pope. But that a pope could turn from grace, betray it, even—somehow he had never singled that thought out in his mind, touched it with the fingers of conscious deliberation. Now that he did, it seemed to leave him for a moment without bearings; in some almost literal sense, it left him without a head—without the authority of the Pope upon which he, like the whole Church, relied in the manner laid down by the Founder; by Jesus. But he realized suddenly the moral strength of men who understood they had to separate the human weakness of the successor and vicar from the divinely ordained function and privileges of that same vicar and successor. Where did men like Wallensky find such strength?

He looked about the room in a sort of inner panic; his eye fell, and remained for a moment, on the place beside Falconieri where Cardinal Lanser used to sit in these meetings. And all at once, it was as though the Jesuit were present again, with all his worldly realism and solid faith.

It was Rico who broke the silence then. His voice was soft, but it filled the room as it might a chapel. "Joachim Lanser used to say that if this is the Church of Jesus, then it will survive; we have Christ's own promise for that. If grace lacks woefully to it now, and if we are reaping Satan's harvest, still there are things we can do. Must do, in fact, more than ever. We must fight, of course. We must do all we can to identify our enemies, to outwit them, to outthink them, block them, fight them bureaucratically, and with our own counterplans—my work of the Apostolate included. And in some way we must try to deal with the things of the world that spawn, say, a Jaime Herreras.

"But most of all, we must pray. And we must do penance. And then pray some more. And do still more penance. Grace is the first fruit of the Spirit Christ sent into the world. If grace has fled, it is because we have made its bearer unwelcome. Now, like John of the Cross, we must work in our very souls to make it welcome again—not as a visitor merely, but as chief resident in this Church.

"Unless we do that, then in all our strategies and plans to outwit our enemies we will be just as they are. And if that happens, there will be no reason any longer to fight them. They will have won, no matter who ends up with the power."

Paolo Lercani hit his head continually against the brick walls the Maestro had built up so well. He didn't give up, of course. He had a little time. The return he could make by his investments of the two or three billion dollars he presently had access to would be enough to allow him to provide for Papa Da Brescia's demands and Pappagallo's too; at least for a while. But just in case he couldn't breach the walls of defense that blocked him at every hand's turn from the major Holy See assets, he began to devise an alternate plan. Foresight. That was the key to his thinking now, as it had been the key to every advancement he had ever made since he had been dumped as a boy into the deep end of the pool of life. It had been sink or swim from the very start.

When Lercani returned to the Isola di Capri restaurant for the first time since his lunch with Senatore Pappagallo, he came alone. And his face was so serious that Gennar Schiavone, the proprietor, began to tremble slightly. He knew he was late with his payment for the latest drug delivery. It was a lot of money, but he hadn't expected Paolo to be on his neck yet.

"By my children's lives, Paolo," Gennar blurted out as the two sat down in a dark corner at the back of the restaurant. "I swear I'll have the money for you tomorrow."

Lercani looked at Schiavone in surprise for a minute, before he realized what the man was blabbering about. Such petty debts were the farthest thing from his mind right now.

"Sure, Gennar, sure. But that's not why I'm here."

Schiavone relaxed visibly. "What then, Paolo?"

"I need an engraver."

"A what?"

"An engraver, Gennar. Someone who knows securities like the back of his hand. Someone whose work is better than the work of the U.S. mint. And someone we can trust like the Pope trusts God!"

[[52]]

It was nearly ten o'clock that morning before Agathi and Keti were ready to drive into the city for some quick errands. Helmut and Guido were already up in the Maestro's study, deep in consultation about some problem or other. Rico was due to join them anytime now.

Keti kissed her son on the top of his head as he sat on the front steps. She gave Tati a little scratch on one ear. "You two behave yourselves. Nanna and I will be back in time for late lunch. It's a lovely day, isn't it?" Keti ranged her eyes over the green Alban Hills. "Maybe we can all go for a walk by the river in the afternoon."

Eugenio thought that was the best idea he'd heard all morning, and he said so, smiling up at Keti with his lovely eyes. He watched his mother step into the back seat of the limousine beside Agathi and blow another kiss back to him.

Sagastume pulled away from the door and was starting down the long drive when Rico's car came into sight. Rico edged over to the side of the drive to let them pass, gave a playful hello honk on the horn, and waved. Keti and Agathi waved back, and were gone.

"Uncle Rico!" Eugenio and Tati ran down the steps to greet him. "Will you race with me? I'll get the bikes out of the shed!"

Tati seemed to understand exactly what was being suggested. She made an excited little run toward the bicycle shed, and then back to Eugenio and Rico, barking and coaxing.

"I wish I could." Rico laughed and reached down to calm Tati with his hand. "I'm late already. But I'll tell you what. I'll walk to the shed with you. You get your bike and take Tati for a run. After I finish with your uncle Guido and your father, maybe then we can have a ride together."

Well, Eugenio agreed, that was better than nothing.

Before Rico let himself in the front door of Villa Cerulea, he turned to watch the boy pedaling slowly down the drive, the dog trotting happily beside him, holding her tail straight up, sniffing at the summer scents, now and then barking up at her master, for all the world as though carrying on a conversation.

Rico thought what a handsome boy Eugenio was. He wore khaki pants and sandals, and a light-blue short-sleeved shirt. His arms were tanned, and his hair was already bleached to an almost white-gold color by the summer sun. Even when the pair reached the gentle curve in the drive a quarter-mile distant, and Rico could no longer make out the blue of Eugenio's shirt or the wheaten hue of Tati's coat, he could still see the sun gleaming off that hair. They turned out of sight then. Rico, hoping he would have time for the promised bicycle ride, let himself into the cool interior of the house, Tati's barking a faint echo in the distance behind him.

It was one of those utterly tranquil mornings when the whole earth seems to breathe calmly. Up the drive, by the side of the house, the gardeners had switched on the sprinkling machines. Eugenio sat with his back against one of the giant Spanish yew trees just off the drive. Tati busied herself chasing a pair of squirrels. The water from the sprayers glistened in distant droplets that defied the sun, like pearls from a land of magic passing unscathed through fire.

This copse was another of Eugenio's favorite places. Yews didn't sough with the wind the way the trees did by the river. But these belonged to him in a special way. His uncle Guido had planted them only weeks before Eugenio had been born. Sometimes, when all the people he loved to be with most were too busy, he liked to come here, where he could see his house and imagine all the important things his father and his granduncle were tending to. He still remembered that birthday—oh, a lifetime ago—when he had surprised his Nanno in the early morning of his birthday and had said he wanted to be old too, just like Nanno was. He still wanted to be like his Nanno and his father one day; he was happy that day was drawing a little closer.

A rustling made him turn his head. Tati was scuffling and sniffing her way back toward him. She knew he was in no hurry. Tati understood so many things; often so much more than the adults did. She didn't need to talk; she knew how to communicate without words. Sometimes she would point with her nose to something she wanted, or to an empty corridor down which someone was just about to come. She knew before Eugenio when Nanno or Papa was returning home; she would put her paws on his knees, fix her black eyes on him—and he understood what she was saying.

She knew about people too. With some, she brightened and made friends—though a little cautiously at first, it was true. With others, she simply kept her distance. And with a very few—people in whom she seemed to "read" something she didn't like—she bristled and growled. Danni Mastrangelo always said that God gave dogs a second sight, and Eugenio decided that must be true. At least for Tati.

She was nearly at the edge of the copse now, eyeing Eugenio, ready for a game they played here. If Eugenio could catch her off guard, he would leap on his bicycle and pedal desperately down the rest of the drive, Tati galloping and barking behind him, until they both came breathless to the door of Signor and Signora Manesco's gatehouse.

"Ay! Tati!" Eugenio gave her fair warning that the game was on. He grabbed his bike and pushed himself off to a running start. Immediately, she was barking furiously, running with all her might to catch him.

It was only when they were almost at the gatehouse that Eugenio noticed Signor Manesco had forgotten to close the entry to the drive after his mother and Aunt Agathi had left. He braked to a quick stop and stood the bicycle against a corner of the house. Nanno would be furious if he knew the gates were open. Lately he had become a real bear about such things.

"Signor Manesco." He called to the gatekeeper as he looked about. There was no answer, and no sign of the man.

They couldn't have left, he thought. Not without making arrangements for someone to tend the entrance while they were gone. Signor Manesco had strict orders, and he always followed them.

"Signora?" He turned toward the stone house. "Signora Manesco!" He knew she spent most of her day in the kitchen, but there was no glimpse of her through the window.

Tati let out a growl.

"Sit, Tati!"

With obvious unwillingness, Tati crouched to the ground, still growling, while Eugenio went to knock on the door.

"Signor Manesco! It's Eugenio! You forgot to close the gate. . . ."

Too late, he looked back at Tati, saw her teeth were bared, knew something was wrong. The door of the stone house flew open. He had a momentary glimpse of a tall figure—the black dungarees, the masked head, the eyes glittering at him from slits, the mouth full of teeth.

He felt the rough hurt of gloved hands catch him by the neck and the small of the back, haul him forward. He saw the blur of Tati racing, flying at his attacker's throat; he saw Signor Manesco as another struggling, fighting blur out of the side of his terrified eyes. He fought and kicked and struggled against the terrific force of the arms that tried to pin his own.

Suddenly there was someone else, another hooded phantom, forcing him backward, grabbing him, or grabbing Tati in a tangle of arms and legs. He pounded wildly at his attackers. Tati gave an unearthly howl as yet another pair of hands tore her from the neck of Eugenio's first tormentor and sent her flying through the air. She hit the wall opposite with a terrible, sickening thud and fell limp to the floor.

"Tati!" Eugenio screamed with all his might, in terror, in anger, in anguish for Tati, for himself. "Papa! Nanno! Tati! Ta—" Suddenly his face was buried in a rag, shoved in it, held. There was a sickly smell in his nose. It turned his stomach, bathed his brain. His screams faltered. He couldn't breathe. He no longer knew where he was or what was happening to him. The only sound was his own mind, still screaming, still calling. "Papa! Nanno! Tati!" He was overcome, in that terror and unknowing, by the darkness of sleep.

Call it instinct. Agathi knew something was wrong. Even before they approached the gates, before she saw they were open, before she saw the great red dripping blotches of paint, she knew.

"Sagastume!"

The fright in her voice made Keti turn to look at her, then out the window of the limousine just in time to see the two painted words BRIGATE ROSSE. They were vulgar, bold, obscene, contemptuous in their brevity. *Red Brigades.*

Sagastume skidded the car to a halt, blocking the open entryway. Moving faster than Keti would have thought possible for such a giant of a man, he was out of his seat before the car was even fully stopped. Agathi ran behind him as if her very life depended on it.

They found the door to the cottage open, the whole place torn to bits as though some terrible army had raged through it.

Agathi saw Signora Manesco, lying face down on the floor. The sight held her motionless for an instant in her horror; but Sagastume, moving cautiously but as quickly as a cat through the rooms, somehow brought her to her senses. She rushed to see if the gatekeeper's wife was alive. A deep moan as of pain itself made her turn, and it was then she saw the gatekeeper. He had been horribly beaten, was streaming blood from a gash on his temple.

"Sagastume!" Agathi's eyes swept wildly around her, as though she were half here and half at some other scene, faraway years removed. "Help me! Get help! The phone! Sagas—"

"Eugenio!" Keti's wild, piercing scream from outside was endless. Even Sagastume froze for a second. But then he and Agathi were both beside her. She didn't seem to see them. She just screamed and screamed. *"Eugenio! Eugenio! Eugenio!"* Over and over she screamed, until suddenly the pain of what she knew was too much. Her eyes rolled back in her head, her knees buckled, and she dropped the sandal, her son's sandal, at Agathi's feet.

The de la Valles did not feel they were the victims of a mere crime. They had been exposed to some ultimate in human evil, to the *anus mundi,* the source of the inhuman stench seeping into the atmosphere of their society.

If Agathi had been the first on that afternoon of horror to know something was wrong, Guido was the first to know, or the first to admit to himself, that they would never see Eugenio again.

The chief investigator was efficient, grim, kind. A fleet of police, detectives, and security experts descended on Villa Cerulea, literally camped out for weeks there, combing every inch of the estate and its environs with dogs and men for any lead, any clue. They questioned everyone.

The only people who had seen anything were the Manescos. They had been overpowered and knocked senseless by four men with ski masks who had come from nowhere, bursting through their door in the quiet morning very soon after Agathi and Keti had left for Rome. Signore Manesco regained consciousness just as Eugenio was pulled into the cottage by one of the men. "I tried to get to him, Maestro." The tears streamed down the gatekeeper's face as he remembered it all. "Eugenio put up a tremendous fight. He was stronger than he looked, Maestro. He gave them more than they bargained for. He is a true de la Valle, Maestro. And Tati! I've never seen an animal in such desperate fury. It's a miracle she survived. The last thing I remember is her awful yowl when they threw her against the wall, and Master Eugenio screaming her name, and yours, Maestro, and his father's. But then two of them were all over me, beating me with something, and it all faded out for me."

There were no fingerprints, of course; not a trace of the assailants except for the can of paint and the brush the authors of that obscene blood-red sign had left behind them; and one bloody remnant of the ski mask Tati had pulled away with her sharp teeth when she had been torn from her attack.

The investigation did piece together a picture of sorts. But it was all hindsight. All too late. There had been a well-prepared and efficiently executed plan. Villa Cerulea had been under surveillance for weeks. Someone had used an aged oak as a lookout from the hillside where Keti had sat watching Rico and her son and Tati that day. Someone had lain in the grass of the hillock looking down on Eugenio's "island bridge" where the wind soughed of God and angels to him through the trees. A car with several occupants had been seen irregularly but frequently cruising about in the area. Danni Mastrangelo remembered passing an empty car parked on a road not far from the postern gate, but that had been some weeks ago. Those and a few other details were all the investigation revealed. Really nothing.

Guido's surface reaction appeared almost lethally cold and rational to some, like the inspector, who didn't know him. By some instinct he knew that the purpose of this insanity was to demoralize, to frighten, to cow, to break them and everyone like them. This was not the work of politicians or of some desperate group of social outcasts, but of evil itself, using the body of a young and innocent boy in a heinous, coldblooded power play. Guido de la Valle, the supreme broker of power, recognized the move. He could not keep Eugenio now. But he would not betray his suffering. He would not let that suffering be used. He imposed a total ban on publicity. There were no press reports, no radio bulletins, no television specials, no *paparazzi.* He would deny the enemy at least the victory of publicity.

Guido left Villa Cerulea only once in the days immediately following Eugenio's kidnapping. Sagastume drove him to the papal villa at Castel Gandolfo, where he spent five minutes with Papa Da Brescia—just long enough to give an account of what had happened to his grandnephew.

The Pontiff received the news with hooded eyes. "The insanity!" He whispered the words in a nearly inaudible breath.

"Yes, Holiness."

The Maestro asked that the blackout on news of the matter be respected. He said he would remain for the foreseeable future in seclusion with his family at Villa Cerulea. In an emergency, he would be available, of course. "We need Your Holiness' prayers."

He waited only a moment for some further response from the Pope. But the gulf between them was very great, even at such a time as this.

He kissed the papal ring, and left.

Only very slowly did the sense of hate and helpless rage and pain loose its hold on each of the de la Valles in turn. An obscene hand had reached into the delicate intimacy of their lives and smeared some moral filth across their souls. Each one of them—Guido and Agathi, Helmut and Keti—had received a wound that would refuse to heal. They would, each one of them in his or her own time, lay Eugenio to rest in their hearts, so that the suffering of his suffering ceased to haunt them. But they would never obliterate the memory of his face, the echo of his voice, the sweet taste of Eden that he, as a child, had given them.

Initially, one of the greatest difficulties affecting those four people who loved each other so much was their inability to talk about what had happened. They were like little isolated islands separated by deep waters and clad in a constant twilight. The brutality of Eugenio's fate and bereavement for his loss deepened each one's sense of inner self. They spoke at first only in staccato and disjointed phrases, usually about practical matters. Except for Rico Lansing, they wanted no one near them. Mariella and Regina kept all the other servants far from the main living quarters. Sagastume made himself scarce. They all attended Don Filippo's Mass every morning and received Holy Communion. They ate together. But whatever they did, they seemed apart except for the agony and patience that bound them.

Even Tati seemed to want to be alone. She recovered quickly from her injuries, as young animals often do. She spent her days in Eugenio's room, occasionally whimpering, or running on sudden impulse to the ground-floor windows to watch awhile for her master. But then she would return to her upstairs vigil. Once, after a particularly harrowing talk with the chief investigator, Guido walked back to his rooms and sat down, trying to calm his raw sorrow, rubbing his hands over his eyes in an effort to ease the sting of pressing tears. He heard a whimper, and looked toward his open door. Tati was standing there, just looking at him. She whimpered again, and then she turned away. She knew: Guido could not console her, could not bring her Eugenio back.

The tower of unshakable strength, cool judgment, and sweetest gentleness that Guido was for Keti and Agathi and Helmut in those days was not a masquerade. In outward appearance, he was all of that. He was their only recourse. It was just that behind those unshaken walls of self-control, a deep turbulence whirled, peeling away the trophies he had treasured from all his victories as faithful Keeper of the Bargain.

Curiously, it was Papa Da Brescia who unwittingly raised that turbulence to a tidal wave. "The insanity!" That was all he had been able to say by way of response to Guido's loss. But even he, the Maestro reflected, with his myopia for reality and his peculiar view of the Church, even Da Brescia could recognize the lineaments of evil once it poked its face naked in his way.

It was poignant for Guido to recall how arrogantly he had himself responded to Papa Profumi's prescient warnings of some evil he saw let loose and looming toward them out of world events. Guido had thought then that he could control it all, ward it off, keep it at bay. Certainly, keep it from touching his own flesh. But it had outrun all his fine calculations.

Guido, like the others in his family, had his own way of dealing with his pain of loss. He went on quiet pilgrimage to Eugenio's "places." The "island bridge." The copse of Spanish yews that were of an age with the beloved boy. The back road where he used to ride with Doni Graziani. The little shed beside the garage where he used to clean and repair his bicycle. And in each one of them, he would stay for a time and talk with Christ, and with Eugenio as Christ's own angel now. He would remind Eugenio that they had made a pact. They would never lose one another, they said. When Christ called Nanno home to heaven, he would still be with Eugenio, watching over him always.

"Now Christ has called you instead, Eugenio. And I, who by all rights should have gone instead, am left to carry on. Be nearer to me than ever now. Help me. And be near your mama and papa. Tell me someday that you are with us. That you still love me." Now and again, he might raise his head, as if to hear the angel sounds in the soughing breeze, as Eugenio had.

For Keti, the pain was unendurable. The cruel moment when she had found Eugenio's sandal was the grimacing tormentor of her first days and nights after his disappearance. She tried to stop herself from living that moment over and over, as if she could, by that act of will, stop the event itself, reverse it in its course. As if she herself had made a mistake somewhere between the door of the limousine and the door of the gatehouse. As if, by correcting that mistake, whatever it was, she could bring Eugenio back.

She began to behave with Helmut as if he were repellent to her, a personal sign of failure and death. Certain that she was doing him a favor, she began to sleep in another room. She chose a small guest room across the hall from Eugenio's old room. She didn't so much decorate that place as change it into something resembling a monastery cell. She slept on a narrow bed, had some bookshelves moved in, a large desk, a kneeler. She hung dark curtains against the light, and some paintings—Christ and his mother and a favorite saint or two. Two photographs of Eugenio hung above her bed, one as a baby in her arms, and one on his thirteenth birthday—his last.

There, she spent hours alone, asking agonizing questions. How much did Eugenio suffer? Had he cried? Had they beat him if he did? Did they feed him? Did they mutilate him? How did they kill him? Were they cruel about it? Did he see the weapon they used? Did he take a long time to die? Her imagination and her love played havoc with her. She spent day after day alone in that chamber of unknown horrors a mother's mind becomes when the child of her womb is stolen and she is sure only of two things: his suffering and his death. She hadn't even the comfort his burial might have given her.

So deep was she in grief and despair that Agathi called for the doctor. All he could do, however, was to prescribe a mild sedative. If she could at least sleep at night, he said, she would come around in time.

Sometimes Rico would visit with her for a while. The nightmare was terrible for him too. He never stopped remembering Eugenio, or that last beautiful look he had given him as he rode off in the morning sun with Tati to wait for their promised ride together on the afternoon that never came for him. Perhaps, Rico thought, if he had only gone with Eugenio as the boy had asked, nothing would have happened. "If" was his tormentor. Never had Rico thought that the memory of such fresh beauty and winsome innocence as Eugenio's could cause such refined pain as he now felt.

Still, he showed none of that to Keti. Their conversations were her only solace. There was no aberration of thought she expressed, no word of reproof to God or revolt against what had happened, that Rico could not hear with his almost infinite patience and that particular gentleness he had. "I teach without noise of words," Thomas à Kempis once wrote; "without confusion of opinions, without ambition of honor, without the scuffling of arguments." Rico was the embodiment of those words for Keti.

Certain though she was that she was doing Helmut a kindness by removing herself from his bed, and as much as possible from his sight, Keti was in fact only doubling her husband's agony. He was without the comfort of sharing, as he struggled with his own memories. How often had he put Eugenio off? How often had his son begged to go along on this trip or that one? How often had Helmut said, "Not this time, *carito"?* How often had Eugenio said, "I won't be a bother. I just want us to be together, Papa." How often did Helmut weep now in solitude, "I just want us to be together, Eugenio."

If Helmut managed to sleep at all, he would wake with a start in an hour or two, and reach across the bed for Keti's hand, for the solace of her touch.

Finally one night, when for the tenth or fifteenth or millionth time he realized how alone he was, he stood up suddenly from bed, went to Eugenio's room, removed one of the photographs of the boy and Keti from his dressing table, and took it back with him. He placed it under the bedside lamp. "I'm alone now, *carito.*" He spoke to it. "Unless you can help, I'm alone now. And so is your mother. Can you teach us to love all over again?"

Agathi's nightmares were all her own. Except for her beloved Guido, no one could guess at their depth. As she watched Keti's pain, though, she began to think she would have to find the strength to live them again. Perhaps she could do that. If it would help Keti, perhaps she could.

When the chief inspector called after weeks of silence to ask Guido and Helmut to visit his office, he had no news of Eugenio to report. Neither he nor the de la Valles expected he ever would. Nor did he know why Eugenio had been chosen as a victim of the Red Brigades.

"We think they are just looking for victims, Maestro, victims of a certain type." The inspector continued talking as he showed Guido and Helmut into a long, narrow room. "How your Eugenio came to their attention we may never know."

"Victims?" Helmut was aghast to think that what had happened to his son might be becoming the routine stuff of police work.

"Yes, Signore. That's why I asked you here. We've been interrogating one of the Red Brigades bastards. Caught him in a bank robbery that turned into a shootout. They left him behind. Too slow, I guess. But he's a stubborn s.o.b. I thought you might want to see what we're dealing with. It's not pretty, though. . . ."

"By all means, Inspector." Guido wanted to put some face on his enemy, even if it had no face, really.

"Please. Sit down, Maestro. Signore." The inspector pressed a button beside the one-way mirror at the far end of the room and turned off the lights. In a moment, two detectives came through the door on the other side of the glass. A single prisoner, his feet and ankles shackled. A third detective came in last.

The inspector threw a switch, and the sounds of coughing and shuffling of feet and the scraping of chairs came through.

"Your name is Pietro Spazza?" One of the detectives began the interrogation—not the first, by the looks of this Spazza.

The prisoner spat on the table in front of him. He was young, perhaps twenty-five, with long hair. There was a look of arrogance on his face that said he cared about nothing—not his chains, or the prison, or his interrogators, or anything.

"You are a member of the Red Brigades?" The detective asked a second question, and Spazza spat a second time.

"Why do you torture and kill helpless people?"

Guido gripped his chair so hard his knuckles were white. Helmut put out his hand and took his uncle's in his own.

"Because people respect only death!" Something more than his own spittle finally came from Spazza's mouth. "The Red Brigades kill only those in authority. That's all we want to do. Break down their morale. The morale of authority. The government's morale. The morale of the corrupt governing classes. When we have killed enough, raped enough, dynamited enough, they will break. All of them. They will collapse. The people will be free! The people will take over!"

"How many children have you killed, Pietro?"

Helmut tightened his hand around his uncle's.

"Try a more intelligent question, pig, if you can find the brains for it!"

The inspector threw the switch and the sound stopped coming through. Guido watched for a minute more the mobile visage of hate that Spazza's face was, as his mouth spewed out soundless obscenities.

He was grateful for the glass of cognac the chief inspector poured when they were back in his office. "Tell me, Inspector. What do we know about these Red Brigades?"

"Pretty much what you heard from Pietro Spazza, Maestro. They want to destroy all authority. Government. Church. Any organized institution. We have collateral evidence that they're being financed by others, who stay in the background but who apparently have the same aim. They have cells of sympathizers all over Italy now. In every city and town. Every university and college. But we haven't been able to locate the source of their funding."

"Perhaps we can help each other in that, Inspector. We will keep one another informed, eh?"

"Of course, Maestro. I am always at your service. I only wish we had been able to . . ."

"I know, Inspector."

With Helmut and Guido both out of the house for the first time since Eugenio had been kidnapped, Agathi felt it was the moment to try to get through to Keti. It was typical of her that someone else's pain galvanized her to surmount her own. And she was beginning to fear that Keti's tearless, barren agony would actually kill her in time; that she would die of her grief.

Agathi went to her own apartment and dug deep down in an old chest, where she retrieved a photograph album she had long ago buried away. Then she went down the wide corridor and, after a last, deep sigh, tapped lightly on Keti's door.

Keti looked up from the chair by the window and smiled faintly as

Agathi came in. The dark curtains were partially drawn, and Keti appeared as a sort of twilight silhouette, the open book in her lap obviously forgotten.

"I wish I had some of your strength, Agathi," she said as though taking up after a pause in some normal conversation.

"You're doing better than I did, sweetheart." Agathi sat down on the bed, made sure Keti saw her put the album on her lap and, with exaggerated interest, begin to leaf through it. She was coaxing Keti with curiosity, the way she had done with Eugenio when he was small and pouting over some hurt.

Keti's hurt wasn't the same, and Agathi didn't pretend it was. It was just that she had to try, and didn't know any other way to begin.

"No, I'm not doing better than you, Agathi. I guess it's because a mother suffers most. I can't seem to cope with it."

Why has she come here? Keti wondered. She just sits there thumbing through those photos. How insensitive she seems. . . .

It was that thought that finally triggered something in Keti's mind, set it to work independently of her will, as it seemed. Agathi was not insensitive. She was the very opposite, and always had been. What was she up to?

"Are those pictures of Eugenio you're looking at, Agathi?" It seemed logical as a ploy Agathi would use to draw her out in her grief.

"No, my darling. Not Eugenio. Joanna."

Joanna? Keti thought and thought, but couldn't remember anyone in the de la Valle family ever talking about someone named Joanna.

"Come." Agathi patted a place beside her on the edge of the bed. "Come see. She was beautiful. As beautiful as Eugenio. She would have been much older, of course. She would have made me a grandmother several times over by now, I expect. If she had lived."

Keti seemed for a moment not to understand. She looked at Agathi; rose slowly from her chair, not minding the book that dropped to the floor. She crossed the narrow space to the bed and, without a word, took the album in her own lap. She began looking at it carefully from beginning to end.

Agathi as a teenager; a little awkward, but already very pretty. Agathi as a young woman, even more beautiful than when Keti had just met her in Waidhofen; the ideal of beauty, in fact. Agathi standing next to a darkly handsome man, holding her hand rather obviously, so the camera would catch the ring she wore.

"Michael was his name." Agathi's voice was little more than a trembling whisper in Keti's ear. "Michael Stavronas. He was from Chios. I met him in Paris. I was so proud of that ring when he gave it to me. And so happy."

"Yes," Keti said. "I can see it in your face, in photo after photo."

The next pictures showed all the pomp and dignity of an Orthodox wedding in a Byzantine church in Athens. And then there were a few of Agathi and Michael waving as they boarded a very handsome yacht; and still more photos, dozens of them, of the party given on board before the two sailed off on their honeymoon.

They filled Keti with nostalgia, all those pictures of happy people, and of the exquisite bride Agathi had been, waving goodbye at the railing, her Michael beside her.

The next pictures, however, were so stark by contrast that they made Keti catch her breath. There weren't many. And they were of Agathi alone. All light and grace had been eclipsed from her face. There was a greenish misery and a forced, false smile. In the last ones of the series, no amount of makeup could hide the bruises. Then there was one last photograph. A tiny, perfect, beautiful infant girl.

"Joanna?" Keti looked up for the first time since she had taken the album from Agathi's hands.

Agathi was pale as death. Her answer didn't seem to follow on the question.

"Michael knew how to make love only in a perverted fashion. He was ill or twisted in some way. I blamed myself. It was my fault. I should have been able, I thought, to bring out the tenderness in him. But he would rage and foam at the mouth. The more I tried to please him, the worse he became. When I was able to think back on it later, I wasn't sure he knew he was even beating me. I was too stupid or too innocent to leave him. I was too foolish to tell my brother, or anyone, what was happening. I just kept thinking it was my fault.

"I did conceive, though, finally. I locked myself away for most of those months when I was pregnant. I wasn't so afraid of the beatings any longer; not for myself, at least. But I was afraid I might lose the child.

"When Joanna was born, Michael was enraged because she wasn't a boy. She wouldn't carry on the Stavronas name. I had failed in that too. He stayed away for weeks.

"I had just begun to hope he would never come back, when he stumbled into the nursery one day in a drunken haze. I barely remember what happened. I know I ran for Joanna. He ran for me. He picked something up and flailed at us both. He killed her in my arms. Crushed her skull."

Tears of remembrance and love and rage and helplessness were streaming down Agathi's cheeks. Keti knelt on the floor so she could see her, look up at her, wipe her tears, comfort her.

"The local judge was an uncle of Michael's." Agathi went on in that peculiar, trembling whisper. "He said Joanna's death was an accident. Regrettable, he said.

"Michael never came near me again. I think he knew I would have killed him if he did.

"And then one day he collapsed. On the pavement not far from the ruins of an old Greek temple. I never even asked what killed him, or if anyone was with him when he died.

"I sent a short note to Guido. I don't know what I wrote, but it must have been half mad. He had known Joanna was dead, but I had asked him not to come then. This time, he wouldn't stay away. Little by little, I was able to tell him most of what had happened.

"He brought me here then, to Villa Cerulea. He never made it seem as if he was rescuing me, or that he pitied me. He made me feel I was essential to his life, to the life of this house; that I was doing him a favor because he needed me. And oh, Keti, I needed to be needed. I needed some purpose, some love, something and someone to make me want to live from one day to the next."

Agathi looked down at Keti then, her eyes shining with the tears. "I never intended to tell you all this. I've never even told Helmut. But I thought maybe—if you knew that someone understands a little what you feel . . ."

She shivered slightly, though the day was warm. "That day in the gatehouse, for just a minute in all the shambles and turmoil, I almost thought I was back there in that nursery; that Michael was—"

"Oh, Agathi! Don't! Please, don't!" Keti was choked with all the tears she hadn't been able to release. That Agathi should do this for her, relive her own deepest horror for Keti's sake. She laid her head on Agathi's lap and wept at last, for a long time, until there were no more tears left in the abyss of her grief.

They talked quietly for a time afterward. Of death and parting and uniting all joy and all suffering with Christ's own. Of what it costs to put tragedy away after a time, and of how memories are kept alive.

Keti's mouth was still trembling when they heard Tati barking, and then some faint sounds downstairs. Guido and Helmut must have returned.

Agathi cupped Keti's chin in her hand and raised her face. "What about Helmut?" She knew Keti understood what she was asking. When would she end this exile from her husband? He loved her and needed her. More now than ever. But she saw in Keti's eyes that she couldn't believe that yet. Like Agathi years before, Keti blamed herself in some irrational way for what had happened.

Agathi kissed the top of Keti's head, much as Keti had kissed Eugenio's that last morning on the steps by the drive.

"Don't wait too long." She spoke in the tenderest, softest voice Keti had ever heard. "There are too few days; and too many regrets when all the days are done."

"That's a change for the better, Helmut!" The Maestro cocked an ear as he climbed the front steps beside his nephew.

They both listened again to be sure. It was Tati! She had finally left her vigil and was barking behind the door, waiting to be let out, to say hello.

The minute they opened the door, though, Tati backed away.

Perhaps she only hoped again that it was Eugenio coming home, Helmut thought.

But no; not this time. She looked straight into Guido's eyes, the way she used to do with Eugenio when she wanted to be picked up.

"All right, Tati girl." The Maestro bent down and scooped her into one hand. "Come, my brave little one. It's time we did something to make Eugenio proud."

Guido looked at Helmut, a little smile trying itself out on his lips, his eyes asking the question in his mind. Are you with me? Are you ready?

Helmut couldn't quite manage the smile yet. But, yes, his eyes answered Guido's; he was ready.

[53]

The de la Valles dated events from that awful day. The loss was built into their lives as a permanent component of their actions and character. Never would any of them do even the simplest things—sit at dinner, walk the estate, see a child running, greet a change of season, feel a ruffling wind—without embracing a sweet shadow memory of Eugenio. Their mutual relationship was colored by what had happened to him, and they regarded the final end of their mortal days as a promise of their reunion with him.

The appearance of winter suited the Maestro's mood. The outrageous assertions of that Red Brigades member, Pietro Spazza, in the police interrogation room became for him a sort of lens through which he began to focus on a wider scene.

Pietro Spazza had ranted about two things: demoralization and destabilization. The actions of Spazza, and of the Red Brigades, were beginning to hang over Italy like a great red blotch. Just the way Jaime Herreras' now hung like a red blotch over Latin America, for the purpose of demoralizing and liquidating the lines of authority there. And as the Northern Alliance actions had for years hung over the Vatican, threatening liquidation of the central authority of the papacy, and the dilapidation and tearing down of the unity of language, of worship, and of belief throughout the Church.

Inevitably, Guido's mind began to trace again through Giulio Brandolini's P-1/P-2 theory. Hadn't the Vatican intelligence chief, after all, been ahead of everyone when he had traced that pattern—that arch of destabilization—on the blackboard in his office? The odds were great against the chance appearance of these nearly identical "red blotches" everywhere at the same time, unless they were all painted by the same hand—by Brandolini's "keystone": by P-1.

If the Maestro's one further theory was correct, if P-1 was in fact the Universal Assembly with which the Keeper's Bargain had been struck, then the direct parts of Papa Profumi's forebodings back in the forties were being vindicated. The long-dead Pope had warned him graphically about the dangers of consorting with Mammon. But all along, the Maestro had thought he could keep things under control, keep the desires of Mammon away from the *impero,* keep the powers of Mammon from damaging his Church and his Pope.

There would never be an opportunity to discuss the Bargain with the members of the Assembly. Obviously, in pursuit of their enmity for Catholicism, they had aided and would go on aiding groups and individuals who had the opposite intention from that of the Keeper, whom they were sworn by the Bargain to aid only in certain financial ways.

The difficulty was that P-1—as Guido began to think of the Universal Assembly in his own mind now—wielded such huge, indeed almost incomprehensible, worldwide power that even the Maestro could not begin to destroy that power without destroying his own. As he had pointed out to Helmut after the Security Two meeting nearly two and a half years before, the *impero*'s far-flung and highly successful activities in behalf of the Holy See's assets were possible precisely because of the universal financial "doors" made accessible through the Bargain.

The corresponding difficulty, however, was that P-1 had now apparently wrapped its fingers of control around the Vatican. Around the papacy. Around the spiritual authority of the Church. Around the sole motivation for the Keeper to keep the Bargain. In this view of things, Papa Da Brescia, with whom the Maestro had been at war for some time already, was merely an instrument being used by others. Like Eugenio, he too was a target—though a far less innocent one, to be sure. A target, not because of who he was personally, but because of what he represented. And if that was so, the deep threat to Church and papacy would not end with Da Brescia's reign.

Well, if the Maestro could not meet with P-1, and if he could not attack its overarching power without destroying his and the *impero*'s power, he could and would go after the lesser fry. Those interest groups at the center of Brandolini's arch, the P-2 elements, had to be his target.

In the quiet of his study, and with Helmut at his side, the Maestro sketched out again a new version of Brandolini's arch of destabilization. It stood to reason, he said, that the most practical common element linking all the conflicting interests that Brandolini had identified—Pappagallo, the Nazis, Herreras—was the financial element. "And who is it," he asked, "who has cropped up most often? Wherever we look, in fact? And now even in the Vatican Bank itself?"

The answer was as obvious to Helmut as it was to his uncle: Paolo Lercani.

"The key to prying the fingers of P-1/P-2 loose from our domain"—the Maestro spelled it out—"has got to be Lercani.

"Up until now, we have waited for him to make some mistake, and for whatever mistake he made to surface in the natural order of things."

"And now?" Helmut was ignited in his turn by the cold fire in the Maestro's eyes.

"Now, nephew, we go after him, this little superman. We use every means at our disposal to find out every detail we can about him and his operations. We use our *impero* associates. We use our international network of trusted men. We use our banks and companies. We use our contacts who know about so-called laundering operations, and we use the contacts of our contacts. We use Security Two, including Brandolini and Solaccio and their contacts and resources.

"Once we know all the details of how Lercani works, it should not be that difficult for us to bring him tumbling down the side of his mountain."

The plan suited Helmut's entire frame of mind. The hardest thing would have been for him simply to go on as before, as though nothing had happened. He wanted revenge. He wanted a target.

The war of the financial titans began, then, with a meeting of the *impero* at Villa Cerulea in November of 1969. Guido and Helmut left no doubt in the minds of their associates about what they wanted, or the urgency with which they were to swing into action. No lead was to be ignored. No possible source of information, however remote, however high or low, however big or small, was to be left aside. They expected, they said, a veritable torrent of facts, figures, names, connections—anything that might be useful—to begin without delay.

The day after the *impero* meeting, Helmut started a series of trips through Europe and the Americas to set up still more avenues of information through the intricate financial network he had developed with a fine hand over the years.

By early 1970, the remarkable empire of Paolo Lercani began to take shape in outline for the Maestro and his nephew. Working together for eighteen and twenty hours a day with the tidal waves of intelligence that washed across the Maestro's desk, they assembled complex charts that became, in effect, the developing portrait of a man who brokered money in exchange for power, and who would deal with any group, any person, no matter how disparate their purposes, to parlay himself, Paolo Lercani, from one level of financial control to another.

The first job Guido and Helmut tackled was to reconstruct the "tools," the physical plant—the actual banks, corporations, and businesses—upon which Lercani's operations rested; and to discover how he had them organized in relation to one another.

The nerve center was obviously his operation in Milan: "Milan Central," as the Maestro dubbed it.

At the next level, there was a series of what Guido called "master banks": world-class banks, about a dozen in number, each one strategically located in a major city and able to deal easily anywhere else in the world on a moment's notice; and in each of which Lercani held control, sometimes through actual equity ownership, sometimes simply through the immense amount of business he funneled through it.

On the third tier down in the Lercani banking pyramid, directly beneath the "master banks,' there began to appear an intricate international system of medium- and fairly large-sized banks, all owned by Lercani, or in which he held majority shares. Unlike the master banks, these rank-and-file or "field banks" could be anywhere in the world. The de la Valle sources uncovered them in cities, towns, and villages in Italy and

Germany, Switzerland and Liechtenstein and Luxembourg, Singapore, Hong Kong, and the Virgin Islands; and in the Americas they were beginning to spread both north and south from Panama. There were none, however, in the United States.

As still more information came to them, Guido and Helmut saw that the most important banking area for Lercani outside of Italy was Liechtenstein, with a list of nothing less than thirty banks, headed by some very impressive names. Very nearly as important and impressive were the banking networks at Lercani's disposal in Luxembourg, Singapore, and the Virgin Islands.

The one big question mark was in Switzerland. They were, for example, able to get some information, despite the secrecy of the Swiss banks, that verified Lercani's dominant position in a few of the more than three hundred banking institutions in Lugano. But of the nearly $4 billion that had been banked in that city alone over the past five years, since 1964, they could only guess that a goodly portion of it was controlled in one way or another by Lercani.

Of course, Lercani's "physical plant" was not confined to his elaborate worldwide pyramid of banks. There was as well an equally intricate and equally far-flung system of nonbanking business establishments that ranged in size and importance from some of the larger in the industrial and postindustrial centers of the world, to hole-in-the-wall operations tucked away in Dijon or Glasgow or Pittsburgh or Ann Arbor. There were interests in steel, chemicals, petroleum, toys, furniture, grain and animal feed, textiles—the list seemed all-inclusive.

As the charts of banks and businesses grew in complexity, certain patterns of particular interest for the Maestro and his nephew began to emerge. Given the nature of the *impero*'s activities, and of Lercani's ambition, it was inevitable that their international investment paths had frequently crossed. Indeed, one of Lercani's "master banks" appeared to be the Banco Agostiniano Milan, which was owned by the Vatican, and whose director-general, Roberto Gonella, had been approved by the *impero* some years before.

Other banks and corporations through which Lercani frequently did business, or in which he held minority shares, were controlled by the Holy See. There were still others, not controlled or owned by the Vatican, whose boards contained at least one representative of the Holy See.

Even before they had assembled all the details of Lercani's "physical plant," his "tools" of operation, the information flowing in to them allowed the Maestro and Helmut to begin to understand the ways in which Lercani used those tools. While there were many variations, in general he seemed to favor three.

First, Lercani had developed to the level of high art a sophisticated system of over- and under-invoicing that made expert use of his business and corporate holdings. In this scheme, one of Lercani's Italian companies—probably one that was buried among the subsidiaries of a larger one—would, for example, export goods to one of Lercani's own foreign companies. The purchase price in the contract would be shown at, say, two or three million dollars, while twice the contract price would actually change hands. The money shown in the contract would be paid and recorded in the proper way by both buyer and seller. The second two or three million, however, which was not shown in the contract, would be paid by the buyer in cash to a Lercani account in Switzerland or another of his banking havens, whose records lay beyond the reach of normal scrutiny.

A second favored device was a sort of variation on the first, except that it primarily used Lercani's banks and money houses rather than his other corporations. This was the systematic use of foreign exchange. Here, a Lercani bank in Italy might buy a few million dollars from a Lercani bank in Germany at an inflated rate of exchange, paying perhaps 10 percent or 15 percent over the trading range. A few weeks or months later, the Italian bank would sell those same dollars back to the German bank at the lower, official rate. As with the bogus billing scheme, the difference between the inflated buying price and the lower selling price would be paid by the Lercani German bank to a Lercani account in Switzerland or another protected haven. Thus, again, a huge, unrecorded cash sum was exported from Italy, the *cedolare* tax was avoided, and still more capital had become both liquid and anonymous, to frolic on the international money scene with remarkable freedom from strictures.

The third method of operation that seemed to be favored by Lercani was a fiduciary account system: the sequestering and investment of money for others, both corporate and private, through his own banking system in such a way as to produce paper profits for the depositors, and —as always—a huge pool of capital in Lercani's hands, which could be shifted out of Italy and into countries where restrictions were less troublesome and further movements easier to accomplish.

In just about all of Lercani's methods, the "pairing" of banks was of primary importance. In fact, as Guido and Helmut saw rather quickly, such "pairing" was one of the principal keys to his entire structure. For every bank where there were strict regulations of one sort or another, there was a corresponding bank in a suitable money haven.

Another striking factor—another key to his success—was the degree of immunity Lercani enjoyed in this international money game of his. The Maestro and Helmut knew of his Mafia connections, of course, which had been a help to him from the very start in Sicily. They had already discovered his connection with Senatore Pappagallo, whose influence both in Italy and abroad had its uses in this regard. Papa Da Brescia had obliged with the immunity of the Vatican by virtue of the contract he had signed with Lercani. And, of course, Lercani's very success as an international businessman, banker, and entrepreneur was a help in itself. He was respected by the money changers of the world, as befitted a man who owned or controlled over five hundred companies worldwide, and who was chairman of the board of his Milan-based Argentking, Inc., the biggest international currencies brokerage the world had ever seen. He couldn't use much of the trillion dollars deposited there, or its annual gross volume of

$200 billion, in his sub rosa money schemes. But Argentking alone brought him more than acceptability; he became *persona gratissima* with governments, major cartels, and anyone of significance he might care to deal with.

On top of that, the Maestro's and Helmut's far-flung lines of investigation reeled in information they had not suspected before.

Lercani, it turned out, had for some time been a clandestine conduit of money into Italy for American intelligence organizations.

"What's *that* all about?" Helmut puzzled over the information when it first came in.

For Guido, the answer seemed obvious. "Just look around you at the chaos setting into our political and social life in Italy. The Left could take over. U.S. funds are coming in to prepare for a possible takeover by right-wing forces. Just as they did in Greece two years ago. With U.S. funds."

"But why in the world"—Helmut still scratched his head—"would American intelligence deal with the likes of Lercani? I mean, for one thing, they must know his Mafia connections and some of his other *dirty* business as well."

Again, Guido thought the answer was right in front of them. "I've no doubt that Senatore Ectore Pappagallo, with his political connections from his days in the Italian government, and with his international business connections now, and his connection with Lercani as well, is the marriage broker there. I don't imagine U.S. intelligence cares about Lercani's pedigree, in any case. He serves their purpose. The result for him is that he handles more money, makes more profit, and gets another level of protection, to boot."

Among the rafts of information Brandolini and Solaccio came up with were the first connections tying Lercani banks to the Red Brigades. The odd man, like Pietro Spazza, had been caught. Mail drops and contacts had been discovered. Such things linked up and led to the matching of sums taken in a kidnap ransom or a bank robbery with a sudden increase in the flow of funds in similar amounts through Lercani's laundering system.

By early 1970, within a month or two of the *impero* meeting, Guido began to address the primary reason for all this information-gathering: he began to look for the weakest points in Lercani's system, areas where a bit of judicious tinkering by the *impero* might work wonders—at least from the Maestro's point of view.

"What is noteworthy, Helmut," he said, while scribbling some calculations on a sheet already covered with numbers, "is that I don't think the money adds up!"

"Come on, Uncle! He's dealing in billions!"

"I grant you that. In fact, he's dealing in more than billions. If I read all these charts and dossiers of information we've assembled correctly, this is one financier who will never have enough. Power is his only god, and money is the offering he makes to it.

"What he's developing here, as far as I can see, is nothing less than a worldwide monetary system with himself at the apex. Step by step, he has been moving toward greater and greater information and control of liquid capital flowing between all nations, north, south, east, and west. Even the Soviet countries are not excluded. Remember the Herreras connection? And the connection with KOR in Poland?

"Unless I miss my guess, that new global monetary system is what he's after. That's why he doesn't care if it's Herreras or the Nazis or the Trotskyites or the Red Brigades or the U.S. intelligence he makes his deals with. He doesn't care if it's kidnap ransoms or drugs or petroleum or shoe leather or currency stocks or bonds or whole companies he's buying and selling. The object—that god he worships—is a program that is petty only by comparison with some grandiose blueprint for conquest of the human race by force of arms, or the conversion of all people to one religious faith. And in the end, it amounts to the same thing.

"I'm as convinced of all that by what we've learned in these past two months as I am of anything. He's not just a petty crook from the *sottogoverno,* as I thought he was when we began this operation. Not by a long shot!

"And now he's got his first finger into the assets of the Holy See! It's my job—our job, Helmut—to cut that finger off. And if we can make him bleed to death when we do it, so much the better!"

Guido returned to his original point: how to start the hemorrhaging of Paolo Lercani. His money didn't add up, the Maestro had said. He proceeded now to show Helmut how this "dance of billions" they had pieced together was really a house of cards.

Lercani was living beyond his means—billions or no. Taking all the visible, legal funds at his disposal—including the $1.4 billion from the Vatican—and making good, hard-nosed calculations about the dirty money—including the funds he laundered for the Mafia—the whole thing came to maybe $2.5 or $3 billion in liquid assets.

"But if you look at these operations,"—Guido held up a whole sheaf of money-flow charts—"he's got about another $2 billion in thin air. Money that doesn't exist. I don't know yet how he does it—I'll find out—but I don't have to know in order to start the offensive. It's just a question of overloading him, flushing him back and back and back until he has noplace left to go. We use our own companies, our own banks, our own controlling interests. We kill a market he needs in one area. We let companies go bankrupt—companies we own or control, ones in which he has minority shares or that he needs for some other reason. We buy out major sources of the raw materials he needs for companies he does own or control. We force the devaluation of stocks. In other words, we close off his options. We squeeze his lines of capital so that the air is forced out. He won't be able to cover himself.

"It won't be easy. He's proved he's no amateur. It will take up most of my time for a while. That means you'll have to carry most of the *impero* load yourself."

That didn't bother Helmut. He didn't even hesitate in his answer. "When do we start?"

At least one of the ways in which Paolo Lercani managed to "live beyond his means" to the tune of billions of dollars came to light at a meeting of Security Two. Through one of his "private sources" who owed him a few "favors," Giulio Brandolini had uncovered an interesting operation involving counterfeit securities. The lines led from certain organized-crime leaders in the United States to certain banking and business connections of Lercani's.

"They're not bad," Brandolini said, passing a sample to the Maestro. "Not top quality, but on the whole, they're good enough for careful use in certain parts of his system."

Once he had this further bit of information, the scheme was so obvious Guido wondered why it hadn't occurred to him as a Lercani ploy. What he was probably doing was buying out various financial interests using these false securities as part of the payment. He might purchase a private corporation worth $7 million, for the announced price of perhaps half its value. The other half of the purchase price would be paid under the counter, in false securities deposited in—where else?—one of Lercani's fiduciary accounts. The odds against several "investors" at once calling on these fiduciary accounts was slim. Lercani always had enough real currency to cover most contingencies. If the occasional fiduciary client discovered the swindle, by then he would be too deeply implicated himself to blow the whistle on Lercani.

The Maestro suggested to Brandolini that this information about the false securities might be of interest to the U.S. authorities. "There's no reason we shouldn't have them working on our side, for a change, putting on a little pressure through investigation."

"Consider it done, Maestro." Brandolini sneezed and smiled, and then sneezed again. "They can't do much to him since he lives here; but maybe they can do a little demoralizing of their own."

The importance of all this financial plotting and planning to undo Paolo Lercani's hold on Holy See assets was not lost on Cardinal Falconieri; but he was far more interested in discussing Rico Lansing's underground educational movement in Poland and the rest of Eastern Europe.

Lansing reported that he was making excellent progress in Poland. "Some fairly good progress in Czechoslovakia," he continued down the list. "Some in Hungary; a little in Romania; a good deal in Lithuania and East Germany. We're getting there. We have growing pains. Cardinal Valeska would still like to include the KOR in our open operations—the study groups and all that—but Cardinal Wallensky and I won't budge an inch on the point. There's continual government harassment, of course. But it's moving forward."

Cardinal Falconieri was generally pleased at that, but he felt Rico's work should move forward even faster: "At double the pace, if you can,

Excellency." It seemed fairly clear to him, the Cardinal explained, that as things were going in the Church worldwide, Catholics—and Christians in general—would live in such a hothouse of secularization that within another decade or so, they would have as urgent a need as the Polish people of some way of thinking and feeling about human life that would be independent of their cultural, political, and social surroundings. "If you can evolve something solid, something visible, Rico—in Poland, for example, where you seem to be making the best progress—it may just turn out to be the model par excellence for the rest of Catholicism."

Rico blinked in sudden and unexpected remembrance of one of his last conversations with Cardinal Krementz years before in Chicago. Rico had just begun his travels in Eastern Europe. They had been talking about the faith and the strength of the tortured and beleaguered people in the Eastern countries. And old Blackjack had wondered way back then if such priests as Rico described to him might not be good models for the fat and spoiled clergy in America. Not long after that, Rico had got the radio message from Lanser that brought him back to Rome, to begin his first clandestine missions for Papa Profumi. Now they were all dead. Blackjack first, then Profumi. Now Lanser too.

"Rico?" Cardinal Falconieri recalled Lansing's thoughts to the present.

"Yes, Eminence." Rico gave a straight answer. If funding could be increased, he was certain that, working closely with Wallensky and Valeska, he could come up with new ways to move ahead, and to test the organization to see if it was as independent and tough and resilient as Rico had built it to be.

"Whatever it costs by way of money," Helmut assured his friend, "we will supply."

"Well, then"—Rico responded in kind—"I can supply whatever it costs by way of human effort."

Try as he might, Paolo Lercani could not get any more information about the Holy See's assets. Neither could Peter Servatius, although he tried—or at least he said he tried. Lercani never doubted that hundreds of billions of dollars in real estate, gold, and other assets were involved; but he could not breach—or even get much of a peek through—the protective brick wall that the Maestro had built up.

That problem put Lercani behind in the timetable he had set for himself, and upon which he based important plans. In making his virtually simultaneous deals with Papa Da Brescia and Senatore Pappagallo, he knew he would shortly be called upon to meet the heavy money demands of both. Hundreds of billions—or even a few tens of billions—in assets at his disposal would have allowed him to meet those demands, and also to make a giant step in his own developing plans, with no one the wiser.

Timetable or no, Lercani could not put off Papa Da Brescia's demands without jeopardizing his hard-won Vatican position. Nor could he put off Pappagallo, for whom failure was betrayal.

A few other difficulties began to crop up as 1970 progressed. An unusual number of clients who had always been patient and reasonable until now began demanding their money from the fiduciary accounts he held for them. That meant a drain on other assets; he simply could not produce all the fiduciary money required at once without either drawing on his other sources or allowing a dangerous crack to develop in his fiduciary system.

In addition, stocks in some of the companies he was deeply invested in had taken a nosedive. It was unforeseeable. Lercani couldn't explain it by anything happening in the markets. But there it was. And at a most inconvenient time.

And on top of all that, he had to be doubly careful about how he moved to repair the damage because, for some reason, the Italian authorities had chosen just this moment to begin sniffing around some of his operations. That was nothing to worry about in itself. But until he could find the right people to pay off, he would have to mind his manners, financially speaking, for a time.

What protected Lercani in this temporary embarrassment for liquid funds was his foresight.

When he had gone to Gennar Schiavone at the Isola di Capri restaurant two years before, he had hoped he would never need to use the mint-quality counterfeit securities he had arranged for. He had thought of it as a sort of insurance policy, to be called on, in his "Vatican work," in the unlikely event that he might fail to lay his hands rather quickly on at least one major pile of Church wealth.

As good as these counterfeit securities looked—and they were far superior and far costlier than the ones he normally used—Lercani's first moves to introduce them into Vatican banking channels had to be careful and calculated. He would start fairly small, with about $5 million. And he would choose his point of entry with his usual nose for the lines along which such arrangements would flow with the greatest ease.

By now, Paolo Lercani was no stranger to the Vatican at a certain intermediate level. What he needed was some congregation or ministry that was hungry for funds, and some prelate who would not be too careful. He knew exactly where to find both.

The Congregation for the Propagation of the Faith, which Papa Da Brescia had renamed the Congregation for the Evangelization of Peoples, soaked up money like a giant sponge. It was responsible for all mission work. It built and maintained hospitals, clinics, leprosariums, maternity wards. It provided medical care for the needy—often for whole populations. It built chapels and churches everywhere they were needed, even in the remotest areas. Poor dioceses whose bishops had no means of raising money were supported entirely by the Congregation for the Evangelization of Peoples. In other words, as Peter Servatius had once said to Lercani, it "earned nothing, spent billions, and, like the Water-Works in Dublin, was always in debt."

The head of the Congregation was Cardinal Fustami. Lercani knew him, but chose another way in. Cardinal Lisserant would be best. He was a tough and crusty old Frenchman who had been made a "consultant" to the Congregation by Papa Da Brescia. "Consultant," as everyone knew, was polite Vaticanese for "fund-raiser." Lisserant was therefore constantly on the lookout for big money contributors, and had several times had Paolo Lercani to dinner for that very reason, and with pleasing results.

Lercani made his move in September, using Peter Servatius—whom he regarded as a bumbling hulk of a simpleton—the way a suitor uses a friend to woo his lady. If someone is going to get slapped, it's best to be second in line.

"This is sheer profit, Monsignore!" Lercani opened his briefcase to show Servatius the first $5 million in securities from Chase Manhattan and Siemens, Inc. "And I suggest we devote it to the Congregation for the Evangelization of Peoples. Perhaps you would like to bring these along to Cardinal Lisserant. I think he would enjoy the actual sight of them before you deposit them."

"Lisserant will be delighted, Signore Lercani. I'll take them to him myself, this afternoon."

Cardinal Lisserant sipped his after-dinner brandy, shaking his jowls and grimacing at the swift pleasure of its bite around his palate. *"Dio!* That's good!" He smiled across the table at Paolo Lercani. The usual angry look was gone from his rheumy, myopic brown eyes. At that moment he reminded Lercani of a benign old bullfrog all flossed out in black and crimson.

It just so happened, the cardinal said, that a new leper station and clinic in Portuguese Guinea would cost the Congregation almost exactly $5 million. The cardinal hardly knew how to thank Lercani. "The Lord has supplied!" he said.

"You had them examined, of course." Lercani didn't know much about the Lord. But he knew a lot about counterfeit securities, and he thought the cardinal might, as well.

"Of course, my dear Lercani. They are works of art! It's only paper, after all, isn't it? No matter who prints it. I presume you always have the collateral, the hard cash, to back us up if there's a pinch."

"Have no fear about that, Excellency. The securities merely permit us to move faster and more freely." Lercani raised his upper lip and poured himself a little more of the cardinal's excellent brandy.

"Well, then." Lisserant held his own glass out. "No one has lost any money. The Church has simply gained a leper station and a clinic in darkest Africa."

That was another point of interest for the financier. He was certain that a consortium of companies he just happened to be involved in would be able to undertake the construction on very advantageous terms.

"Fine, Signore. Fine indeed! Tell me, are you aware of the enormous needs of the Congregation for the Evangelization of Peoples? The outgo always exceeds the intake."

At the end of the evening, Lercani had solved several pressing problems. Lisserant not only had not slapped his face; he wanted $1 billion dollars in top-quality securities for the Congregation. The opening sum of $5 million alone would take some immediate pressure of the Vatican demands off him, and free up some resources for Pappagallo. It would also establish the Vatican's IRA—which enjoyed unparalleled freedom in the transfer of funds—as a worldwide conduit both for false securities and for real assets, including some that needed laundering. And as icing on the cake, any number of companies that Lercani owned or controlled would doubtless be getting a lot of new contracts to perform every kind of work and service for the Congregation of the Evangelization of Peoples.

It would, Lercani reckoned, take until perhaps June of the following year to get as much as $1 billion in such high-quality forgeries.

Perhaps, the cardinal ventured, they could come in stages. One batch in the spring of 1971, for example, and another a few months later. He would leave the details to Lercani. And he would instruct Archbishop Servatius to help in whatever way he could.

"Our missionaries need all they can get, Signore." Lisserant pushed himself onto his short little legs to walk Lercani to the door. "The Lord loves a generous giver."

Paolo Lercani, a man complaisant with evil, a touchstone of destiny for the corrupt and the corruptible, as uninterested in the Bible story as in anything else that did not come over the ticker tape, knew he had found in this red-robed cardinal a willing brother.

"Good night, Your Eminence."

"Until soon, Signore."

[54]

At the opening of 1971, Papa Da Brescia calculated that by the time he reached the young Roman age of eighty-three—this would be within ten years—he would have the governing structure of his Church, together with the outlook and religious practice of his Catholic people, at a watershed point. Almost imperceptibly, the amalgam between Catholics and other bodies of Christians would take place. And as a sequel to that successful play of papal power, there would emerge "new centers of the people of God." The patriarchate of Africa. The patriarchate of India. The patriarchate of China and Southeast Asia. The patriarchate of Latin America. The patriarchate of North America.

All would acknowledge the Bishop of Rome, of course. But as a privileged brother bishop; not as the Roman Pontiff.

It was Papa Da Brescia's papal endgame. And as he played it out, the Holy Father was beset by only two mordant worries. One was the troublesome and highly vocal Archbishop Édouard Lasuisse. The other was the continued lack of progress in Eastern Europe.

Édouard Lasuisse had established himself in neutral Switzerland, had founded his own religious institute just as he had vowed to do, and had begun training young men as priests according to pre–Vatican II theology and liturgy. He remained as voluble as ever in his rejection of Papa Da Brescia's New Arrangement as worthless.

In just a few short years, Lasuisse and his followers had founded their own seminaries in Italy, France, Canada, and the United States. They seemed to have endless funds. They traveled all over Europe and the Americas, celebrating the traditional Roman Mass, and denouncing the New Arrangement as "un-Catholic and heretical."

The numbers of Catholics who rallied to Lasuisse's call was what alarmed Da Brescia. Well over 40 percent of Catholics polled declared themselves in favor of Lasuisse, and in favor of the traditional Mass and theology. No matter what penalties local bishops used to threaten Lasuisse's sympathizers, they continued to grow in numbers and in zeal. Lasuisse himself could not be condemned, for he taught no heresy and created no formal schism.

Lasuisse's warnings, however, were sharp and clear. The danger, he said, was that a vast majority of Catholics would be lulled and suborned until they ceased to think of themselves as Roman Catholics at all. Some may think, he said, of their particular Church as Catholic. Many will think of themselves as quite simply Christian, but only in the merest sense. And there will be a tragic number who will think of themselves as none of those things, but simply as religiously and spiritually minded people in some vague way that has neither definition nor salvific power. That, Lasuisse declared again and again, was the aim and the meaning of Papa Da Brescia's catchphrase "the people of God."

Nor was he any less categoric in his denunciation of "the new breed of theologians, who deny Christ's divinity, deny the Virgin birth, deny the Pope's infallibility, deny the sinfulness of abortion, contraception, homosexuality, fornication."

He pointed constantly in warning to the number of Papa Da Brescia's "brother bishops" who were already "acting as popes on their own." They would obey no order from Rome—whether from the Pontiff or from his bureaucracy. If Rome forbade the giving of Communion in the hand, they imposed it in their dioceses. If they were ordered not to have altar girls, they introduced altar girls. If they were told to fight against divorce, they made it accessible by calling it "annulment." And they let it be known that "no one" agreed with Papa Da Brescia about contraception.

And Lasuisse pointed as well to "the already tragic consequences" of what he termed "this charade of 'renewal.' " The Catholic Church was seeing the numbers of its communicants plummeting. Priests and nuns were leaving in droves. The Catholic ceremonial had become the butt of endless jibes and jokes.

Those last criticisms did concern Papa Da Brescia. And he did discuss the loss in clergy, religious, and lay believers with Cardinal Secretary

Jean Levesque and Archbishop Annibale Sugnini.

"Initial losses we expect, Holiness." Sugnini continued to assure Da Brescia. "It is in the nature of change. But the spirit of Vatican II is mounting."

"We can, of course," Levesque suggested, "strip Lasuisse of all canonical faculties. So that everything he does will be illicit."

Papa Da Brescia toyed with that possibility for a time; but he was never able to escape completely from Cardinal Joachim Lanser's deathbed warning of schism and heresy. "We will talk with Lasuisse one day soon." He put Levesque off. "Let Us be patient."

On the second worrisome point, however, that of his desire for closer ties with the official governments of the Soviet countries in Eastern Europe, Papa Da Brescia's patience had run out.

Richard Lansing had successfully put off and put off final establishment of diplomatic relations between the Holy See and any of the Soviet satellite governments. In all the eight years of Papa Da Brescia's reign, not even one preliminary protocol had been signed.

In April of 1971, however, Lansing had to report to Da Brescia that the Hungarian Communist government was prepared to "ease the tensions" that existed between itself and the Vatican State. Its conditions for that easing had not changed. Cardinal Mindszenty, still a beleaguered guest in the United States Consulate, must be removed from Hungary.

On Da Brescia's instructions, Rico again visited the tough cardinal in Budapest. His conditions had not changed, either. He was old and he was ailing. But he would leave only if Papa Da Brescia would promise to refuse to appoint another Primate of Hungary until Mindszenty himself died; and if Papa Da Brescia would promise further not to appoint Bishop Miklos Sekai as primate even after the cardinal's death. "He's a convinced Marxist, Excellency." Mindszenty told Rico again what both men and the rest of the world already knew. "And he is the man the Soviets want in my place."

On his return to Rome, Rico told Papa Da Brescia and Cardinal Secretary Levesque of Mindszenty's conditions. Papa Da Brescia agreed to them immediately. "Tell His Eminence that We give Our personal assurance that We will appoint no successor while the cardinal is alive in exile. And We agree never to appoint Bishop Sekai."

Following His Holiness' solemn assurances, all the arrangements were quickly made. Cardinal Mindszenty was given full immunity by the Hungarian government, and Richard Lansing accompanied him on the flight from Budapest to Rome.

It was one of those occasions that transmute themselves into media field days. Papa Da Brescia himself met Mindszenty's plane. He embraced the old man and, because the cardinal looked cold in his frayed cassock, the Pontiff removed his own cloak and put it around Mindszenty's shoulders. He wept at the years of lonely suffering the stalwart churchman had endured, and at the blessing of his liberation at last. And a watching world wept with him.

After a short stay in Rome, Cardinal Mindszenty was retired to the Hungarian College in Vienna, there to await his death.

The following month, the Holy Father appointed Bishop Miklos Sekai as Primate of Hungary. He would no doubt be made a cardinal within the year.

The whole affair left Rico bitter in his anger and disappointment. It had all been a charade of hypocrisy and deception. He reminded himself of Cardinal Wallensky's warnings against the open confrontation of many bishops in other satellite countries. And he reminded Papa Da Brescia to his face of the bold and dramatic demonstration the Hungarians had made when Papa Angelica had opened the first session of Vatican II. He described again, lest the Pontiff mistake his meaning, the processions of men and women dressed in prisoners' garb and carrying a cross entwined with barbed wire. If those people had felt obliged to accuse Papa Angelica of betrayal, how much more were the people of Hungary justified in such an accusation now?

The Pontiff was patient with Lansing. The Pontiff had always been patient with this American archbishop. Like most Americans, he simply did not understand all of the wider ramifications of papal policy.

Again, it was the gambit of the fait accompli. What the Pope had done, no one could undo.

John Liebermann was surprised at Rico Lansing's lack of surprise as they walked together in the part of St. Peter's Basilica known as the Confession. It was still early, and their steps echoed in the emptiness of the place. "You mean"—Liebermann seemed a little upset—"that you knew a counterfeit securities scam was going on? Why didn't you say something?"

Rico had no intention of revealing that it was Giulio Brandolini who had, specifically on Guido de la Valle's orders, passed along the information that had set U.S. customs authorities and anti-organized crime units in New York and Washington on an investigation that had so far lasted for eighteen months.

"What's the difference who told whom? You probably would have found out about the securities in time without our help. They're not great-quality stuff, as I understand it. We just decided to push things along a little."

"Wait a minute!" Liebermann suddenly realized Lansing didn't know as much as he thought. "I'm not talking about some run-of-the-mill counterfeit operation, Rico. I'm talking about the best. State-of-the-art stuff. I mean, these securities are so well done that we might never have found them except for dumb luck. Some clerk in the recording department in a bank up in Lugano got a couple of them in the normal run of things. Our people talked to him later, and even he said he almost passed them through. He didn't even know why he smelled something funny about them, so he decided to do nothing on an official basis. Instead, he called an old friend of his—a guy he studied with at Harvard grad school or someplace—who's a securities expert now on Wall Street.

"The friend agreed to take a look. When he got a sample by courier the next day, he practically had to put it under a microscope to tell it wasn't the real thing."

Rico was surprised now. And a little alarmed. "John, are you telling me that these state-of-the-art securities are tied to Paolo Lercani too?"

"I'm telling you more than that, Rico. We triangulated this Wall Street information with information we got from our ongoing surveillance of the organized crime groups that specialize in securities. Thanks to the information your people passed along last year, we stepped up that area of our operations.

"Lercani is involved, all right, no doubt there. But we also have tapes of some phone conversations we tapped into that just happen to concern one billion dollars of high-quality merchandise. The 'guarantors'—the ones who have ordered these securities, in other words—are a cardinal and an archbishop. Their names weren't mentioned on the phone; maybe those clowns don't even know their names. But they know they're Vatican; they made that clear enough.

"There's another bit of fallout from the information your side passed along last year, too. A special and highly secret Senate committee has been formed to inquire into offshore funding of certain American corporations. You won't believe this, but your brother-in-law, Brad Brock, is the chairman.

"Anyway, my guess is that it's all going to link up and blow wide open in the end."

"Can you stop that from happening, John? There's more than just the Church's reputation at stake here. That's important enough. But there's a lot more going on that I can't tell you. Except that Lercani is at the bottom of it, and the Americans can't touch him. He's not an American citizen, and he's not on American soil."

Liebermann eyed Rico with open skepticism. The Americans had believed the Vatican about Hanoi, he said, and got shafted.

"It's not Papa Da Brescia who's talking to you now," Rico answered angrily. "But if you want a reason to back off this thing, I'll give you one. Lercani has been channeling covert funds on behalf of the U.S. government to Italy and Greece for about seven years. You and your people know all about that. But you wouldn't want the American public to know all about it. Call off the dogs, and you have our silence."

Liebermann knew better than to deny Lansing's accusation. They were both too smart for that. "God! You're as tough as the Soviets when it comes to the real crunch. Okay. Let's make a limited deal. I can't call off the dogs altogether. I can probably slow things down for a while and see how it goes at your end.

"As far as the Senate committee goes, that has to be your bailiwick, Rico. Talk to Brock yourself.

"In return, though, we want to know everything you find out about this securities thing."

"And in return, John, you have our silence about U.S. intelligence funds funneled through Lercani. But I will tell you everything I can that touches on federal crimes committed on American territory."

"Always protecting the Church, eh, Rico?"

"Always trying, anyway, John."

On one level, Rico's new information was encouraging to the Maestro and Helmut. Obviously, Lercani was feeling the pinch of the vise Guido was tightening around him. It made sense in the circumstances that he would try to ease the bind by the stepped-up use of false securities.

On another level, however, the Maestro was worried. If Lercani was planning to use the Banco as the channel for his new high-quality false securities, and if the authorities were aware of the plot from the start, it could mean as much trouble for the Vatican and for the IRA as for Lercani.

The Maestro decided to go to Papa Da Brescia with what they had. Even this stubborn Pontiff would have to listen now, would have to see that the contract he had signed with Lercani was being used to place the Holy See in jeopardy.

Papa Da Brescia did not see that, however. *"Non ci credo."* He was categorical in the use of this phrase that Guido had heard so often. "I don't believe it!"

What he did believe was that the Maestro was becoming so desperate, or so jealous of Signor Lercani's papal favor, or both, as to come to the papal study spouting outlandish rumors. Why, the Maestro himself could surely not believe that a cardinal and an archbishop in Vatican service would be involved in such a scheme as he was alleging. Where was the proof? There were not even any names attached to the supposed cardinal and the supposed archbishop who had supposedly been corrupted by Signor Lercani. "Pipe dreams, Maestro! Pipe dreams!" Papa Da Brescia would listen to no more. Angrily, he bid the Maestro good day.

When Guido returned to his office after his brief meeting with His Holiness—the whole conversation had not lasted more than ten minutes—Rico and Helmut could see by his face how badly it had gone.

"He won't budge!" Guido sat down heavily at his desk, shaking his head in anger and frustration. "I tell you, this Pope gets an idea in his head, and it acts like a blinder. He can't see anything else!"

Since the Mindszenty affair, Rico had given up trying to defend Papa Da Brescia. Like the Maestro and like Cardinal Wallensky, he now served the Church and the papacy. If Papa Da Brescia could not be persuaded to take steps, he said, then it seemed to him it was up to Security Two again.

Guido agreed. Step number one was to get the proof the Pontiff required. The Maestro wanted to know who the mysterious cardinal and archbishop were. He could make some good guesses, and surveillance would do the rest.

The Maestro's prime candidate for the archbishop who had been corrupted was Peter Servatius. "He's working under Lercani now, in a sense, since that contract was signed. He has access to IRA banking machinery. He is not an expert in securities. He is just the kind of stooge Lercani would use. The kind who tumbles to things too late, after he's implicated, and can be made to think he has no choice but to go right on down the road to the bitter end. Lercani has built half his empire on the bones of men like Peter Servatius."

The mysterious cardinal, however, was of another stripe, in the Maestro's opinion. Less a victim than a partner. "Lercani doesn't need two Vatican people in this if both of them are stooges. What he needs is a living, walking, breathing imprimatur. An accomplice."

Fortunately, there were very few cardinals whose names Guido felt belonged on such a disgraceful list. He knew the Vatican far more deeply than Lercani did, however, and Lisserant's name was one that came to mind rather quickly.

Guido lost no time in bringing Brandolini and Solaccio into the meeting in his office, to arrange for surveillance of all the suspect prelates.

Rico's information was that the high-grade securities were to be delivered in batches. Apparently the quantity—$1 billion—was something of a problem when they were talking about such high quality. The next batch wasn't expected until the spring of 1972. Brandolini was doubtful that surveillance would give them the kind of proof the Maestro wanted until the securities were actually delivered.

"Keep after it anyway, Giulio. Phone conversations. Meetings here. In the States. I want your best people on this."

In the meantime, the Maestro planned to step up his own offensive against Lercani on the financial front, to try to flush him out before the damage he could cause would become catastrophic for the Holy See. But he decided to change his tactics slightly. Something Rico had said when he reported his conversation with Liebermann gave him the idea. The Americans couldn't touch Lercani, Lansing had said. And that was true. He had no banking operations in the U.S.; and his business holdings were so intricate, it would take years for some Senate committee to unravel them.

"I think we should try to change that situation." The Maestro was thinking out loud, forming details of his new plan in his mind as he spoke. "The laws in European countries dealing with taxes and finances are so full of loopholes that Lercani can probably slip through any trap we set for him without even loosening his tie. But the Americans are different. They take money as seriously as Lercani does. Over there, if you commit rape, maybe you'll get three years. But try embezzlement and you'll get thirty years.

"If we tighten the screws everywhere else first, he might just put himself in harm's way."

Helmut was worried about the possible scandal if Lercani went down in the States. The American press would have a ball. But his uncle felt that was the lesser of the two dangers that faced the Holy See. The Vatican had been through scandals before; and they would do their best to restrain it. After all, the Church was the injured party in this instance.

Rico's mind turned to the Senate committee that Liebermann had mentioned. "My contact thinks I should have a word with my brother-in-law, Senator Brock."

"In time," Guido said. He had rushed to see Papa Da Brescia too fast and with too little information. It had backfired on him. He didn't want to make the same mistake twice. In his view, the American Senate was in some ways like the Italian Parliament. They would move with slow deliberation until they could tell better what was going on, and who would be hurt by it—"no insult meant to your brother-in-law, Rico."

Helmut had only one further question. What if Lercani didn't run? What if he stayed in Europe? Or what if he ran to Latin America or Singapore?

"I'll do my best to see that doesn't happen. But whatever he does, and wherever he runs, I promise I will get him."

Looking at Guido's face at that moment, Rico Lansing was glad it was Paolo Lercani and not himself who was the Maestro's target.

It was midafternoon by the time the Maestro was alone in his office, waiting for Helmut to join him for the drive home to Villa Cerulea, and putting a few more papers he wanted to review into his briefcase.

There was a light tap on his door, and Sagastume came in. "This came by special messenger, Maestro." The bodyguard laid a large, flat box on Guido's desk. "It's marked 'Gift—Personal.' "

Guido snipped the colored twine, removed the wrapping and the cover of the box. Inside, there was another box, a very small one, marked with the initials EDLV in capital letters.

"Now what does EDLV stand for?" The Maestro's voice was sharp and impatient. The day had been difficult enough without some silly joke to end it.

He opened the tiny box and lifted the red tissue paper inside.

"Oh, *Gesù mio!*" The guttural scream was forced from him. His hands shook. At first it was only instinct that told him what he held—the little piece of flesh with its whorls and curves and jagged edges. *"Gesù mio!"* The pain in the exclamation, repeated again, brought Sagastume forward. Guido tried to control his trembling as he stared down at the box in his hands. The poor, wrinkled, bloodstained remnant with the ragged edge was almost unrecognizable. But if you looked at it closely, you could tell. It was an ear. A human ear. "EDLV." Eugenio de la Valle's ear.

The chief investigator rushed the poor remnant of their beloved Eugenio to the police laboratory, while Guido and Helmut waited with Rico in his apartment for the results. Vittorio Benfatti was the perfect valet in this as in all situations. Other than pouring a stiff shot of cognac for each of the three—something he could see they needed—he stayed out of the way.

The inspector returned personally with the report about two hours later. The ear had been crudely refrigerated until just a few hours ago. The forensic experts estimated it had been severed over a year before, but they could not be more exact than that. All the analyses were consistent with the supposition that it was Eugenio's ear.

"Can you tell . . ." Guido's throat was dry, and he had to begin again to get the words out. "Can you tell if the . . . if he was alive or dead when . . . ?"

"Our experts are inclined to think it was done after the person was dead, Maestro."

"That would explain why there was no ransom demand, then." Rico spoke almost like a somnambulist.

"No, Excellency." The inspector disagreed. "The Red Brigades are not above asking for ransoms and then delivering a dead body, or none at all.

"Maestro." The police commander turned to Guido. "What I've given you is all I can say officially. Unofficially, our people are convinced that the ear is Eugenio's, and that the boy is dead." He gave back the little box in a manila envelope. They had put some preservatives in it that would hold for a few days. "We are heartfully sorry, Maestro. Signor Helmut." He turned to each of them. "I cannot tell you how devastated we are for you and your family. We have kept the red tissue paper. We can tell it's of foreign fiber and make. We need time to analyze it further. Do you want to know what we find out?"

Guido removed the little box from the envelope, and wrapped it carefully in his handkerchief. "Yes." His voice was weary and sad beyond belief.

"Yes." Helmut echoed his uncle. "We want to know everything you find out, Inspector. And if you ever find the Red Brigades who did this, I want five minutes alone with them. After that, the law can have what remains."

It took some time after the chief inspector left for Helmut and Guido to decide what to do. They thought it was best to keep the matter from Keti. She still was not entirely back to her normal self, and a shock like this might well be more than she could stand. Later, perhaps they could tell her. Nor would they tell Agathi. Keti seemed to depend on her so much; it would not be possible for Agathi to hide such a secret as this.

It was nearly dark when Guido understood what must be done. "We will bury him," he said quietly.

"Yes." Helmut read his uncle's thought. In both their minds now, the boy's ear was the boy himself; not by proxy, but in reality. "Up in Waidhofen, where Keti and I will be buried. Where you and Aunt Agathi will be buried."

They could not go back to Villa Cerulea beforehand. They hadn't the strength to keep the secret if they should see Agathi and Keti face to face. They asked Rico to come with them, as close friend and to say the Requiem Mass.

Rico agreed, of course. He made arrangements by phone for a charter plane to Vienna, and for a car from there to Waidhofen. He had his Apostolate office call Villa Cerulea to say that Helmut and the Maestro had been called away for a day on urgent business, and not to worry. The Maestro himself called the mayor of Waidhofen and gave him specific instructions.

The mayor listened, and asked no questions. "All will be done as you say, Maestro."

Keti had been edgy all day. Agathi tried to persuade her to go along for a quick afternoon inspection of the sheep farm. With Helmut and Guido not coming home for dinner, they could take their time and enjoy the drive. It would do them both good. But Keti really didn't feel up to it, she said. "Next time, I promise, Agathi."

For as much rest as she was able to get, though, Keti might as well have gone along. The phone in Helmut's study down the hall kept ringing every twenty minutes or so, and the more distant ringing of the phone in Guido's study was like an insistent and bothersome echo.

Finally, in irritation, she got up and strode partway down the hall. Yes, it was coming from Guido's study again. His private line, surely. That's why no one downstairs was answering.

The ringing stopped, and she headed back toward her rooms, hoping whoever it was would have pity on her nerves. As she passed Helmut's study, however, the phone there jangled again, making her jump. On impulse, she opened the door and went in.

A heavy voice she recognized answered her greeting. It was the chief investigator from the central police precinct.

"Is Signor Helmut there, Signora?"

"No, Inspector. He is away for a day or two. May I help in some way?"

"I have just dispatched a messenger to Villa Cerulea with the results of the analysis I promised your husband and the Maestro, Signora. I thought they would want to know as soon as possible. The tissue paper is of a kind made in Lebanon."

"The tissue paper," Keti repeated slowly.

"Yes, Signora. The tissue paper in which the remains of your beloved son came."

"Yes." Keti barely got the words out. "I'll see he gets the report, Inspector. Thank you."

She hung up the receiver and sat down like a limp doll in Helmut's chair. She leaned her elbows on the desk, covering her face with her hands. Strangely, her mind was a total blank, open only to the sorrow that welled up and filled her whole being again with sickness and ailing. She was completely passive and prostrate under its raining blows. She forgot where she was, forgot to think, to pray, to hope, even to shed tears, so enveloping and so brutal was her renewed mourning. She didn't think or say to herself that she didn't care anymore about anyone or anything;

simply, she did not. Nor did she once, in that deep plunge of suffering, question what specifically the police inspector meant when he spoke of Eugenio's remains. She barely thought of Eugenio as the object of her love, or wished Helmut were here to tell her what had happened. She was, simply and finally, it seemed, at the end of her tether, entering that chasm separating those unwilling to die from those unwilling to live. If the human species had been made with some automatic switch that would allow consciousness to cease, and allow an unknowing, forever sleep to begin, Keti would have pulled that switch. It was the nadir of her life. The bottom of the pit where all the snakes of our nightmares hiss and entice us toward the oblivion their venom can invoke.

It was Tati, whimpering and softly rubbing against her leg, that brought Keti back to the feel of her elbows on the desk, her hands shutting the world away from her eyes. Tati seemed to be trying to tell Keti that she was there, that she wanted to be held, that they were both miserable, but both alive.

Keti put one hand down and stroked her. Tati's tongue flicked out, warm and loving against her fingers. She picked the dog up into her lap, and then saw Agathi standing in the doorway.

Her mind began to work again, very slowly. Of course: Tati had been with Agathi; Tati was back; so Agathi was back.

Tati still in her arms, Keti stood up almost like a robot, looking around the study like a stranger.

Once Agathi had helped her back to her own room and Keti was able to pull herself back to the near edge of the chasm, she told about the police inspector's phone call.

Agathi guessed, then, what the urgent business was that had summoned Guido and Helmut away so suddenly, and why neither of them had called. They had gone to Waidhofen. To Sontagberg. To the burial place of the de la Valles.

"Tell me, Agathi." Keti spoke in a sad, soft voice. "What demon is it that keeps us so separate that Helmut and Guido would leave us behind at such a moment?"

When they arrived in Waidhofen, Frau Spoeda had their rooms at the Goldner Hirsch aired and ready for them; but Rico and the two de la Valles made scant use of them. They spent most of the night vigiling in the onion-domed church across the square. Near dawn, they went back to the inn for hot coffee and rolls. They arrived with the first gray streaks of daylight at the mountain chapel of Sontagberg. The stonecutter was already at work in the headlight glare of his own little truck. The persistent musical *tap-tap-tap* of his chisel and hammer followed them into the church.

Rico went alone to the tiny sacristy and changed into the vestments he had brought with him from Rome. As he approached the altar, the morning wind rose and shifted and sighed about the towers. That, and the sound of the stonecutter's tap-tapping were the chorus that accompanied the courageous sorrow of Guido and Helmut, and the sonorous Latin of Rico's Mass for the innocent soul of Eugenio de la Valle.

The tapping became like the sound of the clock of mortal existence. The wind became a lilting regret for mortality's decay. The Mass became, as it always is, the proffering by divinity's hand of salvation and grace and immortality.

"Through him"—Rico raised Host and Chalice high in front of him—"with him, in him, may all glory and honor be yours, God, our Father." In that moment, he stood with Christ. He stood as the Church, through which Christ makes salvation possible, makes grace abound in every generation. It was not Papa Profumi, not Papa Angelica, not Papa Da Brescia, but Christ, using them, who sustained all, finally healed all. It was Christ's real Church, using all his saints on earth, and many who weren't saints, to bring all who could be washed clean in his Blood. That Church could bring a Levesque, a Sugnini, even a Lercani to salvation. That Blood could even quiet the unutterable pain of a father who had fingered the mutilated ear of his dead son; and of a granduncle who had come very close to the breakpoint of his once unbreakable strength.

"Amen." Helmut and Guido responded in unison to the Latin chant, and knelt at the altar to receive the Body and Blood of the Lamb.

The sun washed red-gold over the mountain when they came out from the chapel to stand in the gaze of the Sorrowing Virgin. The stonecutter's tapping had stopped. All was ready.

Guido took the little box from his pocket and held it up very high. Tears sprang to Rico's eyes before he could stop them. Just so had this same man stood fifteen years before, and in just that way had he given thanks in triumphant joy for the gift of the infant Eugenio, the glory of his life. Now he held only as much of his poor flesh as fit in that box.

"Your Son possesses our Eugenio now, Immaculate Virgin." Guido's quiet voice carried on the clean morning wind. "We give him willingly to Paradise."

They turned in to the chapel again. Guido placed the box in the recess that had been opened between the still-covered places where Helmut and Keti would one day lie. Rico said a blessing and a prayer for the de la Valles who were already buried in the chapel walls. The stonecutter stepped forward from beside the doorway and lined the edges of the small crypt with fresh cement. Then, with a final tap-tapping, he gently fitted into place the square marble plaque whose legend he had finished carving as Mass was said.

1956–1969, the inscription read. *Eugenio Guido de la Valle, Age Thirteen, Desired to See God, and Now Sees Him.*

[[55]]

Three weeks before Easter of 1972, Archbishop Giulio Brandolini reported to Guido de la Valle that the expected tranche of high-quality counterfeit securities promised for spring had been delivered the day before, slightly ahead of schedule. Brandolini brought with him a good two hours' worth of reading material—timetables; transcripts of taped telephone conversations; police reports; eyewitness accounts. The names of the underworld characters involved made Guido catch his breath. Two or three of them were on the Interpol list of leaders in international organized crime. There were some photographs, as well. One fact that was made clear beyond any doubt by the evidence now in hand was that Servatius and Lisserant were, respectively, the archbishop and the cardinal hooked into the Lercani scheme.

That the Maestro had been forced to let matters go so far meant that the evidence he held in his hands was a two-edged sword. He had what he needed to convince the Pontiff not to proceed with his Lercani bargain. But the entire securities operation, linked as it was with master counterfeiters in Philadelphia and Los Angeles, had been tracked by the American authorities. They had the same evidence in their hands as Vatican security had, and probably more. And they were ready to close in.

Well, the Maestro would deal with one problem at a time, in rapid-fire succession, starting with Papa Da Brescia.

His first call was to the Pontiff's secretary, Monsignore Delucchi. The Holy Father was to be prepared to receive the Maestro and his nephew alone in the papal study in a quarter of an hour. The meeting was to be of the strictest confidence. The warning note in Guido's voice was clear; no one was to be made aware of the meeting, even after the fact. Delucchi was not one to tempt the Maestro's anger.

His second call was to Helmut, who came to his uncle's office at once, and whom Guido briefed on the way to the third floor of the Apostolic Palace.

The Holy Father received the Maestro and Helmut stiffly. Within ten minutes, Papa Da Brescia had seen sufficient evidence to make it impossible for him to say again, *"Non ci credo,"* or to scoff at the Maestro's accusations as pipe dreams.

The Pope winced. He was tasting real bitterness. It wasn't only that his plan to take control of the IRA was in ruins; or that his trust in Paolo Lercani to disentangle the reins of financial power from de la Valle hands had entangled those reins instead with some of the biggest criminal names in the world. All of that was horrible enough. But why had it to be Guido de la Valle who found all this out?

Papa Da Brescia handed the intelligence dossier back to Guido, his hand shaking slightly from suppressed anger. "What do we do, Maestro?"

That simple question was the Pontiff's first open capitulation in the long war he had chosen to fight with the Keeper.

"What we do, Holiness," Guido answered, "we do quietly. Nothing overt. Nothing that would shake confidence in the Banco, or bring too many questions upon us before we can deal with them." He and his nephew, the Maestro said coolly, would immediately and personally review the IRA records that had been closed to them, to see what damage had been done, and what could be salvaged. Servatius was to be left in place, for whatever help he might be, and because his removal would attract too much attention in knowledgeable quarters of the financial world.

In the normal course of things—as soon as His Holiness published his next list of curial appointments—Cardinal Lisserant was to be stripped of all official duties.

As always seemed to be the case, it was Paolo Lercani who posed the most delicate problem for the Maestro. He had too much of the Holy See's assets in his hands, and knew too much of what had happened in the securities affair, for the Holy Father to alienate him.

"He is not a cleric, Holiness." Guido concluded what were, to all practical purposes, instructions to the Pontiff. "That is, we have no clerical sanctions or control over him. I suggest, Holy Father, that you maintain cordial relations with him, but no more concessions of funding. Your Holiness can simply say the coffers are empty. Leave his ultimate punishment to us."

There was nothing for it but for Papa Da Brescia to agree. But the problem of the Americans did not escape him. "What about the U.S. authorities? Won't the scandal break loose?"

It was a fair question, but one the Maestro preferred not to answer fully. "We will speak with those who can speak to the American authorities. We can't stop them altogether, of course. We can probably prevent a public washing of our dirty linen. It is a matter Your Holiness will leave entirely in my hands."

From the papal study, Guido and Helmut headed for the IRA offices in the Tower of St. Nicholas, with only one detour on the way. They stopped to collect "Sphinx" Di Lorio from his Vatican apartments in German House.

Di Lorio, a cardinal now, had added a bit more girth to his enormous body since his retirement from the Banco. He had remained a consultant for the *impero,* and had lost not one whit of his genius for banking and for quick penetration of even the most complex finances.

Within a half hour of leaving Papa Da Brescia, Guido and Helmut, with Di Lorio between them, swept unannounced into Peter Servatius' large office on an upper floor of the Tower of St. Nicholas, over the Banco. Within five minutes more, Servatius' first flush of anger at being burst upon so abruptly gave way to pale-faced panic. The Maestro showed him the evidence that so clearly entangled him with Paolo Lercani, Cardinal Lisserant, and the affair of the counterfeit securities.

Servatius was speechless. He looked unbelievingly at the dossier. He fingered it gingerly once or twice, as if he hoped it weren't really there, or might disappear under his touch. But then he blurted everything out. He had only guessed at first, from some smart remark Lercani had made, that there was something wrong with those securities. He went to Lisserant, but the cardinal had only laughed at him, called him a naive American, said that all finance was only paper anyway. " *'Drôle d'argent,'* he called it, Maestro. He said we wouldn't harm anyone. Who else could I go to by then? I was in it already up to my hips. If I resigned, left Rome, where could I go? And how could I abandon Papa Da Brescia to face wolves like Lercani and Lisserant alone? There was nobody I could tell. Nothing I could do. . . ."

Guido and the others let him jabber on until it became clear even to the archbishop that his words were as hollow as the sound of the ticker-tape machine rat-a-tatting mindlessly behind his chair. In all the excuses and self-serving rationalizations that poured out of him, the only thing that rang true was his worry for Papa Da Brescia. His love for the Pope, and his concern for him now, were genuine. But they were not justifications. One timely call to the Maestro, or to Helmut, or even to the retired Di Lorio, would have done more to help the Pontiff than all the years of Servatius' Vatican service put together.

Nothing as simple as a phone call to a friend or expert would be sufficient now. With the help of some of Di Lorio's trusted accountants who were still on staff, Guido, Helmut, and the cardinal got their first look at the full accounts since Lercani had signed his midnight pact with Da Brescia. Knowing where to look, and what he expected to find, Guido had his rough estimate of losses within a few hours. It appeared that the IRA was out almost exactly the amount the Pontiff had authorized Paolo Lercani to invest abroad. Guido threw down his pencil in disgust and looked at the ashen-faced Servatius. A little over a billion dollars was gone. How the securities had been used was unclear, but the batch that had been delivered the previous day were already swallowed up—had disappeared into the system. Even Di Lorio couldn't find a clue there. He told the Maestro he would keep after it, follow every lead he could find or dream up. But considering the quality of the securities and Lercani's vast connections, the Sphinx doubted they would be found easily. He shook his head in that familiar way of his, so that the pince-nez bobbled on his nose. "They may never turn up, Maestro."

A report had to be given to the Pontiff. That was Servatius' job, as president of the Banco.

"You tell him, Peter"—Helmut gave the instructions—"that the Holy See has been robbed of approximately the amount Lercani had access to. Tell His Holiness that we intend to conceal the actual amount. After all, if a major corporation had lost $1 billion overnight, it would go into bankruptcy. The Holy See won't—needn't. But neither do we want to create a climate of speculation as to how much the Holy See is worth. There may be no need to say anything at all for a while. If and when the need arises, I suggest we put the public figures at around $200 million."

The Maestro agreed, and added a message of his own for the Pope. "Tell His Holiness that I will make a personal report to him in a day or two; and that we will make up the losses."

Servatius blinked in surprise at the first positive thing he had heard. "How?"

"By external loans, Excellency. His Eminence Cardinal Di Lorio will help, I'm sure. And my nephew will be at your disposal. In fact, you will do nothing without his approval or mine. Is everything clear to you, Excellency?"

Yes, Servatius said, everything was clear. And, indeed, it was. It was clear that Guido de la Valle had regained total control of the IRA. It was clear that for some reason he had yet to figure out, he, Peter Servatius, would not be banished in disgrace. And it was clear that, except for the ordeal of facing Papa Da Brescia, he could breathe a little easier now than he had in what seemed a very long time.

As the Maestro had always understood, Senatore Ectore Pappagallo was a man who was very well connected both in Italy and abroad. It was through those connections that the senatore began to sense a certain clumsiness in Paolo Lercani's normally icy-smooth operations.

His decision, for example, to use the Vatican's IRA to channel some of those false securities onto the international market. If he had asked Pappagallo's advice, the senatore would have warned him he was stepping over an invisible line at his own peril. One of the primary rules the senatore had always tried to follow was never to place himself in open opposition to people who were at least as powerful as he was—in this case, to Maestro Guido de la Valle—until he was certain he had and could maintain the upper hand.

That mistake alone on Lercani's part was enough to cause a certain nervousness in the senatore. But then the way Lercani had handled the matter of the Italian investigation team looking into his affairs had been nothing short of absurd. It was the senatore's guess that the Maestro was mixed up in that investigation too, somewhere behind the scenes; but that was almost beside the point when one considered that, of the six investigators assigned full time to the Lercani case, one had been shot dead on his doorstep; and of the two magistrates scrutinizing Lercani's business dealings, one had been blown up in his car. The logical conclusion would be obvious even to a child.

Not that the senatore was against violence when it served the right cause. But he was against clumsiness. Why, it only made sense to stand several tiers removed from any traceable link to such activities, the way he and his group stood removed, for example, from the Red Brigades. Surely the *Brigate Rosse* were mad dogs, but at least their trail of spittle did not lead to his doorstep.

No doubt about it. Clumsy and heavy-handed. Those were the only words for Lercani lately. Best to stand aloof from him for a while, Pappagallo decided; until he could see more clearly the direction things were likely to take.

It seemed a pity in a way. Lercani had fulfilled his money commitment to the group very well. But doubtless there were others who could serve that purpose. Roberto Gonella, for example, the director-general of the Banco Agostiniano in Milan, seemed a prime candidate. Even Lercani had spoken highly of him. It might not be too soon to begin to nourish a friendship there. Just in case.

There were some who saw Paolo Lercani during the next year or two who said later that he was insane. Or that he was like some wild animal being backed into a corner. The Maestro, however, read him differently. He was certain that the Sicilian superman saw himself as still climbing a pinnacle of power that would make him bigger than the Pontiff, and that would leave a mere Senatore Pappagallo behind like a speck of dust. It was on that reading of Lercani's character and mind that Guido based all his own tactics.

By late summer 1972, it was clear to Lercani that the Vatican Bank would be no further use to him, and that Papa Da Brescia was just another of the pygmies. It was also clear that Ectore Pappagallo had lost his nerve. He refused to take Lercani's calls or to see him. When Lercani tried to reach him in Peru, the senatore was in Italy. When he went to his home in Italy, the senatore was in Peru. Truth to tell, it didn't make that much difference. Like the Pope, Pappagallo created too much of a drain on Lercani's resources and gave too little in return.

Paolo Lercani's best ally, now as always, was his own foresight and daring. The Italian investigation was bothersome. It had forced the closing of some of his banks and other enterprises in Italy. And it did make him decide it would be best to operate from Geneva rather than Milan for a while. But the sum total of the fallout from the investigation was merely to accelerate plans he had made long before for a two-pronged offensive—in Italy and the United States—that would establish him as one of the undisputed premier financial powers in the world.

The first move in that offensive was to gain control of Italy's largest holding company, Lastola, which held equity in virtually all of that country's major industrial companies. Of course, that move would mean reshuffling some of his liquid resources for a time, but he was a master at that, after all. Once he got Lastola, and its predominant equity position, into the palm of his hand, he would virtually control the European markets.

What Lercani failed to realize was that his moves to gain entry into Lastola did more than place another strain on his liquid resources for a time. It put him once again right into the Maestro's backyard. Many of the industries involved with Lastola were already owned or controlled by the *impero;* and those few that were not were at least friendly to the Maestro and his associates. A judicious word here, a revelation of Lercani's operations there, a closing off of contacts at critical points, a blocking by the Italian Treasury of licenses Lercani needed for his purchases, led to his failure to gain even a respectable foothold in Lastola. Instead, his efforts in that quarter caused the government to increase its investigative team to fifteen, and to assign three more magistrates to be in charge of unraveling Lercani's extravagant shell game.

By the time his Lastola venture failed, Lercani decided by instinct that it was time to remove himself to the United States. He had always understood in any case that he would have to make New York one of his major centers of operation. It was the financial capital of the world; it was where he really belonged. They understood the importance of money there; they respected its power. There, he could certainly buy his way out of any fix. And with the right banking base, carefully chosen, he could begin to tap into some of the enormous power of the Federal Reserve. He had not planned to take this step quite so soon, or in just these circumstances. But it turned out to be rather easy to accomplish. Using a fiduciary contract to funnel shares he did not own into one of his holding companies, and selling other companies to Roberto Gonella of the Banco Agostiniano in Milan, he buried large sums in an intricate trail of corporate sales and mergers, coming out at the other end with more than enough funds to buy controlling interest in the Benjamin National Bank of New York, the eighteenth-largest bank in the United States. It cost him a mere $43 million.

By the time the sere hand of that 1972 autumn, like the wanton painter it was, had strewn the parks and paths of Rome with delicately wasting samples of yellow and purple and ocher and pastel green in a thousand shades, Paolo Lercani was comfortably installed with his wife and children in his new luxury apartment in Manhattan's Hotel Maxime, and was busy removing the first $15 million or so from the Benjamin National to cover some of the cracks he had left in his European banks in order to finance his overseas operations. Everything would hold, he knew, as long as the dollar held strong against the other major world currencies.

It had taken some doing, but at last Paolo Lercani was right where the Maestro wanted him.

The U.S. Senate committee chaired by Senator William Bradford Brock had made rather good progress by the spring of 1973. By then, the Federal Reserve was deeply preoccupied with Benjamin National's affairs, as well, due to that bank's sudden and excessive foreign exposure. One question led to another, and those questions led the Federal Reserve officials and the U.S. Comptroller to Senator Brock's committee, asking if it had any evidence that might suggest illegal activities on the part of one Paolo Lercani; and further, if it was true that there were special arrangements between that same Paolo Lercani and the Vatican Bank.

The moment had clearly arrived for Rico Lansing to have a word with his brother-in-law. Armed with a battery of documentary evidence supplied and explained to him in detail by Helmut and the Maestro, Rico called John Liebermann to ask if he could get discreet word to Senator Brock that the senator's brother-in-law had a value in the eyes of the U.S. government.

Liebermann promised he would; it was, after all, no more than the truth.

On the twelve-hour flight from Rome to Washington, Lansing had more than enough time to review yet again the dossier Guido and Helmut had given him. It showed clearly that the only link between Lercani and the Vatican Bank was one by which the Holy See had become an unwitting victim of a swindle. Whatever use Lercani had made of the Banco had been of no benefit to the Vatican, and the brief and ill-advised connection had been entirely cut off.

There was further documentation showing that some of the privileged information about Lercani now in the hands of the U.S. government had in fact come from Rome. Rico himself had funneled some of it through Liebermann, but even he was surprised at the number of ways the Maestro seemed to have at his disposal to make sensitive information accessible to influential and interested parties.

Not surprisingly, there was still further information tracing some of the latest intricacies of Paolo Lercani's offshore investment activities.

Satisfied that he could honestly answer any questions Brad might have, Rico put the dossier back into his briefcase and settled back in his seat. Vatican interests in the States were perfectly legal and legitimate. There was no need for government bureaucrats to go nosing around in them, or to pass laws designed to cripple those interests.

Rico let his mind turn from Brad and the Senate committee to his sister, Netta. In a surface way, they still kept in touch, irregularly, by letter. But in all the important ways, they had grown apart. When Netta wrote now, it wasn't news about Brad and the children, or even about old friends. Usually it was a catalogue of her accomplishments in one or another of the committees she served on, or about the women's activist groups she had joined. Occasionally she ridiculed a Mass she had attended that seemed outlandish even to her. But beyond asking after her brother's health and expressing her shock and sorrow at Rico's news of the death of Eugenio de la Valle, there was almost nothing in Netta's letters that Rico couldn't have read just as well in the impersonal articles of American magazines and newspapers.

He had been wondering for days, and a little nervously, what it would be like to spend a night under the same roof with Netta again. He felt he had lost her as a person close to him.

Unexpectedly, it was Keti who had given him the most solid advice when he had mentioned his worry to her. Keti, who had had so much love stripped away from her so brutally, had gone right to love as the nub of the matter. In his memory he could still see her face turned to him in the dappled sunlight, tilted so she could look him dead in the eye while he told her of the confrontations he'd had with his sister over the years.

"Rico." Keti had been all common sense. "I've known you since 1946.

I've never known any man so gentle, so kind, and at the same time so upright as you are. In most men, as most women find out very fast, there is something savage, selfish, uncaring. But I swear, I have never seen a trace of that in you. At times, though, you become a total prig. It's when you're afraid, I suppose. And you're afraid of contraception, abortion, lechery. So am I. So are most people, finally. But if Netta has been practicing contraception and doing whatever else she may have been up to for all these years, do you think that your telling her again, now, that she's living a life of sin is going to help her?"

Rico had thrown up his hands in frustration. "Keti, I can't tell her she's okay!"

"Don't tell her anything *like* that! Get rid of the prig in you. Let her know you love her. She knows your mind. What she doesn't know is that you love her."

Keti had smiled so lovingly herself, then, that in spite of his embarrassment Rico had smiled back. He promised her he would try.

Rico spent most of the afternoon alone with his brother-in-law in the study of his and Netta's very comfortable "second house" in McLean, Virginia. Brad was quite well informed about the counterfeit securities and about Paolo Lercani, and about a number of other things, as well. He had pretty much guessed what was on Rico's mind even before they sat down together. He read the dossier Rico gave him quickly but thoroughly, frequently asking questions, commenting that some of the information on Lercani was exactly what the feds had been looking for. There was more than enough there to add steam to his committee's unraveling of the offshore investment schemes going on, and to aid the criminal investigation that was focusing with increasing intensity on Lercani. "That guy!" Brad shook his head as he closed Rico's dossier at last. "He's wanted by the Italians for embezzlement, assassination, extortion, drug trafficking, and probably high treason. How he slipped the net over there is beyond me! Anyway, you can tell your people we're going to go after him for his mess over here. He's practically finished. Don't worry about him. Worry about the money the Holy See will never see again."

For the last half hour or so of their confidential meeting, Brad changed both the subject and the mood. He had become quite heavy and was going bald, but he had the unmistakable air of a United States senator, and in the subtlest of ways began to probe for information about Vatican foreign policy. It wasn't so much the Hanoi thing. In fact, it wasn't just Da Brescia. Ever since Papa Angelica's *Ostpolitik* had surfaced, the Holy See seemed to favor the enemies of the United States.

Whether Brad knew about men like Demarchelier and Levesque, Rico couldn't tell. He could only assure his brother-in-law that Da Brescia was a kind man with good intentions who had been caught in grave errors of bad judgment.

"Like the judgment about Lercani?"

The question was too leading; there had been nothing in the dossier about the papal contract. Rico didn't answer.

Brad smiled and changed the subject again. More as a matter of curiosity than anything else, he had picked up on the de la Valle signatures that appeared on some of the documentation Rico had given him. It was a funny thing about them, his brother-in-law observed. "They seem to operate at such high levels of fiscal and monetary circles that information about them is as hard to come by as it is for any of the big-money club members over here."

"So?" Rico didn't at first see the point of the question.

"So they're the only Catholics I've ever run across with that kind of clout. That kind of protection and standing. I mean, most of those guys are highly placed Freemasons. And in case you haven't heard, Richie, there is no love lost between Masons and Catholics—especially when we're talking about Catholic aristocrats who work for the Pope!"

Again, Rico had no answer to give. But he did have a dawning realization of how far, and against what odds, Guido de la Valle had taken his *impero* vision.

Brad locked Rico's dossier away in his safe until morning. He had kept Rico long enough, he said. Netta would have his head if he didn't let her spend some quiet time of her own with her brother. "She's been looking forward to your visit ever since you called last week, Rick. The kids are still away at college. I thought it might be best to let the two of you have dinner without me. I know she has some things on her mind."

Just as he was about to open the study door, Brad stopped for a minute; he did have one more question. "Don't take this wrong, Rick; but do you still love America?"

"Yes."

"I'm not prying, exactly; but we know you work on what's called 'special assignment' for the Vatican. That raises some questions. And you're pretty well connected over there. Your life really isn't centered here anymore. You wouldn't allow America's vital interests to be damaged, would you?"

Rico's mind turned for a minute to John Liebermann—to some of the conversations like this one they'd had; to the understanding they had reached on the difference between Rico's covert work and Liebermann's; and to the help they had given one another over the years. He couldn't begin to reach that stage of understanding with Brad in just a few minutes.

"No, Brad." Rico smiled as he gave his simple answer. Maybe someday they'd have more time to talk about things like that.

"I'll tell you, Rico darling, it all comes down to anger." Netta filled his plate for the second time. She was easy and open with him, as though some switch had been turned that allowed all the old closeness they had once had together to come again to the surface. "All these committees and activist groups I've written to you about. They're all about anger, when you get down to the bottom of it. And they're right too."

Rico had to grant her points all along the way. Men did take women for granted. They did leave it to the woman to prevent conception, and blame it on her if she conceived "inconveniently." If she had an abortion, she bore the pain and the guilt. At the same time, she couldn't even get equal pay for equal work. She couldn't have an equal career, even by putting in unequal effort. She couldn't be as free as a man. She couldn't get credit in a bank or a store or an insurance company. "Wars have been fought over less, do you realize that?"

"Yes, sweetheart." Rico was not patronizing. He knew his sister was leading toward something. He wanted to follow her this time, not interrupt her with thoughts or commentary.

Netta let out a deep sigh and smiled the way she used to when she was up to some mischief. "There's something else about a woman, though, Rico. What she wants out of life is love. Like a man. But as a woman. She wants to love and to be loved. But men have made all the laws about that too, it seems. And so, finally, it all builds up—all the anger and all the frustration. And finally—especially nowadays—she just says to hell with the laws. Civil laws and Church laws. I'm going to be myself, she says. I *am* going to be as free as a man. I'll be a stevedore or a bank president or a priest or a bishop. It's anger that's the fuel, Rico. Anger and injustice."

"But you don't want to be any of those things, Netta." Rico was still trying to see where Netta was leading. "A stevedore or a bishop, I mean."

Netta laughed at the idea of her being a size 10 stevedore. "But don't be so sure about the bishop part. Not for me. But in Chicago I went once with a friend to a thing called 'Womanchurch.'

"It wasn't a church at all, of course, but someone's dimly lit high-rise apartment." Netta went on to describe a "Mass" attended by a few dozen women ranging in age from twenty-five or so to about forty-five. They all wore long white robes and gathered around a table. There were little loaves of white bread, some glasses, and a few bottles of red wine. A cross —not a crucifix—stood at the center of the table between two candles.

"The whole thing was a celebration of something they called 'womanhood' and 'womanlife,' as a 'saving grace once won for us but now denied us.' "

That was a new one even for Rico, and he had heard about most of the aberrations in ritual that had sprung up around the world. He reminded himself forcibly of what Keti had said to him a few days before about being a prig, and about love; but he really was concerned now. "Did you use to go to that 'Mass,' Netta?"

Netta looked across the table at her brother for a long minute. "I went a few times, Rick. And in a way, it was a good thing. It was awful, of course. Idolatry has to be awful. But it made me realize how angry everyone is. And that made me realize I don't want a life motivated by anger. And then that made me remember how you always used to say Christ brings good things out of bad ones. Suddenly, Rico, I was so lonely for you. And for Mom and Dad. And I began to wish I had given our children half of what Margaret and Basil gave us.

"I went home after that last 'womanmass,' Rico, and I just cried and cried. Poor Brad thought I was sick. The thoughts were all jumbled in my head for a while, but I finally got them straight enough to explain to him. We talked all night. And we've talked a lot about everything ever since. I make it sound easy, darling; but it really isn't. It's very complicated."

Netta rested her chin on one hand and lowered her eyes while she toyed with a scrap of meat on her plate. Rico had sense enough not to say a word; just to wait. Wherever it was she was headed, she was almost there.

"No." Netta contradicted herself. "That's a lie. It's not complicated at all.

"Rico." She looked up at her brother again, full in the eyes, much as Keti had at Villa Cerulea. "Rico. I want you to hear my confession."

Brad left for the Senate Office Building, dossier in hand, a little while before Rico had to leave for the airport.

"I don't want to teach Romans how to cook pasta, Rick"—Brad winced at his own bad joke—"but the Church over here is in utter confusion. These clerics don't know what to teach us. They're as ignorant as we are, and differ as much among themselves. Most of those guys connive at abortion, recommend contraception, see nothing morally wrong with almost anything except maybe murder. It's chaos.

"We're doing our best finally, Netta and I. But tell them in Rome, for the love of Christ to do something before there's no Catholic Church left!"

Bad joke or no, Rico said he and others were doing what they could.

The traffic on the way to the airport was awful, but Netta got him there with a little time to spare. She walked him to his departure gate, gave him a big hug, and watched him start toward the exit with those long, sure strides of his.

Rico's head and heart were filled with the richness of the hours he and Netta had spent together. Suddenly, he remembered the one promise he hadn't kept yet. His promise to Keti.

He wheeled around, almost knocking down the poor fellow behind him, to find Netta, but couldn't see her. She was probably already halfway through the terminal, or lost somewhere in the crowd. But no! There she was, just turning away.

"Netta!" His voice lifted over the din, and Netta turned back.

"Netta! I love you!"

"I know!" Her mouth formed the words he couldn't hear, and he saw the tears start down her cheeks.

The crowd pressed around him. The attendant looked at his watch.

"Ticket, please, Father."

[56]

In spite of Paolo Lercani's frenzied use of every possible element in his strained financial network, and in spite of his access through Benjamin National to the U.S. Federal Reserve, he was plainly facing into a rising flood of powerful financial forces. A badly weakened dollar, rising inflation, tightened money markets, the pressure of the newly founded OPEC cartel, the newly imposed governmental controls that were suffocating his moves in industry and finance—these were but some of his worries. Even as much as $1.76 billion in borrowings from the Federal Reserve left Benjamin National alone in need of between $100 million and $200 million to cover its immediate needs.

In May of 1974, the flood turned into a tidal wave. The Securities and Exchange Commission suspended all trading in shares of Benjamin National Bank. In dizzying succession, a series of seventeen European banks, which Lercani had milked in desperate attempts to finance his overseas operations, closed their doors. Six more in Germany and eleven more in Italy soon followed.

By the third week in October, and at a terrible price—the death toll in assassinations of judicial personnel alone had risen to six—the Italian authorities had their case ready against Lercani: the money he had removed illegally from Italian banks to purchase Benjamin National; his private list of over six hundred politicians, industrialists, and *mafiosi* who had smuggled illegal funds abroad through Lercani's banks; his proven links with the drug trade; his participation in the assassinations of government witnesses and investigators.

The Americans decided to jump first. On October 25, 1974, federal officers rang at Lercani's apartment in New York's Hotel Maxime, read him his rights, handcuffed him, and took him away. A federal judge arraigned him on ninety-nine counts of fraud, perjury, and misappropriation of bank funds. He was released on his own recognizance after posting $3 million in bail, with the stipulation that he check in once each day at the U.S. marshal's office. Three officers of Benjamin National were indicted for conspiracy to falsify records of the bank's earnings.

It was afternoon, Rome time, when Paolo Lercani's wife called Peter Servatius from New York with the news of her husband's early-morning arrest.

On October 25, 1974, by the time Paolo Lercani was arrested in New York, Rico Lansing had already been in the Apostolate operations signals room in the Vatican for hours. At 6 A.M., with his best signals expert, Righi, beside him, he received the first coded message from inside the shipyards at Gdansk, Poland. All workers were in the yards. At 6:35 he received a second signal. The whistle to begin work had blown. The gates had been locked. The barricades were up. All the machines remained silent. The "test" strike was on.

The Gdansk strike was in reality not the first but the second challenge of Rico's covert organization to the authority of the Communist government in Poland. This time, they had chosen a social issue: the right of the workers to elect their own union officials.

The first challenge had been to test a purely religious issue; it had taken place a year before at a place called Nova Huta, not far from Krakow.

Nova Huta was a totally Communist town. It had been built by the government holus-bolus, from the cellars of its houses and the storage basements of its production plants, to its rooftops and chimneys, as a model of its expected workers' paradise. There were no religious shrines, no churches, no convents, no religious schools or monasteries. Like Communism, it was godless.

Rico's organization decided to build a church. The issue at stake was double: First, he and Cardinals Wallensky and Valeska were testing the discipline of their own organization. Could they, with the help of their trained cadres, force a church to be built in which the people could worship, without allowing the confrontation to develop into a pitched battle of the sort that had brought ruin on so many movements, in Poland and elsewhere, in the past?

And second, could they in fact break the nerve of the authorities through sheer moral perseverance by the people?

The "disturbance at Nova Huta," as it was officially described in its first few days, began in a seemingly innocuous way on Sunday, the last day of September, 1973. The police report for the day recorded that the Cardinal Archbishop of Krakow, Bogdan Valeska, had celebrated Mass for some two thousand workers and their families on an empty tract of land just outside town. Public gatherings were forbidden, of course. The local police arrived as Mass was ending. The crowd dispersed peacefully. No debris was left. No arrests were made.

The following Sunday, Cardinal Valeska turned up again. This time, a makeshift altar was put up, and some five thousand workers turned out with their families to attend the Mass. Again they dispersed peacefully, but not before they had formed a huge cross of flowers, extending over the length and width of the church they intended to build. For the police commissar, a cross was a cross and no more. He had the flowers bulldozed into the earth.

On the third Sunday, a slightly larger crowd attended Bogdan Valeska's Mass, and then erected a very tall wooden cross on the spot where the cardinal had stood at the altar.

The commissar had an impeccable record of public order in Nova Huta. He saw no reason to jeopardize that record by consulting Warsaw Central about what to do.

"You people!" He bellowed at the crowd gathered around the cross to protect it from attack and destruction. "You are just little bits of dung! You are alone! We can crush you when we like! Do not let me see you and your cross here again!"

Having delivered fair warning, the commissar climbed into his official jeep and motioned to his driver. As his car sped off toward the town, he could hear the cries of the crowd. *"Solidarnosc! Solidarnosc!"* That word was to become the open sesame of his nightmares.

By the time the fifth Sunday rolled around, foundation trenches were underway on that empty tract of land. The *Solidarnosc!* slogan had begun popping up, scrawled here and there on factory walls and painted in the streets. At the same time, all the factories in Nova Huta reported slowdowns in production.

Each worker had been carefully trained by Rico's cadres to break all jobs into as many conscious "pieces" or movements as possible, and to perform each one with the utmost human care. It could take someone trained in the technique more than half an hour to pick up his asbestos gloves, to put one glove on his right hand, to put one glove on his left hand, and to pick up a pair of tongs. When a whole factory practiced such care, the result was a slowdown. "Piecework," the laborers called it.

Now, by any name, a work slowdown was more frightening for the factory managers and the commissar than a sudden outbreak of typhoid. They could lose their pay. They could go to jail. They could be shot.

Concerned now for much more than his perfect record, the commissar called his superior in the capital. "The cardinal has obviously incited the people to put up a permanent building for worship."

"Stop them!" was Warsaw's order. "And get everything back to order!"

By now, that was far more easily said than done. That very Sunday the crowd had grown to perhaps fifteen thousand men, women, and children. They had camped on the Mass site all Saturday night, and by dawn there was no way, short of killing hundreds, even to get to the center of that human phalanx.

To cap it all, Cardinal Valeska remained in Nova Huta now, living in a worker's flat in town, while thousands took to living on the location they had chosen for the new church. Never once, however, was there any unsanitary nuisance or littering or cooking. Everything was organized down to the last detail.

Warsaw Central drafted in some few hundreds of armed soldiers. When an irate Zomo—Poland's official riot police—or one of the soldiers hit or roughed up one of the permanent squatters, there was no reactive violence; the crowds simply closed in around the attacker and his victim. The attacker never persevered. But no one ever laid a hand on him.

By November of 1973, industrial production in Nova Huta had been cut by 75 percent. The church was going up slowly. Mass was being said every Sunday. For the commissar, confrontation was the only weapon left.

When Cardinal Valeska left his flat on a cold Sunday morning and headed toward the church site, he saw the Zomo van, and the army truck and the commissar. He was hardly surprised when a platoon of armed soldiers formed up smartly in his path.

Valeska stopped. He was flanked by two workers carrying a long banner inscribed with a red-painted *Solidarnosc!* A whole procession followed him, including several priests who had come to join in the cause of Nova Huta.

The officer of the platoon barked an order. Sixteen carbines were pointed at the cardinal and those nearest him. "You have one minute to leave this location." The officer's voice boomed through a bullhorn.

For nearly the full minute, there was only silence; until a curious, rhythmic clanging and banging began, rising in volume like some peculiar thunder rumbling in their direction. The road and all the space around them was filled with women—thousands of them—beating with spoons upon saucepans and casseroles.

"Then"—Valeska's booming voice could be heard above the din as he finally answered the Communist officer—"when you have killed us, you will have to kill thousands. And when you have killed those, then other thousands. You will have bodies to bury, and no city, and no work. And the Politburo to deal with."

The police commissar, who had been standing well behind the army officer, was furious but helpless. He stepped forward and snatched the bullhorn. "Say your Mass, and then clear out of here!"

"No!" Valeska boomed back. "After Mass, we go on building our church!"

The officer got on his radio to Warsaw. He put the commissar on. Then he was called back to the receiver himself. After twenty minutes of harried conversation and much gesturing, with the rhythmic din as constant accompaniment, he signed off. At another barked order, the soldiers lowered their carbines as smartly as they had raised them and were marched off. The Zomos retired in their panel truck. Cardinal Valeska said his Mass. And after Mass, the building of the church began in earnest.

From that November Sunday onward, it was a question of little harassments and occasional brutalities.

Cardinal Valeska and Cardinal Wallensky were summoned together to the Ministry of Labor in Warsaw.

The minister was a worried man. He wanted the work slowdown in Nova Huta to stop. He did not care two Silesian potatoes, he said, about the church or Mass.

"Personally, Mr. Minister," Wallensky replied seriously, "I love Silesian potatoes. As to the falloff in production in Nova Huta's factories, I am no labor expert. But I should imagine that if the people were supplied with materials so that they could build their church faster, and if the harassment and the bullying were stopped, the workers would be happier; and it is one of the facts of nature that a happy worker is a good worker."

Cardinal Valeska celebrated Christmas Mass that year in the completed church of Nova Huta. He assigned a permanent complement of priests to tend to the spiritual needs of the new diocese. And the organization Rico Lansing had built and nurtured with so much labor and care had passed its first practical test.

As he sat with Righi on that October morning a year later, monitoring the second test, as he had the first, for hours on end, Rico wished mightily that he could be with his people in Gdansk.

There were broad similarities with Nova Huta, of course. Could they challenge the Communist government without provoking a ruinous confrontation? Could moral perseverance of a large group break the nerve of the authorities? But this time, it was not a religious but a social issue they were addressing. The place was not the tiny town of Nova Huta but the great Polish port of Gdansk. It was not a work slowdown but a full-fledged strike that was in progress. And the strike was not a byproduct but the principal means of the challenge to the Communist authorities. The danger was great; the echoes would probably reach beyond Warsaw, all the way to Moscow.

"Try to relax a little, Rico." Righi understood how Lansing felt. "We've trained our people well. We can do more good here than there. We don't want the government to be able to tie you to these activities."

Rico nodded his agreement; it had all been well thought out. But he didn't relax.

By the time a few Western newsmen were allowed near the shipyards, the strike was already a week old, and their reports were of a crack Polish division surrounding all exits, backed up by tanks. The Zomos formed another cordon all around the place. There were no talks between the government and the strikers.

What the press, and the world outside Poland to which they reported on the "Gdansk disturbance," could not understand was why the crushingly superior government forces didn't just smash through the gates and the barricades, storm the shipyard, and scour it of its striking workers.

There were several reasons why the authorities held back. For one thing, they could detect coded radio messages leaving and entering the shipyards. It became clear that the outside sender was beyond Poland's western border. But they could not break the code, nor was their equipment sophisticated enough to defeat the device that kept them from triangulating the outside sender's location. Doubt was a deterrent.

In addition, while the strike was already damaging Poland's sagging economy, if they had to take the yards by assault, men and equipment would both be out of commission. That would mean inactivity and loss of production far beyond anything the country could afford.

A third reason was related to the second. Industry everywhere in Poland was jittery. There was unrest throughout coal, steel and other areas vital to the economy. That flaming word *Solidarnosc!* kept appearing everywhere. Any uncontrolled spark shooting out from Gdansk could ignite the whole Polish work force of twelve million.

No. There was no question of putting down this trouble with force of arms. Moscow forbade it. That was precisely what their capitalist enemies needed as an excuse to isolate the Socialist countries even more.

"Find another way," Moscow ordered Warsaw, "to deal with this situation."

The Polish government decided to ask the strikers what they wanted.

"Free elections of our union officials by secret balloting," came the answer.

The reply was so surprising in its simplicity that the Politburo immediately became suspicious. They could not believe that was all the workers wanted. It must be a trick. But what trick? Another week went by.

By the dawn of the third week, the Muscovite puppet masters were becoming impatient. The capitalist powers were beginning to smear the news all over the media. Every Western nation had protested to the Soviet minister of foreign affairs in Moscow that the rights of the Polish workers were being violated.

"Get finished with this strike by hook or by crook," the minister of foreign affairs growled into the telephone at Poland's prime minister. "If all they want is their measly elections, so be it! But finish with it! And then come to Moscow. You and your cabinet."

At the close of three weeks, the Gdansk strike was over. The workers had won the right to free and secret elections of their own union officials. Rico's second test had come off brilliantly.

"Sto lat!" he radioed, uncoded, the ancient Polish greeting of joy and triumph—the Polish *Viva!*—to Wallensky and Valeska. In cipher he told them he would be with them soon. *"Sto lat!"* He radioed the happy words openly again, and headed home to bed.

The breaking Lercani scandal reached out in many directions, and touched many lives, some very deeply. One of the people it brushed against, like the passing scratch of a poisoned needle, was Keti de la Valle.

The call from Bill Fleming was an unwelcome surprise. He and Keti had worked together at her Paris syndicate many years earlier, but they had never been friends. Bill had always said he would sell his soul for a good story, and his colleagues had always said he'd rather do that than work for one. He had generally been able to scramble over the competition in a crunch, and while his work didn't win him a lot of friends, in time it did land him the top job in the syndicate.

"I just happened to be in Rome, Kay, and thought we could have a drink together."

That was another thing about Fleming; he had always called her Kay—probably because he knew it irritated her. "Thanks, Fleming." Keti was ready to hang up. "I think I'll pass."

"Listen, Kay. That was a lie I just told." What else is new? Keti thought. "I don't just happen to be in Rome. I came here specifically to see you. There's a threat against your husband, and you're the only one who can head it off."

Keti froze. "What kind of a threat?" Was Bill lying again? With

Fleming, it was impossible to tell. But she couldn't gamble if it meant danger to Helmut.

"I can't tell you on the phone. Can you meet me for drinks this afternoon? Do you know the Caffè Regale on the Via Veneto? Say, four-thirty?"

Bill Fleming hadn't lied. He just hadn't told the whole truth. The threat against Helmut was Bill's own. It was an extravagant scheme, and he smiled a sleazy smile at Keti as he laid it out for her.

Every newspaper and wire service in the States, he said, was trying to get the real story behind the Lercani scandal. He intended to be the one to come up with it. "Not just the mess at Benjamin." He gestured to the waiter for another martini for himself. "The whole thing. Including his Vatican connection."

Keti told him the truth. She was as ignorant as the next person about Lercani. She knew what she read in the papers and no more.

That was no problem for Bill Fleming. She was married, after all, to one of the Vatican's topflight financial managers. What she didn't know, he would.

"My husband never discusses business with me, Bill. The answer is still no."

"Let me give you a good reason to change your answer to yes, Kay." Fleming produced an envelope from his inside jacket pocket. He took some photographs from it and laid them in a neat little row on the table in front of her. They were all shots of Keti and Rico. A couple of them, she saw, had been taken after the opening ceremonies of Vatican II. Paparazzi had been all over the place then, snapping everything and everybody, in the hope that, sorting it all out later, they would end up with at least some material to sell to a hungry world press. All the photos were similar in that respect, taken in public places. There was nothing unbecoming in them, except that they could, taken together, be interpreted as implying great intimacy between them. In one, she was looking up at Rico full-eyed and obviously very happy. In another, he had taken her arm and they were walking close together, their faces happy and smiling.

"Can't you see the captions, Kay?" Fleming was relaxed in his place, sitting back, watching the dawning realization on her face. " 'Bishop Richard Lansing, mystery cleric of the Vatican, seen everywhere in the company of the rich and beautiful wife of financial kingpin Helmut de la Valle.' "

It wasn't hard for Keti to understand how Fleming had assembled this gallery of pictures. Most had probably come over the wire to the syndicate. Others had come directly from the paparazzi peddling their wares. He kept a dozen files with photos of people he knew or could get to; people who might somehow be useful one day, because of this connection or that. It was something he had done even in the old days, but not with blackmail in mind. Or, at least, that thought had never occurred to Keti. Until now.

"This is garbage, Bill!" she hissed at him across the table.

"Precisely, Kay." Fleming agreed. "And there are a lot of publications with good circulation that thrive on just that sort of garbage.

"Look at it this way. All I want is the dirt on a man who is obviously very dirty. Lercani. That's not a lot to ask to keep the very clean names of de la Valle and Lansing from being smeared in muck. It's a simple choice, don't you think?"

Keti snatched up the photographs, her hand shaking in anger, and put them in her bag.

"That's right, Kay." Bill smiled. "You take them and think about them. I have the negatives. They're yours as soon as I get my story.

"It's nearly the end of October. You'll need a little time to get the information. A week. Maybe two. Why don't I come back down to Rome the second week in November? I'll call you. Either I trade you the negatives for a Lercani scoop, or you and your husband read in the gossips about your long-standing affair with Bishop Lansing."

Helmut spread the photographs out in front of him on his desk. Of course Keti had told him all about the phone call; of how Bill had made her believe there was some threat; how what had happened to Eugenio had risen in her mind. And of course Helmut believed Keti about Rico. He loved Rico too, as one man loves another. For his strength. His uprightness. His fidelity. There was nothing physical between his wife and his friend. He knew that was true.

Yet—Helmut picked up one of the photos—there was nothing physical now between himself and Keti, either.

No doubt about it; Rico was happy in this picture. And in the others too. Over the last thirty years he had seen that look hundreds of times in many places.

He studied the figure of Keti in the photographs. When was the last time she had given him that full-eyed laughing glance? Helmut's heart ached with a deep longing.

Slowly, a hatred of Bill Fleming welled inside of Helmut. Another hand was creeping into the deepest intimacy of life at Villa Cerulea. He wasn't worried about Fleming's threat. He could deal with that, and fully intended to. Keti had promised to tell Fleming to call him when he contacted her again.

What did bother Helmut was something less tangible. Not a doubt, really. Even Fleming didn't believe there was an affair between Keti and Rico; didn't even pretend he believed it, according to Keti. But there was something about the suggestion . . .

Helmut's hand flashed out and gathered up the photographs. He was letting his imagination and his own longing for Keti run away with him. Damn Bill Fleming!

He put the photos in an envelope and locked them away in his safe. There were practical things to be done. The first was to get all the information there was to be had on William A. Fleming, and on his syndicate

—board members, corporate structure, owners, stock situation, premises, personnel.

From the moment Ectore Pappagallo got word of Paolo Lercani's arrest and arraignment in New York, it was for the senatore as though the Sicilian had never existed. His usefulness now was nil. The senatore was not even remotely connected to any of the government evidence, and for the past two years and more, he had wisely stood even farther back from Lercani than from most of his "P-2" associates.

Wisely, too, he had cultivated Roberto Gonella as Lercani's replacement. Gonella wasn't nearly so impressive—he hadn't Lercani's force of personality or his sense of power. He was, rather, the most secret-minded man Pappagallo had ever come across; a man who created around himself a curious atmosphere of both mystery and confidence that was almost beguiling.

Gonella had joined the Banco Agostiniano in 1947. He had not risen like a comet in the financial heavens as Lercani had. His record was that of a highly talented broker with occasional touches of genius. He had made a solid climb up the banking ladder. In 1969 he had been made central director of the Agostiniano; the general directorship followed two years later; and this year, just as Lercani's downward slide became precipitous, Gonella became chairman of the bank. That wasn't the same as being the Pope's banker, perhaps. But the Agostiniano was closely associated with the Holy See in some areas of its dealings, and that could prove more useful to Pappagallo in the long run.

For his part, Gonella had believed for a long time that there was some highly secret superclub of money managers who really ran the world. He ardently wanted to belong to that club.

He had once suspected that Lercani might be one of those supermen, until disaster began to dog him. Disaster does not dog the financial managers of the world; Gonella was sure of that.

From the moment Senatore Pappagallo had made personal contact with him—had begun to nourish his friendship and trust, and to intimate his possible membership in a certain nameless group of international importance—Gonella was deeply interested. Cautious. But interested.

By the time he actually entered the large square room, stepped in front of the blinding light, and gave his agreement to the conditions Naja Hanna named, his caution had been satisfied. Roberto Gonella was confident he was headed in the right direction.

Naja Hanna's urgent assignment for his newest member was to replace the now worthless Lercani accounts in Panama. Several would be needed.

Gonella saw no problem with that. Because of Agostiniano's close relationship to the Vatican's IRA, he had easy access to all the money houses with which the Holy See regularly did business. "There are about ten of them in Panama, I believe," he told Pappagallo.

"Very good." The senatore seemed truly pleased. "For the moment, we need to be certain that one Jaime Herreras has access to an account there.

However you do it, engineer funding to him for a while longer. He's still useful to us, though we can already see the time coming when he will have served his purpose.

"When that time actually arrives—within the next five or six years—we will need to have perhaps a billion dollars or more to finance the defense of Latin America against Herreras' planned takeover."

Gonella was not bothered by what appeared to be some setup of this cat's-paw named Herreras; things like that were done all the time; and it was just the sort of major international ploy the real managers of the world would be involved in. But a billion dollars was a great deal of money.

Pappagallo reminded the banker, much as he had reminded Lercani on a similar occasion, that in the group of which he was now an honored and valued member, failure was betrayal; and betrayal was death.

Gonella gave Pappagallo a quick look. There was no need to worry, he said. "The Agostiniano is such a close banking arm of the Vatican that some people have taken to calling me 'God's banker.' Now, tell me, Senatore: How can God's banker fail?"

The thought struck Pappagallo as very funny. Lercani had called himself the Pope's banker. Gonella called himself God's banker. Both of them were willing to lick his bare behind. He threw his head back and laughed until the tears came.

Bill Fleming's call to Keti came two weeks to the day after their meeting in the Caffè Regale. Encouraged by her tone, he jotted down her husband's Vatican number as she repeated it for him slowly. Moments later he rang through to Helmut's private line.

"I find your news very interesting, Mr. Fleming." Helmut spoke coolly. "I think we can come to some arrangement."

"I think so, Mr. de la Valle. Life must go on. Perhaps we can meet in my flat here in Rome. Number 14 Via Como Largo, this afternoon at, say—"

The voice on the phone sickened Helmut. "Say, eleven o'clock this morning, Mr. Fleming. Here in my office." It was not a suggestion, but a condition.

"Just fine, Mr. de la Valle."

"Can I rely on your discretion until then?"

"Of course."

"The last thing we need is scandal."

"My thought exactly, Mr. de la Valle."

"And you will bring the negatives."

"I will have them with me."

William A. Fleming stepped into Helmut de la Valle's office much as a tiger falls into a pit. The police commissioner who had investigated Eugenio's kidnapping was there, together with two policemen, Helmut's attorney, and some Vatican security men.

At a glance from the commissioner, one of the policemen stepped forward and placed a pair of handcuffs on Fleming's wrists. It was a bit theatrical, Helmut thought, but he knew that subtleties would be wasted on this fellow.

Fleming looked in open-mouthed surprise at his manacled hands, then at Helmut, then at the policemen.

"Blackmail, Mr. Fleming"—the police commissioner stepped forward and produced a summons—"is a felony in Italy, punishable by up to fifteen years in prison." He crumpled the official-looking paper into Fleming's breast pocket.

One of the Vatican security men began reading out loud in a clear voice, much as a court bailiff might, from a report on Fleming's private life. A mistress in Paris. A mistress in Rome. Each mistress was kept in quarters charged to company expenses. A bank account in the name of each mistress for funds "apparently not reported to the U.S. government." A wife and children in the States who rarely saw him. A work schedule that came to less than twenty hours a week. A long list of nightclubs, bars, and brothels, all frequented regularly at company expense—"interviews" and "business meetings" were cited to cover them. . . .

Fleming looked as if he was going to be sick. Helmut invited him to sit down.

"I want the negatives of those photographs, Mr. Fleming." Helmut remained standing.

Fleming reached awkwardly into his inner pocket and produced them.

Helmut laid the envelope on the desk behind him. "I'll tell you how this is going to work, Mr. Fleming. If you walk out this door without those cuffs on you, it will be because I withdraw the charge. I will do that, on the condition that you do not repeat your felony. If there is even a hint that you might try anything like this again, I will press the original charge.

"Whether you go free now or not, the charge remains on your civil dossier. You are doubtless aware that everyone in Italy has a civil dossier. In addition, a copy of the charge is being sent to the FBI in Washington. A report of your private bank accounts has already gone to the Internal Revenue Service.

"Now, that may seem a lot to you, Mr. Fleming. But there are things I have not done. I have not had you fired, for example, though I have friends who assure me they would be happy to take that step at the drop of a hat. Nor have I made it impossible for you ever to hold a respectable job in the media again.

"Now, as you do not appear to be a very intelligent man, Mr. Fleming, let me spell the situation out so there will be no room for error on your part. Leave my wife and my family and my friends alone. If one breath of slander surfaces anywhere in the press about us—any of us, ever—I assure you I will assume you are behind it. And I will deal with you the way a housewife deals with a cockroach. I will hound you with the law and with every other means at my disposal. In short, I will make life impossible for you.

"Is your situation clear to you, Mr. Fleming?"

Fleming looked up, his face revealing something close to hysteria, and assured Helmut the situation was clear. He would do whatever was required. He just wanted out of this room. Out from under Helmut's felony charge. Out of Rome.

"And one more thing." Helmut watched the policeman undo the handcuffs. "Not a word to anyone about this meeting. Understood?"

Fleming rubbed his wrists and edged toward the door. "Understood." He nearly flew through the outer office and down the corridor. By the looks of him, he wouldn't stop running until he got to the airport and aboard the first flight he could get that would take him anywhere, as long as it was out of Italy.

In ordinary circumstances, Helmut's victory over Fleming would have been momentarily satisfying and quickly put behind him along with the whole sordid scheme. But life at Villa Cerulea was not ordinary. Not for him and Keti. It had not been ordinary for some time.

He took the pictures out of the safe, to burn them along with the negatives. He looked at the images of his Keti smiling up at Rico. Could it be true? he wondered. Was it so absurd? Could she be in love with Rico and not even know it?

"Damn you, Bill Fleming!" Helmut set fire to the photos and dropped the ashes into the wastebasket.

[57]

The arrest of Paolo Lercani in New York City and the long-drawn-out scandal that unraveled in its wake took its profoundest and most poignant toll on Lercani's most important single victim, Papa Giovanni Da Brescia.

Papa Da Brescia blamed no one. Not even Lercani. He did not for a moment try to deceive himself that, without the secret midnight pact of 1969, any of this would have happened. He certainly did not blame Peter Servatius, who, as president of the Banco, had to deal now with an endless deluge of reporters. It sometimes appeared as if every newspaper, magazine, and broadcast facility in the world wanted an exclusive story or some fresh item of news—something still more shocking than the fact that "the Pope's banker" was one of the century's biggest swindlers, who had linked the papal name and the papal bank with deepest corruption and with organized crime in some of its most sordid aspects. As Papa Da Brescia could see, Servatius rode out the publicity very well; he really had not all that amount to hide.

The Holy Father's earliest reaction to the Lercani scandal that was visible to the papal household, and primarily to his secretary, Monsignore Delucchi, was that the Pontiff was now demanding direct and regular written reports from all over his Church. By whatever norm he used, the picture those reports assembled was harrowing for him. All his plans for a more democratic treatment of the people of God, and for an enhancement of his function as St. Peter's successor, had evaporated, as though they, too, had been embezzled, much as the billion dollars had been embezzled by Lercani.

Instead of the great second spring he had envisioned for his Church, there was only death and corruption and decay. Mass attendance, baptisms, conversions, enrollment at Catholic schools and universities, all were down. By the first half of 1975 alone, over 12,000 priests had renounced their clerical status. Whole convents of nuns had been laicized, and 67,000 left their orders altogether. New vocations, whether to the priesthood or to convents, were still plummeting; in Holland, there were only two seminarians, and one had openly declared that he was a practicing homosexual.

Search as he might for some sign, some small glimmer of renewal, the Pope could not even find what used to be the unified teaching Church. There was now an international band of disorganized theologians and bishops who propagated doctrines that were heretical and false and anti-Catholic. Even the strict Anglican and other Protestant denominations had ceased to be interested in the Catholic Church.

"What interest have they," Da Brescia said with infinite sadness to Delucchi one evening, "in just one more church? Love us or hate us, our only value is as the one, true Church. We abdicated our role."

With this deep, dawning realization of the failure of his policies added to the burden of the Lercani disgrace, Papa Da Brescia was afflicted with a strange and terrible paralysis of will, a freezing of papal initiative. There was little sleep for him, and a vast desire to be done with the papacy. To be done with having to face the men he now felt had become his virtual jailers. Levesque, Sugnini, Fustami, Dell'Angelo . . . There were so many of them. So many hard faces. So many loud voices. So much self-willed, iron determination. So many jailers.

Where was this half-broken man in white to find the strength to fight them? How was he even to know that he had been the target of so many more plots than Lercani's? That Lercani's was not the only or even the largest deception? How was he to grasp that the love that still possessed the heart of the people of God, and still resided in his own authority and mission, was being purposefully hammered on the hard anvil of human affairs? How was he to admit that the hammers pounding the blows were held by so many—the Northern Alliance and the Red Brigades, Pappagallo's P-2 and Moscow's General Control and Jaime Herreras—or that all of them, the best and the worst, saw their own little wills as the only hope of "right" and "justice" and "salvation" left to the world?

Papa Da Brescia was the ultimate victim of the delusion of others. He was trapped between his Apostolic Palace and St. Peter's Tomb, living in the one and longing for the other.

Like a somnambulist, incapable of exercising the absolute power that was his, he received his "jailers" every day in the papal study. Whatever they suggested, he did.

Levesque was determined to condemn Archbishop Édouard Lasuisse; Da Brescia signed the letter Levesque prepared and then leaked to the press. Sugnini suggested reunion talks with "some representative Anglicans," including Bishop Ripley-Savage, who was now a part of the Anglican hierarchy at Canterbury Cathedral; Da Brescia agreed. His own created bureaucracy was in charge of him.

Had Monsignore Delucchi understood Papa Da Brescia as deeply as he loved and revered him, or had Papa Da Brescia found it within himself to communicate his agony and paralysis of spirit to the Maestro or any of the members of the State Council, surely they would have approached the situation that faced them in mid-1975 with a different mind.

They saw, of course, what the Pontiff saw: a hierarchy that was failing on every level to keep faith with the supernatural revelation that Jesus had made to all mankind, and had entrusted to his Church for all ages.

What they did not see was the deep change occurring in the Holy Father himself. There was no way for them to see that.

They had never ceased in their efforts to persuade Papa Da Brescia at the very least to replace Sugnini, who, with the supporters he had succeeded in having placed in key positions, was doing the greatest harm. They constantly pleaded with the Pontiff personally, one by one and in groups. They made sure he saw reports of mangled ceremonies spawned by the New Arrangement. Finally, they hoped for a time when the Lercani outrage, as bad as it was, would make the Pope consider the other dangers he had created.

Despite everything they could do, however, the torrent of documents continued to pour out from the papal office, all reflecting the will of the "jailers," but all signed by Papa Da Brescia. For the Maestro and the State Council members, it appeared to be a continuation of the ruinous, stubborn, and self-willed policies of a pontificate with which they had been at war almost since its inception.

At last, with the Maestro's consent, Cardinals Arnulfo and Ferragamo-Duca prepared and presented two sets of documents at a meeting of the Council of the Vatican State. The first set consisted of papers and articles that had been published by Archbishop Annibale Sugnini, including a series printed in *Messaggiero della Chiesa,* the Jesuit monthly in Florence, in which Sugnini had openly declared his aims to abolish Catholic liturgy as such, and to make every bishop independent of the Pope, with no obligation to conform with Rome, or even with his fellow bishops.

The second set of documents was drawn from the time that Da Brescia had functioned as one of the two ranking members of the Secretariat of State belonging to the Italian Lodge. There was a photograph of his formal Lodge induction; a certificate of membership; several resolutions, minutes of meetings and other such papers, all bearing Da Brescia's signature along with those of well-known Masons.

Cardinal Arnulfo had also prepared a letter to His Holiness, to be signed by the full State Council, if all members agreed with Arnulfo's and Ferragamo-Duca's proposal.

That letter, which Arnulfo read aloud at the meeting, was spare and direct. It advised Papa Da Brescia that publication of the documents revealing his prior membership in the Lodge could only be avoided by the Pontiff's immediate dismissal of Archbishop Sugnini and of his close collaborators in the Curia.

The proposal placed before the Council was that the entire file of documents and the letter all be sent by reliable hands to Papa Da Brescia without delay; and to make good on the threat contained in the letter to publish the Da Brescia–Lodge documents if there should be even the slightest delay in papal compliance with the Council's demand for Sugnini's dismissal.

Cardinal Hoffeldt not only agreed but felt the demand was not sweeping enough. He wanted to see Fustami and Pirandella removed from the Congregations for Bishops and for the Evangelization of Peoples. And he would be happy to see Levesque depart as secretary of state as well. Cooler heads prevailed, as Hoffeldt knew they would. He just needed to blow off steam. Cardinals—and certainly the secretary of state—could not be so summarily dealt with. If the Council's demands were so sweeping as to be beyond reason, Da Brescia would be justified in acceding to none of them. The Curia would be right back where it started.

Cardinal Giacomo Corelli, who had replaced Cardinal Joachim Lanser as the conservative representative on the State Council, was uncomfortable with the proposed plan. It was "duplistic," he said in all candor, to use something Da Brescia had been asked to do as a member of the hierarchy, against Da Brescia as Pope.

Cardinal O'Mahoney of Chicago, however, answered his criticism as Churchill had answered critics of his alliance with the Soviets to fight the Nazis: Any stick was good enough to beat a dog.

"Naturally," Cardinal Hoffeldt agreed.

Cardinal Corelli finally decided to make it unanimous.

The only problem that remained was to get the files and the letter into Papa Da Brescia's hands. It was not something that any of the Council members could deliver personally without, in their judgment, escalating the war between Pope and Curia by their mere presence at such a moment. Nor could they route it by any normal means. Levesque and Sugnini between them scrutinized just about everything that crossed Delucchi's desk, before and after Papa Da Brescia had dealt with it. There was no chance that this curial demand would reach the Pontiff if they saw it first.

Cardinal Ferragamo-Duca was the one who came up with the way. Don Guglielmo, the modest little pastor from the village of Avellino, still visited the Pope every Thursday, as regular as rain. The cardinal would have his own valet drive out to Avellino this very day, with the urgent request that Don Guglielmo put the material personally into the Pontiff's hands.

The matter was decided. Each cardinal in turn signed the letter Cardinal Arnulfo had read. Before the day was out, Cardinal Ferragamo-Duca's portly valet drove to Avellino, delivered the Council's respectful request to Don Guglielmo, and placed in his hands the sealed envelope bearing only the name of its recipient: "His Holiness, Papa Da Brescia."

"Come, good old friend." Papa Da Brescia put his hand on the coarse serge of Don Guglielmo's sleeve. "All during dinner you have seemed like one of those cautious old farm dogs trying to make up his mind to lie down. He goes round and round, following his tail until he's sure he's found just the right spot."

Don Guglielmo was sure the image was apt. He had tried his best to tell about the latest adventures and needs of his parishioners—Signora Cuccia and all the others. He had recited a verse or two of the village poet's latest lampoon of all the town's spinsters; but his heart wasn't in it.

"Settle down now." Papa Da Brescia refilled the old priest's glass with the heavy red wine he loved, and poured a little more for himself. "Tell me. What is it? A message for me? Some news? What?"

"I don't know exactly, Holy Father." Don Guglielmo reached into the inner folds of his worn cassock and produced the envelope. "It must be very important, because it was brought to me by Cardinal Ferragamo-Duca's own personal valet. I don't know why the cardinal chose me. . . ."

Papa Da Brescia sat straight up, spilling his wine on the white cloth. He understood by the very manner Ferragamo-Duca had chosen to deliver his message that it would be yet more trouble for him. He stared at the envelope in Don Guglielmo's trembling hand; but he did not touch it.

The priest laid it down by his plate, the sweat prickling on his scalp. He did not know of great affairs. But he knew pain, and he saw it plainly on the Pontiff's face.

"I know that what you do, Holy Father, you do for the good of the Church. But sometimes the strain seems very great. I think it best if I leave Your Holiness early this evening. . . ."

The Pope seemed not to have heard. He just stared down at the envelope, as if his name on its face were the message it contained, written in some cipher he could not decode.

Don Guglielmo stood, picked up his wide-brimmed hat, hesitated for a moment, and put one hand comfortingly on Papa Da Brescia's shoulder. "Holy Father," he said softly in his rough Tuscan dialect, "I am an old man. I have learned we have only one friend. The Lord Jesus." And then, having given all the wisdom he had to share, he left the Pontiff alone.

The red light on the telephone used by His Holiness to speak with his secretary of state flashed in unison with the loud ringing on the cardinal's bedside table.

"Yes, Holiness." Levesque answered the phone with one hand and groped for a pad and pencil with the other.

"Eminence. Tomorrow you will cut orders for transfers."

"Yes, Holiness?"

"Monsignore Annibale Sugnini will go to Teheran as Our apostolic delegate."

Levesque fought for self-control, seemed unable to make his pencil move.

"Yes, Holy Father. Effective when?"

"Effective January 1 of this present year."

Levesque did not need to take notes; he would remember this conversation. The order meant Sugnini must leave as soon as possible. He would be allowed just about enough time to clean out his desk.

"Anything else, Holy Father?" Levesque nearly dropped the phone as he reached for the water carafe on the night table.

"Yes, Eminence. We will have a full list of thirty names or so on your desk in the morning, together with our instructions concerning each of them. And, Eminence, you are to follow those instructions to the letter, without delay or question."

When Papa Da Brescia hung up the phone in his study, his face was as white as his papal robe. Ordinarily, he would have given instructions of this gravity in person. But he did not think he had the strength left to face Levesque, to contend with the arguments he surely would have made in a personal meeting.

Despite the growing lateness of the hour, the Pontiff rang for Monsignore Delucchi. When he arrived a few minutes later, Da Brescia dictated the names of all of Archbishop Sugnini's close associates and collaborators specified in the State Council's letter, and the new posts to which each would be transferred. All the changes were retroactive, as Sugnini's was.

Papa Da Brescia did not explain anything to Delucchi. He just stared at the Council letter as he dictated in a monotone. He knew publication of his former Lodge membership would destroy his credibility with untold numbers of priests everywhere, and that it would pose yet another subject for scandal among the faithful. It was one more mistake come to haunt him in the nightmare his life had become; unlike the other, the graver, mistakes, it was not one of his choice; but there was little difference in that, and no consolation at all.

The following morning, before Levesque or any of the papal staff had reported for work, Papa Da Brescia had retired to the seclusion of Castel Gandolfo.

Once Peter Servatius' Vatican neck had been saved by Guido de la Valle, and he was schooled by the Maestro and Helmut in how to deal with the constant demands of the press in the Lercani affair, not much bothered him in his post as chief of the IRA. One odd thing did catch his attention, however. The Panamanian money houses used by the Vatican for operations in Latin America had begun drawing heavily on their IRA guarantees. Servatius was not aware of any reason why that should be happening.

This time, he had enough sense to phone the Maestro without delay to tell him of the apparent irregularity.

The Maestro was indeed interested. As soon as Servatius rang off, he decided to call each of his three Latin American *impero* associates: Julio Montt of Peru, Claro Trujillo of Colombia, Aria Potamianos of Panama. It would be best to have the matter looked into at once, in detail and by people he could trust without question.

His first call was to Ari Potamianos in Panama itself. Ari understood the urgency of the situation. He offered to call Montt in Peru and Trujillo in Colombia himself. The three of them together would get to the bottom of the situation quickly and quietly, Potamianos said, and would let the Maestro know if there was anything they couldn't handle locally.

"It's probably nothing, Guido." Ari shouted to be heard over the static of the Rome-Panama phone connection. "We're all nervous and jumpy after the Lercani thing."

"Maybe you're right, Ari," Guido answered. "But let's be sure."

Seclusion brought little rest and no peace for Papa Da Brescia. Even the beauty and tranquillity of the gardens did not seem to help, though he walked in them for interminable hours.

Monsignore Delucchi and the nuns, following the Pope's wishes, saw that he was not disturbed by visitors or by phone calls. They left him alone, but kept a discreetly watchful eye on him. They had cause to be worried. He barely ate enough to keep body and soul together, as Sister Benedetta put it; he frequently seemed to be talking to himself; and sometimes he cried openly.

For the second time in his long and faithful service to Da Brescia, Delucchi considered what nightmares crowded Papa Da Brescia's mind night and day. But this time, unlike the first, it seemed, even after a full week of rest, that the Pontiff did not have the wherewithal to come back, of his own strength, from that valley of depression and regret.

Guido was in his Villa Cerulea study late Friday morning when he was startled by the ring of the white phone. He looked at it as if it were a long-absent friend who suddenly reappears with no warning. That phone had been all but silent during Papa Da Brescia's reign.

He lifted the receiver. "Holiness," he said.

It was not His Holiness. It was Delucchi. The Holy Father needed the Maestro. Had asked for him. Delucchi sounded frightened as he described how the Pontiff's condition had seemed to worsen over the past week. "This morning, Maestro, he was unable to eat after Mass. He has simply sat in an armchair, hardly moving. His only request has been for you to come."

While he was still talking to Delucchi, instructing him to call the Pope's doctor, he rang for Sagastume to pull the car around.

Papa Da Brescia had heard the Maestro's limousine and was standing waiting for him when he entered the papal sitting room.

A single glance at the Pontiff's face was enough; Delucchi had called the Maestro not a moment too soon. Guido kissed the Fisherman's Ring and helped Da Brescia into his chair. He stepped automatically into the role he had been born and trained to fulfill.

He drew a chair up at right angles to the Holy Father's. After a while, Papa Da Brescia began talking slowly, deliberately. His voice rumbled as if it came from deep corners in his soul. His nerves had given way, he said. This morning, he found he could barely move. To get through Mass had been torture. As the morning had worn on, his condition had got worse. Certainly he could not return to the Vatican on Sunday as scheduled. "Maestro, I am afraid for the ship of state."

It was not lost on Guido that this was the first time in all his years as Pope that Da Brescia did not use the papal "We" in speaking to him.

"I do not any longer trust Cardinal Levesque," the Holy Father went on with difficulty. "Yet I cannot control him from a distance. And I cannot have him or any of his"—the Pontiff searched for a word—"his crew come here while I am in this weakened condition.

"What do we do, Maestro? The paper I signed in the Silver Throne Room on the day of my election singles you out as the right hand of the papacy. Now you are needed. I don't matter. Only the Church does."

For the Maestro as for Papa Da Brescia, this was not another capitulation in some war they waged. No longer were there any barriers between the Keeper and this vicar of Christ.

There would, Guido said in a voice that both soothed and gave confidence to the Pope, be no declaration of emergency. His Holiness would take an extended holiday at Castel Gandolfo. All access to him would be forbidden to everyone except a certain few. Monsignore Delucchi and Sister Benedetta could be trusted implicitly, of course. The Maestro and Helmut de la Valle would come each day.

As to dealing with matters of state, he suggested that Bishop Richard Lansing would be the one to keep a tight rein on Cardinal Secretary Levesque. "Lansing can be trusted totally, Your Holiness. And he is the only one with both the expertise in statecraft and the proven personal strength to face Levesque down. He will not be corrupted."

In order to endow Lansing with full discretionary powers to decide grave matters, it would be necessary to make him a cardinal. "But secretly, Holiness, a cardinal *in pectore.*"

It was not unusual to create cardinals *in pectore* when a dire need arose or was foreseen. In this case, the Pontiff knew that no attention could be drawn to the strange situation in which he found himself. To create only one cardinal publicly would do just that, and Papa Da Brescia hadn't the strength to call a consistory to announce the creation of a full complement. And there wasn't time for such formalities, in any case.

There was also the fact, which Guido did not bring up with the Pope, that open announcement of Lansing's status as cardinal would make him a greater target in Eastern Europe than he already was.

"Have Monsignore Lansing here tomorrow, Maestro." The Pontiff rested his head on the back of his chair. "The sooner we start, the better. Have the documents of authorization drawn up for my signature."

There was a light tap on the door of the sitting room. Monsignore Delucchi wanted them to know that the doctor was here.

The Maestro rose from his chair. "I will be back this afternoon, Holiness. And tomorrow morning, of course."

Outside, Guido had a few words with the doctor before he went in to the Pontiff. Then he instructed Delucchi and Sister Benedetta. He told them that he would arrange at once for a special security detail to invest the villa and its gardens. The seclusion of His Holiness must be complete.

Sister Benedetta was deeply concerned for the Holy Father. "How long will all this last, Maestro?"

"Until His Holiness is better, Sister."

Rico still appeared stunned by the abrupt turn of events when he entered the papal chapel at Castel Gandolfo at nine o'clock the following morning, in the company of the Maestro and Helmut de la Valle. He barely noticed the incense thurible moving gently to and fro on its chain, or the sweet-smelling smoke curling upward from its coals. The place itself calmed him, however, as though he had entered a room where angels had been whispering and had silenced their silver voices at the opening of the door.

In the silence of that chapel, Helmut studied Rico's face with a certain intensity, comparing it with his memory of the images in those photographs Bill Fleming had delivered to Keti. No, he told himself. His friend was on another plane. Besides, Helmut knew the man. Why couldn't he just forget? He was just being foolish.

"His Holiness." Delucchi approached Rico and whispered in his ear.

Rico lifted his eyes and saw Papa Da Brescia, his right hand raised, drawing him with a little pulling motion up the center aisle of the chapel to the sanctuary.

The Holy Father was seated on a simple throne placed at the side of the altar. Six tapers burned in the silver candlesticks fashioned by Cellini for Pope Clement V in 1528. The tabernacle door was open; standing before it on the altar was a small gold monstrance, the large Host of the Sacrament gleaming white at its center.

Rico knelt down at the feet of the Pope who had spent so much effort to sweep away the old, and who was seated now in its midst, dependent upon its power and truth. He placed one hand on the Gospels that lay open on the Pontiff's lap.

"My son." Da Brescia spoke softly, but his voice reached Helmut and Guido where they knelt together behind Lansing. "For the glory of God, for the exaltation of our Holy Mother, the Church, for the eternal salvation of men and women, for the good of your own soul, do you swear and do you promise to be faithful to this Holy See of Peter, to serve it and the Church of Christ, even to the shedding of your blood? Do you swear by these Holy Gospels?"

Rico raised his eyes to meet Da Brescia's, and he saw in them more than simple kindness. They wore another sheen, soft but unyielding, humanly appealing, but illumined by light beyond the merely palpable and visible.

Rico's hand tensed against the black and gold lettering of the open Gospels. A gentle shudder, stark in its effect, shook his shoulders and arms. For a tiny instant he held back from this threshold. "I do, Holy Father," he said, and bowed his head in obedience.

"Therefore," Da Brescia answered his consent, "We, by the power of Jesus Christ whose Vicar We are, and with the authority of the Blessed Apostle Peter, whose lawful successor We are, do hereby signify, by the covering of your head, that you, Ricardus Lansing, a cleric in Holy Orders of the Holy Roman, Catholic and Apostolic Church, are now constituted in the order of Cardinal Archbishop. In witness of this, We place this scarlet biretta on your head."

Lansing felt the biretta settled firmly on him by the Pope's hand. After the briefest pause, he removed it, took the Pontiff's outstretched hand in his and kissed the Fisherman's Ring. Then he bent low and kissed the instep of Papa Da Brescia's right foot in the ancient sign of submissiveness of every cardinal to his pope.

"Your Eminence." Da Brescia's voice became hoarse with the effort this ceremony had cost him. "We have conferred the cardinalate on you for specific reasons. You will observe two special commands. First, you are a cardinal *in pectore.* Your identity as such is hidden in Our heart. You will communicate your status to no one until such time as We or one of Our successors on this throne shall decide. The title Eminence will not be used by you or in your regard.

"Second, Maestro Guido de la Valle has explicit instructions from Us in your regard. We have also spoken to Cardinal Secretary Levesque on the telephone. You will follow the Maestro's instructions in all things."

For the eight months of Papa Da Brescia's seclusion, Rico Lansing's schedule was organized totally around the Secretariat of State and Castel Gandolfo. He directed his covert work from afar, depending more heavily than usual on Youn and Righi and the others, and on the radio signals to and from Rome.

Every morning, an icily correct Cardinal Levesque sat in his office and briefed Lansing as he would the Pope. There rarely was a clash of wills between the two. The cardinal secretary observed all the canons of behavior; he was biding his time.

Usually Rico set out for Castel Gandolfo immediately after the morning briefing, and most often he was met there by Guido or Helmut, or both of them together. They sat with the Pontiff according as Papa Da Brescia's strength allowed, transacting necessary current business with him, securing his signature, answering his few questions.

It was a breathtaking chance for Lansing to begin to appreciate the far-flung complexity of Church government, and to begin to realize for the first time the awesomeness of the burdens a pope must shoulder.

The doctor's report on the health of Papa Da Brescia was equivocal. It had been known for some time, though only at the highest levels of the Curia, that the Pontiff suffered from leukemia. A few reports had surfaced in the press somehow, but were quickly denied by the Vatican. It appeared now that the disease was making new inroads. To judge from His Holiness' inability to move quickly, he had undergone a mild stroke. He suffered from severe anemia. At most, the doctor ventured, the Holy Father had perhaps three years to live. Possibly much less.

The plan to maintain normalcy in Papa Da Brescia's pontificate succeeded only partially. Inevitably, as his time of seclusion drew on, a rash of rumors began to surface in the Italian and French press. Papa Da Brescia was dead, some stories accused, and his death was being covered up. He had gone insane, was another theory, and had to be confined. He had been spirited away to a remote prison, and a perfect double was functioning in his place, staying out in Castel Gandolfo while he learned the ropes.

These imaginative rumors were nourished by photographs of Papa Da Brescia when he appeared once or twice on the public balcony of Castel Gandolfo to give his blessing. An enterprising Swiss journalist recorded his voice on one such occasion to prove that it was different than the Pope's voice in previous years, and that obviously an impostor had taken the place of poor Papa Da Brescia.

Rico Lansing and the de la Valles were firm that nothing should be done about all this. When Papa Da Brescia returned to the Vatican, the rumors and lies would die a natural death. Meanwhile, the villa, and above all those gardens he had always loved so much, gave the Pontiff comfort and courage and a slow return of some of his strength. He should soon be able to conduct some papal business himself at Castel Gandolfo, receiving a few Vatican officials, holding an occasional public or private audience, slowly getting back into harness.

In the circumstances, Guido advised the Vatican State Council that it was again time to begin the orderly pre-conclave process.

Before the names of the *papabili* were offered by the Council members, Cardinal Arnulfo summarized quickly the Church whose reins would be handed to the man chosen.

"Many years ago," he said, "we made the decision to let the pus festering beneath the surface of the Church rise to the top so that it could be lanced away.

"Well, my venerable brothers, we have more boils than we bargained for! Most of us at this table will not live long enough to see them all lanced and healed. But we must see that the process is started.

"At the top, the Vatican bureaucracy is now peopled by creatures of

His Holiness who have turned out to be pernicious. The next pope will have to decide if they are to be left to die off, or if he will transfer them to posts where they can do less harm, or preferably no harm at all.

"At the next level, the bishops have cut loose from authority to the point that a good half of them are in schism now, refusing the jurisdiction of the Holy Father in matters of faith, morals, and Church discipline. A large bloc—I would say probably half of the three hundred bishops in the U.S. alone—have no real faith, or a watered-down faith at best. Many are in technical heresy.

"The worst element is the fact that a whole new generation of youth has now been reared in real ignorance of their faith. They don't know what the Church is, what sin is, what a sacrament is. The teaching nuns failed. The teaching brothers failed.

"The next pope must face all of that, as well. But that doesn't even begin to touch on the political situation.

"In his bargain to get them to participate in Vatican II as observers, Papa Angelica made a formal agreement with the Soviet Politburo not to condemn Soviet Communism. Papa Da Brescia has honored that commitment. After all, he was part of that agreement himself. It was he who sent Cardinal Lisserant to meet the Soviet agent in the French town of Metz.

"It is little wonder, then, that all through the Church—but especially in Latin America—the religious orders, along with perhaps a third of the bishops and half of the diocesan priests, openly support Marxist movements. Most notably I would single out the Jesuits, the Carmelites, the Franciscans, and the Maryknoll priests and nuns. Many—diocesan and otherwise—have gone so far as to participate in armed preparations for a Marxist takeover. Whether you look at Chile or the Philippines or South Korea or Nicaragua or Brazil or El Salvador or a dozen other countries, the picture is the same among the clergy and religious.

"That, too, the next pope must deal with."

Cardinal Falconieri looked around the table with a glum face. "The next pope will either have to be a saint," he said, "or a modern and even more ruthless version of Torquemada!"

"Let's seek for the saint first," Arnulfo responded to the observation.

"Before we look for either one"—Helmut interjected a note of starkest realism—"let's face up to the strength of the interests that are now well entrenched against us. Say we find a suitable saint, and on the morrow of his election he lays an ax to the root of the difficulties. What do you think those entrenched interests are going to do? Wait to have their feet cut off? Their achieved positions destroyed? Their arms of power and influence amputated?"

Ferragamo-Duca took the point—or thought he did. "So, Signor Helmut, you're saying we need a saint who is willing to be martyred."

"A true saint," Helmut replied, "is a willing martyr. I'm saying we need two saints. Two strong names decided upon now, before the fact."

It was a sobering proposal, but one with which no one at the Council table disagreed. Coming up with the names, however, took some time.

After about an hour of discussion, the first prime *papabile* was decided upon. Cardinal Serena of Turin, where Corelli had been born and raised, was a man so quiet as to be unnoticed by the wide world. And yet he fit the description of the desired *papabile* almost perfectly. He was a man of extraordinary holiness, a tower of strength, and was aghast at the deteriorating condition of his Church. His age was perfect; he had only recently turned sixty-two.

Cardinal Karajan, who was holy and strong, had to be rejected as the backup to Serena because of his advanced age. At eighty-seven, he would not even be allowed to participate in conclave under the rules Papa Da Brescia had instituted. And, in any event, what was needed now was anything but an interim papacy.

The Maestro, who had been relatively quiet for most of the discussion, suggested that they should not be looking for two identical *papabili,* in any case. He concurred in the choice of Serena as the first—the saint. "But," he went on, "if Serena were to be elected pope, and if our enemies did dare lay hands on him, then we should take that as a clear sign that a new night is about to fall on the Church and on religion. If the evil rampant out in the world can reach in and destroy a pope, then the man to replace him is one strong enough to fight. Someone already trained in surviving the night of desolation.

"I know only two cardinals of that caliber. The two Poles. Except for his age, Cardinal Wallensky would be the better of the two. But Cardinal Bogdan Valeska has proved his worth over the years, and has learned well from Wallensky."

The discussion that met the Maestro's suggestion was a free-for-all. There was some fear on Helmut's part, because of his long talks over the years with Rico, that Valeska would not be able to detach his Polishness from his papacy, were he to be elected.

Hoffeldt was concerned that the election of a Pole as Catholic Pope could be taken by Moscow's Politburo as a direct message—friendly or unfriendly. Would they infer an acceptance or a renunciation of Papa Angelica's secret pact with Moscow?

O'Mahoney was at a loss to guess how the U.S. government might read such an election result.

On and on the discussion went. Could a non-Italian hold the Church in Italy together? What could he do about the Church in Northern Europe and the Americas? Except for brief periods abroad, Valeska had been confined to Poland. What experience did he have of the Church Universal? Did he need such experience? Could he tame the Da Brescia holdovers in the Vatican bureaucracy until he had time to form his own?

In the end it was agreed that Valeska's strengths, which had been proved and were certain, far outweighed speculation about his possible weaknesses.

It was not the first time in her long history that the Church had needed more than a single *papabile* at one time. At her very inception, the earliest years after the martyrdom of Peter, a whole succession of men was customarily readied, because any of them might be whisked away at any time. But it was the first in living memory. Because of the risk Serena would be asked to take, white papers would be prepared for him, detailing the full situation of the Church, much as Arnulfo had laid it out at the opening of the Council meeting, but in greater detail.

The Maestro would prepare as well a paper concerning the Vatican's central economic body, PECA, the Prefecture for Economic Affairs. He would visit Serena in Turin and deliver all the briefing papers personally. At the same time, he would advise Serena of the full Council discussion. In the circumstances, his informed consent was wanted before they began to form pre-conclave consensus.

It was decided further that in traveling to test the consensus for Serena or anyone else, certain Latin American cardinals would not be contacted. Three out of the four French cardinals would be avoided, together with the Dutchman and the Englishman. "We will not need them anyway," Ferragamo-Duca surmised aloud.

In the short term, though the consensus for Valeska would be tested at the same time as that for the prime *papabile,* the Polish cardinal would not yet be told of his status as backup papal candidate. Indeed, everyone prayed that the need to tell him would never arise.

[58]

Papa Da Brescia returned to the Vatican, escorted by Rico and Monsignore Delucchi, on a somber Wednesday evening in October 1976. Guido and Helmut were waiting for them.

No sooner was the Pontiff inside the door of the reception room of the papal apartments than he went down on his knees and kissed the floor. When he stood up again, he had a word to say to this little group of men who had supported his pontificate at the nadir of his strength. It was, they thought, the subtlest of his statements ever.

"I have been Pope since 1963." He looked at each man in turn as he spoke. "But only during this awful time have I realized that to be Pope is not to be me; that it is not to be 'my own' person. I ask forgiveness from each one of you; and through you, from all those whose eternal salvation I may have jeopardized by the policies I have followed and by the arrogance I have practiced.

"Pray for me, so that what remains to me of my life may be a testimony that late, but not too late, I turned to Christ, whose Vicar I am. And to the Blessed Apostle Peter, whose successor I am."

In the ensuing days, the de la Valles and Lansing briefed the Holy Father more fully on a whole array of matters. His Holiness was pleased that the IRA was recovering from the Lercani losses. He was able to discuss some further personnel changes, but confessed candidly to the Maestro that he would not do much in that quarter. "At least not as much as you desire. I am too tired to struggle with Levesque. He is pernicious. He has learned nothing. I have not the strength needed, or the resilience, to enter into prolonged contention. With your help, Maestro, and Richard Lansing's and your nephew's, I will contain him; but I cannot now do more."

Outwardly, life at the Apostolic Palace seemed to resume its normal aspect and flow. The Holy Father received important state visitors again from around the world. He held a full schedule of public and private audiences. He gave his blessing to the people each day from the papal window above St. Peter's Square. The wild press reports began to fade. Don Guglielmo resumed his Thursday-evening visits; the aged pastor was too good, too innocent, too faithful a servant to be hurt unduly by the unworthiness and the misfortune of those whose sins and mistakes had caught up with them at the heel of the hunt. Papa Da Brescia was more grateful than ever for his presence.

Behind the scenes, echoes and ricochets of the contention that had been so much a part of his pontificate went on around the Holy Father as if by inertia. The Northern Alliance was apparently meeting again, and, as a concerned Security Two reported, was continually in touch with Annibale Sugnini as he sulked in his exile within the Apostolic Delegation at Number 92 Teleghani Street, Teheran. Cardinal Secretary Levesque did all he could to mount his high horse again. Within the limits he occupied ex officio, he was his usual tyrannical, autocratic self. But his decision-making powers remained curtailed, censured and limited as they now were by the Maestro and Richard Lansing.

Even with all the increased activity, however, it was clear to Guido and Helmut and Rico, and to the intimates of the papal household, that for all the remaining days of his earthly life, Papa Da Brescia's focus was not upon the here and now, but upon his future life, beyond the reach of mortality and the afflictions of its pains.

Once Guido had visited Cardinal Serena in Turin, and had gone over all the briefing papers with him, explaining as well the mortal danger that might attend the next pope; and once Serena had given his full consent to be that pope, should that be the will of the conclave under the guidance of the Holy Spirit, the work for pre-conclave consensus began without further delay.

The Maestro and Helmut arranged their own travel schedules so that they would not both be absent from the Vatican at the same time. When they and other members of the State Council had completed many of the important visits, it was time to free Richard Lansing up sufficiently so that he could do the consensus work for Serena's candidacy in Eastern Europe. Lansing was not told of the backup candidate. Aside from Serena and the members of the State Council, no one was told about that.

Spacing his travels so that he would not be away from the Secretariat of State for more than a week at any single stretch, Rico began a series of tours of his devotional organizations in the satellite countries, ostensibly to do his usual rounds of preaching.

In East Germany, there was no cardinal; but Archbishop Muller was considered a popemaker, as was the Archbishop of Zagreb, Yugoslavia. Both men were pleased that the Curia was in preparation for a new conclave. They would pray for Papa Da Brescia, they said, and would throw their influence behind Serena as his successor. The Cardinal of Prague in Czechoslovakia was of a like mind; the Curia could count on his support, and on his vote in conclave.

Rico's visit to Hungary was pro forma; he could not omit the area from Apostolate tours without raising the suspicions of a naturally suspicious Cardinal Sekai. His visit with the cardinal was reserved—not only because of the betrayal of Mindszenty, but because Rico knew the conversation, as always, was being monitored and recorded by Sekai's perpetual KGB companion, seated in the next room.

"Eminence," Rico answered Sekai's query after the Pope's health, "please God the Pontiff has many more years to live. But you haven't to wait for the death of a pope to visit us in Rome. You know how desirous the Holy See is to bless the Democratic Government of Hungary."

Sekai gave Lansing a sickly smile as he showed him out. The American was a fool or the Devil himself. Until he discovered which, Sekai would be careful how he treated the man.

In Poland, Cardinal Wallensky and Cardinal Valeska both supported Serena. Their only differences centered on how the next pope should deal with the directives of the Second Vatican Council. Wallensky had not abated in his criticism of everything about the Ecumenical Council. Valeska, however, still felt that the Church should "apply the directives of Vatican II, and curb the excesses of the clergy and religious in capitalist countries."

What consensus work there was to be done in the remaining Eastern countries, particularly in Lithuania, Lansing did through messages sent and received by way of his underground network.

During all these travels and his continuing work with Papa Da Brescia, Rico still directed his covert educational organizations from a distance. The last thing he needed in the complexity of his life now was a midnight call from John Liebermann.

"Can it wait, John?" Rico spoke wearily into his bedside phone.

"I've been trying to reach you for over a week, Rico. I didn't leave messages with your valet for obvious reasons. I'm in a bind, and I need your help. It won't take long, I promise."

Best to get it over with, Rico decided. When Liebermann had a problem, he was like a dog with a bone; he wouldn't let go.

The two met late the following night on the deserted quays of the port of Ostia, about twenty miles outside Rome. Liebermann lost no time in spelling out the bind he had spoken of.

There was grim news for the intelligence community in the States, he told Rico. The new administration had let it be known that, in the name of peace, it intended to dismantle many intelligence networks abroad—

notably in Western Europe, the Middle East, Latin America, and Eastern Europe. The intelligence agency's central core was going to have to face what it hoped was only a temporary eclipse, biding its time and hoping for a better day.

"We can manage the essentials in the Middle East and Latin America." Liebermann gave his assessment. "We can get some help from friends in Western Europe. But we're going to be crippled in Eastern Europe." He proceeded to expose to Rico the details of their network in the satellite countries, and what would remain once the dismantling was effected.

Rico was dumbfounded. "You won't even know what's going on, John, if they do this to the agency. What's the big idea?"

"Don't ask me, Rico." Liebermann shook his head angrily. "I don't know. Maybe we Americans are just plain stupid. Or maybe it's redneck innocence, and naive trust that the Politburo is just a bunch of good old boys who need a chance to show how sweet they really are. Or maybe we've been moled more deeply than we knew by the other side. Whatever it is, my personal view is that the liberal constituency back home is acting like they've wandered into a palace of evil enchantment. The best of them have ceased to know what life means, or how hard most of the world has to fight for it. The worst of them sing rhapsodies about noble causes and love, but seem impervious to the cruelty and hate in our adversaries.

"Why they go along with this at the top, I can't begin to explain. But it's something I have to deal with, Rico.

"What I need now is more than a favor. It's a whole lease on life for some of the agency operatives who'll be left bare naked and vulnerable by all this."

What Liebermann was proposing was that Rico arrange matters so some portion of the curtailed funds that remained to the agency could be channeled to operatives in Eastern Europe, and that they have a reliable mode of communication with home base in the States. And, because of the increased danger, they needed to be as sure as they could about avenues of escape; it was going to be more likely than ever that they would need them.

Rico understood John's anguish, particularly about emergency escape routes. He had needed them himself, more than a few times. But he shook his head. He couldn't do it, he said.

"The services we have rendered each other in the past were isolated and in passing. What you propose is an organizational link. It's not feasible, John. What we've built up has been done with Church funds, on the basis of Church faith, with the Church's spiritual mission and purposes in mind. I can't divert any part of it for purely political purposes, even if I agree with them."

Liebermann isolated himself in silence for a while; but Lansing knew he wasn't going to give up easily.

"Okay," Liebermann began again. "Okay, Rico. I understand what you're saying. But all of this is happening at a really bad time. And we're not the only ones who are going to be hit by it."

The American agent began to open up about links his people had uncovered among the various groups who seemed bent on destabilization of governments "all over the place." What he described to Rico was in essence a repetition of Giulio Brandolini's P-2 theory. They were on to the Pappagallo link with Jaime Herreras and the Nazis in Latin America. Liebermann and his people hadn't put it together as neatly as Brandolini had; and, at least from what Liebermann was willing to say, they didn't posit a single P-1 group pulling all the strings. But John saw as clearly as Rico did that the Church, as one of the primary stabilizing forces in the world, had to be a target for at least some of the groups. "Especially"—he underlined the point—"when you figure this Herreras into the equation. He's got half the priests and nuns in Latin America on the warpath!

"So in a way, Rico, that makes it a spiritual war, right? I mean, that's why you're in this at all! In the long run, the real war is between good and evil. Not all our battles are about that, I grant you. But the war that matters *is* between spirit and spirit. And the lines of that war shift back and forth among people of all faiths and all persuasions. All the good guys aren't on one side and all the baddies on the other.

"I guess what I'm trying to say is that even if someone isn't a Roman Catholic, as you are, and as I am, he's not automatically bad; not even automatically against you."

"I guess what you're really trying to say"—Rico put his hand on Liebermann's shoulder—"is that a lot of your people are going to be killed if we don't help out."

"The lucky ones will be killed, Rico. And the strongest ones may not break under torture. But there are other ways, these days. A lot more than lives can go down the drain."

Rico picked up a rusty scrap of metal from the quay and sent it skittering over the top of the dark, oily water.

"It won't be forever, Rico. This insanity has got to run its course someday!"

"Okay, John. But it's the same drill as before. One on one. You tell me what you need and why. I decide how to handle it. No formal links and no questions asked along the line in your organization. Ever. Take it or leave it."

"I'll take it, Rico! You won't be sorry."

"I hope not, John."

As he swung across the Vittorio Emmanuele Bridge, Rico looked forward to a quiet dinner with the de la Valles at Villa Cerulea, and then a few hours with Guido and Helmut to discuss things in a little more peace than usual. The Maestro was due back from Australia this afternoon; Helmut had already gone to meet him, in fact, while Rico had finished his day with Papa Da Brescia.

As Rico joined the autostrada leading to the Alban Hills, with the street bedlam of Rome banished from his ears, his mind was still focused on immediate concerns. He was worried about Giulio Brandolini's latest intelligence concerning Sugnini in Teheran. Apparently the archbishop had made contact with both the Russian ambassador and the PLO contingent there; neither move had been authorized by the Secretariat of State.

Levesque, meanwhile, had not made Lansing's life a bed of roses. Rico had developed a stone-faced manner of dealing with the cardinal secretary—giving him orders, rejecting his suggestions, even putting him in his place when the need arose. On the other hand, Levesque hadn't made life entirely a bed of thorns, either—and that bothered Rico even more. Levesque was a consummate tactician. He doubtless had no illusions that he could ever take up his battle again for the mind and soul of Papa Da Brescia. But there would be many more battles to fight. Levesque knew how to keep his powder dry while he waited.

Rico branched off the autostrada at Santa Maria di Grasso. His mind opened out with the landscape, leaving the detailed problems of the day for a broader reflection of what his life had become over the last year or so. He was very near the top of the Church hierarchy, touching levers of power as few men ever do. He thought back to his earliest days in Rome, when everything in the Vatican had seemed clothed with glory. Now it seemed banal and sometimes soul-killing, peopled with self-seekers like Levesque and Demarchelier. As hard and lonely and dangerous as his Apostolate work had been all these years, one thing it had done, ironically enough, was to shield him from the dry dust of the normal Vatican routine. By comparison, life now was hardtack. There was no warmth or sensuality; certainly no glory, but only icy winds on the peak where popes reside.

Rico was so much like family that Keti was a little startled at how happy his arrival made her feel. She took his hand, gave him a little peck on the cheek, and led him toward the garden. Helmut had called from the airport, she said; Guido's plane was delayed, so dinner would be late. She was just going to cut a few fresh flowers for the table. "Unfortunately, Agathi and Tati are out inspecting some of the orchards. She'll be furious you came when she was absent."

As though they had planned it that way, as one of their afternoon outings they both missed, Rico took up the basket waiting on the terrace table and strolled beside Keti on the Family Path. "Which one?" he asked.

"Which what?" Keti smiled up at him in puzzlement.

"Which one of them will be furious? Agathi or Tati?"

"Oh, that!" She laughed. "Both of them, of course." For just a second, Keti let her eyes linger on Rico's face. She took in all the details in that quick glance. The auburn hair had streaks of silver in it. The eyes still smiled. The jawline was still firm. It was all set off by the stark white of his Roman collar. There was always such a calm about him. His head, bent slightly to look down at her, gave the impression of a kind of blessing, and of a tallness that had always made him visible in crowds for her.

Keti shivered and turned away, to snip at the flower beds, and fill the basket slowly with her rainbow harvest.

Rico sensed her distraction, but did not know exactly its cause or texture. The damask perfume enveloped them in amongst the trees and flower beds like the continuation of a valued experience they had shared some time before, and that was now theirs again. The sounds around them were quiet ones; their feelings were gentle; the garden seemed made for calm and noiseless enjoyment.

As Keti bent to cut a flower, to peel wilting leaves from this plant or lift the petals on that one, to adjust the prop of some frail living shoot, all her movements seemed deft and at home, as if designed for the very purpose of flicking away the dry dust that had begun to seep into the cracks of Rico's soul. Her voice, when she spoke at all, did not interrupt his mood, but was of a piece with it. Each of her movements was warmth itself; each seemed to remove another hardness in his life.

Keti looked up to share her delight in a minute Alpine rose. "Helmut brought it from Waidhofen," she said; but then she saw the flicker of alarm and surprise cross his eyes and she looked away.

The surge of emotion startled Rico. How often had he and Keti talked about love, he wondered, from those first days when they had walked all of Rome before her wedding day, until her own admonishments to him about Netta and about a woman's need, like a man's, for love. And yet at that moment when Keti looked up at him, he understood that he had never understood about love. The theory of blue is one thing, he thought; but the sight of the sky is quite another.

As if the look in his eyes might violate something sacred, something that now lay within reach of his hand and his heart, he turned his back and faced toward the house. Villa Cerulea blocked the light of the late-day sun, leaving the garden in deepening velvet shadow like a darkling, heavenly meadow. The contours of its four tall towers and its roof and gables were bathed in a gentle halo flame. Its huge stone walls were translated into a mystic home, a sacred place, a shrine where special adoration is allowed.

Keti was glad Rico could not see her face. As long as she was out of range of his eyes, she could think. Keti remembered everything. Knew everything. Sensed everything. She had seen his eyes. She knew that hunger for human warmth that was a twin to her own. Something sprang in her to meet that need, as Rico had always met her need, whatever it might be. Since that first day in Waidhofen when he had, so gently, led her to soften the hardness of her probing questions, to this very moment, he had always been there for her. With almost infinite patience, and that particular gentleness that was his, he had been at the very heart of all that mattered in her life. His thoughts, his movements, his words, always seemed to revolve about a fixed center, some hidden but powerful sun in his own planetary system. He never came off that private plane; but he had often admitted her there. When she had descended, he remained. But she knew he would be there, intact and available for her, the next time, and the next.

Perhaps it was that, she thought, that had always made her feel so safe. He was always there. She was surer of Rico than of anything. She had never lost Rico, the way she had lost Helmut.

The sun, a golden orange, slipped below the treetops. The air was still warm.

"More like August than September," Rico murmured as they turned back toward the house. Keti said nothing.

There was no distraction beyond the crunch of their slow footsteps on the path and the low hum of insects in among the trees. Even the faint echo of someone whistling for a straying dog only served to measure for them their deep immunity from pressure.

The red tendrils of the vines on the wall were drained of vibrant daylight color. The chirruping of the crickets had muted, and the garden waited, almost consciously it seemed, for the first caress of the predusk dew.

Keti walked with Rico, but not quite beside him. In the half-light, half-dusk, he could not read the expression on her face. But he could see her tears, dissolving on a veil of water gleaming over the blue of her eyes.

For both of them, time itself could be annihilated now. Each knew they could be taken up insensibly on the wings of soaring infinity. This moment was immutable, a spacious kernel of living without the husk of mortality. Any word would be a spark. If she should say his name aloud: "Rico"; should he answer: "Keti," they would enter into a place of shadowless ecstasy and joy. But surely shadows, dreadful shadows, would fall on any sacred place they dared to create together.

Rico closed the half-step's distance between them. They walked slowly toward the terrace, toward the house, the home, where special adoration is allowed, where the only law is that you never walk alone, that one never lack the other, lest it be death for all.

Always before when they had walked in this place they had been easy and relaxed, sometimes brushing lightly against each other, now and again linking arms, or touching a hand to a shoulder. But now there was a tiny, sacred distance stretched tautly between them. In its tininess there lay a world, a delicate agony of feeling. No touch, no lightest brushing, could be accidental now.

They mounted the terrace steps. Slowly. In unison. They measured the identity and completeness that bound them, meshed them, as if they had been this close for a long time; as if the separate lives they each had led had mysteriously faded into insignificance and nothingness. And still, the sacred, tiny distance held them in its living tension.

As they entered the Great Hall there was no unease between them. There was a surety that had no name, that was unquestionable and sustained.

Keti crossed to the credenza and put the flowers down.

Rico had been in this room scores and hundreds of times. Exciting times. Tense times. Painful times. Alone with Guido. Alone with Helmut. In private meetings. At crowded receptions. The broad oaken table, the armchairs and divans and ottomans, the chandeliers, the bibelots, the cabinets of precious minerals and exotic shells, everything had become redolant of living memories over the years, like so many luminous mirrors reflecting words, passions, thoughts, vivid experiences. They were Rico's witnesses. Now they had all become deaf and blind, their faces averted from the scene in reverence, like seraphs before the eternal throne. Now only Keti was alive and vibrant for him. Even in the subdued light and with her back to him, she appeared the only living one, luminous and delicately fragile, the most refreshing, the most tenderly soft, the warmest, the only beckoning mystery, the only precious thing he had ever known. Where she stood in the small pool of lamplight, she was his only reality. The surrounding darkness suggested the abysses of lonely dreams.

She turned from the credenza. They looked at one another—Rico for recognition, Keti to grant it.

Eons before their eyes met in that knowing glance, Rico had made vows, as priest, as archbishop, as celibate; he belonged by divine right solely to Christ in his Church. Eons before, Keti had made another vow; by divine right she belonged solely to Helmut as his wife.

Still, there was in their eyes an invisible caress; and it was as if the untouchable goodness of divinity were riding through and consecrating this room for a rite only divinity can evoke or sanction.

They did not lower their eyes. Each knew they would not enter that sacred, shadowless place together; would not ever say the simple words men and women have always used to enter there. The choice was theirs alone. Neither husband nor pope nor any man-made law had forced their hand. A higher transaction had been performed in spirit.

The sudden, surprising sound of car doors banging in the drive recalled them slowly from fantasy to fact, from shadow to substance, from chosen personal inclination back to truth.

As from a great distance, they heard Tati's barking and Agathi's laughter and all the sounds of greetings beyond the door.

"The sweetness will never depart from us." Keti's only words were scarcely more than a whisper.

Rico shook his head gently and smiled at her.

"Great Lord!" Guido appeared in the doorway, with Tati perched happily and wagging her tail in the crook of his arm. "Great Lord, but it's good to be home again!"

[59]

By the opening of 1978, the wanderlust of eternity had infected Giovanni Battista Da Brescia. To those around him in the remaining stretch of his life, he appeared to live every day as if it were his last, measure every week by its separate moments. Every second seemed precious to him.

He redrew his will to make sure all his relatives were taken care of. He chose his casket and the type of lettering to be used on the inscription. He wrote letters by hand, tens of them, to people he had known, asking pardon for faults and sins, petitioning prayers for his soul. He endowed several monasteries of enclosed monks with sufficient money to say Masses every day for thirty years for the repose of his soul.

From Easter onward, as the Pope grew weaker, the machinery of the Da Brescia Vatican began to slow. Normally, Cardinal Levesque, as secretary of state, would have exercised greater power over procedural details, the weaker and frailer the Pope's grip on things became. Normally, too, he would have been at the center of the pre-conclave process; but, mysteriously, he did not seem able to get any toehold in that dizzying spiral of pre-papal election politics. When his friends outside the Roman Church would make discreet inquiries as to how things were going—sometimes not so discreetly underlining their desire to see Svensens of Belgium or Ahumada of Latin America or Pirandella of the Curia put forward as prime *papabile*—all Levesque could do was shrug his shoulders. The situation was beyond him. And Papa Da Brescia never could, or at least never did, give him a straight answer.

By mid-June, visibly shrunken, his movements painful, his eyes blurred, his skin discolored, the Pontiff received Don Guglielmo for the last time.

"Holy Father, please remember Signora Cuccia at Your Holiness' Mass. She passed away last Wednesday."

"But of course, Don Guglielmo. Of course. Poor soul. So. Signora Cuccia is gone home. We serve a loving Lord, Father. He will take me home soon, as well."

Don Guglielmo was nearly in tears, when he thought to mention little Laura Bartoli, and then hesitated, wondering if he should. "I did want to ask Your Holiness to pray for her. The little one was born with a strange disease. A sort of sleeping sickness. Her father is a simple carpenter with no money for those big hospitals and expensive doctors."

The grieved old priest departed before dark with a last gift to pay for a proper examination for Laura, and with instructions to call upon Maestro Guido de la Valle for any further needs the child might have.

"And you, Father," Papa Da Brescia told him. "You must one day soon consecrate the little girl to Our Lady of Fatima. She will look after her as no doctor can.

"Now go well, old friend. God's blessings with you."

"God's blessings, Holy Father."

After that visit—and apart from the doctors and his household staff, the Maestro, Helmut, and Rico—no one saw Papa Da Brescia except the Pontiff's confessor, who came each week, and always left appearing shattered and terrified.

No man's body ever cried out to be gone to its Creator more than the now severely diminished figure of the Holy Father. He wandered from papal study to papal chapel and back again. He could often be heard talking to himself, repeating the words of his faith aloud. Despite the medication administered to him, his physical pain became so great that it sapped the little strength that remained to him. Gradually he slipped into a coma.

It was the hottest, most humid July Romans had known in sixty years when Papa Da Brescia finally came to die. What wind there was came as a fetid blow of offensive air, buffeting face and body with stinging, fine particles of red sand-dust. When frightening thunderstorms tore the skies of Latium with jagged blades of lightning and the waters came down in sheets, the gutters of Rome ran with reddish floods. The witches in their covens out on the Campagna, and the soothsayers on Monte Mario, spoke of the Serpent squeezing the life's blood out of the Victim. "Prepare for the Man!"

On July 29, Papa Da Brescia was anointed with sacred oil for the third time. Two of his brothers were there. The Maestro and Helmut, and the full State Council, were all there. Rico Lansing and Monsignore Delucchi were there. Papa Da Brescia did not open his eyes to see them before he passed quietly home, near the stroke of midnight.

At the Maestro's advice, and with the consent of the State Council, announcement of Papa Da Brescia's death was delayed. Councillors in the finance departments of the Holy See were engaged at just that moment in important and delicate maneuvers that would be jeopardized by news of the Pontiff's death.

Along with the official announcement of August 7 that Papa Da Brescia was dead, the world was also notified that the conclave would assemble on August 25. The solemn funeral Mass would be held on August 10.

To accommodate the vast crowds that gathered for the ceremonies, the simple papal coffin, draped in blood red, was placed out in St. Peter's Square. When all the rites were done, there the casket remained for some hours on its bier, a copy of the Gospels lying open on top of it.

A *grecale* wind from the northwest began to freshen the air. It played with the Gospel pages, flicking them over as if in search of some inspired text that might ease the heartbreak of a pope who had come to his dying and death knowing only part of the damage he had done to God's Church; or as if to find some words from Jesus' mouth to tell those left behind what hopes they might salvage from a second spring that had never come, or what light they might find as they entered the long season after. But the fingering wind reached the last pages of the Book of Revelations without whispering any sound but its own faint sigh.

Vatican officials removed the coffin at nightfall. The ritual burial would be on the following day.

During each formal session of the conclave, the Maestro sat bathed in the soft and eerie blue light of *il Tempio,* listening to the speeches beyond the wall in the Sistine Chapel, tallying the successive votes as Cardinal Ferragamo-Duca, who had been elected cardinal dean of conclave on its first full day in session, read the ballots out one by one.

By nine-fifteen on the morning of the second full day of conclave, Guido knew that the uphill labor was nearing its end. The caucuses had all been held. Every cardinal elector had been sounded out. What the vast majority of Their Eminences thought the Church needed by way of mandate and pope had been made increasingly clear. Levesque and his allies—Svensens, Fustami, Buff of England, Grosjean of France, Artis of Holland, Pirandella—were fighting an angry but losing battle.

Guido looked at his pocket watch as he heard Ferragamo-Duca recognize one more cardinal who wished to address his venerable brothers. By ten o'clock, the Maestro reckoned, the next balloting would begin. By eleven, Cardinal Serena would be asked the ritual question: "Do you accept to be made pope?"

Rico Lansing's hands trembled visibly as he read quickly through the material John Liebermann had just given him. The names that popped out at him were men he knew; men who were among the Maestro's closest and most trusted associates: Franco Graziani; Luigi Garganelli; Aristotle Potamianos of Panama; Julio Montt of Peru; Claro Trujillo of Colombia; the aristocratic Daniel Loredan of Venice; Carlo Benelli, president of the Banco di Venezia.

Lansing's mouth went dry as he skimmed over the summary report Liebermann had prepared for him. Vatican money was being siphoned off in vast quantities through the Banco Agostiniano in Milan and through Liechtenstein, and the brass-plate money houses used by the IRA in Panama. Those funds were being used in a concerted fashion to aid a coup d'état organization whose atrocities were designed to disrupt governments in Europe and the Americas. The means being used were all too familiar, and they again placed the IRA, and the *impero* as well this time, in de facto collusion not only with Senatore Pappagallo and Jaime Herreras and the Nazis in Latin America, but with the top *mafiosi* dealing in the international drug trade, white slavery, illegal arms, and probably every other demoralizing, degrading, destabilizing, stinking activity of organized crime.

Rico paged through the supporting documentation. There were money guarantees, loans, notes of transfer, other certificates and papers Rico didn't examine in detail. Most appeared to make use of long-standing IRA letters of guarantee; all bore one or another of those seven *impero* signatures—Graziani's was on some, Montt's on others, Ari Potamianos' on a dozen more, Loredan's and Benelli's and Garganelli's and Trujillo's cropping up regularly, as well. There were dates and places of meetings linking all seven *impero* members with Pappagallo and Herreras and with the Nazis. Some of the names Rico didn't recognize were identified in the summary as major Mafia figures well known to Interpol. The addresses of those meetings ranged from Florence to Peru and Panama and Colombia and Mexico. It was airtight. And it was damning.

In the cool recesses of the Church of the Twelve Apostles, Rico wiped the sweat from his face. "It's as though Paolo Lercani had never been caught! As though he had never ceased his operations. It's worse, in fact."

Liebermann began to say something to him, to elaborate; or to explain something about how scum like this made the real reforms and changes the people needed and wanted—longed for, in fact—into a grim joke. Rico wasn't sure exactly what he said, didn't really hear the words. There was only one thought in his mind. The Maestro had to have this information. Now. Conclave or no. He was the only one who could stop the insanity, stop these *impero* moguls of his from dragging the IRA and the Vatican and the whole Church back down into the muck all over again. He was the only one who could keep the next pope from the tragedies and scandals of the last one. The only one who had any chance to keep the Church from being riven by yet another lightning bolt that would unleash new doubts, new fear, new apprehension and skepticism concerning the divine mandate of the papacy. Nothing less was at stake.

He fairly flew out of the Church into the morning sunlight, not stopping to thank Liebermann or say anything more to him at all; and not quite sure where he was going. He was halfway down the block, in fact, headed for the Vatican with long strides, before he realized that he didn't have any idea where to find the Maestro. God only knew where he was or what he might be doing. The Vatican—all of Rome—was filled with officials waiting to be among the first to greet the new pope. Guido might be with any one of a hundred of them. But where?

He decided that if anyone would have a clue, it would be Helmut. He looked at his watch. Nine-thirty. By now, if the arrangements made the previous evening hadn't changed, Helmut, Keti, and Agathi would be waiting for him in his own apartment on the Via della Conciliazione, looking out his windows from which the Sistine roof could be clearly seen, waiting for the puffs of white smoke that would tell them a pope had been elected. Rico should have been there too—had intended to keep the vigil with them—until Liebermann had called.

Instead of racing all the way back to his flat, Rico found the nearest public phone and rang his own number. Benfatti answered and, recognizing the urgency in his voice, put Helmut on at once. Without explanation or preamble, Rico blurted out that he had to find the Maestro, no matter where he was.

"Rico," Helmut answered, "what Uncle is doing now is the crux of his work for the papacy. No one can—"

Rico didn't wait for the end of the sentence. "It's the crux of his work for the papacy that's in jeopardy. For the love of Heaven, Helmut, if you know where he is, tell me!"

There was a pause; Rico could hear Helmut's breath through the earpiece. "All right, Rico. In ten minutes' time I'll be in the courtyard of St. Damasus. It's restricted conclave area, but I'll tell the guards to expect you. There's an iron door in the south wall between two pillars. How long will it take you to get there?"

"I'll be right on your heels!" Rico hung up almost before he finished the sentence.

If he lived here for a hundred years, Rico mumbled to himself as he tripped in his haste on the curved iron stairway, he would never find all the hidden corners and passageways in the Vatican. He had never even noticed that door Helmut had opened for him. He hadn't the least idea where he was headed now. Helmut had simply put an ancient key in his hand, gave him a signal to use, and told him to climb until he came to a door. If he had been in a more fanciful mood, Lansing might have felt like a character out of the pages of Grimm or Hoffmann, searching for the giant's treasure in some fairy tale. As it was, no such thought entered his mind.

He groped his way upward by the dim light of some bulb he couldn't discover. He came to a door finally. He figured he must have climbed two stories or more from courtyard level. He knocked lightly with the signal Helmut had given him: once; a pause; then twice sharply. He fitted the bulky key into the lock, turned it, and found himself peering into a small room whose dim blue light came from a sconce near the floor.

At a slight movement to his left, Rico turned his head. "Maestro? Where the . . . ?"

Guido gestured for Rico to be silent, and then motioned him toward the short bench near the table, on the Maestro's right hand.

It was only as he moved a step or two forward that he realized where he must be. He heard the familiar voice of Cardinal Ferragamo-Duca clearly through the far wall droning out one name, again and again, in Latin. *". . . Eminentissimum et reverendissimum dominum Lucianum Cardinalem Serena . . . Eminentissimum et reverendissimum dominum Lucianum Cardinalem Serena . . . Eminentissimum et . . ."* Clearly a conclave ballot had just been taken and Ferragamo-Duca was reading out each ballot for the secretary to record. Rico could see that Guido was keeping his own tally, but couldn't make out if there were other names on the large pad he was marking with each call of Serena's name.

So surprised was Rico by this whole situation that he literally forgot to sit down. Conclave was inviolable. Everyone knew that. Doors were sealed. Surveillance was constant and elaborate. There were guards everywhere. Everything was so secret that even after conclave very little was revealed. And yet here was the Maestro, sequestered in a little room close to the very wall of the Sistine Chapel itself, monitoring every word spoken and every ballot taken!

"Monsignore?"

Stunned as he was, until he heard that half-whisper Lansing had not noticed the Maestro lay down his pen or look up at him.

"Sit down, Monsignore." The Maestro spoke in a hushed but clear voice. He seemed far less surprised to see Lansing here than Lansing was to be here. "I presume your business is nothing less than a matter of life or death, or you would not have been led to me here." The words were not angry or even testy. It was a statement of fact, calmly made. "The vote is clear. Serena will be Pope. So. What is it that could not wait?"

"Maestro . . ." Rico began. But something in Guido's face, the open, benign, unwavering expression, made it impossible for him to pronounce the words, to tell Guido it was all falling apart again, all out of control again.

He reached into his inner pocket for Liebermann's envelope and put it down on the table. "Maestro." He forced the words up from his throat. "You've been betrayed. By your associates. It's all splitting open again. Like Kalikawa. Like Lercani. Worse. Garganelli and Loredan and—"

At the sound of those names, the names of men to whom Guido had entrusted more than his life, his hand shot out and tore the papers from the envelope. He read the summary much more quickly than Rico had, and paged through all the documents, seeming to take them in as a camera records a riot.

Moments of silence passed, in which the only sounds Rico could hear were rustling paper, his own breathing, Ferragamo-Duca's droning voice —"*dominum Lucianum Cardinalem Serena*"—his own heartbeat.

The Maestro read every page. He spared himself nothing. With each paragraph, it became clearer that the lines of corruption ran deep into the *impero* operation. With each document he read, some central underpinning of his life was torn away. This was like no betrayal he had known. This was not Lercani now, or some faceless greedy little bureaucrat in Africa whom he had never met. This was a blow where he had no armor to protect him. He had been betrayed by men whose loyalty to him and to the Pope and to the Church was unviolable; by men who understood and responded with strength to his dependence on them for everything he and his work signified. All of that had been betrayed. Not by the way, as a one-time thing. But systematically, deeply, and over some period. The Church—not just its name, but its substance, its mission, Christ's own very Church—was endangered. And if this much had happened, if this much had been discovered, what else had happened that had not yet been discovered? How deeply compromised were all the achievements and all the plans for which he had risked everything, given up everything? How deeply had his very oath to defend the papacy been violated by this betrayal?

When finally the Maestro's eyelids were raised again like obedient shutters, they looked gold-green in the weird light of *il Tempio.* There seemed no emotion in them. Rico could barely recognize the Guido de la Valle he had known for over thirty years.

Guido tried to release the papers from his hand. Tried to turn his head. Tried to speak. A sound like no sound he had ever made came from his throat, but it was weak and was drowned out by the sound of Ferragamo-Duca's loud question, asked so all in the chapel could hear: "Do you accept to be made pope?"

Rico saw the papers crumpling in the Maestro's hand, saw his fingers stiffen oddly and close in a fist. He saw the mouth open. He knew. It had been too much. Something had given way. Guido's heart. His brain vessels. Something.

Without waiting, almost without thinking, Rico forced the documents from Guido's rigid hand and stuffed them in his pocket. It took all his strength to hoist the Maestro from his chair and, supporting his full weight as he walked with him, move out the door and down, slowly down the long, curving flight of steps.

As he kicked the heavy metal door open and daylight flooded on the Maestro's ashen face, they both heard a great cheer rise to the heavens, and a triumphant voice echo out over all the loudspeakers that had been set up and connected in anticipation of this moment to the microphone on St. Peter's balcony. *"Annuntio vobis gaudium magnum! Habemus Papam!* I announce to you a great joy! We have a Pope! The Most Reverend Lord Cardinal Serena!"

Part Five

THE SEASON AFTER

[[60]]

In a certain true sense, Luciano Serena was what a French theologian and writer once called "one of God's favorites." Long ago in his life as a cleric, he had entered into a personal pact with Christ. Provided that he took steps to curb natural inclinations that disturbed his relationship with Christ—his tendency to hurt others with his wit; his sensuality in food; his jealousy—then a very specific "sense of Christ," an almost permanent consciousness of Christ, was granted him. It could be diminished by lapses in morality. It could be dissipated by infidelities to what he knew was right and required of him. But even then, a muted form of that consciousness remained, mercifully reminding him of what he stood to lose if he did not mend his ways.

In a sense, of course, the pact had not been his doing; or at least, had not been initiated by him. He gave his consent to it; for like everything else in his life and career, it came to him as an offer. And from that time, his whole existence seemed to pass through a series of stages already laid out and prepared, each opening up with mysterious ease and timeliness, requiring of him none of the soul-searching or agonizing choices or consultations with advisers, none of the trial-and-error assays, that mark the erratic progress of most human beings.

After his ordination, Serena was the only young priest in his class to qualify for postgraduate studies in canon law. When he finished those studies, he was posted to teach that subject at the seminary. Fifteen years later, when his bishop died, no one from the lowest clergyman of Turin all the way up to the Holy Father in Rome could think of another man more suitable to head the diocese. Two years later, in 1958, he was made cardinal. For twenty years thereafter, during the hoopla and revolt that shook cardinals, bishops, clergy, religious, and faithful everywhere, Serena ran his diocese with a surety of mind and faith, and with an unthreatening imperturbability, that seemed elsewhere to have fled the Church Universal.

To those who took the time to notice him, Cardinal Serena revealed a universalist view of his Church allied with an unshakable commitment to the papacy as the source of truth in Catholic belief. He was recognized as just, and as partisan to no political point of view. For anyone with the clarity of vision to perceive such qualities, his piety and his holiness were as plain and visible as the nose on his smiling face. And so was his stubbornness. On matters of morality and obedience to the authority of Rome, he was as immovable as a rock.

By 1978, those attributes, and his reputation, clean as it was of all the extraneous accretions that sometimes, justifiably or otherwise, attach themselves to churchmen, qualified him as the only Italian cardinal suitable as prime *papabile.*

From his first working day as Pope, Papa Serena, at the age of sixty-four, acted in the certainty that he had consented to the final stage that had been prepared for him in his earthly pact. And from that day, the same two notes that had marked his life and career until then became the theme around which his papacy would be orchestrated.

First, he seemed to have come ready-made to his papal office. Not only did this non-Roman and non-curial prelate have his mind made up on even the most complex problems; and not only did he have his plans worked out in detail from the very moment they placed the tiara on his head and the Fisherman's Ring on his finger. On top of that, he insisted that those plans be implemented now.

Second, his manner in all this, as in all he did always, was one of a smiling peacefulness such as one would expect in a loving father or grandfather. No matter whom he was dealing with, no matter what commands he gave, and no matter how peremptory and devastating those commands were, he always wore that same winsome cloak of unthreatening serenity and inner joy.

Reactions to Papa Serena eddied outward from the papal study according as people came to recognize, quickly or slowly, that a pope of remarkable caliber and determination was fully in charge.

The first of Papa Serena's peremptory and potentially devastating commands affected the entire in-Vatican bureaucracy that was now in his hands. Aside from his own household staff, and his secretary, Don Diaz, all of whom he brought with him from Turin, the Holy Father did not begin staff changes all at once. Rather, acting through Cardinal Secretary Levesque, the Pontiff did require everyone to tender his written resignation without delay. His Holiness would decide in short order which resignations to accept.

The reaction in the workaday Vatican world was an immediate understanding that this Pope meant business. While it was estimated by some that only about one-third of the personnel were favorably disposed either to the conservative views of the Holy Father or to the sudden clamping down of authority, it was clear to all that the other two-thirds hoped he would leave them in their posts, and that if he did, they, too, would come to like him very well indeed. The machinery of his papacy, therefore, began to hum with an uncommon speed and efficiency.

At the highest reaches of that Vatican machinery, the State Council was delighted with Papa Serena. Even as he received the ritual visits, before most of them departed for their home dioceses, of the cardinals who had elected him in conclave; and received as well the endless delegations from the almost 105 governments that maintained diplomatic relations with the Holy See, he also found time to consult with the State Council members, individually and in groups, in order to refine and deepen his grasp of the information the Maestro had given him before conclave, and of the information that had been covered in the briefing papers he had read and digested before and since his election.

Among the visiting cardinals he received, of course, was Bogdan Valeska. The Cardinal of Krakow had been told in conclave and privately by Cardinal Falconieri of the danger to Serena that had been assessed by the State Council; and he had been told that, with Serena's election, he would be the new prime *papabile.* Valeska had received the news with a somber face. He understood the precaution only too well. His entire ecclesiastical career had been spent in an atmosphere of mortal danger.

The post-conclave interview between the cardinal and his Pontiff touched on many things in the short time they spent together in Serena's study; but neither even hinted at the question of papal succession.

Helmut de la Valle was among the new Pope's more frequent visitors. As acting Keeper, Helmut had been the one to receive Papa Serena in the Silver Throne Room on the day of his election. He had been the one to reveal the full Bargain, and at the same time had explained that the Maestro had been taken ill. Each time the Pontiff called on Helmut for some further bit of information or clarification concerning the assets of the Holy See, he would ask after the Maestro.

"Thank God, Holiness," Helmut was happy to tell him before long, "he is in no danger. Another week or ten days should see him on his feet."

"Indeed, Signor Helmut, We thank God, in Whose hands we all are."

Out beyond the walls and offices of the Vatican, most of the world waited for something more palpable than the general knowledge that the new Pope was, as press reports indicated, "pious and conservative." Such a characterization could have no practical meaning in many quarters until clothed in action. Very few people remembered what it meant to have a pious and conservative pope; it had been a long time ago, and a very different world, when the last of that breed before Serena had been seen.

For the moment, then, bishops and clergy simply went ahead with their own lives and disparate plans. Some in the P-2 organizations, who were better informed than much of the world, realized that Serena truly intended to be Pope, and were neither happy nor resigned to acceptance. The American government was watchful but cautiously optimistic. The Soviet Politburo and hierarchy were nervous, and no more resigned to acceptance than P-2, should their fears prove justified.

Early in the third week of September—never once having lost that note of pleasant, unthreatening peace, despite the strain of the official activities that claim so much of the time and attention of every new pontiff—Papa Serena was already sufficiently in command to hold his first in-depth discussion of papal policies with the secretary of state.

Elderly men with angelic smiles had always made Cardinal Levesque apprehensive. This meeting proved him right in his worry. It was not a discussion at all, but a series of orders.

"We know, you and I," Papa Serena began informally when Levesque was seated across the papal desk from him, "the grounds on which my election was achieved in the recent conclave."

"Yes, Holiness." To Levesque's chagrin, and despite his open opposition, the greater number of cardinal electors wanted a pope who would bring order out of the chaos prevalent in the Church at the death of Da Brescia. The mandate was simple to express, but very difficult and complex even to plan, let alone to effect. In particular, the majority desired some firm declarations and directives from the new Pope about the inroads of Marxism into specifically Catholic teaching, and about how that teaching should be purified.

"Therefore, Eminence," Papa Serena went on, "the most pressing decisions We have to make concern purity of doctrine and belief. Foreign policy will take care of itself—will clarify itself—if We attend to the main defect in the Church."

"Yes, Holiness." Levesque was respectful but noncommittal.

"I know that my predecessor was convinced that the Church had to bend deeply to accommodate the winds of change, and thus to survive." There seemed no note of accusation in that statement.

"And now, Holiness?"

"Now, We have to correct the excesses. You and your office will therefore draw up recommendations under three headings.

"First: how to restate the incompatibility of Christianity and Marxism, with special reference to Latin America, where whole blocs of clergy and religious have adapted basic Christian dogma to Marxism, 'Liberation Theology,' and political revolution. And with special reference as well to those elements of the clergy in North America and Europe for whom social activism and politics, rather than religion, have become the main preoccupations.

"Second: how to correct the errors being taught to our future priests in most seminaries throughout the world.

"Third: what must be done to reform the religious orders—the Jesuits, the Dominicans, and the Franciscans in particular should receive first attention. We can address nuns and other religious soon enough."

There was a fourth heading that the Pope would address, but not with Cardinal Levesque. Serena had been horrified by the Lercani scandal, and had quickly formed a deep distrust of Peter Servatius. He wanted to see what could be done to alter radically the character and stance of the Holy See and the Church as a financial power in the international field. Having read the Bargain in the Silver Throne Room, he knew that the man to help him there was the Maestro.

"Is there anything else, Holiness?" Levesque had finished taking his notes, and clearly expected something more. At the Pontiff's questioning glance, he clarified his own query. "The ongoing work to achieve protocols between the Holy See and the Eastern European countries, Holy Father?"

"In abeyance, Eminence. For the moment, in abeyance."

Levesque scribbled a few more notes, picturing in his mind's eye the reactions of his friends in the Northern Alliance and among the bishops out there in the Church Universal with whom he shared a common mind.

That unsettling smile was on Papa Serena's face again as he rose from his desk. The meeting was at an end. *"Va bene, Santità."*

"I knew it!" Cardinal Levesque stormed into his office some few yards down the corridor from the papal study. He banged the door to his inner office behind him. "I warned them all in conclave! I knew it!"

He threw his notes on his desk beside one of the recent reports analyzing the Soviet Union's "normalization" strategy. His thoughts flew over the possibilities of the situation, words and pictures flooding his mind, all of them tied to that one word, "normalization."

He had understood what those Soviet contacts of his meant from the very first time they had used "normalization" as the buzzword to describe what they wanted him to achieve for the Soviet Union. That had been back in the late thirties, when, as a young French monseigneur, he, like many scions of rich and anciently established families, had drawn close to leaders of the French Communist Party. His motives had been classic—outrage at the sins of the rich, outrage at the high-handed authoritarianism of Papa Profumi, outrage at Italian Fascism and German Nazism, and at the fact that both were tolerated by Profumi.

There had been other motives too; less noble, perhaps, but no less classic. "We can help your career in the Church," his Communist Party friends had said, "if you become our partner. Communism is the wave of the future. Ride with us. Your Church will be safe. Only, with the power we help you acquire, you must achieve normalization of relations between the Holy See and the Soviet Union. Accept that mission, and the future is bright."

By World War II's end, he was deep into affairs he had never envisioned. So deep, in fact, that there was no way out without bringing calamity down on himself. Anyway, things hadn't been all that bad, on balance. Though Levesque's pact was a far different one than Serena's, his career began to open up too. An appointment to the Vatican Secretariat of State; episcopal consecration; a steady rise in the ranks according as his advice proved useful, and his knowledge accurate, about what was going on in Europe, the United States, and elsewhere.

He had been just plain fortunate not only in the election of Papa Da Brescia but in the long duration of his papacy; Da Brescia had been so easy to handle.

Levesque stared hard at those notes he had just taken. Clearly, the smiling "grandfather" who sat in the papal study now was going to be a different kettle of fish. Levesque knew well enough what General Control would say if he let this situation get out of hand, if this Pope's policies were put into effect and allowed to overturn everything the cardinal had achieved over the past fifteen years. Levesque himself would be held responsible. By General Control. And by those American colleagues who had been recruited, as he had been, years before and were well up on the ecclesiastical ladders in Canada and the States. In their eyes, he would have let them all down; he would have let them all in for a holy war on Communism.

"I knew it!" His hand banged the papal notes, as though that might break the papal will reflected in them. He had tried to warn the conclave what disasters would follow if they elected Serena. But no! They would choose him. Let the consequences be on their heads, then.

The cardinal's hand flashed to the buzzer on his desk.

"Monsignore," he snapped when Archbishop Demarchelier stepped in from his own office. "I must send a letter home. About my new ring. It fits badly. An answer is needed."

The Catacombs of Priscilla are always cold. The confusing passageways that descend in their intricate patterns through the tufa are always quiet. Not as the caves are quiet, but in an unearthly way, as though those early Christians whose bones lie behind the plaques lining the tunnel walls commanded unending tranquillity so they, too, might hear the Masses offered continually by pilgrim priests in all the little chapels.

The man who had been his guide through the maze of passages left Metropolitan Nikodim alone in the Chapel of the Virgin. Here, the Russian prelate knew, he was safe from the prying eyes of those who would be happy enough to report him to General Control again for his "lapses of piety."

The chapel was little more than an oval cut into the tufa. There was a marble altar, a tabernacle, a vigil light. Over the altar was the ancient mosaic of the Virgin fashioned in every detail after the description in Isaiah of the "Virgin who shall bear a child, and he will be called Immanuel"—the star over her head as the sign of the Messiah; the Child in her hand; the Christ to her right.

There were no chairs or kneelers in this place. Nikodim stood with his head lowered, not in prayer, but in anger and bewilderment and fear—and because he could not raise his eyes to meet Mary's.

When Rome Station had given him the instructions from General Control the day before, Nikodim had pulled in a quick breath through clenched teeth. It had been one thing—a welcome thing, despite the danger—when he had been told to save Papa Angelica from assassination. But to be told now to murder Papa Serena! It was so outlandish, so impossible to contemplate even for an instant, that Nikodim's reactions had been almost volcanic within him. So outrageous was it, in fact, that Nikodim had suddenly thought that the real plan might be not to murder the Pope but to get rid of Nikodim himself. When he had recovered his poise a little, he had said as much to the embassy official. "This sounds as if I've outlived my usefulness to the family. Is this the way out for them?"

"Not a bit of it," the official had reassured him. "The family is relying on you. The appointment with Serena is already made. You will see him tomorrow morning at ten-thirty. And you will go bearing a gift." The man handed him a handsomely wrapped package. "From His All-Holiness, Patriarch Pimen of Moscow."

The gift, Nikodim was told, was a book, a photo record of Zagorsk Monastery, quite lovely and quite appropriate. Nikodim was to explain that it had been inscribed to Serena personally by the Patriarch. When the Pope opened the book to read the inscription, a small but sufficient quantity of gas would be released. It would all be over quickly. Nikodim was to see that he himself was at a safe distance across the room.

Once the Pontiff collapsed, there would be a great deal of confusion, of course. Nikodim was to make the most of it to retrieve the book and take it away with him.

It was all this that Nikodim confided wordlessly to the Virgin—to "the Mother of all the Russias," as he called her—while he stood in the dark oval chapel in the catacombs. Still, though he remained there for a long time, he could not find the courage to raise his eyes to her, or to look at the altar, or the tabernacle. It was too late. How could a man of such scarlet sins as Nikodim remake his soul?

Moving almost mechanically, Metropolitan Nikodim walked toward the Porta Santa Anna. It was nearly ten-thirty. In the morning light, his face did not look cherubic; rather, it showed the ravages of the two heart attacks he had survived, and the strain of the present time. How he longed for the days of his greatest triumphs, when Papa Da Brescia had received him so affably, so welcomingly. That Pope had been so easy to influence. Nikodim had dubbed him "the Intellectual," because he always had seemed the archetype of the ever self-doubting thinker; the upper-class bourgeois, smitten with guilt for his own origins and for the riches of the Church he headed; the Italian with a modernist French education, essentially weak in faith. He had been easy to get around, the perfect target for Nikodim.

Well, those days were over. As the embassy official had said, "We are dealing now with a man whose belly is sound and who thinks with his heart and his instinct as well as his head. He cannot be derailed, except in this one and final way."

Once inside the Apostolic Palace, Nikodim was immediately taken to the cardinal secretary.

"I bear a personal gift from His All-Holiness, Patriarch Pimen of Moscow, to His Holiness, Papa Serena." Nikodim's voice sounded hollow in his own ears as he spoke to Levesque.

"His Holiness is eager to meet you." Levesque remained expressionless as he rang through to the Pontiff to announce the visitor, and then personally led the metropolitan the short distance along the corridor to the door of the papal study.

"Welcome, Your Grace!" Papa Serena rose from his chair and came around the desk, both hands outstretched in greeting. "Your Grace is very welcome indeed. You do us an honor to break your busy schedule to see us."

"It is my honor, Holiness, and my pleasure." Nikodim bent to kiss the Pope's ring; it was not a customary thing for him to do, and he had not planned it. But he had been startled by Serena's smile, which spoke so immediately of kindness and integrity. Why had no one warned him?

In his momentary bow over the Pontiff's hand, he recovered himself as best he could. As he straightened again, he was relieved to hear the ritual words coming out of his own mouth. "I am deeply grateful for the honor of seeing Your Holiness today. Lest I forget in the joy of Your Holiness' reception of me, please accept this gift from me on behalf of the Patriarchate of Moscow. His All-Holiness has inscribed a little book with his own autograph."

Like a man mesmerized, Nikodim listened to Papa Serena's graceful words of acceptance; watched him reach for a small silver scissors on the desk before they both sat down; engaged in light conversation about a few men of the Russian clergy whom the Pontiff knew, and about whom he asked. "The Bishop of Viborg, Holy Father? Oh, yes, he is doing well. . . ." He watched the scissors clip through the twine. He found his breath coming in short, tight drafts.

"Are you all right, Your Grace?"

At the Holy Father's question, Nikodim raised his eyes to Papa Serena's. They were warm, and they made Nikodim yearn for the happiness he saw in them. "Fine, Holiness. Fine. Just a little tired." A little tired of life. Of deception. Of the threats to his family and of his own complicity and bondage.

The wrapping paper was off the gift. The Holy Father laid his hand on the beautifully embossed bars of gold and silver that decorated the ornate cover of the book. Nikodim's head seemed to bulge with the force of the thoughts that raged at him. It was too much. Even for him. He could not do this.

"Your Holiness!" Nikodim's voice was broken and hoarse. He stood up quickly, jerked his hand forward. "Let me read the dedication for Your Holiness, please!"

Papa Serena put the book into the Russian's outstretched hand, his own eyes revealing something between pleasure at the gesture and concern for his visitor's odd behavior. "Your Grace, would you like a glass of water? Some wine?"

"No, Holiness. Thank you." The metropolitan sank back in his chair and laid the book on his lap. A contradictory medley of thoughts and emotions played through his mind like a tape at high speed. Despite their complexity, it took him only seconds to sort it all out and make his decision.

He was aware that above all else he wanted to fall on his knees before Papa Serena. He wanted confession. He wanted to weep, to ask forgiveness; to ask refuge; to ask advice. He knew that he would do none of those things.

He was aware that he wanted his family to be safe. He wanted blessing and sunlight for them. He knew that whatever he did, he could assure none of that any longer.

He was aware that he wanted Serena to live, and that he wanted not to do murder. He knew that then he, Nikodim, would be killed; and that the men who wanted the Pope's life would try again, some other way.

He was aware that he was the unlikeliest man on the face of the earth to offer himself to martyrdom. But he knew that if he, instead of Serena, should die here this morning, there could be some hope. A tiny one for his own salvation. A slightly better one that, if he did not actually reveal the plot or its authors, his family might be left alone. A hope, whose odds he couldn't judge, that Papa Serena and those charged with his safety would be warned.

As complex as all that was, Nikodim thought with some distant, watching part of his mind how surprisingly fast it was decided. In a few ticks of the clock. A few beats of the heart. A few breaths of air.

Papa Serena could not know what troubled his guest. But with his deepest instinct as a priest, he knew it involved a struggle in which he could not intrude until asked. He waited those few beats of the heart. He watched Nikodim raise the book from his lap, open its cover, lower his head to read the inscription.

Then suddenly, the Russian was looking back at him in alarm, in panic. His mouth was open, but he was not reading, not translating. He dropped the book. His hands flew to his throat. Obviously he couldn't breathe. He couldn't cry out or even whisper or gasp. He fell to one side in his chair, his eyes staring at Serena, his tongue protruding from his mouth.

"Aiuto!" Papa Serena called for help as loudly as he could; he rushed forward and dropped to his knees beside Nikodim. Within seconds the study was swarming with people; just as the embassy official had foreseen, armed guards and security personnel were everywhere. On hearing the Pope's cry, Don Diaz had pressed a silent alarm and then had run into the study himself. Levesque and Demarchelier had both bolted down the corridor at the first outcry and stood now among the circle of men, as horrified as any of them to see the dying Nikodim. What had the fool done?

If Nikodim saw them—Levesque or any of the rest—he gave no sign. It was as though he were on an island of light, and his only companion was Papa Serena, bending down to him, cradling his head. If only he could speak. In these final seconds of his mortal existence, he wanted above all else to make some eloquent appeal for forgiveness and mercy. Why couldn't he make his voice come? He must try. . . .

Nikodim's mouth moved. Papa Serena bent closer to hear, but no words came. Still, with that same priestly instinct, he understood. No man's eyes had ever spoken to him so eloquently of desire for absolution from sins as Nikodim's did.

"Ego te absolvo ab omnibus peccatis et censuris in nomine Patris et Filii et Spiritus Sancti. . . ."

When Papa Serena's hand traced the sign of the cross above his face, Nikodim followed it with his eyes as though it was the most wondrous and miraculous thing he had ever seen in all of creation. The Latin words of his soul's salvation sent cooling mists rising inside him as from the base of a steep fall of water. He breathed once more. His mouth sagged. His eyes closed tightly. When they opened again slowly, they were without life.

It was only some hours later—after the emergency medical team had come and gone, and the Soviet Embassy had been notified, and Nikodim's body had been removed, and security had made its first sweep—that Papa Serena realized that the book Nikodim had brought him was nowhere to be found.

"Somebody must have picked it up in all the confusion, Holiness," was Levesque's opinion. "It will turn up, I'm sure, Holy Father."

"I'm sure it will, Eminence," Papa Serena agreed. But he reported the oddity to security in any case.

The news reports made rather little of the death of Metropolitan Nikodim. For the most part, they cited the official police medical report: a simple heart attack in a man with a history of such episodes. It could have happened anytime.

The ciphered report General Control received was swifter and more accurate; and it left him as enraged with himself as with Nikodim. He should have known better than to trust this, of all missions, to such a piety-inclined weakling who could never jump clearly to one side of the fence or the other.

Well, Control thought to himself contemptuously, Nikodim might have saved himself the trouble. The operation would be rescheduled. And what little time had been lost would be offset by experience gained. He would not make the same mistakes twice.

||[61]||

When the doctors first examined Guido in Mater Dei Hospital, they thought they were dealing with a mild stroke. Through exhaustive testing, however, they determined that the Maestro had been the victim of a transient ischemic episode—what one of the specialists called in by Dr. Sepporis described as "nature's warning ticket for speeding." His body had just rehearsed what penalty could be laid on him if he didn't let up.

Within twenty-four hours, Guido was fully conscious and remembered everything that had happened to him. Within forty-eight hours, he was clamoring to go home, but Dr. Sepporis insisted on keeping him under observation for at least a week.

In true de la Valle fashion, Guido struck a deal with his old friend and personal physician. He would remain in hospital for a week, he said, provided Helmut could see him any time of the day or night.

"You're a hard man, Guido." Dr. Sepporis shook his head, but he gave his consent. He knew it would be a greater strain on the Maestro to be isolated from his affairs than to be certain through his nephew how things were going. Nevertheless, he had his own price to exact in the bargain. Guido was not to have any business papers brought to the hospital, and when he did go home, he was to cut his schedule to some humanly acceptable level.

Guido agreed to the first condition. He would consider the second.

Rico had told Helmut what had happened in *il Tempio* and had given him the Liebermann report he had showed to the Maestro. That report, and its implications for the integrity of the *impero*'s service to the papacy, were uppermost in the Maestro's mind. Once the initial shock of intimate betrayal was over, to begin to deal rationally and positively with the problem was a help to him in every way. He and Helmut agreed that the seven who had got themselves entangled with Lercani were nonetheless, like all the *impero* members, associates for life. The entire matter would have to be discussed openly in a full *impero* meeting, and means would have to be worked out to extricate the Holy See from the danger in which those seven had implicated it.

Guido left it to Helmut to call the *impero* meeting. "About the middle of the month," the Maestro said, "should be right. I plan to be like new by then."

Of equal importance to the Maestro was news of Papa Serena. Helmut told his uncle of the ritual meeting in the Silver Throne Room. Papa Serena had read the Bargain carefully and had understood it. "He accepts it for the moment, Uncle. But he said we must have revisions."

Guido nodded thoughtfully as he sat in his hospital bed. "The Holy Father is right. We will both discuss it with His Holiness when he gets through these first grueling weeks of visits and ceremonials."

The effect of Guido's absence on Tati was visible. The terrier seemed somehow to know this wasn't another of her master's normal absences from her life. Her whole demeanor changed, just as it had when Eugenio had gone. She spent hours in hiding, sometimes under the Maestro's bed, at others in Eugenio's old room. She could not be tempted with food, and ate only very little. No amount of cuddling or caressing could bring her out of her mood, until the day Guido came home.

Had it not been for the Maestro's family, Dr. Sepporis would have had no hope for keeping his patient in tow once he was allowed to leave the hospital. As it was, he enlisted Agathi, Keti, and Helmut in a loving conspiracy to make him retire earlier at night and rise later in the morning than had been his habit before. Helmut persuaded him to work two or three days a week in Villa Cerulea. He brought all papers and reports home to his uncle, and gave him detailed personal rundowns, as well.

In those sultry days of early September, Guido did consent to work and live at a sensible pace. He spent hours on the Long Terrace, a now contented Tati at his feet, working at his papers, speaking on the telephone, planning for the upcoming *impero* meeting, and for as thorough a review of the Holy See's financial affairs as Papa Serena might want. But many a time during those days, he just sat there, looking out over the gardens and the wooded shoulder of the Alban Hills leaning against the sky. He seemed at those moments to be discussing things with himself. During such interludes, Tati would raise her head and watch him for a while. Then, as though she was being left out of something, she would give a little growl and put her forepaws on Guido's knees. He would respond by lifting her onto his lap. There she would lie under his gently stroking hand, content to watch his face with half-closed eyes, occasionally snapping about to catch sight of a bird in flight or to nip Guido's fingers playfully.

If any of the Maestro's associates thought that, because of "nature's warning ticket," he could not manage complex operations, his performance at the late-morning *impero* meeting in mid-September dispelled any such idea. Guido had lost some weight. His movements were slower and more deliberate, as if he was testing his strength. There were new lines on his face, the claw marks of the pain he had suffered and the strain he had fought. He sat at the head of the conference table with his feet raised on an ottoman. But his mind was even more lucid and decisive than ever before.

From the first moment, he left no doubt among his associates that the subject of this meeting was the *impero* itself. Not just the seven who had betrayed their trust, though he named them without hesitation: Luigi Garganelli, Franco Graziani, Daniel Loredan, Carlo Benelli, Ari Potamianos, Claro Trujillo, Julio Montt. He looked each man full in the eye as he named him. He had mastered as many details as could be had beforehand about the complicated situations into which those seven very closely associated friends of his had placed some of the assets of the Holy See. He had made a fair estimate of the sums involved, and understood the banking methods by which those sums had been chaneled. He had a reasonably accurate idea of the profits each of the seven had personally reaped from those clandestine operations. He spelled it all out in excruciating detail, sparing no one, including himself as the one ultimately answerable for the *impero*'s activity and fidelity. And, to give the people involved their due, he also quoted the enormous increments in funds that they had produced for the Holy See by their illicit activity.

It was a tribute to the close feeling of comradeship and affection between Guido and his associates, as well as a demonstration of their very cool and rational mode of treating any crisis, that throughout the Maestro's statements, there was no sharp feeling of discomfort or embarrassment, no glowering or accusatory glances or epithets. The group had a serious problem. They would solve that problem as a group.

"Let's call a spade a spade," the Maestro wound up his introductory summary. "The world, I hope, will never know this; but at present, major assets of the Holy See have been and are being used for purposes diametrically opposed to the spiritual mission of the Holy See.

"We have two questions to answer before we leave this meeting. The first concerns the trust we had between us. Clearly, it has broken down. Can we remake it?

"The second question, which obviously hinges in part on the first, is how to extricate the Holy See's assets from the compromising associations in which seven of us have involved them. For obviously it is unbearable for us to be brokers in illegal armaments, or to fund drug exploitation and launder the profits from it, or to finance horrible and malignant dictators."

When he had finished his general presentation and analysis, the Maestro wanted to hear from the *impero* members. First of all, he called one by one on each of the seven associates who had involved themselves, and therefore the group, in such a mess. Bit by bit, as each explained how he had been drawn into compromising schemes, it became clear that Paolo Lercani had cunningly corrupted each one. He had discovered Graziani's enormous gambling debts, and the overexposure of the others in land speculations and other personal business dealings.

"Lercani was right about one thing." Daniel Loredan spoke in his turn. "He pointed out that eighty-five percent of international bankers and brokers sin in this way. He didn't use the word 'sin,' of course. And I don't offer that by way of excuse. I just hope that the fact will be some degree of insurance that fingers of other money managers won't be pointed at us—that this scandal won't be made public, in other words, by pots who might want to call the kettle black."

"All we can be grateful for"—Garganelli gave his own opinion on the point—"is that Lercani didn't drag us down with him."

Helmut did not want to compromise Rico's source of information, but he did mention in this regard that Garganelli's name, and the names of the other six, were now on Interpol and American intelligence files.

Julio Montt spoke for the seven who had caused this *impero* problem when he said that the question the Maestro had raised about rebuilding trust had to rest with the other *impero* associates. "It's a question of whether you want us to stay, to renew that trust. Guido is right that we can't function as a group without that. So as far as I'm concerned, if you want us to stay, we stay; we put our own affairs in order and we help undo this state of affairs. But if you want us out, we go."

Very quickly all the others agreed that the *impero* must remain at full strength. As far as they were concerned, trust had already been reestablished in the candor with which the erring members had responded to the Maestro's disclosures. Manley of Australia and Kelly of Boston were delegated to meet with Montt, Graziani, and the others to determine what they needed in order to get their personal finances back on even keel. The associates would make loans to them from their own private funds. "It would have been better," the Maestro pointed out, "if you had all come to us in the first place." He didn't have to make the point twice.

After a break for lunch and a short siesta, the most brain-breaking session of their meeting followed. They began to draw up a blueprint to extricate the Holy See's funds from unwelcome entanglements. Of necessity, it would be a long-term project.

One of the first tasks that faced them was to sell off equity control in the Banco Agostiniano. Roberto Gonella's bank had been used, with or without Gonella's knowledge and consent, as a main avenue for the funneling of IRA funds. It was essential to distance the Holy See from such an exposure, and to draw a clear trench between the past and the future.

As to Gonella himself, he might not be the titan Lercani had been, but he was a far better banker. It was simply not yet possible, Guido said, to tell how much he might know. Peter Servatius of the IRA had been as little help as ever in that regard. Until they knew more, the Maestro wanted no direct queries of Gonella himself.

Beyond that, they started the planning for an orderly withdrawal of the Holy See's financial involvement in contaminated areas by a variety of means, taking care in their planning to do nothing that would either create widespread financial panic or draw undue attention to themselves. Over time, it would be a matter of removing their representatives from boards of directors, selling off shares in various companies, calling in certain loans, halting their brokerage activities in areas known to be tainted.

They worked all through the day and into the evening. At the end of it all, for the first time in their history as a group, they established a committee of three—Saramati di Saramate, Potamianos, and Duchesne—to supervise the gradual but steady procedures of disinvolvement.

When they emerged from the Maestro's study at last, some three hours late for the dinner Mariella had tried to keep moist and succulent for them, Agathi and Keti were deeply relieved to see that Guido, far from looking exhausted, as they had feared, seemed instead to be exhilarated.

"We'd better tell Dr. Sepporis." Agathi laughed as she looked into her brother's eyes. "There'll be no keeping our Guido down after this! We'll have to chain him to Villa Cerulea to keep him home even two days a week."

Agathi was only partially right. Guido resumed a heavier workload, but still it was nothing like what it had been before his illness. He continued to work at home for several days out of each week. It was as though he found this intermittent distancing of himself from the Vatican useful for some inner reason he wasn't prepared to share, even with Helmut, at least quite yet.

On one of his days at home, shortly before noon in the third week of September, the phone rang by Guido's chair on the Long Terrace. Tati barked furiously at it for waking her at the Maestro's feet.

"De la Valle here," Guido answered, while calming Tati with a gentle hand around her muzzle.

"Brandolini here, Maestro."

Guido listened without a word while the head of Security Two told him of the curious—"highly suspicious," he called it—death of Metropolitan Nikodim during his visit that morning to the Holy Father. There were details he did not want to discuss by phone. Would the Maestro be up to a meeting of Security Two?

"This evening, Giulio," Guido answered without hesitation, dismissing any thought Brandolini might have that his health might suffer from the added strain. The day he could not deal with matters that affected the safety and well-being of his Pope, that day he would relinquish the Keepership into Helmut's hands.

The first zigzag of late-summer lightning lit up the sky. A few seconds later, a heavy roll of thunder crackled and split the silence around Villa Cerulea. Torrents of rain began to lash at the windows of Guido's study.

"The skies announce the death of princes." Cardinal Falconieri recalled the old Roman saying.

"Not this time, thank God!" The Maestro acknowledged the thought, and turned back to Giulio Brandolini.

The only hard evidence Brandolini had for his suspicions was the tape of Nikodim's conversation with Papa Serena that morning. Because of the assessment of the danger to his life from any number of quarters if he followed the policies set out in conclave, the Pontiff had been prevailed upon by Gian Solaccio to record all but the most highly sensitive of his conversations with visitors. The discretion was the Pope's, of course; but in most cases, including Nikodim's, Serena complied. It wasn't very complex. A button under one edge of his desk in the third-floor study activated a taping system.

Papa Serena had pressed that button just before Nikodim came in. The Russian's voice sounded strained on the tape as Brandolini replayed it now for the members of Security Two; but there wasn't much of substance in it, as far as the Maestro could tell.

"Except," Solaccio pointed out, "that Nikodim's voice nearly explodes, hoarse as it sounds, when he takes the gift book back from the Pontiff." Solaccio backed up the tape and played that part again.

"And except," Brandolini took up, "that the book in question is missing. A thorough search has been made.

"Whatever killed Nikodim—and I don't for a moment believe it was a heart attack—went into action when he opened the book to read the dedication.

"If I'm right—if it wasn't a heart attack—if some lethal mechanism, gas probably, was set in action by merely opening the cover, then it is certain that it was meant for His Holiness."

"And you think Nikodim knew?" It was Rico's question.

"I think so," Brandolini answered, "and so does His Holiness. He described how odd Nikodim's behavior was from the moment he entered the study. In hindsight, it's the only explanation that makes sense. He knew. He got cold feet. Why he decided to kill himself then and there is anybody's guess. But it's my working theory that that's what happened."

"So it's the Soviets." Helmut drew the obvious conclusion glumly. "Papa Serena has been working with Levesque and his staff on the question of the incompatibility of Marxism with Christian teaching. But he hasn't made any public or even quasi-public moves yet. So, with Rico now out of the Secretariat of State, we're again faced with a leak from somewhere in that quarter."

"Maybe and maybe not." Cardinal Falconieri was a little more cautious than the others. "Remember, this is all conjecture. Giulio, you yourself say you're only theorizing. A nervous Russian and a missing book don't prove the fellow didn't die from a heart attack."

"You're right, of course, Your Eminence." Guido agreed. "But I think for the safety of the Holy Father we have to assume Monsignore Brandolini's theory is correct. Someone in the Secretariat has put a simple two-and-two formula together. If the Pope denounces Soviet Marxism explicitly, as it seems he will, that would be a world setback for the Bolsheviks."

The Maestro turned to Brandolini again. "Is there anything you can do to beef up security around the Pope?"

Security was already tight, Brandolini said. Short of sleeping in the same room with the Holy Father, there wasn't much more to be done. He did suggest beefing up security in the Secretariat, "from Levesque on down," and in fact he and Solaccio were already seeing to that.

When the meeting was over and the Maestro was alone in his rooms preparing for bed, his mind continued to edge around the situation.

He didn't for a moment doubt Brandolini's theory; he had too much experience with the security chief's "instincts" not to give them credit. And besides, he acknowledged again to himself something he knew Papa Serena, too, had already acknowledged. If someone really wanted to kill the Pope, whatever the cost, then it could be done. History itself showed that. Nikodim had not been willing to pay the cost in terms of his eternal soul, perhaps. But someone else might. Brandolini and Solaccio would do all that was humanly possible to protect Papa Serena. That was their job.

Guido's job was to prepare for every contingency he could foresee. Inevitably, then, his mind began to examine the possible need for a new backup *papabile.* He was not being coldblooded; merely realistic.

As he settled into bed, Tati gave him a sharp bark as she came skittering across the room. She was not about to be forgotten.

"Come, Tati, lady." The Maestro leaned over and gathered her up onto the bed. "We have some serious thinking to do. And a good many prayers to say for the Holy Father. We will have a little word with our angel in heaven, eh? With Eugenio."

At the sound of Eugenio's name, Tati picked up her ears and cocked her head at the Maestro. But he was already deep in his thoughts again.

[62]

Papa Serena seemed less affected than anyone else by the attempt on his life. Unlike Cardinal Falconieri, the Pontiff had no doubt that Archbishop Brandolini's "working theory" about Nikodim was correct. But once the turmoil of that day receded into the background, and though he now spent a bit more time than usual in prayer and reading—particularly of *The Imitation of Christ,* in which he always found both solace and direction for his life—it became clear that there would be no wavering or faltering on his part.

Even the Pope's private secretary, Don Diaz, who had been with Serena for some years and knew him well, marveled at the Holy Father's self-possession and composure. It was not a question of resignation or pretense; Don Diaz understood that. It was a deep trust born of Papa Serena's intimacy with Christ.

The Pope continued to receive visitors as usual, and managed a full workload at his desk, besides. In the evening, Don Diaz frequently joined the Pontiff for a working dinner in the Holy Father's private, fourth-floor apartments. While Sister Flora served the evening meal, Papa Serena liked to discuss some of the matters uppermost in his mind in a more relaxed manner than was possible during the day.

At one such dinner, on the Friday of the week following Nikodim's death, His Holiness had a number of problems to wrestle with. Cardinal Artis of the Netherlands was one of them, as Papa Serena confided to his secretary. Despite personal blandishments from the Holy Father, the Dutch cardinal was still speaking out openly and frequently in a dangerous way about such practices as birth control, divorce, and homosexuality.

"Perhaps," Serena said on a more positive note, "there is a trifle more hope for the situation in the United States. Have you made the appointment for that American delegation of clergy and lay people coming to discuss contraception?"

"Yes, Holy Father. They will be coming in October. I have filled in the exact date on your schedule."

"Excellent, Monsignore. And the Maestro?"

"Next week, Your Holiness. First thing."

"Good. I have many problems to discuss with him. Archbishop Peter Servatius, for one. And Cardinal Levesque. Both of them are worrisome for me. And then there is the whole question of the Holy See's financial arrangements. The interview will be a long one. See that there will be enough time."

"Yes, Holiness. I have cleared three hours on your calendar for the meeting."

When dinner was over, Papa Serena worked with Don Diaz for a couple of hours longer in his private study. It was nearly ten o'clock when he closed the last folder of documents and handed Don Diaz two newspapers he had been reading the evening before.

"I've marked some articles and columns concerning the recent rush of terrorism, Monsignore. Paste them up for me. They will be useful for my occasional sermons."

"Yes, Holiness. Will that be all? Shall I wait until Your Holiness retires?"

Papa Serena smiled warmly across the desk, mindful of his secretary's concern. "No, no. That won't be necessary. I have some personal letters I want to write. I'll leave them on my desk here. You can send them off for me in the morning."

"Yes, Holiness. Sleep well."

"Good night, Monsignore."

When Don Diaz had left, Papa Serena took pen and paper and began a short note to his brother.

> Dearest Carlo,
>
> It is late and I am tired. I am not sure the illustrious Cardinals knew what they were doing when they made me Pope. God, I am sure, did. In any case, as Thomas à Kempis says, "Whatever happens to you at the hands of friend or enemy is . . ."

Papa Serena lifted his pen from the paper for a moment, trying to remember the exact quote, and chiding himself for his poor memory. As many times as he had read *The Imitation,* and as often as he quoted it to himself every day, he should at least be able to recall its wisdom accurately. Just the evening before, he had read the very passage he was trying to remember.

He shook his head in defeat, and reached for the copy he always kept on his desk. Strangely enough, it wasn't there.

Well, perhaps Sister Flora had put it away by mistake. That would be a little odd, he thought, as he rose to make a search of the bookshelves. She knew he liked to read à Kempis every evening before he retired to his bedroom. Still, odder things had happened.

Oh! There it was. Papa Serena smiled as at an old friend as he reached to pick it off the shelf.

Soviet Colonel Karlis Pelse thought the flight from Moscow back to the port of Riga would never end. When finally his military plane did brake to a stop on the runway, he practically bolted across the tarmac to his official car, ordering his driver, as he got in, to get him home as fast as possible.

Even at top speed, and with no traffic in the small morning hours, it was an endless twenty minutes from the airport to the military governor's house in Akshile suburb. If he looked at his watch once, he did so a dozen times. Four o'clock. Four-o-two. Five after . . .

In truth, Pelse didn't know what time the thing was going to happen. He only knew that General Control had set in motion a nearly foolproof plot to murder Papa Serena by the release of gas from some book the Pontiff read every night before retiring. It might already have been done, for all he knew. Or the whole thing might just be a trap for Pelse, to see what he would do with such information once he had it. If that was true, it was indeed a vile and Satanic trap—one that only General Control could devise. Pelse was sure General Control had begun to suspect him; he had lain low recently on that very account. But General Control knew well how Catholics venerate their Pope. With intelligence like this, if Pelse was a crypto-Roman, he could not lie low. Whatever the consequences, he could not sit on such information and do nothing.

When the colonel let himself into his house at last, and closed the front door silently behind him, it was four-fifteen. He made his way without a sound through the house and unlocked the door to the basement. He removed his cipher book from its hiding place and sat down at the transmitter. With a steady hand, he switched it on and began. "Constantine . . ." He started the message with the signal that preceded only the most urgent messages to Rome. It was the underground code word Rico Lansing had long since established as the top-priority signal for a red alert.

The message was monitored at scores of signal stations that were manned, day and night, by friend and enemy. But only those who had the cipher could make out the message.

When the first word of Pelse's message came through to Rome, Simon Youn sat bolt upright and grabbed his pad and pen. "Call Monsignore Lansing." He barked the order to the clerk on duty with him. "Tell him we have a Constantine signal coming through. Hold him on the line."

In seconds, Youn had the full text down and sent the acknowledgment signal back. A couple of minutes more, and he had deciphered the short, horrid message.

"Rico?" He grabbed the phone from the clerk. "It's from Pelse." He read the text verbatim.

Those Satanic bastards! Rico thought. "Call Brandolini." He gave crisp, clear orders to Youn. "And Solaccio. Then call Captain Berulli at the fire department. He has full set of master keys. Tell him to meet me at the St. Damasus entrance in five minutes. You be there too, Simon."

"Let's hope nothing has happened," Youn said, but he was speaking into a dead phone.

Captain Berulli opened the outer door to the private papal apartments. The light was still on in the bedroom. Rico breathed a sigh of relief. The five men made their way quickly toward the wedge of light that spilled out across the carpet.

"Holy Father." Rico called out at the same time he knocked on the half-open door of the bedroom. "Holy Father." His voice was a little louder, a little more insistent; but there was no response.

When he pushed the door fully open, he prayed to see the Holy Father had fallen asleep, his eyes closed, his chest rising and falling. But on his first sight of Serena, it was Lansing's chest that heaved, as though a fist had tightened around it.

The Pontiff was sitting in the bed. His face was turned toward the door as if to see who might be there; but it was set at a strange and unchanging angle. His eyes were open, as if to peer over his glasses at some visitor; but they had the wide, vacant look of death. His mouth was pulled back, the teeth visible; it was not the hoped-for smile of welcome, but the tightened grimace of frozen pain.

Rico stepped into the bedroom. Without even thinking, his mind took in everything, like a motion picture camera that had been left running. The Pontiff's hands were at his sides, the left clutched tightly around a Rosary. A small, worn copy of *The Imitation of Christ* lay open on the incline of the still chest. Papers were scattered on the coverlet.

Lansing reached down and put one hand around Papa Serena's wrist. The flesh was still warm, still supple. The arm moved easily. There was no rigor mortis. But there was no pulse. No breath. No life in Papa Serena's body.

At a slight stirring behind him, Rico turned. Sister Flora had come in. She was staring in wide-eyed and unbelieving shock, both her hands over her mouth.

At a glance from Rico, Captain Berulli brought a small side chair for her, and Sister lowered herself into it like a robot.

"Sister." Rico came over and bent down beside her. "The Holy Father is dead."

She shifted her eyes from the bed to Rico's face. She nodded her head. She understood. She would be all right in a minute.

Solaccio and Brandolini had gone to the Pope's side by then. With one of his usual supply of handkerchiefs in hand, Brandolini gently removed the book and slipped it into his pocket. The two men glanced through the papers that lay about. They looked at the water carafe; it was still full, and the glass beside it appeared to be clean and dry.

When they came back to the doorway, Rico was quietly asking questions of the nun.

No, she told him, the Pontiff had not been ill. He had not complained of any pains. Don Diaz had worked with him in the study after dinner, but she had not seen the secretary leave. The Holy Father normally retired around ten-thirty or eleven. She herself usually woke him at five-thirty in the morning with a cup of coffee. She was getting ready to do just that when she was surprised to hear noises coming from the direction of the Pope's private apartment, down the corridor from the nun's quarters. That's why she had come in.

"One odd thing, Excellency." Sister Flora looked again toward the dead Pope. "The Holy Father never read in bed. His habit was to do his reading at his desk. And he always left his papers in order when he finished for the day. The last thing he read every night was a few pages of *The Imitation of Christ.* But in the study, Excellency. In the study."

Brandolini went into the private study and switched on one of the lights. Some of the folders on the desk were slightly askew, but otherwise all appeared to be in order. There was a half-written letter to the Pope's brother lying on the blotter, the pen still beside it, the quotation from Thomas à Kempis still unfinished. Brandolini carefully picked up both pen and letter and slipped them into his pocket with the *Imitation.*

When he got back into the bedroom, the others were kneeling at the Pope's bedside. Youn had gone to the papal chapel and brought back a small bottle of holy oil. Rico was just anointing the Holy Father's body. "I absolve you of all sins and censures. In the name of the Father . . ." He traced a cross with the holy oil on Papa Serena's forehead, while the others crossed themselves. ". . . and the Son and the Holy Spirit."

It was all done very quickly. Youn took the bottle of holy oil back to the chapel and Rico assembled everyone in the study. He asked Sister Flora to wait until the rest of them had left. "It's just five-twenty now, Sister. Wait until about five-thirty. Then call Cardinal Secretary Levesque. Technically, he is now camerlengo again, in charge of the smooth running of the Vatican until we have a new pope. Just one thing. Do not tell him anyone was here. As far as His Eminence is concerned, you discovered the body when you came in to wake His Holiness as usual."

The nun asked no questions. She would do as the archbishop directed.

"God be with you, Sister." Rico gave her his blessing, and followed his companions into the corridor.

"And with you," the nun whispered to the door that closed behind him. She was too wise and too experienced in matters of life and death not to guess at the truth.

By all signs and reports, Cardinal Secretary Levesque was the very model of efficiency from the moment he was summoned to the Pope's private apartment by Sister Flora at five-thirty in the morning. By seven o'clock, the first public announcement was broadcast over Vatican Radio: The Holy Father had been discovered dead in bed by a papal secretary. The papal doctor had already confirmed what was suspected, that His Holiness had died sometime before midnight of an acute myocardial infarction.

Even as the news was flashed around the world, Cardinal Levesque had two embalmers at work on the mortal remains of Papa Serena. The papal apartments had been swept clean of all the Holy Father's personal effects. Don Diaz, Sister Flora, and the entire papal household that the Pontiff had brought from Turin had already been dispatched, bag and baggage, from the Vatican.

By that hour, too, Giulio Brandolini had the preliminary report from his specialists on the copy of *The Imitation of Christ,* the letter, and the pen that he had taken from Papa Serena's rooms. According to the report, the *Imitation* had been the means used. It had been doctored. Tests were still going on to determine what had been used.

"So." Brandolini paced in his office while Rico and Solaccio listened. "If Sister Flora's account of Papa Serena's habits held true last night, here is what we are faced with. The Holy Father died from poisoning in his study. He was fully clothed. Someone had to get him into his bedroom. Undress him. Get him into his pajamas. Prop him up in bed. Even put his glasses on him and make it look as if he had been reading.

"The number of people who can get into the papal apartment at night is very limited. I've asked for surveillance reports from all of the guards as to movements anywhere within the palace during the night. There were no visitors from outside. We already checked that. Tapes of all phone calls that may have been made or received during the night are being transcribed."

"In any case"—Solaccio raised his eyes to the photograph of a smiling

Papa Serena that hung over Brandolini's desk—"there's no question this time. It was done from the inside."

Rico got to his feet, his eyes flashing with the anger that burned in him. He had already called Helmut on his private line at Villa Cerulea to tell him what had happened. Ordinarily, he would have called the Maestro, but after the incident in *il Tempio,* he didn't want to give him this kind of news abruptly on the phone. Helmut had said he would tell his uncle, and Rico had promised to come out himself as soon as Brandolini had the early lab findings.

Lansing had called Falconieri as well. The cardinal would take care of informing the rest of the State Council.

"I'd better be on my way." He headed for the door, but then turned back.

If the other two had expected some heavy, hangdog reaction from Lansing, they had soon seen that was not his way. He had been thrown back on his uppers at first, just as they all had. But primarily there was a controlled fury in him that anyone, inside or outside, should have made this direct and lethal attack, not just on the Pope, but on the papacy. It was precisely the harvest of evil that Papa Profumi had spoken of two decades before. It had been slow in reaching so visibly into the very heart of the Church, perhaps; but now it was here; and there was no mistaking its work.

He held up his hand in the old Roman sign of victory, fist clenched, thumb up. *"Cristus Regnat!"* he said. Christ reigns!

Brandolini's eyes flashed back at Lansing. He made the same sign in return. *"Cristus Veniet!"* he answered. Christ will come!

Cardinal Valeska switched off the broadcast that had come through on Vatican Radio. He looked at his watch. Seven-thirty. Pelse's message had not been in time.

Valeska turned in his chair, picked up his phone, and dialed Warsaw. He recognized Wallensky's voice when he answered his personal phone.

"Were you up early this morning, Eminence?"

"Yes." On the telephone, Wallensky dispensed words as a miser dispenses gold; but Valeska understood that Warsaw, too, had monitored the Pelse signal.

"I think we will be traveling soon again."

"Within the week." Wallensky had listened to Vatican Radio, as well; had waited for news he hoped would not come. But now he knew. The Church had lost a pope. And Wallensky would soon lose his protégé to Rome.

Valeska was now prime *papabile.*

[63]

Cardinal Secretary Levesque, acting as camerlengo, sat alone at the center of the long presidents' table in the Sistine Chapel, while the stragglers among the one hundred eleven cardinals took their places for the opening session of conclave. On the dot of 5:30 P.M., he stood to address them; he was all business.

"I will now read the rules governing the choice of the next candidate."

That was as far as he got. The full conclave was as ready for business as he was.

"Eminent Cardinal Secretary and Camerlengo." Cardinal Azande was already standing when Levesque looked up from his papers, annoyance and surprise shooting from his eyes like darts.

Azande seemed not to notice. "Believe us when we tell you this: We, the cardinal electors, were all in conclave a bare five weeks ago. We know the rules. We know the issues. We know our minds. We know Your Eminence's mind. We are the same cardinals who assembled to elect Papa Serena."

"I would remind my Venerable Brother," Levesque shot back in a vicious tone, "that his former choice of a candidate did not take all the factors into account. This office of secretary is acquainted with all aspects of the candidates. . . ."

"Point of order, Eminence." Cardinal Arnulfo did not even bother to rise from his throne. "We are well aware of the acquaintances of the office of secretary. But we are not yet ready to discuss candidates. As our Venerable Brother from Nigeria has pointed out, we were all assembled here just five weeks ago. We made our minds and our choices clear. I move at this time that—as the first order of business is to elect the cardinal dean of conclave and his two co-presidents—we reinstate the three of our number who served in the last conclave. And—as our second order of business is to adopt the mandate, the *impostazione,* that will be presented to the candidate—I move that we reaffirm the mandate of the last conclave."

"I second the motions of His Eminence Cardinal Arnulfo." Azande smiled at Arnulfo's smoothness and sat down.

Levesque threw up his hands. From that point on, conclave was out of his control.

Arnulfo's two motions carried easily, as did Cardinal Ferragamo-Duca's motion, as cardinal dean once again, to adjourn the preliminary session, and be ready to entertain nominations of candidates at the first full session of conclave the following morning. The old Roman hands were at work.

The overnight hours were not filled with intense meetings in corridors and cardinals' rooms, as is most often the case during conclave. Buff and Svensens and Fustami and a few others did their best to "work the cardinals," and they were listened to politely, in the main. But when the morning session opened promptly at nine o'clock, Ferragamo-Duca recognized Cardinal Azande as the first speaker.

The African spoke from in front of the presidents' table this time. He was brief and clear.

"Over the past fifteen years, the Church of Rome has largely passed into the hands of men who want to liquidate it. Now, we have said for the second time in less than two months that we must affirm again, for all the world and for ourselves, that we will redirect this Barque of Peter, revising the abusive practices that have risen out of certain erroneous interpretations of the Second Vatican Council, and that we will work to reaffirm the primacy of the Pope among the Bishops of the Church, and to reestablish the spiritual leadership of the Church in the world.

"It has been plain to see that in one area of the world, these policies have always been in force, and have been effective. I refer, of course, to Poland."

As Cardinal Azande gave a brief summary of the accomplishments of the Polish Church, its hostile environment notwithstanding, Cardinal Falconieri assessed the conclave reaction with a practiced eye. The only electors who seemed surprised were those who had been avoided in the pre-conclave consensus work prior to Serena's election.

Falconieri leaned back and looked over at Arnulfo and Corelli. They had figured it would take one preliminary vote, or possibly two, to draw out the opposition and settle things down. Three votes at most should do it. He nodded slightly at them now. He was confident.

". . . I therefore nominate His Eminence Cardinal Bogdan Valeska of Krakow." Azande retired to his throne.

"I second that nomination, Your Eminence." Corelli's voice filled the chapel.

By nightfall, it was all over. Svensens of Belgium, Sekai of Hungary, Buff of England, all threw in the towel. Even Levesque finally bowed to tradition, virtually throwing his vote to the winning candidate. Bogdan Valeska became the unanimous choice of conclave.

It was obvious from the first moment of his reign that Papa Valeska, like the conclave that elected him, meant business. And like Serena before him, he was stunningly clear about the course he would follow as Pope.

In his very first week, at the papal desk on the third floor of the Apostolic Palace, the new Pontiff sent word with his private secretary, Monsignore Jan Terebelski, that he would be pleased to accept an invitation to appear personally at a meeting of the State Council.

It was unheard of. Popes simply did not do that. But the whole situation of the Church was so odd that the Council members took the suggestion as a very welcome signal indeed. They had been at war with the papal office for far too long. They wanted a frank airing of problems and policies. They wanted collaboration again. Above all, they wanted once more to link the republicanism and the absolutism of the Vatican in the balanced governing of the Holy See and the Church.

From the outset of the meeting, it was Cardinal Arnulfo who provided as much frankness as anyone might want. He outlined the "sorry position" of the Church whose reins were now in Valeska's hands.

"Only two or three years ago, Holy Father, this State Council assessed that roughly half the Church's bishops were in schism; that they rejected the jurisdiction of the Roman Pontiff, in other words, and of his curial organs of government. Now we have to put that figure at fully two-thirds of the bishops worldwide.

"On top of that, we calculate that between one-third and one-half are also in heresy, mainly because they actually teach heresy themselves, or because they allow it to be taught in their dioceses."

As an aside—but an important one in Arnulfo's judgment—he reminded His Holiness and the Council members that even to tolerate schism is to fall into it; and it is to lose one's authority. "In my mind"—the cardinal did not shrink from the thought or the statement even in the papal presence—"it will always be a problem for the Church to decide if Papa Da Brescia did not cease at one point to be a valid pope, so far did his toleration of schism and heresy go.

"In any case"—he returned to the point at hand—"the results are visible in the ever-plummeting supply of priests and nuns, and in the ever-diminishing numbers who frequent Confession and Holy Communion, and respect Church marriage laws. Sacraments are no longer the clear arteries and strong mooring lines of supernatural Grace in the natural world. They have been clogged and snagged to the point that Grace, divine Grace, does not abound in our visible Church."

Cardinal O'Mahoney winced slightly, and wondered if Arnulfo was being a bit too blunt. All watched Valeska's face for some sign or reaction during the cardinal's rundown. They couldn't tell too much; the Pontiff seemed to be smiling with his eyes, sometimes looking at Arnulfo, sometimes studying the tabletop, always with his head inclined forward just a little.

Helmut could read nothing on that strong, round face. He wished they had asked Rico Lansing to attend this meeting. He knew this Pope better than anyone else in the entire Vatican; his contribution to a post-meeting "reading" would have been helpful.

When Arnulfo finished with all he had to say, there was little for anyone else to add; but to be certain, Papa Valeska quickly scanned the faces around the table.

"Bene!" He spoke in his accented but fluent Italian. "You have given me your views. Now I want your recommendations."

On that score, Arnulfo did not have the floor to himself. Everyone had a dozen suggestions to make.

Within the Vatican itself, the most urgent, but not the only, recommendation was the revamping of the Secretariat of State, starting with Levesque and Demarchelier. For the situation out in the Church Universal, recommendations were numerous. Retire certain bishops. Put others under restraining orders. Fire a whole bevy of seminary professors.

Order nuns back to wearing their religious habits, and back from politics into teaching and hospital work. Issue new, stringent rules regulating all phases of Church life. Reinstate the Rosary and other devotional practices.

When Arnulfo recommended changing the apostolic delegate in the United States, everyone chimed in to agree so immediately that Valeska was struck by it.

"Why him in particular, Your Eminences? All the apostolic delegates will be changed in time, anyway, as they are in any new papacy."

"Because, Holiness"—Corelli supplied the answer this time—"Jobert is an unbeliever who has done untold damage to the Church by making bishops of other unbelievers."

When he had heard everyone out, Papa Valeska leaned forward in his chair at last and spoke the words that were to become one of the hallmarks of his style and his attitude. "Here," he said, "is what we will do."

As the letters of resignation requested by Papa Serena from Vatican personnel were still valid, and because the Pontiff agreed that Levesque and Demarchelier, along with some half-dozen others, were inimical at best, it would be a simple matter to be rid of those men.

The Maestro, who was sitting at the far end of the table, looked visibly relieved at the promptness and directness of that papal decision. Like the Council members, however, he was disappointed that Papa Valeska was not prepared to act so soon on the other recommendations. Still, it seemed reasonable for the Pope to take a little time to assess a situation that had taken decades to develop.

Papa Valeska obviously did not want to spend a great deal of time in this extraordinary meeting on matters of personnel. But he would need a new secretary of state without delay.

Cardinal O'Mahoney, who had a good eye for the career bureaucrat, suggested Archbishop Casaregna. He had been in the Secretariat of State since the 1940s. He had worked with Levesque, but had never been in his deep confidence, as Demarchelier and others were. Of late, in fact, he had created a certain distance between himself and the cardinal secretary. Casaregna's loyalty, insofar as he had any, was to the winning side. He knew the ropes, both inside and outside the Vatican.

The Pope nodded his agreement. Casaregna's experience was the deciding factor for him. He needed a man who could move quickly. Loyalty would come with time. It always had for Valeska.

"Now." His Holiness was impatient to get on with the heart of the meeting. "The most immediate and deepest damage done over the past fifteen years has been to the authority and primacy of the Pope. The 'Roman fact' has been endangered."

There were nods of assent from all of the cardinals.

"At the same time," the Pope went on in his rumbling voice, "the entire world is held in thrall and tension in the icy stalemate between the two superpowers. But the superpowers are themselves helpless." He held his two hands out, as if the U.S.S.R. were in one, the U.S.A. in the other.

"They are locked in the ice at the summit of the mountain of nations, unable to move. What we need to do is shift the mountain.

"We all know, of course, that Soviet Marxism is godless. Officially and as a matter of policy. And though it is not 'official'—in the sense that it does not answer on the point to some Politburo system—capitalism is equally godless."

The Maestro looked steadily at Valeska, surprised both at the broad geopolitical sweep of the Pope's mind and at unexpected echoes of Papa Profumi's mentality.

"What we need, in other words," the Pope went on with great intensity, "is a third force, a totally different influence that will curtail the effects and break the stranglehold of both the Soviets and the capitalists.

"And we need a foothold where that third force will begin to be felt.

"First, as to that third force itself: I am speaking purely and simply of moral and religious revival in the sociocultural lives of the men and women of the world. Regardless of the politics and policies of their governments.

"But the foothold for that revival: *that* is the first key we must find." Valeska paused to look quickly around the table. He could see that the seven cardinals and the de la Valles were following his mind. But he wanted more than that, more than intellectual perception of his policies. He wanted to come away with their full support.

"We cannot seek that foothold," he took up again after a second or two, "in Asia. China, which *is* Asia, one might say, is the great enemy of Russia; of all Slavs, in fact. The greatest and longest devastations for them came from the endless waves of Huns and Mongols that swept down from China. They still talk of 'the yellow peril,' and they mean it. What ails Russia above all else is not, as many believe, a paranoia about the West. The Soviets want to secure their borders on the west, true; but they want to do that so they can deal with the east.

"Nor can we look for our new and viable base for the third force in Latin America. That entire continent is an impoverished morass of dictators and misery, with no political or financial stability, no industrial base, and no military strength. It will not be taken seriously at this time except as a victim.

"Africa"—a quick but not apologetic glance at Cardinal Azande—"is roughly in the same situation as Latin America. The most viable country on that continent is South Africa, and it is under attack from nearly every quarter.

"No, Your Eminences. The only foothold possible for the third force is Europe. But by Europe, I do not mean this shrunken, emasculated geographical lump of inertia that Europe has become. When I speak of Europe, I refer to the whole area from the Urals to Calais. And I speak of 290 million people reconstituted from the vegetable state they are in at this moment, into the strong religious and moral stance that *made* Europe, when it was *really* Europe. The industrial, political, and military sinews are still there. But without the faith that once made it great, it is nothing but a pawn. And it will remain nothing but a pawn unless the cruel double moorings that tie it to the U.S.S.R. in the east, and to the U.S.A. in the west, can be cut."

"Holiness." Cardinal Corelli leaned forward slightly. "What Your Holiness seems to be proposing runs directly counter to the most basic policies of both superpowers. It affects the manner in which they live. The whole postwar arrangement will be up for grabs. Out the window. Is that what Your Holiness is proposing to do?"

Valeska gave his answer in one word. "Yes."

"By political power?" Corelli was incredulous.

"No, Your Eminence. It can't be done by the use of political power. But there is no one in Europe—no individual and no government—who does not want to be rid of both superpowers. The only way that can be done is on the moral and spiritual plane."

Corelli was obviously still not convinced, and said so quite plainly.

"I grant you, Excellency," Valeska responded, "that I cannot do this with a single wave of my hand. It must be done in stages. Carefully planned stages.

"The first stage brings me back to what I said when I opened my remarks, about the damage that has been done to the authority and primacy of the Pope. In that regard, I shall set out to visit as many countries as possible, in order to remind people vividly that there is, indeed, a Pope. In order to reestablish the international persona of the papacy, and remind everyone that the Pope is the head of Christ's Church. To embody for them the 'Roman fact.'

"At the same time, I will work to develop a rapprochement with the churches of Eastern Orthodoxy—mainly the Byzantine and Muscovite churches. When I speak of the Muscovite Church, please understand that I am not talking, as Papa Angelica did, of the KGB-dominated patriarchate, but of the flourishing Church of the catacombs in the Soviet Union, with some 130 million people in it."

"And the Soviet Union itself, Holiness? The government, that is?" It was Falconieri's query.

"The central question there," Valeska answered, "concerns the pact Papa Angelica made with the Soviets, and which Papa Da Brescia honored. Namely, that the Holy See would not denounce by name either the Soviet government or Marxism. Until I am ready, there is no point in putting the Soviets on bitter and sharp notice that I am going to wage war against them. That would only make them tighten their grip all the more, and set them against the tack I plan to use."

Guido spoke up for the first time, to remind the Council that Papa Ambrosiano, who preceded Profumi, had put Mussolini on such notice in 1939. "And he died soon after."

On the heels of Papa Serena's death, the point was clear. No one in the higher echelons of the Vatican had any doubt about Mussolini's hand in the sudden death of Papa Ambrosiano just as he planned to make his denunciation of Mussolini public.

There was a fleeting look of surprise only on Valeska's face. He had much to learn about this Vatican. But he went on quickly to address the positive side of his planned policy toward the Soviet Union.

"I plan to deal with the Soviets, not by announcing that we will bury them, but by showing them how to solve the problem that they themselves know will bury them.

"It has been clear to many in Russia since the time of Khrushchev that the closed Marxist economy doesn't work. The only bright spots for them are those places where they have allowed some freedom in economic affairs; where things have been modified to allow something of the free market system to operate. In Hungary and Romania and Yugoslavia, for example. But those countries have not been able to shake off Communist cultural and social control; and the result has been a damping of economic improvement even there.

"The top Soviet economic planners are looking for a solution. They are searching for some model they can show to the Marxist-Leninist stalwarts —to the Gromykos and their sympathizers—that will demonstrate not only that they can still retain military, political, and security control, side by side with a free, open-market economy and cultural freedom; but that they will reap material benefit from such an arrangement.

"Now, the Marxist-Leninists have always been convinced that a man's politics are tied to his bank account. Economics and politics have always been linked. If you let the people have money and access to loans and all the rest of what goes along with an open-market economy, then those people will go political as well; that is the Marxist-Leninist assumption and fear.

"I plan to show them that does not have to be the case. I plan to give them a model where religion, morality, and sociocultural life are totally detached and independent of political control. Political control—the politburos, the parliamentary bodies such as the Polish Sejm, the police and military—will all be left totally in Marxist hands. But all the rest will be decided by the people."

"And that model"—the Maestro now saw clearly where Papa Valeska was headed—"is to be Poland, Holiness?"

Valeska nodded. "Poland has a very special destiny in Christ's plan of redemption for the world. We have already made great strides in developing a whole new mentality in Catholics living under Soviet rule. We have run two highly successful tests. Your Eminences may remember the 'incident' in Nova Huta, and the strike at the end of the following year in the Gdansk shipyards. Both of those were small and highly successful experiments in a strategy for doubling around Soviet control and taking it from the rear, so to speak.

"The time is ripe to make that Polish experiment work on a national level. Everything is in place.

"When the Soviets see that in such an arrangement as I've described, 34 million Poles begin to produce as they were meant to by the Politburo, then we will be ready to expand the "experiment" into Latvia, Lithuania,

Estonia, Bulgaria. Into all the satellite countries where there are already the sinews of a new mentality being fostered among the 100 million or so Catholics living under Soviet rule.

"But more than a model for the Soviets, we will also have produced a model for Europe. We will have demonstrated that culture, labor relations, nationalism—sociocultural life, in other words—can be successfully detached from superpower politics by means of moral and spiritual persuasion. And we will have done it through reeducation of the people themselves."

"Holy Father," Cardinal Hoffeldt intervened. "Does Your Holiness expect everyone in Europe to convert to Catholicism? I mean, Poland is one thing. But all of Europe—from the Urals to Calais, as Your Holiness said earlier—that is quite another!"

"No, Eminence." The Pontiff shook his head. "That would not be realistic; and, for our political aim, it will not be necessary. There is already in Europe a sufficiently strong, vibrant Christian moral and religious outlook among most people. It springs from their very origins as Europeans. Remember, that is one of the primary things that led me to select Europe in the first place—it was its faith that made it what it once was.

"The difference is that in the past, we used that moral and religious outlook to spawn political systems. Now we need to use that outlook to free the people from the two political systems that are crushing them in a vise of inhuman power."

The outline of Valeska's policies was stunning, and its effect showed on the face of every cardinal. This Pope intended to attempt nothing less than a modification of the entire geopolitical face of the world. Once he had demonstrated to the Soviet Union that a neutral but strong Europe was not a threat to its system, it would be reasonable to expect the Americans, too, to talk about pacification and withdrawal from Europe. There would be nothing there to fight about any longer.

Cardinal Hoffeldt was the first to give vocal support to the general plan and aim Valeska laid out. He agreed that all of Europe was sick to death of the superpowers, and that most if not all of his German people would be happy to have the American armaments off their soil.

O'Mahoney was more than ready to "see our American boys come home from Europe." And he felt certain that America would be happy to have Europe and Russia "taken off her back."

Falconieri and Ferragamo-Duca were with Valeska all the way, as the strong leader of the Church they had hoped he would be.

Corelli was wavering, but remained skeptical. Azande said nothing; he felt there was a gap, a flaw, in the pattern the Pope set out, but he couldn't put his finger on it.

Arnulfo, however, was neither wavering nor silent. "It won't work, Holy Father." It was not an attack, not even the slightest bit hostile. "Even assuming that there is some machinery in place for this 'Polish experiment' upon which Your Holiness' plan seems to hinge very importantly, I want to address the very first stage of Your Holiness' plan. The visits Your Holiness plans to make to countries around the world." In Arnulfo's view, such "tripping about the globe" to remind the world of the power and authority of the papacy would backfire. Either Papa Valeska would revive all the old images of Caesaropapism; or he would create a new and cheapened image as just another of the world-class traveling salesmen of ideas.

"In any case," Arnulfo said, "the Pope *receives* delegations and visitors, whether they be statesmen or religious leaders. He cannot travel about sitting on sofas with prime ministers like any signore. The Pope is the Apostle of Peter and the Vicar of Christ. The Rock of the Church, and the Bishop of Rome."

"It *will* work, Eminence." Valeska was not on the attack, either; but he was firm. "It will work because I *am* Pope. Because I know better than to wait for power to be given to me; I will go out and gather it in these two hands. I am a Slav, Eminence. I understand the Soviet rulers. They know I can hold Poland for them, or I can disrupt Poland for them. They know I am neither capitalist nor Marxist. They already fear my spiritual power. They saw it at Nova Huta. We will start from there."

Arnulfo had to concede each of those points. He had no stronger plan to offer—certainly nothing as exciting and flamboyant. In any case, the rest of the Council was visibly with Papa Valeska. Cardinal Arnulfo did not insist further.

On the same day, Papa Valeska had scheduled two more long meetings. Because the Polish experiment was crucial to his policy of creating a third force in Europe, and because Rico Lansing's covert organization was crucial to the Polish experiment, he asked for a special meeting of Security Two to be held in his private study on the fourth floor.

And to discuss a variety of topics, he had already arranged for an early-evening meeting with the Maestro.

Both Valeska and Cardinal Wallensky had known of Security Two's existence from Lansing for some years. They had never been sure, of course, who the other members were. Valeska guessed that the Maestro and his nephew might be involved, because the financing for Rico's covert organization, the "blue card" underground, and the more recent overt Solidarity organization had always been so efficient. Cardinal Falconieri, however, was a surprise to him. And he had never even met Brandolini or Solaccio. He was happy to be able to thank them very warmly for the expert backup they had given to Lansing, and through him to Poland and all Eastern European Catholics for so many years.

As in the State Council meeting, once the preliminaries were over, Papa Valeska was eager to come to the heart of the matters he needed to discuss. The entire hour or so was taken up wholly with planning the Polish experiment.

It was the Pontiff's view that Solidarity—the surface or aboveground organization for Rico's covert cell network and the "blue card" underground—had come so far, and had been so well organized and educated, that it was ready now to be put to the supreme test.

The test itself was simply stated. Could Solidarity do on a national basis, all across Poland, what it had done in the Gdansk and Nova Huta tests? Could it, in other words, parade in the open and wrest a certain valuable amount of autonomy from the Communist superstructure of Poland? And could it do that without violence; without a shot being fired; without a political or military threat to that superstructure? "We will never know if we do not try." Valeska looked steadily at Rico Lansing now. "The Polish model is my hope."

It was obvious to every man present that Lansing was at ease with Papa Valeska. It was not just that the two had been friends for so many years, and had shared so many dangers in their work. It was not even that at last he was again able to share the full knowledge and scope of his mission with his Pontiff, though that had been a felt need in him since Papa Profumi had died. Rather, he had long since come to understand the Slavic mind.

The Slavic mind was marinated in a sense of community, and of community as forming one whole organic mass, and not as made up of separate individuals. Central to that community sense was the instinctual reliance on a leader.

"Holy Father." Lansing spoke in quiet and familiar tones. "I agree with Your Holiness that the aim in Poland must be to do in the nation what we have done in our smaller experiments. But the Solidarity network is not yet strong enough. We need time for the covert cells to screen more leaders for the overt organization. And we must take better precautions than we have until now to be certain that the KOR people have nothing to do with the leadership of Solidarity. KOR cannot be relied upon not to use political and even violent, militaristic means; and they can't be relied on to confine their aims to the religious and social spheres."

Papa Valeska's face flushed. He remembered well how Wallensky and Lansing had so often argued with him about this Trotskyite organization and its anarchistic philosophy. "I personally have talked with the leaders of KOR, Rico." Valeska spoke mildly. "I feel sure they will not bedevil us."

Giulio Brandolini shot a glance at the Maestro, and then spoke up. "Holy Father, it may be that the KOR people would like to help Solidarity. But the people who control KOR have a great stake in the status quo in Poland and all of the satellite countries."

Brandolini proceeded to explain briefly his P-1/P-2 theory to the Pontiff, concentrating on the P-2 level, where he had amassed hard evidence over the years. The funding for KOR, as he reminded everyone, came from Western sources. As with the funding of organizations like the Red Brigades, the connection seemed to make no sense on the surface. But—Brandolini set out his reasoning clearly—one had to ask who in the West would use KOR to beat down the Church, and maintain a Communist Poland. Who in the West would benefit, in other words.

The answer, he said, was some group that saw the Church as an enemy to its own aims; and that benefited from a low-wage industrial area. "For the supercapitalists of the world, Holy Father, every Communist state is a non-strike, low-wage industrial bonanza. Now, one of the purposes Your Holiness has for Solidarity in Poland and elsewhere is to take labor relations out of direct control of the Politburo. If that aim should succeed, if Solidarity wins the right for the unions to elect their own leaders, for example, and to bargain for higher wages, and gains enough strength actually to stop work, as was the case in both Nova Huta and Gdansk, then Poland would cease to be such a valuable area for these capitalist interests—this theoretical P-1 I have posited."

Papa Valeska understood Brandolini's thinking; but he also understood his Poles. He did not even hesitate in his answer. "I think," he said, with a glance toward the Maestro and Helmut, "that we have very good footholds in the highest and most influential capitalist circles in the West. But even leaving that aside, and considering only KOR itself, I know them. I have spent time with them. They are Poles before they are anything else. And because they are Poles, they are Catholics. They will be with us.

"Now, here is what we will do. As those of you know who were in the State Council meeting this morning, I will be deeply occupied for the first year, at least, of my pontificate in traveling widely to reestablish the international persona of the Pope as head of Christ's Church; and in beginning to establish the diplomatic lines that will be necessary for my policies.

"Rico, you say the Solidarity network is not yet strong enough to bear the burden I plan to put on it. I will give you time. While I am 'out in the world,' so to say, you will be in Poland making Solidarity as strong as it needs to be."

"Of course, Holiness." Rico's whole heart and soul was in the plan. And he knew he could rely as always on Cardinal Wallensky's support and canny judgment. Still, he could not help but retain misgivings about keeping KOR under control, once the public experiment was fully underway, without the strong and active presence of Bogdan Valeska within the borders of Poland.

When the Maestro stepped out of the elevator on the fourth floor of the Apostolic Palace that evening, he could tell that he was going to be treated to a Polish feast by the Holy Father. The odors of kielbasa sausage and Polish soups and the sweet-smelling pastries and Polish breads that wafted daily from Sister Martha's fourth-floor kitchen had already become the subject of some light-hearted banter in the very Italian Vatican gossip mill.

"We share everything with the Holy Father," one *minutante* might say to another, "but infallibility does not extend to kielbasa." Or, "Our Caesar never drank cabbage soup." But, generally, it was all said in good humor.

Monsignore Terebelski met the Maestro in the corridor and showed him at once into the papal living room. Papa Valeska came in from his study at almost the same moment. Guido bowed and kissed the Fisherman's Ring, and the two settled comfortably into chairs for a glass of wine before dinner.

The first thing in Papa Valeska's mind touched, as almost everything did, on the plans and policies he was preparing so swiftly to set in motion. He had brought with him from the study two of the several envelopes that Papa Serena had left in the Pope's private safe.

"This"—he held one of them up for the Maestro to see— "is Papa Da Brescia's testimony to Richard Lansing's status as cardinal. My intention is to keep his cardinalate *in pectore.* But I would like your opinion before I decide finally."

"I agree fully, Holiness." The Maestro's feeling was that Lansing would now be spending more time under cover in Poland than ever before, and that it was unheard of for a man "to be walking about Vatican corridors in cardinal's robes one day, and posing under cover as a laborer in Pozna or Blonie or Krakow the next.

"Good," Valeska said, and closed the matter with characteristic firmness.

On their way into the dining room, he broached his second concern. He carried in his hand the envelope, also left in the papal safe, containing all the letters of the famous Sister Lucia concerning the appearances of the Virgin Mary at Fatima. Lucia was one of the three children to whom "the Lady of Fatima" had appeared, and was the only one of the three still living. Much, but not all, of what the Virgin had told the children had been revealed. It was well known, in fact, and the subject of much prayer among pious Catholics, that the Mother of Jesus had asked that the Holy Father, in unison with the bishops throughout the Church, consecrate Russia into her special care.

Now that he had read all of the Fatima letters, Papa Valeska had a simple question for the one man who had known intimately four out of the six popes who had reigned since the Fatima miracle of 1917.

"Why, Maestro, did Papa Profumi, for example, or Papa Angelica, not do what Our Lady asked? Consecrate the Soviet Union by name to her Immaculate Heart, in order to obviate the horrors described in the 'Third Secret'?" Valeksa waved the envelope for emphasis, before he laid it on the dining table by his plate.

"Holiness." The Maestro took his chair opposite the Pope. "Papa Profumi was elected in 1939, just as World War II was breaking out. He was swept up in that maelstrom, and in so many other things as well. He waited until it was too late. He tried to make some amends by defining the Assumption of Our Lady.

"As to Papa Angelica, once he had made his secret pact not to denounce either the Soviet government or Marxism, his hands were tied. Our Lady at Fatima required that denunciation; it would in any case be a necessary element of any genuine consecration of the Soviet Union to her Immaculate Heart.

"Papa Da Brescia observed the pact Papa Angelica had made. And in his case, by the end of his life, when I believe he had a genuine desire to consecrate Russia, the damage to his authority with the bishops was already too great. Remember, she wanted the consecration by the Pope and all the bishops together, collegially, on the same day. He simply no longer had the strength."

The Pontiff nodded to indicate his understanding of the last point in particular. "By now"—he tapped the Fatima envelope—"I could not get even one-third of my bishops to join me in a collegial consecration of the Soviet Union."

"That's clear, Holiness."

"I will just have to wait and watch for my first opportunity. I will have to assess the strength that comes from my policies until I see that the thing is possible. Please God it will be soon."

"Please God, indeed, Holy Father."

The rest of the evening, over dinner and then in the papal study, was taken up with Papa Valeska's questions and the Maestro's answers concerning the financial problems of the Holy See, which many had guessed at since the Lercani scandal had surfaced but which few could assess.

Guido was totally candid. He explained how, since 1969 and the Lercani involvement through Papa Da Brescia, there had been great trouble. To a large extent, the damage could be offset, but it would take time. "There are still left-over relationships from that period, Holiness, and we haven't gotten to the bottom of it all yet.

"We feel, my nephew and I, that the focus of many of those relationships is the Banco Agostiniano. We have divested ourselves of almost all our shares in the Agostiniano, but we still think, for example, that Peter Servatius has relationships through Roberto Gonella, the chairman of the Agostiniano, with institutions abroad from which trouble may yet come. Gonella is one of the cleverest bankers and most secretive characters in the world; and if Your Holiness will permit, Servatius is not the most honorable or the brightest. That is a volatile combination. Until we have things totally sorted out and under control, however, it could still be counter-productive to remove Servatius."

Valeska listened intently. It was his wish to begin to reform the entire setup of the financial agencies of the Vatican. But he could not make that the first order of business. "I need time, Maestro." The Pope was almost fervent now. "I need a peaceful time at home. I will be busy 'out there' for a year or two, traveling and making my presence felt as Pope. You must keep things under control." The Pontiff mentioned Peter Servatius also, but not quite in the same terms as the Maestro had. The American head of the IRA appeared to the Pope to be a big, bluff, rough-and-ready fellow; much like Valeska himself in that regard. Nevertheless, the Holy Father was willing to bow to Guido's judgment as to Servatius' work. And he agreed that if to remove Servatius would cause too much stir in the financial world, he should be left in place "until I can devote more time to financial reform."

When the hour arrived for the Maestro to wish the Holy Father a good night's rest and to make his way to his waiting limousine, he was more hopeful about Vatican affairs than he had been in many years.

Far from being defensive or negative about Papa Valeska's intention to reform the financial areas of the Holy See, Guido himself had been focusing on that need increasingly himself. Ever since Brandolini had first drawn that arch on the blackboard in his office and explained his P-1/P-2 theory, the Maestro had guessed that the balance of power between the two sides in the Bargain had, in the view of the other side, shifted to the point that the Universal Assembly felt an all-out push against the Church could be successful. Acting on his own, and without a strong Pope in place, there was but so much the Keeper could do. Indeed, what could be done, Guido was already doing. He had successfully used the power the Bargain had allowed him to amass to force Paolo Lercani's fingers from around the Church purse strings, and then to undo Lercani himself. And he would continue to disinvolve the Holy See from the rest of the P-2 entanglements. He would, as he had promised Valeska, work hard at undoing the mess and keeping things under control, all the while looking forward to the day when the Pontiff would include the ledger sheets of the Vatican among his top priorities.

At the same time, and though he had explained the Bargain more fully to him, the Maestro was certain that Papa Valeska could not fully realize the ambit of the Universal Assembly. Nothing truly substantive could be done about the Bargain—and therefore about real reform of the Holy See's finances—without the strong leadership of a strong Pope. It would require a Pontiff who could not only reestablish moral authority and spiritual power, but truly and fearlessly use that authority and that power to declare a holy war.

The Maestro was certainly interested to watch the Polish experiment, and Papa Valeska's development of his third force, and all the rest of it. More than interested, in fact; he would do all he could to aid the Pontiff and Richard Lansing. Perhaps Papa Serena's mistake—a mistake that cost him his life—was that he did not tip his papal hat to the needs of governments. Valeska was mindful of those needs, and expert at dealing with them.

Nevertheless, the third force and the rapprochement with the Eastern churches and the persuasion of the Soviets to accept the Polish model, if it was successful—all of that could turn out to be a dazzling series of social and political high-wire acts. What would be the greater test in some respects would be the Holy Father's travels throughout the world to reinstate the figure of the Pope. If he went as the Vicar of Christ, the Pope of all Catholics, the spiritual *Pater Patrum* of the world, then perhaps, just perhaps, there would again and at long last be that strength of purely spiritual and religious force required to fight the battle against the "real insanity" that had taken hold in the world and in the Church Universal.

On the other hand, if Cardinal Arnulfo's worry proved justified, if Papa Valeska only succeeded in—what was that phrase the cardinal had used? Oh, yes, if he only succeeded in cheapening the image of the pope as another world-class traveling salesman of ideas, then the best the Maestro could hope for was to achieve an acceptable holding pattern. In that case, he did not expect to live to see the reign of the pope who would begin the work that had to be done.

[64]

The announcement came over the Italian radio on November 2: Paolo Lercani had been convicted in a United States federal court on ninety-nine counts of fraud; he had been fined several millions of dollars and condemned to twenty-seven years in federal prison.

Franco Graziani switched off the set in the den of his Rome apartment. He walked back across the room, removed a small sheaf of papers from his personal safe, and folded them into his pocket. He had been so sure Lercani would be able to buy his way through the American justice system. But the Maestro had been right again; and clever, as only he could be, in the way he had funneled Lercani over to the States.

Graziani needed time alone to think. He left the flat without stopping for his coat, or to tell his wife he was leaving. He went down to the garage level, got into one of the smaller family cars, pulled out onto the Corso, and headed nowhere in particular.

When he and Luigi Garganelli had first agreed to stick their toes in Lercani's ocean, they hadn't intended to swim out into such deep water, where all the sharks hunted. For them, it had just been a question of getting out of debt. But then one thing led to another. He and his wife had run up some awful gambling debts on top of the ones they already had. Investments Lercani had assured him would pay off went down the drain instead—probably with Lercani's help, now that Graziani thought about it.

The point for him now was that he hadn't told the Maestro and the other *impero* members the truth; not all of it, anyway. For the past three years, he had been a member of Senatore Pappagallo's P-2 organization. Pappagallo had promised to help him out of debt; and it was true that at least he had kept the wolf from the door. But the cost had been high. Graziani was as deep in muck now as he had been in debt before. He had, directly or indirectly, helped Naja Hanna deal with everything from Nazis in Latin America and Bulgarian Communist smugglers, to Red Brigades, political assassination squads, and narcotics dealers in Europe and America. It had revolted him almost from his first visit to the senatore's villa near Florence. He just hadn't thought it would go as far as it did.

He was out of the Rome traffic, well into the countryside, before he was able to get his mind to deal with the present. Both as head of the state-owned Industrial Reconstruction Institute—the famed and powerful IRI

—and as one of Guido de la Valle's trusted *impero* associates, Franco Graziani knew more than most about the Italian government's investigation of Lercani and his affairs. The dragnets the police had thrown out since 1974 had been hauled in teeming with precious catches. But Lercani was the biggest fish. At least, that's what the Italian police thought. He was wanted by now for conspiracy to commit at least six murders, and for bank fraud, embezzlement, importing drugs, violations of currency laws, nonpayment of taxes—Graziani couldn't even remember all the charges.

Graziani knew that the Italian police and Treasury officials had already applied to the U.S. Justice Department for extradition of the big fish. And he knew that, sooner or later, they would get Lercani back. Sooner or later, because of Graziani's association with P-2, where he had masqueraded as Guido de la Valle's "representative," not only the Maestro and the *impero,* but the Vatican's IRA and the whole Church, would be covered with the same muck that made Graziani stink in his own nostrils.

Franco pulled his car over to the side of the road. There was nothing on his languid, aristocratic face or in those eyes of ice to betray the strife of emotions going on inside him.

Until that radio announcement, he had been able to fool himself into thinking that somehow it would all be all right again. Somehow, under Guido's expert guidance, the *impero* would pull itself and the IRA free of the filthy entanglements Pappagallo and Lercani and Gonella had wrapped around them. But he knew now that it had been a fool's dream. It would only be a matter of time before the authorities put all the pieces together. Whatever else he had done, he couldn't let the Maestro and the Vatican be dragged down for things they hadn't done. Even he couldn't go that far. Naja Hanna and his threats couldn't make him do that.

There was only one way Graziani knew to help. It might not undo all the damage he had done. But maybe it would keep things from getting much worse.

Franco gunned the purring engine of his car once, shifted it into gear again, and headed for the Alban Hills and Villa Cerulea.

Much to everyone's surprise, Guido did keep his promise to Dr. Sepporis to maintain a schedule that was less stressful, if not less work-filled, than before.

He still woke up before dawn; that seemed to be a natural reflex that he couldn't change, like breathing or blinking his eyes. As if there were some switch or cable between them, Tati would wake up at the same time; but she would lie still on the coverlet until her master stirred out of bed, ready to start the day.

At the first streak of dawn sunlight across the sky, a thrush or a swallow would send up a few stray calls, like a chorus master rehearsing a difficult passage of grace notes. After a pause, a finch or a starling might try a different melody, or a nightingale would offer to teach them all a thing or two before departing. Bit by bit, as the light increased, the stillness fled before the chirruping, soaring, staccato, sliding, competing birdsongs that filled the morning twilight in increasing volume, until the moment that the topmost rim of the sun peeked over the hills to chase away the last wisps of darkness. Then, as if that chorus master had rapped a baton on nature's podium, the dawn chorus tamed itself into one of the gentler elements among the orderly sounds of day.

Guido waited in every morning's stillness for that chorus to begin. Its sounds seemed to accentuate the peace in which he did so much of his thinking now; and to be part of the assurance he felt that the pell-mell rush of his continued activity in promoting the vital interests of his Pope and his Church would settle him into a wider perspective and a more exalted focus. It was a special grace, he believed, won for him by his angel, Eugenio. The God he had always intended to serve and the Christ whose salvation he fully expected did not wish Guido de la Valle to go into the house of eternity with his will even slightly deflected from submission to the divine will. No matter what his failings had been, or how near he had touched to Mammon, or how often he had fallen from love, in serving Rome he was granted the boon of Rome's perpetual commodity: time. Time enough for God's grace to purify him.

When the dawn chorus was done, Guido would get out of bed, shower, and dress. He would start every day with the Latin Mass said by Don Filippo in the chapel. Then he would breakfast and read the papers.

On the two or three days of every week that he now worked at home, he would spend the rest of the morning in his study, dealing with documents, cablegrams, correspondence, making and receiving dozens of phone calls.

After a full six or seven hours' work, he would join Agathi and Keti for lunch if they were at home, take a short siesta, and then sit on the Long Terrace or stroll about the estate while Tati trotted on ahead as though she knew where he intended to go.

As Guido rearranged his life, Agathi and Keti rearranged Villa Cerulea's days around his new schedule.

Agathi remained as detached and innocent as she had always been of the web of interests and motives that embodied her brother's work. Of international brokerage, corporate alliances, papal displeasures, curial plots and counterplots, the hard coin of competition and infighting within the jungle of industry and finance—of all that Agathi was blissfully ignorant. It was, she knew, a very complicated life her brother still led. But as far as she was concerned, all was well if he was well. And she devoted her own life now to attuning the very rhythm of Villa Cerulea to his needs. She became the angel of comfort for him, watching over his physical condition and his wants, never questioning, never at a loss for a solution, always radiant with that loveliness that the long years and their hardships had softened but never tarnished.

With Keti, it was different. Because of that practical sensibility that had always been so much a part of her, she realized that Guido would need help he could trust if he was to be able to work at home several days a week on a long-term basis.

Keti had never been a secretary; but she reasoned that all the skills that had once made her a topflight journalist could be turned just as well to helping the Maestro. Helmut and Agathi agreed that would be ideal—far better than having any of the Vatican staff trooping in and out of their personal lives.

Guido was delighted when Keti broached the idea with him one morning at breakfast. And so there began between them an association that was useful for them both. Keti would spend hours with the Maestro, going over his mail with him, listening to him reason aloud about confidential bulletins, typing and filing memoranda and letters. Before long, she often anticipated what he wanted to say in reply to this or that communication. She was quick to note where he put the emphasis of his interest. Necessarily she began to form a picture of the literally global business of which he was the functioning center. And, as she became increasingly aware not only of the vast empire of money and influence that Guido regulated and directed, but of his extraordinary tie with the inner workings and public performance of the papacy, she began for the first time to grasp something of Helmut's continual absorption in his work, and his inability to close the painful gap between himself and her. She began to understand a very great deal that she had never understood before.

November 2, All Souls' Day, began for the de la Valles with Don Filippo's Requiem Mass for all the departed members of their family. Guido did not pray for Eugenio. He never did. He was certain that his "little angel," as he frequently spoke of him, was in heaven. He often felt the very presence of the boy, as if he were physically near, though immune now to all weakness and nescience, to all the carping limitations of mortality.

After his usual routine of work, lunch, and a short rest, Guido decided to do some catch-up reading by himself on the Long Terrace. No sooner had he settled on the swinging bench and tucked a lap robe around his legs, than Tati stood up, pointing in classic pose toward the French windows, a slight rumble in her throat.

In a minute, Agathi poked her head through the doors. "Guido, darling, it's Franco Graziani. He didn't seem to want to come out here; a pity, on such a pretty day. He asked if he could see you privately in your study."

When Guido closed the door of his study behind him, Franco Graziani was standing at the window, his back to the room. The Maestro crossed to one of the chairs and sat down. He knew Franco had heard him come in, sensed he wasn't ready to turn around, and knew therefore that whatever had brought his old friend and erring *impero* associate on this unannounced visit was neither trivial nor pleasant.

Guido waited. After that first blow of betrayal in *il Tempio,* and particularly with the curious and almost constant sense of Eugenio's closeness, he felt he could manage whatever it was that lay in store.

Graziani began talking before he could bring himself to turn around and face the Maestro. He started with a question. "Have you heard about Lercani's conviction in the U.S. federal court, Guido?"

"Yes." Guido had had an early-morning call from Italy's President Crasci before the news came over the radio. Again, he waited.

In a few minutes, Franco took in a great breath, as though there were not enough air in the room. A shudder went through him. It required all of the physical strength in his body and all of his will for Graziani to turn around, walk to the chair facing Guido, and look steadily into those blue-green, unwavering eyes.

It took about an hour, but when Graziani was finished, this time he had told the Maestro everything. All the details of his and Garganelli's earliest involvement with Lercani. Their help in corrupting the other five *impero* members. His own worsening financial situation, and how Senatore Pappagallo had seemed to turn up at just the right moment. How he had joined Pappagallo's secret organization, masquerading as "the Maestro's man." How they had tried to get Garganelli in too, but failed. Graziani had been afraid for Garganelli's life for a while, he told the Maestro; afraid Luigi knew too much. "But I guess they've decided his hands are dirty enough from the Lercani association that they can leave him alive. At least I hope so."

He explained in some detail how Pappagallo functioned as Naja Hanna, and the coup d'état nature of his organization, which planned to do away with parliamentary democracy. He told what he knew of the alliance with the ex-Nazis in Latin America, and how the Red Brigades and the narcotics dealers and the Lodge and the Mafia and all the rest fit, one way and another, as unwitting pawns, as nearly as Graziani could tell, into a very big scheme. He told what he knew of the Banco Agostiniano's involvement—its foreign exposure ran beyond a billion by now, and the best thing the Maestro had done, Graziani said, was to sell off the IRA and *impero* shares in the Agostiniano. Roberto Gonella, the bank's chairman, was a member of Pappagallo's organization too. "He doesn't care about destabilization of public life here or anywhere else." Graziani was nearing the end of what he had to say. "He doesn't care about the Red Brigades or the other terrorists, or about Pappagallo's plan for a military takeover. He's sure of a windfall in both power and wealth any way it goes; that's his mind, and his only concern."

"And yours, Franco?" Guido spoke for the first time since he had answered Graziani's question about Lercani. "Your mind and your concern in coming here to tell me all this?"

Beads of sweat were standing on Graziani's brow. He didn't wipe them away. "Paolo Lercani's conviction in open court and Italy's stepped-up efforts for his extradition brought home to me that it's just a matter of time before I become a target for police investigation. Maybe I already am. I'm up to my eyeballs in it. It could lead to—er—others. Because of my association, it could lead to you, Guido; and to the IRA, even though you've had nothing to do with it. That would suit Pappagallo and those other bastards just fine!"

"Need it come to that?" Guido was utterly rational. He knew there could only be one reason why Graziani was here: to try to keep it from coming to that.

"No. It needn't." Graziani pulled some half-dozen folded sheets of paper from his pocket. "Here I have set down the exact location of Pappagallo's villa at Arezzo, with a ground plan of the whole compound. It's the headquarters for his organization.

"There's also a list of names. I've only got a hundred and twenty or so. They're pretty astounding. Biggies. But you have to know that there are more names I don't have. From what I can tell, there are probably well over two thousand, maybe more. I don't know. And there are still more in Latin America. Mainly in Argentina, I think. I'm sure there's a full list somewhere in the villa.

"Anyway, Guido, you can give all this to the authorities. In one fell swoop, they will gather information in that villa that they would spend years seeking and probably never finding. You can trade it for their silence. About the *impero,* I mean. And about the Vatican and the IRA. They'll have to see there's no connection, except for me. Servatius isn't in this. Not really. He's just being used in his stupidity. By Gonella, this time. Sometimes I think they're all being used. The whole lot of them. Even Pappagallo.

"The main thing, though, is that you and the *impero* will be protected. And that Pappagallo will be scuppered. I hope he will, anyway. He's worse than human. He's a devil."

Guido took the papers from Franco's hand and scanned them. He was getting his first real look at the true nature and scope of what Giulio Brandolini had for so long dubbed P-2. There were names on Graziani's list from every walk of Italian life. High-ranking police and military men, politicians, business and industry and financial leaders; some high-ranking prelates were listed side by side with Mafia kingpins and some of the biggest Interpol targets in the world. Almost every name there was known to Guido for one reason or another. A few of the men had even been occasional guests at Villa Cerulea receptions.

In all truth, it was not a list that surprised the Maestro; he had reasoned long ago that P-2 had to be made up of men who were considered to be the movers and shakers in important sectors of Italian life. And because Security Two had linked Pappagallo to P-2 from the very start, he had assumed that the necessary connections could be made. But reasoning about the matter and actually seeing the names were two very different things.

"I'm sorry, Maestro." Graziani had done what he had come to do. He couldn't make himself stay in this tortured situation any longer. He rose abruptly from his chair.

"Where will I find you, Franco, if I need you?" the Maestro called after him, trying not to let the infinite sadness he felt for his friend come through in his voice.

Graziani did not stop in his stride to the door. "At home, Maestro, I suppose. Yes. At home."

Even a cursory study of Graziani's incomplete list of P-2 members was enough to convince Guido that he could not take it to the Central Precinct in Rome. Many regional police heads and military leaders were Pappagallo's confederates. In typical de la Valle fashion, the Maestro went to the top, to the President of the Republic, Benedetto Crasci.

Crasci, an ex-partisan fighter, a genuine lover of freedom, was a man who could be trusted. And he was a man who could be relied upon to make a fair deal.

Crasci understood immediately what was at stake. "We have suspected Pappagallo for some time," he told the Maestro. "But we were working in the dark. Now we know his intent, his base of operations, his weapons, at least some of his supporters, his general plan.

"I just wish this list were more complete. By the looks of it, a lot of the police and military people we would normally have relied on are mixed up in this—what did you call it, Maestro?"

"P-2, Signor Presidente. Problem Two."

If Crasci was asking himself whether that number implied others—a P-1 or a P-7—he didn't bring it up. "Yes. P-2. Anyway, I think we can scotch the senatore in his nest. But we'll have to go slow, be sure of our personnel while we set up this operation. It's got to be good. We've only one shot at it."

Guido spent some time discussing Graziani's case. The president was both understanding and cooperative.

"You have your deal, Maestro." Crasci offered Guido his hand as he walked him to the door of his private office. "Italy owes much to you. Graziani's name will not come up. Nor that of any of your friends who got mixed up with Lercani. Nor that of the Holy See. At the first sign of any trouble for you or your interests, call me personally."

"I hope that will not be necessary, Signor Presidente. But I thank you."

The Maestro's personal bitterness at the situation was deepened a hundredfold when Franco's wife, Giulia Graziani, called in the early morning a few days later. She was in near-hysteria. She couldn't wake Franco up, she said. She was sure he was . . . sure he was . . . She couldn't make herself say the word.

Guido calmed her over the phone as best he could. He would ask Helmut to drive in right away. Giulia wasn't to answer the phone or be at home to anyone until he arrived.

The Maestro had told his nephew about Graziani's visit and had showed him the papers. Helmut guessed what had happened, and lost no time in getting on his way.

The Maestro, meanwhile, phoned President Crasci without delay. By the time Helmut reached the Graziani apartment off the Corso, a Special Branch detail of the carabinieri was waiting for him. They took charge, while Helmut did what he could for Giulia. Doni, who had been so close to Eugenio, was away for a few days. Helmut called him. The following week, a coroner's certificate ascribed Franco Graziani's death to heart failure and other complications. There was no mention of the overdose of sleeping pills that had killed him. There would be no public scandal, no official police inquiry, no follow-up by the media. But as far as the Maestro was concerned, this was yet another poisonous flick of Lercani's scorpion tail; another assassination to be laid at the Sicilian's door.

[65]

Papa Valeska was a man in a hurry. He was like a steamroller, in command of everything, and working himself as hard as he worked any of his staff. "If you are not exhausted by the end of every day," he would often say in his rumbling voice, "then you are not doing enough!"

He received a couple of hundred diplomats and ministers of foreign affairs, who trooped to the Apostolic Palace to pay their respects and establish useful lines with the Holy Father. He planned his trips for the coming year, and the year following. For 1979 alone he had already set dates for major papal visits to Santo Domingo and Mexico in January; if all went well, Poland in June; Ireland in September; the United States in October; Turkey in November. He planned and wrote the scores of speeches he would make during those trips—all of them in the language of the people. He supervised the Secretariat as it made the necessary contacts and arrangements for each of the trips. And after the long workday was done, Richard Lansing could frequently be found with the Holy Father in his private study, formulating, revising, and refining the Pontiff's plan for the Polish experiment.

Bogdan Valeska was the fourth pope Rico Lansing had served. He was certainly the most energetic and physically vital of them all; and in some ways he seemed to Lansing the most willfully determined, as well. Yet, on reflection, each one of those popes had appeared to Lansing to have responded to some engine that drove the main force of his pontificate. For Papa Profumi, the driving force had been to maintain the Roman fact in the presence of some summary evil whose face that Pope had felt he recognized too late, looming up over the horizon of human existence. For Papa Angelica, it had been the Pentecost he had fervently and lovingly hoped would transform the Church and the whole world in its waves of light. For Papa Da Brescia, it had been the transformation of the Church and the world into a vaguely defined "people of God."

In some ways, it seemed to Lansing, Valeska was bringing things full circle. Though he had spent very little time outside Poland, his mind seemed to encompass the same broad geopolitical sweep that Papa Profumi's had. Even the Maestro had remarked to Rico on that similarity. Unlike Profumi, Valeska did not base his policies on political control of any kind; on the contrary. But like Profumi, Valeska did have a profound grasp of the nature and effect of political control. The "engine" that drove him was his intent to undo that control insofar as it separated people everywhere from religious faith and practice, and from the moral values that have their mooring lines only in that faith. The "engine" of his pontificate, in other words, as Cardinal Hoffeldt had said so accurately in the State Council meeting, was nothing less than his intention to modify the entire geopolitical system current in the world.

The heart of that "engine" was Papa Valeska's specifically Slavic perception of people—whether in Poland or in the world—as a community, or a series of groups. "The herd instinct," an anthropologist might call it. Whatever its name, inherent in that perception was the idea of the leader—and of the community focused as one on that leader as its acknowledged head. From the very beginning of Poland's history, the primate or first churchman of the land had been the embodiment of precisely that continuing, unbroken leadership and power; the embodiment of undying community; of Polishness in that sense. One of the oldest titles of the Primate of Poland, "Interrex"—literally, "between kings"—derived from the fact that when Polish kings died, all power resided in the religious primate; and when the next king received his crown, it was from the hands of that primate. The extraordinary moral force of Cardinal Wallensky's power, as both Valeska and Lansing knew, derived not only from his own faith and personality but from the continuing and undying focus of the entire Polish community on him as the Primate of Poland. As Interrex.

Rico Lansing had come to understand all that during his three decades of intimate involvement with the Polish people. And though he and Papa Valeska did not discuss it in so many words, Lansing was convinced that, in his coming world travels, the Pope's intention was literally to "create" a vast cultural and moral community in the world that would be focused on one man—the Pope—as its leader, its Interrex.

Papa Valeska therefore did not eschew the idea of "the people of God"; but for him that phrase had a different and far more concentrated meaning than it had had for Papa Da Brescia. And upon that idea rested the Holy Father's hope to create his powerful "third force" in the world.

Tied to that same view of community-and-leader was Papa Valeska's decision that for the overground organization, Solidarity, which would effect and embody the Polish model, he needed to have a national figure, a worker in many respects like his peers. Someone everyone would know was one of them, was on their side. Someone they could be certain was not a Communist stooge or a mole. Someone backed by the Pope, by the Polish primate, and by the bishops. Someone whose face the workers would come to know as the national symbol of their movement, whose voice they would recognize, whose family was like their families. Someone who would, in effect, speak the mind of Solidarity as it grew into a national movement of cultural—but not political—independence.

Valeska already had in mind the man he wanted. "Do you remember Feliks Moszak?" he asked Rico during one of their late-night working sessions.

Rico did, of course. Moszak had been one of the steadiest rocks in the "Gdansk experiment" of 1975. He had proved himself a natural leader among the shipyard workers. He had an almost instinctive understanding of the fine line between social and political action, and had from the beginning been self-sacrificing in his devotion to the Solidarity concept.

Lansing saw a number of advantages in working closely with Moszak. For one thing, the ability to do aboveground work through one single man in several areas of Poland would make it easier for Lansing himself to stay out of view. In time, as Moszak received more and more exposure and became better known outside his home city of Gdansk, it would also take a certain amount of pressure off a still vital but certainly aging Cardinal Wallensky.

Side by side with such detailed planning with Rico Lansing and others, and along with all his other tireless and energetic activity, the Pontiff set out deliberately, from almost the first moment of his election in October, to establish a direct connection with the Soviets. He wanted, if possible, to bring about some basic receptivity on their part for his policy of an independent and politically neutral Europe.

In December, his energy and hardheaded diplomacy finally prevailed. Like hundreds of other representatives of foreign governments, Andrei Gromyko paid a state visit to the new Pope. Unlike most of the others, Gromyko saw His Holiness alone. There was no need for interpreters; and what Valeska needed to do could best be done without the presence of others.

Gromyko's principal concern was for the pact that Papa Angelica had signed and Papa Da Brescia had honored. Would Papa Valeska honor it, too, the Soviet minister wanted to know; or would His Holiness attack Communism in general and Soviet Marxism in particular?

Papa Valeska clearly understood the Soviet Union's need for reassurance about security in her European backyard. He had no intention of doing anything so grossly disruptive as breaking the pact. He wanted to be friends. But not on Soviet conditions alone.

On what conditions, then? Cautiously, Gromyko pursued the line Valeska threw out to him.

Suppose, the Pontiff conjectured, that they could arrive at a position where Europe would pose no threat politically or militarily or in terms of security to the Soviet Union. Would be no threat, therefore, in terms of raw power; but would remain valuable, or become even more so, in terms of production and economics. Would that not be ideal?

It would indeed be just that, Gromyko agreed. Ideal was the word. But how were they to achieve such a thing?

The Pontiff would, he assured His Excellency, give the matter his personal attention, and would use the means they had now established to be back in contact when there was something more substantial to share.

When the Soviet foreign minister took his leave of Papa Valeska, it was with his assurance that he, in turn, would await further word of developments in the matter from His Holiness.

The Gromyko meeting led most naturally to an equally confidential meeting between Papa Valeska and the Maestro.

Compared to his peers in Western governments, the Pontiff confided to Guido, the Soviet minister was "the only horse shod on all four feet." It was a Polish proverb expressing outstanding excellence. As the Pope explained the situation to the Maestro, Gromyko was now willing at least to consider another alternative for Europe, provided it was benign from the Soviet viewpoint. It would be wise, he said, to sound out the central economist-planners of the Soviet Union, in such places as Moscow, Bucharest, Warsaw, Sofia. "I infer from your ability to channel funds into Poland all these years, Maestro, that you might be able to save me a lot of time. Have you the necessary contacts already established in some of those areas?"

"In all of them, Holy Father. My nephew and some of our longtime associates established lines to the East shortly after the war. It would be a simple matter to arrange meetings. What specifically does Your Holiness want to accomplish?"

The central thing Valeska wanted was assurance that these economist-planners would back a radical modification of labor relations in their areas that would move their stagnating economies off dead center. They should know—without giving them great detail—that the proposed change would increase production and improve the standard of living; and that, for those reasons and others besides, it would defuse political and social tension.

"If their answer is yes, Maestro, as I expect it to be, I will be calling on you to provide bigger loans to satellite countries."

The Maestro thought his *impero* associates would be delighted at the prospect, down the line when he could tell them. It would, after all, mean the possibility of direct participation on the managerial boards of major industries in that sector—something that had been only the faintest glimmer of a hope when Helmut began his first tentative moves toward the East in the latter half of the 1940s.

By the time Papa Valeska set off on the first of his trips in January of 1979, he had already set a huge dynamism in motion, centered around and dependent upon his vision and his activity.

His trip to Santo Domingo and Mexico did, as he had wanted, bring the focus of millions of confused, distressed, and hopeful people upon him as he flew out to bedazzle the world in his white plane and his white robes.

On another front, Helmut de la Valle, together with Jean-Pierre Duchesne of the *impero* and Klaus Fabian of his Geneva office, was well along with his own travels through Eastern Europe and into the Soviet Union itself as the Pope's quietest ambassador for economic reform.

On yet another front—the one that would be the linchpin upon which forward progress toward the third force would depend—Rico Lansing was spending increasing amounts of time on covert missions to Poland. His entire existence now rotated around preparation for the emergence of Valeska's Polish model.

Through combined efforts of his underground network and Cardinal Wallensky's "blue card" organization, Rico and the Polish cardinal worked tirelessly to screen from among the Polish work force of thirteen million, men and women who would expand the elite leadership for the aboveground movement.

As Valeska knew would be the case, Feliks Moszak was totally with the plan, and he quickly became a useful force in grounding the swelling ranks of the Solidarity leaders in the principles of what came to be known, in organizational shoptalk, as "the new social-activist mind."

That mind had no political coloring, no political aim. It was not for or against the Polish Politburo, or the Polish security forces, or the Polish rubber-stamp parliament—the Sejm. That mind, it was dinned into this new leadership, aimed only at independence in cultural affairs, of which labor relations was but one part.

What Wallensky, Valeska, and Lansing had done in Nova Huta and Gdansk in the mid 1970s, Wallensky, Moszak, and Lansing now fostered and prepared on a national basis. Wallensky set the tone, of course: He constantly drummed the idea of the "visible solidarity" of Poland as a tangible fact. "The historical and spiritual personality of Poland for the last seven hundred years," he said again and again, "must now appear in a visible solidarity. Solidarity is our name! *Solidarnosc!* All we want is that we as the people, the workers of Poland, develop again a solidarity among one another based on our rich heritage, our poetry, our painting, our dance, our sculpture, our history, our charitable activities."

The "flying universities" that Wallensky had established long before became again an effective vehicle for the expression and clarification of this new mind.

As 1979 progressed, workers of all classes and kinds in this "workers' paradise" began to form their own councils. In factories and shipyards, on construction sites and in municipal offices, the traditional Communist cells, which had been accustomed to control and run everything, found they had unexpected competition in Solidarity. But any attempts to scotch the new movement at birth were too narrow, and missed the point by too far.

By June of 1979, when Papa Valeska's first visit as Pope to Poland focused the eyes of the world on that country in a new way, Solidarity was a fact. Not only were its organizers and large numbers of workers in every Polish city aware of it. The Polish Politburo and the Moscow Politburo were aware of it, as well.

Richard Lansing's only misgivings were brought to the fore again, oddly enough, as a direct consequence of Papa Valeska's eight-day stay in his native country.

As was to be expected, members of the Trotskyite KOR organization had been attracted along with everyone else to the public call of Solidarity. Inevitably, some of them began to rise into positions of influence in various workers' councils; their ideas and their energy began to be felt, and a few of them—some dozen or so—were admitted to posts of responsibility.

Despite heated discussions with Cardinal Wallensky, and with Rico Lansing too—although he stayed even farther in the background than usual to avoid notice during the papal stay—Papa Valeska publicly embraced the KOR members, just as he had as Cardinal of Krakow. He specifically approved of such appointments as Jaček Kuron's to the key post in charge of Solidarity in Gdansk; and of half a dozen more members of KOR to other key posts.

Rico's greatest fear, and one he expressed openly and frequently to the Pontiff, was that instead of being identified with the nonpolitical Interrex power of the Pope and of Cardinal Wallensky, Solidarity would come to be identified in everybody's eyes—the public's and the government's—with the more fanatical elements of KOR.

Almost equal to that fear was his apprehension that sooner or later KOR would play the tune paid for so readily by capitalist interests in the West. If Monsignore Brandolini's theory was correct—and Rico couldn't remember the last time he had been wrong—the danger lay in the possibility that KOR might push Solidarity beyond any limits acceptable to the Soviet Union.

Papa Valeska, however, never doubted the judgment he had expressed to the Security Two meeting in October of 1978. KOR, like Solidarity, was made up of individual Poles. He was certain they would not betray Solidarity. That certainty seemed as much a part of papal policy as the Polish model itself. There was no way to change it.

When Rico Lansing followed Papa Valeska back to Rome toward the end of June, he carried with him fresh information from Karlis Pelse in Riga. In one way, Rico was relieved when the envelope was brought to him by underground courier. Pelse hadn't been heard from since he had tried to warn Rome of the plot on Papa Serena's life, and his silence had led Rico to worry for Pelse's safety. The arrival of new intelligence from Riga lifted one concern, at least, from Rico's mind.

Pelse's long memorandum, however, brought its own worries with it. Apparently the Pope's recent visit to Mexico had made no difference at all to the revolutionary activities of Father Jaime Herreras. Pelse had learned of a strategic meeting of nine Sandinista leaders—the heads of guerrilla forces in Colombia, Guatemala, El Salvador, and Mexico. Herreras had been one of four priests, two of them Jesuits, who had been at that meeting. The bare bones of Pelse's information about the meeting were summarized in three main points.

First, the central decisions concerned the opening provided by the deaths of the Nicaraguan dictator Somoza and the Archbishop of Managua. Specifically, determinations were made about the purchase of more arms from Havana; the use of training camps in Mexico to build the mechanized guerrilla army in Nicaragua up to a strength of 200,000 men; and the subversion of El Salvador and Guatemala.

Second, Herreras apparently had at least tacit agreement with officials in Mexico that led him to describe that country confidently, in Pelse's words, as an "acquiescent party that will defend revolution in any Central American country." Judging from the first point, "acquiescence" meant going even as far as allowing Mexican territory to be used for the training, and perhaps even the basing, of guerrilla troops.

Third, a special fund called the Green Fund had been established by North American clergy to purchase arms in the United States, and to mount a propaganda drive among North American Catholics, in opposition to any U.S. intervention in Central America.

Pelse drew no conclusions from the information he sent. His job was to report, not to interpret. It seemed clear enough to Rico, however, that in the foreseeable future—perhaps within the next two years—there would be a major push to Marxize several Central American states, with the connivance of Catholic clergy, and therefore with the connivance of the Church.

Before going to see Papa Valeska at Castel Gandolfo, where he was spending the summer, Rico discussed the Pelse memorandum with the members of Security Two. While Brandolini, Solaccio, Cardinal Falconieri, and Helmut were all deeply concerned at the progress Herreras and his people were making in Latin America, it was the Maestro who reacted with a vehemence that was almost surprising. In his view, Jaime Herreras was embezzling the Church's clergy just as surely as Paolo Lercani had embezzled the Church's money. But the results, Guido argued, would be far worse and last far longer, unless Papa Valeska could get Herreras and the others under control. Instead of merely lying about financial connections and money profits, as Lercani had done, the Jesuit priest was, as the Maestro put it, "subverting fundamental Church dogma with his siren song of Liberation Theology."

That same afternoon, when Rico showed the Pelse memo to Papa Valeska, the Pontiff was genuinely surprised at the unabated efforts of Herreras and the other priests in these latest revolutionary plans. He thought he had made some impact in that situation during the five days he had spent in Mexico barely six months before.

Characteristically, however, Valeska was neither discouraged nor pessimistic. For one thing, as he pointed out to Rico, he had already scheduled another trip to Latin America—to Brazil, this time. And for another, as far as he knew, Rome had never spoken out, officially or otherwise, on the subject of Liberation Theology. The Pontiff would ask Cardinal Arnulfo as the leading Vatican expert on purity of doctrine to make a detailed study of it, and to report personally to him with his suggestions. At the very least, he would then take it up with the Latin American clergy, face to face, in 1980.

As to the matter of the Green Fund and the North American clergy, he would be able to deal with that much sooner. His trip to the United States was less than four months away.

Normally it takes a new pope some two years to consolidate his papacy and to put his stamp on the Vatican hierarchy. Not so with Papa Valeska. His personality was so dazzling, and his behavior was such a departure from normal papal standards, that all else fell into chiaroscuro. What pope had ever jogged and swum every day for exercise? Which of them had ever walked every place he went in the Vatican—and at such a fast pace that his cardinals and bishops were hard put to keep up with him? His constant activity was almost mezmerizing. He went through his schedule of visiting diplomats like a scythe through hay. He saw hordes of people, from heads of states in the reception salons of the Apostolic Palace, to groups of seminary students in the papal chapel of his private apartments. He addressed everybody using "I" instead of the papal "We." He refused to wear the papal tiara or use the *sedia gestatoria* even on the most ceremonial occasions. He did not want committee meetings or the reports they generated, but insisted on one-to-one communication.

At the same time, he allowed no one to tread on the toes of his consciousness of himself as Pope.

Quickly enough, however, it became clear to the experienced hands in the Vatican that Papa Valeska's attention and activity were almost entirely outwardly directed. He was focused on Poland, and on his plethora of ongoing and planned excursions into the world outside Rome. In his speech from St. Peter's balcony to the jubilant crowds in the piazza on the day of his election, Valeska had described himself as a man from a far country. The majority in the Vatican felt that those were the truest words he had ever said. They were content to have him troop about the world with his Polish landsmen gathered at his side; for that meant, among other things, that the Vatican was largely free to go its own way.

Cardinal Secretary of State Casaregna, for example, found that as long as he did the needful in such areas as the planning and official preparations for the Pontiff's trips abroad, he could in most other matters run the Secretariat as his own empire. Other heads of congregations and secretariats found the same to be true. As long as they confined their activities to their own official spheres and did not interfere with Valeska's plans as Pope, they were on sure, safe ground. They were happy enough, in such circumstances, to remain in the shadows behind the brilliance of Bogdan Valeska.

Against this background, by the end of 1979, despite some disappointments and failures, Papa Valeska's major policies were making headway. Among his disappointments were certain aspects of his trip to the United States. The concept of liberty and religious pluralism within political unity was something so completely out of his ken—something so contrary to his own experience and his concept of community-and-leader—that he was, in the view of some in the papal entourage, simply bamboozled by the American bishops. When, for example, in private meetings with members of the National Council of Catholic Bishops, Papa Valeska not only brought up the question of Father Jaime Herreras and the Green Fund but ordered his bishops to call a halt to the fund and all related activities, the bishops explained, with expressions of studied pain, all the reasons why they "had no control over the matters." The Green Fund was, they said, something dreamed up by the United States Catholic Conference, which was not made up of bishops, and over which the bishops therefore exercised no power.

For Valeska, that was no answer at all. The Catholic Conference was made up of clergy. The clergy was answerable in obedience to its bishops. And neither bishops nor clergy had the mandate or the right to move into such blatantly political areas—or to drag the rest of the Church with them by implication.

The Holy Father restated his wish. "Yes, Holy Father," the bishops acknowledged his restatement. The Holy Father assumed they would obey him. The bishops assumed the Holy Father would do no more to bring them into line than Papa Da Brescia had done.

In the inelegant but accurate words of Cardinal O'Mahoney, "In the match-up between the Pope and the religious arm of the political left, the Pope got no cigar."

Still and all, there was no denying that the successes Papa Valeska did achieve, and the relatively brief time it took for him to do so, were nearly miraculous. As 1979 drew to a close, Helmut de la Valle had finished all of his consultations with the Soviet economist-planners in Moscow and the West European capitals. Official but publicly unacknowledged Soviet blessing would be given to Papa Valeska's initiative in the satellite countries to renew the interest of the workers, and therefore increase their productivity. The central planners agreed that to achieve that aim—which was primary in their eyes—would also be to improve the standard of living, and defuse political and social tensions.

Armed with that vital information, Papa Valeska put in motion a historic train of activity. He immediately kept his promise to be back in touch with the Soviet foreign minister, Andrei Gromyko. As a result, a draft agreement was prepared in Moscow, amended on both sides, and finally consigned to paper in its final form. In February of 1980, a Soviet delegation led by the ambassador in Rome, Anatoly Adamshin, was received amid the greatest precautionary secrecy in the Apostolic Palace. Papa Valeska's only companion was Guido de la Valle. Valeska initialed the agreement for the Holy See. Adamshin did the same for the Soviet Politburo.

At the end of that brief meeting, Papa Valeska had Soviet sanction at the highest level to proceed with his Polish model. If all went well in the succeeding months, his intention and Gromyko's was that the Pope would make another visit to Poland; but this time he would travel on from Warsaw to Moscow. Success in Poland would open the doors of reality to the rest of Papa Valeska's dream. It would place him in a position to negotiate an overall agreement, based on the Polish Model, for the other satellite countries and for the Soviet Union itself. That in turn would provide the possibility for the catacomb church to emerge over time into the light of day. And it would give the Pontiff standing in the eyes of the political West that would put him in a renewed position of strength with them. Perhaps the most important result of all that would be a huge welling up of hope in the world that would, at long last, penetrate the miasma of fear of a nuclear war that had come of late to grip Europe.

That was the dream. That was the plan. And the center of it all was this Pope who had come from a far land.

[66]

At the onset of spring 1980, if the majority of officials in the Vatican were content to run their little fiefdoms of power and privilege while Papa Valeska was pursuing the multiple avenues of his overall policy, the cardinals of the State Council did their best to develop an explicit picture of the Church, the papacy, and the Holy See.

Cardinal Arnulfo and the other Council members were aware, of course, of the Holy Father's breakthrough with the Soviets in respect of the Polish model. But they were aware, too, of Bishop Lansing's serious concern, due primarily to the presence of KOR, and the possibility that its rude extreme elements could upset the very delicate balance upon which the success of the Polish model depended.

In addition, Cardinal Arnulfo felt that his own concerns, which he had voiced to Papa Valeska in his meeting with the Council in October of 1978, had to be taken dead seriously now. The Holy Father had told the Council plainly that the first element of his strategy, to be effected through his papal travels abroad, was to reestablish the presence and authority of the Pope.

"But that simply has not happened, Your Eminences." The cardinal reemphasized his views for the March Council meeting. In ways, Cardinal Arnulfo was showing the telltale signs of his advancing age. But he was far from crippled and bedridden with the racking pains of rheumatoid arthritis, as Ferragamo-Duca now was. Arnulfo still carried as full a workload as the best of them; both his spirit and his judgment were very much to the good, and highly valued.

"I know," Arnulfo went on, "that we all agreed with His Holiness that he needed a period of preparation at the beginning of his pontificate. But in Poland he has at best prepared a huge and precarious gamble on which too much else depends. And meanwhile his trips have not improved the condition of the bishops or of the Church one whit."

Cardinal Hoffeldt wondered if it was not too soon to make such a harsh judgment. "After all, Your Eminence, His Holiness has now made five formal visits—to Latin America, Poland, Ireland, the United States, and

Turkey. This year he will go to six countries in Africa. He will go to Paris, West Germany, and UNESCO in Europe. And he will go back to Latin America—to Brazil. So far, his trips have been a huge success. There is no other internationally known and publicly acclaimed personage who is as brilliantly exposed and as universally accepted as Papa Valeska. His name is already synonymous with the most cherished wishes of the commonality of men. With human rights and human dignity. And against the unworthy horrors of mass starvation, the arms race, environmental pollution, human slavery, profiteering, the narcotics trade.

"No one has any doubt, either, where Papa Valeska stands in relation to such moral questions as abortion, marriage, sexuality, homosexuality, capital punishment, and religious obligations."

Cardinal Arnulfo was not deterred by such a noble catalogue. That was all very fine, as far as it went. The trouble was, it seemed not to go far enough to make any practical impact. "What concerns this State Council," he insisted, "comes under two headings.

"There is, first of all, the continuing downward descent of all the vital Church statistics. The number of priests, nuns, monks, converts, students, convents, monasteries, marriages within the Church—all keep diminishing. And so do the numbers of people attending Sunday Mass, the numbers baptized, the numbers availing themselves of the Sacrament of Confession. Nothing has arrested this downward plunge. In fact, it is no longer measured on a sloping graph. It is a plumb line, straight down.

"There is, secondly, the increasing isolation of the Holy Father. That is harder to see, perhaps, amid all the publicity and razzle-dazzle that surround him. But we *must* see it!

"It is true enough that Cardinal Secretary of State Casaregna is at least obedient. That's an improvement over Levesque. But it has to be said that Rome no longer rules throughout the Church Universal. Neither in matters of faith, nor in morals.

"Inside this Vatican, there are still scores of holdover personnel from the reign of Papa Da Brescia, who still try to block any attempt at reform. Out in the world, the bishops still have the bit between their teeth. They brook no governance by Pope or Curia. They are full of empty verbal respect; but they are equally full of deliberate disobedience to the Pope.

"For all the public-relations success of the Holy Father's trip to Mexico, nothing has changed Father Herreras and the other revolutionaries. And for all the media coverage in the United States, many dioceses there are still saying Masses that, to a moral certainty, are invalid. In Seattle and Cincinnati, to take just two dioceses as examples, the bishops have done nothing to correct the use of invalid altar breads. And it is also to be doubted that many priestly ordinations and consecrations are valid, because neither the new priests being ordained nor the bishops ordaining them seem to have the proper intention necessary for valid ordination.

"But it's not only in the United States that these conditions prevail. In the teaching at seminaries and universities, in diocesan magazines and newspapers, in instructions and sermons everywhere, heresy and schismatic doctrines are the general rule, not the exception. There is a deliberate diminishment of devotion to the Virgin and her Rosary, to the Sacred Heart of Jesus, to the saints and the holy souls in purgatory. Catechisms in Holland, France, the U.S.A., and Ireland, to name only the most blatant, are sometimes heretical, sometimes even blasphemous, and at all times deficient.

"In other words, the picture we are facing is the dying condition of Catholicism as we have known it. For all his activity, Papa Valeska is tolerating open heresy and schism in bishops and priests. And wherever he goes on his travels, he never announces himself as the Vicar of Christ; but merely as another bishop. So no wonder they feel they can disobey him with impunity."

The cardinals knew Arnulfo was accurate as far as his current summary of the conditions in the Church was concerned. And though the discussion that morning was lively—perhaps heated would have been a better description—the majority could not yet justify taking a Cassandra position.

"After all," Cardinal Corelli put the case, "what this Pope is attempting is so new that there is no way to calculate yet the effects his policies might have. Objectively speaking, he has already got the Soviet Union talking to us, not just on their terms but on Valeska's as well. No Pope has ever accomplished that before.

"If he is successful in his policies in Poland, it is indeed possible that he will have such prestige and such standing that he will be able to make broad changes within the Church just as quickly."

"In any case"—Cardinal Falconieri added a cautionary note—"we have been through too many years of alienation between the papacy and the Curia. There is no question of acting against the Pontiff's policies, and no reason to do so. From the point of view of faith and theology, he could not be better. We must give him our advice. And we must give him time. And I think we must also give him his due. It has been a very long time since any pope has stood before the world with such prestige—and the main thrust of his policies has not yet even taken hold.

"The activization of the Polish model will not get into full swing until this summer. Monsignor Lansing has only just returned to Warsaw. By the end of the year, we will know if Papa Valeska's 'precarious gamble' has paid off."

Aside from some routine business, there was little more on the Council agenda for that day. Cardinal O'Mahoney was taking a somewhat more focused interest in Liberation Theology since Papa Valeska had spoken to the bishops in the United States about the Green Fund and how it was to be used. He caught up with Cardinal Arnulfo on the way out of the meeting to ask if he had given his assessment of Liberation Theology to the Holy Father.

Arnulfo gave a sideways glance to the American. "I gave His Holiness a short report on the subject, Your Eminence. I will give you the same one now, and I hope you will give it to anyone who asks. Liberation Theology should be condemned outright, *sans plus,* for exactly what it is: political modernism."

"Is that what the Holy Father is going to take to Brazil with him, Your Eminence?"

"If he is wise, Kieran, he will do just that. A pope who can face down commissars should be able to face down our own bishops. At least, that must be our hope and our prayer."

By June, Cardinal Wallensky and Rico Lansing did indeed have Solidarity in full swing. Their organizers made successful bids to form labor unions, shopkeeper unions, government employee unions. Communist labor councils that were outvoted in favor of Solidarity sometimes complained to local commissars, or to the commissars in Warsaw; but the answer they got was not the one they expected. "You've been outvoted," the reply came back in essence; "don't complain to us."

In some areas there were bloody clashes, to be sure. But nothing seemed to stop the new mass movement. "Without us, the workers," ran the Solidarity challenge, "this country simply closes shop! So move over. We're going to run our own lives." To that challenge the local Communist cells had no effective reply without the backing of Warsaw Central.

Papa Valeska had arranged his trips abroad so that during the expected peak of the Solidarity push, he would be in Rome. From mid-July to mid-November, he monitored the situation very closely from Castel Gandolfo and the Apostolic Palace.

As early as the end of July, despite seesaw battles in some areas with the intransigent Communist leaders and cadres, the success of Solidarity was already stunning; it spread like a wave through Krakow and Warsaw, Poznan and Gdansk. It was so stunning, in fact, that the Western press began calling it "the Polish miracle." For the first time, Rico Lansing allowed himself to believe that they might really break all the way through, actually achieve the Polish model by the end of the year.

It was around August that a curious note began to be sounded—not from inside Poland but in the Western press. Stories began to appear pointing out that three Soviet divisions were poised outside Warsaw. What most of the stories failed to mention was the widely known fact that those divisions were permanently stationed there, and had nothing to do with Solidarity or the changes taking place in Poland.

Before long, the stories began to scale upward in volume, speculating ominously that the Soviets could not allow what was happening in Poland to go very far. Quickly, the press began to answer its own speculations with its own solution. "The Soviets will invade," the headlines began to scream. "It will be another Hungary! . . . Another Czechoslovakia!"

Some elements of the Western press were as openly puzzled as Papa Valeska by this sudden, negative blast of editorial speculation that seemed willfully to be seeding disaster. In one of the major West German newspapers, a political cartoon appeared showing a hapless and bewildered Soviet premier asking his top military leaders if he was supposed to be invading Poland. Some editors spoke privately of "the political pornography of death in the yellow-sheet treatment of Poland." But nothing stopped the rising wave of negative editorializing. It reached a ludicrous crescendo with the fanciful but alarming report that Papa Valeska himself had warned the Soviets that he would personally lead the defense of his country against any armed invasion. Even outright denial of the story could not deter its spreading from paper to paper and over the international wire services.

At about the same time as these negative, doomsaying stories first began, Western intelligence officers inside and outside Poland suddenly became infected with a similar bug. They disseminated "intelligence" that bore a remarkable resemblance to the press reports. An air force attaché might confide to his Polish counterpart that the Soviets were going to invade Poland. A Western station chief of intelligence in Geneva would seek out his Polish colleague and warn him to get his wife and child out of Poland "while there was time."

One effect of this unremitting blast of publicity in the West and intelligence rumor-mongering within Poland was to convince Rico Lansing that there was a concerted effort about to scupper the whole Polish experiment, and just as Giulio Brandolini had warned, that effort was centered in the West. Still, in this situation, the closed nature of Polish society under Soviet rule worked to some degree in Solidarity's favor. The shock waves that came through were dampened by the constant activity of Feliks Moszak and an unending number of addresses and sermons made by Cardinal Wallensky to the workers of Poland.

What concerned Rico much more was the possibility that the anti-Solidarity campaign—for there was no doubt in his mind that it was precisely that—might create distrust and enmity between the Soviet leaders in Moscow and Papa Valeska. He said as much several times in his constant communication with the Holy Father; but Valeska answered Lansing that he was in close communication with the Soviets, and that there was to be no change in the Polish plan.

Around September, as if on some signal, a new element intruded into the volatile situation. This time it was specifically Polish, and it was exactly what Lansing had feared. Jaček Kuron and other extremist KOR leaders who had penetrated into the top echelons of certain Solidarity labor councils began making political demands of the Polish Politburo. They made speeches boldly in favor of political representation for the workers in the Sejm. They published tracts calling for the disbanding of the Zomos and for changes in the power of the security forces. That new element clearly placed the movement beyond the line drawn in the Valeska-Gromyko agreement; but it was like a spark in dry tinder. It affected not only large numbers of rank-and-file workers, but even some of the seventy-eight Polish bishops, who had suffered so much for so long.

A period of special agony began then for Cardinal Wallensky and Rico Lansing. Despite their stunning success up to that point, they feared that

KOR would force the hand of the Soviets too far—that it was, in fact, their intention to do just that. They would leave the Soviets no alternative but to invade.

Wallensky argued with Papa Valeska to put a cap on all Solidarity efforts for the foreseeable future. The whole situation was becoming overheated. And they needed time to weed the KOR elements out of the movement and to repair the damage done to their education efforts to develop the new mind in the workers.

"We have transcended a hundred years in a matter of months," Wallensky pleaded with the Holy Father. "Better to wait for a short while longer, than to lose everything we have gained."

Valeska's response was brief and determined. "We take our chances," he said. "KOR has violated our agreement with the Soviets. But they cannot invade. They cannot afford that."

Still Wallensky argued. "Neither can they afford to let Poland go, Holy Father. If they invade, I grant you that Poland will be a heavy economic burden around their neck; but that would be the lesser of two evils, from their point of view. It's finished for now. Better to regroup."

"We take our chances," Valeska insisted.

Despite desperate efforts to contain the fire and get Solidarity back on the nonpolitical track that the Soviets had agreed to, the situation steadily deteriorated. In mid-October, Rico called Papa Valeska yet one more time, and put the situation to him in unequivocal terms. It was disaster, he said. If things progressed any further, there would be no way the Soviets could let it go. The Holy Father must get in touch with his contacts in the Polish and Soviet governments, and work out terms by which the situation could be put on hold. It was either that, or see it destroyed by year's end. "We have been the victims of sheer malice, Holy Father," Rico said toward the end of that conversation. "But we have not lost—unless Your Holiness refuses to bend."

Valeska agreed at last to do as Lansing and Wallensky insisted. He sent a message first to Foreign Minister Gromyko. There was no answer, however; that was a clearly ominous sign, and perhaps did more than anything else to convince the Pontiff that the Soviets had already been pushed too far.

Immediately, he was in touch with the higher government echelons in Warsaw. He found their mind to be as one with Wallensky's and Rico's in the matter of the Soviet Union. Unless Valeska could stop KOR, and get his bishops and the rank and file of Solidarity to sink back into a more complaisant and totally nonpolitical stance, then the only alternatives were invasion by the Soviets or martial law imposed from within Poland itself.

Valeska knew he could not tame the Solidarity situation quickly. And he knew that, while he and Polish General Jaruzelski stood on opposite sides of many fences, in one thing they were brothers. They were both Poles.

Jaruzelski's summary of the situation was stark and objective. "For the third time in the same century, Your Holiness, Poland herself is at stake. Unless we want to become another Soviet Ukraine, then the only alternative from your point of view as well as from ours is martial law."

By early November, Valeska and Jaruzelski had negotiated terms. If the situation could not be brought under control by the end of November, Poland would be put under military rule. Solidarity would not be suppressed, but some of its leaders, as well as many of the KOR people, would be imprisoned.

By the second week in November, Warsaw had communicated the negotiated solution to Moscow, and had received a one-word reply: *"Da."* No doubt, the Soviets were relieved to have the situation brought under control.

Cardinal Wallensky prepared his soul for his defeat, and prepared his bishops to accept the coming military clampdown on all civil life in Poland with greater obedience than they had been able to exercise in accepting their first taste of relative freedom.

Rico meanwhile carried out the necessary work of separating his covert cell organization from all overground connections. He sent a few of the Solidarity leaders underground, but he could not do much about protecting them all, without risking almost certain destruction of his entire underground system.

There was not a great deal to do beyond that, except to wait. When Papa Valeska set off on his much-publicized trip to West Germany on November 15, it was not, as he had so fervently hoped, to carry forward some part of his plan for the third force in Europe based on the successfully emergent Polish model. Rather, it was with the sad knowledge that though a remnant of Solidarity would remain, its back was broken. For now at least, he could do nothing either to help his beloved homeland or to move the Germans out of the mold of fearful dealings with the Soviet superpower.

On December 12, General Jaruzelski went on national television. Martial law was declared. The Polish experiment was dead.

Of necessity, Rico Lansing left Warsaw a day or two before the military clampdown. He had spent so much time in Poland over the past twenty-four months that he felt out of place in Rome at first.

One change that affected him immediately was the absence of the little *portiere,* Amadeo Solimando, who had been at the entrance to the Secretariat to greet Rico every day since that U.S. Army jeep had deposited him, bag and baggage, on the deserted piazza in April of 1945.

Amadeo's son Dimo, who was in every way a tintype of his father, swept his beret from his head, just as Amadeo had always done.

"My father went home to God this past summer, Monsignore."

Rico spent a few minutes with Dimo. As long as there was a Holy See, and as long as there was a Solimando family, the eldest son in every generation would succeed his father. It was the Holy See's way of repairing a grave injustice done to that family by a pope four centuries before. But succession was not everything. Rico would miss Amadeo, and he wanted Dimo to know that.

Lansing phoned Papa Valeska from his Apostolate office and spent a quarter of an hour filling him in on last-minute information. The Holy Father asked him to come by early the following week. His Holiness knew all the relevant things about the present situation. It was the future he wanted to discuss. "Take a day or two to get your bearings again and a little rest. We will have dinner Monday or Tuesday. Arrange it with Terebelski."

Rico promised he would. He spent a day at home, catching up on piles of mail, and getting a rundown on all the Vatican news from Vittorio Benfatti. He passed most of one day with Giulio Brandolini and Gian Solaccio on security matters touching on the underground organizations in Eastern Europe. Everything would have to remain dormant now for several months. But the covert operations would be maintained and strengthened.

Brandolini brought up as well the recent changes in the State Council. Benfatti had told Rico that Cardinal Ferragamo-Duca had died. And he had heard even in Warsaw of the death of the fiery Cardinal Arnulfo. Ferragamo-Duca's replacement on the Council by Cardinal Borgo-Mancini would make little difference, in Brandolini's estimation. The two men had been cut from the same cloth.

"But Arnulfo." He shook his head. "That is another story. The Holy Father has named Cardinal Rollinger to replace him as head of the Congregation for the Doctrine of the Faith; and the State Council has asked him to take Arnulfo's chair there. He's a good enough man. Sound in doctrine and all that. But he hasn't the same fire Arnulfo had. The very face of Rome is changing."

Such a eulogy from the hard-nosed Monsignore Brandolini was high praise indeed. By contrast, he was positively curt in his answers to Rico's questions about the onetime cardinal secretary Jean Levesque, and about Monsignore Demarchelier. It seemed odd that both of them had died within less than a year of leaving Rome for their new posts in France, Levesque of a sudden pulmonary ailment and Demarchelier in an automobile accident.

"We saw no point in looking into those matters." Brandolini waved the subject aside. "Or into the deaths of the three French canons who died around the same time. Those dossiers are all closed, as far as Security Two is concerned."

Aside from the day-to-day affairs he had to deal with, Lansing was interested in testing the mood of Rome after the failure of the Polish experiment. He himself felt a bit as though he had been sold down the river, after having warned for so long of the danger from KOR. Still, his covert operation was intact. He would go back into Poland when things quieted down again, and begin to assess the long-term picture.

The Maestro and Helmut largely shared Rico's view of the situation. Guido in particular was quite philosophical about it. The loss of one battle did not mean the war was over. One of the more interesting things for the Maestro in the Polish crisis was Lansing himself. He saw again how strong the American had become. His assessment of the dangers had been dead accurate; his judgment had been sound. Nevertheless, now that all was clear in his hindsight, he did not blame anyone, and certainly not Papa Valeska, for not having listened to him. Those thoughts, however, the Maestro kept to himself.

He remarked to Rico that Papa Valeska seemed to be facing into the situation well enough. Guido was more concerned at the mood of the State Council, which was now dubious about the ultimate value of Valeska's papacy. "They now feel he was wrong," Guido told Lansing, "to put all his energies into Poland instead of into direct reform of the Church. They intend to try to persuade him to stay at home and take care of his own house."

Rico understood the Council's reaction. "But I doubt Papa Valeska will do what they ask, Maestro. I doubt he will stay at home, even now. I haven't seen him yet since I've been back; but I know him. He'll find some way to launch his worldwide effort, with or without the Polish model. I'll be able to tell more about his plans and feelings after I see him next week. But I don't get any sense that the Holy Father sees himself as beaten."

"Well." Wren Reading tapped his ball neatly into the cup of the eighteenth hole. "At least, the experiment has been halted. But these Poles are like rabbits. They just go back underground and burrow away until they can pop up again to make more trouble."

Reading handed his putter to the caddy and walked with his four companions toward the veranda of the Lotos Club overlooking Big Sur, California. A very mild breeze ruffled the tall palms that lined the garden, as though nature itself had joined this exclusive club, and had agreed to abide by its 122-year-old tradition of decorum. All Lotos members were of a certain high financial status, a certain culture and class. And no one who might even remotely be expected to disturb the "Lotos tranquillity" was ever admitted.

Wren Reading and his little group were all honored members and officials of Lotos. They were, as well, very close friends who went back a long way. The three Americans, including Reading, had been in the navy and then on Wall Street together. The Englishman was an aristocrat whose title went back to the days of William the Conqueror. The spare, tall Frenchman came from a distinguished Gallic line, and like the other four, had served his country brilliantly and continually, and still remained part and parcel of a certain level of the West's "intelligence community."

The five men took possession of a table on the enclosed veranda. They nodded to groups at other tables—every Lotos member knew all of the other members personally—and ordered drinks. On any given day, enough business was transacted on the links and in the quiet rooms of the club to finance a good-size government or two. But Reading and his group had come here to transact business of another sort.

They were meeting today as members of an international, capital-based group of power brokers who had made great strides in recent years toward the creation of a new global economic order, a financial hegemony encompassing production, profits, and above all political control on an all-inclusive, international basis. They were, in effect, part and parcel of Monsignore Giulio Brandolini's theoretical P-1 group—the people without whom the contradictory activities of P-2 made no logical sense to the Vatican intelligence chief.

The subject of their relaxed, day-long discussions was Papa Bogdan Valeska. For, unwittingly or not, the troublesome Pontiff was threatening to unsettle the balance of power in the Bargain that had, until recent months, been going very nicely in favor of the Universal Assembly.

"Can you imagine what would have happened"—the Englishman gave a mock shudder—"if his Polish experiment had succeeded? Remember, when this Polish Pope speaks of Christian socialism, he means real socialism. Not the nonsense you have in Sweden or Britain or Denmark. But the real thing, with improved standard of living, and no profiteering. If he had succeeded, in Poland, the thing would have spread to the Eastern satellites, and probably to the hoped-for satellites in Latin America. And *poof!"* He swatted at the air as though at a mosquito. "There would have gone our low-cost labor pools. And all those lovely profits!"

"It would have been worse than that, my friend." Wren Reading sipped his martini appreciatively. "And it still isn't over, as far as I can see. Valeska threatens to reinstate papal influence over politics everywhere. He threatens profits and industrialization and our whole system of management with his childish ideas of justice. He's pushing harder than anyone expected of Rome, and he's going straight to the heart of the matter, trying to erect the struts of religion to buttress civilization of the old order. If we don't watch out, we will have Roman superstition springing up everywhere again, like weeds through cement."

"What I can't make out," the youngest of the Americans said, "is why the Soviets let him get so far in Poland. And why were we the ones who had to stop him?"

"There was a deal." The Frenchman was the one to answer. "And as I understand it, Wren, the other side in the Bargain set it up. The younger de la Valle was all over East Europe in late 1978, talking to the Soviet economic committees." That was meant to be a complaint, but Reading ignored it for now.

"The thing is," the senior American said, "that we didn't really stop him. I'd have been more hopeful if the Soviets had gone in, as we had intended. That would have had some usefulness for us. It would have weakened the Soviets and made them easier targets for us. It would have made a public example of Poland for the rest of the world. And it would have locked up the production area more securely for us. But as it is, that fool in Rome made another deal—with Jaruzelski this time."

There was a lull in the gentle buzz of conversation at the table, until the third American commented that the solution Reading had proposed out on the links didn't answer all the problems.

"Lopping off his head, just like that, won't be much good. They'll just put someone else in his place to carry on."

"We've thought of that." Reading answered the objection. "The purpose is to do more than just remove the excrescence. The purpose is to demoralize. To send a message, in other words. A public example is needed. A very public dirtying of those pretty white robes with a very bloody red."

"Hit them hard where it hurts." The second American nodded his agreement. "They're superstitious as hell, you know. Even the intellectuals among them."

"So"—the Frenchman looked around at his companions—"if we have consensus, and the matter is left in our hands . . . ?" He glanced at Reading again.

"It is," Reading answered the implied question. "I have spoken with our associates."

"Well, then, how do we proceed?"

There was nothing hurried in the conversation. At a certain point, the men interrupted themselves to go to their rooms, shower, and dress for dinner. They continued their talk into the night, as they might have discussed any other transaction—clinically and meticulously.

It went almost without saying that, as in all terrorist assassinations and other destabilization work, suspicion had to be directed well away from the planners. In this instance, the Soviet Union was the most obvious scapegoat. The Soviets had been so heavy-handed in the Serena affair that they would be easily blamed now. The press would doubtless be useful again in that regard.

On that basis, it was decided to work through contacts in Bulgaria. The southern regions of that country had been a veritable smugglers' cove of illegal activity for centuries; it still flourished from the movement of goods and "services" from east to west and back again. There would be no problem about international travel. And since Soviet Premier Brezhnev had made use of Bulgaria himself in past years, he would be easily connected in knowledgeable minds to any plot launched from there against the Pope.

The Frenchman favored the use of a hit man, to be recruited by the Bulgarians, from the Gray Wolves of Turkey. "After all," he reminded his friends, "they issued threats against the Pope when he visited Turkey in late 1979. We will be as assured of their dedication in the matter as we have been of that Jesuit Herreras' dedication in Latin America, and KOR in Poland. And we will be another step removed from any connection. Like Herreras, he can't even know we exist."

The only issue that remained to be discussed was how best to make a public example of this assassination.

Again, it was the Frenchman who had the solution. He had learned from his friend the apostolic delegate in Teheran, one Monsignore Annibale Sugnini, that the Pope planned to make a public announcement of some importance a little less than five months from that very day. "On May thirteenth," he said. "Something to do with all that Fatima nonsense, my friend tells me. The point is that he will draw a big crowd, so our operation will certainly be a public event. And he plans to go down into the square before he makes his speech; so he will be accessible without a lot of elaborate planning."

"And," Reading agreed, "that gives us plenty of time."

There was just one more topic, touched on lightly in the earlier conversation out on the veranda, that needed attention. "Presumably," the Englishman ventured, "if everyone falls into line after the event, there will be no change in the Bargain."

"If." The senior American emphasized the word dryly. "And if not, then we will let all the sludge out of the sewer. One way or another, they will have to go along with the universal policy."

The waiter came around to see if the gentlemen cared for another drink before the bar closed for the night.

"I could use one," the American seated next to Reading said. "I have a helluva day tomorrow."

Reading motioned the waiter for a refill all around. "Oh?" He looked at his friend. "Big business afoot?"

"I wish it were that." The other man flashed a handsome smile. "I promised to take my wife Christmas shopping."

Everyone laughed sympathetically. Most of them faced the same prospect.

[67]

As Easter of 1981 approached, Guido de la Valle looked forward to spring with more hope than he had felt in years. May beckoned with true signs of promise and new beginnings.

Papa Valeska had come through the tragedy and disappointment of Poland in better spirits than the Maestro had thought possible. This was no Italianate traditionalist, no compromise pope elected as the best of two alternative ills, no curial creature or weakling theorist. This was a Pole of the Poles: theologian, philosopher, mystic, robustly healthy; a man with whom other men had to measure not merely their brains and their charm, but the width of their shoulders and the length of their stride. The teeth of this Pope's strategy had only been sharpened by the long knives of the Polish military takeover.

Not long after the Pontiff returned from his two-week trip to the Far East in February, he sent word with Cardinal Rollinger to the State Council that his period of preparation was nearly over. It would shortly be time to tighten and refurbish ecclesiastical controls, begin to correct the errors that had arisen from the Second Vatican Council, and launch a new Catholic effort on a worldwide basis. May 13, 1981, in Papa Valeska's new plan, was to mark the beginning of his fresh offensive. Under the protection of the Woman who had appeared at Fatima on May 13, 1917, the Holy Father would celebrate a Pontifical Mass in St. Peter's. He would go down for a few minutes into the crowds in the piazza, to mingle with them, and to fire them as only he could do, so that they took to his spirit and purpose. And then, from the central loggia of the Basilica, he would announce his intention to call a major consistory in Rome in the coming autumn.

Though he did not intend to say so publicly in his speech, he did inform the Council that his plan was to demand of his gathered bishops, then and there, that in unison with him, they consecrate Russia at long last to the care and protection of the Lady of Fatima. He would no longer be turned aside from that obligation, as Profumi and Angelica and Da Brescia had been. As he himself had been, until now. For he, too, had begun to see clearly what Papa Profumi had seen dimly outlined in the ghostly explosion of Fat Man: An alien power superior to men's petty plans had penetrated deeply into human history. He now believed its only able foe was the Woman described by St. John in his Book of Revelations; the Woman clothed with the Sun of God's omnipotence was the Woman of Fatima.

The reaction of the Council was positive. Any sign that the Pontiff would begin to do what the cardinals thought was vital for the Church was welcome, and would have their full support.

At about the same time that Rollinger brought Valeska's message to the Council, Guido received another piece of good news, this time from President Crasci.

Armed with the information derived from the papers Franco Graziani had given to the Maestro, Crasci had moved with slow and very careful deliberation toward the day when he would be able to intervene in the P-2 situation which, in his view, threatened the existence of the republic. As he had told Guido in their first meeting on the matter, one major concern in formulating his strategy was that he had to be certain the personnel he used in the investigation were not tainted—were not either P-2 or corrupted by people who were. As Graziani's list of members was incomplete, that in itself was a long and delicate operation.

The interval was not all fallow waiting time, however. Though Paolo Lercani had given precious little information to the authorities after his arrest and conviction in New York, he did say enough to lead Treasury officials to begin an investigation of Roberto Gonella and his Banco Agostiniano in Milan.

The Maestro and his *impero* associates had been conducting their own inquiries for some years, trying to trace the whole Lercani system. The *impero*'s main interests were, first, to determine how much Holy See money had been, and might still be, involved in these strangely orchestrated international embezzlement schemes, and to get as much of it back as possible. And, second, to determine, if at all possible, what had been the ultimate destinations of the embezzled funds.

Working closely with President Crasci and the special team of Treasury officials who had been screened to his satisfaction, Guido had assembled about as much of the picture as he would be able to until the government could move in on Pappagallo himself.

Since 1977, Gonella had borrowed several hundred million dollars in the Euromarket. In addition, working through Agostiniano's stockbrokerage affiliate—which was controlled by the Holy See's IRA—Gonella had purchased millions of dollars' worth of Agostiniano stock on the Italian market. He transferred that stock through half a dozen "ghost" companies in Liechtenstein to a dozen brass-plate companies—Sektorinest, Cascadella Marbella, and others, also owned by the IRA—in Panama.

Until 1979, much of the European money transferred to Panama by Gonella had then been funneled to his Agostiniano Group Banco Comercial of Managua. At the defeat of Anastasio Somoza's regime in Nicaragua in July of that year, however, Gonella liquidated the Managua Banco, and transferred the bulk of its assets to a new bank in Lima, Peru—Banco Andino. Its assets of $600 million, and the assets on the books of the Panamanian money houses, were steadily increased in the form of loans funded, in turn, by continuing capital raised on the Eurodollar market by Agostiniano affiliates.

Tracing the lines out of Panama and Lima proved to be possible only up to a certain point. Some funds were traced regularly to the Lugan Bank of Kuwait and thence to the United States. A certain portion was still transferred regularly to Havana's Banco Central. It was not hard to figure out what the Havana funds were used for, or by whom. But what happened to the assets that were fed into the United States was another matter. Who received them ultimately and for what purposes they were being used could not yet be determined.

Roberto Gonella's prowess as a banker and the innate secrecy that was inbred in his character, coupled with the government's own desire not to tip its hand too soon, meant that the investigation had to be carried out in a seemingly routine and not a heavy-handed manner. The Maestro and the Treasury team advised President Crasci that the foreign exposure of the Agostiniano was dangerously high—over $1 billion by 1981—and should be reduced as soon as possible. The IRA exposure through the Agostiniano's use of its stockbrokerage, and through the Panamanian brass-plate houses, led Guido and Helmut to be concerned that Holy See resources were, in effect, on the line again, this time to cover the extensive exposure of the Agostiniano through letters of patronage. Their investigations at the Vatican Banco revealed that all the documents and transactions there were perfectly in order and legally done. They were even profitable on the face of it. Gonella was a consummate perfectionist, and had fallen into none of the impatient mistakes that Lercani had. But the Maestro and his nephew remained concerned.

In an April meeting with President Crasci, the Maestro summarized the IRA situation and put it together with what the *impero* and the Treasury task force had gathered by way of information elsewhere. It was clear that they could go no further until Crasci decided he could move in on the Pappagallo villa, where, as Graziani had said, the senatore's safe probably held a mother lode of vital information.

"It will not be long now, Maestro," Crasci told him at last. "We would have moved long before, had it only been a question of being certain of our own team, though that has been a delicate and difficult matter. It is also that, as has been clear from the very beginning, the shock waves for Italy are going to be very great. My hope is to handle this whole matter in such a way that it will not do more harm than good. Will not, in other words, do this P-2 organization's work of destabilization for them. But we are just about ready, Maestro. I put the date at about the middle of May. I will be in touch, of course."

It was the very hand of God, Don Guglielmo said for perhaps the fiftieth time on that May 13, as he stood in St. Peter's Square with little Laura Bartoli and her parents. Perhaps it was also the hand of good Papa Da Brescia himself, reaching down from heaven, where he surely now lived in God's very presence. Had Papa Da Brescia not arranged for the money to pay for Laura's doctors? Had he not done that act of charity as he himself was dying? Had he not instructed Don Guglielmo to consecrate the ailing child to the Lady of Fatima? How else explain Laura's sudden and truly miraculous recovery from her mysterious sleeping sickness three years later, only days before the Mass Papa Valeska had announced in honor of the Vision of Fatima? The doctors could not explain it; they had said so themselves.

"The very hand of God," the good pastor of Avellino said again, shouting now to be heard over the roar of the crowds as the Holy Father appeared on the steps of the Basilica.

The papal Mass had been celebrated. Rico Lansing, together with Guido, Helmut, some of the State Council, and a few others, began to appear up on the balcony where they would wait for the Holy Father to join them and deliver his short address to the people.

Papa Valeska responded to the shouts of the crowd as he always did; as they knew he would. His face was as shining and resplendent as his white robes gleaming in the late-day sunlight. He stretched his arms wide, his palms turned skyward. His whole being seemed to be one great gesture of welcome and embrace and benediction.

Don Guglielmo pressed forward with Corrado Bartoli, Laura's father, who held the child in his arms. The priest lost Lucia, Laura's mother, for a moment in the press of the crowd, but found her again quickly and was able to clear a way for her. By the time he finally had them all close to the lane the police and security people had cleared through the mass of visitors, Papa Valeska, with Father Jan Terebelski behind him, was already reaching down from the slowly moving white papal jeep, touching hands, responding to the tears and the cries of *"Santo Padre! Santo Padre!"* as everyone tried to get his attention, his blessing, his recognition of them for just one brief second in their lives.

At a certain spot in the piazza, a swarthy, dark-haired young man was as intent on the figure of Papa Valeska as Don Guglielmo was. He watched the papal jeep round slowly through the crowds. Watched how it stopped ever so briefly now and again at a gesture or word from the Pope. Scanned the path ahead of the car. Calculated possible coordinates. Narrowed down the possibilities. When the jeep approached the level of two distant columns, just about where the man stood holding that little girl beside the old priest, he should be ready. He turned his collar up in a prearranged signal to the others; two minutes, more or less, and it would be done.

The jeep curved slowly through the lane. Corrado Bartoli held his daughter up as the Holy Father came closer. He saw her! Bartoli knew it. He could see. The Pope was smiling at her. Had seen the Fatima blue of her dress, the picture of the Virgin pinned to her collar.

"Santo Padre!" It was Don Guglielmo calling out now, certain that Papa Valeska would complete the miracle that Papa Da Brescia had begun; that he would stop and give his blessing to Laura. *"Santo Padre!"*

For a split second, it seemed the jeep would pass, that it wouldn't stop after all. That it would carry the Holy Father right past Laura, his arms outstretched, his body straight. But then, at the tiniest gesture of the Pope's hand, the jeep stopped. Papa Valeska bent down, smiling, and scooped Laura from her father's arms.

He never even heard the shots that slammed into his body—but he heard Laura's scream, and saw her fall back into her father's arms, sobbing in fear. And he felt the impact of the two bullets that drove him down onto the seat of the jeep. Two more bullets, intended to shatter his skull casing, had missed when he bent down to pick up the child. A fifth shot hit a woman in the crowd, and a sixth wounded a young man.

As Valeska fell back, Terebelski flung his body over the Pope to shield him from further bullets. He could see the ugly red stain spreading quickly over the white robes, and through Valeska's fingers as he held his hand against his wounds. And he could hear the Pontiff ask again and again, "How could they do this to me? They must have known. How could they do this to me?"

The jeep sped suddenly forward, sirens screaming, police running to clear the way. And all the while Valeska kept asking the same question, over and over. "How could they do this to me? They must have known. How could they do this?"

It was the one thing that no one had expected. A public killing, a public desecration. Somehow, until it happened, it had been unthinkable. Rico stood transfixed. He saw Valeska slump back in the jeep, saw Terebelski protect him, but didn't realize for a second what had happened. He did not so much hear the shots as remember them at almost the same moment he saw people wrestling a man to the ground.

Immediately he ran down from the Hall of Lights to the piazza. Helmut and Guido were not far behind. Rico commandeered a security car for them, told them he would follow them to the hospital as soon as he could, and set off at a run toward the spot he had fixed from the balcony.

It wasn't until a couple of hours later that he joined Guido and Helmut where they were waiting in the office of the director of Gemelli Hospital.

Valeska's condition was still uncertain, they told him. The Pope had lost a good deal of blood, was still on the operating table. The surgeons had determined the degree of damage done to his internal organs. Probably, a temporary colostomy was going to be necessary. But he was not yet out of danger.

Rico filled the Maestro and Helmut in on what they had been able to find out so far at the Vatican. The man who had been wrestled to the ground in the piazza was the hit man; that much was certain. He had seemed incoherent, but Solaccio and Brandolini were convinced that was deliberate, a fake. They wired his picture through to Interpol and at least had found out who he was.

"Mehmet Ali Agča is his name." Rico sat down in one of the chairs. "His papers say something else, of course. He's a Turk. Wanted for murder and plotting against the state and escape from prison. Belongs to the Turkish neo-Nazi outfit called Gray Wolves.

"He kept jabbering the usual blather about a blow for freedom and all that. First he said he acted alone. Then he talked about the KGB. Then about some Bulgarian connection."

"What does Brandolini make of it?" Guido wanted to know.

"Nothing yet." Rico answered. "As usual, he asks, *'Cui bono?'* Who would benefit? The Gray Wolves hate the Soviets, he says. They wouldn't collaborate with the Soviets any more than the IRA in Belfast would collaborate with the British government in London.

"On the other hand, the authorities have taken a Bulgarian Communist consular official into custody now. If he turns out to be implicated, then that may mean the Communist secret police in Bulgaria had to be involved one way or the other. And that might point to KGB."

"Motive?" Helmut asked.

"For the Soviets? Maybe someone leaked Valeska's plans about the Fatima consecration. They'd do anything to stop that, I suppose. For the Gray Wolves? Hate. They hate us as much as they do the Soviets. For the Bulgarians? Either obedience to the Soviets, or profit, or maybe both. But who knows?" Rico ran his hand wearily through his hair.

It was after eight-thirty by the time one of the hospital surgeons telephoned to tell them Valeska was out of danger. The next few hours would be crucial. He was out of surgery anyway, and in intensive care. There was nothing more to know or to do at the hospital.

Sagastume had long since caught up with the Maestro and was waiting downstairs in the limousine. They dropped Rico off at his apartment on the Via della Conciliazione before heading home to Villa Cerulea.

"One thing, Monsignore." Guido stopped Rico as he was getting out of the car. "Did Brandolini say anything to you about why the Holy Father was taken to Gemelli Hospital?"

Rico thought for a minute. Yes, he said. It was just a passing comment, though, in all the turmoil, and Lansing hadn't paid much heed. Was it important?

"I hope not." Guido sat back against the upholstery. "There is a standing security order for the Pontiff to be taken to Misericordia in case of any emergency. They keep everything in readiness there, including a special blood bank. Who knows what he got at Gemelli?"

Over the next twelve to eighteen hours, Security Two put together the beginning pieces of the puzzle. But they had no answers. For Mehmet Ali Agča to get as far as he did, both a ready supply of friends and large-scale cooperation had to be presumed. Although he was wanted by Interpol, he had traveled with immunity across several European borders, according to his papers. In those circumstances, the complete silence of all European and American intelligence services—the lack of warning from any of them, in other words—was disturbing. In Brandolini's opinion, that was what Valeska had meant when he kept saying in the jeep, "They must have known. How could they do this to me?"

Just as disturbing for Brandolini was the immediate international chorus in the Western media pointing the finger at the Soviets. It seemed to him too much like the KOR incident all over again.

Rico was poring over all the confusing data with Brandolini and Solaccio when the signals room rang through. Righi had just received a "Constantine" message from Riga. It was very short: The matter concerned recent events in Rome; this day week, Lansing was to lunch by himself at the restaurant in the little Polish ski haven of Kuznice. That was all. But the fact that it had come from Karlis Pelse and that it was top priority made it imperative enough.

Rico knew the restaurant Pelse named. It was at the top of the chain lift on 6,500-foot Kasprowy Wierch in the Tatra Mountains. Solaccio got to work at once, arranging Rico's cover—the obvious one was as a Swedish ski tourist—and working out the "windows" he would use to get into and out of Poland.

As Rico was finishing his small feast of roast duck with apples, Cerny, the head chef, came out in his white apron and conical hat to receive the compliments of the guests. Rico watched him make his way through the dining room in as smooth a style as he had ever seen. The man was obviously as good at public relations as he was at the stove.

When he came to Lansing's table, he looked with some satisfaction at the empty plate being removed by the waiter, but his talk was not of the food. "I know you want to view the Tatras from our upper balcony." He spoke softly but did not seem the least bit secretive. "Please follow me."

Once up the stairs and out the roof door, Rico caught sight of a tall figure standing at the guardrail with his back to the building. Cerny closed the door behind Lansing, leaving him alone with whoever this might be.

Rico's boots echoed on the balcony as he walked slowly forward. The man turned in a very deliberate fashion. He wore dark sunglasses. The clean-shaven face was hollow-cheeked and lined, oldened by something more pitiless than age. The hair was gray and bushy. Lansing didn't know the man, but something about his manner or his bearing made the leaves of Rico's memory stir and shift. Lansing stopped a yard or two away and waited. He was totally occupied in watching. This was not his meeting. It was the other man's move.

The stranger reached up with one gloved hand and removed his sun spectacles to reveal dark eyes so penetrating that they seared at once into Lansing's mind and memory. It was Lysenko! Pantelleimon Lysenko! The friend who had taught him Russian! The traitor who had used Papa Profumi's trust, and everyone else's, to betray all of the "lamplight" listening posts so many years before!

It took every bit of self-control that Lansing had taught himself over the intervening years to remain still, to avoid his impulse to throttle Lysenko, to scream damning invectives for the lives he had cost and the suffering he had made inevitable.

"Zdrastvuyte, Monsignore." Lysenko's deep voice had not aged at all, as his face had. "I am Pantelleimon Lysenko, General Control of the Committee for State Security, Moscow. Thank you for coming. Do you wish English, Italian, or Russian for this conversation?"

Lansing resisted the impulse to steady himself on the guardrail. Lysenko was General Control!

Every hard interview Rico had ever been through, every enemy he had faced, every deception he had ever used, and every moment of iron control over his emotions had barely prepared him for this rush of stunned disbelief. And yet, at the same time, he felt this moment had to happen, that he had in some way always expected it. The wheel would not have turned full circle had he never laid eyes on Lysenko again.

"I am Richard Cooper Lansing," Rico answered deliberately. "A priest and prelate of the One, Holy, Roman, Catholic Church. Russian will do. And I thank the Komitet Gosudarstvennoi Besopasnosti for this opportunity." He pronounced the dreaded KGB's full Russian name with the Muscovite accent Lysenko had taught him when they had been friends, as Rico had thought, in the forties. "What is our business?"

The Russian allowed a little smile to appear at the corners of his mouth. He had to admire Lansing's self-control. He wasn't the same explosive young monsignore he had once been. "The attempted assassination of His Holiness Papa Valeska," Lysenko answered the question. "We had nothing to do with it."

Rico's silence was eloquent. Lysenko studied his face for a few seconds; he knew he had chosen the right man for this meeting, and he knew the risk he was taking. Lansing was a skeptical, determined enemy who remembered Lysenko's betrayal, and bore him malice for it. At the same time, he was the most genuine, sincere Romanist Lysenko had ever met. He was no one's pawn, and no one's dupe. And he was the cleverest undercover man the Russian had ever seen. The question was, how to convince Lansing and, through him, the Holy See that the Soviets had not tried to assassinate Valeska. The Russian flung his arms wide. "Why should I come all this way, and reveal who I am to you, just on some false mission?"

"I need proof."

Lysenko turned and leaned his arms against the guardrail. Rico stood where he was.

"First," Lysenko began in his deep voice, "some facts, then. We've heard the same bulletins you have, and a few more besides. About the Bulgarian connection. I'm sure you know it's a simple matter for us to go in there and find out what goes on."

"So?"

"So we have been busy."

Rico could imagine what that meant. The interrogation teams had been working overtime.

"The thing was organized from your side of the water," Lysenko went on. "You'd be surprised how much is arranged with our smuggler friends in Bulgaria by your side. In this case, it took a little more time and the trail was a little longer, but we came up with an interesting name. Wren Reading."

Rico knew the name, of course. Everyone did. Reading was one of the most prominent and respected men in the American establishment.

But why should his name come up in this connection? Why should it be so interesting to Lysenko?

"Our interest isn't in Reading himself." The Soviet stood up straight now and faced Rico again. "Our interest is in his big association. You don't think we're afraid of capitalism as such, do you? We live by it, after all; they finance us willingly.

"But we are afraid of that assembly of powerful men Reading represents, who stand above the United States and above the Soviet Union—above everybody. They are a law unto themselves. They want both of us dead, your side and our side. Our real battle is not with the pygmies. It's with them. The totalitarian, fascist, international, capital-based group that is a hundred times more inhuman than you people think we Marxists are. They know what we know. The Marxist closed economy doesn't work. They want to profit from it while it weakens, and then let it implode. Valeska wants to change Marxism, but not into capitalism. That's why Valeska is dangerous for them. For us, he is valuable."

A little flash of recognition ran through Rico's glance, and Lysenko caught it. He had hit a nerve.

"You know the group, then?"

Rico didn't respond; but what General Control was describing was Giulio Brandolini's P-1—the one group powerful enough to do almost anything, and the one that would benefit by so much of the contradictory insanity that concerned the Vatican's Security Two. Score another one for Brandolini, Lansing thought.

It was Lansing's turn to look away, out over the spectacular view. It was a good theory Lysenko was giving him; but it was only that. Rico needed more. "So you've come all this way to convince me you didn't try to kill Papa Valeska." He tried to sound as though he were chewing over a problem. "Maybe you're telling the truth and maybe you're not. Don't take us for idiotic children, though. You definitely had a hand in the killing of Papa Serena. Why not Valeska? What's one pope more or less to you?"

Lysenko was imperturbable. "That's what this meeting is all about. That Pope, Serena, was going to denounce Marxism and the Soviet Union. If any pope did that, it would ultimately mean war. That's the power that still resides in Rome. In the papacy.

"We also warned you people about the plot on Papa Angelica's life. If you don't know that, you should know it now." Lysenko was speaking with that old intensity and fervor Rico remembered so well. "We *needed* Angelica. We needed the pact he made and Da Brescia honored: no condemnation of Marxism; no attack on the Soviet Union."

"We know that," Rico interrupted. "And the fact that the attack on Papa Valeska came on May 13, right after the Holy Father celebrated a Mass in honor of Fatima, is taken by some to point the finger of guilt straight at the Soviet Union. If you took his act as an indication that he intended to consecrate Russia—"

Lysenko was too impatient with the argument to listen to it. "I wish to God he *would* consecrate Russia to the Virgin. That would probably be a help to us, coming from Valeska. He's a Slav. Unlike Profumi, Angelica, or Da Brescia, he knows us. And unlike those others, he knows neither capitalist nor Marxist is good for his Church, and that neither will survive as long as his Church will survive. He'll have enough sense to consecrate the people of the Soviet Union without condemning the government. Like the Man whose Vicar he is, he wants men and women to be saved. Salvation is his business. And he doesn't want war. We have no fear of Valeska.

"Believe me when I tell you this: Bogdan Valeska as Pope is one of the most important men in the world right now for us. It is very important for him, and for the Holy See, to know that we did not try to kill him. If we had learned about this plot in advance, as we did about the Angelica plot, we would have warned you as we did then. We would have found some way. It's not all that hard, as you must know."

Rico was surprised at what he took to be a close reference to Vatican "moles"; but he knew he'd get nowhere trying to pursue that line. But he was to be surprised again. Apparently Lysenko was willing to go a very long way to convince Rome.

"You know"—the Russian pulled the fur collar of his coat up against the wind that began to blow lightly across the black ravines and sun-struck sheets of mountain ice—"you know we have friends everywhere. Some of them we buy. Some of them we blackmail. Some are just ours by their sympathies. *Nosh,* we call those: ours. They 'belong' to us; not in name, but in sympathy. And some of the easiest *nosh* are clergymen. The World Council of Churches, for example. And a lot of your own kind too. Academics and media people run a close second. We barely have to lift a finger to get them to mouth our very mind for us. They are very sincere. And very convincing."

Rico stirred, whether out of annoyance or skepticism Lysenko couldn't tell; but he decided it was best to get to the point. "We know you people have facilitated the Americans. Fine! But what may surprise you is that in seventy-five percent of such cases, you are betrayed to us. We have our friends within the famous American 'Company,' as they like to call it in their cute undercover games. You should not have to take my word on such a matter. I'll give you a name you can check. They have an agent code-named Saralis in the Kremlin. She's passed a good deal of information to the Americans. What they don't know is that we found her out and 'turned her around.' She's a double agent. Has been for years. Check with your contacts. If the information about her is true, then take this nugget of intelligence about her as a good-faith token on my part that there is no trick in what I am doing now."

Lysenko lapsed into silence. If he had not convinced Lansing by now, then he had no hope of ever doing so.

The rattling of the cable car toiling up from the valley echoed in the crystal-clear air. Rico turned back to the Soviet. There was no disbelief on his face or in his mind. He had known for some time, deep down where men who risk their lives for years in covert work know such things, that Lysenko was not lying. His shock and his anger and his frustration had kept him pounding at the man; but he did believe him. And the pounding had got him a bit of extra information, in any case.

There was still one more bit he wanted before he left. "Was there any cooperation from our side in the assassination attempt on Valeska?" Lansing asked the question in the same level tone.

"Not cooperation exactly." Lysenko answered without hesitation. "Your illustrious Wren Reading and some of his friends *are* intelligence. They were not acting in this instance in any way for the American government. As I said, they are a law unto themselves.

"But at a certain point, you have to talk about permissiveness in the various Western intelligence groups. Maybe connivance is a better word. Whatever you call it, Ali Agča was a wanted man traveling across international borders and meeting with known terrorists. American intelligence and the intelligence organization of other Western countries would automatically be informed by Interpol and by their own surveillance as well. Someone protected him, threw a friendly blanket over the information, you might say. Reading is in it."

In such conversation as Lansing's and Lysenko's, there is never exactly a full stop. There is no *"Adieu"* or *"Auf Wiedersehen."* No "Until the next time." There is only a sudden release of pressure. Each man knows that all the information to be exchanged has been exchanged. They remain what they were before: enemies. They may or may not see each other again. But for now, the truce is over.

Pantelleimon Lysenko leaned against the rail in almost the same spot where Lansing had found him.

Rico took one more full glance at the gaunt, cathedral-like mass of mountains. No wonder Pole, Czech, and Slovak fought for possession of these Tatra; the thought played in some unruly corner of his mind, the way a record plays, automatically.

He turned away and walked back along the terrace. In another few moments, he appeared like any normal day tourist, waiting for the cable car to take him down the mountainside to his hotel.

He glanced up at the balcony of the restaurant. There was no one there.

[68]

Because it occurred in the immediate aftermath of Papa Valeska's brush with death at the hands of Mehmet Ali Agča, the government raid on Senatore Ectore Pappagallo's villa at Arezzo was, comparatively speaking, almost glossed over in the Italian press. An hour before dawn on May 16, the assault was carried out by the combined elements of the carabinieri, the Special Attack Force, and the Anti–Organized Crime Squads of Florence and Pisa. Some shots were exchanged. Seventeen menservants were captured. In two safes, a total of $450,000 in various currencies was found, plus the complete files of P-2 and personal dossiers on some 33,000 Italians, with a sprinkling of foreigners. As careful as President Crasci had been, however, and as leak-proof as his operation was, Senatore Pappagallo himself had escaped.

The villa had obviously been the meeting center for Pappagallo's group, and judging from the robes, hoods, badges, ceremonial instruments, and manuals of rules and rituals that were retrieved, it was organized on a cultic basis around the Indian cobra god, Naja Hanna.

The files revealed that the organization was based in the Argentine. The names that particularly interested the Maestro in the mother branch were those of the twelve former Nazi officers whose transport to South America he had negotiated as part of the Swiss Windfall. The bulk of their funding came from Europe via Panama. The clearinghouses for those funds in Europe used to be Lercani-owned. Since Lercani's collapse, there had been no decrease in funds; they continued to come through the same Panamanian houses; but in Europe, holding companies of Milan's Agostiniano Bank were now being used.

The Italian branch of Pappagallo's organization included about nine hundred names. Full dossiers were found on all of them. Most were Italians prominent in the national parliament, banking, industry, the armed forces, the security and intelligence agencies, and the various ministries of the government. When President Crasci saw those files, he considered it a miracle that he had been able to pull off the operation at all.

Of the names that appeared on the roster of the Italian branch of P-2, the ones of primary interest to the Maestro and the Vatican were: Paolo Lercani; Roberto Gonella; Franco Graziani, now deceased; certain ranking prelates, notably the bishops of Senzi and Dolermo; Monsignore Roman Carnatiu, now deceased; and one obscure monsignore who worked with Archbishop Peter Servatius in the IRA, but who was immediately relieved of all IRA duties.

The rich mine of detailed information secured by the government raid was quickly and carefully sifted and dovetailed with the report of the two-year inquiry that had been conducted by the Bank of Italy; and charges were brought against Roberto Gonella and nine other men for illegal currency exports; specifically, for exporting over 26 billion Italian lire.

Except for Franco Graziani's membership in P-2, which was now moot, tragically enough, and the earlier and more distant ties, which had long since been broken, of the Maestro's errant associates, the *impero* was in no way directly involved or threatened by anything discovered about or connected with P-2, the Agostiniano Bank, or Roberto Gonella. But the Vatican Bank was both connected and threatened.

The connection was the unabated use of IRA-owned money facilities for the international transfer of funds, and the use of IRA guarantees to back illegal loans. The threat was financial, of course, because of the Agostiniano's excessive foreign exposure; but there remained the threat of deep scandal, as well.

The *impero* members had no doubt that the continuing link had to be Peter Servatius, and their certainty was redoubled by the confirmation in the report of the Bank of Italy's investigators that Servatius had, several years before, helped to engineer the passage of the Banca Cattolica through Lercani to Gonella, for a fee of $6.5 million, which, according to the report, was split between Servatius and Gonella. The government-appointed inquirer who had uncovered that deal, Giorgio Ambrosoli, was one of those who had been assassinated at Paolo Lercani's instigation.

By this time, however, Servatius had come to realize that the best defense, both of his position and of his life, in all probability, was that he was too dangerous to touch. If the immunity he enjoyed in the Vatican was important in protecting him, it was also important in protecting the powder keg of scandalous information upon whose lid he sat. He made no admissions or denials to his *impero* questioners. Rather, he asserted angrily that he had done only what banks and bankers do every day—what they are supposed to do, in fact.

Many felt that in time Servatius would be caught; or that he would be killed by someone who feared he would be caught. Meanwhile, he was protected by the very entanglements that made him so undesirable.

In that regard, Servatius was not a great deal different from many of the people whose much more intimate association with P-2 was now undeniable because of the Pappagallo files. At a closed session of Parliament, it was decided to do nothing about most of them, the main reason being a national security one: No government was possible if the people of Italy learned the full truth about the widespread corruption. Their fury would be ungovernable.

Even for Roberto Gonella, the outcome of the entire tortured and drawn-out affair seemed to be mitigated. He was convicted in July of the charges brought against him. He was sentenced to four years in jail and a fine of 15 billion lire. He was, however, released on bail pending an appeal; and while his passport was withdrawn, to the astonishment of more than a few he was quickly back in operation as chairman of the Agostiniano, busily doing his best to reestablish his own and his bank's standing, reputation, and credibility. P-2 evidently still had its supporters. He could rely on them.

About the most promising results as far as the Maestro was concerned —and they were precious few—were, first, that with greatly increased information now in hand, he, Helmut, and the *impero* could begin the long and difficult task of tracing with somewhat more accuracy some of the funds Gonella had transferred abroad. Second, they were able to establish the legally sound function, consistent with their charters, of the IRA-controlled Panamanian money houses that had been used; and they were able to establish as well the presumption, on the part of those money houses, of good usage of the funds involved. And, third, Servatius at least had sense enough, without Helmut having to force him by extreme means that would have been perilous for everyone, to secure a "letter of freedom" absolving the IRA from debts incurred on the basis of the letters of patronage he had formerly granted. The date of that letter of freedom was rather close to the date of at least one patronage document he had conceded to Gonella; but that was hardly a detail to disturb Servatius.

As patiently and hopefully as Guido de la Valle had waited for the government investigation and the windfall of information from the raid on Pappagallo's villa to produce positive results, so just as patiently did he reflect on the puny effects of it all. There was no denying any longer how deep the poison had gone into the arteries of society as a whole. In years gone by, he had been able to convince himself that he could play the world's game on behalf of the interests of the Holy See, without participating in or being sullied by the world's corruption. He had been confident that he could, in the main, keep things under control. But the control he had thought to exercise—and did, for a while—had been possible only because corruption had not yet gone far enough to swamp his efforts.

Now, however, it was clear that corruption had increased geometrically. The *sottogoverno* and the *sopragoverno* had begun to meld and fuse together, so that the government had to withdraw in its attack on P-2, for example, lest too many be killed or brought down or the country's structure implode. The innocent and untouched were too few to form a line of defense any longer. Even the business deals that once would have seemed innocuous were contaminated. Men like Servatius and Graziani and Garganelli were not the disease, but symptoms of the disease.

There was, Guido reflected, on many a long summer day of work at Villa Cerulea, no way that the Holy See could go on playing Mammon's game. Papa Profumi had been right about that. And Papa Da Brescia, to give him his due, had been right in more ways than perhaps he had known, when he observed that Satan's smoke was wafting about the altars of the Church.

The difficulty, however, was that there was no way to repudiate the Bargain—the Church's solid link to Mammon—and survive, by any ordinary means, the all-out, unholy war that the Universal Assembly would unleash on the Holy See. There was no humanly viable way to wage that war. Not even a Julius II, who had spent his entire pontificate riding into battle in his armor, or Sixtus IV, who could hold his Breviary in one hand and lop off your head with the sword in his other, could win such a war. It could not be fought by human means alone.

On the other hand, not one of the popes the Maestro had served as Keeper had ever made a public act based solely on the strength of purely spiritual power and moral authority, unalloyed with the temporal.

Still and all, at least in his most optimistic moments—on sunny afternoons strolling about the estate with Agathi or Keti, watching Tati scramble after darting squirrels—Guido allowed himself to hope that Bogdan Valeska might still prove to be the first such pope in a very long time. On his visits to the Pontiff in the hospital, Guido had seen that the Holy Father's reaction to the attempt on his life had been a spiritual one; the attack had served as a purification of Valeska. His stature in the world was undiminished. His inner life seemed to be enriched. And after all, the Maestro reminded himself more than once, Christian hope had always been born in blood.

The Pope was not yet recovered sufficiently to take on the full burdens of his office and deal with financial reforms besides. But perhaps that day would yet come. In the meanwhile, it remained Guido's responsibility to do as His Holiness had asked: to keep things under control at home and to protect the interests of the Holy See.

Once back in Rome from the Tatra Mountains, Rico was debriefed first by Brandolini and Solaccio. The following day he had a long session with the full Security Two.

It was clear to all that Lansing had come home with a great deal. They now knew who General Control was, for openers; none of them had even remotely suspected it might be Lysenko; but in hindsight, it seemed only logical, and explained the facility with which the Soviets had apparently penetrated the Vatican. Who in the U.S.S.R. would know better than he how to do that?

They also had a greater understanding of the fragility, in a certan sense, of Soviet power, as well as of the extensive power of the Vatican in Soviet eyes; Moscow did not take such a high-handed or even a negative view of Rome in all things as had been supposed. It was a lesson Lansing emphasized to Security Two, and asked Cardinal Falconieri to emphasize to the State Council, as well.

It had been a revelation to learn that powerful elements in the Soviet Union desired to make changes in its economic structure, and that one of the reasons Valeska was important to them was that he had understood this, and could make it possible without touching their political control. The unfortunate thing was that no one in Security Two thought any Western power would value such information, or know what to do with it beyond generating another endless and damaging public debate.

The two most shocking things to learn, at least for Rico, had been the nature of the actual P-1 group, if Lysenko was to be believed—and Rico did believe him, as he made clear; and the extent of KGB information about Lansing himself and his covert organization. There was not a great deal Lansing could do about the first; but the second he intended to deal with himself at a certain level. And very quickly.

"I tell you, Rico, it wasn't our doing!" John Liebermann was nearly shouting. He had seen Lansing angry before, but never had he seen such cold and unremitting fury in him. Liebermann could not seem to get through to him. "We had nothing to do with the attempt on Valeska's life! You must have gone crazy if you think we did!"

"No, John. Not crazy. Let me lay it out for you." Lansing assumed the other man knew all the details that had been discovered concerning Ali Agča, but he catalogued them all out loud, anyway—Agča's background, his travels, his affiliations, his crimes, his international connections, the unhindered facility of his movements around Europe. It was impossible, as the subdued Liebermann well knew, for Western intelligence groups, including Liebermann's, not to know about all that.

But it was possible, Liebermann defended himself, not to know what the man was up to.

"You didn't have to know," Rico pounded back at him. "All you had to do was stop him! Why didn't you? Who told you not to? Because that's what it would take, John! Who told you not to? And why?"

"Dammit, Rico—you know so much, you tell me!"

"I'll give you the whole answer to all the questions in two words, John: Wren Reading."

Liebermann blanched to a dead white. There had been rumors; but he hadn't been able to figure out the Ali Agča puzzle, either; no one had. But now all the pieces clicked into place for him. Just as Rico had known at a certain point that Lysenko was right, John Liebermann knew the same about Lansing.

"I made one mistake, John." Rico was not finished, by far. "I collaborated with you. That's done a lot of damage. I'm not talking about

Papa Valeska now. I'm talking about your own people. The ones you pleaded with me to help. Apparently they went back—their own skins intact, thanks to a lot of brave men and women—and then revealed information about us to your agency. And since your agency is moled, the Soviets know about our people. Or about a lot of them, anyway.

"When I agreed to help you, John, for some reason I thought you were independent in your mind, in your morality. I thought that you saw and understood that men who tie themselves blindly to an organization, and devote their lives entirely to working for it and achieving its aims, end up being molded by it. They abdicate their own identity for the organization's, and they abdicate their personal morality—in judgment and in actions. I thought you saw that and were independent of it.

"Now I see you're not independent. And it doesn't matter whether you're American or Soviet, democratic or Marxist. The process of evil is nourished by you. The sacrilege of trying to kill my Pope could be permitted because, like your organizations, all of you just deal with the 'facts,' as though they had a life of their own, independent of truth and meaning. You gather those facts up like nuggets of gold; you kill for them, if you have to. You catalogue them. You classify them. You encode them. You add and divide and subtract and multiply them. You twist them, neglect them, use them, abuse them. You do with them just what the Communists do. You seek no understanding of what the facts mean. You know about the drug trade; and you truck with it. You know about the Bulgarian smuggler-Marxists and Colombian narcotics kings and Chinese opium masters and Greek colonels and Latin American dictators, and you fatten their Swiss accounts just as the Marxists do. Just facts. To be milked. There's no morality. There's only what's useful for the moment. Or as a payoff for something useful in the past. Or to seed something that may be useful in the future. They way you seeded me, John; and my people through me.

"Well, you're through using me, John. And if I can help it, you're through using the Vatican. As far as I'm concerned, it's immaterial whether you personally knew about the Valeska plot, or whether you personally knew Agča was protected by your side."

There was no doubt in Liebermann's mind that Rico was dead serious; that he meant to cut his ties, to end cooperation. But the move was a dangerous one. Personally dangerous for Rico.

Lansing had considered that. "Carry a message back for me, John. I'll do less damage alive than I would if I died suddenly, or disappeared. At the present moment I have, as you well know, a list of over seventy of your operatives. I'm sorely tempted to use that list, anyway. After all, to allow—even allow—the assassination of my Pope is to sanction the death of a man who is worth more than all your operatives put together. But I'll resist the temptation.

"I also know your mail drops; and I know the location of those radar domes—the only ones of real worth for surveillance of Soviet missilery. I know a lot, John; more than you may have realized. If anything happens to me, however clever it may be, all that becomes public."

Liebermann knew Rico too well to think he was bluffing in any part of what he said. "Anything else?" He was tight-lipped and grim as he spoke now.

"Yes. I want twenty of your operatives out of the East."

"But, Rico . . . !"

"Out of Warsaw, East Berlin, Plzeň, and Bucharest. Get them out in one week. After that, if they're still there, their cover is blown."

"But why? In God's name, why?"

"So you and your agency will never again think you can abuse us with impunity. So you'll never again think that we just do what we're told the way the Nazis did; the way a lot of people do now. And to remind you what it could cost if you ever connive again, or even as much as catch the whiff of a plot, against the life of the Holy Father, and we don't learn about it."

Lansing got up from his chair in the Vatican room he had chosen for this meeting, a clear signal to Liebermann that this meeting, and all cooperation from Rico Lansing, were over.

"I'll give you one last piece of information, John." Rico spoke quietly in the corridors as he walked beside the American intelligence agent for the final time. "Consider it a parting gift. You have an agent inside the Soviet Union. Code name, Saralis."

Liebermann was poker-faced.

"They've turned her around. She's a double agent.

"I think you know the way from here." Rico gestured toward the doors leading to the piazza. "Goodbye, John. Try to keep your nose clean."

Despite their personal shock, the attempted assassination of Papa Valeska forced the cardinals of the State Council to face a cold-blooded fact that they had allowed themselves to neglect. As they had selected a prime *papabile* as backup for Papa Serena, so they must for Valeska. The Maestro and Helmut were in full accord. Indeed, Guido had given a great deal of thought to the matter over the many months since the two conclaves of 1978.

There was general agreement among the cardinals that it was not yet possible to assess the impact of the Valeska papacy on the Church, judging from the message the Pontiff had sent to the Council in the early spring that his time of preparation was coming to an end. The failure of the Polish experiment had not broken the Holy Father's determination to reassert papal authority among his bishops and to bring the Church back to its proper mission of salvation. But there were many questions now about Valeska's health.

It was still very soon after the shooting, to be sure—barely a week and a half—but the doctors at Gemelli reported some metallic poisoning in the Holy Father's system. "They don't seem to be able to eliminate it," Rollinger told the others. The German cardinal, who had replaced the much-missed Arnulfo on the Council, had become one of the very few curial cardinals to enjoy some intimacy with the Polish Pope. "His color is still very pale and he has a slight tremor in his hands. But I think it is simply too soon to tell what lasting effects, if any, this awful experience will have on him: physically, as well as on his will and his determination."

"In any case," Cardinal Hoffeldt put in, "whether Papa Valeska makes great strides in his remaining years as Pope, as we all hope he will, or whether he does not, I believe we all agree on the kind of papacy this Church needs for many years to come. It will take a very long time to undo the damage done by Papa Da Brescia, and to create again that socio-personal ambient in which men and women will see themselves, their homes, their lives, their work, as immersed in the living, shining body of saints and sinners we call the Church, clustered around the See of Peter, drawing strength and instruction and example and commands from the Man in White who sits on Peter's Throne."

That was an uncharacteristically eloquent speech from the normally gruff Hoffeldt, and Cardinal Borgo-Mancini blinked at him for a moment in surprise. Like Ferragamo-Duca, whom he replaced, Borgo-Mancini was not known for his eloquent faith so much as for his ardent Romanism. Nevertheless, he, like all the others present, agreed that Hoffeldt had just given the working "mandate" on the basis of which they should select the most serious papal candidates.

Two possible self-declared contenders had already put themselves forward, in a manner of speaking. Cardinal Pirandella of Rome and Cardinal Buff of Westminster were both "acting much like political candidates running for president." Borgo-Mancini was contemptuous.

"You can forget Pirandella's candidacy, Your Eminence," Guido responded to the comment. "He has been very busy among the cardinals—particularly the Northern Europeans and Latin Americans. But he foolishly tried to enlist the help of the Lodge—apparently thought they could swing some curials and some North Americans in his favor. What it did was to cost him any worthwhile support he might reasonably have expected."

"Do you think he understands that, Maestro?" Cardinal Corelli asked the question. "I mean, do you think he will keep on politicking for himself?"

"Like Da Brescia, you mean?" The Maestro understood the implication at once. "No. He hasn't the base for that. If Papa Valeska hadn't removed him as head of the Congregation for the Evangelization of Peoples, I might worry a little more. But he's basically on the shelf, the way Lisserant was before he died. Pirandella bears watching, but I don't expect much to develop for him.

"Buff is another matter, however."

Everyone there knew both from official reports and from widespread gossip how assiduously the Cardinal from England had been presenting his cause as "a democratic prelate who desired only to live and let live." Lawlor of Boston had been in Rome recently, and had told tales of a so-called spiritual retreat Buff had given for the American prelates. Apparently it had been about as spiritual as a political caucus. Sandwiches and coffee were served every afternoon along with a lot of "dialoguing," as Buff called it, while they all sat around in armchairs.

Still, as Falconieri pointed out, despite his tactics, Buff had some serious support in America—in Chicago and the Midwest. He had even gone so far as to have that American priest-novelist publish a novel with Buff as the hero-pope who saved the Church from "Roman bureaucrats." And he was being taken seriously by some in England, France, and Holland, who were "eyeing him as their man," in Falconieri's phrase.

"Nonsense!" Borgo-Mancini would have none of it. "That's fun and games, not the reality of a papal election."

Cardinal Azande disagreed. The way things stood in the Church today, a man like Buff, working over a period of time, might walk into conclave with a certain amount of serious support, unless the Council could come up with a strong and forceful candidate as prime *papabile.*

None of the Council members had been able to prepare the usual list of potential candidates before the meeting. There just did not seem to be a wealth of cardinals at this time who would even accept, much less have the strength to carry out the sort of mandate Hoffeldt had presented. One German cardinal—if he hadn't been so old—might have suited. There were two or three Asiatic and African cardinals, but all too young for the job.

The comment was made, in fact, that traditionalist Archbishop Édouard Lasuisse, who was carrying on his brave but lonely and isolated fight to preserve the Catholic Mass and the generally neglected deposit of faith, was the only man of any rank who was doing something positive.

"Imagine," Falconieri commented wryly about Lasuisse. "Protestant Switzerland now houses one of Roman Catholicism's most important churchmen, one of the best hopes for Rome's future."

"That's why I support his seminaries," Guido agreed. "But unless Papa Valeska turns things around very dramatically between now and the time of the conclave that will choose his successor, the reality is that Lasuisse could not be elected. And I doubt whether Valeska will make him a cardinal, in the circumstances. He does not share Lasuisse's view that the whole Ecumenical Council was bad news, and he's shown no interest even in seeing, much less in understanding, the Frenchman."

By this time, Cardinal Falconieri, who had worked closely with the Maestro for far longer than any of the other cardinals now on the Council, began to realize that Guido had been sounding them out, testing to see if they could come up with a strong and viable candidate, before he decided to make his own suggestion.

It seemed obvious, Falconieri said, turning toward Guido, that if no strong candidate had been put forward in these forty minutes of discussion, it was time to know the Maestro's full mind.

Guido began by reminding the cardinals that in Da Brescia's final months, and particularly during the time of his breakdown when he stayed out at Castel Gandolfo incommunicado, he had relied heavily on one man in particularly to manage the day-to-day papal affairs, and hold Cardinal Secretary Levesque at bay.

"Archbishop Richard Lansing?" Cardinal O'Mahoney was the only Council member who seemed totally taken aback. "But he's not even a cardinal, Maestro."

"Wrong, Your Eminence. He is. Has been for years." Guido explained briefly that Papa Da Brescia, at the Maestro's suggestion, had made Lansing a cardinal *in pectore;* and how, "for reasons of state," it had been decided not to reveal his status in the intervening years. "Indeed," Guido added, "if Your Eminences agree on Richard Lansing as our prime *papabile,* the fact that he is a cardinal should remain secret. We have seen one pope killed and another nearly killed. It would be folly to make our backup candidate an open target."

From the moment Cardinal O'Mahoney had pronounced his name in such surprise, there was among all the Council members what could only be described as a realization that they had recognized Lansing as their peer for some time, without ever having thought about it in so many words. De facto, he had ascended to a level with them. They had sought his advice. He was as experienced as any man in the Vatican. He had never taken sides in the battles that divided the Church into traditionalist versus progressive, or curial versus non-curial. In fact, they never even thought of him as American versus Italian. He was Roman, purely and simply; and, in a way, they had taken him for granted in almost the same way they took Rome for granted.

Without revealing Lansing's covert work over the years, Guido and Falconieri both spoke convincingly of the judgment and loyalty Lansing had displayed unwaveringly in "many hard situations," while at the same time criticizing actions and policies he disagreed with, in no uncertain terms.

There were some appreciative smiles at that last remark; there wasn't a man present who hadn't had an earful from Rico Lansing, or who didn't know his mind.

At Lansing's request in the recent Security Two meeting, Falconieri had carried back to the Council his message concerning the Holy See's power in Soviet eyes. He brought that message to the attention of the Council again, for a specific reason; and in doing so, he seemed to sum up the view of the entire group with regard to Richard Lansing's papability.

"Even General Control respects Lansing, and trusts him to keep his word. And the point is, he trusts him because of Lansing's faith, not because of his politics. Even Lysenko knows that he is totally and exclusively Christ's man. If Pantelleimon Lysenko can recognize that in Lansing, and single him out for trust because of it, we who have watched and worked with him for so long would have to be blind indeed not to see it more clearly still."

As to the question of secrecy surrounding Lansing's cardinalate, the only risk—one justified by the crisis, in everyone's view—was that the normal work to achieve concensus before the conclave could not be extensively done.

"Except, of course, in the negative sense." Corelli had a mischievous look in his eye. "Against such a man as Buff, I mean."

"If it is agreed, then"—the Maestro glanced at Helmut and began to rise from his chair—"I will have a talk with Monsignore—er, with His Eminence Cardinal Lansing."

"I wish you good luck, Maestro." Azande got up also. "If I know Lansing, he won't be impressed or persuaded by the State Council's decision. He'll make up his own mind. And he might very well not agree to be our *papabile.*"

[69]

After the heavy and increasing strain that had followed for Rico on the heels of the attempted murder of Papa Valeska, it was wonderful to have a few hours' quiet interlude at Villa Cerulea. It was truly like coming home again.

As he sat with the four de la Valles on the Long Terrace that quiet afternoon, Tati perched contentedly on the Maestro's lap, Keti and Agathi both clamored for news of the Holy Father. Rico, they knew, spent as much time in the hospital with Valeska as he could.

The fact that the first blood transfusions given to His Holiness at Gemelli Hospital were from the common blood bank was more than merely disturbing, Rico told them. Papa Valeska had contracted severe hepatitis from those transfusions. That, and the strange metallic poisoning, or whatever it was—doctors seemed to know so little—had put the Pontiff's full recovery in doubt. He would certainly be in hospital for several months, in any case.

One very hard burden for His Holiness was that old Cardinal Wallensky was gravely ill. Lansing's own sadness was evident as he spoke about the imminent death of one of the truest, bravest men he had ever come to know and love.

Had he been physically able, Valeska would surely have gone to Poland to be with his great friend and mentor in his last days. As it was, he spoke frequently with the cardinal in Warsaw by phone. "It's like two old companion warriors speaking from where each one lies in pain," Rico said. "But Wallensky has lost not one bit of that trenchant wisdom of his. He told Valeska that his presence in Poland might have been taken as a signal for general revolt by the suppressed ranks of Solidarity. He's right about that."

The cardinal had suggested his own successor, Archbishop Josef Koczur. Valeska agreed with the choice; but both the Pope and Rico knew that, while the archbishop was a man of quiet strength, with a sense of personal dignity and a profound faith, and while he had all of Wallensky's devotion to the papacy, there was no replacing Wallensky in the true sense.

The day was very near, therefore, when Valeska would be thrust, by Wallensky's death, into the position of chief protector of Poland, and his aloneness as well as the stress of responsibility on him would be increased. "When your real Calvary comes," Wallensky had tried to console his Pope that very morning, "remember that I shall be with God, and nearer to you than ever before."

It was Agathi, true to her nature, who immediately felt and responded to Rico's own pain at the coming loss of Cardinal Wallensky. She guided the conversation skillfully away from that topic, and from anything to do with the Pope and Vatican affairs. She pulled Rico by the hand with her out to the gardens she knew he loved, for a leisurely stroll, and caught him up on all their smaller, domestic dramas of life at Villa Cerulea. And all during drinks and dinner, she managed to keep even Guido and Helmut from lapsing into "shoptalk."

As they all sat chatting easily at dinner, Rico was caught up in reflections on the subtle change that seemed to have affected Villa Cerulea and the people he so loved whose home this was. He couldn't quite tell what that change was, but he felt it unmistakably.

Life at Villa Cerulea was dominated by the presence of the Maestro, of course; but that had always been true. Was it a change in Guido, then? He was aging, certainly. But he had made a miraculous recovery from the ischemic episode that had hit him in *il Tempio.* Even the stress of the past week hadn't seemed too much for him. He did seem more philosophical, though, and less hard-driving in some way than he had been in years past. There was a mellowness about the Maestro now; not a softness—he was still as tough as men come. But a kind of ripeness of understanding and an increase of gentleness was leavening in him.

Precisely because Guido was the touchstone of life at Villa Cerulea, any change in him affected—or was reflected in—the three people who shared his life most intimately.

Keti, for example. Rico looked across the table at her as she glanced toward the Maestro to give a laughing response to some light remark of his. She had been working closely with Guido for these past couple of years; and that had seemed to draw her out of herself, and to make her lose that awful sense she had once had of being locked away from so much that was at the heart of life and meaning for her husband.

And Helmut. Rico looked in turn at his oldest friend in Rome, the first person who had made him feel something more than a stranger here, so many years before. He, like his uncle, seemed mellower, intent on something more than empire building. Obviously aware of the change in Keti, he appeared to have a new appreciation of her that was as deep as his love for her had always been. There was, Rico thought, a harvest of new commonality growing between them, something better than they had had together before the tragedy of Eugenio's violent death had forced them apart.

Between Rico and Keti there would always be the unspoken bond that issued from the lost or, rather, the never-experienced idyll of love they might have had. Such a thought did not disturb the distant slopes of Rico's memory. Rather, the realization that they had violated no trust, neither human nor divine, only increased the sweetness that Keti had wisely said would never leave them. They were bound together by the thread of constancy and of rightful consequences.

Only Agathi seemed never to change. She was of course growing old, as her brother was. And she remained, as she had always been, totally integrated into Guido's mood and condition. But never had she lost that most wonderful, childlike innocence that shone through all her de la Valle sophistication. That innocence, it now seemed to Rico, was the one trait in her that had always made her beauty shine with such captivating radiance—a beauty that still made heads turn to look at her.

"Rico, darling." Agathi was staring at him. "You seem very pensive this evening. Is anything wrong?"

"Quite the opposite." Rico reached for her hand. "I was just thinking how good it is to be here again."

Guido wondered if he would still feel that way in an hour or two.

"An after-dinner cigar, Your Eminence?" The Maestro took the humidor from the table in his study and held it open for Rico.

Lansing accepted the offer and eyed Guido questioningly. Never before had he used that form of address to him, or in any way alluded to his status as cardinal.

"I deliberately use that title in speaking to you." The Maestro sat in one of the comfortable easy chairs and gestured Rico into its twin. "It will not come as a surprise to you, I think, that the State Council and I are convinced that we must have a prime *papabile* in readiness. A backup, in other words, for Papa Valeska. Just as we chose Valeska as a backup when we decided on the candidacy of Papa Serena."

Rico let pass his mild surprise; he had not known that Valeska had been selected with such foresight, so long before the conclave that had elected him; but this was not a time for questions such as that.

"The unanimous agreement," the Maestro went on almost matter-of-factly, "is that you, Your Eminence, are that backup."

Ten years before, Rico would have been thunderstruck by such a statement—would have laughed or looked over his shoulder to see if someone else was meant. But the inner Rico had changed since then, as much as the de la Valles had. He had walked on the peaks of power in Rome; and abroad he had held the destiny of many people in his hands. He knew his value, at least in the eyes of some, as a man big enough to carry the burden, whatever it might be, and farseeing enough to catch the wide vista of world events.

The reaction of such a man as Rico had become, to such news as the Maestro had to give, was not surprise, then, or a false modesty that might lead him to be dishonest even in his innermost response. He did not want to be pope. His answer to the Maestro was as simple and as clear as that.

"What Your Eminence wants or does not want is not the consideration." Guido's tone was not unkind. "We did not choose you as some sort of reward. The papacy is not a prize to be accepted or rejected like a gold watch at the end of a worthy career. If it were, we have holier than you to choose from, just as we have more unworthy. But we do not have stronger that you. You will be Keeper of the Keys, Your Eminence, if Christ wills it. And you will be the prime *papabile.*"

The Maestro spoke now—it was expressed in some way with his whole being—with an air of authority Lansing had seen in him only once before, in those first few moments when he had sought Guido out in *il Tempio,* as Papa Serena's conclave was coming to an end. Rico began to understand that there was something in this whole situation he did not know: some X-factor, some vital piece of information that he was missing. He decided to bide his time in silence, however; he trusted the Maestro to say what was needful.

"In normal circumstances"—Guido rose from his chair and crossed the study to his desk—"I would merely remind you that you are a cardinal, that you have vowed as such even to shed your blood, if need be. Or I would perhaps take your answer and leave it at that."

He returned to his chair, carrying a red, damask-covered folder. "In any case, I would not give you any more information than the State Council's and my decision.

"But these are far from normal times. This situation is critical, and it will only become more so.

"As it is, then, I would like Your Eminence to read the document in this folder."

Without further comment or word of preparation, he handed the document of the Keeper's Bargain to Rico, as he had handed it in the Silver Throne Room of the Apostolic Palace to every pope he had served.

Lansing read the three pages in silence. He read it a second time, and yet a third; not in shock but in a flood of understanding. He studied every word and every papal signature. No explanation was necessary. Everything was suddenly clear to him.

When he finally looked up from the folder, it was not with a question, but a statement. "P-1."

The Maestro nodded. "Yes. P-1."

"It is impossible to go on with this"—Rico glanced down at the papers in the still-open folder—"this Bargain."

Again the Maestro nodded. "I used to think, Your Eminence, that this Bargain I have revealed to you was no different than any other the Church has made in order to get along in the world. What I have only begun to understand in these latter years of my life is that no bargain was ever necessary; and, in fact, that all of them, despite the richness of appearances, were harmful.

"I justified it, of course, and devoted my life to its fulfillment, as a kind of mirror of the Bargain God observes. You've read the Book of

Job, Eminence. Surely there's a bargain there, I used to tell myself. Satan exists, is free, works, and to some extent succeeds. It's all done within the ambit of God's conditions, of course. But God observes His cosmic Bargain, I reasoned; and the Keeper observes his Oath."

The implication of the past tense in the Maestro's explanation was inescapable.

"And now?" Lansing's voice was a whisper.

Without stirring in his chair, Guido fixed Rico in his gaze as though to transmit his very thoughts through that blue-green stare.

"I want you to do something, Eminence. I want you to look back over the last forty years. But try not to see those years as we normally do, as a series of successive events arising from different circumstances, and from the actions of different and separated men.

"You must see them as a whole picture. At first it may look haphazard to you. I confess it did to me—except that something kept nudging my mind to a deeper analysis. Look carefully, and you will conclude that an intelligence has been at work behind all the events of our time. A very fine intelligence. An intelligence larger, more capacious, and more penetrating than any human intelligence. An intelligence that knows beforehand the potential effects of all the material elements that compose the fabric of human life and human society—gold, space, sexuality, health, drugs, prosperity, sickness, atoms, poverty, war, peacefulness, science. Some intelligence has exploited all that—everything material—to bring men and women to this point.

"For, you see, I am presuming that what is bad, what is negative at this point in world history, is due to the foreseeing brilliance and malice of the fallen Archangel; to the Archangel's machinations. Just as I must also presume in my faith the wisdom of my Savior, who is Master of History.

"I read clearly the aim of that Archangel: a totally topsy-turvy, dehumanized world.

"What I read in the other is likewise clear: We have gone too far with our petty bargains; we are not gods. Our age-old, Constantinian Church, and the civilization it made possible, are being swept away. The Master of History has a new thing in mind."

In Rico's faith, he had no difficulty following or accepting the Maestro's sweep of vision, or even its apocalyptic edge. "But does that mean that you merely intend to let this Bargain"—he held up the damask-covered folder—"continue to exist until it is swept away with the rest?"

The Maestro's expression softened just a bit. The American mind was always so practical; Keti was like that too. And a good thing it was, Guido thought to himself; Europeans were always inclined to get trapped in what they saw as the broad sweep, and let too many single days and practical affairs rush past.

"Not exactly," the Maestro answered. "What happens in that regard is not only up to me."

"Maestro." Rico sounded just a bit impatient. "The de la Valle signature is on that Bargain. Surely you have the power to repudiate what your ancestors signed."

"And then what, Eminence? You saw what happened to Papa Valeska when he barely brushed his coattails in the wrong direction—when he threatened the interests of the other side in our Bargain. If we withdraw, just like that, and just as we are, we will be pulverized. We haven't the means to fight them."

Rico shook his head. "That's not good enough, Maestro. You said a minute ago that we're not gods. Well, neither are these P-1 people gods. There must be the means to fight them. We just have to find those means."

"Or refind them, perhaps." Guido had been certain Lansing would react as he had, that he would argue for what had to be done; that was the Maestro's hope, the very reason he had proposed him as *papabile.* He pounced on the opening. "The only means at our disposal, the only thing that will enable us to survive the unholy war that will be unleashed on us by that Assembly if—or when—we withdraw from the Bargain, is something they cannot even see. You can't defeat this thing with money or armies. Remember, they are the lords of the world, the supermen of this age. They have a monopoly on all that. The only challenge is by moral power, by spiritual authority. As Keeper of the Bargain, I have neither. The only one who has that power and that authority is the Holy Father. The Keeper of the Keys.

"It may be, and my hope is, that Papa Valeska will yet rely on those means. If he can do that, then I am ready to begin when he is."

"And if he will not? If he cannot?"

"Then my hope is that you, Eminence, will be strong enough in Christ to do what Papa Valeska may not be able to do."

That was it, then. The Maestro's full mind. Rico thought about all the times they had been at loggerheads over policy, he and Guido. He thought all the way back to that dreadful night when he had come back from the death holes of the Kalikawa mines and, in this very room, had all but shattered the Maestro with his discoveries and his bitter accusations and blame. Back farther still to his own acquiescence—his very first—when he had signed the passports for the Nazis who were now plaguing them as part of P-2. Everything comes full circle, he thought, if you give it time enough. Without even knowing there was a Bargain in any formal sense, any "our side–your side" deal, how often had he argued with the Maestro to take actions that would have gone against that Bargain. And now the Maestro was agreeing with him. The only trouble was, now Rico also began to know the price they would have to pay.

That price was something he needed to know more about. What would be the near-future fate of the Church, for example, if the Holy See withdrew from its relationship of "facilitating enmity" with P-1? "They will, I suppose," Rico himself conjectured, "try to foster complete alienation between the Church and the world around it. They will try to reduce our Pope to the status of the Dalai Lama; and Catholic teachers to the level of popularity accorded to Tibetan astrologers on some of our modern university campuses. In the longer run, they will force us into hiding if they can, I would think; into some new catacomb existence. At the extreme, we could suffer total death and burial as a people—always in the Christian hope of resurrection."

"No, no!" Guido wasn't about to paint any rosy pictures; but he was quite firm, quite confident in what he saw down the road.

"In the worst case," he said, "if Papa Valeska turns out not to be the strong spiritual and moral leader we need and that I hope he will be, then we will adopt a holding pattern, suffering a slow attrition, a slow hemorrhaging of the faithful, a deepening of the schism in bishops and clergy that no one wants to admit is there.

"The more hopeful scenario may seem still more dire. But when the time comes that we do withdraw from the Bargain, it must be behind a pope who can face into this: Down we will go as a body, until we are reduced to an irreducible, hard-core remnant. A Romanist remnant. Until the Church, with its Pope to lead it, achieves a precarious balance of survival and self-renewal."

"It's so bleak, so cold a prospect, Maestro." Lansing closed the folder that still lay under his hand. "Whatever we do, there is no even halfway pleasant path to follow."

"Well." Guido could only acknowledge the observation. "We've had our glorious summers. There's been a plethora of rich, harvest-laden autumns, when we reaped three hundredfold. And we did have our enterprising springtimes—some genuine, some false. But now, come the winter of our wait, we must do just that: We wait, even when mere waiting hurts. As the Poles and the Russians and all the others you have come to know so well already wait. We hold, although at times it may seem there is precious little to hold on to. We live in a sea of indifference and contempt, through every storm of malicious hate. We wait; and we await our Lord."

[70]

When Papa Valeska left Gemelli Hospital in November, life for him had changed forever. He was not yet fully recovered; a man less fit in body and less strong in his will might not have survived at all, so serious were the complications that followed the shooting. As it was, he would not be fully active for several months and he was brought out to Castel Gandolfo.

The most visible change, or at least the only one that the Holy Father chafed at, was the plethora of security precautions that constantly surrounded him. His life became a closely guarded commodity, filled with constant reminders of the deadly enmity that had stalked him once, and might again. Whether at Castel Gandolfo or anywhere in private Vatican grounds, he was guarded by five German sheepdogs, trained exclusively to his voice by an Irish Benedictine monk whose family had been rearing horses and dogs since before Henry VIII had broken with Rome in the sixteenth century. Wherever Papa Valeksa went, he was shadowed by discreet bodyguards. In any motorcade or at the window of his study, he would always now be shielded by bulletproof plexiglass. He was persuaded that he must wear a bulletproof vest on major public occasions. His food was tasted by two others before he was allowed to eat it. His apartment and work quarters were fitted out with hidden electronic eyes and alarms, and were periodically swept for "unfriendly devices."

Those were the visible changes. Among the less visible was, for example, the hush of waiting that fell over the Vatican. At first, on May 13 and the days immediately ensuing, everything had hung in the balance with Papa Valeska's very life. Now all depended on the manner in which he would take up the reins of his pontificate again.

Throughout those summer months, while still in hospital, Valeska had insisted on being informed exactly and regularly concerning his native land. His greatest preoccupation was not exactly how Poland was faring under martial law. Every Pole, including Valeska, knew what to expect. Most of Solidarity's leaders were in prison, as were the dozen most troublesome of the KOR leaders. There were the police brutalities, the iniquities of the hated Zomos, the presence of military personnel everywhere—in the media, industry, parliament, the government ministries. And, of course, there were the few but regular "disappearances" of Solidarity enthusiasts. All of that was to be expected, bad as it was.

What dominated Valeska's concern was the survival of Solidarity's base, that intricate network binding hundreds of thousands together in a living religious and cultural unity beyond the reach of the commissar's whip and the totalitarian decrees of Poland's Communist martinet, General Jaruzelski, who now governed Poland on behalf of Moscow's Politburo.

His Holiness relied heavily on Rico Lansing in a number of areas, but in none more than the work to maintain the difficult high-wire act, the precarious balance by which Jaruzelski had to keep the Soviets happy, and Valeska held the non-KOR elements of Solidarity intact.

Lansing conducted a series of delicate consultations on behalf of His Holiness with the military government of Poland. He formally conveyed the Holy Father's realization that certain elements of Solidarity had gone beyond the limits agreed upon between His Holiness and the Adamshin delegation in February of 1980. He made several covert trips into Poland and satisfied himself and Papa Valeska that his network there, together with its ties to the networks in other Soviet satellites, was intact.

It began to dawn on Rico after a while that he seemed to enjoy a certain immunity on his trips into Poland and the other satellites now. It was almost as though the word had gone out on him, among Polish officials particularly. A visible nod of thanks from General Control? That seemed likely, especially as Karlis Pelse, who had sent the message summoning Rico to the meeting with Lysenko, and who had therefore obviously been discovered, remained untouched. He was able to, and did, send valuable data concerning faith and religious practice—the number of priests operating; the number of baptisms; attendance at worship; abortions. But there were no more dispatches containing military or political data. Pelse, too, had made his deal, Rico guessed.

No sooner was Papa Valeska truly up and around and strong enough to work than he began again his daily round of audiences, and prepared to resume his papal trips.

To the Maestro, Helmut, Rico, and Cardinal Rollinger, Valeska explained his mind. He assured the Maestro in particular that he had not lost interest in the financial reforms they had touched on in the early weeks of his papacy. And he assured Rollinger, and through him the State Council, that he had not lost sight of the urgent need to address the vast problems within his Church. However, his two main offensives—the Polish model and his intentions concerning Fatima—had both been pulled from under him, at least for now. He needed more time to travel, to rebuild the prestige of his papal office, and to use that prestige in talking to the power centers of the world.

It was Rico Lansing who was closer to Papa Valeska than anyone except Father Jan Terebelski, and he was the first who began to suspect the deepest change that had taken place in the Holy Father. The impact of the bullets that had blasted into him went much deeper than the furrows and holes they had torn in his body. There had been an impact on his soul and mind. All the years he had spent in Poland facing down the deadly force of his Marxist enemies had not prepared him for the sudden and unexpected glimpse thrust upon him of the merciless power he was up against as Pope.

He had, after all, been shot on the very day—within the very hour—that he had offered his Mass in honor of the Lady of Fatima; had placed himself and his pontificate and his intentions, in effect, under her protection. How could he not wonder at the significance of that?

Rico broached the subject with Papa Valeska in one of their almost daily meetings. There was very little the Pope did not share with Lansing; on this subject, however, he had said little, and that in itself was revealing.

"Does it not seem," Rico ventured, "that Our Lady did protect Your Holiness out there in the piazza that day? The security people have said that if Your Holiness hadn't bent down when you saw the Fatima picture pinned to little Laura Bartoli's dress, you would have been killed. It was almost as if Laura was permitted to share her own miracle of recovery by being the instrument of saving Your Holiness' life."

Papa Valeska turned to face Rico in that slow, deliberate way that had become his since the assassination attempt. His lips were closed tightly as if he found it hard to control his welling emotion. He said nothing, but the intense suffering and frustration on his face was painful to see.

Lansing bowed his head silently. The Pontiff had suffered betrayal of

Solidarity by KOR, a murderous attack on his person, the loss of Cardinal Wallensky, and his own "rejection," as he might see it, by Fatima, all in less than twenty months. Clearly the waiting time he needed was not only to rebuild the prestige of the papacy, but to rebuild within himself the great fund of moral courage and determination that he had brought with him to Rome. In the meantime, he would do what he knew best to do. He would wait, as the Poles had always waited—and outwaited their oppressors—until God would facilitate a change.

It fell to Guido de la Valle, of course, to continue to "keep peace at home," as Valeska said to him again—to minimize any scandal, in other words, caused by Roberto Gonella's abuse of the Panamanian finance houses, the Italian stockbrokerage affiliate, and his other IRA involvements.

For the Maestro, it seemed evident that the holding pattern he had described to Lansing—that slow decline—would be the order of the day for the foreseeable future. He and Helmut mapped out long-term strategies, to carry at least through 1985, for continuing the work of loosening the grip of P-1 and P-2 on the far-reaching affairs of the *impero* and the Vatican Bank. He met with the *impero* on a more frequent basis; he wanted to ensure that they would avoid all business entanglements that would repeat the excesses of the past, and avoid all tainted deals. "We will still turn an honest penny," he told his associates, "but not as many pennies." And he continued to track the hefty portions of the $1.4 billion that were still missing.

The task of keeping peace at home was suddenly placed in extreme peril when, on June 11, Guido received two phone calls in quick succession, one from a Treasury official and one from Giulio Brandolini, both informing him that Roberto Gonella was missing. He could not be found in his Rome apartment or in his home in Milan. He had last been seen in a car with Nicola Starti at the wheel; that, in Brandolini's view, was a bad sign. Starti, who was now constantly at Gonella's side, it seemed, was a Sardinian building contractor who was both a known paid informant of Pappagallo's and a longtime conduit for underworld funds.

Italian surveillance dead-ended at Trieste. Austrian intelligence reports had Gonella and Starti crossing into that country at Klagenfurt. But there was no trace after that.

Guido's view was pessimistic from the very moment he heard the news. Perhaps there was a slim chance that if intelligence could pick Gonella up again, he would lead them to Pappagallo—for the Maestro didn't doubt that Gonella was headed for a meeting with the missing senatore. The likelihood, however, based on what Guido now knew from the ritual manuals of P-2 that had been retrieved from Pappagallo's villa, was that Gonella was as good as dead.

The banker had spent the eleven months since his release on bail in frenzied efforts to reestablish himself. He had used two main ploys, as the Maestro knew. He sold 2 percent of Agostiniano stock to the ultrarespectable and very Catholic Carlo De Lanieri of Dachtilo Machines. But De Lanieri split away in disgust only a few months later. Then, in January, Gonella announced that his banking consortium had doubled its net profits to 142.3 billion lire, with assets of 24.5 trillion lire; that, however, was almost immediately perceived as "paper juggling."

As far as the Maestro could see, Gonella had run out of options; and Pappagallo, wherever he might be, had surely seen that as clearly as everyone else.

There were only eight days to wait. On June 18, Roberto Gonella was found hanging by the neck from an undergirder of Blackfriars Bridge in London, near Bankside, where the lords and princes of high finance labored at the money trade.

At an emergency meeting of Security Two and the State Council, it was decided that the most "neutral" and the most experienced person the Vatican could send to London was Rico Lansing. They needed as many details as could be had about Gonella's death, and details about his English connections, if any. If Rico found creditors in London, as the Maestro now expected he would, who had been led to believe that in dealing with Gonella they were dealing with the IRA, such creditors were to be told that their money would be made good—in time, and provided the Holy See's financial agencies enjoyed the same confidentiality as before. The scandal must be held within limits. Nobody's hands were clean, least of all the creditors' hands.

Armed with his Vatican passport and letters of introduction to the home secretary, the prime minister, and the head of Scotland Yard's Special Division, Rico spent the best part of a week gathering as much information as possible. Details about Gonella's mode of death were readily available. The major portion of Rico's stay was spent pursuing the tangled web of Agostiniano's creditors and learning as exactly as he could how much money was owing to those creditors. Everywhere he probed in that web, he found three names inextricably linked in it: Lercani, Gonella, and Servatius.

Within ten days of Rico's return, Brandolini and Solaccio had ready for the State Council what they saw as the most plausible reconstruction of Gonella's fate, based on Lansing's findings and all the evidence available from other sources.

The last of "our circle," as Monsignore Brandolini phrased it, to see Gonella alive was Peter Servatius. It was certain that Gonella had gone to Switzerland, and that he had been summoned there by Pappagallo, but that the senatore materialized in London, instead.

"No doubt when they did meet in London"—Brandolini was methodical in his summary—"Pappagallo and the ever-present Nicola Starti formally invoked the rule of P-2 that failure by any member was punishable by ritual suicide. Gonella had agreed to that on the day of his initiation." Brandolini held up one of the P-2 manuals, as if that, or anything, could explain such insanity.

"If he went through with it, his wife and family would be provided for. If he did not, then his family would be taken care of in another way.

"From that point on, it was all ritual. Everything about it was cultic, meant to have a significance.

"The ritual Two Helpers, no doubt *frati,* or 'friars,' of the brotherhood, who rowed him from the bank of the Thames. The ritual choice of Blackfriars Bridge. The names of three men, and $16,000 in the various currencies in which he had dealt, and which he had in the end failed so disastrously to manipulate for the brotherhood—U.S. dollars, Italian lire, British sterling, Austrian schillings, Swiss francs, German marks—placed ritually in his pockets. The very symbol of ritual in Masonry, brick and mortar, stuffed down his trousers.

"Probably he placed the noose around his own neck, and stood of his own volition—if the threat of murder to his family can be thought to leave a man any choice—on the stern of the boat. It remained only for the *frati* to row away.

"Now, to back up for a moment to those three names I mentioned that were found in Gonella's pocket."

"Archbishop Peter Servatius' was one, I understand, Monsignore." Corelli was grim-faced, as were all the cardinals of the Council, including Rico, who knew the details well, and the Maestro and Helmut, to whom he had already confided them.

Silvio Fermaggio, Italian minister of finance, and Alberto Forli, director of one of Italy's largest banks, were the other two whose names were placed on Gonella. "I understand the theory is that these were the three people most significant in Gonella's downfall. I presume that was a warning of some sort to those three?" Corelli looked at Brandolini.

"That would be logical." Brandolini nodded. "But everything is so twisted with the deepest perversity in this killing, that I hesitate to be too logical about anything. It might be that it was meant as some sort of dreadful praise to the failed Gonella's symbolic 'executioners.' Beyond a certain level, who can understand the mind or the intent of men to whom another man becomes merely a chattel and whose life or death is only a means of conveying dreadful things to other people. Because it was a message. Not just to Servatius and the other two, though. But to all those who work at money. Those in Bankside, and all the others associated with them, whether they are in Italy, Switzerland, the U.S.A., or here in the Vatican. All who know how to read such messages have understood the language of the *frati* in that lifeless body of Roberto Gonella hanging over the Thames.

"All I can tell Your Eminences is that there was such intent, so blatant and crude, and so much thought and theory and belief behind this latest desecration, that it cannot have been Mafia; and it was not suicide in any usual sense. It belongs to the world of inverted worship. It bears that mark; and it has that significance."

Roberto Gonella's misfortunes, malfeasance, and miserable fate affected Guido de la Valle profoundly for the rest of his days. He understood that what had happened to Gonella is what happens, usually in subtler ways, to every man who spends his life licking at the drippings from the sweet and hidden power of the supermen. The parabola of Gonella's ambition had reared itself up to human heavens and had run into that straight line of the *sopragoverno* where it joins the curve of infinite evil.

The consequences of Gonella's ambition thrust Guido in spite of himself back into a true *commedia Italiana,* the overall purpose of which was to becloud the main issue on all sides.

The Italian government set up a three-man commission of inquiry. Papa Valeska, with Guido to guide him, set up a three-cardinal commission of inquiry. Foreign creditors hired a team of lawyers. Peter Servatius buried himself miles deep in his diplomatic immunity. The central Italian banks rushed to provide liquidity for the Agostiniano. Guido, Helmut, and several *impero* associates spent many hours talking to them all—Italian creditors, foreign creditors, government commissioners, cardinalatial commissioners, Peter Servatius, Papa Valeska, the prime minister, the president.

It was not the complex organization of the Holy See's defense that caused the Maestro distress; he was at home in such negotiations and planning. It did begin to seem, however, that the scandals and tragedies born of the Lercani–Da Brescia alliance would never end. "Everybody has something to hide," Guido said gravely at a meeting with his associates. "Everyone is jumping all over the Holy See. And we will hide no legal sins, if we find any. But every finger pointed at us, whether it belongs to the parliament or to the banks or to the creditors, has been stuck willfully in the muck. We capitalize on that. We will not be made victims. But prepare your souls. This thing is going to drag on for years."

As usual, his assessment was accurate. Right through the entire first half of the 1980s, Guido continuously mapped out the tortuous paths followed by Papa Valeska in order to minimize the scandal and the debt caused by the IRA's involvement with Gonella. It was he who guided Valeska's tough private interventions with the president of the Italian Republic, and it was he who directed the payment by the IRA of the sum of $250 million to the foreign creditors, "as a goodwill gesture" and not "as a sign of any guilt" in the Gonella embezzlement.

At the same time he set about using the *impero*'s worldwide organization in a new way—to make a different sort of reparation to people far more innocent than those clamoring "creditors," to men and women who had suffered through no fault of their own from Gonella's and Lercani's use of their Vatican connections.

In this operation as in everything he ever did, Guido always stayed well behind the scenes. This was not a matter of public relations, he told Helmut; it was a matter of Christian reparation. The means he used were the subtlest he could find. An obscure pensioner who had invested his life's savings in the Agostiniano, only to find the value of his shares reduced by two-thirds, might suddenly find that his dividends were raised by a comparable or greater amount. A Long Island shopkeeper who had been beggared by the fall of the Benjamin Bank might suddenly find long-term, low-interest credit unexpectedly available to him. A woman widowed by one of the many suicides of those ruined by Lercani or Gonella might be told of a trust fund she had never known about or of scholarships waiting for her children.

The Maestro also began to examine the financial sections of various chanceries of the Church around the world. In any place where he found clerics involved with tainted money or shady transactions, he had them removed.

More than once in all this renewed financial labor that was thrust upon him, Guido remembered how Papa Angelica had once complained to him about the miserable difficulty he had in withdrawing even 5,000 paltry lire from his checking account at the Banco. "I have been convinced ever since, Maestro," Angelica had confided in mock seriousness, "that there are only $10,000 of real money in the whole world, and all the rest of it is monkey money." Guido had laughed heartily with the Holy Father at the time.

The idea of monkey money had been such an innocent joke on Angelica's lips. It was hard to grasp how such an idea, in the minds of such men as Lercani and Gonella, could become the basis for the work of a lifetime, and spawn an epidemic—an international plague—of murders and suicides and corruption and disgrace and ruin. Even by the opening of 1986, the Maestro did not think the plague was over.

While Papa Valeska consulted to some degree with Cardinal Secretary of State Casaregna and found him obedient enough, it was on the Council of State that he relied for overall judgment about his problems with the Church. In the first few years after the most serious attempt on his life, the Council had been hopeful that the Pontiff would build for himself, through his papal travels, a high and unique personal diplomatic status; and that he would use that as a platform to launch his "Christian solution" for Europe, as he had always intended.

Not for a moment did any Council member ever come to doubt Papa Valeska's courage, or his strict orthodoxy in general moral matters such as abortion, contraception, priestly celibacy, marriage, divorce. Or his full belief in the divinity of Christ and the afterlife.

In the matter of his papal trips, however, and his diplomatic efforts, they began to quote to one another Cardinal Arnulfo's stubborn prediction of 1978: "It won't work."

This bitter truth was painfully borne in on Valeska during the occasion of his 1982 visits to Britain and to the Argentine. His trip to Britain had been scheduled almost one year before the day that war broke out between Britain and the Argentine about the ownership of the Falkland Islands—the Malvinas, as the Argentines called them.

A papal visit to Britain under such circumstances would have been taken as a partisan slap in the face to the Argentines. To renounce his British visit would be taken by the British as a rebuff.

Papa Valeska's solution: a visit to both countries—first to Britain, then to the Argentine. Not one bullet was stopped by the visits. No death was averted. No waste of millions on war-making or destruction of property was avoided. Papa Valeska's double visit made no difference. His visit to each side merely confirmed each side in its resolve to teach a war lesson to the other.

By the time Papa Valeska put the total effect of his papal trips into a general pattern containing the Polish failure, the assassination attempt, the Gonella suicide, the Agostiniano collapse, the recalcitrance of his bishops, the continual erosion of faith and religious practice—by then the buoyancy and enterprising élan of his first papal years had disappeared. Every year he still went dutifully on the exhausting trips—to Africa and the Far East, to other European countries, to Canada. But already by 1984 he was speaking of the "apocalypse descending on the human race," and hinting at "the invasion of the Holy of Holies by the Great Whore of Babylon"—a biblical sign of the End Times.

But the end did not come fast for Papa Valeska. He, like the Maestro, like the ever-persisting State Council, like the stubborn followers of traditionalist Archbishop Édouard Lasuisse, like all the hard-core Romanist remnants throughout the lands of Catholicism, were ushered by the blows of events beyond all human control into a holding pattern that lasted year after year.

Toward the end of Valeska's papal reign, the Pontiff's normal life and its conditions were no more than a sustained repetition of the earlier pattern—papal trips, diplomatic interventions, constant preaching of traditional Catholic doctrine to a largely deaf world, the barest control over his Vatican bureaucracy, constant trouble with independent-minded bishops, constant distress over the diminishing vitality of Catholicism. In one of the perennially lugubrious meetings of the State Council, several of the cardinal members remarked on the Pontiff's failure to reassert papal authority throughout the Church over the years of his pontificate.

"Consider ourselves and the Church to have been fortunate," Guido countered. "All these years, we've had a pope who held firm in the middle of universal breakage and through the lashing of storm after storm. *We* wanted a different sort of pope. Evidently, Christ did not. We have had the kind of pope *he* decided we should have. He has made us wait. All of us. Including Papa Valeska."

Later that day, when he and Helmut arrived home to Villa Cerulea, there was still an hour before dinner.

"Let's take a round in the garden," Guido said, looking at the wall clock.

They headed down the Family Path. What he did not express at the State Council meeting, Guido now admitted as he glanced from side to side at flower beds and trees. Of course, he felt a deep disappointment—admittedly personal to him—that Valeska had not been the pope to breathe a new spirit of Catholic commonality into the masses of believers. The divisive devastation of Catholics had never been greater.

"It was so much easier to believe when a great and living and vocal body of believers stood all around us. Nowadays—and this may be what Christ wanted us to learn—each one of us, each small group of us, like this precious family, has to find its own spirit of enthusiasm within oneself, within our small group. Never have I so appreciated this home and this family as I do now. Never was it—Look at that, will you!" He broke off as they reached the pool, and pointed with his cane. "Shh! Don't call out. Just look at them!"

Beyond the pool, and surrounded by shaped cypresses, lay the rose garden. Helmut could see Agathi and Keti inside there, totally silent as they carefully culled roses for the dinner table.

"From the utter gravity and concentration they are putting into this," Guido said quietly, "you'd say there's nothing more important right now in the wide, wide world! Let's wait for them to finish."

Only Tati, lying on the path beside the two women, noticed Helmut and Guido. She raised her head, her eyes shining, tail wagging. Guido silenced her with a gesture to his lips. She stayed in the same posture, looking at him.

"The world outside may be full of all the most horrible things," Guido said, "but look, somehow or other, God must be in his heaven and all must be right with his world, if we still have tranquil beauty and such—"

"Tati, what *are* you looking at?" Agathi had caught the dog's animated attitude out of the side of her eye. She followed the line of Tati's vision and glimpsed her brother and Helmut through the trees.

"Why are you both lurking out there and wearing that same idiotic smile, you two? Come in here and give us a hand. Make yourselves useful!"

As they trudged back to the house, Agathi and Guido carrying one basket between them, Helmut and Keti behind them with another, Tati following them, it seemed to Helmut that there was a whole symbolism in action at that moment. Those two beloved ones ahead of him had for the greater portion of their years successfully borne between them a basket in which they had preserved only the beauteous and the perfumed gifts of life. Keti and he should follow in their footsteps, careful to preserve what beauty and perfumed hope life proffered them.

COME
WINTER

[71]

AFTER PAPA VALESKA died and his mortal remains were buried with the usual pomp and ceremony beside the tombs of the other popes in the crypt beneath the High Altar of St. Peter's, the most frequent commentary among the old Vatican hands who had been on the scene as far back as 1978, and had witnessed the last days of the miserably self-tortured Papa Da Brescia, was that no man had ever sustained life's blows with such peaceful equanimity, with such moral strength, as Papa Valeska. It had been, in the proper sense of that word, a marvel to them all. As, indeed, it should well have been!

Even on the day before he died from the debilitating poison that slowly but irresistibly seeped through his arteries, when asked how he viewed his pontificate and his declining life, he used the same two words that had been on his lips during all the devastating years of the Winter that had clamped down on the affairs of his pontificate and on his Church.

"My czekamy." We are waiting, he would say.

By the day of his death, the words spoke volumes to those who had known him most intimately, for over those years he had used them frequently. If asked for what he waited, he would answer directly, never avoiding the truth he saw. "For the will of Christ about his Church," he would reply sometimes. Or, "For one small egress from the blind alley in which I, and my Church, have been trapped." "For divine grace to abound again and to open churchmen's eyes"; his blue eyes would sparkle at that thought. "For a new strength and force in this precious papacy," he might say, knowing his own strength was ebbing. And, latterly, when his doctors told him the end was near, "For the beloved face of Christ Jesus and an end to my exile."

Yet he never said anything morosely or gloomily or dispiritedly or sadly. It was always with the resonance of unshakable trust and unbeatable hope, no matter what terrible strictures had emaciated the visible body of the Church during the tedious years of that Winter.

The persistence of that trust of Valeska's was a marvel. There was no doubting that, surely: a marvel of divine grace. How else could he have persisted in those endlessly regular papal trips? Every continent and many, many nations saw him arrive, speak, give his blessing, and depart. Yet from it all, neither he nor anyone else could see a tangible result. Even after the much-touted visit to the Russian Orthodox churchmen of Moscow, and the Kiss of Peace exchanged with all the Orthodox at Zagorsk Monastery, the same anti-Roman sniveling continued once he had left. The Soviets did reap some propaganda benefits; but Church unity advanced not a whit.

Or, except for that trust, how could he not have been discouraged, even saddened into apathy, by the now open schism—in some cases, heresy—of his bishops? For, by the time he came to die, the once unified Catholic body had been fractured into multiple, autonomously behaving "churchettes," each bishop a little tinplate pope of his own making. Only sporadic patches of hard-core Romanist and papist communities existed throughout what once was Catholicism's territory. He had a few successes—he installed good bishops here and there. But he also installed bad ones. He had no other choice.

Valeska should, by any normal expectancy, have collapsed into papal solitude, or gone on a head-hunting rampage, or given up. He did none of those things. He simply waited. In trust.

And yet waiting did not mean he was passive. That was not his way either, though many an annoyed prelate was heard to ask why he didn't simply give up preaching against abortion. It obviously did no good, such churchmen said. By the year of his death, the worldwide annual rate was nearly 150 million, counting in the dreadful Chinese harvest of assassinated babies-in-the-womb. Or, faced with the wholesale acceptance of contraception and homosexuality by large sections of his Church and by the world at large, how could he keep on, year in, year out, bombarding it all as utterly unacceptable?

Trust was the answer. That, and the same force of love in him, which enabled him to put up even with the permanent presence of Peter Servatius, now retired from the Banco, but confined to the Vatican for his own physical safety and freedom. Even when he was in severely declining health, besieged by problems of the Church Universal, and battered by the events and developments that were the milestones of that Winter, Valeska was moved to genuine sympathy when the Maestro let drop a passing word about the death of his beloved cairn terrier.

"I hope it was peaceful, Maestro."

"Yes, Holiness. She had been ill. She knew she was going. She died with my hands around her. In peace."

"Surely none of her preciousness is lost but will be found in God in eternity, Maestro!"

"Surely, Holiness."

This from a Pope so beset!

He had done his best. It was little, but his best. He was partially responsible for the agreement between the superpowers to reunite the two Germanys in a totally neutralized federation, and for the military evacuation of all Europe by the United States and the Soviet Union. But then, with the rest of the world, he stood helplessly by as the Soviets substituted China for Europe in a new version of the cold war. He was as helpless as any other man to avoid the "trial" of "clean" nuclear bombs dropped by both the Soviet Union and China on remote populations, as if to demonstrate, like Paleozoic monsters, their readiness to destroy each other. He had been helpless to do anything for the millions who were allowed to die in the widespread starvation manipulated by the rich nations for the sake of population control.

Neither Valeska nor his Church had anything to say to affect the new international monetary system installed by the supermen of finance, or the behavior of the new international managers who, immune in their bureaucracies, now dictated a new zoning of all human activity—work, travel, nourishment, amusement, life span.

All that was heavy enough to bear and continually darkened the skies of the Winter. But it was the state of the Catholic millions of people that grieved him most, because even there, where he had the right by God's own mandate, he could do nothing to cure their spiritual ills. He could not, given the means at his disposal, do anything about the generations settling into adult "success"—the generations born in the sixties and seventies. Their religious education had been nil. They were by and large faithless. There had been no one to teach them. Their children were now immersed in a computerized, "electronic" mode of education in which religion had no place. His Church had no Catholic mode ready to educate people in faith—in spirit and love and salvation—when the only way they knew how to learn was by shrinking themselves to what computers could teach. His Church had no body of Catholic thinking about the new genetics, or about new cycles of human birth-life-death in outer space. His Church had social answers, and went to court like everyone else when they didn't. But they had no Catholic answers to most problems now.

Perhaps it was some small consolation to Papa Valeska that he had done his best to ensure freedom of action for the papacy should the Soviets decide to overrun Western Europe, as seemed to him increasingly likely. All sensitive and secret Vatican documents dealing with religious and political matters were transferred, on his orders, to a safe place in the United States. On his orders, too, extensive shelters against nuclear attack had been constructed beneath the Vatican. Aside from Valeska himself, only six aides—Casaregna was not among them—had ever entered these "communication caves," as the Pope called them. As that name implied, the shelters were fitted with state-of-the-art equipment to enable His Holiness to talk by satellite with his representatives in every part of the world, in any crisis, no matter how catastrophic.

There was some consolation, as well, in the number of priests who had reverted to saying the Roman Mass privately. The Pontiff had failed to reinstate it publicly, but at least the salvage operation originally started by Archbishop Édouard Lasuisse was perpetuated. Few knew it, but when Lasuisse died Valeska paid him the tribute he had not paid him in life. He had his body secretly conveyed to Rome and interred in the private Vatican cemetery. A later generation could, the Pontiff hoped, pay Lasuisse the tribute he had merited but not received from his contemporaries.

The October when Bogdan Valeska was elected Pope had been dark and lowering, like the skies of the prolonged Winter of his papacy. But, in what many saw as a sign of remission and near-future well-being for the gravely ill Valeska, the June in which he died had been a period of extraordinary mildness for Rome. There was none of the humid heat that normally boiled the city and its inhabitants. Instead, hoary Rome glistened in the early sunrise of each morning. Day after day of golden sunlight was succeeded by balmy evenings and nights made lovely by cooling southwest winds.

The mildness of Rome, some said, matched the mildness and forgivingness of Valeska himself. In reminiscing about the past as men do before they die, he spoke no bitter word. Not of Senatore Pappagallo, who had long since been sped to God's judgment by an enemy hand. Not of the bishops and theologians, who had filled his days with bitterness by their recalcitrance and their personal abuse of him. Not even of those who had, in a long-term fashion, brought on his decline in health. About them and all the others he had nothing but forbearance.

"My czekamy."

"The greatest hero of ancient Rome," Guido said the day Valeska died, "was a man the Romans proudly called Fabius Cunctator. 'Fabius, the general who waited but never surrendered.'

"At Winter's end, a very long time from now, Papa Valeska will be gloriously remembered as the Pope who waited but never surrendered."

[72]

Maestro Guido de la Valle settled into his place in *il Tempio* well before the 119 cardinals entered conclave at 5 P.M. that July 15. He took out his gold watch, laid it on the ebony table beside the red phone, and then settled back to wait for the sound of the little silver bell that would call the short evening session to order.

In the years since Rico Lansing had been selected by the Maestro and the State Council as prime *papabile,* the candidates—at least those to be taken seriously—hadn't changed. Pirandella had not been able to remake his fortunes. Buff remained the only opposition to reckon with. Guido hoped this opening session would get as far as a preliminary vote, a first test of strength. If that went well, tomorrow should tell the tale.

At five-thirty, once the doors were double-locked, the electronic surveillance established, and the conclave area sealed off, Cardinal Secretary Casaregna, as camerlengo of the Church, received the members of the State Council. Cardinal Azande handed him a sealed envelope, with Papa Valeska's signature on it, and addressed to the camerlengo. The single typewritten page inside was the required document from the last reigning pope attesting that Monsignore Richard Lansing, who had entered conclave as though he were an aide to Cardinal Rollinger, was actually, and had for some years been, a cardinal.

Casaregna, who had made a career of being on the right side in every situation, went ashen. Not to know a piece of information like that! That a man he had known in the Vatican for years, and had probably insulted more than a few times, was not only a cardinal but might be pope! Well, it was unsettling. Downright unsettling!

"All in order, Your Eminences." Casaregna controlled himself and managed a wintry smile. "I suggest we go in for our first session."

As they walked together toward the Sistine Chapel, he explained to Their Eminences with great amiability the procedure he would follow. Before he began the business of the evening, he would announce Monsignore—er—His Eminence Cardinal Lansing's status. It would be best if—er—His Eminence would wait outside the door until that announcement. He hadn't entered conclave in robes, after all.

"Very well, Eminence." Hoffeldt smiled sweetly. "But comfort yourself. St. Peter never wore scarlet robes, I'm sure."

"Of course, Your Eminence. Of course."

Once in conclave, the camerlengo managed everything smoothly. The announcement of Cardinal Lansing was greeted with murmurs, but by and large it was just noncommittal surprise. Rico took his place beside Lawlor of Boston and Mohunga of Mozambique. Both men gave him a firm handshake.

Lansing was surprised at the absence of any nervousness in himself. Even the wan smile of recognition from Buff across the chapel from him, and the cold-eyed stare of Carberin, who had succeeded O'Mahoney in Chicago, didn't disturb him.

In short order, Cardinal Azande was elected as cardinal dean of conclave, and Ahumada and Corelli as his two co-presidents.

Once they had taken their places at the presidents' long table, Azande read aloud the basic rules of conclave. With that, the preliminaries were finished, and the cardinal dean, consulting the papers Casaregna turned over to him, announced that His Eminence Cardinal Otto Feinstahl of Vienna had been asked to give the opening summary of the present condition of the Church.

Otto Feinstahl was one of the few genuine "characters" in the Sacred College of Cardinals. He prided himself on his nickname, "Feinzunge," for he knew he truly had a "fine tongue." He had a precision of diction, a clarity of phrase, and a natural ability to boil complicated facts down to their essence. At the same time, he could run a verbal saber through you, some said, and make you feel privileged.

It was for his clarity that he had been selected to make this speech, as "a template," he now said, addressing the full conclave, "by which Your Eminences can determine and assess the condition of our Church in order to form a general mandate; and then, with the guidance of the Holy Spirit, select the one among our number who will best use the power and privilege of Peter the Apostle to satisfy that mandate."

Feinstahl's gimlet blue eyes twinkled behind his steel-rimmed spectacles. The Austrian cardinal was a little like the proverbial good sportsman: It didn't matter whether the substance of what he had to say was good news or bad; it was how well he made the speech that mattered.

"Venerable Brothers." He began the litany of bad news eloquently:

"There is not one of us present here this evening who does not know the critical condition of the Church. So pervasive and deep are the divisions that splinter us, and the dissensions that set us upon one another as though we were enemies, that there may be in this conclave as many opinions as to the course we should follow as there are cardinals. But whatever the solution, the facts are undeniable. Painfully clear and undeniable.

"All, from pope to laity, are torn by dissidence. There is no unity in this Church Universal. There is no cohesion between pope, bishop, priests, and nuns—though all of them are supposed to be the official representatives of the Church. There is neither unity of doctrine nor cohesion of discipline.

"No wonder, then—if the governing and teaching structure of our Church is in shambles—that we have fostered in our millions of members ignorance about their religion and confusion about their moral practices; and that we have provided them with such a great array of bastardized methods of worship. It is almost as if we expected that there will be some door prize at the gate of heaven for novelty in liturgical practice and the Sacraments.

"As we offer nothing to the world in this hapless condition except strife—of which the world has a plentiful supply without our contribution—our millions of Catholics are abandoned. And so they in turn are divided. They see themselves not as Catholics, but as haves and have-nots. Not as God's creatures, but as capitalists or Communists. Not as the objects of Christ's Salvation, but as riven between the interests of two superpowers.

"Why, my Venerable Brothers, in Heaven's very name, should there *not* be revolts against authority in the Church in such circumstances? The authority has been abdicated. By us. Hence the clamor for equality, for democratization, for decentralization, for complete liberty of thought, of word, of action. We are fortunate they have not asked for our heads!

"Hence, Venerable Brothers, in short, the shambles of our institutional structure. The Church, as Papa Da Brescia warned us in 1978, is apparently bent on self-destruction.

"And it is in that condition, that mode of self-destruction, if you will, both that the Church faces the world of the new century that stretches before it; and that the world faces its future unprepared for anything that is coming. There is no Catholic teaching or Catholic understanding shedding a tinge of special light on the totally new world on whose threshold we stand.

"Now, Venerable Brothers, why is that, do you suppose?

"Is it, in a word, because we have abdicated our position to the faithless university professors and the novelists and the sociologists and the psychologists and the politicians? Is it because we ourselves have not either found or shown others the way to remain human and godly, in any Catholic—or even the merest Christian—sense, in the world of the managerial system?

"Is it because we have been content to deal with the problems others presented for our attention, that we have, for the first time in the history of the Church, prepared no Catholic thinking or understanding of the world around us? Of the electronic conversion of human activity, for example? Of the scientific domination and control of human genetics? Of life in outer space?

"Compared, my Brothers, to what we face from those factors alone, the blows we have suffered from Marxism-Leninism will seem to have been merely the taps of a clay hammer.

"For, pitifully, we churchmen of Christ have no specifically Catholic mentality. We behave as if our Catholic treasure house were empty. As if we had no supernatural resources.

"And, able to do nothing more than ape our already hapless and baffled contemporaries, we obsolesce. We get more and more out of touch.

"And yet we ask each other how it could be that the world of men and women whose shepherds we were have lost interest in our shepherding!

"It is because we have not shepherded. It is because we have become so preoccupied at picking the bones the wolves have left behind that we have forgotten all about the flock we tend.

"What, then, do we do? How do we heal our divisions? What policies must our next pope follow?

"We know what we do not need. A politician pope. A scientist pope. A financier pope. A humanist pope. A sociologist pope. A media pope. A legislator pope. A businessman pope. A theologian pope. An emperor pope. None of these will do. Nor any combination of all these, merely.

"What do we need, Venerable Brothers? We, who are all lost sheep? We need a Shepherd.

"And that Shepherd's just mandate must be to address the most basic and universal contention within this Church; the contention that has allowed to flourish all the other terrible ills and afflictions I have touched on so briefly.

"That contention is about centralized or decentralized governance of the Church. It is about the Roman fact. The obnoxious dispute is whether or not that traditionally Rome-centered government should be decentralized. For, I assure Your Eminences, if we do not make the settling of that contention the basic mandate of this conclave, the issue will be decided for us. We are very nearly at the point where it has been decided for us. We are very nearly to the point of becoming sheep ourselves, who do no more than follow the voice of oblivion.

"May God have mercy on us, Cardinal Electors. May he send his light into the darkness of our souls."

There was a short round of applause as Cardinal Feinstahl bowed several times to the double row of cardinals surrounding him to his right and left, and a few more times to the double row of cardinals across the floor against the opposite wall. Then he sat down, a beatific smile on his face at the excellent job he had done.

"Eminences." The voice of the cardinal dean quieted the ripple of comment and murmuring among the electors. "Our first task is to agree to the general mandate."

"Your Eminence Lord Cardinal Dean." Carberin of Chicago wanted to be recognized for a clarification. "What is the mandate, please?"

Feinstahl glared at his Venerable Brother. Truly he must be a product of the electronic conversion of human activity. Clearly, the man could understand nothing more complex than a statement of twenty-five bytes, followed by instructions of which button to push. How could one talk of grace and spirit to such a mind? He, a cardinal, was a living example of what Feinstahl had been talking about.

"The mandate," Azande obliged, "is to heal the rift and division in the Church Universal caused by the present contention over centralized versus decentralized Church government."

"Thank you, Your Eminence." Carberin hoped that had cleared away the emotion of some of Feinstahl's rhetoric.

"Unless there is a contrary will in the conclave"—Azande went on with the business at hand—"we can take a simple roll-call vote on the mandate, without a written ballot." He looked up and down the two long double rows of cardinals. There was no contrary will. "Very well. I shall read out the name of each participant here."

It took the better part of ten minutes to conduct the poll. The general mandate was accepted. Among the abstentions were Mohunga of Mozambique, Rollinger, Borgo-Mancini, Hoffeldt, Corelli, Falconieri, and Lansing.

Azande looked at his watch. Not yet seven o'clock. Dinner hour wasn't until eight. Plenty of time. Might as well give the cardinals something to politick about during the overnight hours.

"The next item of business, Your Eminences, is the nomination of candidates."

Cardinal Svensens was on his feet immediately and, when recognized, nominated Cardinal Buff of England, with a short speech extolling His Eminence's long service to and understanding of the Church "in all its many facets," and underlining His Eminence's long-felt desire to heal the very rift that was the subject of the new papal mandate.

As was the custom, the nomination was seconded, without speeches, by two other cardinals, Carberin of Chicago and Grosjean of Paris.

Cardinal Corelli then rose in his place and put the name of Cardinal Lansing in nomination. There was a certain amount of pleasant surprise in some quarters, and of not so amiable eyebrow raising in others, at Lansing's nomination. The phalanx of the opposition—Svensens, Grosjean, Pirandella, four or five more, and certainly Buff—were dismayed, but they had been betrayed by the sudden and surreptitious introduction of this—this American—this Cardinal appointed secretly by a previous pope for ad hoc reasons—this intimate of Vatican power brokers now called on by them to be obedient and do his best for the establishment. Well, his best would not be good enough.

Still, this was not the moment to cross swords. All decorum was preserved.

To the surprise of the majority here, Corelli made no speech in support of his nominee. Lansing had insisted it be done that way. For one thing, he had said, when the cardinals returned to their rooms after the opening session, they would find on their tables a folder with ample information on both candidates. In the second place, no face in conclave would be a stranger to him. He knew a majority of them personally. With some he was on a first-name basis. Some he had met cursorily over the years. With a few—Oceania's Fahimazamahatra; Tanzania's Lokassa—he had merely a handshake acquaintance. But he was a known commodity at some level to them all. Third, and most important, he did not want to *seek* the papacy. He would speak his mind as clearly as he could when the moment came. And if the choice fell on him, he would serve. But if that happened, he wanted it to be the purest will of the Holy Spirit, untampered with by the self-willed politicking of mere men.

There was a greater stirring among the cardinals when Corelli sat down without making the expected speech in favor of his nominee than there had been at Lansing's surprise nomination. Buff gave a bucktoothed smile of satisfaction to Carberin and Grosjean.

Cardinals Lawlor and Mohunga seconded for Lansing.

Once again Azande looked at his watch. Seven-fifteen. There would be time for a test ballot before the preliminary session ended for the night. He reviewed the balloting procedure for the cardinal electors. Each would write the name of his choice on one of the paper ballots on the table before him. Blank ballots would be counted as abstentions. The ballots would then be deposited by each one in the urn at the far end of the presidents' table. As this was a preliminary ballot only, and the seventy-nine votes—two-thirds plus one—required for election was not expected to be achieved, Azande urged a certain dispatch on his Venerable Brothers; and the Venerable Brothers complied.

Within a half hour, all the ballots had been marked. Azande read them aloud; the cardinal secretary of conclave recorded them and announced the results.

"Forty-five votes for My Lord Cardinal Buff.

"Forty-five votes for My Lord Cardinal Lansing.

"Twenty-nine abstentions."

As in so many things, the modern Apostles of the Church of Christ presented a mirror of the world around them. As their vote clearly indicated, they did not yet know which way to turn.

The Maestro negotiated the winding stairs that led from *il Tempio* down to the Courtyard of St. Damasus, where Helmut awaited him in the limousine. He nodded to the chauffeur to begin the drive home; it was odd not to see Sagastume there in the front seat, and odder still the way he had simply packed his things one day and disappeared. It was just as well, perhaps; that giant had become almost surly, as if he had come to disapprove of the Maestro, now that he was no longer fighting for ascendancy among the power brokers.

Well, what did the Maestro need with a giant bodyguard? His days of brave forays into enemy camps were well behind him.

"How did it go, Uncle?"

Helmut's question was not an intrusion on the Maestro's fleeting thoughts about Sagastume.

"Kiff-kiff," he answered. "Even, at forty-five votes each, with twenty-nine uncommitted. The cardinals need more data before they decide."

"No speech from Corelli?" Helmut knew Rico's mind on that matter as on most others.

"No. But our people will make up for that after dinner. The cardinals have a long night of politicking ahead of them. Working a conclave is the *pointe fine* of *romanità.* In that department, men like Falconieri and Borgo-Mancini, and even Rollinger and Hoffeldt, have it all over the unsophisticated glad-handing of Buff and his supporters."

For the rest of the ride home, the Maestro filled his nephew in on the details of the session, and they discussed the possibilities and expectations in quiet tones.

At dinner, there was no mention of conclave, beyond Agathi's and Keti's plans to spend the next afternoon at Rico's apartment, where they would watch from his window for the white puff of smoke, "just in case."

"I'll drop you both there in the morning if you like, *carissima.*" Guido rose from the dinner table. "I'll be leaving at about eight."

"Uncle Guido." Keti laughed as she and Helmut followed the other two up the broad staircase. "Even I know that cardinals at any time are the Lord's most long-winded creatures. And with the condition the Church is in, we'll be lucky if we have a new pope in two or three days.

"We'll drive in after lunch and catch up on all the gossip with Vittorio Benfatti."

It was not the condition of the Church that was on Agathi's mind. "You look tired, Guido darling. Please go to bed without doing any work. Promise."

A tapping on Guido's chest woke him. He opened his eyes, to see Sagastume leaning over him, beckoning him to come along, to hurry. They were already late.

Obediently, the Maestro started to get up—but then he stopped, half raised on one elbow. What place was this? He was not in his own bed. This was not Villa Cerulea. This was . . . This was . . .

Guido forced his mind to concentrate. It was important to know where he was. His head began to ache. The light from that great glass wall over there was blinding him.

Maybe if he could draw the curtains. He stirred again, intent on blocking out that glare; but Sagastume would not allow it, stepped in front of him, forced him back without a word or a touch.

When Sagastume stepped aside again, the glass wall was filled with faces. Why were they all looking at him? Hundreds of faces. Who were they? Why had they come here to stare at him? Who . . . ?

But yes, he knew that one. Wolff, wasn't it? The German officer Wolff, who wanted his Nazis to get to South America. And there was Mussolini, up there in the corner, hanging upside down, staring at him with those terrified, bulging eyes. And oh, dear God, Petacci had come to stare at him too. Claretta Petacci, who had turned her back on Mussolini's executioners and died with her arms around his neck, was screaming, open-mouthed, at Guido. The way she had screamed at the Communist partisan Valerio and his guerrillas on that peaceful day when she had been murdered beside Lake Como.

Was Valerio there too, then? Guido tried to see; but they all began to move, those faces. Wait! He couldn't see them if they moved. They were making him dizzy, the way they careened about, up and down, sideways, pushing and shoving against one another and against the glass of that wall.

The Maestro knew what they wanted. He had always known what they wanted. They were looking for a way in; or a way to get the Maestro out.

There, he could see that one. Lercani, wasn't it? And Gonella, the rope that had fastened him beneath Blackfriars Bridge still trailing from his neck.

He wouldn't allow it! He would not allow them in! He would not go out to them! He had to get to conclave!

"Dear God! Dear God! Send your angels to protect me!" Guido forced his way across the room as though against the counterforce of some darkling current that was having at him with every step. "Dear God in heaven, help me to hold."

The current was entering his body; his skin was no longer an interface. Despair was the name that current wrote across his mind and will.

"My Christ! My Christ!" He could say no more than that, repeat no other words. His whole assurance, his only resistance, his very hope lay there. "My Christ! My Christ!"

The current eddied once more against him, as though to spew him up on some bleak shore. . . . "My Christ! My Christ!" . . . and then receded, sweeping the horde of faces out of sight.

"Nanno? Nanno? Are you all right, my Nanno?"

Guido turned over in his bed. It had all just been a terrible dream, then. Here was Eugenio, come to wake him on his birthday. How fine he looked this morning.

"Nanno, I've been waiting for you. We have everything ready. . . ."

The sound of that voice in Guido's ears again was like balm to his mind and sweet inspiration to his spirit. Lambent remembrances of all past mornings wound gently through his mind. Eugenio creeping in to surprise him. Tati waking up and stretching herself. Don Filippo saying early Mass. The dawn chorus calling daylight down upon the Alban Hills.

He could hear that chorus now, in fact. It was another day. The finches and the swallows and starlings . . .

"Do you hear them, Eugenio?"

"I hear them, Nanno."

"It must be time."

"Almost. I'll go on ahead."

"But where? You mustn't leave; not now."
"I'll wait, then."

"Guido! Guido!" Agathi's hand flew to the bell button hanging on the headboard. Almost at once, Helmut was beside her.
"What's the matter? What's happened?"
"I don't know. I can't wake Guido. When he wasn't down for breakfast, I came to call him. But I can't wake him. Run quickly. Get Don Filippo. And call Dr. Sepporis. Hurry!"
Don Filippo anointed Guido with Holy Oil. Then, with Agathi, Keti, and Helmut kneeling beside Guido's still form, Don Filippo said the Mass of the Angels, because that was the Mass the Maestro asked to be said on Eugenio's birthday every year.
"Do you hear that?" Guido smiled at Eugenio. "Is there any lovelier sound than the words of the Holy Sacrifice?"
"Yes. Nanno. If you'll say goodbye now, I'll show you where. And we'll wait together for the others. Just the way I used to wait in the garden. Remember?"
Don Filippo finished the Mass. Guido's breathing grew slower and stronger. Agathi took his hand in both of hers and kissed it. She kept her head lowered, cradling his fingers against her cheek.
At the slightest stirring—the barest movement, it was—she raised her head. She saw her brother's eyes open slowly. They brimmed with smiling light, telling her of his love; of his gratitude that she had come in time, that she was there; telling her his agony was over; and sharing with her the confirmation of hope eternal.
And then they closed again.

When the cardinal electors assembled for the morning session of conclave, most had had a reasonably good sleep. The politicking and canvassing had gone on until about midnight or 1 A.M., as groups and pairs of cardinals argued and discussed and reflected together up and down the enclosed area of conclave. No one broke the prohibition against canvassing votes; but everyone participating was either making up his own mind, or having it made up for him. Swords were being sharpened. Lines of battle were forming.
Rico had retired early to his room, and had risen before most of the others to say an early Mass while it was still quiet.
"Your Eminences." Cardinal Azande rang the silver bell at nine o'clock straight up. "As Your Eminences know, the trial vote last evening resulted in a tie. Normally, the nominee with the largest number of votes is called upon first to give his answer to the mandate. As it is, we will proceed in alphabetical order." A pause to allow for any objection. As there was none, Azande nodded to Cardinal Buff.
"Here we go," Cardinal Lawlor leaned over and whispered to Lansing. "Dear old Lionel George Dustwaite Cardinal Buff is about to enlighten us."

The gaunt Englishman stood up, notes in hand. Except for his buckteeth, he cut a reasonably impressive picture. He made the ritual bow in Azande's direction, and turned confidently to speak his mind to his brother cardinals.

"Your Eminences, we have arrived at a historic moment in the history of the people of God. I do not share my very eminent brother's pessimism about the general condition of our Church." Buff gave a polite bow to Cardinal Feinstahl; no harm meant, that bow said. "But of course we all share His Eminence's preoccupation to some degree. We do have problems. I do not come before Your Eminences as a Pollyanna. But neither am I a Cassandra.

"Stressing disunity and fraternal friction between pope and bishops and priests and nuns, and with an allusion to the theologians and others in our university, our Venerable Brother Cardinal Feinstahl has told us that the next pope must end the friction, must be a pope of unity, a healer of our divisions.

"With all that I have no quarrel. And I accept with all my heart the mandate to heal the rift and division in the Church Universal.

"The answer is: Remove the cause. What is needed, my Brothers, is a recognition that in our age, the bishops and priests and nuns of the Church have reached a new maturity. And local churches and local communities have been brought by the Holy Spirit to such self-realization that each church and each community becomes, in itself, a focus of revelation and higher spiritual development. It is through still further and still higher development of single communities—all in communion with the Bishop of Rome—that the new era of Christianity, suitable to the century opening before us, will blossom.

"The next pope must therefore end the centralized hegemony of the Church. That was suited to a more immature age, a less democratic age, a less enlightened age, a less Christian age. And, let me say frankly, to a papacy that was imperialist in both origin and outlook.

"The Holy Spirit is now beckoning us to take the next step forward into the fullness of Christ in the human cosmos. Beckoning us to complete the magnificent work of Papa De Brescia, and to humanize the face of the Church so that all will recognize in us their brothers. And, I hasten to add, their sisters; for women now have a new dimension in the economy of salvation."

Buff paused for just a moment. There was a stir among the waiting cardinals. Good. He had them with him.

"I must omit here many details," the cardinal went on smoothly, almost intimately. "Your Eminences will understand that the question of how we can achieve total integration with the human race, and thus achieve the fullness of Christ the Man Savior, is a very large and complex one, involving many important details.

"But as the mandate presented to this conclave concentrates upon the divisions within our Church itself, let me at least touch upon what must be done.

"I assure Your Eminences: if, tomorrow, real and universal decentralization were to take place, there would be an instant and almost deafening hush throughout the Church. There would be no more written and verbal attacks on the Holy See. No more viciously angry women's demonstrations. No more theological tracts published by dissident theologians against the Pope. No more sullen reports by priests' organizations. No more accusations of capitalistic imperialism hurled at the Holy See. No more media blitzes against the Church by the liberal establishment, by fanatical anti-Roman Protestants, by homosexual organizations. No more anti-papal bitterness in Greek and Russian Orthodoxy. In a word, a hush. The friction and contention and scandal would cease.

"Decentralization will mean restoring the See of Rome to its historic role as first among equals.

"But"—the Englishman smiled as at a heavenly vista—"without ecclesiastical imperialism; without a doctrinal straitjacket; with charity towards all; with animosity towards none; without constricting legal power over other equals of Rome throughout the Church.

"These are the main lines along which I would solve the disunity of our Church. As I read that disunity as the call of the Holy Spirit, so I rely, rely on Your Eminences to ratify my policy of decentralization into a concrete mandate. Let us go forward in trust and hope and love."

Cardinal Buff bowed once again to Azande in the total silence that followed upon his stunning performance.

Even before the British cardinal had sat down, Cardinal Carberin was on his feet, claiming the floor, anxious to capitalize on the moment.

Azande nodded, recognizing him.

"Your Eminences, why wait any longer? Our Venerable Brother My Lord Cardinal Buff has offered us a brilliant *impostazione,* one based on our already approved mandate, and one that would knit our troubled Church and all of God's children into one seamless whole. As it should be.

"The alternative candidate has been so contemptuous of this conclave and of its mandate as not even to permit his nominator, His Eminence Cardinal Corelli, to speak of his intentions or his desires or his qualifications to carry out that mandate.

"I propose we vote immediately, therefore."

Carberin took his seat, avoiding Lansing's steady gaze.

It was a gross move, and with Azande as cardinal dean, it failed.

"My Lord Cardinal Lansing," Azande said evenly, "has been duly and properly nominated in accordance with all the rules of conclave. According to honored custom, he will be heard."

Azande turned then to where Lansing sat, his black soutane singling him out in the scarlet-robed assembly of his peers.

Helmut de la Valle fitted the ancient key into the lock, turned it once, and opened the door to *il Tempio.* He stepped inside, turned the switch, stood for a moment in the blue light that shone softly from the floor sconce. He was reluctant to sit in that chair where Guido had been mere hours before. The Keeper's Chair.

He closed the door behind him finally. He allowed himself one more moment, and then took the place he was sworn to take.

As he reached for the red phone, he noticed that the Maestro had left his tally of the trial conclave vote that had been taken the evening before. Beside the orderly count there was a brief notation: "Deadlock possibilities"; and beneath it, the names of two or three men Guido had thought might emerge if the vote did not swing on the next ballot clearly in favor of Buff or Lansing.

Tears swam in Helmut's eyes and he had to wipe them away to see.

"The alternative candidate has been so contemptuous of this conclave and of its mandate as not even to permit his nominator, His Eminence Cardinal Corelli, to speak of his intentions or his desires or his qualifications to carry out that mandate. . . ."

Cardinal Carberin's fiery challenge echoed clearly in *il Tempio,* forcing Helmut's mind to concentrate on what had to be done. He lifted the red phone beside the pad the Maestro had left ready for the next tally of votes.

Even before Azande called on Lansing formally to address the cardinal electors, all eyes had turned to Rico in expectation. Most of the electors had given him rather little thought before this conclave. After all, Monsignore Lansing had always been discreet, retiring, noncombative, part of no bureaucratic cabal, not to be reckoned with in the power rat race.

Most of them were intent in their study of him now—the still-young face, the hair still auburn, but with streaks of gray, thinning a little perhaps, but not receding. Few noticed the small red light winking on the cardinal dean's telephone.

Azande removed his glance from Rico for a moment. He picked up the phone, listened, said nothing, but was visibly affected by what he heard.

In the interim, a few of the more restless cardinals stood to stretch their legs. A few took up whispered conversations with their neighbors.

Azande scribbled out a note, and handed it to the youngest of the presiding cardinals, Corelli, with whispered instructions. While Cardinal Corelli made his way to Lansing's chair, Azande leaned over to the third co-president, Cardinal Ahumada.

Rico nodded his thanks and unfolded the paper Corelli handed him.

> Maestro Guido de la Valle went home to God at 7:35 this morning. The Keeper and his family stand firmly with you.

The words leapt out at Rico, blurring his vision with the force of their impact. In a flash of loving imagination he could almost see the Maestro's face. He could see Keti and Agathi in their grief. His eyes searched along the wall where he knew *il Tempio* must be. It was Helmut who sat there now.

He looked back down at the paper he had crumpled in his hand. *"The*

Keeper and his family stand firmly with you."

"Rico?" It was Cardinal Lawlor, leaning over to him. "Rico. Azande is looking this way. He's waiting for you to give a signal that you're ready. Are you okay?"

Lansing glanced past Lawlor's concerned face, past the presidents' table and the altar behind it, to the face of Christ in judgment painted by Michelangelo to gaze out upon centuries of conclaves that had brought His Church to this day.

"Yes, Bernie." Lansing answered Lawlor finally. "I'm all right." He looked at Azande, nodded his readiness, stood, bowed to the cardinal dean.

"Your Eminences." Rico's voice was hoarse and he stopped for a moment to clear his throat.

"Your Eminences," he began again, his voice and his emotions under control now, his impeccable Roman accent filling the chapel. "So that no one may think later that I had not made myself clear"—a glance at Carberin—"let me state two things categorically.

"First, if I am elected, I shall accept this office. But, of myself, I want in no way to be pope." He faced Buff directly across the chapel.

"I have not made myself available to those looking to make a new pope. I have not, as the saying goes, 'sold' myself as *papabile;* nor mustered the voices of schismatic-minded bishops over sandwiches and coffee; nor solicited media-crazy priests to flog my candidacy."

The shot went home. Buff flushed beet red.

"Nor have I enlisted the favor of prelates placed advantageously with the wielders of secular power who lurk in the background."

Many a brow knit in puzzlement at that; but Casaregna and a few others threw furtive glances at Pirandella.

"Second," Rico went on without a pause, "if Your Eminences do choose me, it will not be on Your Eminences' conditions. I will accept neither the mandate voted upon last evening nor any other that may be voted in its place."

There was a rustle of murmurs as electors looked quickly at each other, trying to gauge the meaning and acceptability of this forthright refusal. Carberin flung his arms up in the air in a despairing gesture, as if to say, "I warned you all!"

Lansing's next words made every head turn back to him. "I will not be your man. Choose me, if you will, against my will, so that Christ, who solely possesses power, privilege, and office, ratify your choice and endow me with the triple power of papacy. That I cannot in conscience refuse. I am and will be only Christ's man. You, of yourselves, have no power to give me, no privilege to confer on me, no office to confide to me."

"Your Eminence!" Azande boomed out in his deep basso. "It is required by immemorial custom that so great a departure from the ritual of conclave as a denial of the mandate be explained."

Lansing bowed his head in Azande's direction. "In any other circumstances but our present ones, probably I could accept a mandate from a conclave of my peers. But now, Eminences, in my opinion, unlike that of

His Eminence Cardinal Buff, we do not stand poised in our spiritual maturity ready to blossom with a 'new era of Christianity.'

"We stand in blind agony, ready to lurch over the edge of a precipice. Our situation is far more critical, far closer to terminal, than I believe many of you realize. We are within sight of the end, as an institution, of what we all have known as the One, Holy, Roman, Catholic, and Apostolic Church.

"I pray there is time for one more move. We are here to decide what move that will be. We can act, as My Lord Cardinal Buff seems bent on doing, so as to topple over the edge into total chaos. Or we can act so as to draw back.

"I have no earthly assurance that your mandate, even if interpreted differently than my Venerable Brother from England does, would not topple the Church over that edge. Nor have you.

"If Your Eminences insist on this mandate, pick another candidate to do your will. I am not willing to take responsibility for that mandate."

"Your Eminence." Cardinal Falconieri was leaning forward in his throne. "Will Your Eminence take a question?"

"I will." Rico nodded.

"Does Your Eminence accept my Lord Cardinal Feinstahl's broader analysis on which he based the mandate?"

Lansing needed little time to consider his answer. "I have, of course, the greatest respect for My Lord Cardinal Feinstahl, as for My Lord Cardinal Buff, as for all of you, My Lords Cardinal. But all of you who accept the analyses we have heard so far have been so thoroughly indoctrinated with the Marxist view of history as to be unaware of it, as you are mindless of the air we breath.

"The Marxist view of everything, like the view given of our Church, hinges on the dogma of 'the class struggle.'

"You have transposed such thinking—this Marxist dogma—onto the plane of Church analysis. We could end all our tatterdemalion status, you say, if we could end this class struggle, or that one. The struggle of priests with bishops. The struggle of bishops with the Pope. The struggle of nuns to be priests or to be bishops or to be Pope or to be married to any of them. Everything is reduced to the image of one class struggling with every other class, some forming temporary alliances from time to time.

"The chief culprit of our ills, in the analyses I have heard in this hallowed place, is 'the Struggle.' 'The Disunity.'

"We can end it all, say My Lord Buff and his supporters, if we do away with one contending side in the struggle. Do away with the authoritative, power-claimant papacy. Leave only 'the people of God' in sole possession of the field.

"That is, of course, much like the Marxist argument proposing to liquidate a different class struggle by liquidating the entire capitalist bourgeoisie, leaving only the 'people' in sole possession of that field.

"My analysis is quite the opposite. Disunity, struggle, disruption—

none of those is the disease that besets us. They are symptoms of the disease. And trying to cure those symptoms with the Marxist-inspired solution to the 'class struggle' is like curing a strep throat with an injection of cancer cells. It is death.

"I have been too close to Marxists for too long to contract any of their dreadful disease of the mind. But I can recognize it when I see it, under any name. And what I have heard here is a formula for creating the de-Catholicized mind which will abandon or forget or betray the fundamental character of the Church.

"We can join the rest of humanity on the meadows of achievement, My Lord Cardinal Buff has said, if we abolish the struggle.

"And yet, Christ did not say, "I will found several church communities, which will each develop autonomously.' Nor did he say, 'You, Peter, will be one bishop among thousands of other peer bishops, a chairman of the board of bishops.'

"What Christ said was this: 'You are Peter, and upon you, as upon a rock, I shall build my Church.

"And that, My Lords Cardinal, is why, from the earliest time, this Church of Christ has described itself with the five titles I have recited once already this morning."

As he repeated each title, he looked straight at one or another of the cardinals who had worked so long and hard to strip those titles away.

"One"—he threw the first title at Buff; "Holy"—that was for Grosjean; "Roman"—for Carberin; "Catholic"—for Svensens; "Apostolic"—he ended with Pirandella.

There were a few isolated shouts. *"Bravo! . . . Ottimo! . . . Bravo!"*

Azande stopped the shouts with a few glaring stares. "Your Eminence." He turned to Lansing. "You have told us your view of the conclave mandate, and that it is falsely based. That it has wrongly taken the struggle and disunity in the Church as its focus.

"What, in Your Eminence's view, should be the focus of our mandate. And therefore of papal policy?"

"Very simply this, Your Eminence: Our struggle is and always has been over one thing—power.

"Not the power of classes. Not ecclesiastical or social or political power. But the very same power St. Paul singled out at the very beginning of Rome's history. The power of one brilliant, fallen Archangel and his hordes. The power of darkness.

"And, as that Apostle pointed out, our struggle with that power can be waged only with the weapons given to us by Christ, whose servants we are. Moral power is ours. Spiritual authority is ours. That is all. And that is enough.

"Your Eminences, I do not wish to make a whipping boy of any cardinal here; and certainly not of any pope. But My Lord Buff has counseled us to complete the magnificent work of Papa Da Brescia.

"I have served five popes. Not from an archbishopric or a bureaucrat's desk, but in the front lines.

"Papa Profumi, the first of those five, saw the reality, the real struggle, the frightening one that lies between evil—a Person resident in the house of human kind—and a divine Person also resident in that house.

"He struggled with that Evil One as best he knew. He was in no way Marxized in his thought; but he was finely schooled in the art of politics and diplomacy, and realized only too late that those are not the weapons to stem the advance of that Enemy. And Papa Profumi died in his regrets.

"Papa Angelica, already the partial victim of the Marxized mind, decided—correctly, I believe—that what was needed in the world was love. It was he who made a pact between the Holy See and the Moscow Politburo. But he had no inkling of what Evil was and is and means. Nor did God give him time to learn. And Papa Angelica died in his regrets.

"Papa Da Brescia, the most Marxized of the papal minds, was the dupe of ruthless apostates and of faithless clerics. He, indeed, believed in the class struggle. And he died in the most poignant and pathetic of regrets.

"Papa Serena, alien to all Marxism, was Marxism's most illustrious and prime victim. But he died in our regrets, because in his death we saw how Evil had so deeply penetrated the Holy See that the Vicar of Christ could be done away with in the safety of the Apostolic Palace.

"Papa Valeska, the most shining figure to occupy the papacy since Pope Benedict XIV in the eighteenth century, or Pope Innocent XI in the seventeenth, fell victim to that same class struggle. For all his papal efforts were bent to solve it. And meanwhile, Evil fattened off his Church like a jackal gnawing at the bloodied carcass left by a sated lion. His 'communications caves' running beneath our very feet are mute witnesses to his desperation in the face of an evil he could not overpower. And, your memories will tell you, Papa Valeska died in his regrets.

"With all respect to Lord Buff, we are not called to complete the work of Papa Da Brescia. Or of Papa Profumi. Or of Papa Valeska.

"Marking the pontificates of each of those men," Rico continued, "was one fatal error: the use of their spiritual office to obtain leverage in the political and diplomatic and civic and cultural worlds; and then using that leverage instead of the spiritual power and moral authority that was uniquely theirs.

"And here, Your Eminences, we are at the root cause of our pain, our struggle, and our deathly peril: our failure, and the failure of our popes, to use the Church's spiritual power to exercise its moral authority."

"My Lord!" Pirandella was standing in his place. "A question." All hostility seemed gone from him. His was not the look of a man ready to throw barbs at an enemy.

"As many as you like, Your Eminence."

"Your Eminence has said you reject the conclave mandate. I understand why. Now I understand. But what mandate have you? How would you carry on this struggle you have described so forcefully?"

For some seconds, Rico didn't answer. He had the oddest sensation.

Not physical. More like a palpable memory; one he could almost touch. He remembered the way the Maestro used to talk about the "presence of my angel, Eugenio." What Lansing felt now was an understanding of exactly what Guido had meant. He felt the presence of the Maestro.

He looked down at the crumpled note he still held in his hand. He smoothed it out and read it again, remembering the night the Maestro had told him he was *papabile;* and the bleak scenario of Winter he had drawn; and the words he had said about breaking the Bargain; and about relying on spiritual power and moral authority alone.

"If Papa Valeksa will rely on those means," Guido had said, *"Then I'm ready to begin when he is."*

"His Eminence has no answer." Carberin was standing, furious at Pirandella's apparent defection to Lansing. "He rejects our mandate and has none other."

"Yes." Rico's voice was strong and full. "Lord Carberin is right. I have no mandate. Except to begin.

"Your Eminences." Rico held up the wrinkled paper with Helmut's message written in Azande's hand. "I hold before you the death notice of a great man. Very few of you ever heard his name: Maestro Guido de la Valle. Fewer of you still ever had the great privilege of knowing him.

"Yet every one among you who rules a diocese handled your diocesan finances through the Holy See. Remember the long-term loans? Remember the low rates of interest? The doors that opened for you in the financial houses in your own countries? Remember the yearly diocesan deficits the Holy See made good? All that was made possible by this one man." Rico held up the rumpled paper again. "He won for the Holy See a position of equality among the managers of our world's money.

"He had achieved that by the mid-seventies. Along the way, he increased the assets of the Holy See from some couple of hundred millions to a figure in excess of two hundred billion dollars. And he won for the Holy See a coveted place at that privileged green-topped table of the supermen.

"Oh, yes, he dealt in power. Raw power. For he was officially Keeper of the Bargain." Rico could see questioning looks, looks of dismay, of consternation, knotted eyebrows, hurried consultations.

"The Bargain?" Merely stating their question for them brought all heads around.

"By 1870, as you all know, the Holy See ceased to have any temporal power, and no real source of income. All the way back then, the popes had forgotten—or had unlearned, perhaps—how to wield their spiritual power without the protection of temporal power. No wonder half the Church's enemies were afraid of her! The other half hated her.

"By 1870, a new race of princes of worldly power had appeared in our world. The men of international money. The supermen who made and unmade governments. Who backed or condemned whole empires. The forefathers of the international money managers of our day, when all—but all—is decided for us by the few who cluster around the green-topped gaming tables of the international monetary system.

"Not knowing any longer how to wield spiritual power and moral authority, the Church's leaders struck a bargain. Not the only one ever. But one so extraordinary it has been known—to the few who knew of it at all—as *the* Bargain."

Rico took from his pocket the only paper he had prepared in advance to carry into conclave. "I have here the text of that signed and sealed Bargain. A bargain with the great assembly of the new international supermen.

"Who signed for the Holy See? A man called Guido the Signer. That Guido died in 1891. He was followed by the next Guido de la Valle, who died in 1924. And he in turn was followed by the Guido de la Valle who went home to God at seven thirty-five this morning. All three were Keepers of this Bargain." Lansing unfolded the crisp sheet of paper. "All three were faithful servitors of the Keeper of the Keys of Salvation. For that, too, was implied in the Bargain; was the whole purpose of the Bargain, in fact, at least from the Keepers' standpoint. But none served so faithfully, so successfully, and in the final days of his life in such a holy aura, as this last Guido.

"My Brothers, I read to you from the Bargain, the statement of its purpose for both sides:

> "To enable two enemies, the Holy See and the Universal Assembly, to engage in mutually profitable business ventures, and still remain enemies.

"What was guaranteed by this Bargain? Again, my Brothers, I read to you:

> "The Universal Assembly guarantees the Holy See all the facilities, easements, favors, privileges, and equality now enjoyed by members of the Assembly.
>
> "The Holy See guarantees that every act of access to such facilities, etc., will be taken only over the signature of one man: the eldest male issue of the same family in each generation, and known to the Universal Assembly. Also guaranteed: two prelates from the Holy See's Secretariat of State, not lower than Monsignore in rank, will be formal members of the Lodge."

Rico paused, then read the two signatures. *"Cesare Sella. Guido de la Valle."*

The effect of this reading was unique in the chronicles of all conclaves. Not one of Lansing's listeners looked at his neighbor, as cardinal electors do in silent consultation. No one stirred in his seat from impatience or eagerness to react. No one made any commentary or remark. For the full meaning and impact of this revelation froze every mind present with the overwhelming ring of truth.

Suddenly, with those three paragraphs, each cardinal present clearly saw his own situation—his compromises; the easements he had enjoyed.

Each saw the situation of his Church clearly—the financial scandals of the seventies and the eighties; the reticence of popes to take bold stances; the strange, godless alliances between churchmen and enemies of the Church; the Mammon of clerics; the unfaith of so many Vatican bureaucrats; the "smoke of Satan" Da Brescia had smelled wafting "in the Sanctuary and around the Altar."

"My Brothers." Lansing read the emotions on many of the faces around him, and shared them. "To add to your confusion and pain of soul, each of eleven Pontiffs was given this Bargain to sign. And each one did indeed sign it." He let that sink in. "Each of these Pontiffs mortgaged the power of Christ's Church to the power of Mammon.

"For, make no mistake about it, my Brothers, what we are discussing in this conclave—the business of every conclave—is no half-boiled theological concept of self-realizing committees and mature autonomous bodies finding new revelations." He spat Buff's ideas out of his mouth as a man spits irritating fishbones on the floor. "We are talking about power. This Bargain is about power. Power is exactly everything and exclusively all Your Eminences are about at this sacred moment. Under the Holy Spirit of Christ, you are here to decide only one thing: on whom that same Spirit should confer the plenitude of divine power, which Christ conferred on Peter the Apostle, and has conferred on all of Peter's successors in this diocese of Rome. Power to forgive. Power to obligate. Power to teach. Power to decide the right and the wrong of all human affairs. Power for the peace of God. Power to war on God's enemies. Power despite weakness. Power in the absence of holiness.

"If any one of our popes, if any of us or those who came before us, had used our power—Christ's power in us—with half the zeal and dedication as the Assembly had used its power, the entire history of the Church and the world in the twentieth century would have been different. And the world we face into as the new century beckons us on uncharted paths would not frighten and cow us, as it already does.

"Once and for all, then, let us refuse to have this sacred conclave diverted by those"—he looked down at Buff and Carberin and Grosjean—"who would have the Church, through us, strike yet another bargain. A bargain with the world. A bargain by which we obligate ourselves to make the Church *as like as possible*"—he raised his voice as he pronounced each of those words slowly—"to the world around it.

"Shame on the authors of such an idea! And shame on those who would accept such an idea!

"My Venerable Brothers, think well on it before you decide to take me as your next pope." Lansing held up the sheet of paper on which the terms of the Bargain were written. "I will not sign this Bargain." He tore the paper in two. "I will not observe the terms of this Bargain." He ripped the two fragments into four. "Because in this whole cosmos of man there can be no bargain, even a temporary one, between God and Mammon, between Jesus and Satan, between Good and Evil. I will admit no Keeper of the Bargain. Because we have one Keeper: the Keeper of our Salvation. Christ, the power of God. Christ, the wisdom of God.

"No bargain exists between God and Satan. Between God's Church and God's enemies." Lansing's voice rang out, sending the blood coursing faster in the veins of tens of cardinals. "A state of perpetual war exists. A long, bitter, wavering struggle, that will go on until Christ steps into the world again with arm upraised to strike evil and dismiss it into eternal perdition."

Lansing stopped. It was not fair—not quite fair—to inflame the hearts of his fellow churchmen, or of anyone, with such brave statements, without warning of their consequences.

"My Lords, just one more moment of your time, and I will, I think, have answered all your questions that I can.

"A few moments ago, I said I could not accept your mandate, because its consequences might push us over the cliff of chaos, into oblivion.

"It may be your turn to say those words to me. The practiced ear in Vatican affairs can see the Holy See's approaching twilight as a worldly power.

"If I as your pope reject the Bargain, that will mean my Church declares itself free to wage Christ's war with Christ's power. There will not be billions at our disposal, as there are now. Nor even millions. Those enemies in whose world the Church has played the game of power can club us to smithereens, because they have worldly power. If you elect me and install me, I may, like Papa Serena, last one month or so before they kill me. And that fate I am willing to accept.

"What I will not accept is any other mandate but this one: to preside over the liquidation of this Bargain, and of every other bargain; yes, over the Moscow-Vatican bargain struck by Papa Angelica, too; and to reinstate the unique spiritual power and the central moral authority of this Holy See, and of its Vicar as the Roman head of the one and only true Catholic and Apostolic Church.

"There will be hardship for us all. For you, in particular. I will not allow you your petty corruptions. I will denounce your shameful alliances. If you fall into heresy or allow heresy to flourish, if you fall away in schism, I will fire you, excommunicate you formally with bell, book, and candle. If you oppose me, I will fight you tooth and nail. I will not permit any use of politics. Any use. I will require a strict accounting from you about money, about doctrine, about moral practice. I will not treat the Church's enemies as friends or even as decent people. And I will not yield to the economic boycott of the financial squeeze of the Universal Assembly.

"So, whatever about the other candidate, my Venerable Brother Cardinal Buff"—Rico bowed in Buff's direction—"know that if you choose me to succeed Papa Valeska, the fullest fury of Christ's enemies—of Christ's Enemy, the fallen Archangel—will be directed at me, at you, and at this One, Holy, Roman, Catholic, and Apostolic Church."

In the hushed and tense atmosphere, every ear could hear the slow ripping sound as Lansing tore the four fragments of the Bargain yet one more time, and let the pieces flutter to the floor at his feet.

Helmut reached the bottom of the stairs and came out into the bright midday sun of June. He squinted for a moment, letting his eyes adjust after the three hours in the dim glow of *il Tempio.* He could already hear the rising hum of the crowds over in the piazza. In a few moments, everyone in the Vatican would be drawn there, as water is drawn to a vortex.

Helmut raised his eyes. "He's done it, Uncle. Be with us. He's begun."

The booming voice of Africa's Cardinal Azande followed on Helmut's gentle prayer, magnified by a hundred speakers, calling out to all men and women of goodwill in the city and the world.

"*Annuntio Vobis gaudium magnum!* . . . I announce to you a great joy! We have a Pope! The Most Eminent Lord Richard Cardinal Lansing!"